THE RANDOLPH CASEY HORROR THRILLER SERIES

BOOKS 1-3

ROCKWELL SCOTT

CONTENTS

THE TENTH WARD

RANDOLPH CASEY HORROR THRILLERS
BOOK 1

PROLOGUE

Although his heart was still beating, Thomas Mowry considered himself dead.

Why shouldn't he? With what the doctors had told him and his parents three days ago, there was no point sucking up any more clean air.

There had been tears and wailing and hysterics from everyone except Thomas himself. He only sat and listened to his mom, dad, and sister cry their eyes out. He'd run out of tears long ago.

Sixteen years old and no longer able to cry. Sixteen and dying.

"How are you feeling?" Thomas's mother asked him for the fifth time that day.

"I think I'll go to the cafeteria." He hopped out of bed, grabbed his portable oxygen, and left the hospital room before she said anything else.

Lunchtime was nearing, so there were a myriad of smells wafting about. Fried food, sweet desserts, and something spicy coming from the international counter. Thomas took a plastic container of his favorite chocolate pudding and brought it to the register, where Mrs. Eloise was balancing the cash drawer before the midday rush.

She looked at him from over her glasses. "You're going to spoil your lunch, Thomas."

"Don't worry, I can always eat more."

She smirked as she pushed the drawer closed with her hip and rang him up. Thomas paid with his quick swipe card, which only employees used, but he'd managed to get one because he was there so often. "Have a good afternoon," Mrs. Eloise said.

"You too."

It was nice to have a casual conversation with someone who didn't know he was dying. She was the cafeteria manager, so she would not have heard the latest news of his prognosis.

He walked down the hallway, wishing he could eat the pudding as he went, but he needed his spare hand to pull the oxygen cylinder behind him.

He passed by the chapel and spotted Father Calvin outside. Thomas wished he'd gone the back way and used the other set of elevators.

The priest gave him a look, one that told Thomas he'd heard the news. "How are you, Thomas?"

"Fine. And you?"

Father Calvin licked his lips. "I haven't seen you here in a few weeks."

"What's the point?"

"I understand things are hard for you right now. But this is the *most* important time to have faith."

"You know I lost that long ago."

"I think you are just having a period of struggling. Please come and attend services. I've been praying for you."

"Thanks, but obviously it didn't help."

Thomas saw that Father Calvin was sad, and that made him feel guilty. But Thomas was also disappointed about all the time he spent believing in and praying to a God who seemingly wasn't there at all. And if God was there, then clearly he hadn't cared much about Thomas to begin with.

So, Thomas grabbed the handle of his portable oxygen and

walked away before Father Calvin moaned any more about his lost little sheep.

Back in his room, he ate the pudding at his desk while surfing the internet. Out of the corner of his eye, he noticed his mother watching him, and he knew she was about to say something, so he put on his headphones and cranked up some loud heavy metal music.

The chirping notification of an incoming video call interrupted the music.

Georgia.

Thomas sucked on the chocolate-covered spoon as the app danced on his screen, beckoning him to answer.

He clicked the red button and the music resumed.

He read a new article announcing the upcoming album from one of his favorite hard rock bands that he would not be around to check out.

The video-calling app chimed. He had a message.

Why are you ignoring me? Please talk :(

Thomas sighed. He clicked the messages and stared at them for a while, wondering if he should reply. Georgia could see he'd read the messages, but regardless, he closed his computer.

That was it. He had to do something.

He had to know for sure what would happen to him. No more of this guessing by the doctors or "hoping for the best" from his parents. He needed real, concrete answers.

And he only had one idea of how to get them.

THOMAS RARELY VISITED the game room at the end of the hall. St. Mary's, having the largest children's ward in the city, meant it was often packed with the youngest patients, so the room was noisy and, honestly, a bit depressing.

He was sixteen, and even though technically still eligible for the children's ward, still felt like he didn't belong.

He pulled his tank behind him. This particular holder had a gimpy wheel that made it wobble. The oxygen filled his nostrils first, and then his lungs, but it still couldn't stop his violent coughing fits.

As he walked to the board game closet, he caught eyes with Kristen, one of the high school volunteers. She was playing chess with Morgan, an eight-year-old, although it didn't look like they were strictly following the rules. Kristen gave him a small, awkward smile that Thomas returned. A month ago he'd asked her out to the movies. She'd shuffled her feet and looked at the ground before reluctantly agreeing. The next day, she'd told him she had plans, and they'd never rescheduled. Maybe she thought his oxygen tank or heavy wheezing would make too much noise. More likely, she wanted to go on a date with a normal boy. Thomas was only a little bit mad about it.

Besides, it was a blessing in disguise. He hadn't realized it at the time, but there was no point in starting a new relationship now.

He went into the board game closet and closed the door behind him just enough to not block out all the light. The bulb inside was dead, and no one had bothered to replace it. Nurse Donna was always going on about budget cuts.

At the back of the closet, Thomas rifled through all the old games shoved into the corner, the ones with torn boxes and missing pieces.

There, underneath them all, was what he'd been looking for. A Ouija board. Just as Georgia had said.

"Weird something like that's in there," she'd told him a week before. "Since this place is so Catholic and all. I bet if they knew they would throw it away."

"Did you tell someone about it?" Thomas had asked her.

"No." Although they'd been speaking via video chat—hospital rules—Georgia still picked up on his interest. "Why? You want to try it out? Those things are bad, you know."

"Nah," Thomas had said, waving his hand.

He hadn't mentioned his plan. She would've gotten mad at him.

Thomas blew off the layer of dust and examined it. The picture of the kids on the cover looked to be from the '80s.

What do I have to lose?

The answer was nothing. So he left the board game closet, making sure Kristen or anyone else hadn't noticed he slipped out with the box tucked under his arm.

THAT NIGHT, Thomas waited until lights out—nine o'clock—before opening his door a crack and peering down the long, tiled corridor. He looked left and right, making sure no one was coming. It was after hours and past bedtime.

If he got caught, his plan would be interrupted.

He closed the heavy wooden door. It did not lock from the inside. Hospital policy.

He'd told his parents he wanted to sleep alone that night. Given his current condition, they were reluctant to leave his side, but they were usually good at giving him his privacy when he asked. They'd said they would return first thing in the morning, and he agreed.

Thomas threw the blanket off his bed. Hidden underneath was the Ouija board.

Loud thunder boomed outside. Rain pelted the window and the hard wind blew against the glass, making it shudder. Whenever the lightning struck, the dark room lit up blue.

He laid the board out on the floor and placed the planchette in the middle.

Knocking.

He pushed the entire thing under his bed just before the door opened. It was Ms. Donna, one of the regular night shift nurses. A nice woman, but if she found the Ouija board, he would be screwed. Thomas knew she was quite devout.

Ms. Donna frowned and put her hands on her hips. "Thomas, what are you doing? You should be asleep."

"I know," the boy said, pretending to be ashamed of himself. "I'll go now."

Ms. Donna forced a smile. Thomas recognized that look. He'd gotten it from all the other nurses who had access to his chart. "You need to rest. Don't you want to get out of here?"

And come right back in a few months? I don't even have that long left. What's the point?

"I'll see you tomorrow for my next shift."

"Good night, Ms. Donna." He feigned his most innocent and compliant voice.

Once the coast was clear again, Thomas took the board out from under his bed and put the planchette back in place.

He sat on the floor and looked down at the array of letters and numbers, a nervous feeling sprouting in his stomach. Although he'd planned it all day long, he was uneasy about the outcome.

"Dear God. Are you listening?" he asked out loud. He stared at the planchette, daring it to move.

It stayed still.

"Did you hear me, God? Are you there?"

He gave the little piece of plastic enough time to act, but nothing happened.

Thomas felt silly. The picture on the box showed more than one person touching the planchette, so maybe that was what caused it to work. But if God was as powerful and all-knowing as Father Calvin always talked about in the chapel, then surely he could nudge a small little board game piece on his own.

"Dear God. You know I stopped believing in you a long time ago. But I figured it was time to give you another chance. So this is your last shot to convince me you're real. Are you here right now?"

He let a long minute of silence go by. He finally released the breath he hadn't realized he'd been holding. Then, as he leaned over to pick up the board and put it away forever, the planchette moved.

It zipped over to YES.

Thomas gasped and stumbled back a few paces, startled. Yes, he had definitely seen it happen. That thing had been in the center of the board, and then moved all by itself.

His breathing quickened. His heart pounded. Thunder roared outside, sounding as if it were right on top of the hospital.

Was he in the presence of God?

Strange. He didn't feel any different. He would've thought being close to the Lord would have caused something out of the ordinary. At least, Father Calvin always made him think so.

However, the room had suddenly grown freezing.

"Who are you?" the boy asked the board.

The planchette moved again, this time darting between the letters.

GOD was spelled out.

"If you're God, tell me my name."

THOMAS

"How old am I?"

16

He backed away from the board as far as he could go, pressed against the wall, not sure if he was frightened or in awe. These were the kinds of supernatural things that Father Calvin talked about. Although he wondered why normal prayer had always resulted in silence.

Maybe Father Calvin should be using a Ouija board to get in touch with God.

"If you're real, then thank you for proving it. I struggle to believe in you sometimes."

The planchette moved again.

I FORGIVE YOU

"I'm afraid, God. They say I don't have much time left and I don't want to leave my friend Georgia behind. Do you know her? She doesn't deserve to be sick. Why are you doing this to us?"

I WILL PROTECT HER

"Do you promise?"

YES

Tears welled up in the boy's eyes. That was all he needed. If he couldn't live, then he just wanted Georgia to be okay. She was a special girl, and he was lucky to have met her, even though their time together had been short.

The next question came to his mind, but he was hesitant to ask. God could know the answer that his entire team of doctors and nurses had been looking for. It had caused him to live each day in uncertainty, walking an agonizing path of confusion and dread.

But his curiosity got the better of him.

"Do you know when I'm going to die?"

At first the planchette didn't move, but then it sprung into action.

17 DAYS

Tears flowed freely down his cheeks now. Such a short time.

But at least he knew.

And if he saw day eighteen, he would be certain God was not real. Or if he was, then he definitely wasn't all-knowing like Father Calvin said.

So, Thomas put the Ouija board back in the box and returned it under his bed sheet.

He climbed into bed and turned out the light. But with the storm booming outside and the sudden foreknowledge of his fate, Thomas found it very difficult to get to sleep.

1

Randolph Casey held up three fingers.

"How many fingers do you see?"

The room was much too large for his class, which made it look sparsely attended even on a good day. Since it was the Friday before a big football game, and the middle of the afternoon, nearly half of his students had flaked.

"Three," someone answered.

"Good." Rand brought his hand down. "Today's lesson will be all about the number three." He clicked the space bar on his computer and the PowerPoint presentation began. The first slide was a big 3 he'd taken from the internet. "Can anyone tell me why this number is important for our purposes?"

He paced in front of the front row of students. The seating was stadium-style, like a movie theater. Each student had two or three desks between them—except the ones who were close friends.

"It's the time this class starts?"

Rand didn't catch who said it, but it received a fair share of chuckling from the other students, as well as Rand himself.

"True," he said, a smile on his face, "and a little bit ironic, now that I think about it. After the lesson today, I feel like you'll agree with me."

He used the remote in his pocket to click to the next slide. All it said was, "Three is a demon's favorite number."

Rand let that information sink in.

"I thought six was the number of the beast?" The girl—Stacy—sat in the front row every time, always enraptured by the subject material. In all honesty, that alarmed Rand more than it flattered him.

"In the Biblical sense, it is. You'll learn all about that in your other Religious Studies classes. But in my class, we focus on *this* number. It's a more practical approach."

The door at the top of the stadium opened. Rand thought he had a latecomer, but instead, a woman wearing a pantsuit entered and took a seat at the desk closest to the exit. She sat up, straight and stern, and laid a folder of papers in front of her.

"Umm." Rand lost his train of thought.

A few students noticed Rand's distraction and turned to look at the woman. She only crossed her legs, pen poised over her paper, and focused on Rand.

Really? We're going to do this on a Friday? He hadn't seen that particular lady before, but he knew she was yet another auditor sent to scrutinize his class.

"Right," Rand said. "The number three. Why it matters."

He clicked his remote again, and the slide changed to another with pictures.

"I'm sure you are all familiar with the Trinity. The Father, the Son, and the Holy Spirit. The three in one. The Christian God is the one God, but he is also all three beings. Demonic spirits hate God, so they will often use the number three to mock him."

The next slide was a smattering of pictures of clocks. Some digital, some wristwatches, and others antique grandfathers. All of them read three o'clock.

"These are some of my personal photos," Rand explained. "Each was taken in the home of someone I've known or consulted with.

Whenever one of these demons was present, their clocks would always stop at three o'clock in the morning."

Rand shot a glance at the woman at the back of his classroom. She stared at the screen now, her note-taking forgotten. She looked confused.

"Why three o'clock in the morning?" Stacy asked, raising her hand, but not waiting to be called on. "Why not three in the afternoon?"

"Great question. It's because demons prefer to operate in darkness. There's still daylight at three o'clock in the afternoon."

Stacy scribbled a note.

"You could have gotten those off Google," said a guy in the third row. Rand knew Garrett. The kid had a C in the class, which was nearly impossible considering he made the course so straightforward. The kid was only enrolled for the easy A and was a skeptic through and through.

"True, Garrett," Rand said. Garrett seemed surprised that Rand remembered his name. "But I didn't."

Rand clicked the remote again. The next slide was of bodies. Lower backs, stomachs, necks, legs. And each of them showed three long, red, and jagged marks gouged into their skin.

"The more violent hauntings usually come with scratches," Rand explained. "Again, these are my own pictures of people I've assisted over the years."

Rand glanced to the back of the class again. The woman used her cell phone to snap a picture of the screen, looking very put off.

Why did she have to choose this lesson? he thought.

Not like many of the others would have been much better.

The group of girls in the center squirmed as they stared at the pictures.

"Could I have also gotten these off Google?" Rand asked Garrett.

Garrett shrugged. "Maybe Photoshop? They are all pretty similar."

"I guess I could have photoshopped them. Except I'm not great at technology. Also..."

Rand untucked his shirt and rolled it up. He turned around and exposed his back to the class. Some students leaned in. "I even have a little souvenir myself."

That had been a painful and violent case. The triple scratch Rand had sustained had scarred. He would carry it for the rest of his life.

As he tucked his shirt back in, the woman in the back seemed appalled.

Maybe I shouldn't be showing skin during an audit. But he always saved his scar for the lesson on the number three.

"Did it hurt?" someone asked.

"Like hell."

"If this kind of stuff happens to you," a girl asked as she raised her hand, "then why do you... keep doing it? Why don't you stop getting involved?"

"Good question," Rand said. "Until you experience it personally —and I pray you never do—you won't understand how frightening it is. And if you ever do, God forbid, you'll be desperate for someone to help you. That is why I do what I do. And I do it because no one else will."

The class fell silent.

"Now," he said, snapping the attention once again to the lesson at hand. "Three. What other tricky things do these bastards get up to? Let's check it out."

He clicked his remote again. Meanwhile, the woman at the back scribbled on her papers, a frown on her face.

2

His office was a cramped space that Rand was pretty sure had once been used for storage. He walked in and dropped his leather bag on the chair across from his desk, then let himself collapse heavily in the other chair behind his desk.

It was four o'clock in the afternoon and the bright sun shone through the single window. Or it would have if it weren't covered in a white, cloudy smudge. Due to the structure of the old building, the window wasn't easily accessible from the pathway that passed by it. Therefore, the cleaners tended to overlook it.

The office was cluttered with papers and books. The place had become his second home, even though there wasn't enough space to keep up with the things that were accumulating. And there was no way he was in line for a bigger office. Not like the ones the department heads got. His class was the most looked down upon in the whole Religion department. He understood.

There was a knock on the door, and the auditor from earlier poked her head in. "Good afternoon, Mr. Casey. May I come in?"

Rand stifled a sigh. *So I guess we really are going to do this on a Friday.* He supposed it was too much to hope that it could wait until

Monday. Without a word, he gestured toward the seat in front of his desk. When the woman found it occupied, Rand quickly removed his bag.

"My name is Doris Galloway," she said, removing the glasses that were resting on the bridge of her nose. "I'm one of the university's head auditors."

"So you're Frank, Susan, and Nelson's boss?" Rand asked, his tone flat. Doris seemed taken aback by that. "They've all visited my class before."

Doris cleared her throat. "Yes, I am their supervisor."

"Got it."

Rand leaned back in his chair. He was no stranger to the auditing process. But this time it seemed they had sent in the big guns to take him down.

People like Doris weren't a problem if you taught freshman algebra or economics. It was the art teachers, music teachers, and paranormal studies instructors who were in constant danger of falling victim to budget cuts.

"I attended your class earlier," Doris explained. She crossed her legs and opened her folder across her thighs. "Very interesting stuff. I took some notes and was hoping to find out more about you."

My official credentials, my teaching experience. Rand had neither and honestly was surprised his class at the university had been allowed to go on as long as it had. He could thank his friend, the Dean, for the job, since he owed Rand a major personal favor. But that had been years ago, and Rand had known it was just a matter of time before the good graces ran their course.

Doris put her glasses back on to keep reading the paperwork. "How long have you been employed at Louisiana State University, Mr. Casey?"

"Rand, please," he said. He folded his hands together and rested them on the desk. "This is my seventeenth semester teaching here. I've found it to be a rewarding experience."

She eyed him over the top of her lenses. "I see. And how many students would you say you have enrolled across all your sections?"

"Four hundred and seventy-eight," he said. "Those are the ones who sign up. Some drop."

"What is your drop rate?" she asked. "Actually, I can look that up to get an accurate—"

"Forty-one percent," Rand said off the top of his head.

"Oh. I see." Doris made a show of clicking her pen and writing the number down in the notes. "I'll still verify it. Why do you think that is? Is your course difficult?"

"No, not at all," Rand said. "It's too frightening."

Doris paused her writing. "I beg your pardon?"

"It's frightening," Rand repeated. "The stuff I teach is real, and it scares the students. Some of them are very interested, and those are the ones I love to have in class. But there are others who can't handle it. I understand."

Doris pursed her lips as she seemed to gather her words. "I don't think I've ever been told that a course is too *frightening*."

"You made it through one lesson," Rand said. "That's better than the students who leave halfway through the first class."

Doris gave a mirthless chuckle. "Perhaps I'm somewhat of a skeptic."

Now she had pushed his button. Dancing around the auditing formalities was one thing, but this was another. "These kids need to know what's out there. Math and economics are part of the real world, sure, but the stuff I teach is just as real, and can be very dangerous for anyone unaware."

Doris stared at him as if he were a crazy person. Good. He was used to that, but he wasn't wrong. The spirits did not discern between age, race, or sex. Doris Galloway, university auditor, was susceptible to their terror, the same as the rest. They did not care if she considered herself a "skeptic."

"I see…" She clicked her pen, but when she brought the tip to the paper, it appeared she could not think of anything to write.

A knock on the door interrupted them.

There stood a young girl, one that Rand recognized from the last section of his class. Stacy Thompson, his front-row fan.

"Hi," she said, hesitating in the hallway. "Am I intruding?"

Doris said, "No, dear. Please, come in. These are Mr. Casey's office hours and *I* am the one who is interrupting. This is your time to speak to your instructor if you need to."

"Oh," the girl said. "Okay. Then..."

Doris vacated her chair and motioned for the girl to sit. She did and moved a piece of blonde hair out of her face and tucked it behind her ear.

"My name is—"

"Stacy Thompson," Rand finished for her. "Section three on Friday afternoons. You currently have an A."

Stacy sat up straight. "Oh. Yeah." She smiled. Even Doris smirked at his memory.

"What can I do for you?" Rand asked.

"I was wondering... for the final exam, is it going to be cumulative?"

The final? They had not even reached midterms yet.

But that was Stacy. He knew the type. Always planning ahead, wanting nothing to threaten her 4.0. He wondered if an A in Paranormal Studies would help someone's transcripts, or just make eyebrows raise.

"Cumulative?" Rand asked.

"Yeah," Stacy said. "Is it going to cover everything we've learned all semester, or is it just the last test? Meaning it only covers material since the test before it."

"Ah, right," Rand said. "Not cumulative. It's just a final test. And it will not be weighted any more than the others."

Doris frowned at that little detail. Other professors in the Religious Studies department always weighted their final exams.

But Rand had always hated weighted and cumulative finals when he was in school. Therefore, in his class—where he was in charge—they were off the table.

"Right. Okay, thank you."

"Is that everything?" Rand asked.

"Yes, Mr. Casey."

She got up and left, casting Doris Galloway a short glance as she went.

Doris resumed her place in the seat across from Rand. "How many students would you say show up to your office hours, Mr. Casey?" she asked, ignoring his request for her to call him by his first name.

"Hmm." Rand wondered if this was a trick question. None of the other auditors had asked him that before. More students coming by could mean they had more questions and concerns about the way he was teaching or grading, which meant more issues. On the other hand, fewer people showing up possibly indicated disinterest. "I have a few trickling in every now and then." Rand shrugged and gave her his best charming smile.

She was unamused. She returned the glasses to her nose and wrote in her papers.

Rand sat across from her in silence for a long time and let her work. He tried to peek at what she was scribbling, but he couldn't read any of her messy scrawl upside down.

Then, Rand noticed another presence outside his office.

One that looked out of a place.

It was a man alongside a woman, presumably husband and wife. They were both middle-aged and most likely not students at the university.

And Rand recognized the looks on their faces—knew them too well. Desperation, terror, and uncertainty.

These people needed his help.

"Good afternoon," Rand said, standing, the audit forgotten. Doris looked up from her work and twisted in her chair to see who had intruded this time.

"Hi," the man said, stepping forward into the office, but only one step. His wife lingered behind him. "We are looking for a Mr. Randolph Casey."

"You've found him," Rand said with a smile. "What can I do you for?"

3

Their nervous demeanor did not change, and Rand felt the smile fade from his face. He saw the urgency in their facial expressions, the tension they held inside.

Doris Galloway, on the other hand, sensed no such thing. "Are you students of Mr. Casey's? Here for his office hours?"

"Oh. No, ma'am," the man said. "But we called ahead and asked when he would be in the office. We were told he would be free during this time."

"He normally is," Doris said, "but if you're not students, then I must ask you to please wait a few minutes. We are having a meeting."

"Oh." He smiled pleasantly, almost masking the pain behind his eyes. "I'm sorry. We'll wait as long as we have to."

"Actually, Doris, I would like to speak with them now." Doris cast him a puzzled look. "Feel free to stay, though."

Doris, not used to being sidelined, eventually rose and took her place on the far side of the office, where she had stood when Stacy had asked about the midterms.

"Please," Rand said, gesturing to the chair across from his desk.

There was only room for one, so the man told his wife to sit, which she did. He stood behind her with a hand on her shoulder.

"My name is Nick Collins." He extended his hand and Rand shook it firmly. "This is my wife, Maria." Rand shook her hand, too.

They were a good-looking couple. Nick was tall and had a firm jaw. His face was barely wrinkled with his age, and the hair on the side of his temples was grey. The rest was brown, and the difference was very stark. Maria looked younger than him, with blonde hair cut short to her shoulders. Her eyes were clear blue, and she wore meticulously applied lipstick on her thin lips. She sat with a straight posture and an air of strength and confidence, but the look of despair on her face ruined her guise. At least to Rand.

"Randolph Casey," Rand said. "But please, call me Rand."

Since Nick was standing, Rand remained standing as well.

Nick's hand brushed the back of his head, rustling his hair. "We uh... we came because..." He and Maria glanced at each other. "We have a problem."

"Sure," Rand said, trying to keep the tone upbeat.

"Well... I don't know how to explain this," Nick said.

"You don't have to worry about sounding silly," Rand said. "Not in this office. Just tell me straight what's going on, and how I can help."

The tension went out of Maria's shoulders, and she slumped forward. That was a common problem when people came to see him— they thought they were crazy for having the issues they were having.

"We have a daughter," Maria said. "Her name is Georgia. She is hospitalized at St. Mary's Medical Center because she has cystic fibrosis. Are you familiar with the condition?"

"I can't say I am."

"Basically," Nick said, "it causes her body to produce too much mucus in her lungs. There's no cure, and she's spent about a third of her life in the hospital for her surgeries."

"I have a picture," Maria said, diving into her purse. She produced a single photograph, which she handed to Rand, the smile of a proud mother on her face for the first time since she'd come into the office.

One glance told Rand everything. Georgia Collins was a lively and vibrant girl. Even in a photograph, her energy radiated out, her smile reaching her blue eyes completely. An oxygen cannula was in her nostrils and the tubes were tucked behind her ears.

"She's beautiful," Rand said. "How old is she?"

"Fifteen."

That hit Rand in the gut. Only a year younger than his own daughter.

"Looks just like her mother."

Maria's smile widened, but then it dropped as quickly as it came.

"Georgia had a friend," Nick said. "A boy she met at the hospital named Thomas, who was also a CF kid. That's what they call themselves. Anyway, about three months ago, Thomas's health worsened, and he fell into a coma. He died a few days after that."

"Oh," Rand said. "I'm sorry to hear that."

"Yeah. He was a good kid, and only sixteen. They say people with cystic fibrosis can have a life expectancy up to their thirties, but sometimes things happen."

"I understand," Rand said.

In the corner, Doris Galloway focused on the couple, her papers forgotten. Rand even thought he could see tears shimmer in the corners of her eyes.

"Georgia's a little trooper," Maria said. "She's almost always positive and happy, and just an amazing young lady all around. But ever since Thomas passed away, she's been in a funk."

"She lost a friend," Rand said. "Perhaps she's considering the same could happen to her."

"Believe it or not," Nick said, "Georgia talks to us often about dying. She says she isn't afraid, that every day is a blessing, and when her time comes she knows she will have lived her best life."

"That's inspiring," Rand said.

"It is." Nick couldn't help but smile. "So Georgia is not afraid to die."

"She sounds like a remarkable young woman," Rand said. "So... what is it that brings you here today?"

Nick and Maria exchanged a glance. Then Nick spoke. "She told us that Thomas's ghost comes to visit her at night."

Now Rand understood where he fit in.

Doris Galloway's brow furrowed. The sad story had—for her— taken an unusual turn.

"Okay," Rand said.

Nick and Maria seemed surprised at Rand's nonjudgmental answer.

"There are child psychologists and sociologists on staff at the hospital at all times," Maria said. "And we've talked to them a lot about these claims Georgia is making. About talking to and seeing and hanging out with Thomas's ghost at night. The doctors are saying it's her way of grieving. She misses her friend and likes the idea that, even after she passes, she'll still be able to live on."

"Right," Rand said, although his first instinct was always to mistrust the opinion of psychologists and sociologists in scenarios like this. Very smart people, to be sure, but they viewed things too clinically. Too black and white.

Sometimes a more open-minded approach was needed.

"We want our daughter to have the freedom to deal with her situation in any way she needs to," Nick said. "Especially in her condition, where we never know what the next day could bring."

Just like what happened to Thomas, Rand thought.

Maria wiped away the tears that suddenly fell from her eyes. Rand grabbed a nearby box of tissues and offered them to her, which she accepted.

"But usually she's so practical and down to earth," Nick said. "This thing with the ghost, though..."

"Do you believe in life after death, Mr. Collins?" Rand asked.

Nick took a few minutes to ponder it. "You know, I never used to. But since we've almost lost Georgia so many times... I have to say it is a very comforting thought."

"Do you think it's possible for Thomas to have visited Georgia from the other side? Do you believe Georgia when she tells you these things?"

"At first, I wasn't sure," Nick said. He rubbed at his chest as he gathered his words. "But ever since, some odd things have been happening."

"Like what?" Rand asked.

"Tell him about the food," Maria said.

"Yeah," Nick said. "One day, the dietary service workers brought around chicken for lunch. Georgia told us not to eat it because Thomas had warned her not to the night before. Maria and I rarely eat the hospital food anyway, but that evening a lot of the kids in the ward got upset stomachs."

"I see," Rand said. For the first time, a hollow feeling of concern sprouted in his belly.

"And the oxygen tanks," Maria prodded.

"They usually drop off full tanks of O2 for Georgia every morning," Nick said. "But for the past few weeks, every morning we'll wake up and find two of them already at the door before the guys make their rounds."

"And they won't be registered," Maria added. "They're supposed to have a code on them so they can be tracked. Oxygen is considered a drug in the hospital, so they need a tag before they go out. It's like someone took them from storage and brought them straight to Georgia's room. And only hers."

"Georgia thinks it's Thomas trying to look out for her," Nick said. "She says she tells him he can't just bring the tanks—that they have to be tagged first—but he doesn't listen."

"What's weird is that when Thomas was alive," Maria went on, "he also griped about how long it took the guys to deliver the new oxygen tanks. He said all the registration and tracking was stupid, and that it was only air—no one freaked out about water like they did about oxygen."

"We've seen these things happen with our own eyes," Nick said. "I don't want to sit there and argue with her if this is what she's using to grieve about her friend's passing."

"I understand," Rand said. "What exactly can I help you with?"

"We need to ask someone who has a different point of view," Nick said. "Someone who is a believer. We are surrounded by skeptics and... we just want another opinion to weigh in."

"I can do that," Rand said. "I am most certainly a believer."

"And, from what we hear, an expert," Maria said.

Rand and Doris exchanged a small glance.

"You could say that as well," Rand said.

"We were hoping you could come to the hospital with us one day soon," Nick said. "Meet Georgia. Spend some time and get to know her and ask her about her ghost friend. She doesn't talk about it much anymore, because she knows people don't believe her. If she knew you believed, then she might open up to you."

Rand nodded. "Sounds reasonable."

"Could you also evaluate the situation?" Maria asked. "Can you tell if there really *is* a ghost there?"

"I would be happy to meet Georgia," Rand said to Nick. Then, he turned to Maria. "And I will check for any signs of paranormal activity."

"Thank you," Nick said, very relieved as if he'd considered that Rand might decline. "Thank you so much. That means a lot to my family. We just... need help."

"I understand," Rand said. "I've assisted many people with their supernatural experiences. And your daughter sounds like a lovely girl."

That made Maria smile.

Rand took their phone number and told them he would call to arrange a time to join them at St. Mary's.

As they left, Nick turned and shook his hand. "Thank you again, Mr. Casey."

"Rand, please."

"Rand. Seriously. It's very hard to track down someone who has knowledge about this stuff, and one that doesn't seem kind of... out there."

"I get it," Rand said. Ghosts and spiritualism were definitely fringe topics, and he was happy to bring some professionalism to it.

It was serious business, after all. Even if people like Doris Galloway didn't agree.

The couple left, closing the door behind them. Rand returned to his desk, thoughts of Georgia Collins and her ghostly friend swirling around in his head.

Instinct and experience told him that Georgia *was* communicating with a ghost. A hospital where terminal children frequently passed away? Where parents constantly lived in grief and fear and doubt? The energy in a place like that would easily attract a lost spirit, especially one that was not yet ready to move on.

Doris Galloway cleared her throat and Rand gave her his attention.

"Oh, right. Where were we?"

She removed her glasses. The papers were in her hand, down by her side. "Is this extracurricular 'investigation' something you do frequently, Mr. Casey?" she asked.

Rand noticed that Maria had forgotten to take back the photograph. Georgia's beaming smile shone up at him from the desk. As if she were not sick at all.

"There's a lot of confusion out there when it comes to this kind of thing, Mrs. Galloway," Rand said. "I always try to be of assistance whenever anyone needs guidance."

"Do you feel this work on the side ever interferes with your focus in the classroom?" Doris asked.

Rand couldn't tear his eyes away from the picture of Georgia. She reminded him of his own daughter.

"Mr. Casey?"

Rand snapped his focus back. "Yes? You were saying?"

Doris only scowled at him. "I think I have all the information I need." She stacked her papers with an air of finality. "Have a good weekend."

4

R and sat at his kitchen table with his laptop open. He wore only boxer shorts and a white undershirt. He had seven tabs open at the top of the screen, each one about Georgia's condition.

Cystic fibrosis.

He scrolled through the articles, becoming more and more depressed at each one he read.

How is it fair for a child to get such a sickness?

And then, on top of it all, to be visited by a ghost. Georgia's picture rested on the table beside his computer. Every time he glanced at it, he couldn't help but smile himself.

He was so lost in his thoughts that a sudden movement startled him.

Rachel set down a cup of hot tea. "Whoa. A little bit jumpy, are we?" She wore only his shirt, her long legs bare underneath the hem.

"Where did you learn to sneak like that?" he said. "And thank you."

She leaned over his shoulder and looked at the monitor. "Studying for medical school?"

"I wish."

Rand closed the laptop and stood. He took her in his arms and looked down into her green eyes.

"You've been quiet this evening," Rachel said. "Everything all right?"

"Yeah. Just a crazy day at work."

She smiled. "How crazy can it be being a college professor?"

He smirked. "You have no idea."

There was an aggressive knock on the door, and then it opened. "Dad!"

It was only then that Rand realized he'd forgotten about Libby.

"Dad!" Libby, his sixteen-year-old daughter, came around the corner of the living room and into the kitchen. She stopped short when she saw Rand and Rachel just pulling out of their embrace.

Libby gave Rachel a quick smile. "Hey, Rachel." Then she glared at Rand. "I thought we were meeting up tonight, Dad."

Blonde-haired and tall for her age, Libby reminded Rand of Georgia Collins. Or maybe the girl had just been on his mind all afternoon.

Rand brought his hand to his forehead. "Libby, I'm sorry. It totally slipped my mind. It's just that work... "

Then Tessa appeared behind Libby. He felt Rachel tense up beside him.

Oh, great, Rand thought. Rachel hadn't yet met Libby's mother, and if it were up to him, it wouldn't have happened until their relationship was much further along.

"So everyone's here," Rand muttered under his breath. "Just what I need... " He rolled his eyes.

Tessa looked Rachel up and down, making no effort to hide it. "I see you have company. Maybe we should come back some other time."

"No," Libby said. "We can't come back. We have to get this figured out now."

"Phones are a thing, you know," Rand told Tessa. "You could've called and let me know you were planning to grace me with your presence tonight."

"We *tried* calling, Rand," Tessa said, putting her hands on her hips.

Rand remembered he was standing there in his underwear. His phone must've still been in his pants pocket in the bedroom.

"I'm Rachel," Rachel said timidly to Tessa, stepping forward and extending her hand. Tessa took it with a limp wrist.

"This is Tessa, Libby's mother," Rand said.

"Nice to meet you. Excuse me," Rachel said, then slipped back into the bedroom.

"Pretty girl," Tessa said coldly. Then to Libby, "I see you've met her?"

"Yeah," Libby said. "I come over here all the time."

"You didn't tell me he was seeing someone new."

"You wanted to know?"

Tessa didn't answer.

"Libby, I'm sorry," Rand said, trying to get the conversation back on topic. "I completely forgot you were coming over tonight. Something crazy happened at work today."

"How crazy can a teaching job be?" Libby crossed her arms. "But you remembered that we're going hiking tomorrow, right?"

That had slipped his mind as well. "Oh."

Libby visibly deflated. "Dad. Come on, you promised. You said you wouldn't cancel!"

"Yeah, I know," Rand said, running a hand through his hair. "But something came up."

Rachel came back into the kitchen. She was wearing her jeans and t-shirt again and had brought Rand his own pants. Rand took them but didn't put them on.

"Something came up?" Libby asked. "What do you mean?" She glanced at Rachel. "You two are hanging out tonight, so can't I have my dad tomorrow for the hiking trip he's been promising to take me on forever?"

Rachel's eyes went wide. "Wait, what? Rand and I don't have plans tomorrow."

"Rachel isn't what suddenly came up," Rand told his daughter.

Libby looked back at him. "Then what?"

"Umm." Rand felt all the eyes on him.

"Randolph," Tessa said, folding her arms. "You've been putting this hike off for a long time. What could possibly be so important?"

"It's something that happened at work," he said. "I'd rather not say."

Libby gave him a look. "You only have one class on Fridays."

"I know. Come and sit." He led the way into the living room and everyone followed him. Tessa and Libby sat on the couch while Rachel continued to stand, arms folded across her chest. Rand had not intended for her to meet his ex that night—or ever, if he'd had his way. But hey, these things happen. He could get it all back on track. No problem.

Libby looked up at him expectantly.

"So, I was in the office today, and I was visited by a couple. They told me about their daughter."

Rand told them the whole story. As he did, he became very aware of Rachel's growing confusion. Libby and Tessa, however, looked bored.

Libby already knew where this was going.

"This is different," Rand told his daughter. "Her parents are emotional right now. I need to go in there and help them set things straight. Understand?"

Libby sighed. "Do you have to go tomorrow?"

"Libby, think of this family and their situation."

"All right," Libby said, without considering for long. She stood and hugged her dad. Rand embraced her back. "I knew you were going to cancel on me because of a case. You haven't had one coming in a while, and I knew you were due for one."

Rand kissed his daughter on the top of her head. "I know. This will be a quick one. In and out, send the spirit on its way. Then we can hike on Sunday."

"I told Bailey I'd hang out with her on Sunday," Libby said.

"Invite her along."

Libby shrugged. "I don't think she'd be into it, but sure."

"So," Rachel said, speaking for the first time in a while. She eyed Rand. "I thought you were a religious studies professor."

Libby rounded on her father. "You haven't told her?"

Tessa smirked and leaned back on the couch, ready to watch it all unfold.

Rand rubbed the back of his head again. "Umm."

"Told me what?" Rachel asked.

"I *am* a religious studies professor," Rand said. "I mean... my class is listed under the Religious Studies department. My actual class, though... is about paranormal activity."

The room was silent for a very long time.

"You mean like... ghosts?"

"Yeah."

Her brow furrowed as if her brain was trying to figure out if it had processed that correctly. "You teach a class about ghosts?"

"Well. Yeah. But not just about ghosts. About the spiritual side of death, resurrection, the afterlife, and how ghosts sometimes get trapped here on earth. And how we can recognize them, and how to deal with them when we encounter them."

"Oh," Rachel said, although Rand could tell he was losing her. "And... people come to you as some sort of expert on this?"

"It's been known to happen."

"You called this a 'case.' Lawyers have cases."

"Right," Rand said. "So yeah, I guess it happens a decent bit."

"And so you're, like, a teacher by day, ghost hunter by night?"

"Well..." Rand searched for the words. "Paranormal activity mostly happens at night. It's the best time to detect them."

"Show her your room of equipment," Tessa said, the smirk still on her face.

Rand shushed her.

"Equipment?" Rachel asked.

In truth, Rand was not embarrassed or ashamed of what he did at all. Quite the contrary. But when it came to his romantic relationships—particularly the new ones—he had to be careful about how he revealed the details. Most of them were skeptics, and their acceptance was usually easier after they had been dating for a while. But he and Rachel had only been seeing each other for just over three weeks.

"I think I should go," Rachel said.

Without waiting, she took her keys from the table and walked toward the door.

"Rachel, wait," Rand began, but without another word, she was gone.

I'll definitely have to do some damage control later, Rand thought.

"I can't believe you hadn't told her," Libby said.

"It's only been three weeks!" Rand retorted. "You shouldn't have brought it up!"

"*You* brought it up," Libby shot back.

"Only because you demanded I tell you why I couldn't take you hiking!"

"I have a right to know why you're canceling on me again! And why don't you put your pants on?"

Rand snatched his pants from the coffee table and shoved his legs into them. He hopped up and down as he yanked them on, almost tumbling over. "The most important thing here is the Collins family. I'm going to meet them tomorrow at St. Mary's."

Libby sighed. "Okay. I'll get over it. Sorry for messing up your evening with Rachel."

"How old is she, by the way?" Tessa asked from the couch.

"Mom!" Libby said.

"Here, take a look at this picture," Rand said, ignoring Tessa and walking to the kitchen. He returned with the photograph of Georgia. "She's your age, you know."

Libby studied the picture for a long time, then broke out into a smile. "She seems so happy."

"I know. That's why it's so crazy that she's sick."

"What does she have?"

"Cystic fibrosis. Ever heard of it?"

"Yeah, but I don't know what it does to you. I'll google it." Libby looked up. "I want to meet her."

"What? Why?"

"Because she seems nice. Take me with you tomorrow."

"I don't know if that's such a good idea. They're only expecting me."

"Come on, Dad. Please?"

"Maybe some other time." He took the picture from Libby and dropped it on the coffee table as if doing that would make her forget her request. Libby could be quite stubborn, and once she got an idea in her head she rarely let it drop.

LATER THAT NIGHT, just before he went to bed, his phone rang. It was Rachel.

"Hey," she said sleepily.

"Hey. You all right?"

"Yeah," she said.

"Sorry about earlier. I forgot Libby was supposed to come over. She usually doesn't bring her mother, though."

"It's no problem. Tessa's very pretty."

Rand ignored that. "And I'm sorry for not mentioning the other thing. It's true—I'm a ghost hunter on the side, for lack of a better term. I still spend most of my time teaching, though." He let the words hang there, but Rachel said nothing, waiting for him to elaborate. "It's just every now and then, the material I teach… word kind of gets around. People start realizing that they've experienced these things before and they get curious, or afraid. So they come to me and tell me they're scared and don't know what to do. Most people don't believe them when they say they are dealing with a haunting. So I feel obligated to step in and help them out."

"I know," Rachel said. "I get it. I've thought about it a lot, and it all sounds kind of crazy to me, but I can get around it. I can find a way."

Rand rolled over in bed, slightly confused. This was usually when women broke up with him. "You're all right with it?"

"Yeah. I mean, you're helping people, right?"

"They tell me I helped them."

"And not hurting anyone?"

"No, of course not."

"And not scamming anyone?"

"Please. I never take money for these types of cases."

"Okay. Then I would love to hear more about it."

"Good. Maybe you can come hiking with me and Libby on Sunday?"

"I think you should spend that time with your daughter. The next night we can go for dinner and you can tell me all about what you found at St. Mary's. I feel so bad for that girl."

"Me too," Rand said. "I'll call you tomorrow, okay?"

"Good night, Rand."

He set the phone down and rolled over again. As he drifted off, he reconsidered the conversation. Perhaps it would've been best if they had broken up.

Although the relationship was new and showed a lot of promise, Rand knew from experience that his investigations and his relationships rarely mixed well. When he got involved with a case, the supernatural tended to affect him along with his client, which meant his past girlfriends had experienced terrifying situations that they didn't deserve. The last thing he wanted was for that trend to continue with Rachel.

This case should be straightforward enough, Rand told himself. *If there's a ghost, send it away, and everyone moves on. In and out. Simple and easy.*

5

St. Mary's was the largest hospital in the city, but Rand had never fully realized just how huge it was. It was the first time he had ever been there, and it was like its own miniature town rather than a medical facility.

Weaving his way into the parking garage, he would have gotten lost had it not been for the clear signs, the bright arrows painted on the asphalt, and the occasional worker wearing a yellow vest, waving him in.

Going above and beyond, he thought, impressed with the ease of finding a spot when the garage was already so full.

The lobby reminded him of the atrium entrance of a large mall rather than a hospital. His footsteps echoed off the high walls, and many hallways branched off that main section. The reception desk in front of him seemed like a logical place to start.

Rand approached a friendly woman, who greeted him with a smile. It was genuine—Rand got good vibes from the woman. "Good afternoon, sir. Welcome to St. Mary's."

"Hi there," Rand said. "I was wondering if you could point me to the coffee shop."

"Certainly. Which one?"

Rand chuckled. He should have figured there'd be more than one in a place this size. "Your nearest."

"The Bean Factory is our own personal brand. We import the finest coffees from all over the world." She pointed toward a corridor that led away from the main lobby. "If you go this way and turn right, it will be on your left."

Rand smirked. Her sales pitch was well-practiced. "Thank you very much."

"You're welcome. Have a blessed day."

Rand followed the woman's directions, looking around as he did. Hospitals usually gave him the creeps, but at St. Mary's he didn't even feel like he was in a hospital. A man in a suit passed him going the other way, an employee badge dangling from his coat. He nodded at Rand when he saw him and wished him a good afternoon.

The coffee shop was exactly where the greeter said it would be. Nick and Maria Collins sat in the corner, talking low between themselves.

When Maria noticed him, she gave him a small smile and stood. Nick followed her gaze, spotted him, and did the same.

"Thank you for coming," Nick said, shaking his hand. "You made it here alright? We figured this would be the easiest place to meet in this huge place."

"No problem at all," Rand said. "Should we get started?"

"You want to grab something before we go?" Nick pointed his thumb toward the counter, where a young girl enthusiastically took orders.

"Had my coffee in the car," Rand said.

Nick looked away as he slowly nodded. Rand saw that he was nervous.

"We can head up, then," Nick said.

"Perfect. You lead the way."

Nᴉᴄᴋ ᴀɴᴅ Mᴀʀɪᴀ brought him deeper into St. Mary's to an elevator, which they rode to the tenth floor.

The doors opened to the entrance of the ward. A single security guard manned the desk, and he smiled and rose when he saw Nick and Maria.

"We're back," Maria said.

"Sure thing." The man nodded and handed them a clipboard where they could sign in.

"This is a friend," Nick said, nodding his head toward Rand. "Wanted to introduce him to Georgia."

Rand extended his hand, and the security guard took it. "Randolph Casey."

"Harold," said the guard. "I'm the main security on duty up here." He was a stout black man, with a round frame filling out his beige uniform. What hair remained on his head was short and grey.

"Pleased to meet you."

"Meeting Georgia for the first time, hmm? Good luck in there, my friend."

"Will I need it?"

"That girl's one of a kind." He couldn't help but smile as he said it.

"So I hear."

Harold took the clipboard away and replaced it with a binder, which he opened. "Simple process for non-relative visitors. Sign in here, then we'll give you a name tag. When you leave, you'll sign out."

"No problem," Rand said. He produced his own pen from his pocket and signed his name. Harold gave him a name tag sticker, with "RANDOLPH" already written in big black letters.

Rand put it on his chest. "Next time, just Rand. It's what friends call me."

Harold nodded and smiled. "No problem, Mr. Rand."

Rand thought he saw a knowing look in the security guard's eyes, and he wondered if someone had told him who he was and what he was there to do.

WHEN RAND FOLLOWED Nick and Maria into room 1019, it was like he'd stepped out of a hospital and into the bedroom of a teenage girl. There were posters of singers on her walls, and around them were photographs of her and her friends. There was a desk in the corner stacked with schoolwork and a vase of flowers. Someone had recently burned a floral-scented candle. The hospital bed had been removed and replaced with a single, narrow bed, with a fluffy pink comforter and a bunch of pillows.

Georgia propped herself against the headboard, a computer on her lap, knees bent up. An oxygen tube ran from her nostrils to a fixture on the wall.

"We're back," Maria said.

Georgia closed her laptop. She and Rand met eyes, and she gave him a beaming smile, the same as in the photograph he had. "Is this the ghost man?"

Rand couldn't help but laugh. "Yes, I am the ghost man. Randolph Casey. Friends call me Rand." He offered his hand and Georgia took it, giving it a single, dramatic pump.

"Georgia Collins. Friends call me Georgia. Nice to meet you, Rand."

"I guess that means we're friends."

She threw her legs over the edge of the bed and sat up. She wore an oversized t-shirt, black leggings, and socks, one that was blue and the other orange. Her blonde hair was wavy.

"You knew he was coming," Maria told her daughter. "You couldn't have put something else on?"

"Take me as I am," Georgia told Rand, spreading her arms.

"Will do." Already Rand felt her warmth and vibrancy.

"Have a seat," Nick said, pulling up a chair from the other side of the room.

"This is exciting," Georgia said, eyeing Rand. "A real-life ghost man."

"I take it you've never met a ghost man before," Rand said.

"All I ever get to meet are doctors, nurses, and psychologists. This is so cool. I hope you know I'm going to tell all my friends about you."

Rand laughed. "Fine by me."

"Come on," Georgia said. "I'll give you a tour of the place."

Maria sat up straight. "Honey, Mr. Rand just got here. I'm sure he doesn't want to walk around the whole place."

"It's fine," Rand said, standing. "I actually would appreciate a tour. I've never been inside St. Mary's before."

That, and Rand already knew he wanted to separate Georgia from her parents if he was going to ask her about the ghost she was seeing. He figured it was the best way to get her to open up fully about her experience.

Georgia unhooked her tubing from the device on the wall, which hissed before she twisted the knob to turn off the oxygen. She hooked up to a portable tank on wheels, which was inside a black bag that looked like a rolling suitcase. Then she donned a pair of oversized and ridiculous purple sunglasses, and said, "Shall we?"

6

.

"This is the tenth ward—for children, so that's why it's got all these kiddie things on the wall," Georgia explained as they strolled. "I'm under eighteen, so they still put me here instead of a normal ward. I'm, like, the oldest person here, I think. Or I am now that Thomas died. Did my parents tell you about Thomas?"

"They mentioned him, yes," Rand said.

"Yeah. He was another CF kid and, like, my best friend for a while. He lived here too, but we only really talked on video chat."

"Why is that?" Rand asked.

They passed by the nurses' station and Georgia waved her hand like she was a pageant queen. "Hello, hello, everyone." The three nurses behind the desk all stopped what they were doing to tell her good afternoon.

Georgia said, "I'm definitely the favorite around here."

"I can see that," Rand said. "So why did you and Thomas only talk on video chat?"

"Oh yeah. It's a CF thing. People with CF shouldn't be around other people with CF. Don't tell anyone, but we totally used to meet up sometimes, anyway. But we'd wear masks, so it's cool, right?

Hospital masks, not like Halloween masks. Although that would've been fun."

"Your secret is safe with me," Rand said.

Harold the security guard sat at his desk near the elevator.

"Miss Georgia," he said when he saw her coming. "Loving those stunner shades."

"I wish I'd known, I would have gotten you a pair." Georgia and Harold high-fived each other over the desk. "I'm heading down for some ice cream with my new boyfriend. Call me on the secret phone if you need help taking down any perps."

"Will do, Miss Georgia."

She pressed the down button on the elevator.

As they waited, Rand said, "You're going to start rumors around here about us."

"Be proud, Ghost Man. I'm quite a catch."

The elevator dinged, and they got inside.

"By the way, I'm on antibiotics right now and it kind of makes me sensitive to bright light. That's why I'm wearing sunglasses. I mean, I'm a freak, but at least I know it's not normal to wear sunglasses inside."

"Doesn't bother me," Rand said. "The sun never sets on being a badass."

Georgia looked up at him for a few seconds. "You're right. I think I'm going to like you."

The elevator opened on the ground floor and Georgia led him down the giant corridor. "The cafeteria here is pretty good. I've had everything on the menu like three times. We're gonna get ice cream, by the way. The ice cream there is totally awesome. It's soft serve. Hey, Mr. Steve." Georgia held out her hand and high-fived a guy in a suit as he passed.

"Looking good, Georgia," he said.

"Have a good day administrating."

"I will."

Georgia said, "That's Steve, one of the hospital administrators. Like, big boss. He asks me before he fires people, though."

"You should tell him I found his parking garage to be easy to navigate."

"I will!" Georgia lit up. "Seriously, that would make him so happy to hear."

The St. Mary's cafeteria was the size of a large restaurant and a myriad of sweet and spicy aromas filled the air. The walls of the dining area were all floor-to-ceiling windows, which looked out over a garden. Some of the employees had taken their lunch outside to enjoy the autumn weather.

"I don't get why they do this," Georgia said, pointing to a podium at the entrance of the cafeteria. There was a plate with the day's main dish—salmon with a red sauce, covered in a clear plastic container. The food already looked like it had grown cold and gross. "I mean, I know they're trying to show it off, but look at it! It doesn't take long for it to start rotting."

"I agree," Rand said.

Georgia led him to the soft-serve ice cream machine. "Chocolate, vanilla, or strawberry?" she asked.

"All three," Rand told her.

"I knew it! We're spirit animals." She grabbed a cup and pulled on the levers one by one.

"Soul mates?"

"Right. What did I say?" She handed the cup to him and then prepared her own ice cream. They walked to the cash registers, where an elderly woman with glasses was ringing people up. "Oh, sweet! Mrs. Eloise is working. Check this out." She elbowed him in the ribs.

"Good afternoon, Miss Georgia," said Mrs. Eloise. "Ice cream for lunch?"

"They brought lunch up to the room today." She turned and winked at Rand when Mrs. Eloise wasn't looking.

"And who is this?" she asked, eyeing Rand up and down.

"My new boyfriend. It's our first date."

"What have I told you about older men, Miss Georgia?"

"I know, but I have to make these mistakes for myself. Duh!"

Mrs. Eloise smiled and pressed a button on her computer, which made the cash drawer open, but she only pushed it closed again. "It's on me."

"Thank you!"

Georgia grabbed the sleeve of Rand's jacket and pulled him away as if trying to move him along before Mrs. Eloise changed her mind.

She took two plastic spoons from the counter on the other side of the register and they sat at a table in the far corner of the dining area.

"Mmm," Georgia said after her first bite of ice cream. "See? It's the best. Even better than those expensive places they have downtown."

Rand tasted the ice cream, and he had to admit it was actually pretty damn good.

"So, like, how much are my parents paying you to come here and talk to me?" Georgia asked.

"They're not paying me anything."

"Really? Wow. You could totally charge top dollar for being the best ghost man in town."

"I'm the only ghost man in town."

"Then you can charge even more. It's like a *neech*."

"A *niche*."

"So, basically, everyone thinks I'm crazy because I see Thomas around. But doesn't it make sense that I would see him?"

"It does, believe it or not," Rand said. "Spirits who linger in our world feel they weren't ready to pass away when they did. Maybe it was too soon, or it was tragic, or they felt like they had unfinished business."

Georgia's mouth fell open as she stared at him. "Wow. Thomas fits all three of those." She took another bite of ice cream. "It's also so cool to talk to someone who believes in this stuff. Everyone else tries to make me think 'rationally.' "

"I'm definitely a believer," Rand said. "It's very real. Do you believe in life after death?"

Georgia shrugged. "I guess I do now. I mean, sometimes I visit the chapel here and Father Calvin talks about God and Jesus and how we go to heaven when we die. Not sure if I only like the idea of it because I'm so close to dying or because it actually makes sense. You know?"

"Close to dying?" Rand asked.

"Yeah. CF people don't live very long. And about a month ago I collapsed and had to go to the emergency room and all this stuff. My parents don't even like it when I walk around—they say I should use a wheelchair because my lungs are so shitty, but I don't like that. The only reason they let me go now is because you're here and they didn't want to get into a fight about it in front of you. So basically I'm using you for free ice cream and to walk on my own two legs like a normal person." She chuckled. "But seriously. They've given me a year, or maybe two. The doctors say I need a lung transplant."

Rand frowned.

"I'm over it," Georgia said. "I've known my life would be short all along and don't have any regrets. I feel like I'm making the most of every day."

"That's good."

"Do you think that's why I can see Thomas?" Georgia said. "Because I'm so close to the end? I read something like that on the internet."

Rand cleared his throat and put his empty ice cream cup on the table. "Sometimes people are more in tune with the spiritual world when they are closer to joining it themselves."

"Wow," Georgia said. "Since you're the ghost man, do you think we'd be able to hang out after—"

"I would like to think you would move on. As you said, you don't have any regrets and live every day to the fullest. What reason would you have to stay behind?"

"To haunt people," Georgia said, dropping her spoon into her empty cup. "Rattle chains and all that stuff."

Rand smiled and shook his head.

"Why are you laughing at me?" Georgia asked.

"I'm not. It's just that you remind me of my daughter."

"Your daughter must be awesome."

"She is. She's sixteen."

"Really? I want to meet her."

"She said the same thing about you."

"No way!"

"Yes way."

"That settles it. You gotta give me her number." Georgia reached into her pocket and pulled out her cell phone. She unlocked it and passed it across the table to him. The screen was cracked so badly that it looked like it had been shot. Rand didn't move. "What's wrong? Don't mix business and personal stuff or whatever?"

Finally, Rand tapped the phone app on her screen and added Libby's number to her contacts. "Her name is Libby. She texts all the time, so I'm sure you'll get a response if you send her a message."

"Sweet," Georgia said, taking her phone back. "Making new friends is awesome. Makes me feel more normal."

"So now that I've made you a friend," Rand said, "why don't you tell me a little more about Thomas?"

"Ah. Nothing for free from this guy, I see."

"Not like that. I'm just interested in your experience."

"Do you want to know about alive Thomas or dead Thomas?"

"Both."

"Hmm." She rolled her eyes up to the ceiling as she recollected. "Well, alive Thomas was cool. He was sixteen, and he stayed on a different floor than me, and the nurses wouldn't let us hang out, but I told you that already. Hmm, what else? He liked rock-and-roll music and college football. He said he always wanted to play, but his lungs were shit. He had a crush on some girl named Kristen, who volunteers on his floor, but she avoided him when he asked her out because I guess she doesn't like sick boys. Ugh." She stuck out her tongue. "Anyway, he deserves much better. Or, he deserved, I guess. He crashed about three months ago. Health just went splat. Went into a coma, they had to operate, but then he never woke up. I cried at his funeral."

"He sounds like a pretty normal teenager," Rand said. "Sorry for your loss."

"Yeah." She sat in her chair with her hands between her thighs, staring off to the side through her dark sunglasses. For the first time, her energy seemed to leave her as she reminisced about her friend. "It really messed me up when he died," she said after a few seconds. "Even though I've totally been at peace with the whole dying young thing… I don't know. I guess when he passed it made my situation all more real."

"I can't imagine it was easy," Rand said.

"But then he came back. Started visiting me in my room as a ghost."

Rand leaned forward and folded his hands together on the table. "When does he visit you?"

"At night. Like, really late at night. Or early in the morning, whatever you want to call it. He wakes me up every time, which is kind of annoying, but then again he's a ghost, so what does he care?"

"Does he speak to you?"

"Not really," Georgia said. "He's mostly just *there*. Watching. It would be creepy if it wasn't Thomas. I try to talk to him, and it looks like he wants to answer, but I can't hear anything. His mouth never moves."

"What do you say to him?"

"Nothing much. Just ask him what he's doing or if he's okay. Once, I asked if it hurts being dead. I also tell him not to watch me shower and call him a pervert."

"I see. What is he wearing when you see him?"

"The hospital gown." Georgia wrinkled her nose. "Which is weird, because Thomas hated wearing those, and never did."

Rand also found that strange. Usually ghosts appeared as they had when they were alive.

"And how do you feel when Thomas is present?"

Georgia looked at him and removed her sunglasses for the first time. "I don't know. Curious? I mean, there's a ghost standing in my room, so I, like, want to know everything about what it's like to be dead. But he won't tell me anything. Which, now that I think about it, is totally a Thomas thing to do. He could be such a punk sometimes." She smiled.

"Does it bring you comfort to have someone watch over you?"

"Yeah. But if he was my guardian angel, then I figured he would be more intentional about it. He just stands there and stares. Shouldn't you be writing all this down?"

Rand tapped his temple. "It's all up here."

"You don't think I'm crazy, do you? Everyone else thinks I'm nuts."

"Not at all," Rand said. "Encountering the spiritual world is a lot more common than you realize. It's a special gift you should be proud of."

That made her smile, although Rand had not been completely honest. Usually it was more of a dangerous liability, as it was in his case.

Georgia opened a flap on her black bag and checked her oxygen tank. "I'm low."

7

When they returned to the room, Nick and Maria were sitting on Georgia's bed, watching the news on television. They stood when Rand and Georgia walked in.

"Hey, now. I know these doors don't lock from the inside, but you should at least hang something on the handle," Georgia said.

"Come on, honey," Maria said. "Not in front of guests."

Georgia unhooked her cannula from the portable oxygen cylinder and reattached it to the wall fixture. She twisted the knob to get it flowing again.

"How was the tour?" Nick asked Rand.

"She's a fantastic guide."

"You can leave a tip," Georgia said.

"It was great to meet you today, Georgia," Rand said.

"Aw, leaving already? I thought we would watch TV. Or talk about ghosts some more."

"I'll come back," Rand said. When he said that, Nick and Maria gave him a worried look.

"Are you sure I'm not crazy?" Georgia asked. "Do I have sanity problems on top of my lung problems?"

Rand laughed. "Of course you're not crazy."

"Tell *them* that, please," Georgia said, nodding toward her parents.

"We don't think you're crazy," Maria said. "It's just… we're curious."

"Right," Georgia said, smirking. "Is this the part where y'all go out in the hall and talk about me?"

"I actually think that's a good idea," Rand said.

Nick and Maria followed Rand out into the hallway. Before the door closed, Georgia shouted after him, "Tell them I haven't lost my mind!"

Nick and Maria stood close to Rand in a small huddle, Maria with her arms folded across her chest and Nick with his hands in his pockets. They wore worried expressions as if Rand was a doctor about to give them bad news.

"Your daughter is quite the character," Rand said. His attempt to ease their tension worked, and they chuckled.

"Hope she wasn't too much," Nick said.

"Not at all. She has an amazing outlook, considering her situation."

"She's always been that way, thank the Lord," Maria said. "No matter what comes, she'll always find a way to smile."

"She seems truly special," said Rand. "And I want to help."

"Do you think she needs help? With this… little problem."

"First, we need to determine if it's a problem at all," Rand told them.

"Okay. And how do we go about doing that?"

"Georgia said that when the spirit visits her, she speaks with him and gets the impression he's trying to respond, but she can't hear anything. He is most likely responding, but she's unable to discern it because of the divide between the realms in which they're existing." Nick and Maria gave him a blank stare. "I know it sounds far out there, but trust me. I've been doing this a while."

"So what do you propose?" Nick asked. For the first time, he looked frightened.

"In my bag, I have an EVP recorder. That stands for electronic voice phenomenon. It's the practice of using a device to pick up voices from the spiritual world. I hope to capture their conversation so I can know what the spirit is saying to her. From there, we'll make the judgment call if its presence is helping Georgia cope with her situation, or if it's harmful."

Nick let out a long breath. "I have to say, this stuff is really weird to me. I almost can't believe I'm having this discussion right now. But with all we've been through with Georgia, I guess nothing should surprise me anymore." Maria put a hand on her husband's arm.

"I know what you mean," Rand said. "And I understand. But your mind is open to the possibility, and that's good."

Nick nodded.

"And another thing. I want to plant the recorder without Georgia's knowledge. If she knows it's there, it could alter the natural results."

"Okay," Nick said.

"I'll come back tomorrow and check the recorder. If Georgia says Thomas didn't appear, then I'll change out the batteries and we'll try again. I'll keep coming as long as I have to until we get a positive recording."

At that, Maria's eyes widened. "I didn't realize this would be such a process."

"With the paranormal, we have to be flexible," Rand said with a shrug.

"And uh…" Nick scratched at the stubble on his beard. "How much do we owe you for your services?"

"Nothing," Rand said.

"What?"

"I don't charge for what I do. I am happy to help."

Nick leaned back and let out the large breath he'd been holding. "It's just, with the hospital bills and the procedures—"

Rand held up a hand to stop him. "I understand. The last thing people need when dealing with the paranormal is having to worry about how they will pay."

"Again, thank you so much," Maria said.

"My pleasure."

They went back inside, where Georgia had resumed looking at her computer and leaning against the many pillows on her headboard. "I hope you said good things about me."

"Of course," Rand said.

"I shot your daughter a text, by the way."

"She'll be excited to hear from you."

Maria said, "Rand, would you like some of this cake? One of Georgia's friends brought it by yesterday, but it's so big we couldn't finish."

"No, thank you. Still full from the ice cream."

"And there's plenty more where that came from," Georgia said, sitting up. "As long as Mrs. Eloise is working, that is. I have to pee."

"Georgia!" Maria chided.

She removed her cannula and shuffled to the bathroom.

As soon as the door closed, Rand reached into his satchel, which he'd left on the floor near the room's entrance, and pulled out the small recorder. He pressed the button on the side and double-checked that the battery was full. Then he hit the record button and placed it under Georgia's bed.

Nick and Maria watched him as he worked.

The toilet flushed. As she walked out, Georgia waved her hand under an antiseptic dispenser on the wall and it squirted some into her palm.

"I have to hit the road," Rand told her. "It was a pleasure to meet you."

"You too, Ghost Man. When are you coming back?"

"Maybe tomorrow. Or the day after."

"Wow. I must need lots of evaluation."

"I'm only in it for the ice cream."

Georgia laughed. She plopped down onto her bed and placed the cannula into her nostrils. "I'll see you then."

Rand couldn't help but smile. Georgia definitely reminded him of his own daughter. He quickly glanced toward the bottom of her bed where the recorder was hidden. The last thing this girl needed was to be bothered by a spirit who no longer belonged in the world of the living.

He found himself hoping, maybe even praying, that his findings would be benign.

8

Although it was an early fall morning, Rand felt no chill. The sun was bright and clear, warming him, and he reveled in the fresh air.

He reached the top of the rock hill he'd been chugging away at, a small amount of sweat soaking his grey t-shirt.

Forty years old and I've still got it. The hiking, along with a consistent gym routine, kept his body more muscular than most men his age. That and his thick black hair consistently made people think he was younger than he actually was.

When he turned, Libby was only halfway up, face buried in her phone. Her friend Bailey struggled, wavering side to side with each step, hands on her hips as if she had cramps.

"What's going on?" Rand shouted down at them. "We're making terrible time."

Libby looked up and shielded her eyes from the sun with her hand. "What's the rush?"

"This needs to at least somewhat resemble exercise."

"Being on the volleyball team at school isn't enough?" Libby asked, resuming her texting. "I don't need to do anything extra."

Rand sat on a rock and tightened the laces on his hiking boots while he waited for the girls to join him. Libby reached the top of the hill first, and Bailey struggled up a few minutes later.

"Y'all go on," she said, panting and face beet-red. "Leave me here to die."

"It's not that bad," Rand said. "Can you tell my daughter to get off her phone?"

"Libby, your dad says get off your phone."

Libby ignored them both.

"Who is she texting?"

"Probably Justin."

"Who the hell is Justin?"

Libby shot her friend a look. "Bailey!"

"You didn't tell him?"

"Who is Justin?" Rand asked again.

"He's no one," Libby insisted.

"He's her *boyfriend*," Bailey said.

"Not a boyfriend," Libby said. "We're just talking."

"Looks like texting," Rand said. "Show me a picture of him."

"What? No. Don't be weird."

"Come on, I want to see this guy."

"Why?"

"Because I can tell everything I need to know just by looking at him."

"You don't need to know anything about him." Libby turned her back, thumbs working furiously on the screen. Something in her texts made her smile.

Rand turned to Bailey. "Bailey." He waved her over.

"Yeah, I've got him on Instagram."

"Bailey!" Libby cried.

Bailey took out her phone, brought up Justin's Instagram, and showed Rand. All he saw was a skinny kid with black hair that was too long, a bunch of pimples, weird glasses, and a guitar.

"He looks like a dweeb," Rand said.

"He is not!" Libby said. "And no one says dweeb anymore."

"Then why did I just say it?"

"Because you're being rude. You've never even met him."

"He really is nice, Mr. Rand," Bailey said.

"Does he play football? Or do MMA?"

"No. Guitar."

"Let me hear some of his songs." Rand stood and led the way down the other side of the hill.

"I don't think he has any."

"Why does he bother playing guitar if he doesn't record any music? What good is that?"

"Dad!" Libby shouted again.

The hill's slope increased and Rand turned his body sideways to get better traction with his boots. He let momentum take him and jogged the rest of the way down the hill. "Lot of rocks down here, so don't stare at the phone," Rand called back to the girls.

"Here's a good way to change the subject," Libby said when she fell in beside her father. "You'll never guess who just texted me. Georgia Collins."

"Who is that?" Bailey asked.

"Yeah, she told me she did," Rand said. "She's a nice girl. Reminds me a lot of you. I think you two would get along."

"She invited me to hang out with her at St. Mary's," Libby said. "That was quick."

"She's really friendly. You should go up to visit her sometime."

"I asked you to take me when you went, but you refused."

"Now that I've met her and assessed the situation, you can go," Rand said.

"I don't need your permission anymore. She invited me herself." Her phone dinged with another message. "She calls you the ghost man."

"Who is this girl?" Bailey asked again.

"Ah, she wants me to tell you she saw Thomas again last night."

Rand halted. "Really?"

Libby froze too, sensing her father's sudden change. "Yeah. See?" She held her phone toward Rand. He took it and read the message.

Tell your dad I saw Thomas last night.

"Who is Thomas?" Libby asked. Then comprehension dawned on her face. "Is that her ghost?"

"Yeah," Rand said, handing the phone back. As soon as they finished hiking, he'd ride over to St. Mary's and retrieve the recorder.

"Is this one of those haunting things you do, Mr. Rand?" Bailey asked. She waved her hands at him. "I don't want to hear about it. Your stories always keep me up at night." She trudged off down the trail.

"Is she okay?" Libby asked, squinting in the bright sunlight. "I mean… is Thomas a good ghost?"

"That's what I need to find out."

Something struck Rand hard on the cheek, just underneath his left eye, and he flinched. The rock that had hit him, about the size of a quarter, landed at his feet. "Ow!" He brought his hand up to the painful spot and felt warm blood trickle down his fingers.

"What the hell? Someone just threw a rock at you," Libby said. They both looked in the direction it had flown from.

They were alone on the trail.

Rand inspected the red on his fingertips.

"Where did that come from?" Libby asked. "That looks bad."

Rand looked around again, but there was definitely no one else in the area. Strange, since it felt like the rock was thrown from close range.

"Do you think it's one of those weird things that happen to you when you're doing a case?" Libby asked.

"Come on," Rand said, ignoring her. "Let's finish the trail."

AROUND ONE O'CLOCK, Rand pulled up in front of the huge house that belonged to Tessa's new fiancé, Bill. Rand hated going there, but Libby and Bailey were going to stay with the couple for the rest of the weekend, so he had to drop them off.

"Dad, your face is still bleeding," Libby said. "Come inside and put something on it."

"I'm fine."

"Don't be like that. Come on!"

"I don't want to go in there."

"It's a nice place, not a torture chamber." Libby yanked on his arm as she opened the car door. Rand sighed and killed the engine.

Tessa greeted them on the porch before they could finish crossing the huge front lawn. When she saw Rand approaching, her arms crossed and her expression grew dark.

"What's going on?" she asked.

"Someone threw a rock at Dad and he needs help."

"And why would anyone want to throw a rock at you, Randolph?" Tessa smiled.

"Hilarious."

"Let me see." Tessa grabbed Rand's wrist and forced his hand away from the cut. He felt the sticky blood all down his cheek, and the gash still pained him.

"Yeah, that's bad," Tessa said. "Come on. I have some alcohol inside."

"The medical kind or the drinking kind?" Rand said. Tessa gave him a look. "You don't have to do this," he added.

"Trust me, I know."

Rand had never been inside Bill's house before. He'd purposely avoided it. The man's living room was the size of Rand's entire home. Tessa sat him on a plush couch he would have happily slept on every night if he owned it.

Tessa returned a minute later with a bottle of rubbing alcohol, bandages, and a wet cloth. The cut stung as she cleaned it.

"Quit being a baby," she said.

"I didn't wince at all."

"You wanted to."

"Hey, did you know Libby has a boyfriend?"

"Justin. Yeah, he's a nice kid."

"You've met him?"

"Of course."

"Why did I not even know about him until today?"

"Because she knows you won't get along with her boyfriends."

"That's not the point," Rand said. "He's a dweeb."

Tessa applied the bandage to his face. "And this is why she hasn't introduced the two of you."

"And he pretends to play guitar just to get girls. I can't believe that worked on Libby. She's too smart for that."

"I admit, he's a bit weird, but he's good for Libby right now."

"What is that supposed to mean?"

Tessa used the wet rag to wipe the dried blood from Rand's cheek. The giant diamond engagement ring that Bill had given her threatened to give him a new cut. "It means we need to keep her dating him as long as possible. Because eventually she'll break up with him and date some bad boy to overcompensate."

"Why do you think that?"

"Because that's exactly what I did when I met you."

"I was *not* a bad boy."

Tessa snorted. "Motorcycle, no money, didn't care about anything."

"That was before the ghosts."

"Now you're just a haunted, semi-reformed bad boy. Don't worry, I found my happy medium."

"Bill is not a happy medium. He's an even bigger dweeb than Justin."

Tessa slapped his shoulder. "Rand, you don't even know him."

"I know the type. Come on."

Just then, Bill appeared at the entrance of the living room. He wore a white tennis outfit with shorts Rand considered far too short and a visor wrapped around his balding head. "Oh. Hi, Rand." His body grew rigid and nervous.

Rand nodded at him. "Bill."

"I'm going to go hit some balls with Frank," Bill said.

"Okay. Have fun," Tessa said.

Bill shuffled out the front door.

"I bet he likes hitting balls," Rand said.

"Shut up. I'm done, so you can leave now."

"You think he heard me earlier?"

"Rand. It's time for you to go."

Rand stood and ran his fingertips over the bandage on his face. "Nice patchwork, Tess."

"You're welcome."

"By the way, remember when I slipped on Adam's Peak in Sri Lanka? Gashed my thigh open from here to here, and no one was around for miles?"

"Yeah, yeah," Tessa said, "you don't need me or anyone else to fix you up. But it makes Libby happy to see it. That's the only reason I do it."

"Not the only reason." He smirked.

She shuffled him toward the front door. "Goodbye, Rand."

"Tell Libby to bring that guy over to my house next week. I have some questions for him."

"Sure thing, Rand." Tessa's tone was flat as she shut the door behind him.

Rand normally would have had no problem lingering a few more minutes to agitate his ex, but Georgia Collins returned to his mind, and the recorder underneath her bed that hopefully contained all the answers he needed.

9

Back at the hospital, Rand went to the tenth floor and greeted Harold. The guard smiled wide and shook his hand.

"How's everything going today, Harold?" Rand asked.

"It's a blessed day," he said. "Here to see Miss Georgia?"

"I am." Rand signed the paper in the binder and Harold gave him a nametag sticker. This time, he only wrote "RAND" on it.

"She's a sweetheart," Harold said, still smiling. "One of the best kids who's come through here. Shame about the condition she's in."

"I agree," Rand said. "Do you spend much time with the children, Harold?"

"I do when I can get away from my post," he said. "I have an open-desk policy around here." He leaned over and opened a big drawer in a filing cabinet behind him. Inside was an assortment of candy and toys. "For the younger ones."

Rand wondered if Harold was this friendly with all the visitors. He also wondered if he knew about Georgia's little paranormal problem.

"Lucky kids," Rand said. "Maybe I'll take advantage of that open-desk policy myself."

Harold laughed. "Be my guest."

Rand found Nick and Maria in the room, huddled together on the couch and reading something on an iPad. The television was on the news channel and muted. Georgia was not there. A chair propped open the door, but Rand knocked on the doorframe anyway.

Nick and Maria looked up and smiled when they saw him.

"Come in," Maria said, standing. Nick joined her.

"Good afternoon," he said, as he walked in. He glanced around the room, but Georgia was gone.

"She stepped out," Nick told him.

Rand bent down and snatched the recorder from underneath Georgia's bed. The battery signal flashed red, but it was still on. He pressed the button, turned it off, and slipped it into his jacket pocket just as Georgia appeared in the doorway, rolling her oxygen tank behind her.

"Hey, it's the ghost man," she said, smiling. She removed her big sunglasses. "You'll never guess who I've been talking to."

"Libby already told me," Rand said.

"She seems cool. We're going to hang out soon."

"Libby is my daughter," Rand told Maria, who seemed confused by the conversation.

"Oh. How old is she?"

"Sixteen."

"What happened to you?" Georgia asked. She stared at the bandage on his cheek.

"Little hiking accident. No big deal."

"You used your face to break your fall?"

Rand laughed. "Something like that."

"Hey, you know Bonnie, the nurse?"

"No. Haven't met her."

"When we walked by the nurse's station yesterday and we waved, there were three there, right? Do you remember the one with the red hair?"

Rand hadn't been paying attention. "No, I don't."

"Oh. Well, she asked me about you. She thinks you're cute. You should get her number."

"Ah, I see. I'm actually already seeing someone."

"I won't tell her that," Georgia said. "I don't like to break hearts." She unhooked her tubing from her portable cylinder and attached the end of the tube to the fixture on the wall. "If you want to hang out again, just give me some time. I need to rest." Georgia's breath was quick, as if she'd been jogging.

"Take a breather, then," Rand said. "I have to step out and make a phone call anyway."

"Sure thing, Ghost Man." Georgia settled in and grabbed her laptop from the foot of the bed.

Rand went back into the hallway and Nick followed him. Nick kicked the chair away and let the hospital door fall into place.

"Is there somewhere private I can listen to this?" Rand asked, patting his pocket.

"There's a staff room at the end of the hall that doesn't get much use," Nick said. "You can try there. May I... come with you?"

"It's best if I listen alone first if you don't mind," Rand said. If there *were* otherworldly voices on the recorder, he didn't want to frighten his client. Besides, there was no telling what they would say.

"Right," Nick said. He already seemed afraid of what would be on there. "Georgia mentioned he came to her last night."

"Then let's hope we have something here."

"Break room is all the way at the end of the hall, on the left."

THE BREAK ROOM had a warm and musty odor to it. When Rand flipped the light switch—only one shimmered to life—he saw that the air vent had been closed. Inside, there was a round table with two chairs, an empty countertop, and a nonfunctioning refrigerator.

Rand slung his satchel off and took out his laptop. He connected the recorder and downloaded the file onto his desktop, then deleted the first hours of footage until he found the material recorded at night. It didn't take long before the audio line went flat, indicating that Georgia had gone to sleep.

Deep into the night, the line zigzagged to life. He placed his beginning point and clicked play.

He put on his large, noise-canceling headphones to listen closely.

It sounded like a distant whisper. He turned the volume on his computer all the way up and used his software to amplify the audio.

After listening to the garbled voice several times, he finally discerned words.

Wake up.

Rand's skin crawled. He had never gotten totally accustomed to hearing the voice of a spirit. The first contact always made him feel very uncomfortable.

Wake up, the voice said again.

There was definitely something visiting Georgia in the middle of the night.

There were long sections of silence. Rand's guess was that Georgia wasn't able to hear the ghost speaking to her. Voices of spirits traveled on different frequencies, which were sometimes difficult for human ears to pick up. They usually appeared much clearer on recordings.

Wake up.

Sounds of Georgia stirring awake crept into Rand's headphones. She most likely sensed the presence.

"Thomas." Georgia's voice was clear, although groggy with sleep and raspy as always. "Tell me what you want."

There was a long bout of silence.

"I can see you're trying to say something, but I don't hear anything," Georgia said.

Thomas spoke again, but Rand could not quite make out what was said.

"My parents think I'm crazy for saying you drop by at night," Georgia told Thomas. "But they brought in this guy. A ghost man.

His name is Rand, and he's pretty cool. He's supposed to be some kind of expert."

And then Thomas responded, but this time he was louder. More agitated. Rand leaned in and paused the audio recording. The words had been unclear at first. He rewound the section and played it again, pressing the headphones into his ears and closing his eyes as he focused.

After listening three times, he thought he knew what the spirit was telling her.

Tell him to leave.

Rand leaned back in his chair and sighed. It looked like Thomas would not be that friendly toward him.

Georgia, of course, did not understand what he said. So she just kept going.

"I try to tell everyone it's fine that you come by. And that you don't hurt anything. By the way, are you ever going to do something besides stand in the corner? All you do is stare at me. It's kind of creepy, Thomas, to be honest."

Tell him to leave!

This time, the command was much more clear.

"And what do you want, anyway?" Georgia asked. She still couldn't hear Thomas. "Shouldn't you be free now? Why do you still want to hang around with CF kids? I'm guessing they don't have CF in the afterlife."

I want you to die.

Rand's breath caught.

"Does it hurt? Does it feel weird? Is there all the ice cream you could ever eat?"

I want you to die.

Thomas sounded angry when he said it. Rand was thankful Georgia couldn't hear the spirit.

"There isn't a lot of time left for me now," Georgia continued. "I realize that. But sometimes I wonder just how long I have left. And when my time comes, will I get to see you? Will I become a ghost like you? I hope not. I've been in this hospital room too much already."

Seventeen days.

Rand closed his eyes and buried his face in his hands. Georgia continued to talk to her friend in his headphones, but he heard nothing else she said.

Rand always taught in his classes to *never* ask spirits about future events. That always seemed to be the first thing people sought to learn when messing around with Ouija boards or other occult practices. And of all the milestones people most asked about—spouses, the number of children, wealth and health—the one thing that should never be asked is the hour of death.

Because these spirits knew. Time was not linear in the hereafter, so lingering presences were privy to future and past events in ways the living were not.

And if you asked about these events, they would happily tell you.

Tears burned in the corners of his eyes. This was why people were not meant to know the future. Rand felt like an intruder in Georgia's forthcoming life—her timeline, knowing something he shouldn't.

Thank God Georgia could not understand Thomas. She had not even directly asked, and still he had told her.

Although she had known this boy when he was alive, Rand knew the ghost was not a benign presence. He was bitter at having died young, jealous of Georgia still being alive, and he wanted her to join him in death. While Rand sympathized with the feelings the spirit had, they were not good for Georgia, and his rightful place was in the afterlife where he belonged.

Rand would have to remove Thomas and send him away. If he didn't, Thomas's presence would get stronger, and his voice clearer. Georgia would learn her fate sooner rather than later.

He'd had clients before who'd heard their day of death from spirits and remembered the madness they'd resorted to in order to change it. Ironically, knowing the end ruined whatever time they had left. Yet another reason why people were never meant to know.

Is it a threat instead of a premonition? Rand thought.

Meaning, would Thomas be the one to end her life in seventeen days? Or was he telling her that was when she would succumb to her condition?

Rand rewound the audio and listened again, but the spirit's meaning wasn't clear.

Rand swallowed the hard lump that had formed in his throat. Georgia's cystic fibrosis destined her for a short life, and no one knew exactly how much time she had left. Seventeen days could very well be accurate.

But if Thomas planned to cause her death in seventeen days, then Rand could save her by sending Thomas away.

He closed his laptop. He knew what he had to do—a cleansing ceremony inside Georgia's hospital room. That should force Thomas to move on to the afterlife.

And hopefully change the fate he'd promised Georgia.

10

R and composed himself and packed his equipment back into his satchel.

Although he had only met Georgia Collins yesterday, he was unnerved knowing that in seventeen days, she could possibly be gone.

And that he was the only one in the world who knew. Not even her doctors could predict it. This was when his line of work was especially difficult.

He returned to her hospital room. Nick and Maria looked up at him expectantly.

"Where's Georgia?" he asked.

"She went downstairs to get something to eat," Nick said. "Did the recording work?"

Rain pattered on the window. The storm had rolled in swiftly.

"Yes." He had to be careful with what he said here.

"And is everything all right?" Nick stood, rubbing his palms on his thighs as he did. "Is there actually a ghost?"

"Yes."

Nick and Maria exchanged a nervous look.

"Are you sure?" Nick asked, his skepticism peeking through.

"I heard it clearly on the recording," Rand said.

"So what will you do?"

"I'll remove it," Rand said. "Once he's sent away, he won't bother Georgia anymore."

And the sooner we do this, the better.

"What do you need from us?" Maria asked.

"Arrange for me to have some time alone in this room," Rand told her. "It won't take long."

"We can request to sign her out for a night and take her home," Maria said, glancing at Nick, who nodded. "This room can be all yours tomorrow evening."

"Can we do it tonight?" Rand asked.

"Um. I'll ask. I guess it would be okay."

"That would be perfect," Rand said. "I would still like to have a talk with Georgia about what's going on and what our plan is."

"She went down to the cafeteria," Nick said. "You can find her there."

"Good. While I'm gone, do whatever you need to sign Georgia out for the night."

<hr />

WHEN RAND TOOK the elevator downstairs, he checked all around but did not spot Georgia. He found Mrs. Eloise at the register, and when he approached she looked at him over the top of her glasses.

"Well, if it isn't Miss Georgia's older man."

"Good afternoon, Mrs. Eloise," Rand said. "Have you seen Georgia? Her parents told me she was here."

"She just came through. Did you check outside?"

Rand went to the far side of the dining area. Although it was storming in full, he spotted Georgia sitting on a bench underneath an awning, watching the rain as it fell into the garden behind the cafeteria. Rand walked outside to join her.

She looked up when she sensed his presence over her shoulder. "Hey, Ghost Man."

"It's a wet one."

"Eh. I like it." She scooted to the left side of the bench, giving him room to sit. Her portable oxygen rested between her legs, and she was wearing her sunglasses again.

"Not feeling well?"

"Just weak today," she said. "It happens sometimes. Didn't get much sleep last night either."

"Thomas came to visit."

She looked at him. "How did you know?"

"You texted Libby and told her."

"Oh yeah."

"And… yesterday, I planted a recorder in your room."

Georgia removed her giant sunglasses. Her green eyes bored into him, and her expression was unreadable. Something between anger and surprise.

"You were spying on me, Ghost Man?"

"Not you. Thomas."

"I should be angrier about that, but I'm too curious about what you found out."

"I was able to pick up his end of the conversation you two had last night."

"Really?" Georgia twisted in the bench to face him, crossing her long, skinny legs. "You heard what he was saying?"

"Yes."

"That's great! Like I told you yesterday, I can always tell he's trying to say something, but I can't understand him."

"That's common," Rand said. "Their words are coming from another realm of existence, so it's hard for our human ears to pick up sometimes unless the presence is very strong. On a recording, it often comes through much clearer."

Georgia looked amazed. Even in awe. "This is such good news."

"How come?" Rand asked.

"Because… Okay, promise you won't tell my parents?"

He nodded.

"Good. I know I can trust you, Ghost Man. The truth is, I've come to terms with the whole dying young thing. I'm mostly over it, but that doesn't mean I don't have difficult moments sometimes."

"I get it," Rand said.

"Some days I'm still afraid to die. Some nights I can't sleep because I'm wondering what it feels like to be dead."

Seventeen days, Thomas's voice echoed in Rand's mind.

Georgia's face, usually so bright, had fallen. Her eyes drifted to the rainstorm. The plant leaves were battered by the falling drops.

"That's why I'm glad you came," she said. "I was hoping you could help me communicate with Thomas. Maybe he can answer some of my questions."

Rand watched her for a long time. He could sense her uncertainty. He knew she was desperate to find reassurance from her friend.

Georgia looked at him again. "Can you help me, Ghost Man?"

Rand took a deep breath and let it out slowly. "I can. But not in the way you want."

Georgia frowned. "What do you mean?"

"I mean I could hear Thomas's side of the conversation. And it isn't what you would expect. Thomas is not happy. He's bitter. And from what I can tell, he's a little jealous that you're alive and he isn't."

Georgia furrowed her brow. "That doesn't sound like Thomas at all."

"That's the tricky thing with these ghosts. Sometimes when they come back, they aren't the same as they were when they were alive. Things change between life and death."

"Then we'll ask him what's wrong," Georgia said. "We need to reassure him. Or make him feel better. Or something."

Rand shook his head, and he could see Georgia's hopes getting dashed. "It's not that simple, Georgia. Spirits aren't like people, and we can't reason with them. They are trapped here because they feel their time on earth is unfinished, or they are not satisfied with how they lived their lives. They don't belong here, like you or I do."

"Then we need to help him," Georgia said.

"I agree. And the best way we can do that is to send him away."

Georgia's face dimmed, and Rand thought he could see tears welling in her eyes. He hated telling her what she didn't want to hear.

"What do you mean?" Georgia asked.

"I mean send him on to the afterlife. To where his spirit belongs."

"No," Georgia said. "We can't do that. I like him here."

"Why is that?"

"Because he was my best friend when he was alive and knowing he's looking out for me makes me feel better."

I want you to die.

"Georgia, he isn't looking out for you."

"How do you know?"

"Because I heard what he was telling you."

"And what did he say?"

Seventeen days.

"I can't tell you that."

"That's bullshit! I want to know."

"You don't," Rand said gently. "Trust me."

"What? Was he, like, cursing me out? Or telling me he always hated me?"

"No, nothing like that." *Much worse.*

"Then I don't understand."

"You need to trust me," Rand said. "I've encountered bitter ghosts before, and even though we think they're our loved ones, they're often not the same. The best place for them is the afterlife."

"I don't *want* him in the afterlife," Georgia protested. "I want him here. He's the only thing I have right now that makes me feel better about dying!" She finally broke, and the tears streamed down her face. "Having him here shows this isn't the end, and that even after I pass, I'll still be able to see my mom and dad." She sniffed, then wiped her nose with the back of her hand.

Rand was quiet for a few minutes and let Georgia cry. He understood her point of view completely, but that was why it was so difficult. It was hard to make her understand why Thomas's presence wasn't good without telling her what he knew.

When she got her sobs under control, she looked up at him again. "I thought you were here to help me."

"I am. But sometimes help doesn't always look the way we want it to."

Georgia shook her head. "I can't believe it. I finally get a break, my friend coming back and showing me that dying isn't that bad. And now you want to take that away from me."

"Please try to understand," Rand said. "Thomas is not the same as before."

"Oh yeah? Prove it. Let me hear your recording."

"I won't do that."

"Then you're just some scammer. Maybe there isn't even anything on your recorder." She stood and grabbed her oxygen tank. "Thanks for nothing."

Then she stormed off.

Rand watched her go. Hurting her now reminded him of the times when Libby thought she knew best, and Rand had to tell her no. He hated to see his daughter upset but had to stand strong and not give in. That was true here as well.

Georgia's reason for wanting Thomas around was compelling, but Rand knew he had to do what was right.

11

R and informed Nick and Maria Collins that he planned to remove the ghost using a cleansing ceremony. Although they both seemed a little skeptical, they were nevertheless on board with the idea.

They got clearance from the doctor to let Georgia spend the night at home, then they signed her out.

Rand had dinner in the St. Mary's cafeteria downstairs while he waited for the family to vacate, not wanting to be present. He knew Georgia would be very unhappy and not want to see him.

Around eight o'clock, Nick called him.

"Okay, we're home," he said.

"How did it go?" Rand asked.

"She was not pleased," Nick told him.

"I figured. I'm not her favorite person in the world right now. But trust me, this is for the best."

"I believe you. Do what you have to do."

Rand returned to the tenth floor, satchel dangling from his shoulder. It was heavy with all the supplies he'd need.

Harold the security guard gave him a strange look as he passed the desk. "Mr. Rand? The Collins family has signed out of the hospital for the evening."

Rand froze. He still wore his visitor name tag, but it probably didn't have much authority when the patient he was registered as visiting wasn't even in the facility.

"Yeah," Rand said. A couple of likely lies popped into his head, but he found he couldn't be dishonest with the man.

Harold wrinkled his brow, confused. Rand knew this was the part where Harold would ask him to leave. But instead, Harold said, "May I have a word?"

Rand returned to the desk and let his satchel drop to the floor by his feet.

The robust man leaned forward and brought his face close to Rand's. "Miss Georgia tells me things. And she told me about you and what you're doing here." Although no one was in earshot, he kept his voice low.

Rand nodded. *So I was right. He does know more about this than he let on.*

"I was the first to know about her little friend coming to visit her in the middle of the night."

"I had a feeling you were a believer," Rand said.

Harold licked his lips and hesitated. Finally, he said, "I am. I've had a few unexplainable experiences in my life, but I try to leave well enough alone. I don't think any good can come from messing with this stuff."

"Wise man," Rand said. How he wished more people felt the same way as Harold. "But not everyone is as wary as you, and they can get themselves into serious trouble."

"A young lady like Miss Georgia has no business dabbling around with all this," Harold said.

"I agree."

"I hoped you weren't here to encourage her curiosity, but I didn't think so. I got a good feeling from you."

"And I from you. I'm here to get rid of it. That's why they took Georgia away for the night."

"Hospital policy says the visitors can't stay when the patient is gone."

"Smart policy," Rand said. "Give me an hour?"

Harold nodded his head. "Make it quick."

———

RAND PLACED candles around the empty hospital room and ignited them. Then he turned out the lights, leaving only an eerie darkness. He took out his incense and lit it, letting the scented smoke drift through the air. He removed his jacket and placed it on the couch.

He'd done cleansing ceremonies countless times, but to him, it would never be a matter of routine. Supernatural entities were far too unpredictable, and for that reason, Rand still got nervous when preparing for an encounter.

The storm from earlier had mostly passed, but the last remains of the thunder rolled in the distance.

Rand stood in the middle of the room and closed his eyes. Embraced the silence. Smelled the incense.

And felt he was not the only one in the room.

Rand was not a clairvoyant, but he had been around enough spiritual activity to recognize when it was present.

"You are here with me," he said out loud. Nothing replied. "I can sense you. Don't worry. I am not here to harm you."

More silence. Rand opened his eyes. He withdrew from his bag a small cross dangling from rosary beads. He held the thing high above his head, displaying it to the four corners of the room.

"It is time for you to move on from this place," Rand said.

A loud crash startled him. A picture frame—a photo of Georgia and three other young girls—had fallen off the wall and smashed on the ground.

Thomas would resist.

But the thing about the spiritual realm was that it had to listen to the commands of those who occupied the mortal plane. They didn't have to like it, but they had to obey.

"I know you can hear me," Rand said, looking around the room, speaking loudly and clearly. "You are loved and remembered here, and we have all grieved your loss. But it is time for you to walk toward the light where you belong. You will be happier there, and the ones you love will remember you fondly until it is time for you all to meet again."

The room's temperature suddenly grew very cold. The presence of a spirit consumed the heat from the room, which caused the room to become unnaturally cold all at once.

Two candles near Georgia's bed blew out at the same time.

"I know you don't want to go, but you must," Rand said.

A vase of flowers on Georgia's desk shifted by itself—Rand saw it just in time. It flew from the desk, right toward his head, but he dodged. It smashed on the opposite wall, sending flowers, glass, and water all over the floor.

This one is strong, Rand thought. Stronger than he'd originally thought. He was right in figuring he needed to cleanse the room immediately.

"I command you to leave this place!" Rand said, voice booming. When the spirits were stubborn, he had to be especially firm. "Walk toward the light! Embrace the next life. You are not welcome here, and you will come here no more!"

The bathroom door swung open and closed by itself, slamming shut. The television turned on, though it displayed nothing but static. Georgia's desk drawers opened and the pens, pencils, and papers inside flew around the room.

It's trying to throw me off.

"Georgia does not need you anymore!" Rand shouted. "You do not belong. I command you to leave this place!"

The doors and drawers stopped moving on their own and the objects being thrown around came to rest on the floor. The tension in the room eased and evaporated, and the temperature slowly returned to normal. Static on the TV was the only sound.

And then, after a few seconds, Rand took a deep breath and

lowered the rosary beads. He closed his eyes and felt out the space for a few moments, to confirm that he was alone.

The room felt empty. Lighter, even.

The spirit was gone.

But it was too easy.

A little voice in the back of Rand's head told him it shouldn't have been that simple. The ghost was stronger than he'd expected, so Rand lingered a few seconds longer to confirm that he'd been successful. He sensed nothing out of the ordinary.

There is no presence here any longer, Rand told himself.

Rand blew out the candles and packed his things. He did his best to clean up the mess Thomas had made—throwing away the pieces of the broken vase and putting the pens and pencils back in the drawers. He threw his bag over his shoulder and checked his watch. The hour that Harold had given him was almost up.

He opened the door, and as he went to step out into the hallway he took one last look over his shoulder. Scanned the room from wall to wall, glancing into the four corners.

Definitely gone. No spirit before had ever withstood one of his cleansing ceremonies.

Thomas was no different.

12

It took Libby fifteen minutes to find the correct elevator. She could imagine her dad getting hopelessly lost in this hospital. *And he would never tell me if he did.*

The doors opened on the tenth floor and Libby stepped out, looking around. The ward now made her feel like she was in a hospital for the first time. Hospitals gave her dad the creeps, but she didn't mind them. When she was younger, she had done some volunteer work at St. Mary's with her mom.

The security guard stood as she approached, giving her a broad smile. "Good evening, ma'am."

"Hello," Libby said. "I'm here to visit Georgia Collins."

"Certainly." The guard produced a binder and opened it for her, where Libby signed her name. She checked her cheap digital watch and filled in the time—5:50 PM.

The guard took the binder back and copied her name onto a nametag. He smirked as he did. "Any relation to a Randolph?"

Libby winced. "Are you going to throw me out?"

He laughed. "I like him. Haven't seen him in a while, though." The guard—whose badge read Harold—flipped a few pages back and ran his finger down the boxes. "Ten days ago."

"Yeah. He's been busy." Libby peeled the sticker off and smoothed it onto her shirt. "I'm his daughter."

"Welcome to the tenth ward. I'm Harold, the security guard up here. Room 1019 is down that way and on the right."

Libby thanked him and made her way past the nurse station and down the hall. She found the door of 1019 wide open. The girl whose Instagram she'd been following the last week and a half was propped on her bed, watching television. The nasal cannula that was always in her pictures hung from her nose.

Libby scanned the hospital room, which resembled a normal bedroom. "I like what you've done with the place."

Georgia noticed her for the first time, smiled, and stood. Without saying anything, she opened her arms wide for a hug, and Libby scooped her up.

"Thank you for coming," Georgia said.

"Absolutely. I heard the ice cream here is amazing." They sat down together on the bed. "Seriously," Libby said, looking around. "This place looks incredible. So comfortable."

"Basically, I moved in," Georgia said. "No idea what the rent is, but my parents tell me it isn't cheap."

"I wanted to paint the walls in my bedroom at my dad's house," Libby said. "I like blue, but right now it's white, which is what it was when he bought the place. But he told me no. Said I'd make too much of a mess and that I didn't know what I was doing."

"*Do* you know what you're doing, though?" Georgia asked. "Do you actually know how to paint a room?"

"Of course not," Libby said. "But I wanted to try."

Georgia chuckled. "You should just do it anyway. Who cares?"

"You're right," Libby said. "He never goes in there. We can make bets on how long it'll take him to notice. Maybe three months?"

"How is the ghost man?" Georgia asked, her voice flat.

"Fine. Busy teaching. Out with his girlfriend. Stuff like that."

Georgia grunted.

Her dad had told her what had gone down with the ghost. In the end, he'd ended up having to remove it, and Georgia was upset with

79

ROCKWELL SCOTT

him about that. It had been a tough call, Libby realized. But Libby knew enough about these ghosts to know it was the right thing to do.

"I like your clothes," Georgia said, her eyes scanning her up and down. "You play volleyball?"

"Oh, this. Sorry, I just came from practice."

"No, that's awesome. Sometimes I watch it on TV. It looks like so much fun."

"Have you ever played?"

"No way. Look at me, I can't even breathe."

"Come with me sometime. We'll hit some balls."

Georgia straightened. "Are you serious?"

"Of course."

"That would be great."

"So what about you?" Libby asked. "What do you do when you're here?" As soon as the words left her mouth, she regretted it. There couldn't be too many interesting things to do in a hospital.

But Georgia only perked up. "This place is so huge. I explore and get into places where I'm not supposed to."

"Oh yeah? Like where?" Libby instantly considered the morgue and hoped that wasn't what she meant.

"You want to see my secret spot?" Georgia asked her. "I didn't even show your dad."

"Absolutely."

"Okay." She nodded toward Libby's gym bag from volleyball practice that she still had. "Bring your gear."

ON THE ELEVATOR, Georgia pressed the button for 15R, which was located between floors fourteen and fifteen.

"I like your bag," Libby said as they rode. Georgia had a nice, heavy-duty carrier for her tanks that had lots of little pockets.

"I'll get you one for Christmas. Oxygen not included."

The elevator opened into an area that they clearly were not

80

supposed to be in. It was not a normal ward, but rather a long hallway that still looked like it was undergoing construction. The walls were wood, not painted, and the nice tile that finished the floor in other parts of the hospital was not there. It was also very warm and humid.

But Georgia led the way confidently, pulling her tank on wheels behind her.

At the end of the hall was a small security station with a man wearing the same uniform as Harold. He stood as they approached. At first, Libby noted that he looked concerned and confrontational, but when he saw Georgia, he softened.

"I told you not to come back, Georgia," the guard said. "You're going to get me in trouble."

"How? I'm literally the best secret keeper ever."

"I know, but it's only a matter of time. If Ms. Shaw figures this out, I'm done for."

"I'll take the fall for you, Sam."

Sam glanced at Libby. "Does she keep *your* secrets?"

"Every last one," Libby answered. Georgia smiled at her.

Sam waved them through. "Okay. Make it quick."

"Yes! Thanks, Sam!"

Georgia tugged Libby's arm and pulled her past the security desk toward a set of double doors. "No one can say no to me," she whispered to Libby.

When the doors opened, a blast of chilly wind hit Libby in the face. The dark hallway disappeared, and they walked outside onto the roof of the hospital. The sounds of the city at rush hour came from far below them, and the sky was orange and purple as the sun fell on the distant horizon.

"Oh my God," Libby said. When she looked up, the rest of St. Mary's fifteen floors towered above her and the platform they were on, making her feel tiny. On the ground was a huge H surrounded by a white circle.

"Pretty amazing, right?" Georgia said.

"Yes. This is awesome!"

Libby took her volleyball from her gym bag and dribbled it. "Want to hit a few?"

"Are you serious? Yes!"

"Do you know how to do it?" Libby tossed the ball in the air and then bounced it off her arms for a few rounds.

"I've seen games on TV," Georgia said. She mimicked Libby with her hand position, and Libby went to her and corrected her placement, folding them correctly to give her a sturdy landing point for the ball.

"Get under it, bend your knees, and focus on where you want the ball to go. You don't need to hit it very hard to have a lot of power. Let's try."

Libby lobbed her the ball, slow and easy and from a short distance. Georgia sent it sailing up in the air with a loud slap from her pale forearms. Libby ran and caught it. The heavy wind around the helipad had taken it off center. "Very nice. Have you done this before?"

Georgia shrugged and smirked.

Libby volleyed it to her again, and Georgia hit it back, this time more controlled and accounting for the wind. Libby returned it to her, and Georgia responded. They went back and forth before Georgia finally dropped it.

"You're so lucky you get to do this," Georgia said, picking up the volleyball before it rolled away.

"You can do it too." Libby hoped to be encouraging, but really had no idea of Georgia's limitations with her condition.

Georgia said nothing, only served the ball to Libby, which she bumped, set, and volleyed back.

They bounced it between themselves, controlled and easy. "See! You're doing it," Libby said. "You could totally do this in a real game."

Libby's next volley was stronger than she'd intended and was swept up by the wind, and Georgia scrambled to get under it. But her oxygen tubing ran out of slack, yanked her face back, and popped out of her nostrils. The tug caused the portable cylinder to fall over, and even though it was in a padded carrying bag it made a loud clank on the concrete.

Libby rushed over, but she relaxed when she saw Georgia smiling.

"I need to commission some longer tubing," she said, stringing the cannula back behind her ears and returning them to her nostrils, panting as if she'd just run a half marathon. She put the portable cylinder right-side-up.

"Let's take a break." Libby was shocked by how quickly the other girl ran out of breath.

"I'm totally jealous of you," Georgia said, placing her hands on her hips to catch her breath. "You're tall, pretty, athletic. You have a cool dad, even though I'm mad at him right now. You probably have a boyfriend."

Libby smirked. "I like you, too."

"You still wouldn't want to trade places with me. I wouldn't let you. What's your boyfriend's name?"

"Justin. Although he isn't my boyfriend yet. We're just kind of texting."

"Lock him down!" Georgia said. "God, I wish I had a boyfriend."

"There's never any rush for a boyfriend," Libby said. "I never thought I wanted one, but then I met Justin and things are just kind of happening."

"I have a legitimate reason for rushing to get a boyfriend," Georgia said, and Libby fell silent. "Do you believe in all the stuff that your dad is involved in?"

"Of course." Libby was glad for the change of topic. "It's hard not to. I've grown up around it my whole life."

Georgia pulled her oxygen along as she walked down the helipad and scooped up the ball. Libby followed her to the edge of the platform, and the heights made her start to feel woozy. Georgia seemed unafraid.

"Did he tell you about me? And my situation?" Libby nodded. "What do you think about it?"

Libby looked away. The streetlights below were twinkling to life with the setting sun. Car horns and the sounds of roaring engines floated up from the rush-hour traffic. Libby took a deep breath, and somehow the air seemed clearer up there. Perhaps that was why Georgia visited. "He did the right thing."

Georgia frowned and tucked a piece of hair behind her ear, and the wind tugged it out of place again. "I miss my friend."

"I know you do." She paused. "Does that mean you haven't seen him since my dad was here?"

"He's gone."

Good, Libby thought. "I know it's hard, but sometimes it isn't a good thing when these two worlds come together." *Oh God, I sound like my dad.*

"I didn't think he was hurting anyone," Georgia said.

"Maybe not at first. But who knows what can happen later?" Libby remembered several of her father's cases that had begun as a benign presence and then escalated. Most people only waited to contact him after things had taken a turn for the worst. Georgia and her family had been lucky. "Can you forgive him?"

Georgia shrugged. "I'm already kind of over it. But still. I miss Thomas."

Libby put her hands on Georgia's shoulders and forced the girl to look her in the eyes. "No one is saying you can't miss Thomas. But it is way better if you stay in the present moment. Focus on life. Not on death."

Georgia's face broke into a smile. Then she nodded. "Okay."

"Promise me."

"Yes, I will."

"Good. I can already tell you're stronger than a lot of the girls in my class. *And* you have your very own helipad. Let's get a selfie because this needs to go on Instagram."

They spent ten minutes finding the perfect angle for the helipad, the sunset, and their faces. Eighty pictures later, Sam came outside. "Just got a call on the radio. Chopper coming in. Bad accident on the Interstate."

Georgia tossed him the volleyball, which he caught easily. "You kicking us out?"

"Do you want to get crushed?" Sam dribbled the ball between his legs as if it were a basketball.

"There are some good ones in here," Libby said, scrolling through her camera roll. "Do you mind if I post them?"

"Is that a serious question?"

13

Georgia tried the chord progression again, but the last one strummed awkward and flat. She groaned and rewound the YouTube video on her laptop.

The girl in the video demonstrated again, and Georgia watched closely. Eventually, she saw what she was doing wrong with the last chord.

Georgia paused the video again and strummed her guitar a few more times, and finally it sounded right. As she repeated the chords over and over, she added in lyrics, singing them underneath her breath.

Singing was hard to do with lungs filled with muck and oxygen running through her nose, but she didn't care. She liked to sing, so she was going to.

Three knocks interrupted her song just as it was coming along. The door opened and Nurse Donna appeared.

"Evening, Georgia," she said.

"Hey there." Georgia twisted in her chair to face the other woman.

"Where's your mom and dad?"

"They went out to eat. They'll be back later."

"Ah, okay. Well, we have a cake out here for Mandy's birthday."

"What kind?"

"Red velvet."

"Mmm. That'll do. Yeah, I'll be there in a minute. Going to rock out for a little longer while I have the room to myself."

Donna smiled. "Sure thing. It'll be at the nurse's station whenever you want it." She left the door open and walked away.

Georgia returned to her guitar. After playing through the first verse and singing along a couple of times, she figured she had it down. She fast-forwarded the YouTube video to the part that would teach her the chorus.

Another three knocks.

"Yeah, just a few minutes more," Georgia said, keeping her eyes on her laptop. "Don't tell me y'all ate all the cake already."

But when she looked toward the door, no one was there.

"Mrs. Donna?" Georgia called.

No answer.

Georgia turned back to her computer and played the video. The girl used a close-up of her fingers to outline the chord progression for the chorus.

A loud slam startled Georgia and made her jump.

She whirled around. The door was closed.

"Mrs. Donna?" she said again, her voice trembling from the sudden fright. She leaned her guitar against her desk and rose from the chair, pulling her oxygen cylinder behind her as she slowly approached the door that had been open moments before.

She tried to open it, but it wouldn't. Hospital doors didn't lock, so it was like someone was holding it closed from the other side.

"Hey!" she shouted, slamming her palm against the wood.

But all the exertion had left her short of breath, and she felt a coughing fit coming on. Georgia backed away and focused on getting her breathing under control. Her coughing fits could last up to fifteen minutes sometimes, and her parents were due back any minute. If they found her coughing, they'd worry about her the rest of the night.

Her breath leveled off. She readjusted the cannula in her nose and felt the pure oxygen filling her lungs.

Then she went to the bed and pressed the Call button on the wall.

Nothing.

Usually it beeped and lit up red. Georgia mashed it a few more times, but it wasn't working.

She then went to the bathroom and pulled on the Call cord that dangled above her toilet. Still nothing.

"What's going on?" she whispered to herself.

Her cell phone was on the bed, plugged into the charger. She was sure she had the number for the nurse station saved in her contacts.

But she stopped short as her room filled with music.

At first, she thought the YouTube video had unpaused itself, but when she looked at her desk she saw it was her guitar.

Playing itself.

The strings pressed down on the frets in flawless chords and strummed, creating a full sound. It was the song she'd been trying to learn. Executed perfectly.

Georgia stared at the instrument, mouth open in awe. And a tightening ball of anxiety began to form in her stomach.

Then, an unmistakable soft breath on the back of her neck.

She whirled around, her hand instinctively going to where the breath had been. But no one was behind her.

"Thomas?" she said, voice trembling.

The song ended with a jarring, dissonant chord and fell silent.

Thomas had played guitar. It would make sense if it were him. *But I thought Ghost Man got rid of him.*

"Is that you?" The only sound in the room now was Georgia's breath. Her pulse rang in her ears. "Please tell me you're still here. Give me a sign or something."

As if on command, the green oxygen cylinder by her bed fell over, landing with a loud clang. The top then burst off, white smoke shooting from the broken handle. The compressed air sent the tank flying across the floor with the speed and force of a torpedo, right toward Georgia's ankles. She leapt out of the way just in time. It crashed into the wall, leaving a spider web of cracks in the plaster. The television toppled off its stand and dropped to the ground, and the wires were yanked from the electrical sockets.

Georgia cried out. Her breath turned to rapid pants, and she was no longer able to control it.

"Thomas! What are you doing?"

The oxygen cylinder by her side was knocked over, the top popping open by itself, just like the first one. It shot across the room, ripping the cannula from her nose as it went. The force was strong enough to pull her off her feet and she face-planted onto the floor. The rogue cylinder crashed against the door and spun in circles as the last of the air inside leaked out.

She coughed and sputtered, a heaviness in her chest cutting off her breath. And there were no more tanks in the room.

"Thomas," she wheezed. "I'm sorry. I didn't want—" She crawled toward her bed, desperate for her phone.

She reached the foot of the bed, breathless, and fumbled blindly across the mattress for her cell.

As soon as she grabbed it, the lights in the room went out.

She whirled around, back propped against her bed, coughing and hacking. It was completely dark inside—even her laptop had shut off by itself. The room was suddenly very cold, frigid as if she'd walked into a freezer.

"I'm sorry," she said again.

She understood if Thomas was angry for being sent away. But surely he realized it wasn't her idea. Didn't he?

Then, something caught her eye. Although it was dark, she could make out the outline of a figure standing in the corner of the room. A person. A boy.

Thomas.

It had been a little over a week since she'd seen him. He stood still and stared at her, even though his features were not clear. Somehow, his shadow was blacker than the surrounding darkness, allowing him to stand out.

She pointed her phone toward the figure and opened her camera app, then pressed the button. The flash went off, blinding her.

As soon as the light faded, Thomas was inches away, having crossed the room in a millisecond to stand over her.

Georgia clenched her eyes shut, covered her ears, and screamed, waiting for whatever Thomas was going to do to her. However, he would punish her.

But then familiar arms were around her. She opened her eyes. The lights were back and her parents were there. Her mom held her close.

"What happened?" she asked. "Why are you screaming?"

Georgia didn't answer. Instead, she only patted her chest, coughing and wheezing. Her dad looked around the room and, finding both tanks empty, ran out into the hallway and shouted for the nurses to bring oxygen.

Nurse Donna and others rushed in, picked her up, and put her on the bed, then reattached her oxygen and tried to calm her down.

As she sucked down the oxygen, Georgia's eyes darted around the room, looking for Thomas. She knew he was still there somewhere, unseen and invisible, hiding from everyone else who had come into the room.

Waiting for the next time she would be alone.

14

It was a Friday morning and Rand drummed his fingers on the steering wheel as he sang along with a Motley Crüe song on the classic rock radio station. It had been ten days since he'd seen Georgia Collins, but she still lingered on his mind.

He ran into the dry cleaners and gave the girl his ticket. She then retrieved his black suit, which was on a velvet hanger and covered in plastic. Rand thanked her and went to Vicky's Alterations down the road. There, he put on the suit and stood in front of a mirror as she measured him and put the pins in the coat and waistline.

"Everything's tighter," she said around the sharp needles in her mouth.

"I've taken up weightlifting the past couple of years." He'd bulked up since the last time he'd worn the suit, especially his thighs. Squats were a killer.

"When do you need this by?" Vicky asked him.

"By tonight. I have a thing."

She glanced up at him. "You know I'm a twenty-four-hour turnaround."

"Do you have an express option?"

She sighed. "I'll do it for you this time, Rand. But don't get used to it."

"I already am."

The next stop was the gym. It was leg day, so he loaded up a heavy barbell on his back and squatted, face red and forehead sweaty, while his headphones blared Motörhead. When the squats were done, he waddled over to the gym's pool, changed into swim trunks, and did some laps.

After he showered, he checked his phone and found a message from Vicky. The suit was finished, so he swung by and picked it up again.

That evening, however, he dressed in his navy blue suit.

He slung the jacket over his white shirt, which he left unbuttoned at the top. Rachel came into the bedroom from the bathroom, her salmon dress tightly hugging her body. She tilted her head as she put on her earring. "I thought you were wearing black tonight."

"Changed my mind."

"After all that? Dry cleaning and tailoring?"

"It needed to be done anyway."

"No tie?"

"Ties are too uptight."

"You'll be the only man without one."

"I'm aware."

At six o'clock, they went to the car.

"Thanks again for coming with me," Rand said as they got in.

"Still a little weird," Rachel told him.

"I know. Don't worry, we won't stay long." He started the engine. The classic rock station from earlier blared too loud, and he twisted the volume knob as Rachel cringed.

"But we can't leave too early. They'll notice," Rachel said.

"If they're noticing my whereabouts at their own celebration, then they don't know how to party."

She smirked as they backed out of the driveway.

Preston Plantation was a manor outside of town surrounded by several acres of land dotted by hundred-year-old oak trees. Like most plantations in the south, it was now used as an indoor reception hall.

Rand parked, and as they walked toward the main building he noticed that, in fact, he was the only one not wearing a tie. He also sensed the heavy feeling within the walls of Preston Plantation. It was an old home, and therefore likely haunted. Wealthy families would have lived there, and usually, they had their fair share of problems, debauchery, and mistreated servants. Plenty of negative energy to attract lingering spirits.

"What's wrong?" Rachel asked. She'd noticed him glancing up at the high ceilings and toward the corners of the room, and at the portraits of the past owners that adorned the wall along the staircase that led up to a darkened, unused second floor.

"Nothing," Rand said, pushing the thoughts from his mind.

He'd attended engagement parties before, but none that resembled an actual wedding. Bill had spared no expense, as usual. The main reception hall was decked out for the occasion, with pink tablecloths matching the curtains of the high windows. A live band played slow songs on their woodwind instruments, which Rand hardly thought was useful if one were trying to throw a decent party, but to each their own. He swung by all the offerings—the roast carvery, the vegetables, the lobster tails, pasta, and even the children's chicken finger stand. Last, but not least, was the open bar.

"I've never seen you eat so much," Rachel told him. Three empty plates had accumulated in front of him before a busboy came to clear them.

"Bill's dollar, so why not?" He leaned in his chair and sipped his whiskey.

They sat alone at a table in the back, separate from the main party. Well aware that he was only there as Libby's father, he kept away and let the others do their thing. Tessa and Bill floated from conversation to conversation, playing host. Libby stood in a huddle with her friends Bailey, Claire, and Samantha. Libby wore a red dress that Rand had never seen before. Justin was with her, looking awkward in his oversized suit, hands in his pockets, seeming like he didn't have much to say to the girls.

"Thoughtful of Bill to let Libby invite her friends," Rand said. Despite Bill being able to afford the extra heads at a dinner like that, there were still a lot of empty seats in the place. Just like Rand's classroom.

"He really is a nice guy," Rachel said. She signaled for the waiter, who swooped in and placed another champagne on the table in front of her, and took away her empty glass. By Rand's count, she was three deep.

"When have you ever talked to Bill?"

"He came by when you were in the bathroom."

Rand smirked. "That rat."

Rachel shoved his shoulder.

Tessa caught his eye again for the fifth time that night. She looked stunning in her blue dress, and the personal trainer that Bill had gotten her for her most recent birthday was really starting to pay off.

In a locked container at the back of his closet, there was a ring in a little black box. No one else knew it was there. He'd bought it years ago and had held on to it ever since. Soon after Libby was born Tessa had made it clear she had no intention of being with him long term, so Rand had never actually asked Tessa to marry him. And even though money had been tight, he'd never sold it.

He drained his whiskey. "Think I'll hit the bar again. Want anything?" Rachel shook her head and nodded toward her full champagne. "And on the way back, I think it's time I meet my daughter's new boyfriend."

"Be nice, Randolph."

"Aren't I always?"

She gave him a look as he rose.

Rand tipped the bartender and carried his whiskey glass to where his daughter and her friends stood. Libby's eyes widened when he approached.

"Evening," he said as he broke into their circle. Bailey and Claire made room for him.

"Hey, Mr. Rand," Bailey said.

"How's the party so far?"

"Music's terrible." Bailey wrinkled her nose at the four old guys on the stage.

"You know, I was just telling Rachel the same thing."

"Right? A DJ would have been much better. And cheaper."

"Money isn't an issue in a crowd like this, Bailey. And look around at these people. I doubt they've ever heard a DJ before."

The party was mostly made up of what Rand assumed were Bill's work colleagues. Everyone wore a stiff, unfitted suit, and conducted themselves as if they were there for business rather than a celebration. Hunched shoulders, serious expressions, and formal head nods.

Rand then focused on Justin and extended his hand. "Rand Casey."

Justin awkwardly shook it, his hand limp like a dead fish. "Justin."

Libby folded her arms and glared at her father with a stiff-lipped warning, which Rand already intended to ignore.

"Libby's dad."

"I know," Justin said. His eyes darted around the floor at everyone's ankles.

"Nice suit. I have one just like it. I'll give you my tailor's number. Tell her I sent you and you'll have it back same day."

"Dad," Libby spat.

"Thanks," Justin said, missing the gentle jibe.

Bailey and Claire stood tensed on either side of him, awkwardly watching a father meet a boyfriend for the first time.

"So I hear you play guitar."

"A little." He ran a nervous hand through his shaggy, unkempt hair.

"Weren't you supposed to wear your black suit tonight?" Libby asked, desperately trying to change the conversation.

"A little? What does that mean? You either do or you don't. What kind of music do you play?"

"Mostly original stuff."

"I'd love to hear it sometime. You know, I used to play a bit myself."

"Dad," Libby said again.

"I was in a band in college," Rand went on. "We played at the bars every weekend. There were four of us, and we called ourselves Amateur Surgery." Rand chuckled, lost in the memory. "Man, we thought we were awesome, but really all we wanted to do was make as much noise as possible. The ladies loved us, though."

"Dad!"

Rand turned toward Libby. She gripped her cell phone, a look of concern on her face. "What?"

"I just got a text from Georgia."

Rand frowned. "Saying what?"

"He's back." The words were a whisper barely audible over the band's interlude. She passed him her phone, and the latest message in their thread was a picture. Rand swallowed.

He recognized the hospital room. And in the darkened shadows, on the edge of the flash from the phone's camera, he could make out the spectral outline of a boy standing in the corner.

It was their first photograph of Thomas. This meant that not only was he back, but his presence was stronger.

"Oh no," he muttered.

Justin and Libby's friends looked back and forth between them, confused.

His own phone vibrated with a call in his pocket. When he fished it out, Nick Collins's name was on the screen.

"Excuse me," he told the kids. "I need to take this."

15

S t. Mary's Hospital was just as busy at night as it was in the morning.

    Rand, Libby, and Rachel approached the Coffee Bean, the same shop where Rand had originally met up with Nick and Maria.

Maria was waiting for them and stood when they neared.

"Oh, I'm so sorry," she said when she saw how they were dressed. "You should have told me you had plans."

"It's okay," Rand said. "How is Georgia?"

"Not well," Maria said. "Whatever happened to her really stressed her out."

"What's going on?"

"Maybe it's better if she tells you herself."

Rand turned to Rachel. "Do you want to hang out here for a bit? I shouldn't be too long."

Rachel shrugged and joined the line to get a coffee. Rand and Libby went upstairs.

Harold the security guard was quite concerned as he wrote out the visitors' nametags. "Apparently there was a huge commotion down the hall about an hour ago."

"Did you see anything?"

"Nothing," Harold said. "Not until Mr. and Mrs. Collins came back and found Miss Georgia on the floor."

In the hospital room, Georgia lay on her bed, covers pulled up to her chin and cannula running from her nostrils. Her father was seated by her side. She groaned when Rand entered.

"I should've known the ghost man would come." Then, she smiled at Libby. "Hey, Libby. Cool dress."

"Hey. Are you okay?" Libby took the desk chair to the side of the bed and sat down next to her.

Georgia looked awful. Her skin was whiter than usual and her eyes were red and puffy from crying. "I'm fine. Probably shouldn't have texted you, though." Her voice was thin and weak. "I should've known you'd bring your dad."

"I know you think he's a jerk right now, but he can help you," Libby said.

"He's already helped me enough."

"Come on, Georgia," Nick said. "Don't be like that. Tell Rand what happened so we can get to the bottom of this."

At the mere suggestion of reliving her tale, Georgia twisted in her bed and squeezed herself into a ball under the covers. Tears rimmed her eyes. Libby reached out and took her hand.

"Where did this picture come from?" Rand asked. "You did well in capturing it, but I need to know the whole context."

Georgia's breathing became shallow and labored, in through the nose and out through the mouth, as if she were running on a tread-mill instead of lying in bed.

"Georgia?" Maria said.

"Okay, okay." She coughed and then told them everything.

Rand's eyes moved around the room as he imagined Georgia's story. There were cracks in the wall and door right where Georgia said the exploding oxygen cylinders hit. The television that had been mounted the last time he visited was now on the floor, the screen broken.

"I took the picture after I saw him when the lights went out," Georgia finished.

"Honey, how could you see him if the lights weren't on?" Maria asked.

Georgia fixed her mother with a rigid stare, one that showed she refused to be disbelieved. "Because his body was darker than the dark around him."

Maria seemed confused, but Rand knew what she meant.

And he was very concerned. The girl had been attacked. However, he didn't want to use that word in front of the family right now and alarm them further.

Nick and Maria looked at him expectantly, as if he had the solution to all their problems.

"I'm sorry you went through this, Georgia," Rand began. "It seems Thomas's presence is stronger than he was letting on at the beginning. These spirits can do this as a way to protect themselves."

Rand had encountered spirits that knew what he was. Someone had once explained to him that it was in his aura. For that reason, spirits attempted to downplay their own energy so as to not be threatened by him.

Georgia rounded on him. "This wouldn't have happened if you hadn't pissed him off." She struggled to sit up in bed. Her mother tried to coax her, but she had none of it. When her back was against the headboard, she jabbed an accusing finger at him. "This is all your fault. He was fine before, but now he's mad. I told you to just leave him alone, and that he wasn't hurting anyone!"

"Georgia!" Nick scolded.

"I want you to leave. You being here is only going to make him angrier." Then she launched into a coughing fit.

Libby looked at him, frowning.

"I understand why you're frustrated," Rand said, "but you and I both know what happened here is not something Thomas would ever do to you. Something triggered this spirit and made it aggressive."

"*You* did!"

"It wasn't me. If he did this tonight, then he was always capable of doing it. That's what worries me."

"Then why did it take so long for this to happen?"

"Probably to get you to trust him. And it worked. Because now you're on his side and against me."

"Well, yeah," Georgia said. "Thomas was my friend. He was only sixteen when he died. Of course he's upset. But instead of being there for him, you come in and try to chase him away."

"Georgia," Nick said, "Rand only did what he did because he thought it was best for you. You heard him before. It isn't good or right for these... spirits to be here. They need to move on."

"I don't care," Georgia said. "All I know is he made everything worse."

"Georgia." Libby spoke for the first time, and everyone looked at her. "Listen. I've grown up with this stuff my whole life. My dad's been dealing with it since before I was born. He's told me all about his past cases, and I've witnessed these things. Sometimes these pissed-off ghosts follow him home and try to take out their anger on him. Imagine being a little girl and having spirits attach themselves to your dad. I've seen so much crazy stuff, and I'm not even the Ghost Man. But he's right. These entities are so unpredictable that you can't have a normal life whenever they are around. You'll never be at peace. You'll always be on edge, waiting for the next thing to fall and break, or have your keys or purse go missing. Trust me, all of that's happened to me. So I know you're mad at my dad. He's easy to get mad at, and he pisses me off at least once a week. But believe me when I say he isn't here to upset you. He wants to do his best to help you. And he can. He's helped so many other people before."

Georgia fell silent as she retreated into herself. It slowly sunk in that she was fighting alone in her own corner. "Fine." The single word was weak, defeated.

Nick turned to Rand. "What do we do now? And this time... it needs to work." His eyes seemed to droop.

Rand already knew his next course of action before even arriving at the hospital. "I want to bring in a clairvoyant."

Everyone stared at him blankly. Everyone except Libby, who had met a few clairvoyants in her short life.

"What is that?"

"It's someone who is sensitive to the spiritual world. I can be sensitive, but there are others who are far more in tune than me. I work with them frequently. They are better able to communicate with spirits, sometimes acting as physical mediums, where the spirit can use the clairvoyant's voice."

Nick and Maria were even more confused.

"Sorry," Nick said. "I'm a little lost. But if you think it's best, I won't argue with you."

"I suggest this because this spirit obviously has more to say," Rand replied. "At first, all the evidence pointed to the fact that it was upset at having passed early. If that was all, then my cleansing in this room should have worked. But there are stronger emotions anchoring him here, and we need to find out what he wants so we are better able to send him on."

Libby nodded along.

"And um… when can we expect to meet this colleague of yours?"

Three knocks sounded at the door, and a nurse entered. "Sorry to break up the party, but visiting hours are over in ten minutes. Anyone not related to the patient needs to leave."

"Thanks, Donna," Nick said.

"I'll make calls first thing tomorrow and come back as soon as I can." To Rand, the case had become urgent. All his cases did when a restless, irritated ghost attacked someone.

And there was still the matter of Thomas's threat. It had been eleven days. Six days left. Rand still couldn't say if Georgia was destined to die from cystic fibrosis or an attack by Thomas. At that point, either seemed likely.

He forced himself to believe Thomas would be the cause. If not, then the girl would perish regardless of what he did for her. He kept that little detail to himself.

"And what do we do until then?" Nick asked.

"Cope. Be together. Keep an eye out for anything strange happening. If you see something, leave." Rand wished he had a better answer.

Nick didn't like the response, but he nodded anyway.

Rand and Libby returned to the Coffee Bean, where they found Rachel sitting alone at a table, playing on her phone with an empty cup in front of her. She looked up when she saw them approach. "How is everyone?"

"Not great," Rand said. "But I'm not out of ideas yet."

She frowned. "You seem stressed."

He shrugged.

"Mr. Rand."

He turned at the sound of his name. Harold the security guard had followed him down to the first floor.

"Harold," he said. "I didn't sign out. No one was at the desk when I went by, but I already threw my visitor sticker away."

Harold raised his hand. "Not a problem at all." He glimpsed at Rachel and scanned their matching formal attire. "Sorry to disturb. You folks seem busy."

"What can I do for you?"

"I was hoping you could look at something."

Rand glanced between Libby and Rachel. Both seemed tired, and it was already nearing midnight.

"It's about what's been going on with Miss Georgia."

"What about her?"

"Well, in the time since I last saw you, there's been some interesting things happening on the security footage. Given what you do, I was hoping you could take a look. I've shown every member of the team, but no one can make any sense of it."

"Paranormal activity?" Rand asked.

Harold winced. "I'd call it... unexplained."

"In Georgia's ward?"

"Not just there. All around the facility."

"And when did it start?"

"A few nights after you were last here."

After the cleansing, Rand thought.

He turned to Libby, who shrugged. "You should check that out, Dad."

Rand dug into his pockets and handed his keys to Rachel. "You two take my car. I'll grab a taxi."

"Is everything okay?" Rachel asked again.

"I have to look into this. I'll see you soon." He kissed her, and before she could protest too much he followed Harold down the corridor.

"I apologize for interrupting whatever you folks were up to," Harold said, "but I really do think you need to see this."

16

Harold led the way down several long hallways at the back of the hospital, then onto an elevator down to basement level 2. All the doors down there required badge access, which Harold had.

"I'm sure it goes without saying," Harold said. "But please keep this between you and me. The general public is not permitted in this area."

"Already figured."

They reached a double door with SECURITY plastered across.

"Wait here," Harold whispered, then went inside, leaving Rand alone in the silent hallway, grey and dim.

The door opened again and Harold motioned for him to enter.

Inside was another security guard, who watched the many monitors, all showing the live streams from the cameras throughout the hospital. The man looked Rand up and down.

"This is the ghost guy I told you about, Jerry," Harold said.

"Ah." Jerry popped his gum. "Glad you're here. Harold's all stressed out, so maybe you can tell him he's crazy."

Harold waved his hand dismissively at his coworker but smiled all the same.

They went into a smaller room on the other side of the main control panel, one filled with computers, metal shelves laden with boxes, and other equipment. A computer was set up on a workstation against the wall.

Harold shut the door behind them. "We can review the videos in here. Have a seat."

Rand lowered himself into the black plastic chair in front of the computer. Harold pushed the button on the monitor and it came back to life.

"A few days after you left, some other staff started going on about weird experiences in their own departments. One nurse even quit over it. I spent my lunch hours down here reviewing the film, and turns out I found a few things. I spliced them together for the next time you came by."

"Okay. Lay it on me."

Harold leaned his heavy frame over Rand's shoulder and used the mouse to click through some files saved in a separate folder.

The first video that Harold pulled up Rand recognized as the nurse station at the front of Georgia's ward. The image was grey-blue, soundless, with the time and date written on the bottom corner in white letters.

"You can follow Nica here," Harold said, pointing to the nurse frozen in the frame. He clicked a button and the footage rolled.

Nica started at the nurse station, where she looked through papers and gathered them together. Then she set out down the hall, carrying her chart close to her chest. The camera angle switched over as soon as she walked out of frame. The colorful cartoon walls were greyed out by the footage's default lens.

"Watch this," Harold said.

The stream blurred. Static dotted the screen at the corners, but the camera continued recording. The picture was clear enough to see what happened next.

Nica's body jerked backward as if pulled by a strong force. She whirled around, startled. When she saw no one there, she clutched her chart against her chest and hurried the rest of the way down the hall.

"Did you catch that?" Harold asked.

"Yeah."

"It looked like something came up behind her and yanked her back."

"Does that static normally happen?"

"I noticed that too," Harold said. "And no, it doesn't. These cameras record in high quality."

That alarmed Rand. Spiritual activity had a tendency to interfere with electronic equipment. Since the glitches began right before Nica was grabbed, that was a bad sign.

"Is there more?"

"Oh boy." Harold shook his head and clicked a few times to load more footage. In the next video, it showed a normal square, carpeted room.

Rand noted the time at the bottom of the screen. Four o'clock in the morning.

"This is the playroom in one of the wards," Harold told him. "Obviously, none of the children are allowed in there at four, and there are no volunteers at that time."

"Right."

The seconds ticked away in the corner of the screen. The closet door opened by itself, painfully slow, as if blown by the slightest of breezes. Then it came to a halt, completely agape.

Static appeared again, causing the entire picture to blank out in zigzags of white and grey. When the video settled, the image had changed.

The contents of the closet had been thrown all over the floor. Game pieces were strewn about, play money covered the carpet like confetti, and the boxes that contained them were scattered. It was a huge mess. According to the time on the tape, it had only taken a few seconds for the closet to be ransacked.

And, of course, there was no perpetrator caught on video.

"When I came in that morning and I heard someone had thrown

the board games all around, I checked the footage and this is what I found. They all thought it was one of the children, but there was no child on the tape. Even when it blanked out, no kid could have messed it up that fast and then gotten away *and* been lucky enough to do it right when the stream cut."

"Exactly," said Rand. "Did you bring this to the director's attention?"

Harold shrugged. "No. Even though the staff said it was one of the kids, they didn't want to point fingers. And besides, the video clearly shows it isn't the kids."

Rand agreed. He'd seen enough paranormal activity caught on security cameras to know.

"I even checked the door that day," Harold said. "It clicks in place when it's closed, so it's impossible for it to slip and open by itself. And if you were to open it just a fraction, then it stays put because the hinges are good."

"I believe you," Rand said.

The next piece of the stream showed Nica the nurse and one of the high school volunteers in the game room a few hours later, appraising the mess. They were talking, but none of the audio was captured.

After a lengthy discussion, the volunteer got down on her hands and knees and picked up the games, matching the pieces to the proper boards and sets and returning them to the closet.

"One more," Harold said. He clicked a few more buttons and brought up another tape.

They were back at the nurse station. The time was 3:58 in the morning on a different night. The seconds ticked by and no one was around.

"Nica does rounds every so often to make sure everyone is still in bed and that all is good," Harold said.

That must have been what she was doing. Then the same static happened again on the screen. It blurred and blanked out for three seconds. Rand watched the clock.

When it was clear, the nurse's station was a mess. Charts were on the ground. Papers had been thrown everywhere. Drawers were open and their contents—pens, paperclips, sticky notes—were all over the floor. Keyboards had been yanked from their computers and tossed away. Chairs that had been behind the desk were now on the far side of the room on their sides.

It would have taken time to create such a huge mess, yet it was all done within a few lost moments on the video.

The seconds ticked by, and eventually Nica walked back into the frame. She stopped short, looking around and scratching at her head. Then she ran away and was gone for several minutes before she returned with a security guard, who also looked confused.

"That's Keith," Harold said. "Works nights. He later told me he couldn't explain what happened, and that no one was there at all. Nica quit a few days later."

As the footage rolled on, it showed Nica and Keith picking up the nurse's station. It would take them the rest of the night, Rand knew.

Harold shut off the screen. "I'll keep monitoring. But I have a feeling it's only going to continue."

"It will," Rand said. "Thank you for showing this to me. This is exactly what I needed to see."

"What happens now? I'm worried for Miss Georgia."

"I am too. Now we deal with the problem. Don't worry, I have a plan."

"Is there any chance that this thing could... you know... hurt us?"

"Regardless, it's best if we remove this spirit as fast as possible."

Harold fixed him with a grim stare.

They returned to the main control room, where Jerry tapped at a game on his cell phone while the monitors streamed in front of him. It was the middle of the night, and there wasn't much activity going on.

"I trust everything has been thoroughly debunked," Jerry said without looking up.

"How I wish," said Harold.

Something on the video feed caught Rand's eye. Something that Jerry wasn't paying attention to. "Is this live?"

"Yeah." Jerry looked up for the first time. "Why?"

"Who's this?"

Rand pointed to the monitor in the corner. It showed the lobby of the hospital, now empty at the late hour. A teenage boy sat on one of the benches in the center of the room.

"It's a kid," Jerry said.

Rand checked his watch. "At midnight?"

"Maybe he's visiting?"

"No one else is in the lobby."

The three men watched the feed in silence. The boy did not move. Not to scratch an itch, not to look around, seemingly not even to breathe. He was like a statue.

"What's his deal?" Jerry said.

"Can you rewind this?" Rand asked. "To see how long he's been sitting there?"

"Yeah. Hang on." Jerry set his phone aside and clicked things on his control panel. He uploaded the feed to the screen right in front of him and rewound.

As the footage went backward, the time stamp in the corner reversed. An hour ticked away, then two hours. The boy had not moved.

"What the hell?" Jerry said. He mashed his finger down on the button and the rewinding sped up.

The time rolled back to five o'clock in the afternoon, where the frame filled with visitors and staff leaving for the day. They all walked past the boy, none acknowledging his presence. Four o'clock, three o'clock, two o'clock.

Then, somewhere between two and one, the boy disappeared within the space of a single frame. No footage of him coming or going.

Jerry looked up at Rand. "What did I just see?"

"Harold, did that kid look like Thomas?"

"Hard to make out on the camera, but yeah, there's definitely a resemblance." The man shook his head. "You have to help us, Rand."

Jerry busied himself rewinding and playing and analyzing the frames where Thomas disappeared, searching for any kind of rational explanation.

Rand knew he would not find one.

17

Rand's eyelids dropped closed as he drove, head bobbing up and down as if his body was trying to force a shut-down. It was one thirty in the afternoon and he'd tossed and turned the night before, thoughts consumed with Georgia. He was fueled only by three cups of coffee and a desperation to help the Collins family.

He pulled his orange Jeep into the parking lot of the elementary school. Children filled the playground, playing soccer or basketball —all form and rules disregarded. Their collective shrill voices carried to where his Jeep idled.

The teachers on duty stood in a huddle near the fence—three women and one man. The man spotted him, said something to the group, and the others turned around. They knew Rand's car. He was the only person in town who owned a bright orange Jeep.

Rand picked out Katie among the teachers. Her eyes lingered on him the longest.

Katie's colleagues murmured to each other for a long time, casting sideways glances at him. Eventually, Katie broke away from the group and went through the gate in the chain-link fence that separated the playground from the parking lot.

She sauntered toward him, arms folded across her body, looking down at the pavement.

Rand rolled down the passenger window.

"What are you doing?" she whispered through clenched teeth. "You can't just show up at my workplace. Especially an elementary school. That's creepy."

"Everyone over there knows who I am," Rand said. "And that I'm not a predator."

"Maybe not a predator towards kids, but you're definitely a predator to me." Her voice was icy.

"That's a colder reception than I anticipated, I'll admit," Rand said. "But you know I wouldn't come unless it was important. I need to talk to you."

"About what?" she shot back. "What could there *possibly* be left for you and me to talk about?"

"Business," he answered. "And business only. I'm hoping you're able to let the personal stuff slide for now."

"I can't let the personal stuff slide, Rand. And our business is resolved."

"Again, I told you I wouldn't come unless I needed to, and I'm desperate. This isn't about me. Can you sit?" He nodded toward the passenger seat.

"Your window is down, I can hear you just fine."

"It would be better if you sat."

Katie rolled her eyes, then opened the door and got into the car. The other teachers on duty watched them with unbroken gazes. None of the kids were paying them any attention at all.

"What's this about?" Katie asked. She pushed up the sleeve of her purple sweater and checked her watch. "Recess ends in six minutes. You have three."

"I'm involved in a case," Rand said.

"You're always involved in a case."

"I need you for this one."

Katie groaned. "Don't tell me that."

"Please. You're the best there is."

"I'm the only one there is."

That was true. Katie held kind of a monopoly on the clairvoyant market in town.

"You know I wouldn't call you if it wasn't serious. It's about a little girl. She's fifteen years old."

"I spend my day with ten-year-olds."

"This one is sick. Very sick. Terminal, actually."

Katie finally looked at him earnestly for the first time. "What do you mean?"

"Over at St. Mary's. Her parents came to me after class, told me their daughter speaks to the ghost of a friend who passed away three months back. They weren't sure if it was real or just her way of dealing with her situation, so they wanted me to get to the bottom of it. Got some EVP of her talking to the ghost, and it told her the day of her death."

"Oh my God," Katie said, her eyes growing wide. Like him, she knew the gravity of asking a spirit about the hour of death. "That's so terrible."

"Here's how it's complicated. Her disease is terminal, and she could pass away at any time. So I don't know if the spirit was talking about her illness or if he was going to do something to directly cause her death."

"So it could be that no matter what you do, you still lose her," Katie said.

"Exactly." Rand sighed. That little detail hadn't failed to gnaw at him in the back of his mind. "Anyway, I did a cleansing in the room and sent the ghost away. Figured I knew the spirit's story—the kid passed too early and he was hanging around, so I didn't bother to call in a clairvoyant. But then, last night, the ghost came back and was upset. It attacked her in her hospital room. Held the doors closed and blew out her oxygen tanks. It's not even isolated to her room anymore, either. It's causing disruption in other areas of the hospital, too. I've seen the security footage."

"And?" Katie asked, suddenly interested.

"The usual. It's throwing stuff around in the middle of the night, knocking things over, making a big mess. You know, just trying to get attention. People notice it now, and if we don't do something about it, then it'll only get crazier."

Katie let out a deep breath and settled in the seat. Her teacher colleagues murmured amongst each other, probably speculating on why Katie was talking so long to an ex-boyfriend—one they had no doubt heard so much about.

"I need to bring you in," Rand said. "I want you to talk to him, find out exactly what he wants, because it seems I misjudged his desires. You can smooth-talk him into the afterlife, send him away, save this family loads of grief in this already difficult time for them, and then, after that… we can never see each other again if that's what you want."

"Of course that's what I want," Katie shot back.

There was no code of conduct in the ghost-hunting business, but if Rand were to ever write one, he would mandate one never sleep with their clairvoyant.

Something about dealing with the supernatural had brought them closer over the years, and they had ended up in a relationship. Since they had worked together so often, that had inevitably ended up in disaster.

"I can't involve myself with this stuff again," Katie said. "Or with you. I have a normal life now. A normal job." She gestured toward the playground. "I love my students and I love what I do. I don't want all that… chaos."

It was true. For many long years, Katie had used her special gift for good. But over time, Rand had seen the all-nighters and the stressful, terrifying situations take their toll on her. She was young, only twenty-seven if he remembered correctly, but she already looked about five years older.

"I understand," Rand told her. "I'm not asking you to go back to it completely. I'm only asking you for just this once. For the little girl. If it were any other client, I wouldn't ask. But you wouldn't believe how cool Georgia is. And how much her family has already been tormented."

Katie took in a long, heavy breath and let it out slowly. "Rand. You know how it is. There can never be just one—this is a lifestyle. And it's not even one that I can choose. I was lucky to get out of it when I did, and if I go back, I'll be roped in forever. My life is good now. It's normal."

"You're denying your gift," Rand said. "You were given it for a reason. And I'll make sure that this is the last case you ever get involved in, at least from me. If you do this, I promise, you'll never hear from me again." He held out his hand.

Katie looked at it, considering. Rand knew it wasn't him personally that was the main problem. It was the life of chasing ghosts and dealing with the spiritual world.

Movement on the other side of Katie caught Rand's eye. A boy was chasing a rolling basketball through the parking lot. He ran up to it and bent down to snatch it up.

"One of your kids got loose," Rand said.

Katie followed his gaze.

The kid had run between the Jeep and the other teachers' line of sight. Yet none of them reacted.

Rand's mouth went dry.

The boy straightened, basketball underneath his arm and pressed against his side. Now that Rand had a better view, he looked more like a teenager than an elementary school child.

And he looked Rand directly in the eyes. Although the midday sun was bright, and he wasn't that far away, a shadow still fell over his face, obscuring it.

Katie looked back at him. "What kid?"

"Shit," Rand muttered. He threw open the Jeep door and ran around the front. But in the split second he'd taken his eyes off the boy, the kid had vanished. He checked between the parked cars nearby, but he wasn't there.

"Rand, what are you doing?" Katie shouted through the passenger window.

He returned to the Jeep and shut the door behind him. Katie

looked at him, worried, but he knew she understood what was going on. "How long?" she asked.

"First time I've seen him."

She swallowed. "So he's appearing to you now."

"I told you it's escalated."

Often, once the spirits realized what he was and that he was against them, they'd switch their efforts to him. Try to scare him off the case. Since that never worked, their attacks eventually turned physical in time.

"At least I know you're not making it all up," Katie said, then sighed. "I'll go with you just this once since you're starting to see apparitions. And when we go, you will not tell anyone about this. And then when it's over, you are not to contact me about any case ever again."

"Deal," Rand said.

"I live with my boyfriend now," Katie said. "You can pick me up from his house. He'll be out of town for business, so he won't know I'm gone."

Funny. He hadn't heard about her getting a new boyfriend. "Sure."

"I'll text you the location. Is your number still the same?"

"Yes."

"A miracle with all the phones you go through."

Spirits liked to smash his stuff when they got mad at him. That was why he couldn't have nice things.

She got out of the car as the bell rang and the children lined up. She rejoined the other teachers, all waiting expectantly for her to tell them why in the world her ex-boyfriend had shown up to her work, but Rand noticed that she didn't indulge their curiosity.

Rand started the engine and drove away, scanning the parking lot one more time for the boy and his basketball.

18

That night, Rand wolfed down the dinner he had prepared for him and Rachel. Chicken thighs and rice. It was one of the few recipes he'd perfected.

"So, let me get this straight," Rachel said, taking another sip of wine. "You have to go back to the hospital tonight?"

"Yes."

"And do a second little ritual thing? This time with a... what?"

"A clairvoyant. She's more sensitive to the spiritual world than most normal people. It's also easier for her to communicate with presences. After we figure out what this ghost wants, then we'll be better able to successfully send it on its way."

"And how do you know this clairvoyant?"

"We used to date."

Rachel choked on her wine, then wiped her mouth with the back of her hand. "Sorry?"

"Well, really we only hooked up. But we hooked up a lot, so does that count as dating? Maybe just a relationship. We had a relationship, yeah, but we never actually went on any dates. If that makes sense."

"You're seeing an ex tonight?"

"Yes, but not like that. She's going for Georgia." He took another mouthful of food.

"I'm... not sure how I feel about that."

"It will be weird for me too. Before, it was like hooking up with someone from work, because we used to team up on a lot of cases a long time ago. But for Georgia Collins, I had to pull her in. She's the most gifted of anyone I've ever met, and the family needs her. That's all it is."

Rand wasn't stupid. He could see that Rachel didn't like that he was seeing an ex-girlfriend, and he knew his casual explanations weren't doing much to assuage her feelings. But the case came first, always. And he didn't like to lie to the people he cared about, so he gave her the blunt truth. If she was uncomfortable with that, there wasn't much he could do. It was the nature of the job.

He finished his food and dropped his plate in the sink. Rachel's food remained half-eaten in front of her.

"I'll be home late," Rand said, kissing her forehead. He threw his keys in his jacket pocket and picked up his bag, already packed with the things he'd need for the night. "This will be the last time I have to go there. I'm sure we can take care of this spirit tonight."

"Yeah," Rachel said, swirling her wine around in the glass.

Just then, thunder boomed in the sky. The clouds opened up, and rain came hurtling down.

Rand frowned. "Great."

"Drive carefully," Rachel said, her voice still flat and unimpressed.

As HE DROVE, Rand tapped the latest text from Katie. She'd dropped a pin—the location of her boyfriend's house. He hadn't looked at it closely when she'd sent it, but now he squinted at the map, his eyes darting between the road and his phone.

The pin was in a very nice part of the town, where the houses were massive and the families were rich.

That couldn't be right. Could it?

Sure enough, Rand followed the pin right to Azalea Lakes, the most prestigious neighborhood in the city, filled with small mansions, huge yards, and three-car garages. Rand had never been inside but had seen plenty of pictures on the internet.

The security guard stopped him at the booth.

"Name?" the man asked, clearly bored. The rain still pelted down, falling into Rand's rolled-down window.

"Randolph Casey."

The man typed on his computer. "Rand Casey?"

"Yeah. Sure."

"Here to see Mr. Albright?"

That must be the boyfriend. "Katie, actually."

"Ah yes, also the residence of Katie Fitz." The security guard cast him a suspicious, sidelong glance. "Does Mr. Albright know you're here to visit his home?"

"I'm sure he has full access to your records of who comes and goes," Rand said, meeting the guard's gaze.

"You're right. He does. Have a good evening, Mr. Casey." His voice was ice cold.

The gate opened and Rand proceeded through, knowing that Mr. Albright would surely hear about his little visit. He hoped it wouldn't cause any trouble for Katie.

Rand pulled up in front of the house and stared at it for a long while. It was huge. He could only chuckle and shake his head. All his ex-women had a habit of springboarding from him to rich, stable, successful men. Men who didn't spend their time chasing ghosts around dark rooms.

The front door opened and Katie emerged, pulling her jacket hood over her head as she ran across the yard toward his Jeep—no short distance. He reached over and opened the door for her, and she climbed in. Despite the coat, she was still soaked. The rain fell thick and accumulated into giant puddles on the sides of the road, unable to drain quickly enough.

"Let's get this over with," Katie said.

"I hear you." He turned around and pulled away from the house. The security guard opened the gate for them on the way out and let them proceed without any questions, but he glowered at Rand. Katie, however, gave him a friendly wave, which he woodenly returned.

"That guy thinks I'm here to cause trouble for Mr. Albright," Rand said.

"He likes Mitch a lot."

"Mitch, huh? And when did you meet Mitch? What's Mitch do?"

"Rand..."

Rand shut up. None of that mattered, anyway. Only Georgia Collins.

19

R and found Harold waiting for him at the Coffee Bean, just as the man had said. An almost empty cup of black brew rested in front of him while he stared blankly at the table, wringing his hands together.

"Evening," Rand said, and Harold snapped out of his trance. "This is my colleague, Katie. She'll be assisting me."

Harold forced a smile and stood to shake Katie's hand.

"You all right?" Rand asked.

"Just nervous."

"I am too," Rand said, not untruthfully. His wet jacket froze to him in the chilly hospital air. "Has everything been arranged?"

"I've talked to the nurses working tonight. They've agreed to give you folks two hours alone time on the ward. This took a lot of convincing; you're lucky that Donna's the shift lead, and that she's had her own weird experiences up there lately."

"Understood," Rand said.

"All these ladies could lose their jobs for abandoning their posts," Harold said. It was the most serious Rand had ever seen him. "Me as well for being part of it. I know you won't, but they've asked me to remind you not to take advantage of all this."

"You have my word," Rand said. A heaviness settled on him, pressing against his heart at asking the man to put his own job on the line for them.

Harold nodded once and took out his cell—a plain flip phone that must have been ten years old. He punched in the numbers, eyes squinting as he struggled to read the tiny keypad. "They're here," was all he said into the receiver before closing the phone. "Donna and the others will vacate. I'll walk you up, then make myself scarce."

"Got it."

Harold offered him a walkie-talkie. "Borrowed this from Jerry. If you need to get in touch with me, I'll be on the other end. Channel nine is never used by the staff, so tune in to that one."

Rand took it and twisted the knob. It flared to life with a burst of static. He clipped the device to his belt. "Anything else?"

"Kick this bastard out of my ward. I'm tired of seeing so many good people go through so much."

The three started toward the elevator. Once inside, Harold pressed the button for the tenth floor.

"Where will you be?" Rand asked.

"I'll head to security and keep an eye on everything from the cameras. Jerry's off tonight and Juan called in sick, so it'll just be me. If anything—"

A tight hand clutched Rand's arm. He turned in time to see Katie stumble backward and fall hard against the elevator's back wall.

"Oh," Rand said, rushing to support her. She leaned heavily against him. "Katie, what's wrong?"

Her palm went to her chest, which heaved with deep breaths. "I can't," she managed between gasps.

"Katie, what is it?"

"I'll get help," Harold said, reaching for his radio.

"No!" Rand held out his hand, and Harold froze, confused and nervous.

"Katie. What do you feel?"

"It's so powerful," she said. Sweat had broken out on her forehead and her eyes welled with tears. "So much."

The elevator chimed at each floor as it rose.

Ding. 6.

Ding. 7.

"I can't go up there," she said.

"You have to," Rand said.

"I've never felt anything so—"

Ding. 8.

Katie's knees gave way, and she slumped to the floor. "Stop the elevator! It's getting worse!"

Harold reached for the emergency button.

"No, Harold!"

The man looked between him and Katie, unsure of what to do.

"Rand," Katie said. "It's too much. There's something big up there. We need to leave."

Ding. 9.

Rand put both his hands on Katie's cheeks, ice cold and slick with sweat and looked into her eyes. "We've never run away before, Katie. It's just not what we do. We have to be strong for the people who can't be. Remember?"

She slowly nodded between his palms. The tears broke and began to stream down her cheeks.

Ding. 10.

The doors slid open.

Harold pressed a button on the panel that froze the elevator in place. As he'd promised, the ward was empty. It was after hours, so half the lights had been turned off, leaving the corridor in a dim light, the shadows edging the colorful cartoon animals and children on the walls. The nurse station was vacant.

"Can you stand?" Rand said. His words were loud against the silent ward in front of them.

Katie sniffed and nodded curtly. She crawled to the other side of the elevator and used the sides to support herself. Once she was steady, she stepped out into the ward.

She froze, then looked around. Brought her hands to her mouth to keep herself from crying out.

Be strong, Rand thought. He had never seen her react so intensely before. Nor had he known her to get visions so fast. *We weren't even there yet.*

Katie walked toward the large area near the nurse station, focusing all around her as if a crowd of distracting people surrounded her.

"What's going on?" Harold whispered.

"She senses something," Rand whispered back. "She can feel what's there. Things that we can't see."

Katie's shoulders shook as she sobbed, but still, she pressed on. She crossed her arms, rubbing her hands up and down her sleeves as if they were crawling with bugs.

"What is this?" she whispered to herself. "How can this be?"

"Should we do something?" Harold asked. "She seems upset."

"Leave her be for now. Let her work."

Katie leapt to the side, appearing to be startled by something to her right. But Rand saw nothing. "I'm sorry," she said through her tears. "I don't know what to do for you. I can't—"

She was speaking to someone. *Does she already hear voices? That's unusual without first going into a trance.*

"Please. It isn't my fault," Katie said.

Rand noted she was looking toward the ground rather than to the corners of the room, where she normally focused. Spirits had a penchant for lingering in the corners.

"Rand, this can't go on," Harold said, no longer whispering. "If you don't do something, I will."

"Please! No!" Katie screamed, then turned and ran. She bounded toward the stairwell, where she banged open the door and disappeared.

"Katie!" Rand called, following her.

Katie's footsteps clanged and echoed off the grey walls of the narrow staircase as she ran down.

"Katie!" Rand's voice boomed around him. Over the railing, her figure sprinted down, winding in a circle along the steps that hugged the wall, like water down a bathtub drain.

"I have to get out of here!" Katie shouted back at him.

"Wait for me!"

Finally, he caught up to her. She sat on the last step by the door that led to level six, her back to him, leaning against the metal handrail and crying.

Rand dropped down next to her and she put her head on his shoulder. He gave her time to get it all out, wondering what on earth she could have possibly seen.

"What's going on?" he whispered to her.

"Rand, we can't stay here."

"You know that's impossible." He kept his tone gentle. "What was it? Was it Thomas?"

Katie looked up at him, eyes wide and red and full of tears. "Rand. The spirits of children on the tenth ward... there are *hundreds* of them."

20

Hundreds.

It took Rand a minute to process what he'd heard. "What?"

Katie wiped her eyes and sat up straight. The anxiety brought on by being on the tenth floor subsided. "There are hundreds of spirits up there. They rushed me all at once. They grabbed at me, cried at me, begged me to look at them. I couldn't hear any voices, but I saw it all on their little faces."

Rand swallowed. "How is that possible?"

No wonder his cleansing ceremony hadn't been effective. Could it be that Georgia was interacting with more than one spirit?

"Surely lots of children have passed on that ward over the years," Katie went on. "Some I could sense have been there for decades. There were *so many*."

"I don't get it," Rand said. "How is it that hundreds of kids could not move on?"

Katie let out her shaky breath, steadying herself. "All of them had harmless energy. They're innocent. But there was one not like the rest."

"One?"

"I didn't see him. But I felt him stronger than all the others. One of them is dark and angry." She looked at him. "And he did not want us there."

Rand licked his lips. "They're trapped," he said. "Whoever this one is, it's keeping the rest from moving on."

"I think so," Katie said, sniffing again. "I could sense that all the kids wanted to do was leave, but they couldn't. They were so desperate and it broke my heart. I'll never be able to unsee that ever again."

Rand clenched his jaw. He never would have insisted Katie join him had he known what they were truly up against. As usual, everyone around him was affected by his cases and his life.

"How do you feel?" Rand asked her.

"A bit better."

"Do you need to go?"

She paused to consider before she answered. "No. I'm here, so we should finish. There's a huge problem on that ward, so I can't in good conscience leave those children there now."

"I'm sorry. I had no idea they were there."

"You couldn't have known. What do we do now?"

"You said there's the one that doesn't feel like the others?"

"Yes. It's very different from the rest," Katie said.

"That's who we need to get in contact with."

HAROLD WAS WAITING for them at the top of the stairs. "Everything all right, folks?"

"Yes," Katie said. "I was just caught off guard with what I found up here. It's been a while since the last time I've done this."

Rand nodded at her little white lie. Despite the rough beginning, Katie would pull through with the strength and determination he'd always known her to have.

Harold, though, seemed skeptical. "You guys sure?"

"Yes," Rand said. "Now it's time to get to work." He checked his watch. They had about an hour and forty minutes left before the nurses returned to their post.

"What do you need me to do?" Harold asked.

"Head to security. We'll take the rest from here." By Rand's side, Katie's eyes darted around the room, likely taking in all the spirits that had desperately hoped to see her return.

"Remember the radio. I'm only a call away."

"Same."

Rand knocked on Georgia's door and Nick answered. He stood aside and let them in.

"Everything all right?" he asked, checking his watch.

"Sorry to be late. This is my colleague, Katie. Katie, this is Nick and Maria and their daughter Georgia." Georgia sat on the bed, hands pressed underneath her thighs. She seemed uneasy.

"Nice to meet you all." Katie had composed herself well, hiding the fact that she had recently been crying.

"This is the… what do you call it?" Nick asked.

"Clairvoyant," Katie answered. "Yes, that's me."

"And you can help?"

"I am confident that I can."

Nick sighed in relief. "Good. We're out of ideas here."

"What about you?" Rand asked Georgia. "How have you been since last night?" She only shrugged. "Anything paranormal going on?"

"Not so far," she said. "But I'm sure now that you're here something else of mine will get smashed." Her television had not been replaced. "If you're the ghost man, I guess that makes her the ghost lady."

Katie smirked. "I can get on board with that nickname."

"Do you piss off ghosts like he does? Because if you do, then maybe we should rethink this. He's already angry enough."

"We're not here to make any ghosts angry," Katie said, taking a step closer. "We are here to clear this place so they will leave you in peace."

"Right, right, I've heard it all before. Can we just get it over with so I can go to bed?"

"What do we need to do?" Maria asked. "Anything?"

"We'll try to communicate with the spirit," Rand said. "For that, Katie will act as a medium and allow the entity to reach us through her voice. She's done it many times before and is quite the expert, so there should be nothing to worry about."

Rand hoped that was true. *There is one not like the rest.*

"Like the movies?" Georgia said.

"In a way," Katie said. "But mediums have existed for hundreds of years before they started appearing in movies."

"I think it would be best to have the room as empty as possible," Rand said. "So, Nick and Maria, are you able to let us have some private time? Maybe head down to the Coffee Bean?"

Nick and Maria were clearly uncomfortable with the idea but were pliable enough. "What about Georgia?" Maria asked.

"She should stay," Rand said. "Since she's been the target, it will be easier to attract the spirit and convince him to open up."

"Like bait?" Nick asked.

"Not bait," Rand said. "More like a familiar face."

"Nothing will happen to her," Katie said. "We promise. The only contact will come through me."

The couple looked at each other for a long time before silently coming to an agreement.

"On the bright side," Georgia said, "if I like this, then maybe I've found what I want to be when I grow up. A medial."

"A *medium*. And please try to be more serious about this," Maria said, kissing her daughter on the forehead. "We'll be downstairs. Call if you need us."

Then they were gone.

"Had I known I was coming face-to-face with a ghost tonight," Georgia said, glancing in the mirror and smoothing her hair, "I would have put on eyeliner."

"We want them to leave, remember?" Rand said.

"Them?"

"Him," Rand said quickly.

He got to work on preparations, first by taking Georgia's desk chair and two extras from her closet, then setting them up near each other in a triangle. On the floor between them, he placed a glass of water, a plate of bread, and three candles from his bag, then lit them. Incense went on Georgia's desk and her nightstand. The sweet, powerful smell quickly filled the small room. Rand opened the door just a crack—open doors were much more inviting to spirits.

Georgia was quite interested in the setup. "Is he supposed to be like a stray? Feed him and he'll come."

"It's best to have offerings ready when contacting the other side," Rand remarked.

"Thomas liked the ice cream from downstairs. But that'll be closed now."

"We don't have to be precise."

"Good. Because that would melt."

"Do you have a picture of Thomas?"

Georgia surveyed the mounted corkboard near her bed and removed the pin from a photo among the dozens already there. It was the first time Rand had ever actually seen Thomas. It was a selfie of him and Georgia, him a few inches taller with wavy dark hair swooped to the side, matching cannulas falling from their nostrils. Rand propped the picture against the glass of water.

With the preparations made, Rand turned off the lights and instructed them to sit in the chairs, Katie at the head.

"Everyone hold hands," she said. When they did, the trio formed a circle around the candles and offerings. The room was dark, and the only light flickered from the tiny flames in front of them. "Remember, what we're about to do is simple and has been done for centuries, but it will only work if we keep our minds open to what we may find. Whatever happens, listen to me, and do not break the circle until I tell you to." She spoke strongly, as she always did when instructing newcomers to her séance. But, even in the flickering candlelight, he could see the fear behind her eyes. "Let's begin."

Rand felt Georgia's hand tighten on his own.

"Beloved Thomas, we bring you gifts from life into death. Be guided by the light of this world and visit upon us."

Georgia looked around the room. But the whole place was just as silent as before.

"Beloved Thomas, we bring you gifts from life into death. Be guided by the light of this world and visit upon us."

Katie's palm in Rand's was clammy and her breathing was nervous and uneven. After a prolonged silence, Rand asked, "What do you see?"

"We're not alone," Katie whispered.

Georgia's head darted left and right, up and down, for the first time uneasy.

"Who is here?" Rand asked.

"So many of them."

The candle flames bent and danced all in the same direction as if blown by a light wind.

"I know that you all are here," Katie said, voice trembling, "but please, give us a sign anyway."

The place erupted in clamor. Rapping and beatings on all the walls and floor surrounding them, like hundreds of hands banging every inch of the surfaces that made up the room.

Georgia gasped and jerked in her chair. Rand clenched her hand, afraid she might try to break the circle.

The noises ceased.

"We welcome you here," Katie said. "But there is one among you called Thomas. We wish to speak to him."

Katie had a sharp intake of breath as if someone had pressed cold hands against her skin.

"What now?" Rand asked.

Katie didn't answer. Again the flames flickered, this time so much that they were almost extinguished. But after whatever movement had caused them to shift ceased, the fire regrew.

"What is it?" Rand asked again.

"They've all gone."

Rand straightened. That was new to him. Usually, you had to struggle to bring spirits to a séance, then had to struggle again to make them leave. "Gone?"

"They fled as soon as I mentioned the name."

"I don't get it," Georgia said. "There's more than one ghost?"

"Let's call them back," Rand said.

Katie shook her head. "They won't come. Not as long as we ask for that specific name." Katie licked her lips. "There is one left lingering, though. She's by the door." Her voice was a soft whisper, as if afraid she would frighten the spirit away.

Rand glanced toward the door, but he saw no one there.

"Can you help us?" Katie asked. "Can you bring us the one called Thomas?"

Katie watched the door, and Rand watched Katie. Long moments passed as she waited for a response. Finally, Katie deflated. "She ran away too."

"Call out for him directly, then."

Katie fixed him with a hard look. "I have a bad feeling about that."

"This is who we need to speak to."

Katie took a deep breath. "We wish to speak to the one called Thomas. If you are here, please make yourself known."

Nothing.

"Thomas, please join us here. We have come to speak with you. We want to know what troubles you so we can help you. Do not be afraid."

They waited for a long while. Rand found his heart went from beating to pounding, and while he hadn't been involved in a séance in a while, it was far from his first. *Why am I getting uneasy?*

"He's coming," Katie whispered, clenching his hand. "He's in the hall now."

Her eyes traced the wall over Rand's shoulder. On the other side of that wall was the outside corridor. Katie's gaze drifted along it as if she could see through the wall. Then rested on the door. "He's here." Her voice was thin and terse.

"What do you see?"

"I can't see him. But I can feel him. And it's not good."

Rand glanced at Georgia, who looked frightened and full of questions.

"T-Thomas. I sense you are here. But please, give us a sign."

There was a single, huge rap from the ceiling as if all the pipes and fixtures were about to burst through the plaster and crash to the floor.

She hesitated before continuing. "Thank you for coming. We're here to help you. Tell us what you need us to know."

Katie let the silence linger on. Raw nerves clawed at the inside of Rand's stomach; he could not remember the last time he'd been anxious in the presence of a spirit.

Katie only frowned. "Thomas, there must be something we can talk about."

Her eyes were still at the door, and she looked upset.

After another long pause, Rand asked, "What's going on? Is he talking?"

"He refuses to say anything," she said.

"He's silent?"

"No." For the first time since Thomas had arrived, she took her eyes from the door. Even in the dim candlelight, Rand saw that her tears had returned. "He's speaking. But refuses to answer my questions. He says there is only one person here he will deal with, and it's you."

Usually, the spirits were happy enough to communicate through Katie. But Thomas had been stubborn up until then. Perhaps it was because Thomas was already familiar with Rand from the last cleansing ceremony.

Or angry at Rand for trying to get rid of him, more likely.

"Okay. We can do that. I'm listening."

"No," Katie said. "He's only got one message for you. He keeps saying 'follow me.' "

21

A new wave of dread crashed into Rand.

"Follow him?"

"He's not saying anything else," Katie said. "And he won't leave until you do."

"Don't do it," Georgia whispered. She looked utterly terrified. "Or let me at least come with you."

Katie shook her head. "He wants Rand alone."

"Right," Rand said, pushing away any fear that may have crept in. Thomas would be able to sense it, so he had to remove it. "No problem. I'll follow him."

This means he has something to show me, Rand thought.

"First, though, we need to end the séance properly," Rand said.

To the room, Katie said, "Spirits, thank you for coming. You can return to your own world." Then to Rand and Georgia, she said, "We'll let our hands go on the count of three. One. Two. Three."

They broke the circle all at the same time. Katie blew out the candles.

As soon as she did, the door creaked open by itself, all the way.

"Guess I'll get going," Rand said, standing from the chair.

"Call if you need us," Katie said, and for the first time in a long while, looked concerned about his wellbeing.

The lights flickered in the corridor outside. The hallway was long and straight, the nurse station at the end abandoned. It looked like the power had gone out and only the backup lights were on, but even those blinked off occasionally, plunging Rand into complete darkness as he stalked down the tiled floor. It was like he'd stepped into a new dimension.

Something knocked on the wall, once just near him, again farther down, and then a third time at the end of the hallway, which echoed back to him.

He followed the sounds, moving cautiously, trying to look everywhere at once. The smiling and innocent cartoon characters on the walls looked a lot more menacing in the blinking light like a twisted audience watching him walk toward a terrible fate.

Often, instead of speaking, spirits wanted him to follow them. They were known to lead him to any possibility of things—sometimes the site of the tragedy that kept them bound to earth, and other times it was the location of their unmarked grave no one had ever discovered.

So when a spirit beckoned Rand to follow, he knew he had to.

The radio on his belt came to life with static. "Rand, everything all right?" Harold asked.

Rand had forgotten about it already. He unclipped it and brought it to his mouth and pressed the button. "Yeah. All good."

"I've got you on camera in the corridor by yourself. What's going on?"

Rand was glad to have eyes on him for this. "Playing a little round of follow the ghost."

No response for a few seconds. "Your time's almost up. Hurry and do what you need to do."

Halfway down the hall, Rand heard the unmistakable sound of bare feet pattering on the tile floor behind him. Running straight for him.

He whirled around just as they came close, only to find no one there. Then, laughter from the other direction where he'd been walking before. When he turned back, again there was nothing.

So we're going to play games.

He reached into his pocket and withdrew the same small recording device he'd planted in Georgia's room and pressed the button to record.

Rand approached the beginning of the corridor, where it opened into the round nurse station area. The circular desk created a cubicle filled with computers, charts, and papers. The only sound was a telemetry machine that beeped as the lines of the heart rhythm dipped up and down, remotely monitoring a patient some-where else on the ward.

Rand shivered as the temperature suddenly plunged to freezing as if he'd walked into a meat locker. His damp clothes clung to him, jabbing tiny, invisible icicles into his skin.

"I know you're here, Thomas," Rand said to the empty room. "Show yourself." He tightened his grip on the recorder in his hand.

Something moved in his peripheral. He turned just in time to see a young boy duck below the counter on the other side of the nurse station, out of view. Rand rushed around the circular desk, but when he got there the boy had vanished.

"Enough playing around, Thomas," Rand said.

Beep. Beep. Beep.

The telemetry machine picked up its pace, the heart rate increas-ing, the beats per minute shooting up impossibly fast.

Beep-beep-beep-beep

Then the machine shut off and the screen went black. The room was silent now.

Rand brought the radio to his mouth and pressed the button. "Harold, are you still watching?"

"I'm here. What's up?"

"Are you seeing anything on your cameras?"

"Nothing besides you running around like a crazy guy."

"There's an apparition. He's messing with me. Wants me to follow him."

A rack of charts tipped off the desk and crashed to the ground, sending papers everywhere.

"That's enough, Thomas," Rand said. "Just talk to me without being destructive. You have my attention."

"Holy moly," Harold breathed into the radio. "I saw that."

The door to the stairwell that Katie ran into earlier opened. He turned in time to catch a small figure disappear through it before it fell back into place.

"The door just opened and closed by itself," Harold said.

"Looks like I'm heading for the stairs."

Rand followed the apparition to the stairwell. He stood in place for a few minutes, waiting for further instruction.

Up or down?

Someone fell from above like they had leapt from the upper story, their body disappearing in a flash past Rand's line of sight and startling him, causing him to jump back.

Rand rushed to the rail and looked down, but the jumper had vanished.

Down.

No matter how softly he stepped, his footsteps clanged and echoed through the narrow room. Round and round, down the stairs, on edge, waiting for the next sudden appearance of the apparition. He kept a tight grip on the cold handrail. Rand had encountered a spirit or two that enjoyed sending hapless victims tumbling down steps—falling victim to it more than once.

The radio gave a sharp burst of feedback.

When Rand came around to the sixth floor, the sign unhooked and fell, turning into a nine. He paused. It swung back and forth on its remaining screw, squeaking until it came to a halt.

"Why'd you stop?" Harold asked.

"He wants me on six."

There was silence for a moment, and then Harold came back in a burst of static. "That's out of bounds."

"I never assumed he'd take me to a public area."

"You don't have badge access."

As soon as he said it, the door creaked open by itself.

"Thomas does. Can you check if I'm clear?"

"Hold on."

Harold disappeared for a few minutes. As Rand waited, he stared at the door, waiting for something else to happen. The room on the other side appeared abnormally dark for a hospital ward.

"No one's around," Harold said. "Place is usually quiet after hours. But here's the thing: the power's out."

"Power's out?"

"Yeah. Sixth floor is on generator power. Same as the tenth. But wards seven through nine are fine."

"That's not the storm, then." *Only the places where Thomas has been are affected.*

"Just be careful, Rand."

Rand opened the door all the way and went into the sixth-floor corridor. As Harold had said, the hallway was dark, only lit by the scant backup lights.

A second later, the door to the stairwell slammed shut behind him. Rand pressed against it, but it didn't budge. Locked. Or something was holding it closed from the other side.

"You should be able to open it from that side," Harold said.

"It's stuck."

"Wait a minute. I can give you remote clearance from here. Okay, try now."

It still would not budge. "Don't worry about it. That way is going backward."

"Yeah, but I'd like to know you have a path out of there if you need it."

"We're moving forward. What's on this floor that I—"

When Rand turned, there was someone on the far end of the corridor. With the backup lights, it only appeared as a black figure. A child's silhouette, his hand gripping an IV pole.

Rand froze. It was the longest the apparition had appeared to him, and it had changed form. Now it presented itself as a patient.

"Rand?" Harold said.

"Are you seeing this?"

"Seeing what?"

"He's staring right at me."

"I don't see anything. But…"

"But what?"

"The video feed is distorting. I might lose you."

The presence is stronger now.

"Thomas," Rand called down the hall. His clear voice echoed all the way. The dark figure did not react to the name. Nor did he move.

Rand took one step forward, wondering just how close he could get to the apparition. But as soon as his foot landed, the boy turned and walked out of sight around the corner. The IV pole's wheels squeaked as he went.

"Thomas, wait!" Rand broke into a run, but when he rounded the corner, the boy had disappeared.

"I know where he's taking you," Harold said.

Rand brought the radio to his mouth as he slowly proceeded down the hall. "Should I be afraid?"

"Don't go, Rand," Harold said. "Turn back. Your time's up, anyway."

"I can't do that. I'm close."

"I'm begging you. There has to be another way."

A boom sounded on Rand's left as if something heavy had fallen over. It had come from the other side of the door he'd just passed.

The sign on the wall said MORGUE.

22

R and's breath caught. *I should've known.*

"I see what you mean," Rand said into the radio. "I'm guessing I need badge access."

"Of course."

"Help me out, Harold."

"Rand..."

"For Georgia."

The man was silent for a long time, and Rand wondered if their connection had been broken. But then, without a word from Harold, the badge scanner near the door handle blinked from red to green.

The light flickered on when he entered, motion activated. A metal examining table stood in the center of the room. Shelves of square boxes lined the walls like drawers in a filing cabinet. Each had a label with a name and identification number. Rand shivered—at first because the place gave him the creeps, but then he saw his breath frosting in front of his lips, and he knew he was not alone in that small room.

He circled back to the door and pushed against it. Stuck. Trapped inside. And this time, there was nowhere else to go.

"Stuck again, Harold," Rand said into the radio. "Maybe you can head down this way and let me out. I have a feeling by the time you get here I'll know what I need to know."

Rand looked around the room again, waiting for Thomas to make his next move. "I'm here. Show me what you want me to see."

Silence.

"I'm losing my patience with you. Enough of these games."

A loud, crashing sound came from behind him.

Rand whirled and saw the walled-in office of the morgue through a glass window. Everything had been swept off the desk and onto the floor by an invisible force.

"Trash the place if you want, Thomas, but you're not scaring me."

The hair rose on the back of his neck. He got the unmistakable impression he was being watched.

And when he turned, the apparition stood on the other side of the examining table, maybe six paces away. It was the boy from Georgia's picture, and he wore a simple hospital gown and gripped an IV pole with his right hand. A single line ran from his vein to the dripping bag that dangled above him. He stared at Rand with a blank expression, almost a glare.

"You don't need to be afraid," Rand whispered. "I'm here to help you."

The boy didn't budge. Rand still held the recorder, ready to pick up any speaking that came from Thomas.

It was then that Rand realized he'd never heard back from Harold.

"Harold," Rand said into the radio. "Are you there?"

"I'm here."

Thomas continued to stare at Rand, holding impossibly still.

"I need you to come let me out. We should be done by the time you get here."

"Can't do that," was all he said. The radio gave static feedback so thick it was hard to discern Harold's words.

Rand licked his lips. "Why's that?"

The feedback grew, and Rand tried to adjust the channel. It

didn't help. The whole time, he kept an eye on the apparition, waiting for it to make a move.

"Harold, I'm losing you."

"Randolph Casey," Harold said through the noise, and his voice no longer sounded like his own. "Why don't you go fuck yourself?"

Thomas turned and put his back to Rand. His untied hospital gown hung open, revealing a gaping wound from Thomas's head to the top of his buttocks. His flesh was open, showing his bloody spinal cord, his guts, his organs.

And Rand knew he was in the presence of evil.

"In the name of Shindael," the radio said in a dark voice, and then he began speaking a language Rand had never heard before. It was not Harold. The entity before him was speaking through the radio.

"Leave here!" Rand shouted at Thomas's back. "I command you—"

Thomas's head twisted around. His eyes glowed blood red, and his face contorted in a grimace.

The voice on the radio spoke faster and louder, jumbled and nonsensical words. Rand drew back and threw the radio right at Thomas, but the boy batted it away with impossible speed and strength. It shattered against the wall of freezers.

The drawer it hit sprung open by itself. Then another. Followed by a third.

Thomas's face no longer resembled a human, but a creature. Red eyes, razor teeth, and scaled skin replaced the guise of an innocent boy.

The drawers opened with such force that the bodies flew from their tables, landing on the floor like stiff, frozen blocks. Naked corpses rained around the room, tossed about by an invisible force.

A table containing a neat arrangement of medical instruments leapt an inch off the ground and fell. Rand spotted it just in time. He gripped the examining table and toppled it onto its side, dropping behind it.

An instant later, the instruments were flying right at him.

Razors, speculums, needles, and scalpels. Their sharp points clanged on the other side of the examining table, some soaring over and hitting the wall behind him.

Although the radio was smashed, the entity still shouted at him in the unknown language. It had changed from Harold's voice to one that spoke with a growl, barking from a creature that did not exist in the natural world. It got so loud that Rand had to cover his ears, feeling like his eardrums would burst at any second.

He couldn't hear himself scream or speak or think. Could not put together the words needed to command the entity to leave.

The lights in the morgue flickered, and then blew out in a rain of sparks, plunging him in darkness.

And in that moment, the oppressive force of the creature in the room with him was too much. He'd never felt such weight, such despair, such *evil*. His only thought was that this must be what it was like for an insect as it was crushed.

And Rand knew he'd lost. It had happened so quickly, and—despite all his knowledge and experience—he'd finally met his match. Whoever this monster was, it was not Thomas, and it was stronger than Rand had ever anticipated.

Hands gripped Rand's arms, which he was using to cover his face. He knew the creature had grabbed him and would now drag him to hell, or eviscerate him, or dismember him. Maybe all three. He fought back against the strong grip, knowing eventually he would lose.

"Rand!"

It knew his name.

But Rand also knew its name. It had told him on the radio. "Shindael!" he shouted. "I command you to leave, Shindael!"

Cold palms gripped his face. "Rand!"

Rand slowly opened his eyes and blinked. Harold came into focus, the big man kneeling over him.

And as Rand regained his composure, the tension left his body, but he still shivered and trembled.

"What—"

His mouth was desperate to move, but he could not form words.

"Come on," Harold said. "Let's get you out of here."

The next thing Rand knew, he was scooped up like a baby, surprised by Harold's strength as he was thrown over the man's shoulder and carried away. Rand tried to protest that he could walk, but it only came out in a jumbled mess.

Because, in that moment, his brain could only process one singular name.

Shindael.

23

Time seemed to skip ahead. The next thing Rand knew, he was in a room he didn't recognize. Bright lights shone overhead. He was on a mattress, one that was soft but not comfortable.

His head ached and throbbed. There were people around. Gradually, his clarity and thoughts came back to him and images of the morgue and the entity flooded his mind.

He shot straight up, only to feel hands on his shoulders, pushing him down.

"Whoa now," Harold said. "Not so fast."

"Relax for a minute, Rand," Katie said.

He looked around. He was in a small hospital room, lying on a stretcher. Only Harold and Katie were with him, and the curtain was drawn over the entrance. He had no idea what time it was, or how long he had been there.

"Katie," Rand said.

"Shh," she said. "You've been hurt."

"What..."

"Our connection cut out as soon as you went—" Harold checked over his shoulder and lowered his voice. "Into the morgue. When I couldn't get you to answer, I came running. Had a feeling something was off—more off than usual—and I was right."

Rand remembered how the entity had impersonated Harold on the radio, and the mysterious language he had spoken. "Thanks for that. I think you saved my ass."

"Looked like it," Harold said. "Never seen a mess like that in my life." He shuddered. Rand recalled the stiff bodies thrown around the room.

"Save those security videos for me," Rand said.

Harold shook his head. "Already tried to play them back. All blank. Destroyed. Whatever was in there with you took care of that."

Katie put her hand on Rand's arm, a soft and comforting touch. "Rand. What happened?"

"It isn't a ghost," he said, wiping at his face. It was slick and greasy as if he'd been sweating a lot. "Never was."

"You mean—"

"We have a demonic presence here."

Harold looked back and forth between Rand and Katie, confused. "Excuse me?"

"Makes sense now that I think about it," Katie said.

"Yeah. Something strong enough to keep the spirits of the children trapped here. Powerful enough to levitate things around Georgia's room. Not to mention its ability to mimic Harold's voice, tamper with electronic equipment, and speak unknown languages."

"I don't get it," Harold said. "What's the difference between a ghost and a demon?"

"Where do we even begin?" Rand's brain pounded from a headache that had settled in the bottom of his skull. "There is no Thomas. It was a demonic entity pretending to be Thomas. He was trying to gain Georgia's trust, and he almost did."

"Until you came," Harold said.

"Yeah."

"Do you think you'll be the new target now?" Katie asked.

"Most likely." In all previous cases he'd worked on involving demonic infestations, Rand had become the target of the entity. That was fine with him. As long as the creature no longer concerned himself with Georgia Collins.

"Where am I?" Rand asked.

"In the emergency room," Katie told him. "Georgia's in the waiting area outside. She's worried about you."

"How nice."

"Rand," Katie said. "What do we do now? We have to get rid of this thing."

She was right. And now that they knew they were dealing with the demonic, their plan of attack had to change.

"We have to cleanse the children's ward and bless it. An exorcism."

"Exorcism?" Harold said, eyes wide. "That's a real thing?"

"More real than you'd probably like to believe," Rand told him. "It's not just for people, though. We use it to remove these entities from places as well." Then Rand remembered something. "My recorder. I lost it in the morgue."

"You mean this?" Harold held it up.

"Ah, good man." Rand took it from him and pressed play. He rolled the recording through the captured audio, hoping the demon's presence hadn't ruined the device. The recording was still intact, thankfully. "Listen to this," he told Katie. He found the part from the morgue, and the heavy, guttural voice came through the speaker. The garbled tongue of an unknown language.

Katie winced at the demon's words. "He must have been close. You can hear him without any amplification."

"That was the closest I've ever been to one," Rand said, shuddering at the memory. "And this one is powerful."

Shindael.

"And... he told me his name."

Katie frowned. "What?"

"Yeah. You heard me."

"Did you command him to tell you?"

"No. That's what's weird about it. He told me on his own like he wanted me to know."

Katie gave him a strange look. "I don't know, Rand. There's something off about that."

A demon's name was one of its biggest weaknesses. If you knew it, it was easier to take control over him and banish him back to hell. Demons went to great lengths to hide their names from those who sought to fight against them.

So why would he volunteer his name so easily?

The curtain was pulled aside, and a doctor entered carrying a chart of papers. "Mr. Casey, I see you're awake." Rand nodded but said nothing. He wondered what reason had been given for his check-in. "Have you ever fainted before?"

"No."

"I wouldn't worry too much. Probably just stress and fatigue. Take some time off work and relax a bit. If it happens again, make an appointment with a neurologist. I'll get your discharge papers ready."

The doctor and Harold exchanged a knowing look before he disappeared on the other side of the curtain.

"Fainting?" Rand asked him.

"Should I have told him you were attacked by a demon, instead? Besides, he knew why you were *really* in the hospital tonight."

"How many people around here know who I am and what I do?" If the word got around too much, that could interfere with his work.

"I told you, Rand. Many people in the hospital are experiencing things now. Whatever you saw in the morgue is getting stronger."

The curtain pulled open again, but this time it wasn't the doctor. It was a woman that Rand had never seen before, dressed in a brown pantsuit and her chestnut hair tied in a bun on the back of her head. She did not seem at all pleased to see him. Rand glanced at Harold, who looked at the newcomer with astonishment, which told Rand this lady was not on the same page. "Mr. Casey?"

"Who's asking?"

She took one step into the room and lifted his wrist. Someone had placed a white hospital wristband on him, stating his name and date of birth.

"I need a word with you, Mr. Casey, if we could have some privacy."

"I don't want to keep secrets from friends." Rand didn't like the intense and abrupt way in which the lady had conducted herself so far. She reminded him of Tessa's mother.

"I insist," she said. "Or, if you prefer, we could go ahead and call the police."

24

Katie eyed him, and Rand nodded. She stood and left. In that moment, he wished he still had access to Bill's open bar. He had a feeling he was going to need it.

"That will be all, Harold. Thank you," the woman said. "You can return to your post."

"Yes, ma'am."

Once they were alone, the woman pulled up the chair Katie had occupied. "My name is Fiona Shaw. I'm the director of the children's ward here at St. Mary's."

Her lips were pressed into a thin line and her cold blue eyes pierced him with a hard gaze. Rand figured all her subordinates cowered underneath that stare.

"Randolph Casey," he said, struggling to sit up on the stretcher. "My friends call me Rand. Religious Studies professor at—"

"I know who you are, Mr. Casey," Fiona said. "And what you do."

"Ah. A fan." He tried his best charming smile, but it did nothing to melt Fiona's frozen exterior.

"Hardly. I'll make this quick. After Dr. Carter has assembled your discharge papers, you will leave St. Mary's and not come back."

"Isn't that always the hope when one leaves the hospital?"

"Mr. Casey, I am very serious. I have added you to the blacklist and you are now banned from this facility. Your name has been distributed to all security and staff, and if you ever show your face here again the police will be called, and you will be arrested."

For the first time, Rand frowned. "Why are you doing this?"

"I'm doing what is best for this hospital and the patients."

He paused and met her gaze for a long time. She did not budge, as if they were playing a staring game. "And what is it you think I did to deserve this?"

"You are responsible for exacerbating rumors that this facility is 'haunted.' " She spat the word as if it tasted bad. "That is not true, and continuing assertions that it is cannot go on. We have lost too many staff members over these crazy tales, and more importantly, should news of this ever get out, it would be very detrimental to the institution. St. Mary's is known in the community as a faith-based healing center with a strong Catholic support system. We can't have the staff thinking ghosts are running around the place."

"Are you a practicing Catholic?" Rand asked. For the first time, Fiona Shaw let her rock-solid shield slip. But only for a moment. Rand took her reaction as a yes. "And you believe in spirits and demons, don't you?"

"This has nothing to do with me."

"It has everything to do with your hospital. Your healing center. Your patients are being tormented by a demonic entity. It has attached itself to Georgia Collins."

"Enough, Mr. Casey. You sound like a crazy person."

But Rand could see how her eyes darted when he'd said the D-word. Saw the way her hands wrung in her lap.

"I'm here to help you. And Georgia."

"Myself and the other directors have already discussed it. If Georgia Collins and her family keep spreading these rumors or engaging in this activity, we'll have to relocate her to a more appropriate place to continue her treatment."

"What? That's not fair. You can't punish her for this."

"This isn't punishment. It's protection for all the patients."

"Don't do this," Rand said. "I get it, you have a hospital to run. But you're letting your job get in the way of your better judgment." Fiona Shaw looked away again. "I'm the only one who can help you. If you don't address this now, it will only get worse. You already told me you know who I am and what I do, so trust me."

Fiona Shaw eyed him hard for what seemed like an eternity. Then she stood and pulled the curtain aside. "I'll check with Dr. Carter and see what's taking him so long with the discharge papers. Remember what I told you, Mr. Casey. I'd hate for us to have an incident in the future."

Rand fell back onto the stretcher and rubbed at his eyes. The headache wouldn't go away and fatigue coursed through every inch of his body. He knew he needed to sleep, but he also wouldn't be able to until the job was done.

The job, which had gotten much more difficult now that he was no longer allowed inside St. Mary's. Rand was accustomed to getting kicked out of places, but this time his banishment was dangerous to others. Without him, Georgia Collins was vulnerable. And since the demon was out of hiding, his attacks would only become more vicious.

Shindael.

When the doctor returned, Rand snatched up the discharge papers and didn't wait around to hear what he had to say.

Katie and Georgia met him in the waiting room. "Who was that lady?" Katie asked.

"We need to make a plan, and now," Rand told her. "We don't have much time."

25

R and wobbled down the hall on rubbery legs, the feeling still had not fully returned to his body. Aches and pains lingered with him, and Fiona Shaw's banishment had been the final kick to put him down.

But he would not lose hope.

"A demon," Georgia said as she and Katie followed behind him. He was limping, like an injured fighter after a beating, and they kept pace with him patiently. "So, you're saying it wasn't Thomas at all."

"No," Rand said. "You were never talking with your friend."

The hospital was starting to wake up. Night-shift nurses were on the way out, looking tired and haggard. The early visitors had appeared, and The Coffee Bean was brewing the day's first batch. A pleasant smell wafted down the corridor, but the thought of having a coffee only made Rand's stomach churn.

"But... it looked just like him."

"They can imitate well," Rand said. "But never perfectly. There is always some kind of flaw." Rand remembered the gashed-open spinal cord from the morgue.

"Now that you mention it," Georgia said. "I could never see his legs. When he appeared, he seemed invisible from the waist down. But why pretend to be Thomas?"

"To gain your trust."

"And after that?"

Rand halted when he walked by the chapel. The door was open, and the inside was dark, like a portal to a different holy dimension within the hospital. And in that moment, Rand felt its strong draw.

"That's the chapel," Georgia said. "Remember? We passed by it the first day you came."

"Are you going in?" Katie asked, concerned. She knew how every time he encountered the demonic, the only thing he wanted to do afterward was get into the presence of God.

"Yeah. I have to."

"Didn't take you for a big man of faith, Ghost Man," Georgia said.

"It's something I have to do. I'll be in touch with you later, okay? Keep your phone charged."

"Am I in, like, a lot of trouble?"

"You're in danger," Rand told her bluntly.

Georgia chewed her lip. "Can you help me?"

"Yes, but first I need to prepare. Then I'll come back as soon as I can."

"But they banned you."

"Does that seem like the kind of thing that'll stop me?"

"Good point, Ghost Man. Just please don't forget about me here. I'm officially scared now." She fist-bumped him and walked away, rolling her oxygen tank behind her.

"Nice girl," Katie said when she was gone. "Now I see why you're so serious about helping her."

"So when I come back, will you join me?"

"I have to," Katie said. "This one seemed to take a lot out of you. It's a powerful presence, and you can't do it by yourself. Or maybe you're just getting old."

"I've never felt anything like it before," Rand said, trying to keep the memory from surfacing again. The presence alone had been so intense it may have killed him if Harold hadn't come for him. "This shouldn't take long," he said, pointing a thumb at the chapel. "Wait for me in the coffee shop—have breakfast or whatever. Then I'll bring you home."

"You want anything?"

"The last thing I want right now is to eat." He placed a hand over his belly, which felt like he had ingested a large stone.

Inside, the chapel resembled a miniature Catholic church. There were pews on either side of the aisle, five on each. At the back was an altar, a table, and a wall-mounted crucifix with Jesus looking down over the sanctuary.

No one had stopped by for morning prayers, giving Rand a welcome solace. The room was colder than the hallway outside and had a pleasant smell of finished wood. Stained-glass windows along the sides depicted Bible scenes. The lights were pleasantly dim in the early hours.

Rand limped down the aisle and sat on the front pew, looking up at the cross and the statue of Jesus.

Rand's involvement with religion had always been complicated. He'd been raised Catholic by a strict mother, lapsed in high school, and forgotten all about it until he'd gotten involved in his current line of work. Now, his relationship with God was strained. He wondered why, if God was all-powerful, he allowed the demons to torment innocent people. Surely with a wave of his hand, he could eradicate them forever. Still, he chose not to. His own life had been irreparably altered. This left him angry at God, but whenever he encountered the demonic, as he had a few hours ago, nothing felt right until he fell before the Lord and sanctified himself.

That made him feel like a hypocrite who only needed God when he faced true evil and thought he could handle all other problems on his own.

But Rand owned that completely. He had seen the minions of hell. After that, it seemed benign to pray about anything else that happened in his life.

"There is evil here," Rand whispered to the statue in prayer.

"Give me the strength needed to save this girl and her family. I ask that you help me help her."

Although he was experienced, Rand always felt self-doubt when going head-to-head with the demonic. There was no force on earth more unpredictable.

"Good morning."

The strong voice startled him from behind, interrupting his prayer. Rand stood and turned. There, he faced an older man who wore a black suit and a white clerical collar around his neck.

"Good morning," Rand said.

The man strolled down the aisle, appraising him. Rand got the feeling that the priest knew who he was.

"Do you know me?" Rand asked.

"No," he said. "But I know what you are."

The headache still lingered in the base of his skull. "A lot of people have been telling me that. I'm worried that it'll soon go to my head."

"People talk in this hospital. You come to visit Georgia Collins, and I'm aware of the things she's been seeing. It's been a long time since she's come down to Mass."

"I'll remind her that going to Mass is highly recommended during times like this." He held out his hand. "Randolph Casey. Friends call me Rand."

The priest clasped it, almost too tight, as if he'd been desperate for another human's touch. "Father Calvin. I understand the family brought you in because of the ghost stories."

"Yes."

"And that you did indeed find a ghost."

"I wish," Rand said. "What I found was worse. A distinguished man of God such as yourself should know what I'm talking about."

Father Calvin only stared at him, a hardness coming across his face like a shield going up.

"She needs you," Rand said.

"I cannot help her." He looked away.

"You must have sensed what was here long before I ever came. Felt it."

"I don't feel much of anything these days," Father Calvin said. "My job is here in the chapel."

"The real job will never be just inside this chapel. And you know it."

"I don't meddle with such things anymore," Calvin said. "I did once in my youth, and it was then that I learned I am not strong enough."

"You are responsible for these patients," Rand said. "There must be something you can do."

Calvin looked at him for a long while, hard and silent. "Let's speak frankly, then. You are talking about an exorcism."

"Yes. This hospital is infested with a demonic spirit. It seems anchored to the tenth ward, specifically—drawn there. It's grown stronger over time, and now that I've come and challenged it directly, it will only become more dangerous."

"I cannot help you," Calvin said.

"Why?"

Calvin sat down in the pew as if he were suddenly too weak to stand. "Twenty years ago, I assisted in an exorcism. It was the only one I have ever been involved with. It was a little girl possessed by a demon named…" He trailed off. "No. I will not name him. But I will never forget the name, or the face of the girl as it invaded her body. He beat her and broke her, pulled out her hair, scarred her. The vulgarities and blasphemies that came out of her mouth were unlike anything I'd ever heard. It took four full days of constant fighting to cast that monster out of her. After that, I knew I could never do it again. It was just too much. I was so weak, so demoralized. For days afterward, I had dreams of hanging myself or jumping off the roof of a tall building. I decided that kind of work was not for me, yet I felt horrible because it seemed it was the highest calling of any man of God. Here I was, content to sit inside a confession booth or give sermons on Sundays. Meanwhile, the real God-fearing men were out there tackling true evil." Calvin looked up at him, and Rand got the impression he was the only one to have ever heard this tale. "But what could I do? I tried once, and it nearly forced me to end my own life. I am not carved from stone like those other priests. God did not give me the same constitution, and surely he would not require it from all of his devoted disciples."

Rand sat in the pew across the aisle. He felt for the man—truly did. He remembered his first brush with the demonic, all those years ago. He'd gone through the same trauma, the same pain, and had come out on the other side as a changed person. He'd known he could no longer go through life ignoring the evil that lurked in the corners of the most innocent and unsuspecting places.

"How did you pull through?" Rand asked.

"Through the grace of God alone."

"So you're okay sitting back and watching the demonic encroach on your territory? On your patients and your flock?"

Father Calvin said nothing. Only looked at the floor between his feet.

"Would you try again? For Georgia and her family?"

"I don't know *what* I'm willing to do anymore," Calvin said. "I've considered that maybe there is nothing we can do. That things will happen as they may, without our control."

"Isn't that called God's plan?"

"Yes, if you're the cynical type. I've seen so many patients come and go in this hospital. Some walk out, some never leave. No matter what prayers I say, very little seems to get answered in the way we ask. So what's the point? Maybe there really is no one listening."

"Now is not the time to lose faith," Rand said, although he felt ridiculous saying it. At the best of times, his own belief was about as solid as a house of cards, something he only cashed in on during situations of desperate need.

"No one chooses to lose their faith, Rand. So I imagine the timing is even more out of our control."

It was hard for Rand to argue. Watching patients die after praying so earnestly for their healing had to take its toll. Such were the mysteries of God, though. Some lived while others died. Some walked and others were crippled. And all the while, inhuman evil spirits ran wild on his flock.

Rand stood from the pew. "I'm coming back soon. When I do, I will remove this spirit from this place. The more people we have fighting for Georgia, the better. I hope I can count on you to join and that you can muster up enough faith for this. It could be the biggest battle of your life."

Father Calvin's face was heavy and sad as he frowned. He looked like he wanted to say something, but just couldn't find the words.

26

The bell jingled over the door when Rand walked in.

The used bookshop was in disarray. Boxes of paperbacks were open and resting in the walkways, big cardboard tripping hazards. Other stacks of books weren't in boxes at all but piled on the tables and the floor and even by the cash register. A thin layer of dust lingered in the air, tickling Rand's nose and threatening to make him sneeze.

He made his way to the counter while stepping over the boxes, making him walk like he was in quicksand. Something crashed to the ground in the closet behind the counter, and someone muttered a curse.

"What's the point of having the bell over the door if you ignore it?" Rand said.

"What's the point of shouting at me when you can clearly see— oh." Miller stuck his head out and finally saw who had entered his stop. "Rand Casey, the one and only." Miller dropped whatever he was holding with a crash and dusted his hands off as he walked out of the closet. "I didn't know you were coming so soon."

"You got my message, right?"

"With all those audio files? Yeah, of course."

Rand looked around at the disorganized state of the place. "Have you had time to look into it, or have you been distracted with all this spring cleaning?"

"It's fall. And I'm not cleaning. You know how much I hate to clean. I'm just trying to reorganize. The stacks have gone crazy on me."

"Or you've been negligent."

"If it weren't unethical to charge for my side gig, I wouldn't have to worry about running this dump."

"So you had time to look at the files?"

"Let's step into my office."

Miller Landingham was a head shorter than Rand and far more overweight than the last time Rand had seen him. His neck and chin sported a healthy orb of fat that spread his already-thin stubble. His black hair was disheveled and greasy, matching the thick rims of his glasses, which made his eyes pop. He almost always wore a button-up, plaid, short-sleeve shirt and khaki pants, and he walked with a deep limp from an injury that Rand had been present for long ago.

The two never would have become acquaintances in real life if Miller's unfortunate brush with the demonic hadn't brought them together years before.

"Even after all this time, the stuff you send me still freaks me out."

"Come on. Where's the professionalism?"

"Don't tell me it doesn't get to you, too. Keep in mind I'm listening to this by myself in here after hours."

He opened the door to the bookshop's back office. It was uncomfortably warm inside, and besides the usual desk and computer and overflowing filing cabinet, there was a brown mattress pushed against the far wall with a single bedspread and a flattened pillow. Crumpled fast-food wrappers and empty soda cans were accumulating around it.

"You're really committed to the overtime."

"Larry spiked the rent on my place last month. Can you believe it? The man's always been a dirtbag."

"So you live here now?"

"I'm crashing until I figure something else out."

Miller sat heavily in the chair at his desk, making the cracked leather groan and letting out a puff of air from the seat. He jiggled the mouse and the computer came to life. "So this Shindael. Yeah, there's a lot on him. He's been busy the past couple of years. Where did I put it?"

Miller rummaged through a pile beside the monitor—invoices, shipping receipts, and overdue bill notices—until he found a stack of papers he'd paper-clipped together. "Here it is. Printed out every instance where I ran across his name on the web."

Rand skimmed through the documents. The printouts were from message boards, online forums, and niche websites that Miller owned and moderated—places where people recounted their own personal accounts of the demonic.

Rand knew well that Miller did not want to face a demonic entity again in person, but he wanted to help out after Rand had rescued him from an intelligent haunting a few years before. The way he did that was by scouring the darkest corners of the internet for information people posted on their own encounters, then saved it all in a large file. It contained eyewitness accounts and personal experiences, and he cross-referenced them for similarities and grouped them together. If one account determined a demon's name, then Miller could match it with other similar stories and discover a type of "MO" for that particular demon. Knowing whom you were dealing with gave you the upper hand in any battle with the demonic.

He also used this information to create a database of known demons and their names—as well as their appearances when someone was unlucky enough to glimpse one in their true form. All of it was like a modern-day grimoire, he'd said once, and Rand had to admit that the data had been useful to him on more than a few occasions.

"And you've vetted the crazies?" Rand asked.

"As much as I could. You'll see all those accounts have at least a few similarities. There are three or four mediums who managed to speak with him. Apparently, he is quite talkative and receptive and usually shows up quickly when called by name." Miller shivered. "Freaks me out just to think about."

Rand thumbed through the pages. The stories were long and drawn out, so he'd have to sit down and read through them later.

"The short version is, he's a high ranker," Miller said. Rand looked up at him. "Yeah. The real deal. There are several demons that are under him, or are his slaves, or servants, or whatever. I saw one account of someone who was able to send away Rakhon-om simply by threatening to invoke Shindael. You remember Rakhon-om?"

"He's a rotten piece of work. But why would Shindael tell me his name?" Rand said, flipping the stack of papers closed. "That doesn't make any sense. These bastards do anything they can to keep me from learning their names. But this one, Shindael, he wanted me to know."

"Because he's an arrogant prick would be my guess," Miller said. "He commands other demons. He ranks in hell. Wouldn't you think you were awesome too?"

"Perhaps."

"Also, get this. Those recordings you sent me..."

"Yeah? You figured them out?"

"It wasn't so simple as Latin or backward English. I had to ship that off to my linguist friend at the university, and then she had to pass it along when even *she* couldn't place it."

"And?"

Miller leaned back in his chair, proud of himself. "Ancient Sumerian."

Rand stared at him.

"I thought you'd be confused," Miller said. He spun and made a few clicks on his computer. He played the audio file Rand had sent him—the recording of Shindael yelling in his deep voice in the morgue, the words unrecognizable.

"Sumer was a civilization in Mesopotamia around three thousand BC," Miller said. "Modern-day Iraq. One of the first to exist. They spoke their own Sumerian language, but it only lasted about a thousand years before intermingling with other civilizations caused Akkadian to become the primary spoken language in the area."

"So in other words, he's showing off."

"That was also my conclusion."

Shindael was probably trying to impress upon Rand how timeless he was. Show how long he'd been watching humans, tormenting them.

"How's the girl?" Miller asked.

"All right for now," Rand said while rubbing at his eyes, exhaustion setting in. "They kicked me out of the hospital, so I have to find a way back to her if I'm going to help."

"Hang in there," Miller said, standing from the chair. "Read those Shindael encounters I printed out for you. See if you can get any useful information."

"Will do."

"And be careful. If this gets nasty and you need any assistance, give me a call."

"But you hate the front line."

"I do. But I have a bad feeling about this one, this Shindael. He seems like a real son of a bitch, so just... watch your back."

27

Stacy Thompson was the last one to hand in her quiz. She always checked and rechecked it, making sure her answers were correct. Rand didn't even have to grade her work against the answer key to know she got a hundred percent.

The girl seemed oddly interested in this stuff. Not something he would have ever expected from someone like her.

She rose from her usual desk at the front of the classroom and passed her paper to him. "Thank you, Stacy," Rand said. "I'm sure it's an A as always."

"I don't know," she said, frowning. "This was harder than the rest."

It wasn't. It was one of the easiest quizzes on his syllabus. As long as she hadn't overthought it, she'd be fine.

He stuffed her quiz in the stack along with the others and shoveled them into his bag. He closed his laptop and put it inside his case. Stacy didn't move.

"Anything else I can help you with?"

"No, sir," she began, although Rand could tell she had something she needed to say. "It's just that... you seem off."

"Off?"

"Yeah. Distracted, spaced out. I don't know. Is everything all right?"

No. Everything was not all right. Stacy was quite perceptive. Georgia Collins and the case at hand had dominated his thoughts lately, as they tended to do, and he was trying his best to keep that from spilling over into his lectures.

"Just some stuff going on right now," he said.

"Like what you talk about in your class?" She gestured toward the screen where he projected his photos of previous cases, hauntings, and demons.

"Yeah."

"That sounds scary," Stacy said. "Please be careful."

"Thank you, Stacy."

Once he was alone in the classroom, he scooped up his stuff and bounded for the door.

He almost ran into someone as they were coming in.

"Excuse me," Rand blurted out and tried to maneuver around the lady in his way.

"Mr. Casey."

A familiar voice. He turned and saw that the person he'd almost bumped into was Doris Galloway, the woman who'd audited his class and wanted to remove it from the university curriculum.

"Afternoon," he said, trying to keep his tone pleasant, but he couldn't afford to think about this right now. "Sorry I ran into you. I'm in a hurry, actually. Is there any way this could—"

"This isn't about the audit," Doris said, stepping closer to him and keeping her voice low. Her face was not stern and inquisitive, as it had been in their previous meeting.

"Oh. What can I help you with, then?" Rand checked his watch.

"The little girl," she said, glancing around them as if she did not want to be overheard. "The one who that couple came to see you about?"

"Yeah?" Rand said, curiosity piqued.

"Is she… okay?" She looked genuinely concerned.

"Not yet. But I'm working with her."

Doris nodded as if she'd been given a bad health diagnosis. "Right. Sorry, it's just that ever since then I've been thinking about it. And about her."

"It's complicated at the moment."

"I understand. Well, I don't, but... I'm just hoping you can help that family."

"I appreciate your concern." Rand smiled.

Doris nodded. Then she straightened herself and her professional mask returned. "That will be all, Mr. Casey."

LIBBY STEPPED out of the elevator on the tenth floor, expecting to be greeted by Harold's friendly smile, but instead it was another man at the security desk.

"Where's Harold? Is he off today?" she asked as she signed in.

"Harold's been suspended," said the man—whose name was Jerry, according to his badge.

"Oh." Libby frowned as she placed the name tag on her shirt. She surmised that had happened because he'd helped her dad.

Libby had never before gotten so involved with one of her dad's cases. But something about Georgia was different. She was a girl Libby could see herself being friends with after this whole mess was over. No one ever deserved to be tormented by a demonic spirit, but Georgia was an especially vulnerable victim. She found herself eager to help in any way she could, so when she'd gotten a text from Georgia an hour before asking her to come and visit, she'd called Justin and canceled their date so she could go.

When Libby entered the nurse station, she stopped short in her tracks. Georgia Collins, her parents, Nurse Donna, three more nurses, and four other children—patients, Libby assumed—formed a circle near the desk, hands joined, heads bowed.

"And lead us not into temptation, but deliver us from evil," Nick Collins intoned. "For thine is the Kingdom, and the power, and glory forever."

Georgia caught Libby's eye and gestured with her head for her to come and join them. Libby walked over and broke into the circle between Georgia and a nurse and clasped their hands.

"There is evil here, Lord," Nick continued in prayer. "We have all been affected by it, and some have seen it. Please intervene and reclaim this place in your name. We are your children, and we dedicate our lives to you. Please rescue us from this creature from hell and give us the courage needed to see through its deceptions."

As Mr. Collins prayed, Libby felt Georgia's hand squeeze hers tighter and tighter, as if afraid to let go.

It had been a long time since Libby had prayed, and in a way she felt as if she did not belong in such a devout circle. But she understood the desperate times these people were facing and kept her head bowed respectfully.

That was until a sharp voice interrupted them from the other side of the room.

"That will be enough."

Nick Collins's prayer was cut short, as if with a knife. There stood a tall and ferocious-looking woman wearing a brown pantsuit, with dark hair tied into a tight bun. Her eyes were ice as she approached the circle, her heels clacking against the tile.

"Miss Shaw," Nurse Donna began, but the woman only held out her hand.

"You know I support prayer and prayerful gatherings. But they are to be done in the appropriate venue and at the appropriate times. There is a very nice chapel on the first floor available to all of our patients." She eyed Donna and the other nurses. "And prayer times should be restricted to your one-hour break. Doing this while on the clock is negligent to the other patients."

Donna looked like she had a great deal of things to say to the frigid woman, but in the end, she acquiesced. "Yes, ma'am."

The prayer circle fell apart like a wilting flower. The nurses returned to the desk and the other children meandered back to their rooms.

Libby had heard about this woman from her dad. Fiona Shaw,

the director of the children's ward, had confronted him and banned him from the hospital.

Fiona stood her ground and watched everyone fade away. Then, she fixed Georgia Collins in her stern gaze. "I'm glad to see you getting back into your faith, Miss Collins," Shaw said as she approached. "Father Calvin has noted your absence from his services lately. But as I said, there is a time and a place for that. There is an appropriate way to go about it." As Shaw spoke, Georgia stared daggers at the woman, standing straight and defiant, as if her condition did not leave her body weak and broken. "And I do not appreciate you spreading stories that scare the staff and the other patients."

"They're not stories," Georgia said, her words sharp. "I know what I've seen, and everyone here knows what they've experienced."

Nick put his hand on his daughter's shoulder and squeezed, but it did nothing to make her back down.

"I'm sorry," Nick Collins offered. "We've spent so much time here that this place almost feels like our living room. We'll keep the prayers inside from now on."

"I'm *not* sorry," Georgia said. "I know what's going on here, even if you refuse to believe it."

"Georgia," Maria said, a warning tone in her voice.

Georgia let out a loud groan, grabbed her portable oxygen cylinder, and stormed off down the corridor.

Fiona Shaw then fixed Libby with her steel-blue eyes. "And you —Libby Casey, according to the visitor log. I won't hesitate to ban you from this facility if you cause even a fraction of the trouble your father stirred up. You can consider this your first and final warning."

With that, Fiona Shaw turned and left.

"Nasty woman," Libby said when she was out of earshot.

"She just doesn't understand," Nick Collins said. "Come on."

They caught up with Georgia in her room, where she was replacing her empty oxygen tank with a full one.

"I don't get it, Dad," Georgia said as soon as they walked in.

"Why do you act all weak in front of her? She's the worst, and she doesn't believe anything that's happened!"

"It's her ward, Georgia," Nick said calmly. "We have to play by her rules."

But Libby remembered what her dad had told her. Shaw had threatened to remove Georgia from the hospital if she kept scaring the other patients. Surely Nick and Maria had been warned as well.

"There *are* no rules anymore," Georgia said. "Not when something like this is going on."

Her anger spike caused her to lose her breath, and she started to cough. She sat down, weakened by the spasm, and hacked her lungs into a tissue for several minutes before she could get her breathing under control.

"Don't wind yourself up too much," Libby said, rubbing Georgia's back. "Everything will work out okay."

Georgia wiped the tears from the corners of her eyes. "How? Your dad isn't allowed in here. How's he going to help me?"

"I don't have an answer for that," Libby said. "But one thing I know for sure is that my dad has never given up on a client. Not ever. No matter how bad it gets, he always wins. Now, let's forget about that Fiona Shaw lady and go downstairs for some ice cream."

Georgia took deep breaths and seized control of her breathing again. "You know just what to say to cheer a girl up. How did you know her name anyway?"

"Because my dad had plenty of terrible things to call her when he got home yesterday."

"I'm sure every word was true. Come on. If we hurry, we can get there before Mrs. Eloise's shift is over. Then the ice cream will be free."

28

Thunder rolled heavy and loud in the distance. The glass rattled in the window panes from the vibrations.

Rachel pulled the curtain aside and looked out into the dark night, a worried expression on her face. "What are the odds that your power will go out?"

"I think we'll be good," Rand said, not entirely sure if it was true.

"Because I really want to watch this movie with you," Rachel said. "I've been waiting a while, but you've been so busy lately."

Rand grabbed her and guided her down to the couch. "Nothing is going to stop us from watching this movie tonight," Rand said.

Rachel had been the unintended recipient of everything that had happened so far. Rand only had one goal for the night, and that was to make Rachel comfortable, put her mind at ease, and settle her frazzled nerves from all the stories about Georgia Collins.

Regardless, he knew the girl and her family would remain at the forefront of his thoughts.

During the first scene in the movie, Rand's phone buzzed.

"Who is that?" Rachel asked.

"Libby. She's hanging out with Georgia tonight."

Rachel frowned. He shouldn't have brought it up. "Is everything okay?" she asked, even though Rand knew she didn't really want to know.

Rand did not reply. He laid his phone face down and leaned back on the couch with Rachel as they watched the movie. She cuddled into him, burying her face into his chest. He put his arm around her shoulders, holding her tight, but after watching for a few more minutes, Rand looked down at her and noticed that her eyes were not on the screen.

"What's the matter?" he asked.

"I don't know," Rachel said, sighing. "I have to pee." She got off the couch and disappeared into the back hallway.

The movie would not make her feel better. It wasn't enough of a distraction from everything that had been going on.

He lifted the remote and paused the movie. The only sound in the living room was the wind outside and the coming storm.

Then three loud knocks on the door.

Rand sat up straight, suddenly alert, an anxious feeling clenching inside his stomach. He stood and crept to his bag, which rested against the far wall, and pulled out a wooden crucifix, the one he brought with him to every investigation.

He held it out toward the door, staring it down, waiting to see if whatever was on the other side knocked again. He gripped the doorknob and flung it open.

There was nobody there.

He stuck his head out. The front yard was shrouded in the dark night, the sky marred by rolling, grey storm clouds.

His palms grew clammy. These occurrences were very familiar to him.

Rand went back inside, then closed the door and locked it. The only light in the room came from the luminescent television screen, the movie paused in a single frame.

Suddenly, Rand got the impression he was not alone in the house. Not because of Rachel in the bathroom. No, someone or something was with him in the living room. He felt eyes on him.

"I command you to leave here," Rand said, turning in circles, the cross still raised, keeping his attention on all corners of the room.

Loud thumps overhead. As if someone were running along the roof.

This demon was escalating things faster than usual. It had taken no time at all to follow Rand home.

This was a standard occurrence. Once Rand stirred up a spirit enough, the entity would always come after him rather than his initial target. That was good. If the demon left Georgia Collins alone for at least a little while, she would get a reprieve.

Then there was a loud crash at the back of the house, and his heart leapt into his throat.

Rand rushed down the hall and threw open the door on the right —his office.

Inside, he found the entire room ransacked.

His desk was overturned, books had been thrown from the shelves, and pictures had been torn from the walls, the frames smashed on the ground. The window that looked out into the back-yard was open as if a burglar had snuck in.

Just like the nurse station at the hospital.

Then Rachel screamed.

Rand rushed to the bathroom connected to his bedroom. He turned the knob, but the door did not open. He tried to force his way in, but it would not give. Something was holding it closed from the other side.

"Rachel!" Rand shouted as he banged on the door with his palm.

"Rand, help me!" she shrieked.

Rand stood back and kicked the door as hard as he could, cracking the wood and sending it flying open.

He ran inside just in time to see Rachel levitating in the air before she fell. Before the demon dropped her.

Rand caught her as best he could, and they both went down together. She wrapped her arms around him, squeezing him tight, her tears rubbing along his cheeks. Her chest heaved as she panted, her face red, her skin covered in slick sweat.

He clutched her tightly, knowing that he had brought this upon her. The entity was using Rachel to take revenge on him for provoking him.

"Rand—what was that? What's going on?"

Rand stroked her back as he held her. He still gripped the crucifix in his other hand.

She flinched.

"What?"

Rachel pulled the shirt down off her left shoulder, and he gasped at what she saw.

Three jagged wounds, red and glistening, resembling claw marks. Almost identical to his own scars on his back, an everlasting memento from a demonic foe.

"Rand, what the hell is this?" When she tried to touch them, she only flinched again, her fingers darting away from the pain as if the marks burned her.

Rand stared at the scratches, his jaw set, anger rushing through him for the first time.

Come after me all you want. But leave the others alone.

However, this was how it always worked. These entities knew him well, and often the best way to get to him was to go after his loved ones. Libby had had a very tumultuous childhood.

"I don't want to be here anymore," Rachel said through her tears.

"Come on. I'll take you home." Rand stood and helped her to her feet. She wobbled like her knees were made of jelly. Rand remembered how he felt the night he'd first encountered Shindael in the morgue.

You son of a bitch. As soon as I drop her off, I'm coming for you.

This demon was strong, and he was fast. There was no lurking and waiting with this one. He had to be removed tonight. There would be no peace until it was done.

I t was eight-thirty in the evening, and the first floor of the hospital, which was usually crowded with patients, visitors, and medical professionals, had grown thin.

"How have you been?" Libby ventured as they walked. Georgia only shrugged in response. "I see you've ramped up the prayers."

"I'm not the only person having experiences anymore," Georgia said. "The nurses are all complaining. He keeps trashing their desk and throwing their charts all around. Someone grabs them and pushes them when they're walking down the hall at night, but there's no one there. A nurse named Nica already quit over it."

Libby remembered her dad telling her about Nica. He'd seen security footage of her getting tormented by the entity during her night shifts. It didn't help that Nica had already been a deep believer in the spiritual and supernatural.

"And now Fiona is on a rampage. I've never liked that woman."

"She seems kind of mean," Libby said.

"Yeah. And she totally believes us when we tell her these stories —I know she does. But it's all about the hospital image. All about the reputation. All about burying the problems so she doesn't get in trouble. And now she's banned your dad from ever coming back."

"I wouldn't worry about it too much," Libby said, trying to be consoling. "If you can believe it, my dad's banned from a lot of places." Georgia chuckled. "He always finds a way in."

Just then, Georgia stopped dead in her tracks. She stared straight ahead, her eyes growing wide and her mouth falling open.

"Georgia?" Libby followed her gaze down the corridor but saw nothing.

"Do you see him?" Georgia whispered.

"Who?"

Libby looked again, and then she saw.

A teenage boy dressed in a hospital gown. He gripped an IV pole next to him, and there was a bag of fluids running from the tube into a cannula in his arm.

Libby pulled Georgia close. She'd seen apparitions plenty of times in her life, and it was something she'd never gotten used to. A dark aura exuded from the boy all the way at the other end of the corridor.

"What do we do?" Georgia whispered.

Neither of them took their eyes off it as it glared at them. It held impossibly still. A standoff.

"It'll leave," Libby said, hoping that was true. Her mind raced with all the ways her father had taught her to order a spirit to depart.

"Make him go away. Do something."

Command him, Libby thought at last. *Give him a command in the name of God and he has to listen.*

The lights in the corridor shut off and the backups came on, leaving them in a shadowy prison. There was no one else around, even though the area they were in was public. It was as if the demon had singled them out.

And then the boy walked toward them. The only sound was the squeaky wheels of his IV pole, steadily growing louder as he neared.

Georgia trembled against Libby's body and they clasped each other's hands. "Do something," she whispered again.

As the boy drew closer, Libby found her voice. "In the name of Jesus Christ, I command you to leave!"

He only smirked.

So there was only one thing left Libby could think to do—run.

"Come on!" She pulled Georgia's hand and forced her to turn around to run.

But as soon as they whirled, the boy in the hospital gown was there, a single pace away from them, the same smirk on his face.

The two girls let out a scream and stumbled backward.

The boy spoke to them, but the words were in a language that Libby could not understand. His voice was deep and unnatural, like a recording that had been ruined.

Libby pulled Georgia's hand as they ran the other way. This time, the boy did not appear in front of them. But as they fled, his words followed them down the corridor, booming after them. And although Libby could not understand, she also knew she did not want to.

Libby hoped they would find someone else who could help them. But the place seemed impossibly empty as if they had been transported to another dimension. Their hands remained clasped together, Georgia's oxygen cylinder bouncing up and down on its wheels.

They turned the corner and stopped short. The boy was there, except this time his back faced them. A gaping wound from his head to the top of his buttocks exposed a bloody spinal cord.

Georgia coughed. A hand went to her chest, her eyes bulged.

Libby knew they couldn't keep running away. Georgia's lungs wouldn't take it. Maybe that was what the demon wanted. Chase them until she dropped dead.

"Where's the chapel?" Libby said.

"I can't breathe," Georgia said between pants.

In front of them, the boy had turned around and stalked toward them again, the same grin on his darkened face.

"The chapel," Libby said, grasping Georgia by both arms. "We'll be safe in there!"

Georgia nodded. "This way."

They ran away from him again, Georgia mustering her breath as she led the way. They turned another corner, only to find the boy had appeared in front of them again.

But Georgia ran straight toward him while Libby followed. Libby panicked, hoping that Georgia knew where she was going. Then, Georgia yanked her into a room on the right.

The chapel was empty and dark. Libby slammed the door closed.

Surely we are okay in here. They can't enter holy places. At least, that was what her dad always told her.

Georgia fell onto her hands and knees, coughing and hacking. Libby crouched beside her, rubbing her back and stroking her hair. "It's okay. We're safe in here." She spotted the large crucifix mounted on the wall behind the altar. On it, Jesus looked up and away, lost in a daze of pain and defeat as he hung from the cross.

"Shit," Georgia muttered. She fumbled with the knob on her oxygen tank. The needle on the meter was in the red. "I can't stay in here for long."

"But... I saw you get a new one upstairs."

"I did! Something's wrong with it."

Libby figured the entity had something to do with that. "I'll call someone." She pulled out her phone.

"Are we really safe?" Georgia whispered.

"Yes. Demons can't come inside a holy—"

The door burst open as if hit by a wrecking ball. Both girls screamed and whirled around. The boy stood at the edge of the threshold into the chapel, his smile gone and replaced by an angry scowl.

He shouted at them again in the same mysterious language.

"Help us!" Libby called at the top of her lungs.

The boy pointed at them. Then, the stained-glass windows on either side of the room shattered all at the same time. The cushions in the pews ripped open by themselves, clouds of cotton drifting into the air, and the mounted Jesus statue unhooked from the wall and fell forward, crashing into the altar, and then to the ground, breaking into pieces. The lights above blew out, raining down shards of glass.

Amidst the destruction, Libby and Georgia hugged each other and dropped down. Libby threw herself over Georgia as the chapel fell apart around them, trying to shield the girl from any flying debris. She clenched her eyes, doing her best to pray for God's protection, but the commotion and the demon's chanting were the only things that filled her head.

Only after the room finally fell silent did Libby open her eyes. The chapel was completely trashed. No piece of furniture had been spared. Even the paint on the walls had been marred, covered in sets of three gouges like a giant claw had scratched them.

The boy was gone.

Libby helped Georgia to her feet. "Are you okay? Are you hurt?"

Georgia looked at her without seeing her, dazed. She stared for several long moments as if trying to think of what to say. Then she whispered, "It's over."

"What? What's over?"

Georgia collapsed into Libby's arms. The girl was dead weight, and Libby lowered her gingerly to the ground. "Georgia?" Libby gripped her shoulders and shook her. "Georgia, wake up!"

But she was unresponsive.

Libby did not know what to do. Start chest compressions? Shake her until she opened her eyes?

In the end, she ran out of the chapel and into the hallway, screaming for help.

30

The rain pelted down on them as they jogged to Rand's Jeep in the driveway. Once inside, Rand could no longer see the tears on Rachel's face mixed in with the rainwater.

As they drove, Rachel said nothing for a long while. The only sounds were the drops pattering on the windshield and the thunder roaring in the distance, farther away now.

"How do you do it?" she asked.

"Do what?"

"Live like this."

"It's not like it happens all the time," he said, trying to make it sound not as bad. "Just... whenever there is a particularly difficult case."

She wiped at her eyes. Her hair was damp and disheveled, her makeup streaked. She even looked like she'd aged a few years. "When you first told me about this, I wasn't sure what to think. As long as you were helping people, I didn't care. But..."

"Now you believe?"

"How can I not?"

Rand ground his teeth. "I'm sorry. I never meant for you to get involved."

"You weren't the one who attacked me in the bathroom."

"Yeah, but—"

"Rand. What was that thing?"

"You don't want to know."

"It picked me up and scratched me. It made me feel so bad... Like it wanted me dead."

Shindael. Hearing the desperation and sadness in her voice made him despise the demon even more. *First Georgia, now Rachel.*

"It's not something you need to worry about."

"Can you get rid of it?"

His phone vibrated in his pocket. He wondered who would call him so late at night, and then he remembered that Libby was visiting Georgia.

He fished the phone out of his jeans and checked the screen. As he thought, it was Libby. He swiped his thumb to answer.

"Rand! Watch out!"

It all happened in a split second. Rand looked up just in time to see a man run out in the middle of the road. He stopped right in front of Rand's path and held out his arms as if he were trying to catch the oncoming Jeep.

Rand slammed on the brakes and jerked the steering wheel. The car hydroplaned on the wet road and spun out of control.

They skidded in circle after circle, the smell of burning rubber filling the car and smoke swallowing the Jeep. Rand's seatbelt latched hard into place and pinned him to the chair. He squeezed the wheel with both hands, praying they would not flip.

When they settled, he tried to relax, but his entire body was trembling and his breath came in short gasps.

"Are you okay?"

Rachel looked at him in complete terror. Fresh tears were in her eyes. "Did we..."

Did we hit him?

Rand threw off his seatbelt and opened the door. He stepped out into the rain, which quickly soaked through his jacket and jeans.

He jogged back to where the man had leapt out. But there was no sign of him at all.

He turned and saw Rachel following, arms folded across her body.

"There's no one here," Rand said.

"That's impossible," Rachel said. "He couldn't have run off that fast."

"And because of the way I swerved... I didn't have time to miss him. He should have been hit."

Rachel nodded.

Then, it occurred to Rand what had happened. "Oh."

"What?"

"He wasn't real."

Rachel eyed him, the rainwater dripping down her face. "Wasn't real?"

A loud crash came from the Jeep, startling them both.

The front driver's side tire rested on the ground, the Jeep leaning its weight into the wheel-less corner.

Rand jogged back over and found all five lug nuts unscrewed and scattered in the puddles. "Shit," he muttered.

"How the hell did that happen?" Rachel said. But when Rand looked at her, she understood. "You mean that thing can do this kind of stuff too?"

"It can do whatever it wants, almost." Rand threw open the trunk and pulled out the jack.

"But we could have been killed!"

"I think that's the idea."

Rachel wrapped her arms around her body. Before, she had been afraid, but now Rand could tell she was also becoming angry.

Rand got down on his hands and knees and shoved the jack into place. "I'll put this back on and then drop you off."

Rachel said nothing. She only went to the passenger side, retrieved her umbrella, and opened it over Rand as he worked.

His phone rang again.

It chimed from somewhere inside the Jeep. He'd forgotten that Libby had tried to call him just before they'd spun out.

Rand straightened and found his phone underneath the car seat where it had fallen.

"Hey," he said. "Sorry about before. You're never going to believe—"

"Dad! Come to the hospital!"

He'd never heard his daughter sound so upset. "What's wrong? Are you all right?"

Rachel looked at him, concern washing over her face.

"It's Georgia! You need to get here now!"

31

R and left his Jeep at the front of St. Mary's main reception door, not caring if it got towed. He and Rachel rushed into the hospital.

The ICU was on the third floor, and the elevator opened into a large visitor waiting room. It was mostly empty at that time of night, but Libby met him there. When he saw his daughter, he could tell she'd been crying.

"Libby!" he said, running up to her. "What's wrong? What happened?"

"She just fell. Collapsed."

"What were you and her doing?"

She gave him a look. One of frozen terror.

"Libby—"

"He attacked us."

"The demon?"

"Yeah. He came for us in the hallway when we went down to get ice cream. We tried to run away, but it kept appearing in front of us. So we ran into the chapel to hide. But then he burst open the door and trashed the whole place. After, Georgia just fell down and I couldn't wake her up." Recounting the story made tears fall from her eyes again.

"Okay," Rand said, pulling her close to him. "You did well. Running for the chapel was the right thing to do."

"But it didn't work! He still hurt her. He did this to her."

"Come on. Let's go see her."

"What should I do?" Rachel asked.

"You should go," Rand told her.

"I don't want to leave you," she said. "What if the same thing happens as before? Like last time?"

Rand hated to see how worried she was for him. "It won't get the best of me again."

She nodded, but Rand could tell she wasn't so sure. Regardless, she took a seat on a couch and tried her best to calm herself.

Libby used her ICU visitor badge to scan the reader by the door to get into the ICU. But as Rand tried to follow her in, a nearby security guard placed a strong hand on his chest, holding him back. It took Rand a moment to recognize him, but finally, he did—Jerry, Harold's colleague.

"Evening, Jerry," Rand said, trying to put on his best charming smile.

"You know I can't let you in here," Jerry said quietly, looking around them. Libby stood on the other side of the ICU's threshold. "I'm supposed to call the police, but I don't want to do that, Rand. You should just leave."

"This is for Georgia," Rand said. "Please. Just give me some time."

"Harold also gave you some time, and look what happened to him. Suspended. He's in there now, with the girl, and I wasn't even supposed to allow *that* to happen. Please, Rand. Don't put me in a tough position."

Rand met Jerry's eyes and held his ground. "I can't leave and you know that. You saw what was on those security videos. It's gotten even stronger, and now it's attacking her." Jerry let his gaze drop to the ground. "I'm the only one who can help her."

Jerry placed his hands on his hips and looked around as if

checking to see if anyone was watching. "Damn it. For as much as you claim you're here to help, you sure do stir up a lot of trouble."

"My daughter and her mother would both agree with you," Rand said. "But listen. After tonight, this will be all over. Everything will go back to normal."

Jerry sighed heavily and stepped out of Rand's way.

THE ICU WAS A LARGE, circular room. All the patient rooms were on the periphery of the main section so that the patients could be seen at all times by the staff. Georgia was in room 316.

Inside were Nick and Maria, Father Calvin, and Harold, dressed in plain clothes.

Georgia lay on the bed, still and peaceful. Her body was straight and relaxed, arms down by her side, a thick, white blanket pulled up to her chin. She looked like she was sleeping.

She also looked dead. Rand had to tear his eyes away.

"Oh, Rand," Maria said, hugging him. "Thank you for coming."

"I drove here as soon as I could. Libby told me what happened."

Nick shook his head. "I could hardly believe it."

"The chapel is destroyed," Father Calvin said. "The girls were only in there for a few minutes while I stepped out." Calvin took out his cell phone and opened his camera roll. He showed Rand the pictures.

They weren't kidding. The entire place was ransacked and turned upside down. The stained-glass windows were smashed, the cushions in the pews were torn up, the carpet was covered with dark marks that looked like blood, and the statue of Jesus had fallen, the face broken to pieces.

"I came back to the chapel and heard screaming," Father Calvin continued. "That's where I found your daughter and Georgia. Georgia had passed out and we could not wake her up. I pressed the code-blue button on the wall, which thankfully still worked, and now we're here."

Rand looked at the girl in the bed again and ground his teeth. All of the trauma. All of the attacks. It had to end. She was too young and too sick to go through something like this. He despised the demons and how they chose their targets. They always picked on the vulnerable and unsuspecting.

"The doctors are saying coma," Nick said. "But they can't figure out why. All of her other vitals are normal."

"They don't know why she won't wake up," Maria said, wiping away a tear.

Seventeen days.

It was now the night of the sixteenth day. The demon was making good on his promise.

Rand took in a slow, deep breath. "Right. Then there is only one thing left to do."

There came a knock at the door. When Rand turned, he saw Katie slipping in, visitor badge in hand and looking worried. "How is she?"

"Coma," Nick said. "And they don't know why."

"We have to get rid of this demon," Rand told Katie. "Tonight. It attacked her and Libby, and that's why Georgia's in the coma."

And because the time limit is up.

Katie nodded. She was the only other one who knew of Georgia's ticking clock.

"Will you help?" Rand asked Calvin.

The man tensed at the suggestion, but after feeling all the eyes in the room on him, he finally said, "Whatever needs to be done for Georgia."

Rand hoped the priest would find the same courage he'd mustered for his encounter with the possessed girl all those years ago. "Do you have any holy water?"

"There are a few bottles in the chapel that weren't smashed."

"We'll need as much as you have. Can you get them now?"

Calvin nodded and left.

"Wait a minute, Rand," Katie said. "You want to do it in here? In the ICU?"

"Where else? This is where Georgia is."

"There are people around. Doctors, patients, nurses. Everyone."

"So?"

Katie looked at him incredulously. "So, it's an ICU. You can't kick all the staff out of here. The patients are really sick."

"What other choice do we have?"

"You know how destructive this demon is," Katie went on. "There could be more damage. Vandalism. Especially when we challenge it. This is a very dangerous place for an exorcism."

She was right. But there wasn't much use in doing it in the parking lot when the demon was attached to Georgia in the ICU.

"Can we bring her to another room?" Maria asked.

"They won't let us move her when she's comatose," Nick said.

"Why not? She's our daughter. They should allow us to go anywhere we want."

"Excuse me."

The sharp voice belonged to a thin woman at the door, wearing a white coat. Her name badge read Vanessa Clarke. "There is a visitor limit in the ICU for a reason," she said, eyeing everyone in the group sternly. "There are really sick patients up here and we can't have too many people around."

"Right," Nick said. "We were just leaving, Dr. Clarke."

Dr. Clarke looked as if she didn't quite believe him, then turned and walked away.

"We'll leave you and Katie here," Nick told Rand. "And Father Calvin. You three... do what you need to do."

Rand nodded. "Sounds like a plan."

The machines attached to Georgia Collins started beeping and going haywire.

"Oh my God," Maria said.

The alarms triggered a flood of nurses into the room, which pushed the group out like displaced water. Rand and the others waited outside 316 while Dr. Clarke rushed over and supervised the four nurses who pressed buttons on the machines, analyzed Georgia's heart rhythms, and checked her pulse and breathing.

Maria Collins started crying. Her husband pulled her close.

"She's not crashing," Rand whispered to Katie. "It's just our little friend messing with us."

The nurses who were investigating the equipment looked back at Dr. Clarke, shrugging.

"The machines aren't reading accurately," one of them said.

"Why?" Dr. Clarke asked. "What's wrong with them?" No one had an answer. "Swap them all out."

The nurses nodded and Dr. Clarke left the room, the equipment still beeping and blaring wildly behind her.

"What's going on?" Maria asked her.

"Your daughter is fine," Dr. Clarke said. "No change. The machines are reading stats that aren't correct."

Nick and Maria looked at Rand. He saw in their faces that they'd put two and two together, now silently asking him if it was the demon who was causing the malfunctions.

Dr. Clarke followed their gaze and settled her eyes on him. "There are a lot of rumors going around about Georgia Collins," she said. "Are you that man everyone's been talking about?"

"Probably."

"If I'm not mistaken, you're not allowed in this hospital anymore."

"I'm here for the same reason as you, Doctor," Rand said. "To help Georgia."

"Then why don't you leave it to the professionals?"

A loud *crack* came from Georgia's room. One machine had blown out, a rain of sparks falling onto the ground as the screen went black. The nurses all jumped back, startled. Even Dr. Clarke stared in amazement before regaining her composure.

It's escalating, Rand thought. *He's near.* He wouldn't be surprised if an apparition appeared soon. *We need to begin.* But Dr. Clarke was interfering.

"Get those things out of there!" she shouted at the nurses, and they moved double time to obey.

"Do you know why that equipment is doing that?" Rand asked. "Have you ever experienced something like that in your career?"

Dr. Clarke set her jaw and did not respond.

Father Calvin came through the ICU door, carrying a box with him. He approached the group while eyeing the chaos happening in Georgia's room. "What's going on?"

Rand ignored him for the time being. "Let me do what I need to do," he pleaded to Dr. Clarke. "What do we have to lose? You still haven't figured out what's keeping her in a coma."

"What do we have to lose?" Dr. Clarke rounded on him. "Everything! Our reputation, our accreditation, our *patients*. You threaten all of those things by being here."

"The demon doesn't care about any of that."

Dr. Clarke winced at the word. "You sound like a crazy person. I have to ask you to leave. If you don't, then I will call security." Then she walked away.

Inside Georgia's room, the nurses had powered off all the medical equipment that surrounded her and were rolling it out.

"What are we going to do?" Katie asked.

Rand watched Dr. Clarke go. "We're not getting any support here. I think we just need to go for it." He turned to Nick and Maria Collins. "It's probably best if you two wait in the visitor area outside."

They looked at each other, frightened and hesitant to leave.

"Come on, folks," Harold said, putting his hands on their shoulders. "Let's go get some coffee."

He led them out of the ICU, Libby following close behind them. She turned and gave her dad a saddened, hopeful look.

Because they both knew if he couldn't remove the demon now, it was likely to be beyond his ability. In his past cases, Rand had been beaten, thrown around, and scratched. He'd witnessed past clients on the verge of madness, driven insane by the unexplainable terror happening around them. But in the end, he'd always won. For the first time, though, the possibility that he could be in over his head entered his mind. He remembered the morgue, and how helpless he'd been, saved only by Harold's arrival.

This one is strong, he thought. *I have to be stronger.*

There was no one else to save Georgia Collins.

"It's time," Rand said.

Calvin looked around the ICU nervously. "There are too many people and patients."

"I told him the same thing," Katie said.

"You're right," Rand said. "We need to clear them out."

"How? You can't just tell the doctor to move a bunch of sick people out of the ward. It would take hours to relocate them safely."

"If I can't convince them, then I know what can."

It took Calvin and Katie a few moments to understand what he meant.

"No," Katie said. "Absolutely not."

Rand's idea was against his better judgment. He knew it was dangerous, and it was not something he would have normally ever done.

But he was out of options and out of time.

He went to the center of the ICU and bellowed at the top of his lungs, "Shindael!"

32

All the nurses stopped short and stared at him like he was a crazy man. They weren't wrong.

"Shindael!" Rand bellowed again. "Show yourself! In the name of the Lord, I command you to come here!"

The room was silent and still, all the ambient noise created by the staff doing their jobs halting as they stopped to stare at him and look around at each other, wondering which one of them would be the first to step up and speak out.

That person was Dr. Clarke. She zipped over to him, a patient's chart in hand, glaring. "That's it. I'm calling security and the police."

Rand ignored her. "Shindael! You coward!"

"Stop screaming in here!" Dr. Clarke said through clenched teeth.

When nothing happened, Rand knew it was time to play dirty. He went to Father Calvin and grabbed a bottle of holy water from the box he still held. He bit off the cork and spat it onto the ground, then walked to the entrance of Georgia's room and tossed the water over the door in the sign of the cross. He'd learned it was sometimes better to go on the offensive. Anything holy was sure to provoke the spirit into action.

"In the name of the Lord Jesus Christ, I command you to make yourself known!"

All of the lights flickered. In response, the backup lights on the generator flared to life, and then those also lost power and went dim.

The nurses looked overhead, confused and frightened. Dr. Clarke, who had raised a phone to her ear to call security, paused and glanced around, unsure of herself.

That's it, he thought. *You hear me now.*

Rand returned to the center of the ICU and threw more holy water in the sign of the cross on the floor. "In the name of the Lord Jesus Christ, I command you to show yourself! Come out of hiding. We're here for you."

You can't disobey when commanded in the name of God.

The ICU filled with the incessant sounds of medical equipment going haywire. Beeps, alarms, and chimes all went off in every room of the ICU as if every patient had suddenly crashed at the same time.

Dr. Clarke looked around. The colored lights above each patient room flashed with an alert. "Everyone!" she called out to the frozen nurses. "Get with your patients! Close the blinds!"

The nurses moved all at once. Each one darted into a patient room, closed the door, and lowered the blinds over the windows.

The alarms dinged and the lights flickered on and off. Then, Rand experienced the unmistakable heavy feeling. The same one from his night in the morgue when he'd encountered Shindael for the first time.

He's here. He's coming.

"Shindael!" Rand shouted again.

"What is going on?" Dr. Clarke demanded, grabbing his arm, phone and police forgotten.

"I'm saving your patient," Rand said. "That's what's going on."

Everything went silent when all the alarms stopped at the same time. The room fell into darkness, with only a few backup lights giving off a dim hue in the large room.

The temperature of the room plunged. Rand looked around, expecting Shindael to appear behind him.

And when Rand looked in front of him again, he had appeared—the boy from the morgue. The boy he'd followed around the hospital, dressed in a patient gown and holding an IV pole. He looked at the ground, his face obscured in the dim room.

Shindael disguised as Thomas.

"Does everyone see him?" Rand whispered.

No one around him said anything. They only nodded. Katie, Calvin, Dr. Clarke. Shindael had materialized for all of them. He stood only a few steps away.

Which meant he was done hiding. He was ready to fight.

And so was Rand.

"Shindael. Your time here is finished. We don't want you here anymore, and you need to leave."

The boy looked up at him, a knowing smirk on his face. His eyes were only two pools of black that Rand could not bear to look into.

"In the name of Jesus Christ, I command you to leave," Rand shouted at him.

The boy glowered. "No!"

The voice that came from him was deep and rough, not human. Rand's entire body tensed, remembering the morgue and what the entity was capable of.

"You must do what I command of you in the name of the Lord. You are powerless against God."

"Bullshit!" he shot back.

"Our Father, who art in heaven," Father Calvin prayed, "hallowed be thy name."

When removing a demonic presence, it was a good approach to have at least one person pray unceasingly. Invoking the presence of the Lord was a powerful strategy.

"Shut up, old man!"

"That's enough, Shindael!" Rand shouted. He raised the bottle of holy water and cast it toward the demon. When it landed on Shindael, he acted as if it was acid searing into him, crying out in pain.

Then, the boy changed.

His body grew into a terrible being that stood twice the size of Rand. His head almost reached the ceiling. The face changed from that of a human to one that resembled a bat, its mouth filled with razor-sharp teeth. His ears became pointed and his skin was black and scaly.

The body morphed into some sort of reptile. Skinny arms, bent at the elbows, and disproportionally large hands with three sharp claws at the end.

The eyes were completely black.

Rand's body told him to take a step back, told him that this creature was large enough to bite him in half and destroy the entire hospital.

"And lead us not into temptation, but deliver us from evil," Calvin continued to pray. Tears streaked his cheeks as he forced himself to look at the demon—forced himself to remain faithful.

Although it was terrible to look at, Rand knew this was progress. He had gotten it to reveal its true form. No more disguises. He looked upon the real Shindael for the first time, and while his heart pounded in his chest—while his legs ached to run—he stood his ground, facing down this powerful being.

So, this is you, he thought. *So large and evil, targeting a girl as young as Georgia.*

As Calvin continued to pray, Rand did not let up on his commands. "In the name of Jesus Christ, I command you to leave this place!"

Again he threw holy water onto the demon, making the sign of the cross. It stumbled back, angry and sneering, acting as if it was burned by the fluid.

Rand pushed forward. "In the name of Jesus Christ, I command you to leave this place!"

Shindael shouted something back at him, but Rand could not understand. Ancient Sumerian, he assumed.

"You are not welcome here, demon," Rand said. "Return to hell where you belong." Rand used his hands to trace out the sign of the cross in the air, forming a barrier between him and the demon. "And we will hear from you no more. You will leave this place alone, and you will not torment the patients anymore. You will free the spirits of the children you have held here, and they will move on to the afterlife. Then, you will return to hell."

Shindael roared at him one last time as Rand used the rest of the holy water. "Leave now! In the name of Jesus Christ, *leave this place once and for all!*"

Shindael fell to his knees as if punctured and deflating. Then his body morphed into a large cloud of black smoke and seemed to disintegrate into thin air.

The room fell silent. The only sound was Rand's heart pounding in his ears.

After a few long moments, he let out the breath he'd been holding. *He's gone. Sent away. It's over.*

The lights of the ICU returned to normal. The temperature rose, melting away the icy chill the demon had brought along with it.

Rand looked around the room, searching for any trace of the lingering demonic spirit. *You're safe now, Georgia.*

"Amen," Father Calvin said behind him.

ONCE THE PLACE WAS QUIET, the nurses came out from where they had holed themselves up in the patient rooms.

Katie gripped Rand's arm.

"Rand."

When he saw the look on her face, he frowned. "What's wrong?"

"He's still here."

"What? How can that be? We saw him leave."

The apparition, then the dematerializing, then the vanishing. It was all by the book. That's what happened every time he'd successfully banished the demonic.

"I don't know, but something is off." She looked around the

room as if waiting for the silence to speak to her. Her brow furrowed. "Something's wrong."

"Are you sure?"

"I always get that clear, pure feeling after we remove an entity from a place. I don't have that now. In fact, it keeps getting worse." Her face twisted as if the feeling was weighing down on her painfully. "Rand, we missed something—"

And then he heard a voice from inside Georgia's room.

"Randolph Casey!"

Through the glass windows that looked into her room, they all watched as comatose Georgia Collins shot up straight in bed.

And turned her head toward them.

Her eyes were completely black, and she smiled a sharp-toothed grin that sent chills down Rand's spine.

33

She's possessed.

The final stage of any demonic encounter. Once inside her body, the demon could control her and cause serious harm.

"We need to restrain her!" Rand grabbed the nearest nurse and pushed him into Georgia's room. The nurse resisted, afraid, but Rand forced him. "Now!"

A possessed person was completely controlled by the entity inside them, so it was paramount that they be tied down.

The nurse found the patient restraints at the bottom of the hospital bed and deftly wrapped the first around Georgia's left wrist. Rand watched him and started to do the same on her right, but Georgia yanked her arm away. Rand pulled it back, trying to slip the restraint onto her wrist. Georgia snapped her teeth at his hand, trying to bite him. The nurse helped straighten Georgia's arm and they managed to tie her wrist, then fastened the restraints together below the bed.

Her body writhed and her wrists pulled against the restraints, while she glared at the nurse with her black eyes. "Let me go!" she spat with a dark voice that was not her own. The nurse froze in terror, then turned and fled.

Her face was scaly, ears pointed, taking on some of Shindael's features.

Rand took a step back and looked at the girl. The demon turned his attention to him, staring at him through Georgia's body.

He has her now. I thought he was gone, but...

Possession was a demon's ultimate goal. Georgia being in a coma was the perfect opportunity. She had no control. No willpower or mindfulness to defend against it.

That was why he put her in a coma in the chapel. To prepare her for this.

Rand stared at her, helpless and crushed. He thought he'd won, but actually—

"You've lost, Randolph," Shindael told him, his voice an unnerving mix between his own and Georgia's. "The girl is mine, just like she was always meant to be."

Not yet. I can get her back. "We'll see about that, you son of a bitch."

Shindael only grinned at him.

Rand went outside of Georgia's room and closed the door, isolating the demon from the rest of the ward.

Katie looked ill. Calvin stared through the glass at the girl, face fallen. Tears leaked from the corners of his eyes. Rand felt exactly the same, but he'd run out of tears for these situations long ago.

"What is going on in here?"

Fiona Shaw stormed in and her stony gaze came to rest on Rand. "How did I know you'd be here?" She crossed her arms over her chest, rubbing them with her hands, shivering.

"You knew it was me because you know what's going on in this hospital," Rand said.

"Please listen to him, Miss Shaw," Calvin said. "It's serious, and it's real."

"Enough," Fiona spat at him. "I'm surprised at you, Father, that you would allow—"

"Randolph!" the demon's horrible voice pierced through the walls.

Fiona stared at the door of 316. "Who was that?" When she went to open the door, Calvin went to stop her, but Rand only held him back.

Fiona threw open the door to Georgia's room. Shindael growled at her through Georgia's body, his sharp-toothed mouth open wide.

Fiona immediately slammed the door back into place, trembling. All color had drained from her skin.

"W-w-what…"

"He's possessed her," Rand said. "And now we need to exorcise."

"What did I just see?" Fiona asked him. Her eyes began to fill with tears.

"You know what you saw," Rand said. "Now please let us do our job."

Fiona only brought her hands to her face, looking away from him. Unable to say anything else.

"This is the strongest entity I've ever faced, for sure," Rand told her. "We chased him from this room, and so he went inside Georgia. She was susceptible because of the coma. But if we can expel him from her body, he'll have nowhere left to go."

Calvin swallowed heavily and nodded, crossing himself.

An ear-splitting roar sounded through the ward.

"RANDOLPH!"

Shindael's voice pierced them like knives, the sound waves reverberating like they came through a hundred amplifiers. The glass in the windows of all the patient rooms shook, and then shattered, bursting into a cloud of shards. Ceiling tiles came loose and fell to the ground. Rand and the others dropped low, hands over their heads as the debris crashed down.

When everything had fallen, the only sound in the ward was Shindael's gleeful laughter.

They stood. Tears now streamed down Fiona's face. "What is going on? I've never seen anything—"

Rand grabbed Fiona by the shoulder. "I can save her. You just have to trust me. Evacuate the ICU. All of the patients. It's not safe as long as the demon's still here."

She stared at him for a few moments, seeming to not comprehend. Then, she slowly nodded and pulled out her cell phone.

RAND PACED NERVOUSLY BACK and forth in the main room of the ICU, crucifix in one hand and cell phone in the other. The broken shards of glass and debris from the ceiling crunched underneath his shoes. He sent a message to Miller Landingham:

Head bat, body dragon.

Knowing a demon's appearance was always helpful. Hopefully, the man could dig up some more information on Shindael. Maybe give them a reason for why they were making no progress in banishing him. At that point, anything would be helpful.

Then Rand started praying.

"God, please be with me now. Give me the strength to cast out this demon."

Father Calvin did the same. Rand noticed that the man could not stop trembling. That was normal, and Rand felt for the man. *Time to face your fears. Time to reconcile what happened to you twenty years ago.*

Patient transporters had arrived and systematically worked to roll the ICU patients from their destroyed rooms. Some of the patients were conscious while others were not, on ventilators that breathed for them, oblivious to all that was going on around them. Fiona Shaw supervised the movement while Dr. Clarke inspected each patient on his or her way out the door.

The blinds in Georgia's room were pulled down, but since the windows were broken, they could clearly hear Shindael's voice.

"You've already lost, Randolph. Ha ha ha." A patient was pushed by Georgia's room. "Oh, there goes Mr. Gilbert. He's not going to make it. So sad."

"Go," Fiona told the transporter, and ushered him out the door.

The demon rambled on, talking to himself, taking pleasure in the sound of his own voice. "Randolph Casey, I thought I called for you." More laughter. "Do you want to fuck little Georgia? I promise I'll lie still for you. Ha ha ha."

Trying to get a rise out of me, Rand thought. It was a classic ploy. *Not going to work.*

Calvin approached Rand. "Are you ready?"

"Yes. How about you?"

Calvin did not answer.

"You need faith," Rand told him. "Be strong. You've done this before. And you were successful last time."

Calvin looked down at his feet. "You're right. For Georgia."

"The patients are all gone," Fiona said, coming up to Rand. Harold was with her.

"Good." Then, to Harold, he said, "How are Nick and Maria?"

"Worried," he said. "Far worse than that, actually. They heard all the commotion."

"Do they know that Georgia..."

"No. Of course not."

"Stay with them, please."

Harold nodded.

"Will you three be all right in here alone?" Fiona asked.

"Yes. Now go with Harold. The next time you see us, this place will be back to normal again."

Rand could tell Fiona wanted to believe that but was unsure. She and Harold left, and Rand, Katie, and Calvin were the only ones who remained in the deserted, destroyed ICU.

"I'm getting lonely in here," came the voice. "Won't someone come and play with me?"

This was it. If Rand couldn't cast the demon out now, then he'd lose her for good.

"Let's kick this bastard out of here," Rand said.

34

Miller Landingham sat on a folding chair in his back office at the bookstore, flipping channels with the remote in one hand and his take-out noodles in the other. He slurped down another pile as he thumbed the channel button.

Soon, if things kept going the way they were, he'd have to cancel the cable to the store. It was probably something he should have done a while ago, but he loved television. Strange for someone who owned and operated a used bookstore.

He passed by the news, which was on the screen just long enough for him to see BREAKING on the bottom ticker. He went back up.

The reporter stood in front of St. Mary's. It was being evacuated.

That's where that little girl stays. The one Rand was taking care of.

"A couple dozen ICU patients are being transferred to a nearby facility," the woman was saying.

"And is there any more word on the problem?" asked the man in the studio on the other half of the split screen.

"All we could get was 'a widespread electrical malfunction.' We assume it's serious enough to threaten the safety of the patients."

Behind the reporter, several ambulances and police cars were parked with their lights on.

In his gut, Miller knew this had something to do with his buddy Randolph.

"All right," said the man on the television. "Keep us updated as the story develops."

The female reporter disappeared off the screen as the man started talking about a celebrity scandal.

Miller's phone beeped with a text from Rand.

Head bat, body dragon.

So Rand had finally gotten a clear glimpse of what he was dealing with.

Miller knew what it meant. In their natural form, demons often resembled combinations of real-world animals.

Noodles forgotten, Miller went to his computer and opened the database he'd been building for years.

Head of a bat, body of a dragon.

Rand had mentioned the name Shindael. Miller had found a few stories from those who had encountered Shindael, but none of them had ever described his appearance.

Miller ran a search for bat and dragon. A few possible candidates showed up. None of whom were named Shindael.

"It isn't him," Miller muttered to himself.

He searched again.

Head of bat. Body of dragon. Sick people.

It turned up nothing. He had no information on a demon of that description who particularly enjoyed preying on sick people.

"We've received word that upwards of thirty patients have been evacuated," the voice on the TV said behind him. "If you're just joining us for this breaking story, a widespread electrical malfunction at St. Mary's Medical Center has forced the evacuation of their ICU."

"St. Mary's..." Miller said to himself, remembering what Rand had told him about there being hundreds of children's spirits trapped in the ward there. He typed in a new search.

Head of bat. Body of dragon. Children.

This time he had one result.

It was a story from an internet forum he'd copied and pasted many years ago, but one he had no recollection of. It was a long block of text recounting the writer's experience with a supernatural haunting in a home they'd just moved into.

Allegedly, they'd purchased the house in 1985 for a bargain. Once there, they'd experienced the usual occurrences that Miller was used to reading about. Missing valuables, strange bumps in the night, cold spots, feelings of dread when in certain rooms.

Then, the writer's children complained of a monster that lived in their closet. At first, the writer explained, he thought it was just his kid having normal fears. But then the writer began catching glimpses of the creature in the periphery of his vision.

When he looked into it, he discovered that the house had been built on the site of a tragedy ten years before. A preschool had burned down, and thirteen children had perished in the fire.

Miller leaned in close to his computer screen as he read, feeling he was on to something. *Burned down preschool.*

The writer explained that he'd brought in a priest to bless the home and remove the negative energy, and whatever was living there had fought back. He saw it for the first time and wrote that it looked like a mixture between a bat and a dragon or lizard. Maybe a dinosaur.

The priest had commanded the entity to reveal its name, which he said was Karax. He used the name to send the demon away, and for a few weeks it seemed to have worked, and there was peace again. But then the strange occurrences happened again. The family eventually had to move out of the house.

Miller leaned back in his chair. This was why he farmed the internet daily for people's accounts of their hauntings and kept a record of them. With enough shared information, cross-references were possible.

Karax, Miller thought. He ran a search for the name, but still, the only result was the story he'd already read.

The physical description and the habit of going after children were two identifying factors that were too strong to pass up.

Miller picked up his phone and tried to call Rand. It went straight to voicemail.

"Come on, pick up," he muttered as he tried once more. Since the ICU had to be evacuated, he knew his friend was probably in the middle of an all-out battle.

But he needed to get through. Rand was using the wrong name.

The demon meant to fool you, and it worked.

35

Rand led the way into the room, pushing open the door and going to stand at the foot of the bed. Calvin was behind his right shoulder, Katie at his left.

Georgia looked even more like the demon. Her hair had changed from blonde to white and the flesh over her entire body had turned scaly and reptilian.

Shindael gave his fanged grin. "Oh. Is it time?" Father Calvin was the first to move. He held his Bible out toward the demon, who recoiled from it, the grin replaced by a glaring scowl. "Fuck off!"

"Lord in heaven," Calvin said, continuing his bombardment of prayer, "deliver Georgia Collins from this servant of evil. Reclaim her for your kingdom and expel this wretched creature from inside her."

"Not going to work, Father!" Shindael spat at him, although Rand could see that the prayers still pained him.

"Shindael, I command you by name," Rand said. "Depart from the body of this girl."

Shindael turned his attention to Rand. "Who the fuck is Shindael? Ha ha ha."

"You are. You are a liar and a coward and a monster, and you must do what I command of you."

"*I command you to fuck this priest!*" Shindael threw his head back and roared in laughter.

Rand had heard all the clever comebacks before. He held the crucifix out, which instantly made Shindael cease his laughing. He stared at it as if waiting for Rand to plunge it into his heart.

"Yeah, you know what this is," Rand said. "And you know what it means. It has power over you."

Shindael regarded the cross for a few moments before turning to Katie, acknowledging her presence for the first time. "Aren't you pretty," he muttered.

Rand knew what was happening. When faced with something that made him feel threatened, a demon would always try to exploit some other weakness in the room. Demons he'd faced in the past usually assumed Katie would be the weakest among them.

Katie did not flinch when the black eyes landed on her. "I'm not afraid of you," she said, not a hint of fear in her voice.

"Maybe not," Shindael said. "But they are." He nodded his head, gesturing past Father Calvin and out into the hall.

Katie looked and froze. Rand had seen that look before. He followed Katie's gaze out to the main section of the ICU and found nothing. But he already knew what she saw.

The other children. Shindael knows they affect her.

"Yes, you see them now, don't you? I called them here. They do whatever I say. They are my slaves."

"They're here," Katie whispered. "All those kids."

"I collect them," Shindael said. "They die, and I capture their souls. They belong to me because they're weak and stupid." He laughed again.

A sudden fury coursed through Rand, reminded that Georgia was not the only one at stake.

He's trying to make us angry. Provoke us.

He held the cross out toward Shindael again. He stepped around to the side of the bed, bringing the crucifix closer. Shindael recoiled away, not wanting to be burned. Rand gripped it, knuckles turning white. Anger flared through him at the thought of all the children who had not been allowed to move on because of this creature. "In the name of the Lord Jesus Christ, I command you to leave this place and free these spirits from your hold."

"No! They're mine!"

"They do not belong to you. They belong to God."

"Then tell him to come and get them!"

Shindael turned toward Father Calvin, who had been praying ceaselessly since he'd begun. "The forces of hell are of no match for you, Lord, and we have faith that you will intervene and protect us from this evil."

"Shut up, old man!" Shindael shouted. "I've heard enough out of you!"

"This demon, Shindael, is a servant of Lucifer, and has no power here where your Kingdom reigns."

"You'll hang yourself after this," Shindael said. "You'll finish what you started twenty-five years ago. Because you are weak and pathetic, and your God knows it too!"

Calvin's prayer hit a sharp bump.

"Don't listen to him," Rand said.

"Little Betty. You remember her, don't you? She was never the same after that night. She's dead now, you know. No, you *don't* know, because you never cared about her. Only about yourself!"

"Lord, please—"

"Enough of that. Where was your God when you last did this? Where was he when you wanted to kill yourself? Where was he when he let Betty get taken?" Shindael laughed. "Not there. He doesn't care about you. You remember my friend Ezu, don't you?"

At the mention of the name, Father Calvin ceased praying. *Ezu.* Rand figured that was the demon who'd Calvin had encountered before.

"Yes, you do remember. And he remembers you very well."

"You're a liar," Calvin said, voice trembling.

"Am I? Come with me to hell. You can meet Betty and Ezu and be one big happy family."

"That's enough," Rand said. If he let Shindael go on about Calvin's past, he knew they'd lose ground.

But Shindael only looked to Katie, fixing her in his cold glare. His dried and broken lips spread into a menacing grin. "And what are you doing here? Did your old boyfriend drag you into this?" He chuckled.

"I won't listen to you," Katie said.

"Did you ever tell him the truth?"

Katie's mouth pressed into a thin line. "There is no truth that could ever come from you."

"Fine. Be selfish. Don't tell him about your miscarriage."

Katie's entire body tensed.

"Why haven't you told him? Don't you think Daddy deserves to know?"

"Stop it!" Katie shrieked. But Shindael only laughed.

Miscarriage? She was pregnant?

"Oh yes. It was yours, Randolph, and she never told you," Shindael said, as if reading his thoughts. "Then she lost it. Now that baby is down in hell with me. I know because I've seen it. A little boy."

When Rand looked at Katie, he saw the brokenness in her eyes. The guilt was clear on her face, and Rand knew that everything Shindael had said was true.

The memories came flooding back to him. The abrupt end of their relationship. She'd called it off with no explanation, disappeared, and stopped returning his calls. Then when he'd finally gotten in touch with her months later, she'd told him she could no longer work as a medium.

His own tears formed in the corners of his eyes. Pictures of him with a son, a baby brother for Libby, flashed through his mind. A future that was possible, but he'd never known. *Because she kept it from me.*

"Rand, I'm so sorry," Katie said through her sobs.

Seeing her despair snapped him back into the moment. He saw

what Shindael was trying to do. Anger coursed through him so strongly and so suddenly that Rand shoved the crucifix onto Shindael's forehead. It sizzled like raw meat on a frying pan, and Shindael wailed in pain. Smoke billowed from the spot where the wood pressed into his skin.

"In the name of Jesus Christ," Rand said through gritted teeth, into the demon's ear, "I command you, Shindael, evil spirit, to leave this girl forever. Go back to hell."

"Fuck you!" Shindael shouted through his cries.

Rand pulled the cross away. It left a red mark on the black, scaly skin.

Shindael recovered from the pain of the burn and glared at him. "Give it up, Randolph. It isn't going to work. This is the end of the road for you."

Georgia's body looked less and less like herself as the demon spent more time inside her, taking over.

He's right. It's not working. This bastard isn't budging.

Rand caught the negative thoughts in his head and pushed them away, hopefully before Shindael could sense that he was having them.

"Rand..." Calvin said.

Rand could see that Calvin was thinking the same thing. Nothing was working. They needed a new approach. A new idea.

Then Katie fled from the room, crying, the trauma of her secret being exposed getting the best of her.

My team is falling apart, Rand realized.

Shindael only chuckled. "You're a failure, Randolph. Now, can you untie me so I can play with myself before I kill the girl? Ha ha."

Ignoring him, Rand left the room, pulling Calvin along with him to the main section of the ICU. The lights were out now, leaving them in a shroud of darkness.

"Rand," Katie said.

"It's okay," he said, though he wasn't sure just how okay it really was. *It has to be. We cannot change it. Shindael wants us to get emotional.*

"I'm so sorry," she said. "I didn't know what to do. It was years ago. I was—"

"You don't need to explain," Rand told her gently. "We can talk about that later."

"Nothing we do is working," Calvin said. "Shindael seems immune to all prayers. He won't budge."

"He's very strong," Rand said, keeping his voice low, not wanting Shindael to overhear.

"We must be missing something," Calvin said.

Rand scratched at his chin. The priest was correct. The demon was showing a huge amount of resilience, a level that Rand had never encountered before.

I can't let the self-doubt into my head.

Because once that slippery slope began, there was nothing left but a glide to the bottom. Then, he might never get Georgia Collins back.

Miller, he remembered suddenly.

He fished his phone from his pocket and saw a bunch of missed calls from Miller.

Odd. He hadn't felt it vibrate. His phone must have been messed up along with all the other electrical equipment in the ICU.

Rand tapped the screen and called him back.

"Who are you calling?" Calvin asked.

Miller answered on the first ring. "Rando! Thank God!"

"Is everything all right?"

"You tell me. You're doing an exorcism at St. Mary's, aren't you?"

"Yeah. How did you—"

"They've evacuated and it's all over the news."

"We're dealing with a full-on possession now," Rand told him. "He's so strong. Nothing seems to—"

"Rand, it's not Shindael." Miller spoke fast and breathlessly as if he'd just run a mile.

Rand turned to face the other two. "What?"

"It's what I've been trying to call you about. That demon is *not* Shindael."

Rand paused for a moment. "How do you know?"

"I searched the description you sent me. A cross between a bat and a dragon. Bat head, dragon body."

"That's it," Rand said.

"His real name is Karax. He's a known servant of Shindael, one of hundreds. And he likes to hurt children. I found a story of another priest who encountered him at the site of a preschool that burned down a decade ago."

That bastard, Rand thought. *He gave me the wrong name.*

"It's the only thing that makes sense," Miller said. "Why would he have given you his name? Because it's the *wrong* one. He gave you his master's name, not his own. So if you've been trying to command him to leave by invoking the wrong name, then you're not using your full authority."

"Karax," Rand said, the word tasting like poison on his lips. Calvin and Katie exchanged an uneasy glance.

"That's it," Miller said. "Next time you face him, try commanding him with his real name."

"All right, I'm going back in there."

"Good luck, Rando. Be careful. Have faith."

Rand hung up and glared at the door of room 316. The blinds were drawn, but he could still hear the demon muttering to himself.

"Who was that?" Calvin asked.

Rand stormed over, crucifix gripped in his hand.

"Rand!"

"You two wait out here." He knew his anger was getting the best of him, that he should not face down this creature alone. But Karax had already gotten into their heads and thrown them off.

Rand stepped through the door and threw aside the curtain.

"Welcome back," the demon said, grinning at him, an evil mirth in his blackened eyes. "Are you here to untie me now?"

"I don't believe we've ever met before, Karax."

And for the first time, the smile faded from the demon's lips.

36

His eyes bored into Rand and a low growl rumbled from the back of his throat.

"Karax," Rand repeated.

"Don't say that!" he snapped.

"Why not?"

"Because—"

"Why don't you want me to say it, Karax?"

"Fuck you! Eat shit!"

"Not today, Karax." Rand walked around to the side of the bed, getting closer to Karax, who, for the first time, looked afraid in his presence. His black eyes went to the cross in Rand's hand. "This is over."

"You're right," Karax said, his voice low and dark. "I'm done. But I'll take the girl with me. I can stop her heart whenever I want. I'm inside her, remember? And it'll be all your fault that she died."

Now that Rand knew Karax's name, the demon was running out of defenses. He had to end this now, or it would be too late.

Rand held up the crucifix and Karax recoiled. "In the name of the Lord Jesus Christ, I command you, Karax, to leave the body of this girl."

Karax had nothing to say in return. He trembled underneath the presence of the cross.

Rand reached for the nearby box Calvin had brought from the chapel. He took a bottle of holy water and yanked the cork out with his teeth.

"No," Karax said. "Look at the door!"

Rand ignored him, figuring Karax was only trying to distract him. But then movement at the entrance of the room caught his eye.

Oh my God...

The ghostly apparitions of children filled the room like a solemn procession. Their bodies were a soft blue light, half transparent, their expressions hollow and empty. They seemed to glide through the air rather than walk. They surrounded Rand and the bed, crowding him.

Some were tall, others were short. Some looked to be about fifteen, while others were as young as four or five. Some wore hospital gowns, and some wore clothes from the '70s and the '80s, as well as the present day.

Rand had never seen so many apparitions at once. They all seemed so lost and hopeless.

There are hundreds of children here, Katie had said. Now he fully understood why she had been so upset that night.

"All of them are mine," Karax said, grinning again. "Some have been here for decades."

The faces of even more apparitions peered at him through the window outside the room. All looked longingly at him, as if desperate for his help.

They are, Rand thought. *I'm their only chance of moving on.*

Rand tore his eyes from those of the ghostly children and glared at Karax. "You will free these souls. They belong to God."

"Wrong again!" Karax shouted. "They stay because God does not want them. Ha ha!"

Rand threw the holy water at Karax in the sign of the cross. Georgia's body trembled and writhed under the fiery pain.

"I can go inside you next!" Karax's voice was now high and shrill, a desperate scream. "I'll make you a pedophile! I've done it so many times before. It's too easy!"

Rand knew it was an empty threat. Karax was finally feeling cornered.

"In the name of the Lord Jesus Christ, I command you to let these children go and to leave the body of this girl!"

Rand threw the holy water again. He touched the cross to Georgia's heart, and the demon convulsed underneath it.

"Take it away! Make it stop!"

"You know what you have to do if you want it to stop," Rand said.

"Fine! Fine!"

"Do it, Karax."

And then the apparitions of the children around Rand turned into balls of blue light, little orbs that hovered in the air. They lingered there for a moment before blinking out like a flipped light switch.

They're moving on.

They disappeared one by one until they were all gone.

"There!" Karax shouted.

"And now you," Rand said, the crucifix continuing to burn the demon. "Leave here now, and your pain will end."

Karax, amidst his bellowing, found new strength and broke the restraint on his right wrist. He swatted the cross from Rand's hand and it clattered to the floor on the other side of the room.

Karax used his free hand to tear the other restraint, and in an instant, he was loose.

No!

"Take them all," Karax said, his voice low and grumbling. He glared at Rand through his black eyes. "I don't need them anymore. But the girl is mine. Her time is up."

Rand's mouth went dry.

"That's right," Karax went on. "You know what I mean. Seventeen days. Why do you care so much, Randolph? No matter what you do, the girl will die anyway."

"That's not true," Rand said, although he knew it could be. When he'd first heard Karax on the recording, there had been no way to know if he'd meant Georgia would die from cystic fibrosis or be killed by him in seventeen days' time.

And he still didn't know.

Karax must've seen his thoughts on his face. "You don't know. You can't know. But I do, and I'm not going to tell you. All of this could be for nothing." He smirked.

Karax leapt upright on the bed, lithe and nimble like an acrobat, then jumped through the air, landed, and ran with blinding speed out of the ICU.

37

Rand grabbed the crucifix from where it had fallen onto the floor and took off after the demon. He only caught a glimpse of Karax fleeing before the demon bounded through the main doors of the ICU.

Rand sprinted after Karax. The situation was bad enough, but having a demon-possessed girl running loose through the halls of the hospital was far more dangerous than anything else. Karax had all but destroyed the ICU, and he could easily extend that havoc to the rest of the hospital.

In the hallway, Rand's eyes darted from side to side. He spotted the door to the stairwell falling closed. When he burst through, he found Karax crouching on the steps leading up.

"Give it up, Randolph!"

Rand ran up the stairs, but Karax only leapt away from him, clearing entire floors with a single jump. Rand had to take three steps at a time just to keep up.

"You can't have her!" the demon's voice echoed down to him through the stairwell.

You're wrong about that.

Rand rounded a corner on level 15R and saw the door falling

closed. He followed Karax through it and found himself in a hallway that looked like it was under construction. Definitely not the main part of the hospital.

It was a long corridor with plywood for walls. At the end, near a set of double doors, a security guard crouched by the wall, eyes wide and trembling.

"Where is she?" Rand asked the man.

"W-w-what was that thing?"

"Where did she go?"

The guard lifted a shaky finger and pointed to the doors on Rand's left. Then he rose to his feet and ran away in terror.

Rand pushed through the doors and stopped short. He was outside, the cool air and heavy wind slapping him hard in the face. The rest of St. Mary's upper floors loomed above him. Red lights flashed in a circle on the ground.

The hospital helipad.

He spotted Karax on the far end of the helipad, standing right on the edge. The wind whipped at Georgia's whitened hair and hospital gown, so strong it should have blown her over the side. Only the demon kept her footing sure.

He means to throw her off. That's how he wants to finish her.

Rand and Karax eyed each other from opposite ends of the roof. He was maybe thirty paces away from Georgia. But the landing pad was wide between them, seeming miles in that moment.

Rand ventured a step forward, hoping Karax would not drop himself off.

The demon did not move. So Rand pressed on, crucifix gripped by his side.

When he was halfway there, Karax finally spoke. "This place was special to her. There's no better location for her to die." He smiled.

Proud of your own theatrics, Rand thought. He stopped advancing, letting the standoff continue.

"Since you care so much about her, I assume you'd like to share her fate," Karax went on. "You can lead the way down!"

Karax broke into an inhumanly fast sprint, closing the distance between them in milliseconds. He pounced on Rand, knocking him backward and wrestling him to the ground with ease. The crucifix spun away and out of reach.

Hands went to Rand's face, jagged thumbs aimed at his eyes. Georgia's fingers had elongated, topped by long, yellow fingernails. Rand caught his wrists just in time and fought back against them, but the demon was lending Georgia's body powerful strength.

"The girl dies tonight," Karax growled at him. "And I'll take you with me. All three of us in hell together!"

Karax leapt off of him and broke free of his grasp. He gripped Rand by the front of his shirt and pulled him to his feet, the seams ripping as he did. Rand tried to resist, but the demon dragged him to the edge of the helipad, slung him around, and pressed his back against nothing but the empty air. The wind whipped at him, and the lights from the police cars and ambulances that had arrived to evacuate the patients flashed what seemed like miles beneath him.

Rand held onto Karax's wrists, but the demon could let him topple over the side whenever he wanted.

He's so strong. So quick.

Rand had never encountered anything like it before. No matter what he did, he always seemed to be at Karax's mercy.

Karax's black eyes bored into him, studying him. Then his lips parted into a sharp-toothed smile. "Shindael will be pleased I brought you down with me."

Karax released him, and Rand toppled backward. His entire body felt like one of those dreams where he was falling, only to wake up at the last minute.

Just before he fell out of reach, Karax caught him again, pulling him back to the edge. It was the closest to death Rand had ever been, and his body knew it. Everything felt numb as if it had all shut down to accept it.

Karax squealed with laughter. "You should see your face!"

A sound from overhead.

A helicopter lowered over the landing pad, stirring up a heavy wind that ripped at Rand's clothes and Georgia's hospital gown.

The demon twisted its head to look at it. The white, stringy hair blew in the gusts from the spinning blades.

One last chance. Rand had only a moment while Karax was distracted. He slipped his hand into his jacket pocket and gripped the last vial of holy water.

Karax looked back at him just in time for Rand to smash the vial onto his scaly face. The glass broke, the shards stabbing into Rand's palm.

Smoke erupted from Karax's forehead where the bottle had broken. Rand pushed forward at that moment, the momentum knocking Karax off his feet while he screamed in agony.

Rand dragged him back to the center of the helipad, the whipping sounds of the chopper blades drowning all the cries of the demon.

"Clear the helipad for landing!" Someone was dangling out the door of the helicopter, a megaphone up to their mouth. The chopper hovered in the air above them, stuck in limbo.

Working on it, Rand thought.

Rand threw Karax down onto his back in the center of the helipad. Rand's bloody palm stained the front of the hospital gown. He picked up the crucifix and pressed it to Karax's forehead. It burned and sizzled like the holy water.

Rand brought his face close to Karax's so the demon could hear him over the sound of the chopper blades. "In the name of the Lord Jesus Christ, I command you to leave the body of this girl!"

Rand moved the cross to Karax's chest and his body convulsed. "You have no place here anymore! Leave this girl's body and never return. Karax, the Lord commands you by name to *depart from this place.*"

Karax's scream erupted like a volcano, a deafening shout that threatened to blow out Rand's hearing. Every instinct of his wanted to curl into a ball on the ground and guard his ears from that horrible sound.

But he stayed firm. Held the cross to Georgia's chest. Watched as Karax threw his head back, eyes clenched, bellowing.

It's finally working.

And then a black mass of smoke spewed from Georgia's mouth, like a cloud of evil that seeped from her insides. It rose into the air, formless and dark, and then scattered as if a wind had carried it away.

Rand knew that sight well. It meant victory. *He's gone.*

Georgia's body lost all tension. The scaly skin softened into pale flesh. Her white hair changed back to the blonde curls. Her face relaxed and became peaceful. The transformation reversed right in front of Rand's eyes.

Yes. Come back to us, Georgia.

"Clear the helipad immediately!" the man shouted from above.

In the final moments of his fight, Rand had completely forgotten they were about to be crushed by a landing helicopter. He scooped Georgia up, arms under her neck and knees, then carried her inside as the helicopter landed behind him, the powerful gusts threatening to topple him over.

He placed her on the floor, where she opened her eyes and stirred awake.

"Georgia?"

"Where am I?" She blinked a few times and looked at him. It took a few moments before recognition dawned on her face. "Ghost Man?"

Rand broke into a smile. "Yes. It's me."

Georgia pushed herself to a sitting position, and Rand supported her back with his hand. She was weak and wobbly but managed to find some strength.

"How do you feel?" Rand asked.

She assessed herself briefly, and then said, "I'm starving. I want a cheeseburger."

38

Ten minutes later, Nick and Maria reunited with their daughter in the ICU. A quick assessment by Dr. Clarke and a team of nurses determined that nothing was wrong with Georgia. Her cystic fibrosis remained, but the coma had come and gone with no rational explanation. At least, not one that modern medicine could provide.

Rand stood outside her hospital room and watched through the broken windows. The family sat together on Georgia's bed. Rand knew from experience that Georgia would have no recollection of her possession. No one ever did. That, in itself, was a blessing.

Maintenance crews had appeared to clean up the glass and plaster that covered the floor. A second team brought ladders to replace and repair the blown-out light fixtures overhead.

Fiona Shaw oversaw the restoration, eyeing the patients as they passed her by, asking the maintenance men about the severity of the damage and how long it would take to fix. Once, she caught Rand's gaze, and she nodded. Rand thought he saw just the hint of a smile on her thin, tight lips. And he figured that meant *thank you*. It was good enough for him.

Rand slung his bag over his shoulder and walked toward the

exit of the ICU, feeling like he was in the way as everyone around him worked to put the place back together. He considered stepping into room 316, but he stopped short and lingered on the threshold. The family huddled close, Nick and Maria sitting on Georgia's bed, and they talked low amongst themselves. Maria cradled her daughter against her chest. None of them noticed him there. So, without saying a word, he left them to be with each other.

He already knew the next twenty-four hours would be the hardest of anything so far—at least for him. It would be nothing but waiting. Karax was gone, but the demon's original threat still remained. *Seventeen days.* The prediction could still come true. After everything, they could still lose Georgia to her disease.

All Rand could do was pray and hope.

In the hallway outside, Father Calvin leaned against the wall. His eyes were red, face fallen into despair.

"You all right, Father?" Rand asked.

Calvin only shook his head. "How do you do it? How do you face down evil like that over and over and feel nothing?"

"I definitely feel something."

Calvin looked as if he didn't believe him. Rand felt exhausted, hopeless, and empty, like he was on a treadmill that would never end. In a way, he was. Removing Karax from St. Mary's was well and good, but there would always be another demon, another haunting, another victim. He supposed the feelings he had after every encounter were locked away deep inside him, a coping mechanism that kept him stoic and steadfast for the next battle. Because if he wasn't there to be strong, who else would be?

"Thank you for saving her," Calvin said. "You did what I could not."

"I couldn't have done it without you," Rand said. The man's prayers had helped rebuff the demon, keeping it from becoming so much worse.

Calvin didn't seem to believe that either. He looked like he needed a long vacation. Or maybe a stiff drink. Possibly both. "I hope to see you again, Rand. But I pray it will be under different circumstances."

Rand left him and went into the ICU visitor area, where Nick, Maria, and the others had weathered the storm. It was empty except for Katie.

She looked at him from the couch when he came in. "How is everyone?"

"Happy. Like a family again."

"I'm sorry I never told you," she said. "That wasn't fair to you."

Rand sat next to her and set his bag by his feet. "It's okay."

But he wasn't sure he believed those words. Thoughts of a son came into his mind again. For so long, Libby had been his only family. But after knowing there had been the possibility for one more, the idea had latched onto him. Taken root and given him a desire he didn't know he had.

A second child.

But it was a dream he could never claim. It would not be fair to expose another child to the life he lived.

"I hate that thing for bringing it up," Katie said. "I should have known it would."

Demons were not bound by time or place. They knew everything about everyone, and they would use it against you if they felt threatened.

"I should leave," Katie said.

"I'll bring you home."

"No. Your daughter and girlfriend are waiting for you in the hall. Go with them."

He found Libby and Rachel where Katie had said they would be, surrounded by maintenance men going in and out of the ICU with equipment and tools. They both wrapped him in a tight hug.

"Are you okay?" Rachel asked. "I was so worried. Those horrible sounds coming from there…"

"Everything is fine. It's over."

"And Georgia?" Libby asked.

"She's back to normal," Rand said.

"Did you see it? The demon?"

Rand put his arm around her daughter's shoulder. "You know there's no point in talking about it now."

Out of the corner of his eye, Rand spotted a man among the working maintenance crew. He stood out because he was standing still against the wall while all the others were moving around him. Rand got the feeling he was being watched, but couldn't quite see the man's face from the cap pulled low over his eyes.

"Should we go now?" Rachel asked, breaking his concentration.

"Yeah."

"Can I say bye to Georgia?" Libby asked.

"She's with her family. Leave them be for now."

They walked toward the door but halted when Rand stopped short. "I forgot my bag. I'll run and get it real quick."

Rand returned to the ICU visitor area. It was empty now—Katie had gone. He looked beside the couch where he knew he'd left his bag when he'd spoken with her, but it wasn't there.

Someone must have picked it up.

The security station where the visitors signed in was unattended. He checked behind the desk to see if the guard had put it there, but it wasn't there either.

The elevator on the side of the waiting room dinged. The door slid open and no one was inside. However, Rand's bag was propped against the wall of the elevator, as if placed there.

What the hell?

The doors should have closed long before then, but they remained open. It was the service elevator, so it was larger than a normal one—big enough to carry ladders, machines, and other equipment around the hospital. Rand figured it was being used by the repairmen in the ICU.

He walked inside and to the far wall of the elevator, then snatched up his bag. As soon as he touched it, the elevator dinged again, and the doors began to close.

Rand rushed to stick his hand between them so it would open

again, but the door ignored him, sliding closed and threatening to crush him. He moved it out of the way just in time.

He pressed the buttons on the control panel, but none of them responded. Next, he tried the red help button, but it did not light up or activate.

Rand's pulse quickened. He gripped the handle on his bag. *I've taken the bait and fallen into a trap.*

He felt the hairs rise on the back of his neck. And he knew that whatever had brought him there was behind him.

He turned. The man he'd spotted earlier among the maintenance crew had appeared out of thin air.

But it was his face that stood out. He resembled a person, but his flesh seemed stretched too tight and was a light shade of blue. The eyes were small and completely filled with black.

Randolph.

He heard the demon's voice in his head, communicating telepathically. His mouth did not move.

And Rand knew who he was.

"Shindael."

You are well known where I come from. The demon's words were a whisper in Rand's mind, almost soothing. But also threatening. *You have met and bested many of my servants.*

Rand swallowed hard. "What do you want?"

I want you. And I will have you.

Shindael glared at Rand through his tiny black eyes. Rand wondered how many demons he'd faced in the past that had served Shindael directly.

Deep down, he'd always known that the more powerful demons would eventually come for him. Rand figured casting Karax out of Georgia was the final straw, and now Shindael was here.

I vow to torment you until the day you die. I vow to destroy your family. I vow to end your life. I will send all the angels of hell after you until both your body and soul are broken.

Those words settled into Rand's mind, and he knew he would

never forget them. He also understood it was true. Shindael would keep his word.

That declaration cemented the rest of his life as a never-ending battle with the demonic. Like a diagnosis of a terminal illness, it filled him with fear. Even regret—he'd played with fire too many times and had finally gotten burned. There was no going back. But Rand was determined to stay strong in the presence of his nemesis.

"I guess I'll be seeing you again," he said.

Rand wasn't sure, but he thought there was a shadow of a smile on Shindael's face. Surely he knew how hard Rand was fighting to maintain his composure.

The elevator dinged and the door opened behind him. Rand turned his back on Shindael and left.

When he got down the hall, and then looked over his shoulder, the demon had disappeared.

39

Rand woke at six o'clock the next morning when Rachel got up for work. She showered in his bathroom, did her makeup, and dressed quietly.

"You all right?" Rand asked her as she headed for the door. He propped himself up on his elbow in bed.

"Yeah," she said. "Didn't sleep that well." She left without another word.

Rand frowned. Neither had he. All the events from the hospital the night before still lingered in his mind. That, and Shindael's threat.

He threw off the covers and pulled on a pair of sweatpants before he went to the kitchen. He found Libby sitting at the table. She had put on a pot of coffee, and the aroma drifted through the air.

"What's up with Rachel?" Libby asked. "She walked by, but didn't say much."

"She said she didn't sleep well last night."

"Ah." Libby eyed him for a few moments. "You don't look that great either. Did you two have a fight?"

"I just woke up, Libby. Of course I don't look great."

"No. It's not that. You seem… worried."

Rand busied himself at the refrigerator so he didn't have to make eye contact with his daughter. Sometimes it freaked him out how well she could read him.

"Dad? Is everything actually over? With the thing?"

"Yes, it's over."

"Then why—"

"I don't know," he said, more terse than he meant to. "Maybe I'm just tired."

Libby didn't seem to buy his answer. "Fine. Go back to bed, then. I'm heading to school."

She swiped a banana and a granola bar from the counter and hustled out the front door, returning his coldness.

After she left, the house was silent and still. Too quiet. Rand had to find a way to occupy himself, to take his mind away.

Sixteen days had passed since Karax had told Georgia when she was going to die.

It was now the seventeenth day, and Rand knew it would be one of the longest of his life.

He felt helpless and hopeless. Like an inmate sitting on death row waiting for the final hour. If Georgia was meant to succumb to her illness on the seventeenth day, there was nothing he could do to change her fate.

At least what I did was not in vain, he told himself. *If it does happen, I still gave her peace for her last day on Earth.*

Although the thoughts did little to comfort him.

Around six in the evening, he heard a car pull up in front of his house. When he drew the curtain aside, he saw it was Rachel. Odd. She hadn't mentioned she was coming back after work.

He opened the door as she walked across the yard. When Rand saw the look on her face, he knew something was wrong.

He had seen that expression many times before.

"You all right?" Rachel asked. "Have you left the house today?"

"You didn't say you were coming over."

"I know," she said. "I was on the way to the store. Thought I would stop by for a minute."

It was a beautiful fall evening and the air chilled him. The sun was setting over the trees. The two of them stood rigid, and Rand waited.

"I wanted to talk to you," Rachel said, suddenly very serious.

Rand set his jaw. "Go ahead." Although he already knew what was coming.

Rachel took a moment to form her thoughts. "I'm sorry, but I don't think I can do this."

He'd heard many break-up lines in his life. That one in particular seemed to be the most popular.

"It's my work," Rand said. Not a question.

"Yes. I know you help lots of people with what you do, but it's just too much for me, especially this past week. All that weird and crazy stuff happening. I can't take it."

"I'm sorry it affected you like that," Rand said. "It's the nature of the job, and these things happen." Still, that didn't make it okay for her to be collateral damage.

Rand remembered Shindael's promise—how the rest of his life would be a war with hell that would affect everyone he cared about. The safest thing for Rachel would be if they stopped seeing each other altogether.

"It's just too much for me," Rachel said. "I know I can't ask you to stop doing it."

Rand swallowed a hard lump in his throat. *She's right. She can't.* Even if he wanted to give it all up, it was too late for that. Shindael had already made that clear.

Rand reached out and stroked her arm, and she leaned into his touch. "I get it. This is not for everyone. If you feel unsafe with me, then there's no other way. You have to take care of yourself first."

"So you're not mad?"

"Of course not. Sad, definitely. I care about you a lot. But if what I do is too much, then it's best for us to head our separate ways."

Rachel looked like she might cry. It was a shame he was so accustomed to the women he cared about leaving him because of the supernatural monsters that attacked him. There was a time when women ending relationships with him had upset him, but he'd become numb to it long ago. Ever since Tessa had left him, no other breakup had had quite the impact. Honestly, that worried Rand. His life of fighting the demonic was eroding the things that made him human.

Rand walked Rachel back to her car. As she got in and drove away, he wished her the best. She deserved to find a normal, great man who wasn't followed around by evil spirits wreaking acts of terror.

In a different life, he could have given that to her.

For a moment, he imagined what it would be like if he gave it up. A new life, settled down alongside someone, without the fear of the demonic.

But people needed him. They depended on him. There would always be another case around the corner.

And when he remembered Shindael's words, he knew that wasn't even an option anymore. So he didn't dwell on the fantasy for too long.

Rachel drove away. He stood at the edge of his yard and watched her turn out of the neighborhood.

On top of his feelings of dread and uncertainty, he now felt worse. *Not her fault. She had no idea that today was significant.* The only person he had told about the seventeen days was Katie.

When he went back inside, he had a text from her, asking if he'd heard any news.

Not yet.

She responded a minute later.

I've been praying.

Rand knew he should have been as well, but was also aware it wouldn't change anything.

He forced himself to get into bed at ten o'clock. He called Libby before he turned his lamp off. She was staying with her mom, and they chatted for a bit.

"Oh my God. She broke up with you?"

"Yeah."

"Really? I thought she could handle you for the long haul."

"Apparently not."

"I'm sorry, Dad. Are you all right? Do I need to come over there?"

"I'm used to it."

"That isn't a good thing."

"I'll live."

They said goodnight and hung up. Libby hadn't brought up Georgia.

That's good. She would have mentioned something if she had heard.

Rand tossed and turned all night, drifting in and out. When he finally managed to fall asleep, Shindael's face filled his dreams, scaring him awake again.

Around seven in the morning, he trudged out of bed and into the living room.

Day eighteen. If she was meant to go, she'd be dead now.

That was why he'd gotten his black suit altered and dry-cleaned before Tessa's engagement party—so he'd have it in the event of an unexpected funeral.

He thumbed his cell phone, debating on whether or not to call Nick Collins. He would say he was calling to check on Georgia and see how she was doing after her ordeal. Then he would know for sure. No more wondering.

But he couldn't bring himself to do it.

Not yet.

His heart was heavy, sitting like a stone in his chest. If the worst had happened, he just wasn't ready to hear it.

That day, he only had morning classes. So, he headed over to campus, did his thing, and then ducked out after the lessons were over so he wouldn't get held up by anyone.

When he got home, Libby's car was in the driveway. It wasn't her day to stay with him, and even though he and Tessa didn't adhere to a strict schedule with her, Libby usually told him when she was planning to come over.

He found her lying on the couch. "What are you doing here?"

"Nice to see you, too."

"That's not what I mean. Normally you give a heads-up. I don't think I have any food here."

"I figured you'd want company after what Rachel did."

"No need," he said, setting his bag on the floor beside the door. He dropped his car keys on the nearby table.

"But I also brought you a gift," Libby said, sitting up on the couch.

"I don't want gifts, either. You know how I am. I'll get over it after six or seven beers."

He walked toward the kitchen to grab the first of those beers from the fridge, and then a figure caught the corner of his eye, startling him.

It was her.

Georgia.

She stood off to the side of his kitchen, out of sight from where he'd come through the front door.

"I was supposed to scare you. Did it work?"

As he stared at her, an oxygen cannula dangling from her nose, he couldn't help but break into a huge smile. He almost started crying. He walked up to her and wrapped her in a tight hug.

Georgia's body was rigid and awkward. "Uh. What did I do to deserve this?"

"You're still here."

"What is that supposed to mean?"

Rand let her go and looked down at her. She gave him a curious, suspicious look, but it only made him laugh. "Nothing. It's just good to see you."

"You're not sick of me yet?"

Libby joined them in the kitchen. "She's your gift, by the way." To Georgia, she said, "He never greets *me* like that."

"You must not bring enough demons into his life."

Day eighteen and she's still alive, Rand thought. His entire body lost the tension that had built up over the last twenty-four hours.

"Come on," he said. "This is a celebration. I'll cook something. What do you two want? I don't have any food so, Libby, you'll have to go to the store to get some stuff."

"What are we celebrating, exactly?" Libby asked. She and Georgia both gave him a weird look.

"We just are."

Beer forgotten, he pulled out his pots and pans to prep for dinner. Georgia Collins showing up in his house had made him happier than he'd been in a long time.

For now, at least, he could forget about Shindael and Karax and all the rest. They'd be back on his mind in the morning, for sure, but that evening, he was a free man.

People like Georgia were the reason he would never give it up—people who were helpless and confused, and had nowhere else to turn.

They were why he fought. They were why he lived. They were why he served.

———

THE PERFECT POSSESSION

RANDOLPH CASEY HORROR THRILLERS
BOOK 2

PROLOGUE

Fear was a foreign thing to Hoby.

     He'd been big his whole life, taller and more built than most other people he knew. There was never any reason for him to be afraid of anything.

So why now?

It was nearing midnight, and Hoby strode through the dark halls of the old mansion, doing his final round before he could retire for the evening.

The job that Hoby had been hired for was the same as all his previous jobs. He was needed for only one thing—his size, strength, and protection.

The old man who owned the mansion—Hoby's employer—was paying Hoby handsomely to be a private bodyguard, while also adhering to a few odd requests.

The first was that Hoby had to live inside the mansion.

Second, the lights were to be kept off inside, even at night, forcing Hoby to use a head torch just to see where he was going.

But more important than anything else, the employer was not to be disturbed when he was inside his study.

The evening patrol was all that Hoby's employer required before

Hoby could take the rest of the night off. Normally, that would be easy work, but making the rounds of the run-down mansion always made Hoby feel uneasy.

He didn't like the way his heavy footsteps echoed off the grey, empty walls, which made it sound like he was always being followed.

There were random spots in certain rooms that were colder than others for no reason that Hoby could discern.

Even more disconcerting were the times Hoby swore he'd heard voices. He would spring into action and follow the sound to its source, only to find no one. Those instances made him wonder if his imagination was getting the better of him.

In those moments, Hoby would stiffen up and remind himself that he was strong and powerful.

As Hoby treaded through the quiet halls, he couldn't help but wonder why his employer felt he needed protection in the first place.

The house was empty, mostly devoid of furniture and appliances. Even if someone were to break in, there was nothing of value to steal. That, and the old man was loved around town, so it was hard to imagine that he had a single enemy.

But that night, when Hoby approached the old man's study, he found the door slightly ajar, which was unusual. He paused, feeling his curiosity bubble up. His employer had made it clear that he was to *never* be disturbed while he was inside his study.

Hoby decided he would not be doing his due diligence if he didn't at least check to make sure his employer was all right in there. Deep down, though, he knew he was more interested in finding out what the old man was hiding.

He crept toward the open door, switching off his head torch so as not to be noticed. The study was illuminated only by the light of the fire that the old man kept roaring in the hearth every night.

Hoby peeked into the room. The old man was bowing on his knees in front of the fire, speaking in tongues as he prayed to the flames.

Hoby listened for a long time, but none of the words were intelligible to his ear.

I'll leave him be, Hoby thought.

Hoby turned and stepped quietly away from the open door, but then he heard the old man finally say something that he could understand.

"The time has come."

When Hoby looked back into the study, the old man was still on his knees, but now his back was straight as he gazed into the fire.

"We have been waiting a long time for this," the old man said. "It is clear that you have ordained this moment. I will carry this out for you. I will serve you."

The fire swelled in the hearth, bursting and expanding as if someone had thrown gas on the flames.

Hoby leapt back from the door, startled by what he'd seen. The old man had not moved a muscle, unafraid of the sudden burst of fire.

It was like the fire had responded to the old man's promise to serve.

Hoby had seen enough. If he wanted to stay sane on the job, it was best to ignore what the old man did in the privacy of his own study.

Hoby tore himself away from the unusual sight and continued his patrol within the dark corridors of the mansion.

Still, the horrible tension within him remained—his body's way of telling him that something was very wrong.

1

ny questions so far?"

Randolph Casey scanned the sparse collection of students. A quick head count gave him twenty-two, which was a decent turnout. The classroom they'd assigned him was still too big, which highlighted that his class was severely under-attended.

"Good," he said, turning his remote to the screen and clicking the button. The slide changed to display a single word in a large font.

MIMICRY.

"Today, we'll talk about mimicry. Does anyone know what that means?"

The students stared at him, a few of them nodding.

"To pretend to be something," said Stacy Thompson. She was his constant front-row fan. Rand knew she was gunning for a 4.0, and that was why she worked so diligently in his class, not necessarily because she was interested in the subject material. Not that she had to work hard. His tests were the easiest in the entire Religious Studies department.

"Exactly. Its meaning in context to what we're learning today, though, is that mimicry is a common weapon of evil spirits. They use it to gain our trust, confuse and frighten us, and even impersonate."

Rand clicked the remote again and changed the slide.

THE CANTON FAMILY

"I think it was..." Rand looked at the ceiling as he tried to calculate the time in his head, "... maybe four years ago? Yeah, four years ago I met the Cantons. They were a family of five, with three daughters. The mother came to me because they were experiencing strange occurrences in their house. It all began with the youngest child—as it always does." He clicked the remote and Laura's name appeared on the slide. "She was five years old, and at least once a week she would tell her mom she'd seen one of her sisters somewhere in the house when they were really at school. Maybe in the bathroom putting on makeup, or in the bedroom flipping through clothes in the closet. She claimed she'd even spoken to them, and they'd answered her back. But her mother, Frances Canton, told her it was not possible, because the girls were at school, or out visiting a friend. When Frances checked the bedroom or bathroom, there would be nobody there. At first, Frances thought her daughter was just confused, or imagining things because she missed her sisters, but then the situation got weird."

Stacy Thompson shifted in her seat. A few of the other students exchanged nervous glances. Rand's past stories often frightened his class. There were, of course, the token skeptics who leaned back in their chairs, amused grins on their faces, waiting to hear whatever nonsense he came up with next.

"The middle child, Ashley, was thirteen at the time and told her parents one day that she had spotted her mother in the garden. When Frances came back an hour later with shopping bags, Ashley was confused. Frances told her daughter that she had been at the mall, and had not been in the garden all day. Ashley burst into hysterics and swore what she saw was real.

"This all came to a head when Frances became the target. She was a stay-at-home mom and would spend a lot of time alone in the house. Several times, she heard her husband saying her name, or her daughter Laura calling out for her in the back of the house, or one of the bedrooms, clear as could be. It was unmistakably their voice. She would rush to the room, wondering what they were doing at home—especially since she herself had dropped her daughters off at school, or watched her husband drive away to work. She would find no one in the house."

Stacy Thompson cringed as if watching an unnerving scene in a horror movie.

"That was when she came to me. Sure enough, my team and I sensed a presence in her home, and we were able to remove it before too much damage was done. Usually, people let this supernatural activity go on for too long because they don't believe in it, and then it gets too strong. But Frances was a believer, and luckily she got in touch with me in time."

Stacy Thompson raised her hand and didn't wait to be called on before she said, "What's the point of the spirit mimicking people?"

"To cause confusion and to frighten. Put yourself and your family in the Cantons' shoes. If this kind of activity went on for a long time, you'd think you were crazy, right?" Rand let the question linger and got a few nods in return. "Imagine the arguments it could cause. Your brother or sister insisting you were home, yet you weren't. Or spotting your father in the garage when he was supposed to be out of town. You see someone you know appear in places that don't logically make any sense."

"And it's a spirit pretending to be these people?" Stacy asked.

"Precisely. It causes division in the family by making them argue and doubt each other. Then it's easier for the spirit to take over and destroy them."

Stacy shivered. His skeptics in the back row didn't seem impressed and likely thought there was no such thing as the Canton family.

But Rand remembered them well. Laura, the youngest, had drawn him a picture after he cleansed their home, and he still kept it in a frame in his home office. That particular spirit had put up a tough fight.

Rand clicked his remote again to move to the next slide.

MIMICRY TO GAIN TRUST

"Not all demons mimic people to scare and divide. There's another tactic I've encountered, where they'll do it to gain your trust. In this instance, the demon will appear to someone and pretend to be a child or a teenager, and make up a tragic story about how they died. The person communicating with the spirit will often want to help the 'lonely ghost' or be his friend. At that point, the demon has gained trust. This happens when people play with spirit boards or do other kinds of séances or rituals to talk to spirits. How many of you in here have ever used a spirit board?" A few hands went up. The class knew well by then how their teacher felt about spirit boards. "I hope you cut that out. People go into it wanting to contact someone specific, like a relative who's passed. What they get is something completely different. And you have no idea who it is you're talking to on the other line."

Rand changed the slide to move on, but Stacy Thompson's hand went up again. "Wait. Do you have any stories of times you dealt with this?"

"Yes, of course," Rand said. "Recently, actually. It was..." He trailed off, flipped the remote around in his palm as he fidgeted, and lost his train of thought for a moment. "Um. Yeah, it was a sick teenage girl in the hospital. She saw the ghost of her friend who had died a few months before of the same condition." He looked at the floor between Stacy's feet as he spoke. "But that ghost was not who he said he was. He was impersonating her friend to gain her trust, and it worked. And by the time I was called in to remove it, things had escalated very far."

He swallowed the lump in his throat that came from thinking about Georgia Collins and her case. He hadn't talked to her in a while, but his daughter Libby followed her on social media and reported she was doing well.

"But you removed it, right?" Stacy asked, eyebrows going up.

"Yes," Rand said.

And when he looked up, someone else had joined his class, sitting in the chair in the topmost corner of the stadium.

Shindael.

The demon's frame was thin with light blue skin that made him look frozen. His face was smooth, featureless, without a nose and ears, except for small, pure-black eyes.

Rand stared at him for a long time, his mouth going dry and his skin turning to ice.

Stacy Thompson even followed his gaze, but was confused. She saw no one there.

Rand clenched his eyes closed for a few seconds and opened them again.

Shindael was gone.

"Mr. Casey?" Stacy asked.

Rand snapped back to reality. "I think that'll be all for today. You can go."

No one moved. They all stared at him blankly, some of them exchanging nervous glances with each other.

"Go on!" Rand said, louder and snappier than he'd meant to. All his students jumped into motion at once, closing their notebooks, picking up their bags, and streaming out the door.

Rand leaned on the podium, and the remote dropped from his loose grip. A sudden fatigue had taken over him, leaving him winded and weak, as if he'd run a mile with the flu.

That was typical when in close proximity to Shindael. The demon had appeared to Rand many times in the last several weeks. He knew Shindael was making good on his promise to torment him.

Stacy Thompson stayed behind after everyone else left, concern on her face. "Are you okay?"

"Yeah. I'm fine." Although he knew he didn't sound convincing at all.

"It's just... this is the third time you've canceled class in three weeks."

"Really?"

"Yeah. You're normal at the beginning, then you start to look pale and sick. Then you kick us out."

"Nothing to worry about," Rand said. "Just a bit under the weather."

"For three weeks?"

Rand closed his laptop, gathered his books, and shoved them into his bag. He slung it over his shoulder. "I'll be all right."

"Just making sure," Stacy said, like she saw right through him.

"I appreciate it," Rand said, walking away from her and up the stairs of the stadium classroom. "Have a good weekend, Stacy."

It wasn't like him to turn his back and run out on a student—or anyone—but he had to get out of that room. It felt tainted by Shindael's momentary presence, closing in on Rand, suffocating him.

2

Rand found fresh air outside as he strolled through campus. It was Friday afternoon, and he blended in with the hundreds of students who moved in crowds all around him. A grey sky ahead threatened rain, so all the kids had a certain quickness in their steps that usually wasn't there on sunny days. The grounds were notorious for rapid flooding, even during the shortest of rainfalls.

Rand ran through a mental list of things in his office and decided he had all he needed for the weekend, so he could go straight to his car and beat the afternoon traffic. And save himself from getting caught in the rain.

Although so late in the week, the Student Union was a hive of activity. Tents, trailers, tables, and chairs had already been set up as the tailgaters prepared for tomorrow's home game. It didn't matter to these die-hard fans if the sky opened a torrential downpour on them. Nothing would cramp their football season.

There was a light chill in the air, the first hints of a coming winter, a reprieve from the hot southern summer. Rand threw on his jacket—one so casual that it clashed with the slacks and the nice shirt he wore to work.

But the tailgaters weren't the only ones out in full force. Apparently, that day was also chosen by the campus's religious zealots who dropped in once a week.

There were about ten of them, and Rand slowed to read their picketing signs.

SALVATION FOR THE SAVED, HELL FOR THE SINNER!

GOD HATES SINNERS!

REPENT NOW! THE END TIMES ARE NEAR!

YOU ARE SINNER SCUM! JESUS IS THE ONLY WAY!

The words were painted in big black and red letters, decorated with what resembled fire and blood. These guys must've spent hours working on their signs and they still looked like bad art projects. Did they really have nothing better to do than come out on campus and yell at everyone?

A tattooed skateboarder zipped by Rand, nearly running over his toes. One picketer spotted him as he went past. "Your body is a temple, and you've desecrated your gift from God with all that trashy ink! Hell is the only thing you have coming!"

The skateboarder glided along as if he didn't hear and disappeared into the crowds.

A little girl, no more than five years old, walked up to Rand and meekly handed him a flyer. Saying nothing, she rejoined her father, whose sign read NO HOPE FOR GAYS AND FORNICATORS.

The flyer was black and had simple instructions for him written in red text. It declared he was a sinner and bound for hell, and that Jesus was the only one that could save his filthy soul. Then there was a list of Bible verses, all from the book of Romans, that instructed him on what he could do to be saved.

The Romans Road, Rand thought to himself. A series of passages in Romans that laid out the path to salvation. He knew it well and was surprised these guys recommended it. Usually, they preferred to beat people over the head with threats.

Rand crumpled the flyer in his hand and continued on. But he spotted a man sitting opposite the picketers in a simple folding chair. A second chair was across from him as if he was waiting for someone to sit with him. In his hands, he held a small, white placard, and on it was a single word.

PRAYER?

Rand saw the zealots every week, but he'd never seen this guy before. Sometimes the more religious-minded students would engage the fire and brimstone guys, getting into loud and passionate debates that went nowhere because no one was changing their minds. But this man… it seemed he wanted to take a more Christlike approach to combating the insanity.

It was then that Rand realized he'd been caught staring.

"Won't be long before the hellfire gets extinguished." Rand gestured toward the cloudy sky, which now had taken on shades of black. Thunder rolled in the distance.

"It won't stop these guys." The man smiled at him. "Why don't you have a seat?"

"Ah. Not in the market for any prayer at the moment, and I'd hate to take up a spot for someone who needs it."

"You're always in the market for prayer."

Rand figured he was the only person to give this guy any attention all day long. So he dropped his bag and lowered himself into the folding chair.

"Patrick Perryman." He extended his hand.

"Randolph Casey. Friends call me Rand." Rand squeezed Patrick's hand.

Patrick Perryman looked to be about his age. Although sitting, Rand could tell he was short, with sandy brown hair and small, wire-rimmed glasses. His jeans were faded and years old and not from any named brand, and he wore a tan jacket over his plain white t-shirt.

"Are you a teacher, Rand?" Patrick asked.

"Yes."

"Are you saved?"

"You don't like to waste time, do you?"

Patrick only shrugged and smiled. "I know what's important. My priorities are straight."

"Do you get much success out here? With these hooligans shouting and yelling?" Rand pointed his thumb over to the guys with signs.

"It's important that everyone knows our God is a God of love, not hate. Screaming to people that they're going to hell won't help anyone. We're not meant to scare folks into their faith, but demonstrate the love of Jesus to them."

"Right."

"Are you saved?" Patrick asked again.

"I would say so," Rand said.

"That doesn't sound like a confident answer. Maybe you are saved, but have drifted away from God."

Rand started to regret sitting down with Patrick Perryman. After the ordeal with Georgia Collins, and the lingering threat of Shindael, Rand had considered rededicating himself to God. But he still couldn't reconcile how a loving God allowed demons to prowl the earth, terrorizing the innocent and unsuspecting.

A single image of Georgia appeared in Rand's mind, possessed by the demon Karax, and the way those black eyes had stared at him.

Rand clenched his eyes shut and forced the memory away.

"Maybe you're angry at God for something," Patrick said, his smile faltering.

"Things are complicated in that area," Rand told him.

"I understand. My faith was weak my entire life. When I was in college, I didn't believe at all. I smoked dope and drank for three semesters and eventually dropped out. Never could keep a job. Had no direction at all."

"And now?"

"Now I've found my mission. To reach people for Christ."

"Does it pay?"

Patrick chuckled. "Money is of little consequence when we're talking about eternity. Listen, Rand. Maybe you haven't found the right church yet. Maybe you haven't discovered a place that gives you the proper connection you need to get all the way there in your heart."

"I was never a fan of church hopping," Rand said. "I always figured people who did that were looking to make themselves happy rather than have a legitimate religious experience."

"Wise man," Patrick said. "You know what you're talking about. I can tell you've dipped your toes in and out of faith. So for someone like you, I know what you need."

"Assuming I'm interested," Rand said. He wanted to keep a healthy distance from this man he'd just met.

But Rand had stumbled upon Patrick at the same time Rand was considering giving God a second chance. Was that some kind of miracle? Divine intervention? God's timing?

"Of course," Patrick said. "I won't force you to do anything. But I sense you want this on your own and were seeking something before you ever sat down."

Rand did his best to hide his surprised reaction to the correct pseudo-prediction.

Patrick reached into a plastic shopping bag by the side of his chair and pulled out a flyer. He passed it to Rand.

"More flyers," he said, taking it without looking at it. "Just like those guys."

To his right, a college girl walked by, and one of the sign holders caught sight of her short skirt.

"Respect yourself, whore!" he shouted at her. "Fornicating women will spend eternity in hell. Turn to God so he can clean your soul and save you from your life of sin."

The girl only put headphones in her ears and quickened her pace.

"You should already know this is different," Patrick said.

Rand looked at the flyer. It was a brochure for whatever church Patrick attended, although curiously enough, he couldn't find the name. Instead, the advert was all centered on a specific person.

"Pastor Deckard Arcan," Rand read out loud.

"Pastor D," Patrick said, a smile lighting up his face as if Rand had asked him about his father. "That man saved my soul. He put me on the right path and changed my life. Awakened in me a passion to reach people for the Lord who were lost like I was."

"I see."

Pastor Deckard Arcan invites you to his Sunday Service. All are welcome. Come worship and hear divinely inspired teachings and learn what God has in store for you.

Every Sunday at 10:00 AM. Located five miles down Highway 38 in Finnick.

"Join us for our service this weekend," Patrick said. "I think you'll like what you see."

"Finnick is two hours away from here," Rand said. He'd heard of the small town but had never been.

"It's worth the drive. Trust me."

Rand didn't trust him that it would be worth the commute. But at least the guy felt he was doing something right. Rand stood and folded the flyer into his pocket alongside the one given to him by the little girl.

Patrick rose with him. "Although you didn't ask for prayer, I'll still pray for you. And I hope to see you this Sunday, Rand."

He extended his hand, and Rand took it. "Don't delay the service on my account. Take care, Patrick, and try to keep dry."

Overhead, the blackened clouds edged open and the first raindrops fell among the thunder.

3

Rand drove home through the heaviest downpour in recent memory. He parked in his driveway, which inclined just enough to dump the water into the street. The drains couldn't keep up with the huge amount of rain coming from overhead. Although he ran the short distance to his front door, he was still soaked by the time he made it inside.

His house was uncomfortably cold. He checked the thermostat to make sure he didn't leave the air conditioner running. He hadn't, so he figured it was his wet clothes.

Rand emptied his pockets on the kitchen table—wallet, keys, and the two flyers he'd collected, each suggesting radically different ways to reclaim his faith—and went straight to the bathroom for a shower.

Even after he'd finished, he lingered in the hot water, letting it wash over him for several minutes. He knew after he got dressed, his mind would wander again. Although his house was not large, it still felt that way when he was there alone. The place was always so quiet, and it was in that silence that memories came back to him. Georgia. Karax.

Shindael.

Sometimes he would even spot the bastard in the periphery of his vision. A shadow that peeked at him around corners, disappearing as soon as he looked. Making him feel watched and pursued.

He turned off the water and snatched the towel from the rack. He dried and pulled on a clean pair of underwear. That was when he heard a sound from the front of the house.

He froze and listened, his entire body tensing.

Footsteps. Something being picked up and put back down.

Who's in my house? he thought.

Rand opened the bathroom door, the icy temperature of the bedroom chilling his steamed skin. He crept down the hall, listening for any clue as to who was there.

He rounded the corner into his kitchen to find a figure walking straight toward him.

And leapt back and howled. So did Libby.

She fell backward, hand on her heart. "Dad, what are you doing sneaking up on me?"

"What are you doing in my house?" he shouted, still numb from the scare they'd given each other.

"I can't come over? Fine, I'll leave."

"No, no. I meant I thought I was here by myself. When I heard you, it freaked me out."

Having Shindael on his mind so often kept Rand on edge.

"Doesn't mean you need to sneak up on me." Libby took a few breaths to steady herself.

"We scared each other, so now we're even."

"Whatever." Libby rolled her eyes. "Why do you never wear pants?"

"I was just in the shower."

"This is weird. Normal people wear pants most of the day."

"It's my house and I'll walk around naked if I want to. I paid for the place."

"In that case, I'll give back my key." Libby picked up one of the flyers from the kitchen table. "I saw this when I came in. Where did you get it?"

Rand walked over to the fridge and pulled a bottle of beer from the door. There were only four left, and he'd recently bought a crate. "Have you been drinking my beer?"

"No, Dad," Libby said. "You've just been drinking a lot lately."

He winced. That was true.

"I asked you a question. Where did you get this?"

Rand used the magnetic bottle opener on the refrigerator to pry off the cap. He took a long swig. "The religious fanatics were out on campus today."

"No, not that. *This.*"

Both flyers were black and looked similar, and Rand realized she was talking about the one he'd gotten from Patrick. "There was another guy there. Not with the crazies. I sat down and chatted with him for a few minutes and he asked me to come to his church. Then he gave me that."

"You know Justin goes to this church, right?"

Rand took another sip of beer. Justin was Libby's boyfriend, and Rand had only met him a grand total of one time, briefly. He seemed like a nice enough kid, but Rand still wasn't that impressed. "Really?"

"Yeah. Like, every Sunday."

"I didn't take him for the religious type."

"You don't know anything about his type because you've never gotten to know him."

"You never bring him over."

"I don't bring him over because you'll give him a hard time."

"Then don't be mad at me for not knowing him. And you're wrong, by the way. I don't have to know him to know his type. Guys have *types* and I can peg them coming from a mile away."

Justin was a soft-spoken, introverted, and introspective musical guy. All girls fell for one of those at some point in their lives, and apparently, it was Libby's turn. Rand was glad she was going through it now instead of later. She was getting it over with, like chicken pox.

"Whatever, Dad," she said. "So… are you going to go?"

Rand was taken aback by that. "Seriously?"

"Yeah."

"When have you ever known me to go to church?"

"Whenever you need it."

Rand knew what she meant, and she was right. After fighting head-to-head with a demonic entity, Rand almost always felt the need to recover somewhere holy.

Like what I'm going through now, he thought as he stared at the beer in his hands. *I went through a whole crate in less than a week.* He hadn't even noticed until then.

"Your last case with Georgia took a bigger toll on you than the others," Libby said.

"Yeah."

"Do you still see him?"

Shindael.

"Every day. And in the most random places."

Libby chewed her lip. Rand could see the worry on her face. He hated to put her through this. "Let's go to church this Sunday and see what it's all about," she said. "I'll come too, so I can get Justin off my back. He's been begging me to check it out, and I'd much rather do it if you were there."

Rand sighed and looked away as he considered it. It wouldn't hurt and it could only help. His only plans for Sunday were lying around and finishing the crate of beer if he didn't manage that on Saturday.

"Fine," he said. "But you realize it's a long drive, right? Down by Finnick."

"What's Finnick? Is that a town?"

"You've proved my point."

"It's a date then."

"Must be one hell of a church if your boyfriend will travel two hours there and back just to go."

"He says it's incredible." Libby had never been a church girl. She took after Rand and her mother.

"We'll see."

Then Libby said, "Now can you please put pants on?"

4

After a long and silent drive, Rand edged his Jeep onto the Interstate exit and followed the highway until he came to a crossroads marked by two signs.

Turning right would bring him to Finnick. Going straight would take him to Highway 38.

Highway 38 was paved for only a mile until it turned into a dirt road that was mostly mud. It had rained the entire weekend, and even now the skies were still grey. Rand had checked the weather before leaving, and the weatherman warned that there were more showers left to come.

Libby rode in the passenger seat wearing a black and blue dress she'd bought for fifteen dollars three years ago. She called it her "recycled dress" because she wore it whenever she needed to look presentable, but didn't feel like going all out. Rand had donned a navy suit, shirt unbuttoned at the collar.

Justin Tidwell was in the back, having spent the entire drive staring out the window into the grey morning and saying nothing. His black hair was overgrown, shaggy, and dangling low into his eyes. Whenever he tossed his head to throw it out of his line of vision, it revealed a garden of zits on his forehead. He'd also pierced his ears, which Rand was dying to comment on, but knew it would only earn him a sharp punch from his daughter, who had grown quite strong in her mere sixteen years.

The zealots that came to campus would have threatened Justin with hell if they'd seen the way he'd desecrated his temple with the small hoops that dangled from his earlobes. That meant this church —and the pastor—were much more liberal and inviting.

When the muddy road turned into a copse of dense magnolias, Rand said, "Are you sure we're going the right way?" His Jeep's tires skidded, and he felt like he was off-roading through a forest.

"Yeah," Justin said, his voice cracking. "Keep going."

There were tire tracks through the mud as they went, so Justin must've known what he was talking about.

When the dense trees gave way to a clearing, Rand found himself in an open field filled with cars and people. Rand pulled up along-side them and killed the engine. When he got down from the driver's seat, though, his nice brown shoes sank into a couple of inches of mud, water, and slime.

"Ugh." He'd assumed that the church would have a parking lot like any other building, but apparently not. He'd just shined the damn things, too.

Libby wobbled in her heels as they went, planning each step before making it in order to land on the sturdiest ground. Justin lent her a hand to keep her steady. The overgrown grass was still wet, leaving dark marks on the bottom of Rand's pants.

As they fell in with the other churchgoers, Rand noticed that he and Libby were way overdressed. These guys looked like they'd come straight from their manual labor jobs, or their lounging clothes, or even their pajamas. One woman had curlers in her hair. Another man, about eighty years old, wore a camouflage getup as if he'd planned to hit the deer stand as soon as church was over. Knowing small-town Finnick, he probably was.

Libby had also noticed the motley crowd around them, and she and Rand exchanged a silent, confused look. Justin was not put off at all. Rand would've thought the kid might have mentioned it was a casual church.

"Justin!"

A woman approached them. She wore faded jeans and a plain yellow sweater.

Justin broke into a smile and halted as the woman caught up with him. "Happy Sunday, Chloe."

"Happy Sunday to you, too. How was your week?"

Rand figured Chloe was about his own age, but she looked much older. Her skin was leathery, wrinkled, and sagged. A bandana covered her bald head, and when she rolled up her sleeves, she had purple bruises around her thin veins.

"Chloe, this is my girlfriend, Libby. And her dad, Mr. Rand."

"Hi, nice to meet you," Rand said. When he shook her hand, it trembled involuntarily.

"How are you feeling today?" Justin asked.

"Oh, you know," Chloe said, still smiling. "The doctors say all kinds of things, but what it sums up to is that each day is a blessing from the Lord." She glanced at the sky as if God was listening. "I am thankful for every hour."

They walked together while Justin and Chloe chatted about her treatment, her daughter who'd come to visit, and her cat. Libby eyed her dad and only shrugged.

Justin's more plugged into this place than I assumed, Rand thought. Apparently, Libby hadn't known it either.

And then Rand saw what they were walking toward.

A huge tent was erected in the field. It resembled an old circus tent with bright stripes, all colors of the rainbow. Its flamboyance clashed against the grey, stormy sky.

"What in the world…" Rand halted. *It's a tent church.* "Did you know about this?" he asked his daughter.

"No."

"What's wrong?" Justin asked them both. He and Chloe looked concerned.

"Nothing," Rand said. Although these southern, pop-up tent revivalist preachers tended to be far more charismatic than Rand was comfortable with. They spoke in tongues and played with snakes, and the highly emotional congregations loved every minute.

"This isn't for me," Rand whispered to his daughter.

"Come on. We drove for two hours. We can sit through a sermon."

"No one's going to sit through a sermon in a place like this," Rand told her. "Watch. They'll jump around all over the joint, hollering and crying."

Libby jabbed his ribs and pulled him along.

Justin and Chloe only smiled, ignoring his obvious hesitation.

Although the tent was open on all sides, everyone seemed to file into one designated entrance area. And there, greeting people with a warm smile and a "good morning" was Patrick Perryman.

Justin lit up when he saw the man, and he introduced his girlfriend and her father.

"Oh, I know Rand," Patrick said, smiling.

Justin wrinkled his brow. Libby must not have told him about the flyer.

"I knew I'd see you here today," Patrick said. "I prayed all weekend for the Lord to move your heart."

"Yeah, yeah," Rand said. "You should've prayed for the rain to stop while you were at it."

As the procession moved inside the tent, Patrick abandoned his post and walked with Rand. "We have special spots up front for our guests. I'll show you."

"Actually, I'm a back row kind of man," Rand told him.

Patrick smirked. "I could've guessed that. Always the troublemaker in school, huh?"

"Something like that."

"But Mr. Rand," Justin spoke up, "the front is the best. You need to try it." It was perhaps the only time Justin had ever addressed him without being asked a question first.

"I appreciate it, but I'll hang back."

Libby gave him a look. She wouldn't be able to refuse. She and Justin disappeared into the crowd toward the front of the tent. There was a small raised platform that served as a stage and a single podium on top.

"I'll ask you to take the second to last row," Patrick said when they had gone. "We prefer to save the back for our special needs guests."

"Special needs guests are given the back? Aren't they supposed to be in the front?"

Patrick's cheery demeanor faltered for only a moment before he recovered it. "Come. I'll show you where you can sit."

Patrick directed Rand there like an usher, despite being capable of finding it on his own. The seats were nothing more than wooden benches, similar to what would be found on picnic tables. He slid in and went all the way down and sat next to a large woman dressed in a baggy white dress. She smiled at him.

Although it was a cool autumn day and the storm clouds made it even colder, it was warm inside the tent now that all the people were crammed together. Rand definitely regretted wearing the suit. He estimated there were about a hundred and fifty people there, maybe two hundred.

Already the bench was uncomfortable. The uneven planks bit into Rand's ass and he rocked back and forth, trying to find a comfortable way to sit. There was nothing to lean on, so a dull ache formed in his lower spine.

Rand checked his watch. By ten o'clock, everyone was seated, and Patrick Perryman walked onto the stage and took the microphone. "Good morning and happy Sunday," he said, his voice projecting through speakers mounted to the thick poles that kept the tent propped up.

"Happy Sunday," the congregation said in unison.

Rand hadn't taken Patrick for a public speaker. It seemed he was a big deal in this church and not just an enthusiast and evangelist.

"How's everyone doing this morning?"

A jumble of murmuring.

"Are you all ready to celebrate life with the Lord?"

That earned him a more hearty response. The woman next to Rand let out a noise that was a mix of a yelp and a cheer.

"Then let's not waste any more time. There's a great message in store for y'all today, and it's life-changing stuff. So give a round of applause for Pastor D!"

The congregation burst into claps and shouting, and everyone stood. Rand rose with them so he could get a look at the guy.

Pastor D wore a suit—grey, tailored, with the coat buttoned and a fluffy purple tie. Rand guessed the pastor was about sixty-five years old with a head full of silver hair, combed and styled to the side. His eyes shone when he looked out on his flock.

Another tall, broad-shouldered man wearing a black suit took his place at the front of the stage, hands folded gently in front of his body, like a bouncer.

This guy has his own bodyguard? Rand thought.

Pastor D took the microphone from Patrick and surveyed the room. Everyone returned to their seats and quieted down and waited for him to speak.

"What is the will of God?" he asked into the microphone. No one answered his rhetorical question. He held a folded piece of paper that he glanced at. "Is it God's will that we be unhappy?"

"No!" Half the crowd responded.

"Is it God's will that we have nothing?" For an older man, he had a clear and powerful voice.

"No!" More this time.

"Is it God's—"

Pastor D stopped short. He lowered the microphone and scanned the room, letting the tent fill with an awkward silence he seemed to relish. All eyes were on him, all attention was his.

So we're getting a show as well, Rand thought.

Then Deckard Arcan tore his sermon notes in half and let the two pieces float to the floor. A few people murmured in concern, including the lady in the white dress next to Rand. She'd taken a fan out of her purse and fluttered it near her face, and Rand appreciated the residual breeze.

"I'm looking around and I see a lot of new faces today," Pastor D said.

"Praise Jesus!"

"I had a sermon prepared, but I've just received a new word from the Lord."

Oh, here we go, Rand thought.

Deckard let the silence linger, presumably as he listened to a clearer message from God. Rand figured it wouldn't be a proper tent church without a dramatic performance.

"I feel led to give my personal testimony," Deckard said. "I know some of you long-term members have heard it a few times by now, but do you mind if I share it again for the newer folks?"

"Do it, Pastor D!" someone shouted. Others clapped and cheered.

"I won't bore you with all the details, but believe me when I tell you that my whole life, I was a godless sinner. No direction, no love, no hope. If it's listed as a sin, I've done it. But we all know what God can do with sinners, don't we? We know how he can pull them out of their own pits of despair, and in a single day, or a single hour, reset the entire course of their life and turn them into powerful warriors for him."

He jabbed a finger toward the sky, and that elicited several cheers from the crowd. A few people even shot from their chairs and stood, eyes closed as if in prayer as they listened.

"I'm reminded of the Apostle Paul. Do we remember his story? He was first called Saul, and it was his mission to persecute early Christians. We know God is powerful enough to strike down someone like that, but what did God do? God said, 'I have a better idea.' And an angel appeared to Saul, and to demonstrate the mighty power of our Lord, blinded him and changed his name to Paul. Paul was so moved by this that he completely reversed direction and became one of the greatest missionaries of all time. All because God stepped in.

"I was a drug addict. I was forty-five and in and out of prison.

The security guards greeted me by name each time I came back. Let me tell you, folks, if there's anything on earth that's close to hell, it's prison.

"About three years ago, I was released from my fourth stint and I was broke, homeless, and alone. What did I do? I decided I needed some heroin to keep me company. It had been so long since the last time I'd gotten high, but I knew exactly who to call and where to go to score.

"But that deal went wrong and things got heated and nasty. I jumped into my buddy's car and we sped away from them, driving a hundred miles per hour. But those guys weren't going to let me go.

"They ran me off the road and the car flipped. I wasn't wearing my seatbelt, of course, and I landed outside with the car on top of my legs." Deckard laid his hands on the tops of his thighs. "Pinned down, all the bones broken. I remember lying underneath that car, destroyed and bloody, and seeing those bad guys walk up and look down at me. They were laughing. I was waiting for one to pull out a gun and finish me off. In fact, at that moment, I wish they had. But they didn't. They just left me for dead.

"I was found by a good Samaritan who was passing by, and he called the police. They rushed me to the hospital where I was told it was a miracle I was still alive. But they also said I would never walk again.

"I had never felt so low. Everything in my life had taken me up to that point, and it was all my fault. As long as I kept on living, the more I would suffer." Deckard's voice turned low and heavy.

"So I called a friend and made a request. He brought a bottle of mixed-up pills to my hospital room and I told him goodbye. I swallowed every last one and waited for the end. And as I lay there, waiting to die, a profound change came over me.

"I don't know how to explain it, but at that moment, something overwhelmed me. An inner peace I had never known before. And I knew I needed to live, that I had made a mistake.

"I prayed in that hospital bed. I said, 'God, if you let me survive this, I will dedicate the rest of my life to you. I need a new master, and I don't even care if my legs are gone.'"

"Amen!" someone shouted. Rand assumed they were familiar with the story.

"And folks..." Deckard choked up. The energy with which he spoke escaped him as he remembered the wonder that had supposedly happened in that hospital bed. "Folks, God heard my prayer that night. He accepted me into the kingdom of heaven. And like the Apostle Paul, he sent an angel down for me. Azora came and spoke to me, telling me I was now a servant of God. He even healed my legs."

He beat on his thighs, showing off how sturdy they were, and the crowd around Rand cheered.

Azora? Rand thought. That name didn't ring a bell, not from the Bible or any other Christian tradition he was familiar with.

"And when I walked out of that hospital, the doctors were stunned!" More cheering. "And I wasted no time starting the new mission God had given me. I told those doctors that this was the power of God, stronger than any medicine on earth!"

Now most of the people in the congregation were standing, blocking Deckard from Rand's view. But Deckard's voice grew louder over the microphone.

"And the next day I started this church," Deckard declared. "Back then, I had no idea how to run a church, and I didn't care. All I knew was I wanted to reach others for the Lord. What began with just a few has turned into the congregation you see around you today."

"Amen, Pastor D!"

"And I couldn't do any of this without you. You all keep me strong and balanced. And the Lord reminds me every day why I do what I do."

By this time, the people were cheering for their pastor as if he were a rock star. Rand sat still, mind spinning. Deckard Arcan moved around the stage more lithely than a man half his age, yet he claimed a car had toppled over him and crushed both his legs. Then God had healed him.

Rand's alarm bells were ringing. The most likely situation, he noted, was that Deckard Arcan's testimony was true, but the bit about being crushed by a car was a fabrication. There was no way for anyone in that tent to prove it. All they had to go on was his word. And when a charismatic preacher ratcheted up the emotions in the room, people who didn't have the same shields as Rand were prone to believe anything.

Preachers did it every day all over the world. They used their high-emotion sermons to lure a large congregation, usually to take their money. On the other side, the followers left feeling spiritually fulfilled, all sorts of loopholes triggered in their psychology to feel satisfied and ready to come back the following week. To Rand, a spiritual experience with God should be simple, direct, and personal, but to each their own.

For the first time since Pastor D had started talking, Rand stood, but not to join the congregation in their worship. He wanted to get out of there and wait by the car for the service to end. If Justin hadn't been with them, he would have grabbed Libby and pulled her along. He knew his daughter was having the same thoughts as him.

"And that's what brings us to this very important day," Deckard said into the microphone. His high-energy voice lowered. "Everyone, please quiet down."

The audience halted their cheers, and a confused silence filled the tent. Even Rand froze in place. Why work so hard building up the emotion only to kill it in a few seconds?

Deckard Arcan gripped the microphone with both hands. A solemn calm had come over him now. His eyes were closed and his lips were moving, although he spoke no words. Praying.

"Please be seated," he said, almost threateningly.

The congregation obeyed. Rand's curiosity was piqued. He looked at the exit, so near since he was in the back row. But in the end, he returned to his spot on the bench.

This guy's good. He can even get me interested.

"I've been praying about this for a long while," Deckard said. "I never knew when the right moment would come, but I kept my heart open to the instructions of the angel Azora. And I believe today is the day. With so many new people here, it's time we witness the power of the Lord at work."

He closed his eyes again as if listening to God. The congregation waited in total silence to see what he would do next. Thunder rolled in the distance, the newest wave of the storm coming in quickly.

"Is there a man here today named Gerald Roberson?"

5

Deckard Arcan kept his eyes closed. Everyone in the room looked around.

Oh no, Rand thought. Now Deckard was trying to divine something.

"Gerald Roberson," Deckard repeated, louder, as if commanding him to show himself. "I know you are here. I feel your name in my heart."

"Here!" someone shouted, and all heads turned. The person pointed at an elderly man at the back of the tent. He sat in a wheelchair.

"I'm Gerald Roberson," the old man said, raising his hand, nervous.

"Happy Sunday," Deckard said to him. "Please join me up here."

Gerald Roberson hesitated, but eventually, the will of Deckard Arcan won out. Gerald rolled himself down the aisle, the wheels struggling through the grass and mud.

It took time, but no one spoke as he approached the altar. It appeared cruel—Pastor D remaining at the front while forcing the old man with the useless legs to do all the work.

Now Rand understood why the special needs guests were relegated to the back of the tent instead of the front. It was all part of the show. When they were summoned, they had to demonstrate an effort to approach Deckard.

Once the old man was close, Deckard looked down, analyzing Gerald, then stepped off the stage to be closer to the wheelchair.

"The Lord has put your name on my heart this morning," Deckard told the man, speaking into the microphone so everyone could hear. "You and I have never met, is that correct?" He held the microphone out to Gerald's mouth.

"No, sir," Gerald said, his nervous voice projecting from the speakers.

"Then the only way I could know you were here is if God told me. Would you agree?"

Gerald considered, then said, "I suppose so."

"You were fifty-five years old when you had your accident. You are sixty-nine now, so you have not walked for fourteen years. You were on a ladder, cleaning leaves out of your gutter. Your wife Paula begged you to hire someone, but you can be stubborn sometimes. You lost your balance and fell. The broken ribs healed, but the nerve damage in your spine meant you would never walk again."

Deckard held the microphone toward Gerald, but the old man said nothing. He stared at the pastor, at a complete loss for words. Finally, he found some. "How did you know?"

"Because the Lord knows the number of hairs on each of our heads, Gerald. He knows everything about all of us, our pasts and our futures. God showed me you, and he showed me all about you. And..." Deckard softened his voice. "I have seen Paula too. Beautiful woman. Her four years in heaven have been filled with joy and reward, and she can't wait for you to join her."

Gerald Roberson wiped a tear that had fallen from his eye.

Deckard placed a hand on the man's shoulder. "Gerald. Do you believe in God?"

"Yes, sir. Of course."

"But do you *really* believe the creator of the universe, who made you in his own image, loves you and has a plan for you?"

"Yes, sir."

"Do you believe God is without limits and has the power to change our lives?"

"Yes, sir."

"Even to heal us, as he once healed me."

"Yes, sir."

Oh, no, Rand thought. A tight ball of nerves formed in his stomach when he realized what he was about to see.

"Do you believe the Lord can return your ability to walk?" This time, Gerald hesitated. Only his breathing filled the microphone, so Deckard took it back. "You must have *faith*, Gerald. This won't work unless you *do!*" His voice rose, and other members of the congregation called out, cheering Gerald on. "I asked you, Gerald Roberson, if you believe the creator of the universe is powerful enough to make you walk again!"

"Yes!" Gerald shouted into the microphone. The cheers and clapping had grown around him, pushing him over the threshold. His energy spiked, joining with the emotional high of his surroundings.

"Tell us all, Gerald," Deckard shouted at him. "Tell us all what you believe!"

"God can make me walk again."

"Louder!"

"God can make me walk again!"

Deckard removed his hand from Gerald's shoulder and lifted it to the sky, clenching his eyes closed. "Then in the name of the Lord, I command you, Gerald Roberson, to walk again and feel no more pain!"

Deckard's raised hand dropped onto Gerald's shoulder again and he tumbled out of the wheelchair as if pushed by an unseen force. The applauding congregation gasped and rose from their seats as the fragile man fell. Even Rand stood to see what was going on.

Gerald rolled around on the ground, his clothes soaking through with water and mud. He looked like he was having a seizure.

And then Gerald Roberson stood.

He jumped up and down several times, waving his hands in the air. The congregation cheered and hollered and shouted, celebrating along with him. In a fit of overwhelming joy, he ran down the aisle toward the back of the tent, running like a marathon man. Tears streamed from his eyes as he went. "Praise God!" he shouted. "Praise God!"

Amidst all the celebration, Rand felt his own legs give way. He lowered himself onto the bench, drowning in a loud sea of cheering and applause. He'd never seen a miracle healing live before—only on internet videos—and every time, he was sure that there was some catch. It was easy enough for Gerald to be a paid actor, but even then, the sixty-nine-year-old was running around like he was sixteen again. Still hard to believe.

Rand was the only one who was not celebrating. It became too much, so he rose and pushed through the crowd, which was well on its way to becoming a riot. People had abandoned their seats and now engaged in full-on worship, thanking God for his healing powers and praising his name. Rand left the tent, the cool autumn air giving him rapid relief from the sweat that had broken out all over his skin.

Once he'd put some distance between himself and the tent, he turned and looked back. The celebration that was going on in there would last quite a while.

Deckard Arcan, he thought. *Who are you? Where did you come from? How did you do it?*

So many questions had to be answered first before Rand could ever concede that the old man had actually been healed by God.

6

On Monday morning, Libby drifted through school, existing only in body, but not in mind.

She found it hard to stay awake during first-period Chemistry. She hadn't slept well the night before, tossing and turning over what she'd seen at the church the day before.

History class wasn't much better.

She finally woke up in fourth period, just in time for Math, but instead of focusing, all she could think about was Pastor Deckard Arcan and how that old man had run around the tent.

She and her dad and Justin hadn't spoken much on the drive home. Libby's guess was that they were also very stunned. She'd asked Justin if stuff like that happened every Sunday, and he'd only shaken his head.

Once the celebration of Gerald Roberson's new legs had quieted down, baskets for an offering were passed around, and by the time it came to Libby, a mountain of cash was already there. She'd sent it along without contributing.

After, she'd found her dad outside the tent, and she guessed he'd left after the healing, knowing he probably didn't believe it was true.

And no matter what, Libby knew she didn't believe that the man had been healed. Something tricky was going on. It must have been planned beforehand. Gerald Roberson had to be an actor.

She heard her name.

Libby realized that Mrs. Granger was speaking to her and that all the other eyes in the classroom were on her, waiting.

"Sorry?"

"I've called on you three times," Mrs. Granger said.

"Oh."

A few snickers from the back of the class.

"What did you get for number seven?"

Libby looked down at her notebook, but it was closed.

"We're going over homework right now."

Libby flipped her notebook open to the work she'd done last week. Number seven was blank, with a giant question mark drawn next to it. "I, uh… didn't know how to figure that one out."

"Steve?" Mrs. Granger said impatiently, looking at Steve Kerry, who sat behind Libby. He rattled off the solution, which was correct.

The sudden attention was not enough to snap Libby back to the present. Instead, she remembered Justin, and that she hadn't heard from him all day. They had no classes together, but usually they would have texted by then.

Libby waited until Mrs. Granger looked to the other side of the classroom, then she slid her cell phone out of her pocket and checked the screen. There were a few Instagram notifications, but that was it. She unlocked her phone and opened her messages, wondering if maybe the notification had failed to go off or if she'd missed it at some point.

Nope. Justin had not texted her. That was unusual.

Now that she thought about it, Justin hadn't messaged yesterday after church, either. Libby hadn't noticed at the time because she'd been busy with her mom, working in the garden behind Bill's house.

She checked again to see if Mrs. Granger was looking, then fired off a message without looking at the screen.

Hey. You all right?

By seventh period English, Justin had not responded. Libby also remembered that she was supposed to drive her boyfriend home after school. She texted him again while Mrs. Collier wasn't looking.

Hey. Am I still bringing you home today?

He waited until the end of class to message her back.

Yes please.

They met in the parking lot, and Libby could already tell that Justin was off. Instead of lighting up when he saw her, as he usually did, he merely walked with a frown, eyes on the ground.

"How was your day?" she attempted as they climbed into her car.

"Fine."

Libby took that as a sign to quit trying. Boys were like that, and she'd learned it from her father. If something was bothering them, even if you wanted to help, just let them come out with it in their own time.

So she drove, and when the silence got too awkward, she turned on the radio, tuning it to one of Justin's rock stations he preferred.

Halfway to his house, during her wandering thoughts, she remembered she'd forgotten her Math textbook at school.

"Crap," she muttered.

"What?"

Really? That got your attention?

"Nothing. Just forgot my Math book and I have homework." She sighed. "After today, Mrs. Granger's going to be mad when I turn up with it not done."

"I have mine in my room," Justin said. "You can come in and borrow it."

"Oh. Thanks."

A solution to her problem *and* Justin had started speaking to her again. Progress.

She parked on the road outside his house and they went inside and upstairs. Libby noticed something about Justin's bedroom was different.

Libby scanned the walls as Justin searched for the textbook

underneath the pile of mess on the desk. The room used to be covered with posters of rock bands, but no longer.

"What happened to your posters?" she asked.

Justin found the textbook and handed it to her. "Pastor D gave a sermon two weeks ago about listening to evil music. I figured I should take a break from my usual bands for a while."

"Are you okay?" she asked, unable to hold it in any longer. "You've been acting weird lately."

"How?"

"Quiet. Stand-offish. Maybe a little unhappy. Did I do something wrong?" Even though she already knew she hadn't.

"No," Justin said.

She gave him a few seconds to offer more and then shrugged. "All right. Well, see you tomorrow, I guess."

She went to leave.

"You never said anything about yesterday."

She stopped with her hand on the doorknob. Apparently, he was ready to talk about it after all.

"What do you mean?" She turned back around, and this time Justin looked truly upset.

"I mean, how could you *not* say anything about what we saw?"

"You didn't say anything about it either."

Justin thought about that for a minute. "We watched a man get healed. Right there in front of our own eyes. He couldn't walk, and then he was running around the tent."

Oh no, Libby thought. *Here we go...*

She looked at the floor, unable to think of what to say.

"You *do* believe he got healed, don't you?"

"I... I don't think so."

Justin seemed to deflate. "What?"

"So you actually think that man was healed?"

"Are you serious? Of course! We were sitting like four feet away from them when it happened."

"But Justin..." She was surprised she had to explain this. "People get caught faking this stuff all the time. They hire actors, and..."

"Why would Pastor D have an actor?"

"Because..." She remembered the offering baskets that were passed around, stacked high with cash. "I'm sorry. It's just not something I believe in. But if you do, then that's fine."

"I thought you believed in God."

"I do," she said. How could she not believe after all the horrible things her dad had faced in the past?

"Then if you believe in God, then you believe he healed that old man."

"Not necessarily."

Justin furrowed his brow, seemingly unable to put the two concepts together.

"Look, you've been going to this church for a while now," Libby said, "and that's good if it makes you happy. I don't mind going to church sometimes, but ones like that are a little much for me, you know? I prefer them simple. Sing some nice songs, listen to a sermon, then head somewhere for lunch afterward."

"So you like fake churches."

"Fake churches? What does that even mean?"

"A church where God is not really present. Pastor D has warned us about them."

Pastor D. She hadn't realized how deeply this church and that preacher had gotten under Justin's skin. She glanced again at the empty walls where the band posters used to hang.

"Can we talk about this later?" Libby asked. "I don't want to have a fight right now."

I don't want to have our first fight, was what she could have said. Of all the first fights couples had all over the world, she wondered how many of them were over the validity of a miracle-working preacher.

"Fine," Justin said, turning his back on her.

She left him in the bedroom and went downstairs, textbook tucked under her arm.

"Hey, Libby."

She turned toward the living room and saw Justin's dad on the couch, legs crossed, iPad in hand.

"Oh. Hey, Mr. Tidwell. I didn't see you there."

Mr. Tidwell set the iPad down and stood. "How have you been?"

She shrugged. "All right. School and all that."

"Yeah, I hear you. When I was your and Justin's age, I hated school. Never wanted to go, and I skipped a lot. Almost flunked out my senior year."

"Really?" She didn't know much about what Mr. Tidwell did for a living—something in business—but judging by the family's lifestyle and sizable house, he seemed successful. "You must have turned everything around."

"Yeah, sure did."

His small talk was short and stilted, and Libby shuffled her feet, ready to head home and get started on her homework, but didn't want to be rude. She got the impression there was something specific he wanted to ask.

"How's your dad?" Mr. Tidwell asked.

"He's fine. We all went to church together the other day."

"We should get together sometime. Have dinner."

"Yeah," Libby said, struggling to imagine just how she'd pitch such an occasion to her father. "That would be good."

"How about tomorrow night?"

Libby froze. "Oh. That's so soon."

"Yeah, it's short notice, but Janet is planning to cook her salmon. It's her grandmother's recipe, and it's incredible. Besides, I haven't met your dad yet, and I think it would be nice."

"Well. I'll ask him." Libby chewed her lip. "I don't know what his plans are. If tomorrow night doesn't work for him, then maybe another time."

"Sure," Mr. Tidwell said as if he didn't particularly like that answer.

She lifted the textbook. "Got a lot of homework."

"I understand."

Libby turned and left him, feeling weird about their discussion. She opened the front door, but before she could leave, she heard her name again.

Mr. Tidwell walked toward her and closed the door. He glanced around the room and up the stairs, making sure they were alone.

Libby's stomach sank.

"Listen, Libby," he said, his voice low. He gazed into her eyes, and Libby couldn't help but stare back. "It would mean a lot to me and Janet if we could... meet your father. Preferably tomorrow. If he can't make dinner, then let me know another way to speak with him. Please."

"Is there something specific you need to speak with him about?" Libby asked.

Mr. Tidwell glanced up the stairs one more time, then looked back at Libby. "Yes. I've heard a thing or two about this church that Justin's been going to, and I'm worried. Justin's also told me a bit about what your dad does, and I think he's the perfect person to talk to about this."

Libby swallowed. Apparently, Mr. Tidwell was concerned about Justin's involvement, and Libby was not surprised. She herself was worried after the conversation she'd just had with her boyfriend.

And Mr. Tidwell was right. When the supernatural was involved, there was only one person in town to call.

"I'll tell him," Libby said.

7

Miller Landingham sat in a chair near his cluttered desk, his considerable weight straining it as he reclined. Rand paced in the small office while he recounted his story, trying not to meet his friend's eyes as he spoke; he knew they were narrowing in skepticism.

Miller worked—and now lived—in a used bookstore downtown. Business had been hard, so the man had moved out of his apartment and into the rear office. A mattress with dirty sheets was shoved in the corner, surrounded by old fast food wrappers and empty soft drink cans. Boxes of books and sales invoices were stacked along the edges of the room, making it feel even smaller than it already was. And Rand did not have the heart to tell his friend that the cave had developed quite an odor.

"So yeah," Rand finished. "The guy just got up and ran around all over the place."

Miller had his hands behind his head. He blinked several times through thick-rimmed glasses. He was silent as he considered Rand's story. Ever since he'd called Rand in to remove a haunting a long time ago, Miller had committed to helping Rand with his future cases whenever possible. That meant, over the years, Miller had heard some weird stuff.

"Nah, not buying it," Miller finally said. "No way."

"I figured you'd say that."

"You mean you actually think it was real?"

Rand only shrugged. "I guess I *want* it to be real. We've both seen ghosts and demons and the power they have. On the other end of the spectrum is God. God is even more powerful than demons. So something like this could potentially be real, right?"

"The deal is, Rand, that this miracle healing business has been going on since the beginning of time. So many preachers have gotten rich off this kind of thing. They all eventually get busted. Research it and you'll see."

Rand chewed on the pad of his finger. "You're probably right."

"I'm definitely right." Miller leaned forward in his chair. "Look, man, I know you're hurting since your case with the young girl. That one banged you up badly. And you've mentioned before you think it's time to reconcile with the big man upstairs. But don't get caught up in some showman."

"I won't," Rand said. "It was just weird. I've never seen anything like that before."

"What did Libby say about it?"

"Same as you. Absolutely no way, it was all staged, it was a performance, all of that."

"She's always been very clever."

"The problem is her boyfriend is super into that church."

"And what does he think?"

"Not sure. I didn't ask. He didn't say anything on the ride home. I think it blew his mind just as much as mine."

"But you said it was the first time this preacher ever healed someone?"

Rand pulled up a sturdy box of books and sat on it. "The way he talked made it sound like it was the *only* time he'd done it. Saying he'd been waiting for this day, praying for the right moment, stuff like that."

"Ah. Okay."

"But as you said, people have been miracle healing since the beginning of time. I tend to believe in things that have been happening for that long. Like ghostly presences, spirit sightings, demonic possessions. You're saying it is *impossible* that someone could be healed? Isn't that the same as a bunch of people saying it's impossible to be possessed by a demon?"

Miller thought about that for a minute. "I guess since I believe in God, I also have to believe it is possible for God to heal a person through someone else. But it's suspicious when some old man in Finnick, of all places, shows up out of nowhere and does it."

"So a healthy skepticism."

"It's the only way. If you bought into everything you saw, you'd be just like…"

"Everyone inside that tent."

"Yes. And that's not you. Or me."

Rand let that tumble around in his head for a few minutes.

"Are you going to go back?" Miller asked.

"I don't know. If I do, do you want to come with me?"

"Not particularly."

"Figured."

Miller stood from the office chair and it creaked, happy to be free of his weight. "Listen, man. You're fragile right now. It's probably best if you stay away from that place until you get your head back on straight. When people go through these hard times, that's when they're more prone to fall for tricks and scams."

"True."

"Are you still seeing what's his name? That shadowy bastard." Miller lowered his voice as if Shindael could hear him. Truthfully, the demon probably wasn't too far away.

"Every day," Rand said.

"Have you been praying?"

"Every time I see him."

"And he leaves?"

"Yeah."

His phone chimed with a text message from Libby.

Where are you? I need to talk to you about something.

He frowned as he typed back. *Is everything okay?*

Yes, but can you please come home? It's important.

"Pray even when Shindael doesn't show up," Miller said. "Do the usual stuff. Command him to leave in God's name. Take baby steps into the religious world rather than jumping all in with some revival-tent miracle healer."

"Yeah," Rand said. "That makes sense." He sighed. "Even when I command Shindael to leave, he will, but he'll always come back. Karax was strong, and he serves Shindael, so that can only mean Shindael must be one of the elites in hell."

"That means you're one of the elite on Earth, my friend," Miller said. "You've got those demons trembling. But remember. You are stronger, and God is stronger. There is nothing they can do to you."

Rand appreciated his friend's encouragement, and in a way, Miller was right.

But in other ways, he was wrong. There was a hell of a lot Shindael could do to him, and Rand couldn't help but think the demon was just biding his time, waiting for the perfect moment to strike.

8

R and got home and parked his Jeep next to Libby's brand-new, sky-blue Mini Cooper. He grimaced every time he saw the thing. Bill, Libby's mother's fiancé, had plucked it off the lot and given it to Libby without any discussion with Rand. That had annoyed him.

"She needs a car, Rand," Tessa had told him.

"It's more than just a car," Rand had told his ex. "It's freedom and expenses and risk."

"You don't trust your daughter? You don't have to worry about the expenses."

The conversation still rattled in his head every time he saw the car, but he pushed it away.

He found Libby at the kitchen table doing homework. "What are you doing here? Monday is your mother's night."

"I told her I was here."

"What's up?"

"You and I were invited to dinner tomorrow evening." She closed her textbook.

"You came all the way here to tell me that? With whom?"

"Justin's family wants to meet you."

Rand groaned. "Absolutely not." It shot out of his mouth before he knew what he was saying.

"What? Why?"

Rand had known this was coming. Libby and that kid had been dating for a while now, and when Justin's parents inevitably heard that Justin had already met him and Tessa, they would get antsy and want to know why they weren't taking part in all the fun.

Honestly, he was surprised he'd gotten away with it for this long. "Because what's the point?"

"The point is he's my boyfriend."

"Yeah, but not for long."

"Give it up. I know you don't hate him and you're just putting on that clichéd dad act you see on TV, but it isn't working anymore."

Rand went to the fridge and grabbed a bottle of water. The remaining beers on the door shelf caught his eye, but he ignored them.

"I was putting on that act before, but I'm serious this time. He's into that crackpot church, which makes me concerned for you."

Libby said nothing for a minute and Rand wondered if he'd upset her with that one. She twisted in her seat and looked at him. "I think they want to meet you *because* of the church."

Rand took a sip of water. "What?"

"Justin told them what happened there yesterday."

"Okay..."

"And... they're worried about him."

"They should be."

"I agree. But the way Mr. Tidwell asked me, I could tell he didn't just want a friendly dinner. He said if you couldn't make it tomorrow night, he and Mrs. Janet would meet you wherever."

Rand licked his lips. This was making more sense. "They want me to figure out what's really happening there."

"Yeah. Ever since Justin started going to that church, something's been off. He's been changing. And now, after yesterday, he's totally bought into it."

"So Justin thinks that guy was healed."

"We sort of had a fight about it earlier. He believes it, but I told him I didn't, and that I thought Gerald Roberson was an actor or there was some other trick."

"That's my girl."

"But this is what you do, Dad," Libby said. "You help people who can't understand the supernatural things around them."

Rand said nothing.

"I care about him a lot, and I'd hate to see him tricked or misled. Or hurt. Please consider Justin a client."

And there was that magic word. *Client.* As soon as someone became one of those, Rand would stop at nothing to get to the bottom of their situation.

He had planned to never go back to that church. True miracle or no, it had nothing to do with him or his renewed search for God. If he was going to get right with the Lord, it would not be with the help of Pastor Deckard Arcan.

But Mr. Tidwell wanted Rand to figure out what was going on with that church, so it looked like he had Sunday plans.

9

Despite all his initial dread, dinner at the Tidwells turned out to be a pleasant affair.

Rand had finished two portions of salmon, the second one forced on him by Janet, who was a lovely woman. Charles Tidwell was a man that Rand could see himself getting along with. Charles was a bit older, was a successful owner of a chain of tanning salons around town, and had even recently expanded into other nearby cities. He had a clear head on his shoulders, which was why Rand predicted he had such trouble accepting his son's choice to frequent Deckard Arcan's church.

Justin spent much of the dinner in silence. He answered questions, but the rest of the time, his eyes were on his plate. Rand noticed Libby nudging him a few times, but he only grew exasperated. The church never came up in the table conversation.

Mrs. Tidwell served a homemade cheesecake for dessert, and when there was only one slice left on the tray, which everyone was too polite to accept, Charles Tidwell leaned back in his chair and rested his hands on his belly.

"So, Rand," Charles said. "You ready for a second dessert?"

"You mean Janet's made more?"

Charles chuckled. "No, sir. I'm talking about whiskey and a cigar. In my office."

Rand grinned. "You lead the way."

Charles Tidwell's office was a large room at the back of the house, containing a huge mahogany desk and book-filled shelves lining the walls. One portion was like a lounge, with black leather chairs, a table between them, a chalice of whiskey, glasses, and an ice bucket.

"On the rocks or neat?" he asked.

"Neat, please," Rand said, surveying the books on his shelf. Almost all seemed to be nonfiction regarding business, history, and economics.

Charles made two of the same drinks and handed him one. Then he opened his cigar box and trimmed the ends off a pair of thick Cubans.

The men sat and lit their cigars. Rand relished the mouthful of cigar smoke and let it out easily. He followed it with a sip of smooth, aged whiskey, and for the first time in a while, felt totally relaxed. "Been too long since I've had a night like this."

"I'm no doctor, but I recommend it twice a week," Charles said.

"I bet this is good for you and Justin. If I had a son, I'd do this with him as often as possible."

Charles blew out a plume of smoke and sighed. "Justin's more into the heavy metal thing. Which is fine. I just wish he practiced it more. I think it's a phase, anyway."

"These things typically are."

"Yeah, but then it's just a bunch of wasted time. If he followed through with the music, then he could start a band and make something of himself."

"Usually parents prefer their kids to forget that kind of dream. You wouldn't want him to follow in your business footsteps?"

"Not if he doesn't want to," Charles said. "There are plenty of ways to build a life, and my path isn't the only one. I want him to do whatever makes him happy, but I'd also want him to stick with it and not give up on it so fast."

"Wise words," Rand said, taking another sip of whiskey. He'd promised Libby he'd lay off the alcohol for a while, but it would have been rude to decline. She would smell it on him later.

"So Justin's told me about you," Charles said, tapping the ash of his cigar into a tray on the table beside his armrest. "And about what you do."

"As a professor?"

"Yes, that. But also your side gig."

"Not sure what he's told you, but I hope he didn't make me sound crazy."

Charles raised his eyebrows and shook his head, eyeing his whiskey glass. "It makes you sound *fascinating*."

"Are you a believer?" Rand asked.

"In what?"

Rand shrugged. "Anything, I guess. Anything that requires faith."

"No. Never have been."

"Fair enough." Rand crossed his legs.

"Obviously you don't share that opinion."

"I don't. But I understand that you and I have had different experiences, which are both valid."

"True. My disbelief has caused me a lot of trouble in my life." Charles inhaled from his cigar. "My father was a preacher. A very popular one. We lived in a small town not too far from here. He was very strict with me, so of course, I rebelled. You've heard the story a hundred times. I almost flunked out of high school, and barely scraped by. Then I went to college because according to Dad, that was the only way to become something."

"Things must have changed with you soon after that," Rand said. The room they were in, and the whole house, was evidence of his business success.

"One day, when I was walking to my freshman Biology class, I realized how damn cold it was. It was seven in the morning and everyone around me was freezing. I remember thinking about how I wanted hot chocolate. That was when I had my idea. After class was over, I ran down to the store and spent all the money I had buying supplies to make hot chocolate. The next day, instead of going to class, I set up a stand and sold it for fifty cents a cup. I ran out in twenty minutes. The day after that, I bought twice the supplies with the money I made, and again, sold out. I did that until the weather warmed up. I failed freshman Biology, but I made a ton of money.

"After that, I dropped out of school and started a textbook hustle. I would sell people's used textbooks for them and keep a percentage of the money, their fee for not having to deal with it. Then when the weather turned cold again, I paid someone to sell the hot chocolate for me. I made money without even having to be there.

"It wasn't long before I started other businesses. By the time I was twenty-three years old, I was worth more than my father."

"He must've been proud," Rand said.

Charles grunted. "You would think that. He accused me of idolizing money, which according to him, was the root of all evil. But I was actually quite frugal. I never bought nice cars and clothes. We grew up poor, and those money-saving habits were ingrained in me. No matter how much I made, I never forgot the value of a dollar. The one thing I wanted to do with the money I made was give it back to my parents. Get them a nicer house, or give them something to invest for retirement, but Dad refused. Funny how after a lifetime of preaching, he never realized how prideful he was being."

Rand puffed his cigar and eyed the other man as he recounted his story. Charles's eyes lingered on the floor, lost in the memory of the past.

"When I was twenty-six, they found a polyp in Dad's colon. They said it was benign, but it could become cancerous, and they wanted to remove it. Dad refused, saying if it was God's will, then God would heal him."

"Oh," Rand said. "One of those."

Charles nodded. "And so, as you'd expect, within a few years he was dead. Wouldn't accept treatment, and my offering to pay for it just made him even more stubborn."

"Sorry to hear that," Rand said.

"His faith was the only thing he held on to, and it seemed to give him a reason to wake up in the morning. But after all that devotion and commitment, he died from something that could have been prevented with a simple procedure, especially since we caught it in time."

"How about your mother?"

"Mom accepted my financial help after Dad was gone. I moved her into a better place, got some live-in help when the time was right. She passed away about four years ago. She eventually told me she'd lost her faith when she saw how it drove a wedge between Dad and me, but she never admitted it to him."

"It doesn't work for everyone," Rand said. "And it seems like you've done well for yourself without it."

"When I knew there was no God who would bless me and give me stuff just for praying and obeying, it meant I had to go out there and build a life on my own."

"I get it."

"And so I never forced religion on Justin. Never brought him to church, never told him what to do. I answered his questions as best I could when he was eight or nine—that was when all his friends who went to church would tell him he was going to hell if he didn't believe. I would've thought those kids would be too young to hear all that, but apparently, their Sunday School teachers didn't waste any time. I figured that age was only about singing songs about Father Abraham and coloring pictures of Jesus."

Rand had known Charles would eventually steer the conversation of church and religion to Justin. As they neared the topic, Charles seemed troubled.

"How do you feel about Justin's involvement with the church now?" Rand asked.

Charles Tidwell took in a deep breath and blew it out through puffed cheeks. The ash on the end of his cigar had built up. "If anything, it keeps him from drinking and drugs and all that nonsense. He's a good kid, you know."

"Sure."

"But... when he came home and told me what he saw on Sunday," Charles met Rand's eyes, "and I could tell that he believed it hook, line, and sinker..." Rand nodded along. "What about you, Rand? You were there. You must've seen it."

"I did."

"What do you think?"

Rand hesitated. He knew what he *wanted* to believe, but he also knew what was probably the truth.

"My tendency is to lean toward a rational explanation," Rand said. "They say the Lord works in mysterious ways, but a tent revival in rural Louisiana seems a bit too mysterious for me."

"My thoughts exactly," Charles said. "I know you're a man who's interested in the unexplainable."

"More than just interested."

"Right." Charles leaned forward. "Janet and I have been talking about having you over for a while now. But I also wanted to pick your brain about whatever's going on at that church."

"I understand."

"I know we just met. But if I asked a favor of you..."

"You want me to find out if it's real."

"I already know it isn't real," Charles said. "But I would like you to find proof. Hard evidence. Justin won't listen to me, but he'll hopefully listen to you since he knows what it is you do."

"Hard evidence." Rand finished the rest of his whiskey. "Shouldn't be too difficult. This Deckard Arcan fellow seems clever, but he's no magician."

"Do all your investigations lead to supernatural things?" Charles asked.

"Of course not. Actually, less than half of them do." Rand remembered the person who had come to him claiming to hear scratches on the walls at night. Their dog would also go crazy and bark at something that no one else saw. Those were two common signs of a spiritual presence, but Rand discovered what they actually had was a rat infestation inside the walls.

"Then you're an expert debunker as well as a ghost hunter," Charles said.

"You could say that."

"Look, Rand. My goal is to get my son out of that crazy church. I don't care much about what the other people do, or even if this preacher man keeps going. I just want Justin to know the truth." He peered at Rand with a strong, blue-eyed gaze.

Charles Tidwell wanted Rand to prove that Deckard Arcan was a charlatan and did not, in fact, have supernatural powers. Rand officially had a new case.

"As the Bible says," Rand said, "the truth shall set us free."

10

The week passed and Sunday came.

Instead of dressing in a suit, Rand pulled on a pair of nice jeans, a black V-neck t-shirt, and his usual casual jacket. He packed his satchel full of his standard equipment—recorders, cameras, and crucifixes—just in case. This was a different kind of investigation, but still, he never went investigating the unknown without his gear.

The two-hour drive was nothing but silence as Rand turned over in his head what his plan might be. He needed evidence that Deckard Arcan was a fraud and not gifted with miraculous abilities. He'd have to make sure his eyes and ears were in tune for that kind of thing.

Despite Rand forcing himself to remain rational, a small piece of him still wondered if Deckard Arcan could be for real. Perhaps that was the part of Rand that longed to get back into the embrace of God. Maybe Pastor D was the one God sent to show Rand the way. And here he was, trying to sabotage the work of the Kingdom.

When Rand arrived, the field that served as a parking lot was even fuller than the week before. Although the skies were still grey, the rains had halted, and the trek to the tent was less muddy.

Rand fell in with the people who flocked to the church. There were at least twice as many as before, maybe three times. Word of the miracle healing had apparently gotten around.

"Rand!" He turned and found Chloe, the woman who had known Justin. "Happy Sunday!"

"Happy Sunday, Chloe," Rand said.

She gave him a beaming smile and reached out her hand, which Rand shook. She had barely enough strength to hold it and she trembled even more than the week before.

"I'm so happy you're back," she said as they walked together. "Such divine planning that last week was your first!"

"You can say that again."

"Look at all these people," Chloe said. "Amazing. All of Finnick has heard about Gerald, and now they've come to see Pastor D. When the Lord moves, he *really* moves."

Rand had to slow his pace for Chloe as she limped along. Rand offered her his arm, and she slipped her hand through the crook of his elbow.

"Such a gentleman."

Ahead of them, the multicolored tent came into view. The seats inside were already full, and the excess people were standing on the outside. Church had not even started yet.

"Look at all these people," Chloe said, excited. "So many looking to hear the good word."

"Praise be to God," Rand said flatly.

Chloe squeezed his arm. "I don't know what Pastor D has planned for today, but I've been praying all week that there is more healing. I realize it sounds selfish, but I hope the Lord moves him to choose me." Rand looked down at the frail woman, whose smile had faded. "The doctors say there's nothing more they can do. All that's left is to make sure I'm comfortable and that my affairs are in order. I've been coming here to listen to Pastor D ever since they told me that, and now I'm no longer afraid to die. He has done me a great service already. But... I can't help but be hopeful. After seeing what he did for Gerald... maybe the Lord will lead him to heal me next."

Rand's heart broke for the woman. He felt her helplessness and her desperate hope at the same time. And he'd only come for the sole purpose of poking holes in the one thing that gave Chloe peace.

"Looks like standing room only," Chloe said as they reached the entrance of the tent. "Praise Jesus."

"Come on." Rand pushed through the crowds, pulling Chloe along with him. The sea of people parted for him until he was inside the tent, where he guided Chloe to the bench in the back row. A middle-aged man sat at the end.

"Excuse me," Rand told him. "Good morning, happy Sunday. Would you mind giving up your seat for my friend here? It's hard for her to stand for a long time."

The man took one look at Chloe and beamed. "Absolutely. No problem at all."

He stood, and Chloe struggled to lower herself onto the bench. Once she was down, she looked up at Rand with soft eyes. "Thank you," Chloe said, clasping Rand's hand in both of hers. "You are a good person."

Rand stepped back and merged with the crowd. He checked his watch, and at ten o'clock sharp, Deckard Arcan walked onto the stage to an intense standing ovation. Just like the week before, his bodyguard took his position at the front of the stage.

Deckard stood there, basking in the adoration, making no effort to calm the crowd down. He wore another fine suit, this one navy, with a pink bow tie. It was well-tailored and pressed—the man had an impeccable eye for fashion.

When the congregation settled, Deckard took the microphone and said, "Happy Sunday."

The congregation answered back in unison.

"Well, well. It seems we have a lot of new faces here today." He scanned his audience, eyeing all those who were standing on the outside of the tent, rising onto their tiptoes just to get a glimpse of the miracle healer.

"I know I said the same thing last time, but praise be to God for the new people who have come to hear the good news."

"Amen!" called out a few voices in the crowd.

"Yes, my friends, God moved among us. That really happened. Perhaps some of you have had the chance to speak with Mr. Roberson during the week." A few people cheered. "God made him new, and God can do the same for you. Pray with me, please."

The congregation all bowed their heads in unison, and Deckard closed his eyes.

"Dear Lord, we come before you humbly and ask that you move into this place—"

And then he began speaking in tongues.

Rand glanced around the tent, but no one reacted to Deckard's rapid, nonsensical words. It must've been something he did often.

Rand knew the spiritual gift of tongues was mentioned in the Bible. Someone praying would be so overcome with the presence of God that they would speak in languages that were not known on Earth, only in heaven. Rand also knew the Bible instructed that if someone were to speak in tongues, it was required to have another person there to interpret for the listeners.

It was a small detail that most churches with tongues missed out on, and this one was no different.

Rand slid his cell phone from his pocket, opened the camera app, and switched it to record. He made a video of the rest of the prayer, the rapid sounds flowing from Deckard Arcan's mouth with no effort.

"Amen," the pastor finished.

Rand stopped recording and texted the video straight to Miller. Once it was gone, he typed out a message.

Preacher man speaking in tongues. Can you verify?

A minute later, Miller sent back a thumbs-up emoticon.

"I sense there is a good portion of you here today because you heard of the miraculous things that occurred here last week," Deckard said, looking over the crowd. "Maybe you've never stepped foot in a church before. Maybe you used to attend church, but your faith has drifted. Maybe you don't believe in God, and you're only here to be entertained. Whatever your motive, whatever your past, you are welcome here. The things that happened last week were done precisely to gather you all together so you can witness the awesome power of the creator of the universe. I have spent the last week in prayer and silence. And I have been spoken to. I have been told that there is more good work to be done today."

The congregation cheered for Deckard. He waited for it to die down again.

Deckard raised the microphone to his mouth again, but before he could speak, someone stood from their bench and called out to him.

"Pastor D! My arthritis!" The man lifted his hands into the air. "It's gotten so bad I can't even drive anymore!"

Then a lady on the other side of the aisle stood. "My doctor told me I can't get pregnant! Can you pray for me?"

Then a man in the back, not too far away from Rand, called out, "They found a mass on my kidney! Please, Pastor, can you make it go away?"

Deckard looked at each one of the people as they called out to him, appearing pained by what they told him.

Two or three people stood at once, shouting at him at the same time. Their complaints drowned each other out.

Deckard held up a hand, and everyone fell silent at once. The people who had stood to request prayer lowered themselves back down, disappearing into the crowd once more.

"A lot of you are experiencing great trial and sickness," he said, speaking low. He looked around, and he genuinely appeared heartbroken. "If I could, I would lay hands on each of you and take away your pain. Perhaps the Lord will permit me to do that one day. But it is up to God who will be spoken to today."

Deckard lowered the microphone, lifted his head, and closed his eyes. "Lord, guide me. Tell me who you wish to bless today," he shouted, loud enough to be heard without his microphone.

The only sound was the tent material flapping in the chilly wind. Rand pulled his jacket tighter around him, shivering. He was waiting on edge just as much as everyone else.

Entire minutes passed in silence. Deckard remained still, as if in a trance. His eyelids fluttered but never opened. He appeared to listen intently to a voice that only he could hear.

Then he brought the microphone back to his mouth. "There is a man here today named Randolph Casey."

11

Rand's mouth went dry.

The silence continued, except now everyone looked around, waiting for the man called to identify himself. Waiting to see if Deckard's prophecy was true.

Rand said nothing.

Deckard opened his eyes and joined everyone else by looking around the room. "Randolph Casey," he said again. "The Lord has laid your name on my heart."

No, he didn't, Rand wanted to say. But in that moment, he wasn't sure *what* to believe.

The silence lingered on. Rand already knew he would not come forward. No amount of curiosity would push him to approach Deckard. Perhaps Deckard would back down. Maybe he'd find another name from God since the first one wasn't interested.

"Randolph Casey," Deckard said again, this time firm, almost angry. "Your God has called you forth. Do not deny him."

"Come on!" someone shouted.

"He's there!"

A man in the front row stood and pointed directly at Rand. It was Patrick Perryman, the guy Rand had met on campus.

Hundreds of heads turned to face him at once. The people next to him took a step away as if he had a disease. But of all the eyes, none of them pierced into him more than those of Deckard Arcan.

"Randolph Casey," Deckard said to him. "Please come forward. You have been called."

Rand struggled to find words in his tight throat. "I'm not sick. Thank you, though."

Someone booed.

"It isn't about being sick, Randolph," Deckard said, his voice soft, almost paternal. "I never said there would be a healing today. I only said the Lord would move. And he will move through you. Please come forward."

Everyone's stares continued to bore into him, and Rand felt surrounded. Even if he tried to turn and leave, he had a feeling the wall of people behind him would not let him through.

So Rand broke from the crowd and walked down the aisle toward Deckard Arcan.

Patrick must have given Deckard my name, he told himself. *He saw me come in, but I didn't see him. He told Deckard about me because of our conversation the other day.*

It made perfect sense to him.

Rand stopped a few paces away from Deckard, and the two men watched each other for a long time. Deckard's gaze went from welcoming to something else—perhaps confusion. It was as if the other man realized he had no tricks to perform with the person he had chosen. Rand felt the tension in the room tighten.

"Last week we saw a healing," Deckard said into the microphone, never taking his eyes off Rand. "That is because God is loving and merciful. He gives generously to his faithful children."

An "amen" rang from somewhere over Rand's shoulder.

Deckard went on. "But the Lord is also powerful and just. As with Israel, his own chosen people, he allowed them to be conquered when they did not obey his commands. There can, and will, be judgment."

Rand felt his insides twist.

"The Lord has told me about you, Randolph," Deckard said. "You are a man who is followed by darkness." Gone was the comforting, welcoming voice of a pastor. Now he spoke as if every word produced a bad taste in his mouth. "You have spent your life dabbling in things that no one has any business touching, and yet you persist. This evil has now attached itself to you and is always a step behind. You know exactly what I'm talking about."

Shindael.

Rand clenched his jaw and met Deckard's hard gaze with his own, refusing to back down.

"That's nice and all," Rand said, "but anyone can say that about anyone. It's called cold reading."

A wave of murmurs coursed through the crowd. Deckard eyed Rand hard. He had a feeling this was the first time the man had ever been challenged. To Rand's surprise, Deckard Arcan did not seem ready to back down.

"Cold reading, huh," Deckard said. "So you do not believe."

"In God? Sure. In you? No."

The murmurs grew into louder conversations.

Deckard raised his hand, and everyone shut up all at once.

"If you think I'm cold reading, then maybe we should dive a little deeper," Deckard said. He took a step closer. "Randolph Franklin Casey. You are forty-one years old. You do not go to church regularly. You only come back to God when you need something from him. You are a sinner. You have fornicated with thirty-two women outside of wedlock, the first when you were only fifteen years old. Two of them got pregnant, one of them miscarried. The daughter who was born has lived a tortured life on account of you and your penchant for dabbling with dark spirits."

Deckard stalked closer to Rand, and he unconsciously took a step back.

"You resist God because you are angry with him, but in reality, you are immature. When you get depressed, you drink heavily. You're going through one of those times right now.

"You were here last week and witnessed a miracle, but still you do not believe. In fact, you came here today for the sole purpose of revealing me as a fraud and a liar."

As Deckard's strong presence pushed Rand farther down the aisle, he felt compelled to back away. Out of the corner of his eye, he spotted Justin sitting on one of the benches, his mouth hanging open in disbelief.

"Just because you have no faith, you think you can steal the faith of others. Well, that is not how it works, Randolph Casey. God is much too strong for people like you."

Now the crowd grew more animated. Some started shouting at him. Others booed. Rand saw angry faces all around him.

"The Lord will always accept those who repent, but that is between you and God. Acceptance is not something you'll find from me," Deckard said. "Today, you are not welcome here. You are attacking the faith of hundreds, and that cannot stand. Come back when you have forgiven yourself and asked God to forgive you as well."

"Get out!" someone shouted.

"God have mercy on your soul!" cried another.

Everyone in the tent erupted into loud shouting, chastising Rand. It was as if the crowd was one second away from attacking him.

Rand did the only thing he could think to do. He turned and ran. As he forced his way through the crowds, he felt slaps and kicks on his arms, torso, and hips. He tripped and almost went down, but caught himself before straightening and quickening his pace.

He burst through the sea of people outside the tent and sprinted down the path, leaving the shouting mob behind him.

The last thing he heard as he left the church in the distance was Deckard Arcan's voice over the microphone. "Praise Jesus!"

12

R and slammed the door of his Jeep and locked it. He peered through the windshield, half expecting the angry mob to chase after him.

But there was no one there. Now that the skeptic had been expelled from their midst, Rand assumed they were ready to continue on with church as scheduled.

His chest heaved from the running. He hadn't sprinted like that in a long time. Although it was a cold autumn morning, sweat beaded on his face and chest, staining dark spots on the neck of his t-shirt. He peeled his jacket off and threw it into the backseat.

"Holy shit," he whispered as he caught his breath.

Deckard Arcan had nailed him one hundred percent. That was *not* cold reading. Cold reading was purposely vague, causing the target to twist their mind to find ways the words could apply to them.

No. That man had intimate details of Rand's past and present.

And Deckard had rebuked him for it.

He started the Jeep and drove down Highway 38. Deckard Arcan's cold, steel-blue eyes were still burned into Rand's memory. The way the pastor had looked at Rand—such disgust.

He had known.

Known precisely what Rand had come there to do. And had played him perfectly.

Rand came to the crossroads. One way led him to the Interstate that would take him home, back to the city. The other way would take him to Finnick, the nearest small town, and presumably the home of most of the congregation in Deckard's church.

Rand idled there for a moment, glancing back and forth between both signs.

Home was where he wanted to go. His nerves were still shocked and rattled. His heart still pounded in his chest.

But he remembered Justin. The boy was still back there in the church, soaking up every ounce of whatever Deckard told him. Charles Tidwell had wanted Rand to prove to Justin that Deckard was a sham, but after that little incident, there was no telling how credible Justin now thought Deckard was.

But it was more than Justin. Rand knew that something fishy was going on. Patrick Perryman could have told Deckard to call on Rand, but Patrick could *not* have told Deckard all the details that he'd known.

Rand was going to get to the bottom of it. He always did.

He turned left and drove toward Finnick, foot heavy on the accelerator.

ALTHOUGH THE SERMON elicited strong and favorable reactions, Justin Tidwell could not concentrate on any of it. Pastor D had preached vehemently and with conviction. Deckard and the others seemed to have already forgotten about the heretic who had been expelled from the congregation.

But Justin had not. In fact, Mr. Rand remained on his mind the entire sermon, blocking any of Pastor D's words from entering.

Is Mr. Rand really that sinful of a man?

Justin also wondered if he himself was guilty of associating with such a family. Libby was not the same person as her father, but they were still close. Mr. Rand had the potential to influence her a lot.

The event nagged at Justin too much. He had to know if his relationship with the Caseys would interfere with his walk with the Lord. And there was no better person to ask than Pastor Deckard Arcan himself. After Pastor D's amazing feat the week before, Justin was sure that everything Pastor D had said was true. If God gave Pastor D the ability to heal, then certainly God also gave the man divine knowledge.

So after church was over, Justin hung back while the crowd dispersed and headed toward their cars. Pastor D had disappeared through the rear exit of the tent after his sermon as he usually did—otherwise, a mob of adoring fans would rush him. Justin assumed he wasn't welcome to search out Pastor D, but he figured his motives were pure and that Pastor D wouldn't mind.

He walked past the raised platform on which Pastor D gave his messages and through the tent flap behind it. On the other side was the rest of the field, a few cars, and the man himself.

Pastor D spoke to Patrick Perryman. They stood near a sleek black sedan, where the big bodyguard that always hovered like a statue beside the stage waited to drive Deckard away. Justin was acquainted with Patrick but didn't know how Patrick had come to be so close to Pastor D.

He walked toward them, the butterflies springing up in his stomach. It was like approaching a celebrity, knowing how they acted in public, but not one on one. The last time he'd felt that way was when he'd initially asked Libby out.

Deckard saw him first, and he ceased his conversation with Patrick as he approached. Patrick followed Deckard's gaze.

"Justin Tidwell. Happy Sunday."

Justin flushed. *How did he know me?* Probably the same way he knew Mr. Rand. Then it occurred to Justin that perhaps Deckard also knew every sinful thing Justin had ever done. He was suddenly a lot more nervous.

"H-h-happy Sunday."

Justin realized he didn't know what he would say. He had no plan. He just needed to speak with Pastor D. He regretted wasting the time of such an important man.

"You seem distressed," Pastor D said, his voice gentle—a completely different tone than the powerful one he'd used to expel Rand from the church.

"A little," Justin admitted.

"You felt the need to tell me about it. Come, then. Do not be afraid. What's on your mind?"

Justin shuffled his feet, considering not saying anything at all. But if he wanted to become a true disciple, then these were the hard conversations he needed to have.

"That man. From earlier. The one you said was evil, that ran away from the church."

Deckard's face hardened. Only a bit, but it was enough that Justin noticed. "Randolph Casey."

"Yes. He's my girlfriend's father."

"Is that so," Deckard said, flat and unimpressed.

Patrick also gave him an incredulous look.

"And what is it you have come to tell me?" Pastor D went on. "That I am wrong? That the things I said about the man were not true?"

"No!" Justin said quickly. "I actually don't know him well at all. I've only met him a few times and have barely talked to him."

"Do you believe they were true, Justin?"

"Yes," he found himself saying. "I've seen the things you do and I believe in you."

"Good. I have heard the truth from the angel Azora, and we should not have such a dark man in our midst. Redemption is possible for all men, and I will pray that Randolph Casey finds his way out of the darkness. He can come to me alone for guidance, as you have done, but being in a crowd of saved people is not the right place for him now."

Justin digested those words. He was glad to hear that there would be a second chance for Mr. Rand. He liked the man, although he always got the feeling that Mr. Rand did not particularly like that he and Libby were dating.

"You have come here to ask if I think it is right or wrong for you to continue dating the daughter of an evil man," Pastor D said.

Justin was shocked, even though he was starting to realize he shouldn't be. "Yes."

"We each have a responsibility to lead good and clean lives," Pastor D said. "We should flee from any sin and darkness, especially those related to hell and dark magic. This is what Randolph Casey is involved in. How can you be sure that his daughter, your girlfriend, isn't as well?"

That couldn't be possible. He'd been with Libby for a few months now, and surely she was not like that.

But when Justin looked into Pastor D's eyes, he saw a stern, challenging look. One telling him to think and discern for himself. On top of that, Justin got the feeling that Deckard knew something he didn't. Yet another piece of hidden information divined from God. Deckard had been right about Mr. Rand, after all...

"I guess I never considered that..."

"Consider it now," Deckard said. "I won't tell you what to do, but you are a smart young man. You know what you need to do to get your life back into the light. Have a good week, Justin."

With that, Deckard climbed into the backseat of the car. His bodyguard closed the door for him and went around to the driver's side. Patrick Perryman joined Deckard in the rear, but before he got in, cast Justin a quick look of disgust.

That was strange. Justin had known Patrick for a while and thought they were friends. Was the news of him dating the daughter of an evil man something that would make Patrick angry? Shouldn't he respect that Justin was coming to Pastor D for guidance?

The car drove away, leaving him alone. Pastor D had been right —Justin knew what he needed to do. If he wanted to be a true disciple, the best thing would be to end his relationship with Libby. Because who knew if Mr. Rand would ever stop dabbling with evil spirits?

But the idea pained him. He cared about her, and they'd had many good times together. Honestly, he never thought he'd ever date someone like her. She was way out of his league, as his few friends reminded him of often. They were right.

Why does the perfect girl have to have an evil father?

Later, on his drive back to the city, Justin felt tremendous guilt over his conflicting desires. So far, all other sacrifices—his music, his movies, his books—to lead a more faithful and obedient life had been easy. But Libby? He wanted to hold on to her tightly.

If he let her go, he knew he'd feel totally empty.

13

Rand had never been to Finnick, Louisiana, before. When he got there, he discovered why.

It was a country, nothing town. At first, he wasn't even sure he had arrived. But when the farmlands gave way to buildings, he slowed down to read a sign and realized he was on Main Street.

It was Sunday afternoon, and only a few people were about. As he cruised through, those he passed craned their neck to stare him down with no consideration of being rude. Surely everyone knew everyone, and no one recognized his orange Jeep.

First things first, he thought. *Gerald Roberson.*

It seemed the best place to start—determining if what had happened to the man was real.

He came out on the other end of Main Street and ended up in farmland again, so he did a U-turn in the middle of the road and headed back into town. About halfway down Main Street, he spotted a bar called the Flat Tire. If he was correct in assuming that everyone knew everyone, then someone there would know where to find Mr. Roberson.

Besides. He needed a drink.

He parked on the street and went inside. It was a small country joint filled with empty tables and a few locals sitting along the bar. There were video poker machines in the corner and a pool table nearby, the balls racked in the shape of a triangle on the table.

Rand pulled up a stool among the others and ordered a whiskey from the bartender, a girl who looked much too young to be working there. She eyed him curiously as she poured it—probably the same look she gave everyone who came in that she didn't recognize.

He downed it in one gulp and asked the girl to refill it. That earned him stares from the others at the bar—old men who most likely went there every day just to get out of the house.

Rand knocked it back, and the bartender passed him a third without waiting.

"Careful, son," said the elderly gentleman next to him. "Whatever she's done to you can't be that bad."

"I wish it was as simple as woman trouble."

"You're not from around here, are you?"

"What gave it away?"

"I've never seen you before."

"I'm looking for an old buddy of mine," Rand said. "Gerald Roberson. Do you know where he lives?"

The other man's smile faltered. "You're not the first person who's been looking for him. Everyone wants to see if it's true. If what happened to him was real."

"And was it?"

"Of course. Gerald couldn't get around town without that wheelchair."

"I'd still like to talk to him."

The old man sneered. "Let him be. He's been through a lot and has finally caught a lucky break. Doesn't need to be bothered by skeptics like you."

Then, a loud crack sounded behind Rand—the noise of someone powerfully breaking the racked pool balls.

He turned. No one was there. The balls lay just as they had been when he'd arrived.

The door to the Flat Tire opened and another man walked in. He looked about fifty, khaki shirt tucked into his matching pants. A shiny silver star was pinned to his front pocket.

He ambled up to the bar, where the young girl met him and gave him a shot of whiskey without even asking him what he wanted.

"Afternoon, Sheriff," said the man Rand had been talking to.

The sheriff, whose name was Jones according to his tag, tossed back the drink and wiped his mouth with his hand.

Gotta love small-town law enforcement, Rand thought.

Jones placed the empty glass on the bar. "How are you, Phil? Didn't see you in church this morning."

Phil only shrugged. "Speaking of church, this fella here's looking for Gerald Roberson."

Rand wished Phil hadn't called him out like that.

Jones fixed his attention on Rand for the first time. His eyes narrowed. "*You* were there earlier. Runnin' your mouth about how you don't believe Gerald was healed."

"Afternoon, Sheriff." Rand put on his best smile.

"I already know you're trouble," Jones said, bringing his face closer. Rand could smell the whiskey on his breath. "I suggest you head back to the city, or wherever it is you came from. We don't need people causing problems for folks like Gerald Roberson. He's a good man."

Another loud crack from the pool table. Rand looked again.

And this time, he saw Shindael. Blue skin like a frozen corpse, black eyes staring right at him. The balls scattered all around the table, each sinking into a pocket until none were left.

Rand's heart pounded.

"Are you listening to me?" Jones said.

Rand turned back to the man. He knew the sheriff could not see Shindael. Demons only revealed themselves to those they wanted to be seen by—even in a crowded room—and usually at the most inopportune moments. Shindael was trying to make Rand seem crazy in

314

front of the sheriff; Rand resolved to keep his cool. "Yes, sir. No trouble from me."

Jones snorted as if he didn't believe it.

He shouldn't believe me, Rand thought. He had every intention of poking around town to get the answers he needed.

The young bartender girl watched their tense conversation. She didn't seem nervous, though. Perhaps she was used to seeing barroom arguments.

"You've been warned." Jones dropped a few bucks on the bar and walked outside. Rand watched through the windows as he got into his cruiser and drove away.

He looked back at the pool table. Shindael was gone, and the balls were racked again.

"You heard the sheriff," said Phil. "Best you head home."

Rand followed suit and put some cash on the bar. He could tell when he wasn't wanted. The sheriff's untimely visit had ensured that he wouldn't get any useful information from the Flat Tire anyway.

He went out into the chilly afternoon and pulled his jacket around his body. The whiskey had done little to warm him, but it had taken off the edge that lingered since the episode at church.

"Excuse me." He turned to see that the bartender had followed him outside. "Eight-seven-five Albert Street."

"Sorry?"

"Gerald Roberson lives at eight-seven-five Albert Street. My grandma was friends with Mrs. Roberson before she passed away."

Rand nodded. "I appreciate it very much."

She pulled out a cigarette and lit it. She looked about Libby's age, maybe younger, and Rand felt a twinge of anger. He remembered Georgia Collins and how much she would give to have normal lungs. And here was this girl, voluntarily destroying her own. "I'm like you. I don't believe he was actually healed. I think everyone has gone crazy over nothing. So hopefully you figure something out and set the record straight." She took a long drag.

"I'll do what I can," Rand said.

"Just be careful," she added. "Sheriff Jones is kind of an asshole. He's arrested my boyfriend like three times."

"Noted," Rand said, although there was likely a decent reason for those arrests.

He returned to his Jeep and punched the address into his GPS.

14

R and followed the driving instructions and soon found himself at 875 Albert Street.

The house was small, despite being two stories. The white paint was flaking off and the posts on the front porch were cracked and looked ready to collapse. One strong hurricane might be enough to blow the place over.

Rand parked on the road and walked up the driveway, now mostly mud and puddles. The porch floorboards creaked underneath him as he approached the screen door.

He rapped on the screen door's window. The interior door was open, allowing him to see into the dark house.

When no one came, he knocked again. Still, there was no answer.

I'll come back later.

He was walking down the porch when an old red pickup truck turned into the driveway. The tires splashed through the mud, then stopped at the side of the house. The cab door opened and out came Gerald Roberson. No wheelchair, walking on his own two legs.

"Morning," Rand said.

Gerald did not return the pleasantry. He analyzed Rand as if trying to remember where he'd seen him before.

"You're the man they ran out of the church earlier today," he said.

"Ah. Should have known you'd be there."

"After what God has done for me, I'll be there every Sunday until the day he takes me to heaven."

Rand waited for Gerald to demand that he leave since Mr. Roberson was likely tired of the gawkers that Sheriff Jones had said had been pestering him.

Gerald walked toward Rand, and as he did, Rand kept his eyes on the man's legs. Not a single hint of a limp or joint ache. They didn't even match his upper body movement—his arms hung rigid and stiff by his side, his back slightly hunched. It was like he was young in his lower half, old in his upper. To Rand, it looked very unnatural.

"You're just like everyone else," Gerald said. "Can't stop looking at my legs. Makes me feel like a supermodel, you know."

"You must understand," Rand said. "People don't see that every day."

"I get it," Gerald said. "So, is what Pastor D said about you true? All that stuff." Rand said nothing. "I imagine so. He got all that information straight from an angel named Azora, you know."

"So he said."

"How else could he have known?"

That's what I'm here to figure out.

"Well, we can stand out here and freeze our bottoms off, or you can come inside." Gerald walked up to the front porch. "You're maybe the hundredth person who's come in the past week to see if my new legs are real or just some trick. You'd think I'd be tired of it by now. But I understand why the Lord blessed me like this. Not so I can walk, but to be living proof of the Gospel. So come on in. I'll make you some coffee."

Gerald went straight for the kitchen and Rand followed. At the bottom of the stairwell, there was a motorized chair Gerald could use to ride to the top.

"What you looking at?" Gerald asked.

"Nothing." Rand caught up with him in the kitchen. "You live here alone?"

"Yeah. Ever since Paula passed." Gerald filled the pot with water. "It's a quiet life. The kids come by now and then. Heading out to hear Pastor D has given me a lot to look forward to."

"Have you always been a believer?" Rand asked.

"It was Paula who led me to the Lord," Gerald said, putting ground coffee into the top of the machine. "She was big into it and she dragged me along to church. We used to go down the road to that place where old Simon Cole preaches. Mount Grace Church."

"Don't know it. I'm not from here."

"Nice church, but simple. Haven't been back since I found Pastor D. Honestly, a lot of the people who went there now head out to the tent. Not sure if there's anyone left for Simon to preach to. Paula's buried in the cemetery behind the church."

Rand made a mental note of the information. *Simon Cole. Church near the cemetery.*

Gerald served his coffee, smoke rising from the mug.

"I guess you're here because you want to know if the miracle was real," Gerald said, walking into the living room. Rand followed him. There was only a couch and a recliner, beside which was a table stacked high with paperbacks. The seat cushion was very sunken and there were stains in the blue material. Gerald lowered himself in without a hint of struggle.

Rand settled on the couch, though he sank lower than he'd expected. "I guess you could say that."

"I'm glad you came. Yes, the miracle was real. It was all a gift from God."

Rand sipped the coffee. The man had made it very strong, just as Rand liked it. "You'll understand why I struggle to believe it."

"Don't understand it too much," Gerald said, his thick southern accent coming out. "You saw it with your own two eyes. What more do you need?"

Rand chuckled. If only it could always be that simple.

"I know what you're thinking. You think Pastor D hired me as some kind of actor or something. Does this look like I'm an actor?" He gestured around the living room. The inside was even more run down than the outside, years of neglect adding up. "Did he pay the whole town of Finnick to tell people I wasn't able to walk, and now I can? Come on." Gerald sipped at his coffee.

"I suppose you have a point," Rand said.

"There can only be one explanation," Gerald said.

"The Lord," Rand finished for him. *And his angel Azora, supposedly.*

Gerald nodded and smiled. "You got it. I suggest you take Pastor D's advice and get right with God. We do not know the hour of our death, and I would hate for you to have witnessed his power first-hand and still miss out on eternity in heaven."

"I'll consider that," Rand said.

This was a dead end. Gerald was not backing down from his story, and there seemed to be no clues in that barren house as to how the old man was suddenly able to walk again. Rand would have to search elsewhere.

"I think I've taken up enough of your time, Mr. Roberson," Rand said, finishing his coffee and standing.

"You need more convincing," Gerald said, his voice becoming low and grave.

Rand lowered himself back onto the couch. "Sorry?"

"I can't in good conscience let you walk out of this house without all the information. I'd be doing a disservice to God and the way he used me to bring you here."

Now Rand's curiosity was piqued. "Okay. What did you have in mind?"

Gerald eyed him for a long time, pursing his lips in and out as he considered. It seemed as if he was rethinking his offer. Finally, he said, "Come back tonight."

"Tonight?"

"Yeah. Eleven o'clock."

"Okay. Then what?"

Gerald set his coffee cup on the table next to the stack of books.

He leaned forward in his chair. "Between you and me, the legs aren't the only thing God has given me." He spoke low, secretively.

"What else has he given you?"

"He has allowed Paula and I to be reunited."

Rand swallowed. A solid lump had formed in his throat. "You mean your wife who passed away a few years ago?"

He nodded. "She visits me now. Every night at the same time. We chat, and she tells me what it's like to be in heaven. She has the most amazing stories, and now I can't wait to join her there. She'll tell you, too. Then you can know it's all real."

Gerald was smiling, but Rand had a terrible feeling about what he was hearing.

"So you're telling me your wife's spirit has visited you every night since you were healed?"

Gerald frowned. "I should've figured you wouldn't believe me. If you don't want to see, then fine."

Rand quickly backpedaled. "No, no. I want to see."

Whenever someone claimed to be visited by a spirit, Rand had an obligation to investigate. But what did Gerald's healing have to do with him being visited by Paula's ghost?

Maybe coming here wasn't a dead end after all.

Gerald scowled at Rand as if trying to decide whether to rescind the offer. Finally, he said, "Eleven o'clock tonight. Don't be late."

"I'll be here at eleven and not a minute after."

15

Back in the Jeep, Rand used his phone to look up a place to stay for the night. There was a small motel about fifteen minutes away. It had four reviews that averaged a rating of one and a half stars, but it was his only option. So he punched the address into his phone's GPS and drove away from Gerald's house, following the highlighted path to the motel.

The Finnick Inn was a ramshackle joint, looking like it had been built in the '60s or '70s and not updated since. The Jeep rumbled as Rand drove through the potholed parking lot and pulled up to the front office.

The reception area was marred by a nasty shade of yellow-green wallpaper and a similarly colored carpet. A magazine rack was filled with old issues, their covers showing headlines for news stories that were years old.

No one was at the desk, and Rand searched around for a bell. A single voice came from the rear office—someone talking on a telephone.

"Hello?" Rand called.

Whoever was there stopped speaking, then resumed their conversation.

So Rand waited. But it seemed like the guy was happy to have him wait there forever.

"*Hello?*"

"Let me call you back," the man barked into the phone. Then he appeared at the desk, looking agitated. "Help you?"

He was an older man, his skin wrinkled, weathered, and tan. He wore a dirty camouflage cap and a collared red shirt that hung loose on his skinny body. A plastic name tag said he was Keith.

"I was hoping to get a room."

Keith grumbled as he snatched up a key hanging on a rack behind the desk. "Forty-three bucks for the night. Cash only." His southern accent was thick.

"Avoiding the tax man, I see." Rand smirked as he dug into his wallet and found the money. "I like your style, my friend."

Keith did not respond to Rand's quip. There was no register, and Keith instead tossed the money into a drawer and made his change. "Follow me."

Outside, the evening had grown colder and the clouds had darkened, threatening more rain. The storms were far from over.

Keith walked with an arched back and his head forward, like a chicken. He wobbled from side to side, as if he had knee problems. He led Rand to a door that had the number 11 nailed into the wood.

Keith inserted the key and jiggled it a bit, but it was stuck. "Son of a bitch," he muttered as he shook it, rattling the whole door on its hinges. Finally, it gave way. He pulled the key out of the knob and handed it to Rand. "Gets caught sometimes. Wiggle to the left while pulling in, and it'll give, eventually."

One and a half stars seems generous, Rand thought.

"Got it," he said.

Keith spat on the ground. "There's only five minutes of hot water in the tank. Trying to get the repair guy out here to take a look, but he's apparently sick. Something with his prostate. Oh, and the phone don't work. Only calls the front office. You got a cellular, right?"

"Not a problem at all."

"Good." Keith marched off without another word.

Rand chuckled to himself as he watched Keith walk away.

The room was about as basic as he'd expected. There was a single bed, hard as a board when he pressed on the mattress, two flattened pillows, a thin red comforter, and a brown carpet with dark stains. The place smelled of cigarette smoke and the air inside was humid and damp.

"Not exactly home," Rand muttered to himself. He'd stayed in worse places while working on cases before, though.

Rand fiddled with the air conditioner and it roared to life, blowing icy air in his face. It hummed and vibrated as it worked. Sleeping with that on would be like trying to fall asleep next to a running lawn mower.

Rand lay on the bed on top of the bedspread. His mind and body were heavy after everything he'd been through that day.

Right. Quick nap, then meet Gerald Roberson, and find out what's going on...

It wasn't long before his eyes closed and he was fast asleep.

RAND WAS awoken by a loud crash. He shot up straight, heart pounding, and looked around the room. It sounded like someone had kicked in the wall.

There was no light shining through the thin curtain. Rand pulled his phone from his pocket and checked the time. Nine-fifteen at night.

How did I sleep for five hours?

The room was freezing now, so he got up and cut off the AC, which plunged the room into silence. He heard the pattering of rain outside.

And what the hell made that noise?

A crash again, startling him. It was coming from the room next to his. The thin wall shook, and the stock artwork rattled and almost fell from its mount.

Rand approached the wall and placed his ear against it. He could make out voices on the other side.

"The hell is the matter with you?"

"I'm sorry!" A woman's.

"No you ain't!"

Then something hit the wall again near where Rand was pressed against it, listening. He leapt backwards. Then the woman started crying.

She's in trouble, Rand thought.

He went outside and approached the room next door—Room 12. Rain dripped off the overhead awning in heavy drops.

Another loud crash came from inside.

"Son of a bitch! I thought I told you not to do that anymore!"

The woman cried louder.

Rand pounded on the door of Room 12. "Hey! Leave her alone!"

He expected the man to shout back at him, or fling open the door and confront him. But neither happened. The man inside only continued to shout while the woman cried and begged.

Rand banged on the door again, this time louder, but that too was ignored. He tried the knob, but it was locked.

I have to help her, he thought. He looked toward the front office on the other side of the rain-slick parking lot. *Keith will have the key.*

Rand hurried across the lot, stamping through puddles that had collected in the potholes. He burst into the office, and once again, the manager was nowhere to be seen.

"Keith!" he called. No answer. "Keith!"

Then Keith appeared, looking alarmed. "What?"

"Something's going on in the room next to mine. Let me borrow the key."

Keith narrowed his eyes at him. "What do you mean?"

"It sounds like there's a fight. There's a man yelling and a woman crying. I need—"

"No there ain't," Keith said. "You're the only one here."

Rand paused for a moment, then said, "How could that be? I

know what I heard." But even as he said the words, Rand remembered that his Jeep had been the only car outside.

"Don't bother me again," Keith said. "This reception ain't a twenty-four-hour service desk." He turned and disappeared into the office.

Rand looked at the rack of keys behind the desk. The key to Room 12 dangled from the hook. All the room keys were there, except for 11. He leaned over the desk and snatched the key from its hook.

Rand rushed across the parking lot but stopped short when he heard the phone ringing on the bedside table in his room. He'd left the door wide open in his urgency.

What the hell?

He glanced at the office. According to Keith, that phone only connected to the front office, but Rand didn't see Keith standing at the phone through the window.

Rand sensed that something was very, very wrong.

Rand went inside and hovered over the phone, watching it for a few seconds. It continued to ring.

He snatched the receiver up and brought it to his ear, but said nothing. The line was garbled and filled with static.

"Dad?" Libby's voice.

"*Libby?*"

"Dad, where are you? Are you coming home?"

A cold spike pierced Rand's heart. *She doesn't know I'm here. It's impossible for her to call.* He slammed the receiver down and stepped away from the phone.

That voice had sounded like Libby, but it was not his daughter.

He's here, he realized. There was only one who could play such tricks on him. *Shindael.*

Another loud crash on the wall.

And now that Rand realized what was going on, he knew what he'd find inside Room 12.

He went next door, then used the key in the lock.

Empty.

The room was exactly like his, except mirrored. The lights were off, the bed made, and no one was inside.

It was all fake. All mimicry. He's definitely here.

And when Rand turned, he saw a black figure standing on the other side of the parking lot near the road. The figure was under a streetlight, the yellow beam doing nothing to illuminate his dark features. The rain fell all around him as he stared at Rand.

"Shindael, you son of a bitch," Rand whispered to himself.

Then a presence to his left startled him.

"What the hell are you doing?" Keith had appeared. He snatched the key from Rand's hand and slammed the door of Room 12 shut, then locked it. "Are you crazy? I told you no one was in there. You can't steal the keys, you maniac."

Rand glanced toward Shindael. He was closer now, half the distance than before.

"He's coming closer," Rand whispered to himself.

Keith followed Rand's gaze. "What the hell are you looking at?"

Shindael, when he appeared, had always been at a distance—usually across the room. Rand knew from experience that when demons neared, especially after they had always maintained space, it meant they were planning to attack.

"Who's closer?" Keith demanded. "Look at me when I'm talking to you!"

Keith gripped Rand's arm and forced Rand to turn toward him.

And in that split second, Shindael appeared just over Keith's shoulder. Smiling with his jagged, razor-sharp teeth, the demon placed his clawed hand on Keith's shoulder, but Keith gave no indication that he felt it at all. Rand knew Keith wouldn't. Shindael was invisible to the man.

He's threatening him.

"Leave him alone!" Rand shouted at Shindael.

Keith glanced behind him, then looked back at Rand. "You're a crazy son of a bitch. I want you out of my motel."

Shindael had made Keith a hostage right before Rand's eyes. The demon certainly had the power to bring Keith great harm.

"He hasn't done anything to you. Don't hurt him." Rand said.

But Shindael only gave a soundless laugh and then disappeared.

"I'm warning you," Keith said. "If you don't leave…"

Shindael's presence has become much stronger, Rand thought. *I'm getting close to something.*

Something that Shindael did not want Rand to discover. He was certain of it.

"You hear me?" Keith shouted at him. "Get out!"

Rand snapped out of his thoughts. Keith was right—Rand had to leave. Shindael had threatened the man, and as long as Rand was there, Keith would not be safe.

Rand swallowed hard. "Sorry to cause you trouble," he croaked out, unable to think of anything else to say.

"I'm calling the sheriff."

"No need for that," Rand said quickly. He grabbed his stuff from the motel room and went straight for his Jeep.

16

Rand could barely keep his Jeep straight as he drove away
from the motel. His hands shook too much.

Finally, he pulled over so he could gather himself.

He was so close...

The only time Shindael had been that close to him was the night
they'd met, right after Rand had defeated Shindael's servant, Karax.

But ever since then, Shindael had always kept his distance. He
would appear at random times—when Rand was teaching, when he
was out to lunch with his daughter, or sometimes materializing on
the side of the road while driving—but always far away.

But this time, Shindael was close enough to touch.

That horrible face over Keith's shoulder. He'd been rude, but
Keith definitely did not deserve to be touched by a demonic entity—
he would likely discover some mysterious markings on his shoulder
the next day and have no idea where they'd come from.

I'm getting too close to something, Rand thought. *Shindael may have
threatened Keith, but Shindael was actually using him to warn me.*

The clock on the dash read 10:21 PM. Rand was meant to meet
Gerald Roberson at eleven, the time his deceased wife's spirit
supposedly visited.

Shindael doesn't want me to go there, Rand thought.

Shindael had not appeared close until Rand had made a plan to meet Gerald. If Rand wanted out of the case, to leave it all alone, now was the time. He could heed Shindael's warning and return home.

Rand didn't even pause to consider that option.

He put the Jeep in drive and headed toward Gerald's house.

ALTHOUGH THE HOUSE WAS LARGE, Patrick Perryman had been relegated to a small room on the second floor that served as his bedroom.

It was enough. He did not need much. God warned against the dangers of materialism. All he had was a simple bed, a closet for his tiny wardrobe, and a desktop computer.

It was about nine o'clock at night, and he browsed Facebook. He'd found the profile page a few days ago, and he'd viewed it every night since then.

Libby Casey. The girl who had come with Justin Tidwell to church the previous week. She'd caught his eye instantly, and in that moment, he realized she was something special.

Things were starting to make a lot more sense. The more faithful he was, the better he had become at noticing God's plan for his life in the little details. The day he'd met Rand, Patrick knew the professor was a hurting man, struggling with his faith.

But since Libby Casey came to church, Patrick understood that God was up to much more.

Patrick navigated to her profile, which he had bookmarked. For the first time since he'd found it, she had updated it with a few new pictures. These were of her and some friends from her volleyball team at practice. Libby and two other girls posed for the camera, arms wrapped over each other's shoulders, smiling brightly. Her blonde hair was tied up and her face was flushed and sweaty, but Patrick thought she was stunning. He allowed his gaze to linger on the tight shorts of their uniforms before forcing his eyes away, reminding himself that it was sinful. Still, he felt a primal urge stirring inside him.

There was nothing else new on the page. Libby didn't seem to get on Facebook as often as he did.

So instead, he concerned himself with going through the pictures he'd already scrolled through every night: she and her friends while they were out for dinner somewhere. He especially liked the one where she wore the black dress. If he had a printer, he would have printed it out. There was another of her and her dad hiking. Then a few with a woman who resembled her, which Patrick took to be her mother. There was another man in the pictures with the mom, and they looked friendly with each other. Patrick surmised that Rand and Libby's mom were not together. Maybe they had never been. That would make sense. Pastor D had said Rand Casey was a sinful man.

He scrolled all the way through, taking in the photos he had memorized by then. His body flushed with desire, and he closed his eyes and tried to pray away the temptation. It didn't always work. He had succumbed last night, and he'd spent the day praying for forgiveness. He knew he would eventually have to confess to Pastor D.

Patrick checked the clock on the computer. It was now 9:16, and his appointment with Pastor D was in fourteen minutes. It was better to be early than late, so he minimized Libby's Facebook profile and left the bedroom.

The old mansion on the outskirts of Finnick had been built fifty years ago by a wealthy businessman, but after he died alone in the house, it was vacant until Pastor D purchased it. Perhaps he was the only man in town who could afford it.

Patrick descended the stairs to the first floor, gripping the handrail so as not to tumble down the steps. Pastor D ordered that the house remain dark after sundown—he did not like any artificial light. He'd never explained the reason, but Patrick knew Pastor D was close to cutting off the power. Patrick had convinced him not to, because if he did that, Patrick would not have his computer.

Patrick turned off the main foyer and toward Pastor D's study, where he spent every evening. The door was ajar, and Patrick peeked into the expansive room beyond.

There, he found Pastor D kneeling in front of a roaring fireplace, on all fours, head to the ground. He was speaking to himself, chanting in a language Patrick did not understand. Pastor D spoke in tongues often, especially when he spent his evenings in prayer. That was when he communicated with Azora, the angel of the Lord who gave him his information and blessings.

Patrick lingered by the door, not wanting to interrupt. Pastor D did not like to be disturbed.

Even though they lived in the same house, Patrick still had to make an appointment to meet with Pastor D during the evenings and nights. That was just how Pastor D needed it to be. He was very particular about his time since he dedicated most of it to prayer and communicating with Azora.

So Patrick remained in the hallway, watching the man in his nightly ritual. Pastor D straightened from his bowed position and sat upright on his knees, looking at the roof, then into the fire, speaking incoherently.

Patrick had always been envious of the man's spiritual gift for tongues. If he could have chosen, that would have been the one he would have picked. Whenever Pastor D spoke in tongues, he looked like he was enjoying a deep connection with Azora, while Patrick, a spectator off to the side, felt left out.

"I know you're there, Patrick."

Patrick straightened at the sound of his name. Pastor D had not turned around, and he was sure he had been quiet enough to not disturb the man in his prayers.

Nerves suddenly clawed at his stomach.

"You can come in."

Patrick pushed open the door to the study and entered. It was uncomfortably warm inside because of the massive fire. That was another of Pastor D's quirks. He liked it hot, to the point of sweating.

As Patrick approached the center of the room, Pastor D stood and looked at him for the first time. The older man wore nothing but a robe and his chest and face were slick with sweat from the heat.

"Sorry to interrupt," Patrick said. "I didn't think I'd made any noise."

"We had an appointment," Pastor D said.

"But I was early."

"It's okay." Pastor D sat in the plush chair and crossed his legs. He wiped at his face with his hands, but that did little to clear the moisture from his skin. It was the only chair in the mostly empty study, which left Patrick standing like a subject before his king. "What did you want to see me about?"

Patrick swallowed. The heat and his nervousness caused sweat to break out on his forehead and back. He'd rehearsed this over and over in his head many times before, but still, it never seemed to be right.

"I've been thinking a lot lately," Patrick began.

"Thinking or praying?"

"Both."

Pastor D nodded.

"Every night, actually. As you've instructed."

"Good."

Patrick never got on the floor, bowed down to a fire, and spoke in tongues like Pastor D did. But Patrick was not privy to the voice of Azora.

"I think the time has come," Patrick said.

"What time is that?"

"The time for a wife."

Pastor D eyed him and said nothing for a long while. The flames created shadows that danced on the side of his face, giving him an eerie glow. Patrick couldn't decide if Pastor D was angry or just thinking it over. He swallowed again.

"How old are you, Patrick?" Pastor D asked.

"Thirty-eight, sir."

"And how much have you prayed about this?"

"Every night for a long time."

"Why didn't you tell me until now?"

"Because I did not want to concern you with something that I was not sure was clear from the Lord," Patrick said, and it was the truth. He always tried to tell Pastor D the truth. "But lately... He has laid it on my heart."

"This is a big decision, as you know. Do you feel you are ready to love another for the rest of your days? Or is this something you want only to satisfy your desires?"

Patrick winced. Pastor D was very wise and could read him like a book. Sometimes he thought Azora told Pastor D precisely what was going on inside Patrick's head and heart. It would not surprise him if that were the case.

"Both," he said, opting for honesty. "My desires cause me to fall into sin sometimes. But I always pray for forgiveness. More than that, though, I know I am prepared to love someone else. To care for them. And I feel the Lord is ready for me to move into the next part of my life."

Pastor D watched Patrick again, saying nothing, and he felt as if the preacher was waiting for him to say more.

"Of course, me being married won't change anything when it comes to you and the church. I'll be just as loyal as before, just as present and dedicated. I plan to allow my marriage to help me grow in my faith and to become a better man."

"This is a big decision," Pastor D said. "Do you really think you can stay committed to the church and your faith after you have a wife?"

"Yes, sir," Patrick said firmly, standing straight. "I do." His sweat dripped down his cheeks and soaked through his shirt now. As usual, the heat did not seem to bother Pastor D at all, even though he was also drenched.

"And who is this lucky lady?" Pastor D asked. "Do you have anyone in mind?"

The way Pastor D said it, Patrick suspected he already knew, the info given to him by Azora.

"Her name is Libby Casey," Patrick said. "She came to church the other week. Whenever I saw her... I don't know. It's hard to explain. The Lord just spoke and has not stopped since."

"You were filled with lust."

"No!" Patrick shot back. "It's not like that."

"Patrick..."

"Well... maybe a little. But as I said, I avoid temptation as much as I can and pray for forgiveness when I fall." Patrick was committed to the truth, but he feared if he made himself sound too weak in the face of sin, Pastor D would forbid him from seeing Libby Casey.

"She is sixteen years old," Pastor D said.

Patrick knew from her Facebook that she was in high school and had figured she was sixteen or seventeen. What he couldn't figure out, though, was how Pastor D knew. Again, it was probably something from Azora.

"I'm willing to wait a few years."

"We all know the laws of God are greater than the laws of men," Pastor D said, "and if God has willed for this girl to be in your life, then there is no reason to delay any further. I can perform the ceremony and the two of you will be man and wife until the end of your days."

Patrick's heart fluttered. For the first time, Pastor D had given him hope that he would accept his request.

"But I will do my own praying about it," Pastor D said. "I do believe that your commitment to me, the church, and the Lord will not waver because of your marriage, Patrick, but things *will* change. I must find out if the timing is right. I hope you understand. From now on, I promise to include this in my prayers to Azora, and I will let you know what he tells me."

And that was that. There was nothing to argue with. "Thank you,

Pastor D." It was just about the best outcome he could have hoped for.

"Now, Patrick, go to sleep," Pastor D said.

Patrick left him in the study, the chilled air of the hallway feeling great against his slick skin. His heart still pounded from the adrenaline rush of their conversation, but his boldness had paid off. Pastor D would pray about it, and that was amazing news. God truly knew what he was doing.

Patrick returned to his bedroom and changed out of his sweaty clothes. Pastor D had told him to sleep, but he was too excited. The buzz of his success was still too fresh in his mind. Patrick Perryman hadn't been successful at much during his thirty-eight years.

He brought Libby's Facebook page back up. He couldn't wait until God revealed to her what his plan for her life was. Likely, she did not know yet, and he was excited for her. All young girls wanted to get married, and he would be the best husband she could ever hope for.

As he perused her pictures, he felt a lustful temptation again. So, he clicked off the page and onto a list of random names around the state. He scrolled through the profiles and chose one of a girl whose profile picture was a selfie that was much too revealing.

Patrick sent her a message.

Cover up! God hates whores.

And he sent it.

He scrolled again and found another girl whose pictures were of her making out with a guy. When he clicked her profile, he saw she was unmarried. He sent her a message as well.

God hates fornicators. Repent and be saved.

Sending out warnings to the lost did a lot to calm his temptation. He had learned that from Pastor D. Whenever one feels cornered by the thought of sin, just do the Lord's work, and everything will be better.

17

Rand pulled up in front of Gerald Roberson's house and idled his Jeep. The rain still pattered down, tapping on his rooftop. He stopped the wipers and water began to gather on the windshield.

It was ten minutes until eleven.

The man's house was dark except for a dim light that crept through a window on the first floor. It almost looked like no one was home, but Gerald's truck was in the driveway, obscured by the rainy night.

Rand wasn't completely sure what he'd discover inside, but he had a feeling it wouldn't be good. The man had told him the spirit of his dead wife was visiting him every night. Even worse, the visitations had begun *after* Deckard Arcan had restored Gerald's ability to walk. That couldn't be a coincidence.

Plus, Shindael did not want Rand there, and had tried to warn him away.

Rand killed the engine and grabbed his bag of gear from the backseat. As he crossed the yard, the damp grass squished underneath his shoes.

The front door opened before he got to the porch and Gerald stepped outside.

"This weather is something else," Gerald said. "Colder than it usually is this time of year, and the rain just won't stop."

"You can say that again."

Rand wiped his dirty shoes on the mat by the door and followed Gerald inside. The house was toasty, a nice feeling compared to the chilly air outside.

There were no lights on, just a fire roaring in the living room fireplace.

"Have a seat," Gerald told him. "I'll get coffee."

The last thing Rand needed was coffee. He was already on edge about whatever spiritual activity was happening inside Gerald's house late at night.

Rand returned to the couch, the same spot he'd sat earlier that day. He dropped his bag on the ground at his feet and removed his jacket, the warmth quickly becoming stifling. Sure, it was cold outside, but Rand wondered why Gerald needed it so blazing hot inside the house.

Gerald was gone for a while but finally returned with two mugs. He had also changed into a suit and tie, which Rand thought was strange. Gerald handed Rand a mug and Rand sipped it. The coffee sent a jolt of energy through his body.

Gerald sat in his recliner. The sweet scent of his cologne mixed with the smell of coffee.

"Interesting pair of pajamas you have there," Rand said, nodding toward his suit.

"I try to look my best when Paula comes."

"Does she come every night?"

"Yes," he said. "Ever since Pastor D gave me my legs back. At eleven thirty-nine at night, just like clockwork."

"Why is that? Is the time significant to you?"

"It's the time she died," Gerald said, taking a sip.

"Oh." Rand checked his watch. It was 11:23.

"But it's strange. She died at eleven thirty-nine in the morning."

That gave Rand pause. And he suddenly had a very bad feeling about this.

"What?" Gerald said. "You look sick."

"I'm just cautious about spirits that reverse times."

"So, you do believe in something after all," Gerald said. "What's wrong with the time?"

"If your wife passed away at eleven thirty-nine in the morning, why wouldn't she choose that time to come to you? Why does she reverse it and come at the same time, but at night?"

"Beats me. I never asked her." The firelight flickered on the side of his face.

Because it prefers to come in darkness, Rand thought. That was never a good sign.

At 11:37, Gerald finished the rest of his coffee in a single gulp and Rand did the same, then placed the cup aside.

"Won't be long now," Gerald said, straightening his tie.

"What should we do?" Rand asked. He felt as if the man were leading him in a séance. He'd been involved in plenty before, but none like this.

"We wait."

The only sound in the room was the popping and cracking of the fire. As the silence lingered on, Rand grew nervous.

He kept his left arm on his lap so he could see the seconds tick by on his watch.

When the second hand reached the twelve, his watch froze, as if the battery had died.

Rand sensed a presence behind him. He twisted on the couch and looked, but saw only the wall.

"Paula, sweetheart," Gerald said. He stared into the fire. "Are you there?" Rand waited for a reply, but none came. "There's no need to be afraid, dear. We have a visitor tonight, and he is very excited to meet you. He wants to know about heaven and what eternity is like."

They sat in silence for a minute. Then Rand got the unmistakable sensation of a third presence in their midst.

"I feel something," Rand said.

"She's here," Gerald said, not taking his eyes off the fire. "Watch. I do this sometimes." He cleared his throat. "Paula. Can you give me a sign that you are close?"

Loud thumps boomed from the ceiling overhead, as if someone were jumping up and down.

"That's her sewing room," Gerald said. "She spent every evening in there before she went to bed. Paula loved to sew." A sentimental smile came to his lips.

The thumping stopped. Rand looked to his left and right, and then behind him. He felt surrounded, eyes on him from all directions.

"Don't leave our guest confused, sweetheart," Gerald said. "He's come to meet you."

The room, which was stifling hot, now turned cold—it was as if someone had just opened a window and let the autumn air inside. The flames stirred like a strong gust of wind had blown, even though there was none.

The frozen watch. The unmistakable feeling of eyes on him. The unnatural chill in the air. There were too many classic signs that Rand had experienced time and time again.

A demonic presence was in Gerald's home—one that he mistook for his wife's spirit.

Rand knew that he and Gerald were in danger.

"Gerald," Rand began.

"Shh." He stood from his chair and walked to the center of the room, not looking away from the fire. "Yes, it's cold, but that's normal. Paula always loved keeping the house cold, even in the winter. I was the opposite and liked it warm. So she makes it cold in here when she comes, even though I have a fire."

"Gerald... I don't think Paula is here."

Gerald took his eyes from the fire and pierced him with a hard gaze as if Rand had insulted him. "You said yourself that you sensed her."

"What I mean is that I don't think you've been talking to Paula."

He rose from the couch, looking around him, the feeling that they weren't alone growing stronger.

"What are you talking about?" Gerald said, suddenly angry. "I know my wife. You don't."

Rand saw it.

A shadow shaped like a human. Darker than black. An empty space in reality. It crawled along the ceiling like an insect with long arms and legs. Its head twisted around, and Rand saw glowing red eyes glaring down at him.

There it is, Rand thought, body stiffening in fear. He had to remain calm and remove the creature that Gerald thought was his wife.

Rand reached for his bag at his feet with a trembling hand, never taking his eyes from the demon overhead. If Rand moved quickly enough, he could remove the evil presence from the house.

Gerald followed his gaze but did not react. "What are you looking at?" He couldn't see the shadow.

"Don't move," Rand told him.

"What are you talking about?"

Rand's hand went inside his bag and he felt around for the crucifix he always kept there. As soon as his fingertips brushed against it, the demon dropped from the ceiling, deftly turning and landing on his feet right behind Gerald.

The shadow stood a foot taller than Gerald. The red eyes remained on Rand, glaring over Gerald's shoulder. Tendrils of blackness streamed from the shadow's head like long, flowing hair caught in a breeze that was not there.

The demon stood in the same threatening position Rand had seen earlier, mirroring what Shindael had done with Keith. The parallel was not lost on Rand, and his flesh crawled.

"Leave him alone," Rand commanded the demon.

"Who are you talking to?" Gerald said.

The demon twisted his head and brought it close to Gerald's face as if whispering in his ear.

And Gerald froze. Listened.

"Don't listen to him!" Rand said. He gripped the crucifix and pulled it from his bag, straightening up and holding it out toward the demon.

The shadow reacted instantly, backing away to the far end of the living room.

"What are you doing?" Gerald said, looking at the cross.

"I'll take care of this," Rand said. "Get behind me."

"No." Gerald's voice was firm and resolute.

Rand looked at him. "You need to trust me, Gerald. There is something dangerous inside your home."

"I know. It's you."

Rand was taken aback.

"I heard Paula's voice," Gerald continued, snarling. "She told me you're a very bad man, and if you don't leave, she'll never come back."

It was a typical demonic lie, one easily believed by someone who already trusted that the entity was who he claimed to be.

"Don't listen to him," Rand said. "He's not your wife. He's something else entirely."

"You need to leave," Gerald said. "Right now."

"Don't do this."

"I *won't* take any chances of losing Paula again."

The demon started moving toward Gerald, red eyes glued to him, hand raised and ready to strike.

Rand saw this and bolted around Gerald, holding the cross out toward the shadow. "In the name of the Lord Jesus Christ, I command you to leave—"

"Stop!" Gerald shouted, gripping Rand's arm. "I'm calling the police—"

Rand pulled out of Gerald's grasp. "You are not welcome here," Rand said to the demon. "Leave this man alone. I command you to return to hell and never come back."

The shadow backed away, moving toward the front door, cowering underneath the power of the cross. Rand advanced further.

The demon's back pressed against the wall near the door. Then he climbed up the wall and onto the ceiling to get away from Rand and the crucifix. The red eyes bored into Rand, clearly ready to attack as soon as he faltered or let the cross drop, which Rand had no intention of doing.

Rand threw open the front door, a burst of cold wind coming inside.

"I command you to leave this house, demon, in the name of the Lord," Rand shouted. "You are compelled to obey. You are not welcome here. Depart!"

The entity on the ceiling contorted and twitched, the blackness seeming to cave in on itself. He turned into a dark, unshapely mass and drifted to the door. The shadow disappeared into the rainy night outside and Rand slammed the door behind him.

Immediately, the temperature of the room rose, and the tension decreased.

They were alone again. Gerald was safe.

"What have you done?" Gerald whispered, voice trembling. He approached Rand in the foyer near the front door. "I don't feel her anymore. She's gone."

And then Gerald lost his balance. He waved his arms around, flapping them wildly as he fell over.

Rand got to his side just in time, catching him before he hit the ground. "Are you okay?"

Rand lowered Gerald to the floor, where he sat up straight, gripping his thighs. "What is this?" He struggled to stand, but couldn't.

"Hang on," Rand said. "Relax. Take it easy."

"What's going on?" Gerald shouted. "My legs! They gave out!"

"Just rest for a minute."

But Rand already knew what was happening. That demon was what had given Gerald the ability to walk again.

"You did this to me." Gerald looked up at Rand with a desperate, simmering rage. Tears ran down his cheeks now. "Paula is gone. My legs are gone. Why couldn't you just leave me alone?"

343

Rand wanted to explain the truth. He even opened his mouth to do so, but only managed a dry croak.

It wasn't your wife. It was a demonic spirit. He mimicked your wife so you would trust him. He used his power to make you walk again so you would be loyal.

But Gerald Roberson would never understand. All he knew was what he wanted to believe.

"I'm sorry," Rand said gently. "If you let me explain—"

"Just get out."

Rand knew that, in that moment, leaving was the best thing he could do. Gerald wouldn't listen to anything Rand had to say.

Rand went to the living room and grabbed his bag. When he returned to the foyer, he was struck by the broken man sitting on the floor, unable to move, probably in shock at losing the blessing Deckard Arcan had given him.

Rand knew removing the demon was the right thing, but in that moment, it was hard to feel like he'd done Gerald any favors.

"Is there anything I can do?"

Gerald lifted his hand and pointed toward the door. "You've done enough."

18

fter leaving Gerald's home, Rand climbed into his Jeep, but he did not start the engine. Melancholy fell over him as he watched the rain drip down the windshield.

That was awful...

Rand knew he'd never forget the look on Gerald's face for the rest of his life: the look of a man who'd lost his ability to walk for a second time.

Demonic entities were pure evil, but were not above bestowing positive supernatural gifts on humans to gain their trust and loyalty. Those gifts always came with a price, and sooner or later the debt would be collected. Gerald Roberson would never understand how Rand had helped him. Rand couldn't even convince himself that he'd done the man any lasting good.

But Gerald was only the beginning.

That demon he'd expelled from Gerald's home had to be a servant of Shindael. Shindael had known what Rand would discern once he went to Gerald's house, which was why the demon had warned Rand at the motel.

And where did the new entity inside Gerald's house come from?

Deckard Arcan. It all made sense now. The preacher's supposedly divine knowledge, the ability to heal others—classic signs of someone influenced by supernatural evil.

But that only confused Rand. Deckard Arcan himself showed no symptoms of a diabolically possessed person.

Rand thought back to Georgia Collins, his most recent case of possession. Her skin had become scaly, and her eyes had gone black. Her voice had changed to that of Karax—the demon inside her—and her personality had disappeared. Whenever possession occurred, a person's soul was displaced by the possessing entity.

But Deckard Arcan seemed entirely like himself—a normal man. Yet still, he had the ability to wield demonic power.

Rand had never seen anything like it before. And it terrified him.

I'm dealing with something new.

That meant he needed help.

Rand remembered Gerald mentioning the other church in town, the one everyone attended before Deckard Arcan's tent came along.

What was it? Mount something...

Rand searched it on his phone, and it gave him his result.

Mount Grace Church.

Right. Maybe the pastor there will know more about Deckard. I can talk to him tomorrow.

Rand also felt he could do with some time in a holy place. He always liked to retreat into the presence of God after an encounter with a demon.

Rand checked his watch. It was well after midnight, and the two-hour drive back home did not appeal to him. He decided to find a place to park and sleep in his Jeep—he surely wasn't welcome back at the Finnick Inn. Rand had never been opposed to sleeping in the car—he'd done it plenty of times when he was younger.

Might even be nostalgic, in a way.

As he drove away, he took one last glance at Gerald Roberson's house and hoped that the man would eventually come to understand.

PATRICK WAS in a deep sleep when he heard a soft pounding from somewhere distant.

At first, he thought it was part of his dream. As he woke, though, he knew it was real.

He lay in bed in the dark room, listening. The noise echoed from the first floor of the mansion.

Someone was at the front door.

He checked the digital clock on the bedside table. It was two o'clock in the morning.

What in the world...

Visitors came by sometimes, sure, but in the middle of the night? Never.

Maybe they'll leave.

The poundings boomed out again, louder than before. They were insistent.

Patrick flung the covers off. He had to get down there before they made more noise. Pastor D was in the midst of his prayers, just as he was every night, and Patrick did not want him to be disturbed.

Patrick descended the stairs. Whoever was on the other side of the door had started shouting.

"Pastor D! Someone help me!"

He didn't recognize the voice, but whoever it was sounded crazed and desperate. They'd have to be to show up in the middle of the night like that.

God, protect me if this person is dangerous, he prayed.

He opened the door to find a man lying on the front porch. As soon as the door was open, the man crawled inside like a soldier pulling himself through a trench.

"Patrick!" shouted the old man.

"Mr. Roberson?"

"Please help me!"

He wore a dark suit, wrinkled and covered in mud. Tears and sweat streaked his face.

"What happened to you?" Patrick knelt down beside him. He glanced back outside and spotted a wheelchair at the bottom of the porch steps, abandoned.

"That man!" Gerald shouted. "He came to my house!"

"What man?"

"That one from the church. The man Pastor D said was a sinner."

It took Patrick a minute to place what Gerald was rambling on about, but then it clicked.

Randolph Casey.

"What is going on in here?" Pastor D appeared from his study, wearing his robe. His voice was loud and stern, and he was clearly angry about the interruption.

"Oh, thank God," Gerald said when he saw him. "Please help me, Pastor D!"

Gerald reached out for him, but Deckard did not return the embrace. He only watched the man critically, as if disgusted by the begging and groveling.

Why is he not concerned? Patrick wondered.

"Explain, Mr. Roberson. What happened to you?"

"That man from the service this morning," Gerald said. "You called him to the front and convicted him of his sin."

"Randolph Casey is his name," Patrick added. Pastor D nodded.

"He came and found me. He wanted to know if the miracle was real or fake. I told him it was real, but he still seemed unsure. I figured this was a perfect opportunity to use my blessing to save another soul, so I invited him to my house to meet with Paula when she visited. But..." The man started to cry. "I don't know what happened. He tried to claim it wasn't Paula, then he did some kind of black magic and now Paula is gone and I cannot walk anymore. Pastor, he reversed your miracle."

Patrick looked over to Pastor D. "We need to help him."

"Take him to one of the spare rooms," Pastor D said. "Lay him down and let him rest."

"Will you heal him again?"

"Do as I say, then come and see me when it's done." He'd never heard Pastor D speak to him, or anyone else, that sharply before.

Pastor D only turned his back and returned to his study.

Patrick retrieved Gerald's wheelchair from outside, helped him into it, and pushed him to the other side of the mansion to a spare room that was rarely used.

"Have faith, brother," Patrick said as he left him. "Pastor D will take care of everything. I am sure of it."

Gerald still sobbed and said nothing. Patrick wanted to say something else to console him, but came up empty.

Patrick imagined himself in Gerald's shoes—the loss of his legs and his wife had both surely been traumatic the first time, but the second...

Randolph. What did you do?

Patrick returned to Pastor D's study as instructed. He was in his chair, watching the fire.

"This man has been sent by the devil," Pastor D said without taking his eyes from the flames.

"When I first met him, he seemed harmless."

"Lucifer is a master deceiver, as you know. His servants come in all forms, shapes, and sizes. He has hurt one of our members, and he needs to be dealt with. Are you willing to help me?"

Patrick wished Pastor D would be clearer about how exactly Randolph Casey should be dealt with. But he knew in that moment there was only one answer. "Yes, sir. Of course."

"Good. Now go to bed. We'll address this in the morning."

Patrick had a hundred more questions. Could Gerald Roberson be healed again? Would Paula Roberson come back? Had Azora already given Pastor D a plan to "deal with" Randolph Casey?

And would these new developments interfere with his desire to marry the man's daughter? He thought the instruction had come straight from the Lord, but why would God direct him to marry the daughter of an evil man?

To save her.

It was the only explanation.

Begrudgingly, Patrick tore himself away from Pastor D and returned to his bedroom as he was told, like an obedient child. Although it was late, he knew he would get no more sleep that night.

19

The atrium of the high school's gymnasium was like a museum of the past. Floor-to-ceiling glass cases displayed the trophies, plaques, and medals won by the various sports teams.

Justin walked by them all and stood at the entrance of the actual gym. The volleyball team was practicing. The sounds of shoes squeaking on the polished floor, balls bouncing hard, and the coach's constant whistling echoed off the high walls.

He spotted Libby behind the net, getting low and waiting to return a serve from her teammate. Justin slung his backpack off and sat in the bleachers.

She was great at the game, and she loved it. He'd seen her play many times, and even as a junior, she was better than some seniors. In fact, it was her goal to play in college.

That was one of the main reasons Justin liked Libby. She had goals. Had something to work toward. Justin wished he had things like that in his life. Sure, there was guitar, and he'd always wanted to be in a band, but so far it hadn't worked out. Either he couldn't find other guys to play with, or he didn't feel motivated to write any new songs. Usually, he just got addicted to the latest video game that came out.

Now he had his church, and that had given him a sense of purpose more than anything he'd had prior. And as he watched Libby maneuver around the court, darting and volleying the ball back to the other side, he felt such regret that their lifestyles were completely opposed and that he needed to end things.

The coach blew the final whistle, signaling that practice was over. Libby still hadn't noticed him sitting there. It was her friend who spotted him first, and then whispered to her as she toweled off. She looked over, surprised he was there.

She would be. They hadn't talked much since their discussion in his bedroom about the miracle healing.

The girls filed into the locker room, but Libby crossed the gym and went over to him. He stood up to meet her.

"You look good out there," he said. He'd spent the entire practice trying to think of the right thing to say.

"What are you doing here?"

"I wanted to talk to you."

She tensed up. The last time they had talked, it had been an argument about Gerald Roberson.

"My mind hasn't changed, Justin."

"It isn't about that."

She tucked a loose piece of hair behind her ear. "Okay. Then what is it?"

"It's just that..." Her face was flushed and sweaty, but she still looked beautiful. He'd thought he'd come in with a plan, with the words all mapped out, ready to do what was right. But conversations with girls like her never went by the book.

"It's what?" Libby said, a bit firm, maybe even challenging him. As if daring him to break up with her.

Does that mean she doesn't care? Does she not like me anymore after what happened?

The thoughts came, and Justin knew they shouldn't matter. Ending their relationship was the right to do. But they still made him feel terrible. It reminded him that even though it was morally correct, it was not something he wanted to do.

"Why was your dad at church on Sunday?" he blurted out. He couldn't bring himself to say the words that would break them up, so he went with the question that had been nagging at him.

"What do you mean?"

"Your dad was at church on Sunday. You didn't know?"

Libby shrugged. "No."

"Why not?" He found that strange. Surely it seemed like something Mr. Rand would have told her. *Unless they're in it together, whatever he was up to. She could be lying to me.*

"Because I haven't seen him," Libby said. "You know I live with him only half the time. I've been with my mom."

"Right, but I just thought—"

"I figured you would have liked him to be in church." She crossed her arms.

"Well..."

"What is it really, Justin?" She'd lost her patience. "You've barely spoken or texted me since Sunday and now you're here. What do you need to say?"

He hadn't expected her to turn the tables so quickly. He thought he'd walked into the conversation with all the power. He supposed he'd given that power up when he chickened out at the last minute.

"I just wanted to know why your dad was suddenly so interested in Pastor D and the church. Because before—"

And then a realization struck into his head like lightning. So quick and unbidden that he wondered if it was what Pastor D felt when Azora gave him divine knowledge.

Mr. Rand *had* been uninterested in the church after the first week. But then he'd come for dinner a few nights later and spoken to Justin's father in his office for quite a long time.

"My dad is interested in a lot of things, Justin, and he's all over the place. I can't even begin to keep up with every little thing he does. If you want to know so badly, why don't you ask—"

"My dad put him up to it," he said.

Libby stopped speaking. "What?"

"Yeah. That night y'all were over for dinner. My dad pulled him into the office and they talked about me."

Libby's demeanor changed completely. She went from agitated and impatient to looking like a child who'd been caught doing something naughty.

"I'm right, aren't I?" Justin pressed.

"Justin—"

"And you're in on it."

"No! How could I be? I was with you the whole time my dad and yours were together. How could I have known what was going on in there?"

"I just know you do. I have a feeling."

Libby rolled her eyes. "Whatever. I didn't ask what they talked about. If you're so concerned, then maybe you should talk to your dad, or even mine."

Justin studied her and still felt like she wasn't giving him the whole truth.

"I have to get changed. I'll see you later." She started walking away.

It made too much sense. Justin's father was not a believer. Could it be possible that his dad had enlisted Mr. Rand to expose Pastor D as a fraud?

Good luck with that, Mr. Rand, Justin thought. *Pastor D is definitely the real deal.*

"We need to break up," Justin said toward Libby's back.

She stopped in her tracks, then turned around to face him again. She gave him a stony look. "Did your pastor also tell you to do this?"

How did she know?

"I just… think it's best."

"Whatever, Justin. Do whatever makes you happy." Then she turned and left him.

Justin picked up his backpack and slung it over his shoulder.

I did the right thing. I know I did.

Libby, Mr. Rand, and his own father were in a conspiracy to interfere with his growing faith.

Pastor D was right. Only bad things can come from a relationship like this.

Justin trudged out of the gym. He'd handled things with Libby, but now he needed to know how to approach his own father. He decided to ask Pastor D for advice on Sunday.

The man was quickly becoming one of the few people Justin could trust.

20

The path was a single dirt road through a field filled with old oak trees. The early morning sunlight barely broke through the thick branches overhead. Rand's Jeep rocked back and forth as he went, the big tires dipping into holes in the earth. The shaking hurt the crick in his neck—he must've slept funny.

Maybe my car-sleeping days are over, he thought.

Regardless, Rand was happy to have skipped the drive home—and his own bed—in favor of getting an early start on the day. The sooner he could figure out what was going on in Finnick, the better.

Rand checked his phone's GPS several times, wondering if the thing had crossed signals and was taking him to the wrong place, but it seemed to be working. Apparently, Mount Grace Church was dead ahead.

The building was simple and possibly one of the oldest in town. The paint on the wood had long since flaked off the structure and it looked ready to topple over from the next gust of strong wind. A cross on the top was cocked to the side as if it had fallen off and been hastily nailed back on.

Right beside the church was a cemetery more expansive than Rand had expected.

He pulled up to the front and got out of the Jeep. The morning was chilly, and he zipped up his jacket. There were no signs of life around, which made Rand feel eerily alone.

The cemetery was delineated by a rusted metal fence that reached to Rand's waist. A larger structure denoted the entrance, but it was bent, faded, and the gate looked like it no longer closed. The grass was overgrown between the headstones, which went as far back as he could see. Rand figured the people of Finnick were still being buried there.

Movement among the graves caught his eye. A man ambled in the distance, approaching the church. As he neared, Rand saw the man walking with a limp and leaning heavily on a cane.

He was a frail black man dressed in an oversized suit. Thin, gray hair covered his head, and his dark eyes were soft and gentle.

"Morning," Rand said, smiling.

"Good morning," the other man said. He walked through the gates and passed his cane to his left hand as he extended his right. "Simon Cole."

Rand shook Simon's hand. "Randolph Casey. Friends call me Rand."

"You're not from around here," Simon said, eyeing the orange Jeep parked in front of the church.

"That easy to tell?"

"I know everyone in this town," Simon said. "Been here a long time, and I've never seen you."

"You're right."

"What brings you here? Services are on Sunday, and that was yesterday."

"I was in church yesterday," Rand said. "Except I went to the big tent."

Rand watched Simon Cole carefully when he mentioned the other church, and all at once, the friendly expression on the man's face changed. His mouth turned into a frown and his eyes seemed to fill with fear.

"I take it you know what I'm talking about," Rand said.

Simon Cole looked him up and down before answering. "You don't seem like the typical person you'd find there."

"You're right again."

Simon Cole nodded. "Please, let's step inside the church. It's cold out this morning."

Simon led the way into the church's foyer, where the only light was from the open door. A series of random paintings adorned the walls—the only decoration. Another set of doors opened into a simple sanctuary, flanked on both sides by rows of wooden pews. A statue of Jesus oversaw the stage and altar at the front of the room. Simon labored as he walked down the aisle toward the altar.

"I was hoping you could give me some information about the tent church," Rand said.

"There's not much I can tell you about that place," Simon said.

"What about Deckard Arcan?"

Simon looked away, as if the name pained him to hear. "Him either."

"Then what *can* you tell me?"

"That my church was the only one in Finnick until Deckard showed up. I hear his fans call him Pastor D. It was earlier this year when the tent first appeared off Highway 38. Slowly, over time, my meager congregation grew even thinner. They all attend *his* sermons on Sunday, now."

"Competition."

Simon shook his head. "It isn't about competition. As long as people find the Lord, it doesn't matter who leads them there—at least in my opinion. I care only for the souls of those in Finnick. Deckard Arcan's church brings in many more folks than my own. When that started happening, I was okay with it, at first. He was doing the Lord's work. Although he is about my age, he still has strength and vitality. I do not. I figured perhaps the Lord brought him here just in time. I considered maybe my time was coming."

Rand thought that was a bit grim. "You are speaking about before. Do you not believe these things anymore?"

"Over time, my doubts about the man grew."

"I was there when he healed Gerald Roberson," Rand said.

Simon wrung his hands together on top of his cane. "Gerald Roberson has been in that wheelchair ever since he fell off the ladder," he said. "That is well known around town. And now he's walking with no issues."

"What do you think about that?" Rand asked.

Simon shook his head. "The Bible is clear that miracle healings are real. Peter and the other apostles utilized them in the Book of Acts to spread the early church."

"Can they still happen today?"

"Anything is possible with the Lord."

"True. But what is your take?"

Simon met Rand's gaze and straightened. "Tell me why you're here."

Rand realized he'd put Simon on the defensive. He had a good feeling about the man—there was more power in the old pastor's voice than Rand had expected, and Simon seemed stronger than his frail body let on. They were both suspicious of Deckard Arcan, so Rand chose transparency. "I came back to town to discover the truth about Gerald Roberson. To see if he was actually healed, or if it was all a trick."

"And what did you learn?"

"More than I thought I would."

"Meaning?"

Rand wasn't sure where to begin. This whole thing went deeper and darker than Simon Cole was probably comfortable with.

"Let me start over," Rand said. "I am a Religious Studies professor. But outside of that, I'm a demonologist and paranormal investigator."

Simon Cole set his jaw and digested the information for a few seconds. Then, he said, "Where were you when I needed you?"

That caught Rand off guard. "What do you mean?"

"It's a long story, but Finnick is no stranger to the demonic."

"Really."

"Oh yes."

"So you believe?"

"How can I not? A demon gave me this." He patted his bum leg. "And another tried to possess a young boy that lives in town. It all came to light when a woman arrived searching for her deceased brother. It was quite the ordeal, but we prevailed."

Rand turned around and lifted his shirt to show Simon the three gashes that had scarred his back years ago.

"A frontline fighter, I see," Simon said, not particularly impressed by the marks. If he'd had encounters before, then he was no doubt familiar with scratches that came in sets of three.

"You can say that," Rand said. "I've been asked by the father of someone caught up in the church to find out the truth and get to the bottom of this."

"And what have you found?"

Rand told the story of the night before. How he'd gone to Gerald's house at the man's request to witness the visitation from his wife, but instead, a demon had appeared. As he spoke, Simon's face fell and his forehead wrinkled, but he listened without interruption.

After Rand finished, Simon stared at the floor as if lost in thought.

Finally, Simon said, "So, whatever Deckard did to Gerald that allowed him to walk again caused Gerald's home to become infested with a demonic presence."

"Yes," Rand said. "And when that presence was gone, Gerald once more lost his ability to walk."

"All of this makes much more sense now," Simon said. "You have brought me the missing piece of the puzzle. Deckard Arcan wields demonic power, and that is how he is able to perform these miracles in the name of God." The old pastor seemed truly unsettled. Rand didn't blame him.

"There's another missing piece, I'm afraid," Rand said. "There is something more going on, but I can't place my finger on it."

"What do you mean?"

"Deckard shows no outward signs of possession. I'm sure you know what I mean. He has no altered appearance and no strange or erratic behavior. Everything about the man seems normal, except for his supernatural abilities. It's like he gets all the benefits of possession, but none of the downsides."

As Rand spoke, Simon slowly lowered himself into the nearest pew, as if his body had suddenly lost all its energy. His expression showed he was very distressed about what he was hearing.

"Are you all right?" Rand finally asked.

"It's all so clear," he said, lost in thought. His words were barely audible.

"What do you mean?" Rand asked, stepping closer. "What's clear?"

Simon looked up at him, eyes wide. "It seems we're dealing with a perfect possession."

21

Rand blinked. "Beg your pardon?"

"A perfect possession," Simon repeated. "You're not familiar with the term? Ah, I suppose not. You said you've never witnessed anything like what Deckard Arcan is demonstrating."

Rand lowered himself into the pew behind Simon, eyes transfixed on the man, and readied himself for what he was about to hear. It wasn't often that Rand learned something new when the demonic was concerned, but he was not foolish enough to proclaim that he knew everything.

"A perfect possession is when the evil spirit and the soul of the victim are so entwined, so complementary of each other, that the two almost become one," Simon explained.

"Become one? How?"

"Desire and a will to submit." The words dropped heavily from Simon's mouth.

"Like when someone invites the spirit to possess him," Rand said. But that confused him. He'd had cases before where someone had invited a demon into their body, and they still demonstrated the usual signs.

"Yes and no. From what I've seen, the willingness to submit needs to be there, but there is also something more. The subject has to be... *useful*, for lack of a better term."

"Useful?"

"Useful to the entity."

"Can't demons make use of all humans they possess?" Rand asked.

"When I was younger, and had first begun encountering these types of spirits," Simon explained, "I was involved in a spiritual battle alongside my mentor at the time. The victim was a state senator, and one of his staff had approached my mentor, concerned with the changes that had happened in the man over time. The woman who worked for the senator was a spiritualist, and she sensed the senator's negative energy as it grew. He became cold, mean, and seemed to delight in the intentional mistreatment of his workers.

"When we first met the senator, he seemed like a normal man. But it did not take much provocation from my mentor to get the possessing entity to reveal itself. The spirit was deep inside, and we had to draw it out before we could remove it. The two had been working as one."

Rand stood and paced down the aisle between the pews as he reasoned things out. "I've always compared a possession to a puppet and its master. The master pulls the strings while the victim dances." Rand remembered Georgia, her body no longer her own once Karax had taken over. "But what you're telling me sounds more like two co-pilots in a cockpit."

"You could put it that way, yes."

"Working together in harmony to achieve... what, exactly?"

Simon's face grew grim. "This was a state senator—someone who had influence and authority." Simon now stood, though it obviously took effort, one hand on the back of the pew and the other on his cane. "Think of historical figures like Adolf Hitler. Or serial killers like Ted Bundy. They were fully human, but committed heinous acts that make even the most vicious men shudder. How can someone plunge into such a depth of evil? I've heard it claimed many times, and I'm inclined to believe, that these men were examples of perfect possession."

Rand ran a hand through his hair. "High-profile individuals inviting demonic possession as a means of increasing their power and influence."

Simon nodded.

"A regular person being possessed harms that person only. But a powerful and influential person being possessed could mean death, destruction, and chaos on a much larger scale."

"You've got it," Simon said. "I thought Deckard Arcan was just another revivalist preacher. His congregation grew because of his energy and fervor. After what you've told me, though, I'm afraid for this town."

Rand remembered his first visit to the church when Deckard had given his testimony. He'd claimed he was on the edge of death and an angel of the Lord had offered him a second chance.

That was it. That was the moment he invited the spirit into him. It was a demon disguised as an angel. It was a deal with the devil with the classic fine print.

"Do you think Deckard has realized that it wasn't really an angel?" Rand asked.

"I am certain he has," Simon said. "This spirit spared Deckard's life, and now he continues to use this demon's power to spread darkness into the lives of many, all while Deckard's own influence continues to grow. Gerald Roberson was only the first, and you know how popular these miracle preachers can become."

It wouldn't be long before Deckard's spectacles were filmed and posted on the internet. He would eventually move out of Finnick and into the big cities. His audience would grow, and those that he healed, like Gerald Roberson, would be making their own unintentional deals with the devil.

As Rand considered the growth potential of Deckard Arcan's reach, he understood the gravity of the situation.

"We have to stop him," Rand said, voice barely a whisper.

"You're right," Simon said, eyes boring into him. "Any help you need, I will give you. That poor woman I told you about earlier... after she went through what she did with her brother, I was brought back into this spiritual battle against my will. But I believe it was God's plan to bring me back into the fight. Just as I believe it was God's plan to bring you here today. The Lord knows what's happening in this poor town, and he knows you are the one to end it."

Rand's pulse quickened. Perhaps Simon was right. Maybe God wasn't as silent as he always assumed.

His phone buzzed in his pocket.

Miller.

"Hey," Rand answered, voice cracking.

"Rando. What's up?"

"More than you think." Rand resumed pacing up and down the aisle as he spoke. "Lots of crazy stuff has been happening."

"Where are you?"

"Down in Finnick."

"Still? Anyway, listen. I watched the video you sent me a bunch of times. You know, of that preacher speaking in tongues. It wasn't Latin or backward English. You remember that happened last time you showed me something? So I sent it straight to the same person who confirmed the last language, and they said the same thing— ancient Sumerian."

"Karax also spoke Sumerian."

This proves the demon within Deckard is another servant of Shindael.

"Miller, have you ever heard of a perfect possession?" Rand asked.

"No. What is it?"

Rand met Simon's eyes and saw the pastor was watching him with interest.

"It's..." But the words caught in Rand's throat. The rush of new information from Simon jumbled in his brain. "Miller, can I call you back?"

"You all right, Rando? You sound... afraid."

"I'll call you back." And Rand hung up.

"You have a team?" Simon asked him.

"In a way. It's always good to have support."

His phone buzzed again in his hand. Rand answered it. "Miller, I need—"

But the voice on the other end of the line was not Miller Landingham. "Hello, Randolph."

It was familiar, though it took Rand a few seconds to place it.

"This is Deckard Arcan."

22

*I*t's like he was listening to us.

Rand cleared his throat and tried to make his voice sound natural despite the fear. "Good morning, Mr. Arcan."

Simon's eyes went wide.

"It turns out I was right about you," Deckard said.

"What are you talking about?" Rand asked.

"Mr. Roberson came to my house last night. I've never seen someone so upset in my entire life. I don't know what you did to reverse his blessing, but I realize now that you are working with the devil."

Although Deckard likely knew a demon had saved him rather than an angel, he was apparently still dedicated to playing the part of a preacher.

"Why are you calling me?" Rand asked. "How did you get this number?"

"I got your number because I prayed for it," Deckard said, sounding impatient. It was another unexplainable occurrence chalked up to God. "Azora provides me with what I need to do his work, and now I believe I have a task bigger than any I've had before."

Azora. The possessing demon—surely it's a false name.

"And what might that be?"

"To save your soul."

The way he said it sounded like a death threat. But Rand knew this could be his opportunity.

"If you want to give it a shot, be my guest," Rand told him.

"Your arrogance is astounding. God always humbles the prideful in his time. And I believe yours is coming soon."

"Okay, then. What should we do about it?"

"Meet me tonight," Deckard said.

"Where?"

"At my church. Come at midnight and come alone."

The words sank into Rand. It sounded like it could be a trap. Almost certainly was. But if he wanted to remove the demon that possessed Deckard, then he needed to see the preacher face to face. And this was his chance.

"I'm looking forward to it, Pastor D," Rand said.

The line went dead.

Simon took a few steps closer to him. "What's going on?"

"He wants to meet me," Rand said. "At midnight at the tent. Alone."

"You can't go alone. I'll come with you."

"Are you sure? There will be trouble."

Simon nodded. "What will you do until then?"

Rand glanced up at the statue of Jesus on the altar. "I originally came here to be in the presence of God after what I experienced last night."

"As you should. Now, it is more important than ever." Simon checked his watch. "It is just after ten. Midnight is fourteen hours away."

"When should we begin preparing?" Rand asked.

Not all of Rand's past cases allowed him time to sufficiently prepare for a spiritual battle. But when he did have the luxury of knowing beforehand that there would be a fight, he liked to take advantage of it.

"We will begin now," Simon said. "A perfectly possessed individual is a whole new challenge. The subjects are valuable to the demon inside, and he won't free his victim easily. It worries me that you are inexperienced in this matter."

Rand frowned. "Still. This is what I do. If not me, then who else do you have?"

"You are correct. That is why we will prepare for this encounter now. I only wish we had more time."

"Fourteen hours?"

Simon fixed Rand with a stern look. "Already you are underestimating this particular servant of the devil."

Rand swallowed hard. He always prepared when he could, but he had never done it for fourteen hours straight.

"Okay. Show me what we have to do."

23

"First, we begin with personal prayer and confession," Simon explained. "I will retire to my quarters behind the sanctuary, and you will remain in here. Submit yourself before the Lord. Ask God to fill you with his spirit. Confess all ways that you have sinned against him. I will do the same. Only after this can we move on."

Rand had his way of doing things and did not like being told what to do, especially when religious matters were concerned. However, taking on a perfect possession was new territory for him, so he figured he'd best cooperate.

After Simon left him alone, Rand sat cross-legged at the foot of the altar and peered up at the statue of Jesus.

It's been a while since I've done this...

Simon's simple instruction felt, in that moment, like a monumental task. All at once, the heavy feelings Rand had been wrestling with lately bubbled to the surface: that God had abandoned him in his mission, that he was only a mere plaything for the devil, and that no matter what he did, his family and loved ones would suffer and die at the hands of Satan's servants.

This is how I feel, Rand prayed. The statue of Jesus on the cross looked down at him. *But I know I am doing your will. I must continue to be faithful. Forgive me for the times when I am not.*

But it was hard to ask for forgiveness. It was hard to accept that after all the work he'd done—the exorcisms, removing evil spirits from homes, ushering lost souls to the afterlife—that God had still been so mysteriously silent and absent in his life.

Next, he confessed. He dug deep, strived to remember all the times he had done wrong in his life: the times he had been unfair to Libby, the times he had been cruel to Tessa, the angry thoughts toward students that tested his patience in class, the women he'd caused pain with his inability to maintain a relationship.

As Rand rattled off these shortcomings, his chest tightened and tears came to his eyes. It was a feeling he hadn't experienced in a very long time—being broken before the Lord. His pride had prevented it. That pride came from his belief that even without God, he could take on the devil. He didn't want it to be that way, but as long as God was silent, then it had to be.

You're silent in my life for a reason, Lord, Rand prayed, the tears growing thicker. It pained him to admit it. *But all I do, I do for you. You have chosen me for this life.*

And as the time passed, Rand found himself going even deeper. *God, I am thankful for meeting Simon Cole, because he forced me to sit down and do this. But I am not doing this only because he told me, or because of what's to come tonight. I'm doing it because I want to change. To be the best I can be for you. To serve you better with this task you appointed me here on earth.*

Rand had no idea how much time he spent in prayer. It did not matter. The reconnection with God was long overdue, and already he felt a lightness in his spirit at finally having faced the baggage that had grown over time.

Simon Cole emerged from the room behind the sanctuary. He carried a box, which he set on the altar near Rand. Simon withdrew several long candles, which he placed on the altar's table, and lit them. Rand counted seven.

Without saying a word, Simon limped over to each window on

the side of the church and drew the curtain. Each curtain he closed plunged them further into darkness. When he was done, only the smallest slivers of daylight peeked into the room.

Simon returned to the altar and took out two old Bibles, each the size of a tome, their leather covers worn from age. He stacked them on the edge of the table.

Next came a loaf of bread wrapped in a white cloth, an unlabeled bottle, and a chalice. Simon filled the chalice with red wine from the bottle.

Rand had never gone so all-out in his own preparations. He usually only prayed and lingered in a holy place, such as a church. Simon's thoroughness was inspiring.

"What's all this stuff for?" Rand asked.

Simon held the loaf of bread in both his hands. "I trust you know the Lord's prayer."

"Of course." It was a prayer Rand found most effective in removing unclean spirits from haunted places.

"Join me," Simon said.

Together, they recited it.

"Our Father, who art in heaven, hallowed be thy name. Thy kingdom come. Thy will be done, on earth as it is in heaven. Give us this day our daily bread; and forgive us our trespasses, as we forgive those who trespass against us; and lead us not into temptation, but deliver us from evil. For thine is the kingdom and the power and the glory, forever. Amen."

Simon tore a chunk of bread from the loaf and offered it to Rand. Rand cupped both his hands and held them out to receive the bread. Simon placed it in his palms. "The body of Christ given to you."

Rand consumed the bread. Simon then removed a portion for himself and did the same.

He set the bread aside and lifted the chalice of wine. "The blood of Christ shed for you."

Rand sipped it, then Simon.

After that, Simon handed Rand one of the Bibles. It weighed

heavy in Rand's hands, and he couldn't remember the last time he'd opened the holy book.

"Do you know the Litany of the Saints?" Simon asked.

Rand exhaled. "It's been a long time."

"Open the cover."

The Bible's spine creaked as Rand opened it. Right behind the cover was a folded-up piece of paper that looked as old as the Bible. Rand unfolded it and found the familiar prayer from his youth handwritten in curvy script.

Rand's father had dragged Rand to church every Sunday when he was young, and if he didn't read aloud with the rest of the congregation, he'd receive a stern, sideways glare from his dad.

"Lord, have mercy," Simon began.

"Lord, have mercy," Rand answered.

"Christ, have mercy."

"Christ, have mercy."

"Lord, have mercy."

"Lord, have mercy."

"Christ, hear us."

"Christ, graciously hear us."

Simon recited the Litany impressively by memory as Rand followed along on the paper, answering the invocations as instructed. It made him feel insufficient—perhaps God was right to be silent in his life.

"Holy Mary," Simon said.

"Pray for us."

"Holy Mother of God."

"Pray for us."

Then Simon recited the Patriarchs and Prophets, then Apostles and Disciples, then the Martyrs.

Simon finished with, "Lord God, you know our weakness. In your mercy grant that the example of your Saints may bring us back to love and serve you through Christ our Lord."

"Amen," Rand said, glad to be finished. It had brought up too many memories of his childhood—ones that weren't as buried as he'd like them to be.

Rand found this preparation a bit too thorough for his taste. He'd done much less in the past and was still victorious over demons. But he knew Simon would not want to hear any protests.

"Now, please turn to the Book of Psalms."

Rand opened the Bible to the halfway point, remembering the approximate location of the book among the others. He ended up in Proverbs and flipped back a few pages to the beginning of the Psalms. The pages gave off a musty scent as he turned them, reminding him of the old hymnals from his father's church.

"Blessed is the man that walketh not in the counsel of the ungodly, nor standeth in the way of sinners, nor sitteth in the seat of the scornful," Simon read aloud. After he finished the first verse, he glanced up at Rand. "Please read with me."

"Oh," Rand said.

Simon continued, "But his delight is in the law of the Lord; and in his law doth he meditate day and night." Rand joined him a few words into the sentence and kept pace with the man's steady reading.

They read aloud from the Book of Psalms for a long time, and Rand quickly realized that Simon intended to read the whole thing.

Really? Rand thought. *Is this necessary?*

As Rand stood, the heavy Bible in his hands, his legs and back grew sore. His mouth became dry and his throat parched. But Simon showed no signs of fatigue, or of ceasing his Bible reading. Rand didn't want to be outdone by a man twice his age, so he strengthened his resolve and kept up.

Rand did not know how long it took them to read the entire Book of Psalms out loud, but he knew they'd been going for multiple hours. Rand had to wonder if reading it silently—and faster—would have been more efficient. Maybe a nap would have been a better use of his time.

When it was done, Simon said, "We will stop for five minutes. There is a restroom behind in the foyer."

Rand was thankful for the bathroom break. After he finished, he sat in a chair in the foyer and rested his aching legs while massaging his thighs.

Rand sighed. They were meant to face a perfectly possessed person—supposedly a formidable foe—and all they were doing was making themselves tired. They'd said the prayers and read aloud from the Bible. How much more was needed? Wasn't there some value in showing up to the fight energized and rested, also?

"Rand," Simon called from the sanctuary. "We must continue."

Groaning, Rand pulled himself off the chair and left the foyer.

He wished he could sit for longer, but he also did not want to delay Simon's process.

Rand found the old man standing where he'd been before, and Rand realized that Simon had only allowed a break for his benefit.

"You didn't have to pee?" Rand asked, joining him. "You deserve a medal for your endurance."

"Please turn to the Gospel according to Matthew," Simon instructed, ignoring his quip.

Rand found it, and just as he expected, Simon began to read aloud. "The book of the generation of Jesus Christ, the son of David, the son of Abraham. Abraham begat Isaac; and Isaac begat Jacob; and Jacob begat Judas and his brethren..."

This is too much, Rand thought. *This is insane.*

After Matthew came Mark, then Luke, and then John. In the rare times Rand glanced up from the pages of the Bible, he noted the vanishing daylight from around the edges of the curtains.

Despite Rand's physical discomfort, a new sensation started to bloom inside him. It began sometime during the reading of the Sermon on the Mount, in the Book of Matthew.

He felt peace, protected, like his entire body was covered with a shield. Maybe that was what the Bible spoke of when it mentioned the armor of God. The rituals, prayers, and readings stirred a latent zeal in him that seemed from another life entirely. He truly felt like he could do all things through Christ who strengthened him.

The strain of standing and reading for so long slipped from his mind—perhaps because his body was growing numb or because God was giving him strength.

By the time they began the Gospel according to Luke, Rand actually felt strengthened by reading the words of Jesus aloud.

When they reached the end of the Gospel according to John, Rand waited for Simon to begin Acts of the Apostles, but he was met with silence.

Rand looked up at him. The room was darker now that night had fully set in. The candles had burned down to mere stubs of wax with the melted remains filling their holders. Soon, there would be nothing left to support the little flames and they would be extinguished.

"How do you feel?" Simon asked.

Rand was pleasantly surprised by the truth. "Strong. Ready. I thought you were crazy, but maybe you do know best how to prepare for spiritual warfare."

Simon closed his Bible gently. "Now we will have rest and more personal prayer. Again, I will go to my room and you will remain here."

Once Rand was alone again, he began praying, and this time did so from a position of power.

I will remove this demon in your name, Lord. Thank you for Simon and for rejuvenating me with your holy presence.

After some time, Rand's thoughts were interrupted by the lights suddenly coming on in the sanctuary. Simon Cole stood near the door that led to the back. Rand had not heard him come in.

He approached Rand and handed him a bottle of water and two apples, which Rand quickly consumed.

"Thank you for leading us," Rand said after he'd finished eating. "I would have never thought a fourteen-hour marathon ritual would work, but I feel… good. And very ready for what's to come."

"Good," Simon said. "Because it's time."

24

Highway 38 looked much different at night. Rand turned his high beams on, but they barely cut through the darkness. The field that served as a parking lot was empty, so Rand plowed through the footpath that people used to access the church.

The tent was a large monstrosity, a darkened shadow against the light of the full moon. There were no other sources of light, so Rand left his front beams on.

He and Simon got out and approached the tent. Rand had his bag slung over his shoulder, which contained his usual supplies for situations such as this: crosses, sage, holy water, and a Bible.

Rand found the place eerie during the night when there weren't several hundred people around.

"Have you ever been here before?" Rand asked.

Simon shook his head. "I preach to the few who remain at my church on Sundays."

Rand dug into his bag and pulled out a flashlight. He used it to scan the rest of the tent. "I just noticed there are no crosses in here. No religious icons at all."

Simon looked around. "You're right. That's very telling."

A noise came from Rand's left, and the two men whirled to face it. Rand jerked his flashlight in that direction, but only saw trees and bushes on the edge of the church property. The foliage rustled in the wind.

Rand grew nervous, his stomach clenching.

"Good evening."

At the entrance of the tent, Deckard Arcan stood as a darkened shadow, backlit by the Jeep's headlights. He had another man with him—Patrick Perryman.

"Simon Cole," Deckard said, walking toward them. Patrick followed a step behind. "I'm surprised to see you here."

"We have something very important to discuss," Simon said.

"Agreed. To be honest, I'm not trying to purge your church of all its members, but I am interested in saving their lost souls. If they find that in my church instead of yours, then so be it. Surely you understand."

"We are not here to talk about saving souls," Simon said. "We are here to talk about saving you."

Deckard neared them in the aisle. He wore a suit as if it was Sunday morning. He turned his attention to Rand. "I told you to come alone."

"You brought your man." He nodded toward Patrick.

"True. I figured you would do the same. But of all the people you could scrape up, Simon Cole was the last person I would have predicted."

Rand reached his hand into his bag that hung at his waist. Deckard seemed not to notice—or if he did, he made no mention of it.

"I have asked you here tonight because you have brought harm to a member of my congregation," Deckard said. "I cannot let that stand."

"What harm would that be?" Rand asked, although he had a good idea of what the man was referring to.

"Don't play dumb with me," Deckard said. "You went into the

house of Gerald Roberson and did a dark ritual to reverse the blessing brought upon him by God."

"That was no blessing," Rand said.

"I had hope for you. All men are lost at some point in their lives, including me. But almost all can be found. I believed I could reach you, but it seems like you are intent on battling God and pushing your own agenda." Deckard frowned as if the words pained him to say.

And in the small amount of light that came from Rand's flashlight, Rand could see that Deckard earnestly believed he was being guided by God. He had no clue that the entity that held sway over him was anything but holy.

"You have to listen to me," Rand said. "The spirit speaking to you is not God, nor is it an angel named Azora."

"And what would a sinner like you know about the voice of God?"

"Because I fight those spirits," Rand said. "Let us finally get to know each other. My name is Randolph Casey, and I have removed and cast out countless demons from the lives of ordinary people. I know how they act and how they behave. More than anything, I know how they deceive."

Deckard's face grew grim.

"The miracles you perform. The things you learn in prayer that you can't possibly know. Where does it all come from?"

"From God."

"Are you sure?"

"Who else could reveal these things to me?"

"From a servant of the devil. They are timeless and know all things about all people. They are also masters of deception. That is why you think an angel named Azora is speaking to you. Think back to when you had that near-death experience. Of course you would have accepted help from any supernatural being that offered it. But in that moment, when you were at your most vulnerable, it was a demon that slipped inside and possessed you. I know this is hard for you to hear, but I can prove it."

Deckard only glared at Rand. The pastor was half a head shorter, but he had no problem looking up and meeting Rand's steady gaze.

Behind Deckard, Patrick took a step back, as if the growing tension was too much for him.

"These are the ravings of a sinner," Deckard said. "A shame. I hoped better for you. But as it stands, I cannot allow you to come near my congregation again."

Rand's hand found the crucifix at the bottom of his bag. In one quick motion, he pulled it out and pressed it to Deckard's chest.

With blinding speed, Deckard leapt back and slapped the cross from Rand's grip, sending it flying away with a power greater than any mere human could have.

Rand's hand throbbed.

Deckard looked at his own hand, amazed at his strength, confused. He touched his chest where the cross had been and rubbed as if trying to ease away the pain.

"What was that?"

"You see what I mean?" Rand said. "You cannot stand to be touched by the cross. The entity that follows you won't allow it."

Deckard considered it for a moment, but he only set his jaw. "Impossible."

"Would you like to try again?"

"No!" he barked back at Rand.

"Why not?" Rand asked. "You're not thinking for yourself, Deckard. Why are you so averse to being touched by a cross?"

"You don't know what you're talking about," Deckard snarled.

A change came over the man. Gone was the formal calmness, the cool and collected nature. The facade was cracking. Even Patrick Perryman seemed afraid of him.

"Look at you," Rand said. "You're losing control."

"No—"

"All over a simple cross. Why are you afraid of the sign of your Lord?"

"Shut up!" Deckard shouted, his voice booming. "You are wrong. You are the one who is possessed! People like you are the reason

Azora has given me his blessing. He is the one who gives me the strength to resist you."

"You don't need to resist me," Rand said, taking a step back. Deckard's body tensed, and he looked ready to attack. "I am here to help you. Listen to me, and we can get you on the right path to God."

"I will never listen to you!"

Deckard Arcan gripped the end of a wooden bench. Rand watched in amazement as the old man lifted it off the ground as if it were nothing more than a stick.

The bench was at least ten feet long, but in Deckard's hands, it looked like it was light as a feather. He brought it over his head.

Rand saw that Deckard's eyes had changed. They glowed blood red.

Deckard swung the bench like he was batting with a tree trunk.

Rand dropped flat and felt the thick wood whoosh over him. Simon and Patrick fell away from Deckard, stumbling far out of his range.

Deckard lifted the bench over his head and hammered it down where Rand lay. But Rand rolled out of the path right before the wood embedded itself in the soft earth.

Rand sprang to his feet. *Here we go. God, give me strength.* He rushed toward Deckard, ready to tackle him.

But it was not Deckard. Those glowing eyes told him he was running straight for the dark entity that held the pastor.

Deckard reached out to him first, shoving both hands into his chest. Rand felt a burst of pain in his ribs as if he'd been hit by a wrecking ball. The force lifted him off his feet and sent him hurtling backward through the air and out of the tent. He landed hard on the ground near his Jeep and rolled, the breath knocked from his lungs. His chest throbbed. Was his sternum broken? Caved in?

Superhuman strength was a common symptom of possession. Rand had been struck by these individuals before, but he'd never been hit so powerfully before.

He coughed and sputtered and tried to stand. Deckard approached him quickly, and Rand tried to crawl away.

He's too strong.

Rand felt firm hands on his shoulders, flipping him onto his back. Deckard leaned over him, face inches from his, red eyes glaring into him.

"You've gone too far this time," Deckard said. His voice had changed. It had taken on a rougher, demonic edge. "Shindael has marked you for death, and it will come."

Deckard reached out his hand and grabbed his throat. His grip was a vise. Rand tugged on Deckard's wrist with both his hands, but it was not going anywhere.

Deckard clenched Rand's windpipe closed. He struggled and kicked his legs, but Deckard was a rock, sturdy and powerful.

And Rand realized that despite all the prayer and preparation, God was not there to protect him from the servant of Shindael.

Then a loud siren blared in the distance. Red and blue lights flashed through the night.

The glow from Deckard's eyes faded, and he released Rand's throat. Rand gasped and crawled away, forcing air into his lungs.

"Police!" someone shouted.

Rand coughed and sputtered and rubbed at his neck where the demon had tried to crush it. A few seconds more and he would have lost consciousness.

There was shouting, but Rand was too dazed to make out what any of it was.

All he knew was that someone had come to save him. The cops. They had seen Deckard attacking him and were there to rescue him.

But then he felt strong arms grab his right hand, then his left, and force them behind his back. Cold metal clasped on his wrists and clicked into place.

"Randolph Casey. You are under arrest."

Rand was yanked to his feet. He was face to face with Jones, the sheriff he'd met when he'd first arrived in town. "What are you doing?" The words only croaked out of his mouth.

"You are under arrest for breaking and entering into Gerald Roberson's house."

Jones grabbed his elbow and forced him toward the police cruiser. Rand turned to look back and saw Deckard Arcan and Patrick Perryman standing together, watching him go. Even further in the distance was Simon Cole, looking on helplessly as Rand was led away.

The sheriff shoved Rand into the back of the car.

"Wait—" Rand began, but Jones only slammed the car door in his face.

It was a setup, he realized.

Deckard Arcan had baited him there and called the police. Gerald Roberson must have gone to Deckard and told him Rand had broken in.

Something happened there, however, that not even Deckard had been prepared for—the demon came out. And Rand realized that by arresting him, Sheriff Jones had inadvertently saved his life.

25

It was Wednesday morning in math class, and Libby could not leave her phone alone.

The last time she'd heard from her dad was Monday evening. He was knee-deep in a case, so she had resisted the urge to contact him on Tuesday knowing she needed to give him his space.

But now it was Wednesday morning. Two entire nights had passed. Usually, his fights with the supernatural took place over the course of a single night.

Everything okay?

The last message she had sent him lingered in her app, delivered but not answered.

When class let out, she went into the hallway and called her dad. He did not answer.

Next, she called her mother.

"Are you at school?" her mother asked when she answered.

"Yeah."

"What have I told you about using your phone at school? You've gotten in enough trouble for that already."

"Have you heard from Dad?"

Tessa paused. "Since when?"

"Since the weekend."

"No, I haven't."

"Oh. He's doing a case right now."

Tessa huffed. "He's supposed to tell me."

This was about Justin—a case that was more personal and close to home. It had sprung up quicker than most, so her dad probably hadn't thought to tell her mom. But it was true. Rand kept Tessa up to date about these matters. Her mother didn't like to admit it, but she still worried about him.

"I'll try calling him," Tessa said.

"I've already tried. Calling and texting. He hasn't answered for two days."

"Hmm. Well, you know how these... *things* can mess with his phone and electronics. Or whatever."

"Yeah. True."

"I'm sure he's fine," Tessa said. "But if he keeps canceling his classes like this, they're going to fire him."

As far as Libby knew, he'd only canceled his classes on Monday while he poked around in Finnick.

Libby hung up with her mother and moved to her next class, where she resorted to Plan B and texted Justin.

Hey.

Her last message to him had gone unanswered as well, and she'd been too annoyed to try any harder. He'd broken up with her a few days before, presumably because she didn't believe his pastor had healed anybody. That, and Rand was investigating the man as requested by Justin's dad, so talking to Justin during that time almost felt like a conflict of interest.

But she was getting desperate. Maybe he or Mr. Tidwell had heard from Rand.

The class wore on with Libby barely paying attention, and the bell rang. The next class came and went without a message from anyone.

She ground her teeth and waited for school to let out for the day. She went down to her car in the parking lot and tried calling her dad on the way. Nothing. She called her mom back.

"He hasn't answered for me either," Tessa said. "Do you think we should call—"

"No," Libby said quickly, knowing what her mom was thinking. "You know what dad says. When he's on a case, never get the police involved, no matter what."

If her dad was caught up in something crazy, one of the worst things they could do was call the police. She'd learned that the hard way once when she was younger. As counterintuitive as it was, it was always best to trust her dad and his abilities.

Libby drove to Rand's house. His Jeep was not in the driveway and three newspapers lay near the mailbox. Libby picked them up and threw them in the recycle bin around the side of the house.

She used her copy of the key to let herself in and poked around, noting that everything seemed normal.

Nothing was out of place.

She opened her backpack on the kitchen table. She'd work on some homework while she waited. Although she didn't know what she was waiting for. Anything from her dad.

But within five minutes of opening her books, she knew it would be impossible to concentrate.

The phone rang, a shrill, electronic jingling that caused her to jump.

It was the house phone. She couldn't remember the last time they'd used it. Her dad always gave out his cell number to people.

She crossed the kitchen to where the portable landline rested on its cradle. The green light flashed as it rang.

Libby picked it up and checked the caller ID. Unknown. She pressed the button and brought it to her ear.

"Hello?

"Libby." It was her dad.

Libby let out a huge breath she hadn't realized she'd been holding. "Dad. What the hell? Where have you been?"

"Libby. I need your help."

Her relief suddenly evaporated. "Are you okay?"

"Yes, I'm fine." He said something else, but the line filled with static as if he were in a bad reception area.

"I can't hear you. You're breaking up."

The line cleared. "I said I need your help. Can you help me?"

"Yes, of course. What do you need? Should I call Mom or someone?"

"Come to Finnick," her father said. "I need you here."

"Okay... Why? Is everything—"

"Just come now, please. I'll explain when you get here."

"Fine, all right. But where?" She hoped he wasn't about to say the giant tent church. Even thinking about that place gave her the creeps.

"It's called the Finnick Motel."

"Right. Finnick Motel." That must have been where he was staying this whole time. But why not call and check in earlier if he had been at a motel?

I'll know as soon as I see him and he fills me in.

"Are you coming now?" her father asked.

"Yes. Are you sure everything's okay? Do you need me to bring anything?"

"I'm sure. Everything's fine. Just come now."

Then the line went dead.

Libby hung up the phone. Her dad didn't sound desperate or in danger, so why was he so insistent that she meet him urgently?

Maybe something to do with the case.

Libby packed up her books and slung her backpack over her shoulder. As she walked to the car, she typed "Finnick Motel" into the GPS on her phone and dropped a pin. It would take her just under two hours to get there.

Hopefully, she could get there and back to town before it got too late in the day. And have her dad in tow with her, case complete, and everything resolved.

As she backed out of the driveway, she called her mom. "Hey, just talked to Dad."

"Really? What's going on?"

"Not sure. But he wants me to meet him."

"Meet him where?"

"In Finnick."

Tessa paused. "Why there?"

"That's where he's working."

"Right, but why? Did he say?"

"No. But he told me everything was all right, just that he needed my help. I'll go meet him and then come back later tonight."

"All right." But her mother still seemed unsure. "You sure he said everything was all right?"

"Yes, Mom. I talked to him."

"Okay. Keep me updated, please."

"I will."

She hung up her phone and laid it in her lap.

Although Libby was relieved to have finally heard from her dad, she now found herself frustrated. *We need a new rule. If cases take multiple days, he should call and let me know everything's okay.*

She planned to give him an earful when she saw him.

Libby cranked the radio and pressed the gas pedal to shave time off her drive.

26

The Finnick Inn was a run-down dump if Libby had ever seen one. The sun was just starting to set and an eerie, purple-and-orange light peeked through the storm clouds that had taken root overhead the past week. The sign in front tried to light up, but it only flickered on and off. There were no cars in the cracked and pothole-filled lot, and she got the feeling that merely stepping inside any of the rooms would have her walking out with a disease.

So basically, it was the kind of place she'd expect her dad to stay. Hunting ghosts and fighting demons hardly had him rolling in dough.

Libby parked and killed the engine. She picked up her phone and called her dad to tell him that she was there and ask him what room he was staying in.

He did not answer.

She tried texting him.

Hey, I'm here at the motel. Where are you?

She let that linger unanswered for several minutes before she decided she'd have to go to him. When she found him, she planned to give him a verbal thrashing for being so crappy at communicating.

Libby glanced around the area. No shady or shifty characters from what she could see.

She got out of the car and went to the front office. The man behind the desk was a grubby old dude who looked like he hadn't showered in a week. His name tag read Keith.

Keith stared her down a bit harder than she was comfortable with.

"How can I help you, sweetie?" he said, his smile slimy and sketchy. His eyes scanned her entire body up and down.

Libby wanted to vomit. "I'm looking for my dad."

"No one's staying here at the moment," he said, southern accent thick and rough. "You need a room for the night?"

"No. As I said, I'm looking for my dad. He told me to meet him here, so I assumed he was staying here."

Keith only shrugged. "Just cause he said to meet him here don't mean he's staying here. No one's checked in tonight, and I would know. I'm the manager."

Libby took out her phone and found a picture of her dad in her camera roll.

"This man." She showed it to Keith.

Keith donned a pair of glasses from his pocket and stared at the picture for a few long seconds. "Ah yeah. I do know that guy." He removed his glasses. "Was here…" He rolled his eyes up toward the ceiling as he thought. "Sunday night I think."

That long ago?

"That's it? Just Sunday night."

"Wasn't here for very long," Keith said. "Started acting like a crazy man."

The unsettled feeling returned to Libby's stomach. "What do you mean?"

Keith scrunched up his face as he tried to recall. "Came here and checked in. Everything was fine, then he ran in here telling me there was something going on in the room next door. But there wasn't, because he was the only person staying here that night. Still, he kept saying there was. Stole the key right off my rack and broke into the other room. Lo and behold, nothing there, just like I told him. Man was hearing things, I think. Then he started seeing things, or at least it seemed that way. Kept freaking out and looking around like he was hallucinating. I don't know. I don't need that kind of crap in my business, so I threw him out. Ain't seen him since."

Libby took in the story and swallowed hard. "You don't know where he went?"

"No. Honestly don't care, just as long as he ain't here. What about you? I'll hook you up with a room if you need one, just as long as you ain't crazy like your old man."

"Thanks for your help," Libby said flatly, then turned and left the office.

Sunday night.

That was seventy-two hours ago. Why would her dad ask her to meet him at a motel where he hadn't been in three days?

She took out her phone to call her mom, but hesitated. She considered calling the police first—the one thing her dad asked her to never do when he was on a case.

But something just wasn't sitting right this time.

As her fingers moved over the keys, a beat-up truck pulled into the gravel lot and slowly coasted over. It parked next to her car and the driver switched off the ignition. The door opened and out stepped a man that Libby knew she'd seen before, but couldn't place.

He wore faded jeans and had a clean white t-shirt tucked into them. His straight brown hair was swooped to the side and he gave her a smile as he walked over to her.

"Libby," he said.

"Have we met?" she asked, even though she knew they had, and wished she could remember where.

The man laughed with genuine humor. "In a way. My name is Patrick Perryman, and we bumped into each other at church. I'm friends with Justin." He extended his hand. "Nice to meet you again."

"Yeah," Libby said, taking it weakly.

"Listen, your dad asked me to come," Patrick said.

Libby perked up. "My dad. Where is he?"

"He's with me, at my house. He wanted me to come and get you. Told me you were coming to meet him here."

"Why couldn't he meet me himself?" Libby asked.

"He's been crazy busy," Patrick said.

"Is he okay?" Libby asked.

"Yeah, he's totally fine," Patrick said. "Sorry, I didn't mean to worry you, but yes, everything's okay."

"This is all just a little weird," Libby said. "And not really like him at all."

"I understand," Patrick said. "But you know how these things can be with your dad."

That was true, which made Libby wonder just how much Patrick knew about her father. The man was involved with the church, so it made sense that her dad would have sought him out in the investigation. Maybe Patrick Perryman was just as worried about the place as Justin's dad was.

"I'll take you on over to my house. Rand's waiting for us there."

"I'll take my own car," Libby said.

Patrick only shrugged and smiled. "Okay. You can follow."

The two got into their cars and Patrick pulled out of the motel parking lot, Libby close behind.

Along the way, she tried calling her dad again, but he did not answer.

Why send this guy? Dad, what are you involved in?

Libby called her mom again.

"Did you find him?" Tessa asked.

"Not yet. He sent someone else to meet me."

"Who is it?"

"His name's Patrick. I've met him before, actually. I still don't know what's going on down here, but I think Dad's working with this guy."

"Libby, you should come home," Tessa said.

"I will. I'll find out real quick what's going on with Dad, then I'll come back."

"Are you sure everything is fine? Especially with this guy?"

"He's one of Justin's friends from church."

"Why is Justin's friend working with your dad on a case?"

"Long story." Neither she nor her father had told Tessa the details of Charles Tidwell's request. "I'll fill you in on the whole thing after I talk with him."

"Promise?"

"Yes. I promise."

She hung up just as Patrick's truck left the main part of town and meandered down a side road. The neighborhoods turned into farmlands, and after a few more miles, even the houses dropped away.

They came to a single house that was far from town or any other homes. It was a mansion—the last thing she had expected.

Patrick parked in the yard and Libby pulled up behind him. Patrick got out and signaled for her to turn off the car.

She got out of the car but left the engine running.

"You live here?" Libby said, raising her eyebrows. Surely Justin would have told her if he had a friend who was super wealthy and lived in a mansion.

"Yes. Come on. Your dad's inside and waiting for you."

Patrick started up the steps of the large porch, but Libby hesitated in the yard.

Patrick turned around. "What's wrong?"

"Sorry, it's just that I don't know you. I don't want to go inside your house."

Patrick looked genuinely confused. "But I'm a friend of Justin's. You and I even met at church." He gave a smile, but it seemed forced.

"Look, can you just go inside and tell my dad to come out? Please. I want to see him first."

Patrick's smile faded. His lips tensed into a thin line, and he glared at her.

That's it. I'm out of here.

Her entire world became dark as something was pulled over her head. She tried to scream and run, but strong arms clasped her body and covered her mouth, stifling her.

Then Libby was lifted several feet in the air and carried effortlessly toward the house. She tried to thrust her arms outward to break from whoever grasped her, but they were too strong. She flailed her legs, kicking her tall captor's thighs as he walked, but it did not stop him.

Libby tried to scream, but a large hand covered her mouth and stifled her.

27

The jail cell was a box of bars that Rand estimated was ten feet by ten feet. It was located in the back of the police station, behind the desks and offices, in the far-off corner by the rear exit of the building.

"Sleep tight," Sheriff Jones told him after locking the cell. "I'll deal with you in the morning."

"You can't just leave me alone in here," Rand called after him as he left.

Jones ignored him. Once he was gone, the entire police station was eerily quiet.

Rand was galled when he realized he was the only soul in there. There wasn't even a deputy to keep an eye on him.

This has got to be against some protocol.

Rand sat on the hard ground with his back against the bars. Illegal or not, he had no choice but to wait until Jones came for him in the morning.

Deckard Arcan had arranged for his lock up, and Rand was starting to realize there was nothing he could do about it. It was Deckard's word against his, and in a small town like Finnick Deckard's word would always win. Especially since Sheriff Jones was a member of the congregation, and had even witnessed Gerald Roberson's healing.

In the silence, Rand had plenty of time to reflect on what had landed him there. He realized just how short his confrontation with Deckard had been, and how quickly the man had overpowered him —and nearly killed him.

You forsook me again, God, Rand found himself thinking. *After all that prayer and Scripture reading. Was fourteen hours straight not enough for you? How long until you actually back me up?*

Rand pressed his fingers into his temples as if trying to physically force the thoughts from his mind. His heart wanted to sustain his faith, but his brain wanted to remind him just what faith was: belief in something without any proof that it was true.

And when he found his eyes tearing up, he realized he was more upset than he'd originally thought. Once again, God had hung him out to dry. On top of his emotional pain, he'd had his ass kicked by a perfectly possessed man. His chest still throbbed where Deckard had hit him.

He was without any way to communicate with the outside world. Jones had taken everything—his bag of supplies, his cell phone, his wallet. No one knew he was there except for Simon Cole.

Come on, Simon. Get me out of here. Surely the old pastor was doing everything he could to get to Rand.

His stomach rumbled and his mouth was dry. The full moon's light spilled through the windows, and Rand spotted a sink next to a vending machine on the other side of the room. That cruel sight exacerbated his hunger and thirst, making him feel like a man in the desert who couldn't quite reach the oasis in front of him.

Just hold on until morning, Rand told himself. They may not release him, but they would surely feed him. *Won't be long now.*

Rand checked his watch. It read 11:43.

That's not right. We met Deckard at midnight. It's way later than that.

The moonlight didn't illuminate much, so Rand clenched his eyes shut, trying to adjust them to the darkness. But he had not misread the time. He held it up to his ear, but it was still ticking. It was not broken.

Then something occurred to him.

He twisted his wrist, making the watch face away from him. Then, a few seconds later, he returned it face up and checked the time.

It now read 2:08.

Oh, no.

Rand turned his watch away again, then back.

7:23.

Time distortion.

People who'd had close encounters with demonic entities reported this phenomenon; Rand himself had experienced it himself a time or two. Demons were not bound by time and space, and therefore could insert themselves into any point in history they wanted—even the past. As such, they had the ability to put humans through a distorted sense of time.

Both Rand and Miller had searched for an explanation for this occurrence, but they had only come up with hypotheses. Some claimed the victim was temporarily brought into a parallel dimension that was close to reality as humans knew it, and that was where the supernatural was active. Others suggested it was literal time travel—forced upon the person by the demon to disorient them and make them further question their own sanity.

It was similar to the experience described by lucid dreamers—people who could control their dreams. They said time did not exist normally in dreams, which was why dreams seeming to last three days could occur during a thirty-minute nap. Further, these folks always claimed that if they looked at a clock in a dream, and then immediately looked away and back again, it would read an entirely different time.

Regardless of what was true, Rand knew one thing: he'd be there until Shindael decided to relent.

He had no doubt Shindael was behind this. Rand had figured out that Deckard Arcan was perfectly possessed and confronted him.

Gotten too close. And now Shindael had him locked in a box with a jumbled sense of reality.

Rand twisted his wrist back and forth, flashing his watch dozens of times. Each time, the watch hands were in a completely different position.

He dropped his head back against the bars, the metal clanging against his skull. He sighed deeply. "Come on, Shindael," he said out loud. "I know you're close, and I know what you're doing. Just get on with it. Make your point."

But he knew it was useless. Shindael would let the attack go on for as long as he wanted.

Without a reliable watch, Rand had no idea how long he sat in that cell. Eventually, he knew it was long enough that the sun should have started to rise, but it never came. With time distortion, the night would last infinitely, as if the earth had stopped rotating.

The only indication of how much real time was elapsing was the weakening of his body. His hunger compounded, and the roars coming from his stomach filled the silent room. His mouth tasted as if it was stuffed with cotton. A sharp headache snuck into the top of his brain, brought on by dehydration.

He laid down and tried to sleep. He dozed a bit, but never for long.

Eventually, his mind began to wander into horrible places. *What if he keeps me like this for years? Decades?*

He imagined Shindael freeing him, only for him to find that Libby had grown up and gotten married. Like he'd been in a coma that lasted a third of his life.

She would have spent that entire time not knowing what became of her father. All she knew was that one day he'd driven away for a case and never came back. She would resent him for having never given up the supernatural work when he had the chance.

He sobbed as he imagined that scenario. The possibility of it all hurt him worse than anything he currently felt—more than his hunger, more than his thirst, and more than God's betrayal.

Rand tried to make himself stop thinking about it. He knew

Shindael was close and could see his thoughts, and he didn't want to give the demon any ideas about how to torture him. Shindael had once assured him that his death was not enough—that release would only come after he'd truly suffered.

Rand's dozing felt like sleeping in the middle seat of an airplane. Just as real sleep started to come, his head would droop and jolt him awake again. After that happened many times, he opened his eyes to find that someone was standing just outside the bars of his cell.

He blinked many times. His eyes burned and watered and his vision blurred. At first, he thought he was hallucinating, but no. Someone was there.

Rand was sprawled on his back, and it took all his strength to push himself into a sitting position.

He lifted his head up to see who was there.

Black eyes looked down at him.

Shindael.

The fear that Rand normally felt when Shindael was near never came. His body simply had nothing left to produce it. Instead, he felt relief. Finally, this could end.

Even if it means he kills me...

Rand struggled to push off the floor. His back popped as he straightened it. Then he stood on wobbly legs. With no strength or energy left, it felt like trying to stand on the surface of a planet that had ten times the gravity of Earth.

But regardless of the effort, Rand had just enough mental fortitude left to know he needed to face his nemesis on two feet.

"Now what?" Rand's voice was gravelly and stilted, having not spoken in however long.

Whatever I want. You are my plaything, remember?

Shindael's words were a voice in his head. Telepathic. It was deceptively smooth and gentle, different from the demonic voices Rand was used to hearing.

Rand shuffled forward, the soles of his shoes never fully leaving the ground. When he reached the bars, he leaned against them, having run out of energy to stand. He was inches away from Shindael now, closer than he would have normally put himself, but he needed something to happen.

If you want out, there is a way.

"So we're going to play games?"

No games, Randolph. I'm offering you an escape. Behind you.

Rand slowly turned and looked over his shoulder.

Shindael had caused a noose to materialize. It dangled from the roof, just high enough to give him the room to hang himself. Rand reached out and grasped the cold bars to steady himself. As he stared at that rope, so neatly tied, it occurred to him this may be his most merciful exit.

But then Rand remembered the story of Jesus in the desert when he and Simon had recited the Gospels. Jesus had fasted alone for forty days and has been tempted directly by Satan, but never gave in.

"I won't do it," Rand said.

It's so easy. Just slip it on.

"No."

I'm offering you a deal, Randolph. If you do this for me now, I promise to leave your family alone.

"I don't make deals with monsters like you."

Smart man. You are right. You shouldn't make deals with the ones that work under me. But me, I am different and you know it. If I tell you I'm going to do something, you know I'll do it.

Shindael then vanished and reappeared a split second later inside the cell, even closer to Rand than he had been before. Their faces were inches apart, and Rand's breath caught. He wanted to back away, but did not have the energy. He could feel Shindael's heavy, evil aura radiating off of him.

I have watched you every day since the first time we spoke. Sometimes I allow you to see me, just to remind you that I am close. But it is not just you I keep track of. I watch Libby. I watch Tessa. I watch everyone you care about. I know everything about them. I know how they spend their time, where they sleep, and exactly what they think about you.

Rand began to tremble. He didn't know if it was from fear or weakness. But his anger rose at his body betraying his brokenness to Shindael.

I can kill them any time I want. Easily. But I don't. Because it's far better to use their misery to torment you. To make you pay for all the times you have interfered.

"Leave them alone. They've done nothing to you."

You are right. But you have, and that is good enough.

Shindael's dark eyes absorbed him like black holes consuming everything.

I will make you a deal. And I will keep my word. If you give yourself, then I will leave them alone forever. All we care about is you. End it all now, and they will be freed.

Rand looked past Shindael at the noose still dangling from the ceiling.

You understand that there is no hope. If you refuse, then you are only hurting them more than you already have. In the end, you know you will die by my hand. It is inevitable. The only question is when and if you will take your family down with you.

No matter how much Rand tried to deny Shindael's words, he knew the demon spoke the truth. He hated to admit it to himself because he knew Shindael could hear his thoughts as if he'd spoken them aloud.

He could push and fight as much as he wanted. He could banish every demon in hell three times over, but they would always return to haunt another. The work would never end, never be complete. And after Shindael had had his fun, after his minions had inflicted enough chaos and psychological scars, after Shindael had grown bored with toying with him over the years... only then would the demon end it. And once he was gone, Shindael's servants would be free to attack the earth at will.

So why let it go on? Why not end it now and spare his family? Why not take the deal?

You are finally thinking clearly for the first time in your life, Randolph.

There was just one thing Rand could not get his head around.

Never, ever, under any circumstances, should a human make a deal with the devil. No matter how sweet it sounded, there was always a twist, always a lie. Even in his weakened, desperate state, Rand knew this was the absolute truth.

"No."

Shindael almost seemed amused by his refusal. The demon's face didn't reveal much, but Rand thought he could see the hint of a smirk on those thin lips.

It seems you *have chosen to play games, Randolph. You'll remember this night for the rest of your life. Every time your actions and resistance hurt you or someone you love, you'll remember the time I tried to help, and you refused the offer. Every misfortune that befalls you now is entirely your fault.*

A sound. Rand turned and watched as the cell door unlatched and slowly swung open by itself, the rusty hinges creaking.

Let the games begin, Rand thought. He looked back toward Shindael, but the demon and the noose had vanished.

He'd rejected the deal. Now, there was only one thing to do. He had to persevere. Pick up where he'd left off. Continue fighting, no matter how weak he felt.

Rand stumbled over to the sink and drank heavily from the stream, dozens of gulps filling his stomach. With each new mouthful that went down, he felt more and more alive.

He had to find out how long he'd been trapped in Shindael's time loop. Had to see if there was still a chance of stopping Deckard Arcan.

Rand bumbled through the dark police station on rubbery legs, finding the door and bursting out into the cold night.

No phone. No car. Only his determination and the clothes on his back.

His nearest ally was Simon Cole. Rand had to get to him.

28

Libby sensed she was being carried inside the mansion and up some stairs. It was completely dark inside the bag that covered her head, and the more she screamed, the more the air seemed to grow thin inside of it.

Despite her breathlessness, she kicked and squirmed, looking for any give in the strong arms around her body. But they only seemed to grow tighter, forcing her elbows into her sides and causing stabbing pain.

She was dropped into an uncomfortable chair and her hands were bound together behind the back of the chair. Her ankles were tied to the legs, leaving her completely captive and helpless.

She heard footsteps walking away, a door opening and then slamming behind them.

"Let me out of here!"

Though she could not see, she knew she was alone in the room.

She pulled on her restraints.

Stupid, she thought. How could she have been lured all the way here? Even her mother had tried to tell her something seemed off about the whole thing. She didn't listen. She had been too eager to find her dad.

He's hurt.

Mauled by a mob of angry church people.

He's captured.

Tied up just like she was.

He's dead...

Libby pulled against her restraints, which cut into the soft flesh around her wrists. The ropes around her ankles weren't budging either.

I have to get out of here and help him. Somehow.

The more she struggled, the more tired she became. Her breaths came in short, shallow gasps. The limited air inside the sack over her head made her dizzy.

Her adrenaline finally gave out, and she slumped in the chair. Then the sobs surfaced, though she fought hard to suppress them.

Dad wouldn't cry right now.

Libby had never felt so far away from her father in her life. No one knew where she was. This was what she got for interfering with her dad's case.

How many times had he tried to warn her? Never interfere. Never act. Even if he got himself killed.

This was why.

She had no idea how long she sat in that chair, tied up like a prisoner. But after what seemed like an eternity, she heard the door open again.

Footsteps.

They fell differently than the ones that had left her there—less heavy. Light and hesitant. Still, they circled around her and came to rest right in front of her. Libby felt the presence standing only inches away.

"Please let me go," she said, voice muffled by the sack over her head.

A hand gripped the sack and pulled it off, and she relished the cool air as she took her first proper breath since being captured.

In front of her stood Patrick Perryman.

The bile rose in Libby's throat and her anger flared. She had a vivid image of tearing his oversized head from his puny body. But all that aggressiveness had not helped so far, so she forced herself to remain calm.

"Good evening," Patrick said.

"What is going on?" she said. "Why have you done this to me? Where is my dad?"

"I see you are calmer now," Patrick said. "I'd like to untie you, but you have to give me your word you'll behave."

Libby swallowed all the insults that sprung to her mind, all the things she wanted to say to this creep who insisted she *behave*. Instead, she nodded.

"Good girl." Patrick went around to the back of the chair and began working on the ropes that bound her wrists.

The ropes fell away and Libby rubbed at her scraped wrists. Then she placed her hands in her lap and forced herself to stay still as Patrick got down on his knees and worked on freeing her ankles from the chair legs.

Libby looked around the room. *Is there an easy way out of here?*

She was in a darkened attic with a low, pointed ceiling and wooden walls. There was a bed, a couch, and an empty baby crib on the far side of the room. Despite the furniture, it didn't look like anyone lived up there, but it did seem to be prepared for someone who had yet to arrive.

There was a small, square window in the far wall in front of her —a potential point of escape. She saw no door. *The only one must be behind me.* That's where she'd heard Patrick come from.

Once she was free, Libby tried to stand, but Patrick only put his hands on her shoulders and forced her back down.

"Not so fast. You're tired and hungry and thirsty."

All of those things were true, but none of it compared to her desire to escape.

"Welcome to my home." He smiled.

Welcome? You kidnapped me.

"Technically Pastor D owns it, but he graciously allows me to live here."

Keep him talking. Make him comfortable. Then I can find a way to escape. "That's nice," Libby said, rather unenthusiastically. "Who else lives here? Just you two?"

Patrick only smirked. "Soon you will too."

The casual way he said it made her second guess if she'd heard that right. "What did you say?"

"I said this will be your home soon."

The room was dark, but Patrick was standing uncomfortably close, so Libby could make out the glee on his face.

This guy is crazy.

"And um..." Libby cleared her throat. "Why, exactly, would I want to live here?"

"You will be my wife and bear my children."

Yep, I'm definitely hearing this right.

"Excuse me?"

"You have been chosen by Azora to be among his first women," Patrick said. "This is a high honor, and one that Pastor D and I have been looking forward to for a long time. I have seen you clearly in my prayers ever since that first day you came to church. God spoke to me immediately and told me you were the one. The angel Azora has confirmed this to Pastor D."

Libby didn't know what any of that actually meant, but the bullet points were good enough. "Are you fucking crazy? Are you sick? What the hell is wrong with you?"

Patrick knelt down in front of her, shushing her like she was a child throwing a tantrum. His face drew closer, and she recoiled. "I know it's a lot to take in right now. But please don't worry. We will begin teaching you the ways of Azora soon. Before you know it, you'll realize your purpose. I remember when I first learned—"

"My dad will come for you. People know that I'm here. This isn't going to work."

"Your dad has been dealt with," Patrick said flippantly. "He is no longer a problem."

Dealt with...

Her fists balled up, ready to strike. "What have you done to my dad?"

"After you have been introduced to Azora, you won't even remember Randolph Casey. So there's no point in talking about it now."

His refusal to answer filled her with a rage so hot she felt tears coming to her eyes.

"Try to get some rest," Patrick said. His clammy palm snaked up her thigh, and she tried to shake it off, but he only squeezed her so tight it hurt. "Your first prayers with Azora will begin soon. It won't be long before you realize the truth and joy that he has planned for your life."

He stood and walked toward the attic door at the far end of the room. Before he left, he turned back to her. "And do try to be on your best behavior. Trust me when I say if you try to do anything rash, you won't like what happens to you. I'd hate to have to do this the hard way." He gave her a simple smile.

After he'd gone, Libby heard the door lock behind him.

29

ealt with.

She couldn't get the words out of her head.

Calm down, Libby. Pull it together. First things first, I need to get out of here.

The attic was larger than what she would have considered normal. But then again, she was inside of a mansion. The room looked like it was used for storage—some furniture stood in the center of the room, covered in a thin layer of dust. The bed and baby crib gave her the creeps. Presumably, those were meant for her.

No chance in hell, Patrick.

She tried the door even though she already knew what she'd find. It was locked.

But on the other end of the attic, on the far side of the room, was a single window. The glass was dirty, and when she tried to peer through it she couldn't see anything because it was nighttime outside.

Libby tried to open it, but it was locked. But then she found the latch.

The small window opened and she stuck her head out. The cool air hit her, a stark contrast to the dank attic room, and the wind blew through her hair.

After her eyes adjusted, she could barely make out the mansion's roof that surrounded the window. She leaned out and explored with her hands, finding rough shingles. The slope of the roof was very steep, and the darkness would make climbing on it even more dangerous.

I have no choice. I have to get out of here right now.

The wind rustled the leaves of a nearby oak tree. She could see the movements of the branches from the light of the full moon, one of which scraped against the roof like a giant claw.

If that branch was thick enough, she could use it like a bridge to the tree's trunk, then slide down. She'd have some scrapes and bruises and maybe a hard drop at the end, but at that moment she would have taken a lot worse just to escape.

Libby threw one leg over the edge of the window and planted a foot on the sloped shingles.

Once, when she was younger, she'd insisted on helping her dad clean out his gutters. She'd climbed the ladder and followed him onto the roof, leaning against the slope as he'd instructed, but she still remembered the way the ground had loomed far below her. The feeling had made her light-headed, and she'd chickened out.

That was the last time she'd ever been on a roof. She tried not to think about that now that she was two or three times higher up.

Both feet on the shingles, she leaned heavily to the left to keep her balance. She gripped the windowpane with one hand as she took small steps toward the tree branch.

In order to get there, she'd have to let go of the window and walk without its support. She took several deep, steadying breaths.

You can do this. Come on. Dad needs my help.

And just as she was about to let go, she heard a noise from inside the attic. It sounded like a loud thump, maybe a slammed door. She gasped and looked back through the window, thinking Patrick had returned. But she didn't see anyone.

If he caught her going out the window, then he'd tie her up again for sure. This was her only chance. She had to make a break for the tree branch and get away now.

But when she looked back toward the tree, to her escape, she was not alone. A high-pitched shriek burst from her mouth.

A figure had appeared on the roof, a monstrous shadow that was darker than the night. He stood on all fours and appeared to have long hair that blew in the wind.

And his eyes. They glowed blood red as they glared at her.

Libby froze in his presence, barely remembering to hold on to the edge of the windowpane. Her foot scraped an inch down the roof's slope, sending a nervous jolt through her stomach. She cried out again and found her balance just in time.

The shadow's negative energy bored into her, weighing her down, making her feel like she was being crushed.

Libby knew what she was looking at. Her dad had taught her what kind of creature this was.

The shadow took a step closer, walking on both his hands and feet like some sort of animal.

Then he opened his mouth. At the back of his throat, a ball of bright fire formed. The flames lit up the darkness around her, and Libby felt the blast of heat on her face.

He breathes fire. Like a dragon.

Libby knew if she stood there much longer, she'd be toast. Literally.

As quickly as she could, Libby pulled herself back into the attic and tumbled through the window.

She landed hard on the floor, the back of her head bouncing off the wood, a sharp pain shooting through her skull.

This demon. This is what my dad must have discovered.

The source of all the crazy things that happened at the church.

Trust me when I say if you try to do anything rash, you won't like what happens to you, Patrick had said.

Libby shot up and threw the window closed, then locked it again. She backed away just as the demon's face appeared in front of the glass, the red eyes glaring through at her.

A silent warning to stay put. To not try that again.

All of a sudden, Libby understood what was going on.

This preacher thinks he's speaking with an angel.

But now she'd seen the creature that was really pulling their strings. Her dad must have discovered the same thing.

Where are you, Dad? Libby thought, unable to tear her eyes away from the demon's. Finally, the shadow moved away from the window, leaving her alone. She knew that if she tried to escape again, it would only reappear. The ultimate prison guard.

She sat down on the bed, her rear nearly missing the edge of the mattress.

I'm totally stuck. There's no way I can get around that thing.

Her only hope was that her dad would come for her. And it needed to be soon. She didn't know what kind of "prayers to Azora" Patrick had in mind for her, but she did know she didn't want to find out.

30

R and trudged down the path that led to Simon's church. His legs were barely able to carry him and wanted to give out now that he'd reached his destination. He stumbled side to side as he forced himself a bit farther. He figured that, from a distance, he looked like a zombie from one of his favorite movies.

The church came into view. His Jeep was parked in front and Rand remembered he'd left the keys in the ignition to keep the headlights on during his meeting with Deckard Arcan. Simon must have driven it back after Rand had gotten arrested.

Rand burst through the doors of the foyer and fell into the dark sanctuary. "Simon!" His voice boomed all around him. "Simon!"

Noises from the back. A door on the side of the sanctuary opened and the old pastor came out, leaning on his cane and looking worried.

"Rand." He flipped a switch on the wall and the dim lights above flared to life. "Where have you been?"

"Simon," Rand said. He tried to walk down the aisle, but he nearly collapsed. He had to catch the edge of a nearby pew to break his fall.

"Whoa," Simon said, limping over to him as quickly as the old man's body would let him. "Easy. You look terrible." Simon slid underneath Rand's left arm and supported him. The old man was surprisingly strong for someone who required a cane. "Come on. Let's get you in the back."

"Water," Rand gasped.

"I've got everything you need. Just work with me here."

Rand allowed Simon to assist him to the room behind the sanctuary.

The back section of the church was a small kitchen, further cementing Rand's suspicion that the old pastor lived there full-time.

Rand collapsed into a chair at the meager table, all his limbs feeling as if they each weighed a ton. Simon busied himself at the counter and soon brought Rand a simple sandwich on a white plate and a pitcher of water. Rand drank straight from the pitcher and devoured the sandwich without even tasting it.

"Oh. I'll make you another sandwich."

"I'm fine," Rand said, but Simon ignored him and continued. He brought the plate back, this time having made three more. While Rand ate, Simon refilled the water jug and also brought a blue sports drink. Rand wrenched off the top and downed the entire bottle in a series of unbroken gulps.

"Have you been hiding out somewhere?" Simon asked.

"I've been in prison."

Simon furrowed his brow. All the sandwiches were gone, and now Rand leaned against the chair as they roiled in his stomach. He'd eaten too fast.

"Yes, but only for half a night."

Rand looked at him. "What?"

"You... escaped."

Rand blinked, trying to figure out what he missed. "Yeah, but... when?"

"Three days ago."

Rand shook his head. "I got out maybe an hour ago."

Simon leaned forward, standing with his cane in the space

between his thighs. "After you were arrested, I drove your car to the police station, but no one was there. I woke early in the morning and planned to go back to speak with Sheriff Jones about your release, but Jones came here before I could leave.

"He told me you'd escaped and questioned me about where you'd gone. I honestly didn't know. He searched the entire church up and down, thinking I was hiding you, but found nothing. He came back two days later to look again."

"There was time distortion, Simon," Rand told him. "These past three days were one long night to me. No one ever came to the police station. My only visitor was my little demon friend. He tried to make me kill myself, but I refused. He eventually released me."

"Demon friend?"

"Shindael," Rand said. "My own personal demon who follows me around." He waved his hand. "Long story."

"I'm sorry this all happened to you," Simon said. "You are truly doing the Lord's work."

Rand choked on the water as he drank more. "I don't know about that." He wiped his mouth.

"What will you do now?"

"I have to go back to Deckard. I need to remove the demon that's possessing him before he hurts anyone else."

"You can't go tonight," Simon said.

Rand looked at him. "Why? I have to. If we wait, worse things could happen."

"Think about it. Your demon friend freed you from the jail for a reason. He wants you to rush back in. You'll be playing right into his hands."

Rand thought on that for a moment. The old pastor had a point.

"You're in no shape to battle the demonic," Simon went on. "You know this. State of mind and strength of body is everything and right now, you have neither."

Rand took a deep breath and accepted Simon's reasoning. "Okay. What should I do?"

"You *know* what you should do. Go home. Get some rest. Sleep and pray. Recover. Then return, and we will both be stronger to fight another day. These demons want you weak because they know how powerful you are at full strength."

Rand nodded slowly. He hated leaving a job undone and postponed. "Okay. You're right."

Simon leaned forward and patted Rand's shoulder. "You're a good man, Rand Casey. I wish I'd known you before when I was having my own encounters with these things."

Careful what you wish for. Knowing me doesn't make for an easy life.

"I appreciate it."

He suddenly remembered Libby. "Do you have a phone I can borrow?"

Simon pulled his old flip phone from his pocket and handed it to Rand. He dialed Libby's number from memory. The line only rang a few times before her voicemail picked up.

"I guess it is late," Rand said. His daughter had not heard from him the entire time he was locked up and was surely worried. In the past, he had gone long stretches of time without getting in touch with her when he was involved in cases. It worried her, sure, but she knew it was the nature of the beast. He felt bad putting her through it every time. "I'll just head home and call her tomorrow."

"Are you well enough to drive?"

"Yeah." Although Rand wasn't entirely sure that was true.

"You can sleep here if you want."

"I appreciate it, but I best get home." He'd have to gather his backup spiritual cleansing supplies and get a new phone. The belongings confiscated by the sheriff were likely long gone.

"Just be careful, Rand," Simon said. "This town needs you."

"When the time comes to face Deckard Arcan again, can I count on you?" Rand asked.

Simon seemed offended by the question. "Without a doubt. I know how important these matters are."

"Thank you for the hospitality. And for all your guidance."

Rand left him there and passed through the sanctuary on his way out of the church. In the sanctuary, the statue of Jesus on the cross caught his eye and gave him pause.

"Where were you when I was locked up?" he whispered. "Why did you allow a demon to come instead?"

Am I just a sacrifice? Like you were?

Was his entire mission to fight the demonic just a hopeless mess? Destined to end in doom and failure for him, his family, and everyone he tried to help. If Shindael was to be believed, it was.

But it sure would help if God spoke to him even half as clearly as the devil did.

31

For the first time in a long time, Patrick actually felt cooped up.

His bedroom was small, sure, but he did not need much. Pastor D had been very generous with allowing him to live in the mansion at all. He'd never felt ungrateful, or that it was too little, or not what he needed.

But that night, he felt the walls were closing in on him. That he couldn't breathe. That he couldn't focus on his prayers to Azora.

It was probably because his beloved was now in the house. She was up one flight of stairs, on the third floor. Waiting to be introduced to Azora. Soon after that, she would become his wife.

The prospect excited him. Made him giddy. He was thrilled that Azora had willed this girl into his life, and he could not wait to get started on his new path with her.

Hopefully, Pastor D would allow him a larger room once they became man and wife. There was a spare bedroom on the first floor that he'd been scoping out for a while, one that was large and empty, never used.

Patrick walked into the hallway, feeling stuffy in his own

bedroom. The air was clearer in the hall and immediately started to ease his senses. It was night, and as usual, the house was still and silent. He wondered what Libby was doing upstairs.

He adjusted his glasses and smoothed his hair. Every bit of him wanted to go upstairs and see her, but Pastor D had warned him about spending too much time with her before she had been properly taught about Azora. She would only lead to sin and temptation, he had said, more than she already had.

Patrick knew Pastor D was right. But still, his body squirmed with anticipation. He took a deep, steadying breath and tried to remind himself that their marriage, and subsequent consummation, was near. If he could only be strong for a little while longer, then Azora would bless him.

He went downstairs into the large foyer of the mansion. He peeked in on Pastor D's study and found the man in prayer before the fireplace, huge flames roaring and creating an uncomfortable heat inside. Patrick left him there and headed toward the front door. He needed fresh air.

Although the night was dark, Patrick froze when he saw a figure lying on the steps of the porch, as if both legs were broken and they'd been trying to crawl up the steps before their body had simply given out.

"Help me," came a woman's voice, barely audible.

Patrick rushed to the figure and crouched down. Once he was closer, he saw who it was.

"Chloe?"

Patrick knew about Chloe's advanced cancer and poor condition, but the woman had always walked into church on her own two feet, ready to give her all to the Lord. Now she was unable to even stand.

Did she crawl all the way here?

The sickly woman looked up at him, barely able to keep her eyes open. Her lids fluttered. She appeared as if she'd been trying to cross a desert and had run out of water. "Oh, Patrick. You're here. Thank the Lord."

"Chloe, are you okay? What are you doing here?"

"I'm dying, Patrick," she said, smiling. "And I need healing."

"Come on," Patrick said. He scooped her up, arms under her legs and neck, and carried her inside. She threw her arms around his neck and held onto him feebly, looking up at him as if he were saving her from a burning building.

Once inside, he kicked the door closed behind him, then gingerly laid her on the floor, unable to hold her longer.

"Please," she said, "I want to see Pastor D."

Patrick glanced uncertainly toward the study door. "He's... busy." But it felt terrible to say to a woman in Chloe's condition.

"Please," she said again. "I've come all this way."

Pastor D had always instructed Patrick to never interrupt him during his nightly prayers. Patrick didn't know how angry Pastor D would be because Patrick had never done it. But surely Pastor D wouldn't mind being interrupted when one of his congregation came to him in the middle of the night.

He'd come out to meet Gerald Roberson. Why wouldn't Chloe be the same?

"Wait here," Patrick said, touching Chloe's cheek. It was slick with sweat. "I'll bring him."

"Thank you so much." She smiled as best she could.

Patrick rushed to the study and hesitated at the door. It was cracked open, as it always was, but that did not mean people were welcome inside. He waited there for a few minutes, watching Pastor D on his hands and knees before the fire as if worshipping it. Sometimes Pastor D was able to divine his presence. In those cases, Patrick did not feel like he was interrupting. But this time, Pastor D continued on, chanting in an unknown language that only he knew, oblivious to Patrick being there.

Patrick heard Chloe cough and groan in pain from the foyer.

He raised his hand and knocked lightly on the door. Pastor D's head snapped up then slowly turned to the side. "Who is it?"

"Patrick."

"What do you want? I'm praying."

Patrick cleared his throat. "It's Chloe. She's here."

"Bring her to one of the spare bedrooms and let her stay the night."

"It's more than that, sir. She's very sick. She's requesting to see you."

Pastor D was silent for several long moments as he considered.

Surely he would not turn away one of his flock, Patrick thought.

Pastor D rose to his feet and fastened his robe around his waist. He left the study, brushing by Patrick without a word. Patrick followed him back to the main foyer.

"Oh!" Chloe cried when she saw the pastor. She still lay on the ground, her arms reaching out to him like he was a vision sent from heaven.

Pastor D crouched over her, the stern expression Patrick had received having melted into one of genuine love and concern. "Chloe. What are you doing here at this time of night? Is everything all right?"

It struck Patrick how quickly Pastor D could switch gears. The demeanor he'd had with Patrick and the one he now showed Chloe was completely different. It even frightened Patrick a bit.

"Something is wrong," Chloe said, gripping both of Pastor D's hands. Her own looked like the shriveled claws of a vulture. "It's finally happening. I'm dying."

Pastor D put a hand on her cheek and supported her head off the floor. "Then why did you not go to a hospital?"

Chloe only smiled. "Because my faith is stronger than that. I know that God's power can allow you to heal better than any doctor in the world."

Pastor D smiled. "You have a great faith, Chloe. And you will be rewarded for that."

Chloe began to sob. The woman, although dying, appeared so happy.

Pastor D stood and looked down at her, saying nothing for a long while. Patrick realized he was holding his breath, waiting to see what the man would do next. Would he pray over her? If so, would she be healed? Would she get up and walk out of the house just as Gerald had risen from his wheelchair in the tent?

Instead, he only turned to Patrick. "Take her to the attic."

"I'm sorry?"

"Take her upstairs. I will be with her shortly. I need time to prepare."

Patrick wondered how much more preparation he needed—Pastor D had been in the study all night, just as he had been every night.

"But…" Patrick was no doctor, yet just by looking at Chloe he knew the woman didn't have much time left.

"Do as I say, Patrick." He walked away from them and disappeared down the hallway and back into his study.

Chloe still cried tears of gratitude. "He's going to help me. I'm finally going to be free."

"Come on, dear," Patrick said, scooping her up the same way he had when he'd found her on the front porch steps. "Let's bring you upstairs so you can rest. You can wait for Pastor D up there."

Hopefully he comes in time.

LIBBY WOKE to the sound of the attic door opening.

It was Patrick Perryman, and he carried someone in his arms.

"Move!" he barked.

Libby shot up from the bed just before Patrick dumped the limp form right where she had been lying.

She recognized the woman, but it took Libby a few moments to place her—Chloe, from the church. She knew Justin.

Her illness had been evident before, but now she looked even worse. Libby wasn't sure she'd ever seen someone so frail.

"What's going on?" Libby asked.

"She's very sick," Patrick told her. "She will wait here until Pastor D heals her."

Libby stared at him in disbelief, although she wasn't sure why she'd expected anything sane to happen anymore. "Are you serious? Look at her. She needs a hospital!"

"She needs prayer," Patrick said. "She will stay up here with you. Try not to disturb her too much. Pastor D will see her soon."

Then he left, locking the door behind him.

Libby knelt down at the bedside. Chloe's eyes wandered, but finally seemed to find Libby. Recognition dawned.

"I remember you from last week. At church. It was your first time. Libby, was it?"

"Yes, ma'am. What's wrong? Are you in pain?"

"Just my cancer," Chloe said. "But soon enough, it will be gone. I have faith in God and Azora and Pastor D."

"We need to get you to a doctor," Libby told her. But Libby was trapped there, helpless.

"No doctor, dear," Chloe said, resting a bony hand on Libby's arm. "I came here by choice."

Libby could not fathom the level of belief the woman had in Deckard Arcan. But then again, after seeing him make that man walk—or so they all believed—perhaps some people were willing to believe that he could do anything.

It made tears well up in her eyes. Deckard had deceived Chloe, and she'd bought in. Preying on the diminishing hopes of a dying woman.

Libby stood and pulled the comforter up to Chloe's chin and tucked her in. Chloe gave her a wan smile. "Thank you, dear." Then she closed her eyes and fell asleep.

Libby paced around the room, wracking her brain for some way to call for help. Not just for herself, but to get Chloe the medical care she needed.

The night passed and no one came, not even Pastor D. As the sun rose and the light of dawn shone through the single attic window, Libby eyed the sleeping woman in the bed. For the first time since she'd arrived, she appeared truly at peace and not in pain.

Libby pressed two shaky fingers to Chloe's throat. She waited in silence, trying to feel for a pulse.

Nothing.
She'd passed in the night.

32

T he dawn had come, chilly and grey, by the time Rand made it home.

When he got there, Tessa's blue SUV was parked in the driveway. She was out of the car and pacing around the lawn, phone to her ear, while Bill looked on.

When she spotted his Jeep, she immediately hung up.

Rand got a sinking feeling in the pit of his stomach.

He parked and threw open the Jeep's door. "What's going on?"

"Where the hell is our daughter?" Tessa shrieked at him.

"What?"

"Our daughter!" Her face was hysterical, and she shoved his chest. "She said she was going to meet you and I haven't heard from her! Or you! Where is she?"

Rand's mind raced as he tried to find words. "I don't know."

Tessa's eyes slowly went wide when she realized what he'd just said. "You don't know? What do you mean you *don't know?*"

"I haven't spoken to her since Sunday."

"Yes, you have! She called and told me she talked to you and that you told her to meet you in Finnick!"

Rand's mouth went dry. He looked back and forth between her and Bill. "It... wasn't me."

"Then who was it? She said it was you!"

Anxiety coursed through Rand's entire body. It slowly turned to panic as he put together the pieces of what was going on.

The demon mimicked me.

Rand knew it in his gut.

"Where the hell have you been?" Tessa demanded.

"On a case—"

"What the fuck does that have to do with our daughter? Why is she involved?" Tessa gripped his shirt, shaking him back and forth. A seam in the collar ripped.

Bill stepped in and tried to pull Tessa away, but she resisted.

"Tessa—" Rand began.

"Why is she caught up in this? What does she have to do with all these freaks and weirdos you deal with?"

"If you—"

"Why do you keep doing this?" Tessa continued to scream at him. Bill was not strong enough to restrain her. She beat on his chest, his face, his shoulders, and Rand stood there and took it. "Can't you see it doesn't affect only you? It's ruined your entire family!"

Shindael's words came through Tessa's mouth. He deserved every bit of beating she gave him.

Finally, when he'd had enough, he caught her wrists in his hands and gripped them tight, subduing her. She tried to pull out of his grasp, but eventually she exhausted all her energy. Her face was streaked with tears.

"How long ago did she say she was going to meet me?"

"Wednesday."

Rand looked at Bill. The man had tried to be calm and impartial during the whole thing, but he still looked sick with worry.

"She said I told her to meet me in Finnick, right?"

"Yes!" Tessa shouted. "Where the hell have you been? Why don't you have a phone?"

"Okay." Rand released Tessa's wrists, and she finally started to calm down. "I'm going to get her."

"You don't even know where she is!"

"I will find her. Trust me."

"I *don't* trust you, Rand!" Tessa shouted. "I can never trust anything you do or say when you're doing a case because of all the weird stuff that happens! I'm sick of it, and this time you've gone too far. Libby has been *missing* for three days!"

"Tessa—"

"I was one minute away from calling the police. I don't give a shit about your 'no police' rule! If you want to go and get possessed by demons or abducted by aliens or whatever the fuck it is you do, then fine! But you have no right to keep involving Libby."

He's behind this, Rand thought. And as he pictured Deckard Arcan luring his daughter to him, the same rage that filled Tessa consumed him as well.

He walked away from Tessa and toward the front door of his house.

"Where are you going?" she shrieked. "Are you listening to me?"

Rand unlocked the door and rushed to his bedroom, where he threw open his closet, shuffled some clothes aside, and found the empty shoebox that he knew was there. He threw off the lid, revealing his small black handgun. He grabbed it, tucked it into the back of his waistband, and lowered his jacket over it.

It was something he never would have brought on a case. Never had before.

But Deckard Arcan had crossed the line. Rand wasn't going to take any chances.

Rand returned to the driveway. Then, he climbed into the Jeep and started the ignition. "I'm going to get her. If you don't hear from me by tomorrow morning, then you can call the police. But until then, don't get them involved."

Calling the police whenever the supernatural was involved *always* made things worse. He'd learned that lesson the hard way.

He closed the door and rolled down the window.

Tessa only stared at him in disbelief, her face completely streaked with tears. "Sometimes I think you are the worst thing that's ever happened to me, Randolph."

"Give me your phone," Rand said, sticking his palm out the window.

"What?"

"I need a phone because I lost mine. Give me yours so I can keep in touch."

"Here," Bill said, digging his own phone out of his pocket and handing it to Rand. "Take mine and call us as soon as you find Libby. The passcode is Tessa's birthday."

Rand reversed out of the driveway and tore off down the road. Although his body was still weak and fatigued, new energy crashed through him, and he knew it would not subside until he found his daughter.

Deckard Arcan, he thought as he quickly exceeded the speed limit. *You've gone too far with this one.*

33

Rand drove furiously through the roads of Finnick, remembering only at the last second to slow down. If he were pulled over, there would be trouble. Surely the sheriff was on the lookout for him after his miraculous escape from the prison cell.

He had not slept. There was nothing left in the fuel tank of his body. He was driven only by adrenaline, anxiety, and anger.

That man has my daughter. I know it.

There was no time. He could not afford to stop. He had to press on. Had to find her before it was too late.

He found the dirt road that would bring him to Mount Grace Church. He gunned the gas as his big tires threatened to get caught in the mud that still lingered from all the heavy rainstorms.

When he pulled up in front of the church, Simon Cole came outside the front doors of the foyer, giving him a curious look.

Rand dropped out of his Jeep and hurried over to him.

"Rand," Simon said as he approached. "Why are you back so soon?"

"I need your help," he said, the words spilling out of him faster and more desperately than he'd intended. But it was how he felt.

"Rand..."

"They have Libby. My daughter." When he was near enough, Rand grabbed the older man by the elbows and thought he saw a hint of fear in Simon's eyes behind the concern.

"Please, Rand," Simon said, voice gentle as always. "You need to sleep and rest."

"No!" he snapped. "I can't! There's no time. Deckard has taken my daughter."

Simon pulled out of his grasp with surprising strength. "I'm not going anywhere until you calm down." He spoke firmly, as if scolding Rand.

And although Rand knew he was desperate and acting like it, he realized that if anything would get done, he needed to settle down. Usually, he remembered this, but when his daughter was concerned...

"You know I will help you," Simon said, speaking gentler now. "But we need to do this correctly. Please come inside."

Simon kept a comforting hand on Rand's back as they walked together into the church. It was toasty in the sanctuary, a stark contrast to the chilled air of the early morning.

He was pretty sure he stank of body odor. His hair was matted and greasy, and his eyes were heavy and dry in his skull. He hadn't changed clothes in days. Simon Cole didn't know him—the man had every right to consider him an insane vagabond and toss him out.

"You're okay," Simon said, rubbing his back and guiding him to sit in the pew. Rand went down, his body thanking him for allowing it to rest.

But Rand's mind snapped into overdrive. "I'm sorry, Simon, but we don't have time. They have Libby."

"How do you know?"

"Because when I got home, her mother told me she came here looking for me, that she'd gotten a phone call from me to meet me in Finnick. But I was locked up for days."

Simon's face turned grim as he listened. "Mimicry."

"Exactly. Whatever demon has taken Deckard has lured Libby here."

"Right," Simon said. He was quiet while he thought it over. "I do not think they mean to harm her."

"I don't either," Rand said. "They only want to get to me. It worked." He stood, no longer feeling comfortable sitting and talking. He was ready for action.

"What are you intending to do?" Simon asked, giving him a strange look—as if afraid of the answer.

"Do you know where Deckard lives? Can you take me there?"

"He won't be at home," Simon said.

"Why?"

"Because it's Sunday morning."

Rand digested that information for a few moments. *I've been at this for an entire week already? That time in the jail...*

He'd have a lot of explaining to do to his boss as well. He'd missed work for cases before, but never for this long.

"Fine. We'll confront him at the tent. Will you come with me?" Without waiting for an answer, Rand started walking toward the door.

"Rand."

He stopped and turned. Simon had not moved to follow him. "What did I feel in your waistband?"

Simon's eyes bored into him, and Rand knew it was a rhetorical question. He'd almost forgotten it was back there. Simon must have felt it when he was comforting him.

He reached behind and withdrew the handgun, showing it to the old pastor.

Simon looked worried, and Rand did not blame him. Still, the man kept his composure. "A curious thing to bring to a spiritual fight."

"I'm well aware, but this has crossed a line. They have my daughter. I'll do whatever it takes to get her back."

"If we go to the church right now, who will you shoot?"

"No one."

"Then why do you have it?"

Rand and Simon stared at each other for several long, silent moments. He had no good answer. He'd grabbed the gun in a wave of desperation and confusion and unclear thinking. He'd been highly emotional—and still was—but Simon was calming him down.

But he already knew he would bring it with him. And brandish it in Deckard's face if he had to.

"I'm going now, Simon," Rand said. "You're either coming with me or you're not."

"Promise me you won't do anything rash."

"It depends on what Deckard does first."

Rand turned and walked out of the church. He was almost to his Jeep when he realized that Simon was actually following him.

"Give me your keys," Simon said. "If you're going, you can't just walk right up to the tent. Not after everything that's happened."

"You know a better way?" Rand asked.

"A side entrance." Simon held out his hand.

Rand considered it for a few moments before dropping his key into the man's palm.

Simon drove the Jeep while Rand sat in the passenger seat. The gun was tucked back into his waistband, covered by his jacket and poking into his spine.

"You don't want to confront Deckard when the entire congregation is around," Simon said. "This matter with your daughter is a private and personal one."

Quite personal, Rand thought.

He still did not know what he would do when they got there. He already figured he'd feel like rushing in and tearing the man's head off his shoulders, but that was why Simon was there—to keep him from doing anything too brazen.

Simon parked in the lot of an old thrift store.

Rand looked around. "Where are we?"

"Finnick is such a small town. I'm surprised you still haven't learned your way."

"I haven't been focused on the geography."

"Follow me."

Simon led him across the lot and behind the store into a thick copse of trees. They trudged over the foliage, sticks cracking and leaves crunching underfoot. Rand pushed low-hanging branches out of his face, and the rough bark caught onto the sleeves of his jacket as if the trees were trying to physically keep him from proceeding.

Rand remembered the area surrounding the tent church and already knew where they would come out.

When they arrived at the edge of the woods, he saw the clearing. They were to the right of the tent, and since all sides were open Rand could see the gathered Sunday-morning crowd sitting on the benches and standing in the back and along the edges, everyone eagerly waiting for their pastor.

The two men stayed hidden behind the trees. Rand checked his watch, but the hands were still stuck at an incorrect time.

He scanned the crowds, although he could not make out much from where he crouched in their hiding place. "I don't see Libby."

"If she's not here, then she might be at Deckard's home," Simon said.

Rand shuddered to think what that could mean. Was she tied up? Drugged? Worse?

"Good morning and happy Sunday." the voice sounded through the microphone. Patrick Perryman stood on the stage.

Rand ground his teeth. *That little runt. I wonder if he had anything to do with this.*

"Happy Sunday." The congregation responded in unison.

Rand noticed there was a table on the back of the raised platform with something on top, covered by a sheet. Rand strained his eyes to see, but his fatigue made his vision blurry, and his desperate situation was probably causing his imagination to run wild.

It looks like a covered body.

He stared at it, trying to convince himself that wasn't true.

Surely it was like seeing a shape in the clouds—you saw only what your brain was already thinking about on some level.

He refused to entertain the thought that Libby was under there. Even a millisecond of consideration was inappropriate.

But still. Whatever was under that sheet resembled a body.

"I won't stay up here long," Patrick went on. "This is a very exciting morning, one that Pastor D has been praying about for a while. I say that every Sunday, but this time it's serious." The crowd chuckled. "No, seriously. You all know what to expect from Pastor D and Azora by now, and today you're going to get even more of it."

There was a round of applause, and Patrick placed the microphone back on the stand and left.

Then, Deckard Arcan came. He wore a light blue tailored suit, silver hair combed and perfectly in place, beard trimmed, and a beaming smile. The congregation erupted into cheers when he took the stage. He stood for several minutes, basking in the standing ovation, before signaling everyone to calm down and listen up.

"Good morning and happy Sunday," he said into the microphone.

"Happy Sunday," the crowd intoned back, louder than the rendition they'd given Patrick.

"Patrick was right," Deckard said. "This is a *very* special Sunday. I have spent many nights in prayers with Azora, and I have always known deep in my heart that this day would come. And now today is that day."

Another round of cheers.

"Pastor D!" someone shouted and stood from their seat. The man waved to get Deckard's attention. "My gout has gotten to be too much. I can barely do my work, and I could lose my job."

Deckard held out his hand, and the man quieted. "I hear your pain, brother. But I assure you that you are thinking too small. Today is different. It's a day where you will all witness and remember the true power of Azora."

What is he talking about? Rand thought. The last time he'd promised that, the fiasco with Gerald Roberson had happened. What did he have up his sleeve?

Once Deckard had the congregation silent again, he said, "Brothers and sisters, I have some bad news and some good news. First, the bad. Our sister Chloe Baker has passed away." Murmurs through the crowd. Deckard spoke over them. "For those of you who didn't know, Chloe was a member of this church since the beginning. She was diagnosed with pancreatic cancer, and it only got worse over time. Still, she remained faithful, and her dedication will pay off."

"You could have healed her!" someone shouted at him. It was the first form of heckling Rand had ever heard toward Deckard Arcan.

Deckard rounded on that man. "Where is your faith in the plan of Azora? Have you spent *your* nights speaking with him? I think not. Now listen."

The scolded man shut up.

Deckard let the congregation linger in silence for a few moments before he said, "Patrick and Hoby. Bring her."

Hoby was apparently the name of the big bodyguard who never seemed far from Deckard. He and Patrick returned to the stage and each gripped an end of the table and lifted it like two men moving furniture. It tipped toward Patrick as he struggled with the weight. The pair brought the table to the forefront of the raised platform, the object on top of it remaining covered the whole time. Once the table was lowered, they disappeared on either side of the stage.

The congregation remained silent as they waited, as did Rand. His nerves twisted violently in his stomach. Whatever was on that table looked like a sacrifice on an altar.

Simon seemed ill as he watched what was happening.

"You are all very fortunate to be here this morning," Deckard said as he went to stand behind the table. He faced the audience. "You will be the first to witness the true power of Azora. This is something that hasn't been seen since Biblical times."

That was the moment that Rand thought the crowd would have

cheered, but no one made a sound. He figured that, to them, perhaps the shape underneath the sheet also looked like a body.

"Only the angel Azora can give life back when it has been taken away," Deckard continued. "I have heard this in my prayers, and I have seen it in my dreams and in my visions. Today, it shall be."

Nervous murmuring in the congregation.

Deckard raised his hands and spread them, similar to that of Jesus on the cross. "Azora!" he called, his voice booming. "Come down and join us here. We are ready to be witnesses to your awesome power."

"This can't happen," Rand said. "She's under there. Chloe."

"What is he doing?" It sounded like Simon knew what Deckard had planned but just didn't want to believe it.

Rand had witnessed a lot of crazy stuff in his life, and most of it would never be believed by anyone who sat and listened to his tales. But this... this was something completely different. He had never seen this attempted before, not even by the craziest of people who had gone down the occult rabbit hole.

"Rand, what is he doing?" Simon asked again.

"Necromancy."

34

Simon shook his head. "It can't be. It won't work." He looked at Rand, his eyes wide and afraid. "Will it?"

"I've never seen it happen, nor have I known anyone to ever try it."

"What do we do?" Simon asked.

Then Deckard's voice changed. He spoke in a different tongue, a language that Rand did not recognize at all. The man's mouth moved, vomiting incoherent words over Chloe's body. His eyes were closed, lost in a trance. It seemed he believed wholeheartedly that what he was doing would be successful.

"We have to stop this," Rand said.

"There's no way this will actually happen," Simon said, placing a hand on Rand's arm and squeezing. "Right? That lady will not come back to life."

"Remember Gerald Roberson?"

"But…"

"We can't just sit here and insist that it isn't going to work," Rand said. "We have to do something. These people can't see this."

The words spilling from Deckard's mouth affected Rand in a way he couldn't pinpoint. Merely hearing them made him feel sickened, afraid, and like he wanted to turn and run. The people in the congregation must have felt the same—those who stood took several steps back. The ones sitting looked away as if they could not bear to watch.

And Rand knew he was hearing a voice from hell. Whatever demon that had entered Deckard spoke through him. Rand had already seen the power the entity lent to the preacher, and if he let this go on, then Chloe was going to come back to life.

The sheet moved. As if the body underneath it gave a short twitch with its hand. The crowd gasped in unison. Some stood, ready to flee.

"Hold strong and do not be afraid," Deckard commanded his audience. "Azora is here. It is almost complete." Deckard looked down at the covered body in front of him. "Chloe Baker. Return to us. Your time was ended too soon by a disease you did not deserve. Return and live out the rest of your natural life in the light of Azora."

The sheet moved again, stronger, like a leg kicking back to life.

More shocked cries came from the crowd.

"Rand," Simon said, desperate.

"I'm stopping this." Rand rose from where he crouched and started walking toward the tent.

He knew these people couldn't witness a body raised from the dead by a demonic ritual. If they did, they would believe in Deckard forever and be cemented into his cult. At the moment, he only had one idea of how to break up this madness.

He pulled the gun from his waistband. He clicked off the safety, pointed it toward the sky, and fired a single shot.

35

The gunshot cracked, echoing off the trees on the edge of the clearing.

The entire place erupted into chaos. The crowd screamed and ducked, dropping low and putting their hands over their heads.

Deckard's presentation ceased and he recoiled backwards. Rand watched as Hoby leapt to Deckard's side and tried to pull him off the stage, but Deckard resisted.

Rand fired again, another shot that somehow seemed louder than the first. The people of the congregation scattered in every direction. In only a few moments, the tent was empty.

Only Deckard and Hoby remained. Deckard was on the raised platform, glaring at Rand.

Rand met Deckard's gaze as he walked to the tent's opening. The two men stood off, waiting for the crowds to finish scattering.

About a minute later, the clearing was quiet. Everyone had fled.

"Randolph Casey," Deckard said, stepping down from the stage, never taking his eyes off Rand. "You have gone too far this time."

Libby.

Rand raised the gun and leveled it at Deckard. Deckard stopped advancing, although he did not seem afraid.

Rand had never pointed a gun at anyone before—ever. But as he faced Deckard then, he saw a man who threatened his family, and it was the only thing he knew to do.

"What are you planning?" Deckard said. "You want to shoot me? Go ahead. I'll be a martyr for Azora. I have faith the angel will make quick work of you after you ruined the greatest miracle he's ever done."

"I'm here for my daughter, Deckard," Rand said. "Give her back."

There was movement over Deckard's shoulder, but it did not distract him. Patrick Perryman appeared from behind the raised platform where he'd probably been hiding.

"You heard me," Rand said. "Libby. Now."

"Your daughter came to us willingly," Deckard said. "She was interested in the teachings of Azora, and—"

"*Deckard!*"

The man fell silent, snarling at Rand. Then he finally spoke. "You want the girl? Fine. You can have her."

Behind him, Patrick Perryman looked shocked. Maybe even a little upset.

"Where is she?"

"She's at my home. Not far from here. I'll give her to you, but only on one condition."

"And that is?"

"That you take her place."

What is this, a hostage negotiation?

"You don't make the terms. I'm the one with the gun."

"And I'm the one with Azora. You remember what happened last time you tried to attack me, don't you?" Deckard smirked. "If you want to try again, then go ahead and shoot me. I have all the faith in the world that Azora will protect me."

Rand had already fallen victim to the incredible strength the demon gave to Deckard. It very well could be that a bullet would not hurt him. Also, it was possible that the demon would do nothing, and the shot would kill Deckard, making Rand a murderer. Rand definitely could not shoot him. And Deckard knew it.

The gun had been helpful in disrupting Deckard's demonic ritual, but it was useless against a perfectly possessed man.

"You understand now that this is ridiculous," Deckard said. "And surely you realize that I don't care about your daughter—only you. So put the gun down, and let's sort this out like the gentlemen we are."

Just as Rand figured. They were using Libby to get to him. And it had worked. *Of course it had.*

Rand lowered his weapon.

"That's the right move. Good. Go ahead, Hoby." The big man advanced on him. Hoby gripped Rand's wrist and confiscated the gun from his hand. Hoby tucked it into his inside coat pocket, then spun Rand around to frisk him for any more weapons. Finding none, Hoby grabbed Rand's shoulder, squeezing it hard enough to hurt him, and pushed him forward, forcing him to walk ahead. The man was so strong that Rand couldn't have broken out of the grip, even if he wanted to.

"Hoby will drive you to my house," Deckard said. "He will let your daughter go. Then you will remain behind."

As they walked, Rand caught Patrick's eye. The man looked frightened and confused.

Forget him, Rand thought. *All that matters now is getting Libby back.* And he prayed Deckard would keep his word.

36

J ustin heard the shots at the same time as everyone else. His first instinct was to duck low, hands over his head. Everyone around him did the same. Then, in the next split second, everyone scattered. He followed suit almost involuntarily.

In the ensuing chaos, he bumped into people running in every direction. They almost knocked him off his feet. Justin flailed his arms, nearly spilling to the ground.

Pastor D.

The shooter had come to assassinate him. *But why?* He ventured a quick glance over his shoulder and saw that Pastor D was with his big bodyguard, still standing, but Justin did not wait around—he only kept running.

Then he caught a glimpse of the shooter.

Mr. Rand.

Libby's father held a pistol upright, having fired into the air instead of the crowd.

What in the world is going on?

He slowed his run, then stopped. He ducked behind the trunk of a thick tree, hidden from view.

Justin thought of all those shootings he'd read about online. At the time, they'd all seemed so far away, like something that couldn't possibly happen to him.

Within seconds, the entire tent and the surrounding clearing were empty of all people. Everyone except for Mr. Rand, Pastor D, and his bodyguard.

Justin knew he should have kept running, but it was Mr. Rand with the gun. Surely he didn't intend to hurt anyone.

He was trying to scatter everyone. He didn't want them to see the rest of the resurrection.

Justin watched as Mr. Rand and Pastor D had a conversation, although it looked more like a stand-off.

On the raised platform, Chloe's body was at rest. It no longer moved like it had before.

The stand-off ended. The big bodyguard approached Mr. Rand, took his gun, and then led him away like he was being arrested.

What in the world is going on? Something is very wrong with all this.

Justin ducked back behind the tree and lowered himself onto the hard roots. He wiped at his forehead and rustled his hair, trying hard to make sense of everything he'd seen.

Especially what he saw a few minutes ago—when Pastor D was moments away from making a dead corpse live again.

He felt ill. Giving Gerald Roberson back his ability to walk was one thing. But what was the point of raising people from the dead? Weren't people supposed to die eventually? Wasn't Chloe in heaven, happy and healthy? Why bring her back?

The power of Azora.

But there had to be a line. A limit. Why use the power of Azora to do things that were not good?

Mr. Rand must have understood that. That must have been why he broke up the crowd, even by doing something as reckless as shooting a gun. And then, because of it, he was taken away on Pastor D's orders. The man that Justin thought he trusted. What if he planned to hurt Mr. Rand?

This is because of me.

The realization dawned on Justin like it was one of Pastor D's divinations. His father had told Mr. Rand to prove that Pastor D was a fraud. Justin had no idea what Mr. Rand had discovered, but all of this had started because of Justin.

He'd been misled. He didn't know the half of what was truly going on. Because whatever it was, it had caused Mr. Rand to get taken.

He pulled out his phone and called Libby. They had not spoken since their conversation in the gym and, unsurprisingly, she did not answer. She was probably frustrated with him, and for good reason, but it was a terrible time for her to not pick up the phone.

Your dad is in danger, he thought.

Something had to happen, and soon.

Before he knew what he was doing, Justin was up and running toward his car. There were several cars left in the area, abandoned by people who had chosen to escape on foot.

He fired up the ignition and pulled out. He was heading toward Pastor D's house. Mr. Rand was in trouble, and it was all Justin's fault. He had to help the man.

37

t the rear of the tent was a sleek black car, brand new. Hoby pushed Rand toward it, then bent him over the hood of the car, smashing his face into the metal.

"Ow! Easy, man," Rand said.

Hoby ignored him. He yanked Rand's wrists behind his back as if arresting him. Rand felt them bound by something hard, then cinched up tight.

A zip-tie.

Hoby grabbed Rand by the neck of his jacket and straightened him.

"Really? You just have those on your person? How many people do you kidnap in a week?"

Hoby spun Rand around, glaring at him. He was a good foot and a half taller than Rand. "It would be wise to shut your mouth." His voice was a deep baritone.

After letting the message sink in, Hoby opened the car door and shoved Rand in. He tumbled sideways, hands bound behind his back, causing him to fall awkwardly and then struggle to get up. Hoby got into the driver's seat and soon they were on their way.

"Why do you let those guys boss you around?" Rand asked as they drove. "I mean, look at you. You're a big dude. No one should tell you what to do, right?"

Hoby kept his eyes on the road, not letting on that he'd heard a word.

"How about this," Rand went on. "Free me and my daughter, and I'll help you out. How much are these guys paying you? I can't pay you that, but I can get you a real job. My favorite bar is always looking for bouncers, and you're a perfect fit."

The big man remained focused ahead, hands at ten and two on the wheel as he drove slowly through town.

"Surprises me you'd be in with people who hurt young girls. You seem better than that. Whenever we get to where we're going, I expect my daughter to not have a single scratch on her. If she does, I don't care how big you are—I'll rip your fucking head off."

Hoby finally acknowledged him, glancing in the rearview mirror before turning back to the road.

They turned off the main drag and onto a dirt driveway that led to an old mansion. It looked like a miniature plantation home and, from what Rand could tell, was the only house in the vicinity.

"Putting the tithe money to good use, I see," Rand said.

There was no real driveway since the house was so old, so Hoby parked in the front yard and went around to yank Rand out of the backseat. The big man squeezed Rand's arm extra hard, probably for the head-ripping-off threat.

He dragged Rand across the yard and made him stand a few paces from the porch, then he released him.

"Stay," he said, his voice deep, commanding Rand like a dog.

Then the big man turned, climbed the porch steps, and disappeared inside the house, leaving Rand outside by himself.

There was not another soul in sight. He was unsupervised and could easily escape. But he refused to go anywhere without Libby.

He waited in the chilly morning for several minutes before the door opened again.

"Libby!"

"*Dad!*"

She bolted down the steps and plowed into him, throwing her arms around his neck and almost knocking him off his feet. "Oh my God, oh my God, what the hell is this place? What's going on? These people are insane!"

"Libby," Rand said. He wished his hands were free so he could hug her back. But he knew he only had seconds.

"What is this?" Libby said, noticing his bound wrists. "Why are your hands tied?"

"Libby, listen to me."

She whirled around to face Hoby. "Hey, let him go, you son of a bitch!"

"Libby, listen!"

Hoby closed the distance and seized Rand again by the arm. Hoby pulled him toward the house.

"I said let him go!" Libby struck the big man on the chest, but it didn't faze him at all.

"*Libby!* Mount Grace Church in town," Rand blurted out. He was powerless to resist Hoby's strength pulling him to the front door. "Find Pastor Simon Cole. He can help you."

"I'm not leaving you here, Dad."

"Do what I say! Find Simon Cole!"

She looked ready to cry. It was that look he'd seen before, many times—one of helpless frustration.

He tripped on the porch steps and went down. Hoby pulled him back to his feet, half dragging him up the stairs. "And Miller. Call Miller!"

"Dad—"

"I'll be fine. And remember, no police! Never the police!"

Then he was inside the mansion and Hoby slammed the heavy door shut.

ALTHOUGH IT WAS MIDMORNING, the inside of the mansion was shrouded in darkness. The windows were covered with sheets to block out the light. A musty smell dominated the air, and the lack of furniture made the main foyer look even more expansive than it was.

Hoby dragged Rand to a nearby room, one devoid of anything except for a large armchair and a fireplace. He shoved Rand to the ground and he landed hard, the wind knocked from his lungs.

"Easy," he said, rolling onto his side.

Hoby stood over Rand, studying him with a stony expression.

"She looked all right," Rand said. "Looks like I don't have to tear your fucking head off after all."

Hoby was unamused. Without a word, he turned his back on Rand and left him there, closing the door behind him.

Rand lay there in the dim room, relief flooding over him. Libby was okay, and now she was free. She would find Simon and round up Miller and, hopefully, between the three of them, they could get him out of here.

Not that Rand was in any rush to leave. He and Deckard Arcan had unfinished business. Specifically regarding the demon he'd allowed to cause chaos in Finnick.

Deckard kept his word. No trickery, no bluffing. It was a straight exchange—Libby for himself. Honestly, that scared him. The man was confident, and he had a plan. Rand had taken the bait.

Not like I had a choice.

Luring Libby there had been the perfect trap.

He tightened his abs and crunched his way up to a sitting position, then stood. He scurried around the room, looking for something he could use to cut the zip-tie from his wrists. He was in a study or library, lined with bookshelves, but there was not a single book on them. Or anything else. There was only a plush, red armchair in front of the fireplace.

Deckard's lair sure is bleak. He wondered if this was where he received all his visions from "Azora" that he loved to brag about.

Just for the sake of completion, Rand tried to open the door. It was locked.

No problem. I can wait.

He was certain it was only a matter of time before Deckard Arcan came for him.

38

Libby stood frozen as she watched her father dragged off by the big man into the mansion. The door slammed, leaving her alone in the front yard.

She sniffled and wiped at her eyes. She hated feeling helpless, and at that moment, she felt like there was nothing she could do.

Her first instinct was to run back to the door, pound on it until her fists were bloody, and hope someone let her in so she could rescue her dad. But he had traded places with her, and that would only be a waste of his sacrifice.

Simon Cole. Mount Grace Church.

She figured she could trust that her dad knew what he was talking about and decided to find the man he'd told her to look for.

A noise came from behind her—the sound of tires on the dirt path.

Oh no. I need to—

She looked left and right for somewhere to hide. Anyone driving up to the mansion could not be friendly.

Her dad's bright orange Jeep came into view from around the curve in the road, and she relaxed. "Who is this?" she muttered to herself.

The Jeep ambled up, and when it neared, the driver's window lowered. An elderly black man was behind the wheel.

"You must be Libby," he said. "You have Rand's eyes."

"Who are you?"

"My name is Simon Cole."

"Why do you have my dad's car?" But the thoughts darted from her mind and she jabbed her finger toward the mansion. "They took my dad inside. We have to help him."

Simon looked ahead at the house, completely calm and lacking urgency.

"Hell-o, did you hear me?"

"He traded himself for you. I figured they'd bring him here, and it looks like I was right."

"I know," Libby said. "But I don't think he realizes what kind of danger he's in. I've seen the demon. It's…" She trailed off as the thoughts of her escape attempt a few nights before came back to her. How that black creature had blocked her path, glaring at her with blood-red eyes.

"We cannot do anything for him now," Simon said. "We have to prepare before we encounter the demonic entity inside Deckard Arcan."

Libby stared at the man for a few seconds. It was something her own dad would say. "Are you a believer?"

"We can't rush in," Simon said, ignoring her question. "We'll go to my church and I'll ready myself for the fight. Then we'll return tonight and get your dad out of there."

It was more of a plan than Libby had, so she got into the passenger seat of the car. Although, she didn't like how they would have to wait until nighttime to come back for her father. That was hours away, and anything could happen in that time.

As they drove, Simon told her how Rand had shown up at his church the week before and filled her in on all that had happened.

"In jail for three days?" Libby said, aghast. "How…"

He'd been a prisoner too, just as she had been.

"The entity possessing Deckard Arcan is very powerful. Through

450

him, it has influence over many people in this town, including the sheriff."

"Ugh. I don't think my dad has ever dealt with something this big before."

Then Libby remembered the other part of her father's instructions to her. *Miller.* "Do you have a phone?"

Simon leaned to the side and dug into his pocket as he drove. He handed her a flip phone that must have been at least ten years old.

"Who are you calling?" Simon asked.

"One of my dad's friends," she said as she dialed Miller Landingham's number. The man was an annexed family member at that point, and she'd had his digits memorized for a while. "He should be able to help."

"Hello?" Miller answered after the fifth ring. His voice was low and suspicious. Libby figured it was because he didn't recognize the caller.

"Miller, it's Libby."

"Libby? Did you get a new phone? I almost didn't answer because I thought you were a bill collector."

"Listen, my dad's in trouble."

"When is he not?"

"He's been kidnapped and being held inside a house down here in Finnick."

"By that preacher?"

"Yes. That preacher is being controlled by a demon."

"Your dad started telling me about it the last time we spoke. Something about a perfect possession, but he couldn't give me more info."

"I can," Libby said. "I've seen it."

There was silence on the other end for a while. Even Simon looked over at her, concern filling his eyes. They turned off the main road and onto a smaller one, passing a sign that read MOUNT GRACE CHURCH.

"Tell me everything," Miller said.

"Completely black," Libby said. "Very large body, darker than a shadow, as usual. But this had... I don't know, black things that came off his head, like long hair. His eyes were red and..."

"And what?" Miller prodded.

"Fire," Libby said. "It can breathe fire, like a dragon." She remembered how the demon had threatened her as she'd tried to escape. There was no doubt in her mind that if she had persisted, she'd have been burned alive.

There was a scratching over the other end of the line—Miller writing what she told him.

"Okay. These are good details. I'll look into this and see if I find anything."

"Miller," Libby said, but the man didn't respond. He probably knew what she was going to ask him. "Can you come?"

"Umm."

"I know, Miller, you only work behind the scenes. But this is different. I don't know if my dad will be able to get out of this one on his own. Can you please come to Finnick and help?"

There was a long silence on the other end of the phone. "Okay. I'll research what you've told me and then drive down." He sounded terrified, and Libby hated to ask him to do this, but she was out of options. She knew Miller would come for her and her dad if they were truly in trouble.

"Where are you?" he asked.

"A church called Mount Grace." Beside her, Simon nodded. They pulled up in front of the church—a dilapidated building that had seen better days. The adjacent graveyard looked like it was hundreds of years old.

"I'll look up directions online," Miller said. "Are you safe?"

"For now. I'm with the church's pastor. But my dad isn't safe, and we need to help him as quickly as possible."

"Okay. I'll see you soon, Libby."

"Thank you, Miller."

They hung up and Libby handed the phone back to Simon as they got out of the Jeep. She followed him inside the church. The old pastor walked slowly and leaned on a cane as he limped.

"I'll spend time in prayer," he said to her. "We can return to Deckard's home once your friend gets here."

Libby didn't want to say it, but she wondered how long Simon could withstand a fight with the demonic when he was already so frail. She'd heard her dad's stories about him being thrown around the room by these monsters, sustaining some terrible bangs, cuts, and bruises. How could Simon tolerate the same?

But right now, Simon Cole was the best she had.

The church was dim and warm inside, and smelled a little funky because of its age. Simon wobbled down the aisle toward the altar, overlooked by a hanging statue of Jesus on the cross.

"What should I do?" Libby asked.

"You should do the same as I am," Simon told her. "Pray. Prepare. Ask God to equip us with his blessing and protection. The monster you described is a formidable enemy. I've already seen what he can do."

With that, Simon disappeared into the back of the church, leaving her alone.

Libby chewed her lip and looked again at Jesus. She didn't pray often, but if she was ever going to, then this would be the occasion.

Please hurry, Miller. I don't think we have much time.

39

Justin arrived at the dirt road he remembered would take him to Pastor D's mansion. He'd been there one time, early on when he had first started attending the church. It had been a special Sunday where Pastor D had invited the entire congregation to his home for the service instead of meeting at the tent.

He figured he shouldn't drive up the dirt path, since he could be spotted. So, he parked on the side of the road and went on foot, walking through the trees that lined the path.

When he came to the mansion, everything was silent and still. Not a sign of life. But Mr. Rand was somewhere inside.

Justin crept around, surveying and looking for a way in. All the windows, even the ones on the second floor, had bars over them.

He went along the side of the house and into the backyard. There, at the edge of the woods that lined the property, he spotted something shrouded by the trees. And as he drew nearer, he got a better look.

Libby's blue Mini Cooper.

Oh my God...

It looked like someone had tried to hide it, but hadn't cared enough to put it completely out of sight.

Is she here too?

Was Libby also held captive? Was that why he hadn't heard from her in days? A newfound resolution to get inside bloomed in him.

But there seemed to be no way in besides knocking on the front door, which he knew wouldn't do any good.

On the side of the house, though, he noticed a third-floor window that did not have bars. It was the only one.

But how in the world am I going to get up there?

He used his imagination to trace a path. There was a steep, shingled roof that surrounded the window. Along the edge, an overgrown oak tree had branches that scraped against the side of the house. One of those branches looked sturdy enough to support his weight. Justin followed the oak down to its roots, noticing the strong limbs that were within reach of each other.

I can climb.

He hadn't climbed a tree since he was a kid, but that didn't stop him. Perhaps it was his desperation to get into the house that drove him. The rough bark bit into his soft palms, but he only tightened his grip and maneuvered from branch to branch, getting farther and farther away from the ground as he went.

When he reached the mansion's roof, he made the mistake of looking down. His stomach turned over when he saw the drop below him. One wrong move and he'd have a broken bone for sure.

He inched himself along the branch that extended to the roof. It bent underneath his weight and wasn't as sturdy as it had looked from the ground. Still, he pushed forward, his body and shirt scraping against the bark. He focused on keeping his balance, not wanting to lean too far to either side. Doing so might send him toppling down.

He reached out and laid his hands on the black shingles, transitioning from branch to roof as carefully as he could. He leaned into the roof's slope as he shuffled along, easing to the window.

When he made it, he peered through the glass, but it was dirty and smudged, and the room on the other side was dark. There was nothing he could see.

He tried the latch, but it wouldn't move. He pushed and pulled, but it was either stuck or locked.

I didn't come all the way up here just to go back down.

He would have to break it. But the thing was, he would have to shatter the glass in his first attempt. If he didn't, the force of bouncing off the window would send him rolling down the roof and tumbling to the ground.

The image of him sprawled in the grass, broken and bloody, came to his mind, sending waves of fear through him. Justin shook it away, though. He had to do this for Libby and her dad.

He positioned himself and drew back with his left hand, mustering all the strength he could. He clenched his teeth. *This is going to hurt.*

Then he punched forward, crashing his fist through the glass. It broke, and he snaked his arm in and grabbed hold of the other side of the window to keep himself from falling.

Cuts burned his forearm. A wetness dribbled down toward his hand. He fished around inside and found the latch, which he turned. The window opened.

He crawled into a darkened attic, a room that looked like it hadn't been used in a long time. The shards of glass crunched underneath his shoes. He tried to inspect the wounds on his arm as best he could in the dim light. Red lines ran down his skin where the glass had cut him, and the deepest one was dripping blood.

A bed and baby crib were against the wall near the window, which Justin thought was odd. There were also a few other pieces of neglected furniture. He spotted a door on the other side, and as he walked toward it, he passed a box of old bed linen. He took a pillowcase and wrapped his bloody arm as tightly as he could.

Justin reached for the doorknob, and just as he was about to touch it, someone started unlocking it from the other side.

He gasped, but reacted quickly. He dove to his left and dropped behind a dusty chest of drawers just before the door opened.

"Put her on the bed, please, Hoby." Deckard's voice.

Heavy footsteps crossed the attic. Justin braved a peek from the edge of his hiding place. Hoby carried Chloe in his arms, though she was still covered by the white sheet, and laid her down on the bed.

Deckard Arcan stood near the door, blocking Justin's only hope of leaving the attic.

They've come home, Justin thought. *And they've brought Chloe with them.*

He eyed the covered body as it rested on the bed.

"We'll leave her up here for the time being," Deckard said. "We have more urgent matters to deal with now, and I need to have a word with our *guest.*" Deckard spat the word with disgust.

He must mean Mr. Rand, Justin thought.

Hoby went to the other side of the bed and adjusted the blanket to make sure Chloe's body was completely covered. Then, a piece of glass crunched underneath his shoe.

Justin's breath caught.

Hoby froze and looked down, then followed the trail of shards to the broken window.

"What is it?" Deckard asked.

"The window is broken, sir."

Oh no.

But Deckard only waved his hand. "It must have been the girl. She's clever, so of course she tried to escape."

Libby... she was here.

"Please be sure to lock this door behind you. I have a feeling Chloe will be quite restless."

Deckard left, but Hoby remained behind for a moment. He scanned the attic, and Justin dipped back down behind the chest of drawers, lungs aching from holding his breath.

If he searches, he'll find me.

Then, after what felt like ages, Hoby crossed the room, his heavy footfalls pounding on the wooden floor. Justin heard the door close and lock.

He let out his breath, feeling like a drowning man that was finally able to resurface.

Once he calmed himself, he thought about what Deckard had said.

Mr. Rand is here. Libby is also here, or was. He said she tried to escape, which meant she was held here against her will.

Justin stood and went to the attic door, just to check. Sure enough, it was locked.

He had to find a way out of there. He had to help Mr. Rand—and Libby, if she was still in the house.

Justin heard a noise behind him. Old bedsprings squeaking.

No...

Impossible. It couldn't be. Mr. Rand had interrupted the ritual.

I have a feeling she'll be quite restless, Deckard had said.

Justin slowly looked over his shoulder.

The sheet-covered body sat upright.

And then Chloe turned her head directly toward him.

40

C hloe's body struggled to stand from the bed, moving like someone who did not have full control of her limbs.

When she was finally upright, the sheet slipped off and crumpled to the floor at her feet.

Chloe's eyes were empty and unseeing. The right was rolled upward, the left looking too far to the side. Her mouth was open, frozen agape.

Deckard's ritual worked, even if no one saw it.

The woman ambled toward him.

"C-Chloe—"

Her legs were rigid, toes pointed in, which made walking difficult. Still, she managed through the rigor mortis. And as she neared, she lifted a stiff arm, as if wanting to grab him.

She lurched forward, closing the remaining distance between them faster than Justin expected.

Justin dodged to the side just in time, and the dead hand barely missed him.

Chloe's wobbly corpse crashed into the door, bumping off it. Unaffected, she turned and staggered toward Justin once again.

Justin backed away, but his shoe caught on a loose floorboard and he fell, landing hard on his back.

Chloe's unsteady gait seemed to speed up as if she had grown even more urgent to get her hands on him.

Justin didn't know what she would do when she did. But he knew he didn't want to find out.

He sat up and shuffled across the dusty floor until he backed into a wall. Nowhere else to go.

To his side was a wooden plank propped against the wall—likely a piece left over after completing construction.

Justin stood and grabbed the wood, holding it in both his hands like a baseball bat. "Chloe. Don't come any closer."

The woman did not hear him. She came forward.

So Justin drew the plank back as best he could and swung it as if he were going for a home run. The wood struck Chloe in the side of the face, and Justin heard a sickening crack of her skull. She went down hard, hitting the ground with a thud.

She lay motionless.

Justin looked down at her body for a while, plank ready in case she got back up again. But she did not stir.

What did you do to her, Deckard? he thought. She should've been buried and laid to rest, not resurrected into some half-dead monster.

If Deckard could do that to her, Justin shuddered to think what the pastor could do to Libby and Mr. Rand.

I have to get to them.

41

Hours passed while Rand was trapped in Deckard Arcan's study. He sat in the red chair, figuring that as long as his hands were bound behind his back, he might as well be comfortable.

Libby. I hope you found Simon and that you're okay.

The lock clicked, and then the man himself entered. Deckard Arcan. He still wore the same three-piece suit from earlier.

He closed the door and sauntered over to face Rand, studying him as if he were a disgusting rodent.

"Happy Sunday," Rand said.

"I bet you are thrilled with yourself," Deckard said, voice low and sinister.

"What were you doing with my daughter? Why was she here?"

Deckard only smirked. "She came willingly. She wanted to learn the secrets of Azora and begin her new life."

"Go to hell."

Deckard waved his hand. "Forget about the girl. This was never about her. It was only about you and me and Azora."

"There is no Azora. It's a demon mimicking an angel."

"Quiet!" Deckard snapped, his face twisting. As before, Rand saw that Deckard couldn't even bear considering the idea. "You do not understand the gravity of what you have done. You have intentionally interfered with the will of Azora. The resurrection this morning was a long time coming, something that Azora has been preparing me for. And because of you, no one witnessed it."

Does that mean it worked? Did he actually bring Chloe back to life?

Rand pushed the thought away and focused. "If Azora is all-powerful, he could have told you I would show up."

"You think this is funny, don't you?"

"That you kidnapped my daughter and practice necromancy to convince people to join your cult? No, Pastor D, it's not funny at all. You are in a huge amount of danger, and if you let me, I will help you."

An involuntary chuckle escaped from Deckard's mouth. It was one of astonishment as if he couldn't believe what he'd heard. "You think you can help me? The man who dabbles with evil spirits from hell?" He inched closer. "I am the one who tried to help *you*. I revealed your sin to you to give you an opportunity to redeem yourself. And what did you do? You interfered with the blessings of Azora. First Gerald Roberson, and now Chloe!"

"How powerful is Azora if a dumbass like me can undo his miracles?"

Deckard backhanded him and Rand's vision went black around the edges. Deckard's unnatural strength left him feeling like he'd been hit with a brick.

"Your name and face have filled my prayers and visions lately," Deckard said. "The message from Azora is clear. You are a problem and you need to be removed."

Rand eyed Deckard, waiting.

"Tonight, at midnight, I will give you to Azora."

"Give me? Will he come pick me up? What does he drive?"

Deckard narrowed his eyes. "Give you to Azora's fire."

Flames erupted in the fireplace to Rand's left, a bright burst of yellow that sent waves of heat throughout the room. The light danced on the side of Deckard's face, casting the other half in shadow.

"Nice little parlor trick," Rand said, although he knew there was no timer or trigger. The man had the powers of the demonic entity that held sway over him.

Deckard pointed a finger at Rand. It was inches from his nose. "Midnight. Azora's chosen hour. If you have anything to say or pray about, I suggest you get started."

He left Rand alone in the study, closing and locking the door.

Rand stared into the fireplace. The fire burned intensely, although there was no wood or tinder underneath it, sustained by some kind of black magic.

He had no clue how much time he had, but he knew he had to free his hands and get out of there.

At midnight, Deckard planned to burn him alive.

42

Libby was alone in the old church, growing more anxious as the time ticked by.

Simon Cole had disappeared into the back room and had not come out since. She had to trust that his process was necessary before encountering a demonic entity.

That meant Simon Cole was a believer. Her dad didn't encounter many believers, but she should've figured that if there was one in town, Rand would have found a way to meet him.

She stepped outside for some air. The afternoon had grown chilly.

I hope Dad's all right...

Although it had only been a couple of hours, it felt like much longer since they'd been separated. There was no telling what horrible things could happen to him in that house.

Libby heard tires rolling up the dirt path that led to the old church.

She recognized the yellow, beat-up pickup truck coming around the curve. He drove slowly as if the car couldn't handle the simple off-road terrain. He was probably right—Miller had had that car since before she was born.

She went to him as he parked and got out. He wore khaki pants and a blue plaid shirt, buttoned up. He had a duffle bag over his shoulder.

"You're going to chip in some gas money for that two-hour drive, right?" Miller asked.

She threw her arms around him and hugged him tight, surprising him. "Thanks for coming. Everything is so messed up. We have to get my dad back."

"We will," he said, patting her shoulder. "We always do."

"You need to meet Simon."

As they walked back inside, Miller surveyed the old church. His eyes were magnified by the thick prescription of his glasses—Libby had tried to convince him for years to try contacts.

"Who is Simon?" Miller asked.

"The pastor here. He's fought the demonic before and he can help us."

"Thank God. Does that mean I don't have to?"

They entered the dim sanctuary. Libby was startled when she saw a figure in the shadows, but then realized it was only Simon emerging from his back room.

"I heard a car," he said.

"This is my dad's friend Miller. Miller, this is Simon."

"Libby tells me you've had... experience in these unfortunate matters," Miller said.

Simon nodded. "I've been praying and preparing all afternoon."

Miller shook the duffle bag hanging from his shoulder. "And I've brought some gear. Crucifixes, Bibles, holy water, some sage."

"Did you find out anything?" Libby asked him. "From what I told you earlier."

Miller adjusted his glasses. His skin seemed to grow paler than it already was. "I believe you are dealing with a demon named Hazul."

"You were able to discover the name?" Simon asked. "How?"

"From what Libby described to me about his appearance, and from his behavior so far. He gains the trust of humans by giving them gifts in the form of healing and strength. Even allows them to bestow those gifts on other people. Sounds like what your preacher has gotten wrapped up in."

Simon's eyes drifted to the side as he paused to think.

"But there is always a price," Miller continued. "Lifelong servitude, and any attempt to break the contract results in death."

Simon took in a deep breath. "Right. Hazul…" He spoke the name with disgust.

"It's good that we know his name," Miller said. "That will give us an advantage." He paused. "Where's this guy holding Rando?"

"Inside his mansion on the other side of town."

"And I guess that's where we're going?" Miller's whole body was tense. Simon only nodded. Miller glanced between Simon and Libby. "Who's driving?"

43

Patrick Perryman stood in the mansion's foyer, eyes on the door of Deckard's study. Randolph Casey was inside, tied up and kept prisoner, and Pastor D was in there with him —they'd been talking for a while.

How long is he planning to be in there with him?

Already Deckard had spent more time speaking with their enemy than with Patrick that day. Every minute that passed, a hot anger boiled higher within him.

He'd returned to the mansion with Pastor D, certain that he had been bluffing to Rand.

But then, when they got home, Libby was not there. Hoby had released her, true to Pastor D's word.

Patrick knew he was always supposed to have faith in the man. But for the first time in a long while, he felt that resolve slipping.

Did Pastor D ever mean to allow me to marry her? Or did he plan to use her as bait all along?

The questions tumbled through his mind, and he could not stop them. But he also could not find a rational explanation for them.

Unbridled anger had been a big stumbling block for him before he'd met Pastor D, but ever since he'd dedicated himself to the church, it had not been an issue. Now it washed over him again, a familiar and unwelcome feeling, yet one completely out of his control.

What is happening? I don't want this.

But it felt so involuntary.

Images of him pummeling Pastor D's face flashed across his mind—he quickly forced them away, embarrassed and ashamed. And afraid, because Pastor D had the uncanny ability to see into his thoughts and soul.

The door to the study opened and Pastor D emerged. When he saw Patrick standing there, Deckard regarded Patrick with a cold, blank gaze, one that he was not used to seeing. Usually, the pastor's eyes were filled with warmth when they were together.

Without a word, Pastor D turned to walk down the dark corridor to the back of the house, apparently not intending to say anything.

"Pastor D," Patrick said, his voice weak and pathetic, even to his own ears.

Deckard tensed and faced Patrick. "What is it?"

Is he angry with me? Pastor D would have a good reason to be, especially if he could sense how upset Patrick was over Libby.

"It's just... I'm confused."

"When are you not, Patrick?"

The terse reply struck him like a blow to the face.

"What are you doing?" Patrick demanded. "Why are you spending so much time with him if he's so evil? And why did you let my bride go?"

He wished he could take the words back as soon as he'd said them. Pastor D gave him a look that made him feel tiny and afraid. It was the same glare he gave Randolph Casey, and Patrick inched backward.

"You are thinking much too small," Pastor D said, walking toward him. "How is it that all you can think about is your desire for a bride when that man in there has ruined everything Azora had planned for us?"

It was the first time Patrick had ever seen Pastor D lose his composure.

"There are far more important things at stake here. Surrendering the girl to have Randolph Casey in our custody is a trade I would do over and over again, no matter how much you lust after her."

"But—"

"You need to decide how dedicated you are to the will of Azora. I told you that a bride would blur your commitment. You swore it would not, but I knew it would. You are proving me correct. Get your head on straight. Remember all I have done for you and how Azora has changed your life. Because right now you are spitting over everything that has been given to you."

But... you promised. You broke that promise and that is why I'm upset.

He opened his mouth to say the words out loud, but his courage failed him. Pastor D had never spoken to him like that before.

"Head up to your room and pack your things," Pastor D said. "Tonight, at midnight, we give Randolph Casey to the fires of Azora. Then we will leave Finnick."

"Fires? You mean... b-burn him alive?"

"There is nothing left for Azora here," Pastor D said, more gently now. "We must move on and start anew someplace where evil men such as Randolph Casey won't meddle with us." He then turned his back on Patrick.

When Patrick was a boy, his father used to sever the discussion in the exact same way. The conversation was over when Dad said it was, and that was that.

Patrick had no bride. His leader was angry with him—and perhaps had never respected him in the first place. Which meant he'd only kept Patrick around to use him.

And he will burn a man alive.

Patrick agreed that Rand was evil, but did they need to do that? Wasn't there redemption and grace?

And Libby. If we do this, she'll be gone from my life forever. Maybe she already is.

The thought of never seeing her again was too much, and tears quickly sprang to his eyes. He knew from his prayers and his gut she was meant to be his for the rest of their lives.

Now all of that was ruined.

There was one last chance to get it back. Pastor D would kill Patrick if he was discovered doing what he was about to do, but Patrick would go for it anyway. Years of obedience and subservience had earned him nothing, and it was time for his reward. Pastor D always took what he wanted, so why couldn't he?

Patrick went to his room and opened one of his drawers, taking out a ring dangling with several keys. A while ago, he'd secretly made copies of each key that Pastor D used: for the house, the car, and even the study where their prisoner was now being held. It was likely Pastor D knew Patrick had the keys, but if he did, he'd never brought it up.

He took the keys downstairs and headed for the locked door. He needed to have a word with Randolph Casey.

44

Miller drove Rand's Jeep to the mansion. Simon Cole rode up front while Libby was in the back.

Simon directed him down a dirt road off the main highway. Something caught Libby's eye. "Miller, stop!"

Miller slammed on the brakes, which sent her forward since she didn't have her seatbelt on.

"What's wrong?"

Libby peered through the window at the car parked along the road. *What the hell?*

"That's Justin's car!"

"Are you sure?" Miller asked.

"Yes! He's got the cross hanging from the rearview mirror."

"What's he doing here?" Miller asked.

"I don't know," Libby said, suddenly more nervous than she had been before.

"Is he in on it with them?"

Libby chewed her lip. She didn't think so, but maybe he'd gone off the deep end, angry at her for not accepting his truth. Was he inside with Deckard, helping to keep her dad prisoner?

"Go." She tapped Miller's shoulder. "Let's hurry."

Miller stepped on the gas and drove up the dirt road, kicking up a cloud of dust behind them.

The mansion came into view ahead of them. The sight of it made Libby sick all over again. It felt like madness having escaped there only to come back. But this time, she had her team.

There were no lights coming from inside, and it seemed as if no one was home. But Libby knew better.

They parked and Miller crossed himself before leaving the car.

Simon said to Libby, "You should stay here and keep the car running. We may need to flee after we get your dad back. You should be ready."

"Getaway driver, huh? I can do that."

Simon climbed out of the car and Libby shuffled over the center console to sit behind the wheel.

"Hey," she said through the rolled-down window, and Simon looked at her. "Be careful. But please kick that guy's ass." He smirked.

Simon and Miller strode toward the mansion. One man was squat and overweight, the other elderly and limping. She would've thought that, by now, if her dad planned to keep engaging in life-threatening supernatural battles, he would've assembled a real team rather than a rag-tag band of misfits.

"Good evening, Simon," boomed a voice from above.

The columns on the front porch supported a balcony on the second floor, and Deckard Arcan stood on it, looking down at them.

"Your friend Randolph has agreed to accept the will of Azora," Deckard continued. "You need to leave."

"We are not leaving without him."

Simon's voice boomed assertively. Libby reconsidered what she'd thought earlier. *Maybe these two aren't the misfits I thought they were...*

"You and your friends have caused me enough trouble already," Deckard said. "I'm finishing it tonight. I do not want to hurt you, but if you insist on pushing me, I will have no choice. Azora does not stand for being disobeyed."

"We aren't going anywhere," Simon shot back. "Let us in and we can talk about this."

"You know the time for talking is over," Deckard said.

"Come on, dudes," Libby whispered to herself. "All this rambling is useless."

Libby pushed her back against the seat and closed her eyes. She felt her heart pounding, and her breaths came in short gasps. "Come on, Dad," she whispered. "You can do it."

45

Rand heard someone inserting a key in the study's lock.

Is it midnight already? No way...

But it wasn't Deckard Arcan who entered the room. It was Patrick Perryman.

The slight man closed the door behind him and walked over to the armchair where Rand sat.

He didn't lock the door, Rand realized.

He couldn't attempt an escape when Deckard opened the door earlier—the preacher was too strong. But Patrick was a different story...

The look on Patrick's face frightened him. It was a mix of desperation, fear, and uncertainty.

When he'd met the man on campus, he'd seemed nice enough, if a little in the clouds. Now Rand had to wonder just how deep into Deckard's dogma Patrick was.

Rand was just about to spring from the chair and make a break for the unlocked door when Patrick spoke.

"Why did you do that?" Patrick asked.

"Do what?"

"Ruin the miracle."

Rand licked his lips. "Do you believe resurrecting a dead person is a good thing?"

"Of course. It was the will of Azora finally coming to fruition. We have been waiting for this day for a long time."

"We? Do you mean you and Deckard? Or is it just Deckard? Because you sound a lot like him. Do you actually agree so strongly with him?"

"He has demonstrated his abilities over and over again."

"Has he?"

Patrick was silent. The way he spoke so far, Rand knew what was going on. The man's faith was fragile. He was doubting the things he had seen. Wondering how much of what he had experienced was true or just smoke and mirrors.

Rand had been through similar crises himself. Maybe that's why he recognized what was happening to Patrick in that moment.

Even with his hands tied, Rand knew he could overtake Patrick if the small man tried to stop him from escaping.

The unnatural fire that roared in the hearth had driven the heat in the room far past bearable levels. Rand was sweating through his clothes, and now Patrick's face was dripping.

"Libby was meant to be my bride."

He said it so resolutely, a statement of fact. The flames danced in the reflection of his glasses.

"What was that?" Rand asked, although he knew he'd heard correctly. Anger flared within him.

"Azora told me in my prayers that she was supposed to be my wife. Pastor D was to marry us soon. Azora led her here to be with me."

So you were the one who lured her here. Sick bastard.

"Pastor D let her go. Traded her so he could have you. He should not have done that. After everything, I deserve her!"

That was too much. Rand leapt from the chair and head-butted Patrick in the face.

He yelped and collapsed immediately, glasses broken. His hands went to his broken nose, blood running through his fingers.

Rand gave him a swift kick in the stomach, which caused Patrick to cry out even more.

"I'd love to rough you up more, you little freak," Rand said, "but I have to deal with your preacher."

Rand went to the door and used his bound hands to open it, then entered the mansion's foyer. The cool air was a refreshing blast on his slick skin.

Patrick still rolled around on the floor behind him. Rand thought he heard the man crying.

I'm free, but I can't do anything here on my own, or with my hands tied.

The front door was to his left. He had to leave and reunite with Simon, and then return later.

But when Rand managed to get the door open, he saw Simon Cole and Miller Landingham standing in the mansion's yard. His Jeep was behind them, Libby in the driver's seat.

Libby's done it.

Simon and Miller spotted him at the same time.

"There he is!" Miller cried.

Miller jogged across to him as best as his pudgy body would allow. Simon Cole followed, wobbling with his cane.

"Deckard's upstairs," Simon said, once inside.

Miller patted the duffle bag that dangled over his shoulder. "I've brought supplies. Are you ready, Rando?"

Rand turned and showed Miller his bound wrists. "Can you help me out?"

"Oh." Miller dug into his khakis and pulled out a pocketknife. A moment later, the zip tie fell away.

Miller dropped the duffle bag and unzipped it. Inside, Rand saw all the gear he'd need. "Will Libby be all right out there?"

"She's ready with the Jeep so we can make a quick escape," Miller told him.

Rand would've preferred her to be farther away, but he supposed a getaway driver was a useful thing to have.

"I've had just about enough of you."

Rand followed the voice. The staircase went up from the foyer and split off to the right and left. On the right side, Deckard Arcan glared down at them.

Patrick Perryman stumbled out from the study, holding his bleeding face. Deckard's eyes immediately snapped over to him.

"Patrick! You let him go!"

"No!" His voice was distorted from his injury.

"Of all people, *you* were the one who betrayed me."

"It wasn't me!"

"After everything I've done for you. How could you?"

Patrick started sobbing, seemingly growing smaller and smaller under Deckard's anger. Finally, when it was too much, he bolted. Rand watched as Patrick fled down the darkened corridor and toward the back of the house.

Deckard turned his attention back to Rand.

This is it, Rand thought. *Face to face again. A rematch. I won't go down easily this time.*

46

The chest of drawers was heavy, but once Justin got it sliding along the dusty floor, he was able to keep up the momentum.

He pushed the heavy furniture to the door that—although locked —seemed quite weak. Like a battering ram, it slammed into the door and the wood splintered. Justin fell atop the chest, waist driving painfully into the edge. A loud crash echoed through the attic.

I hope no one heard that, Justin thought as he rubbed his burning hip bones.

Regardless, he had to get out of that locked attic. He couldn't do anything if he was trapped inside, and spending more time with Chloe's corpse didn't appeal to him.

Justin pulled back the drawers and inspected his demolition work. He'd damaged the locked door pretty well.

He gave it a few solid kicks, and the wood around the latch splintered and cracked, allowing the door to fly open.

There was a narrow hallway beyond, and on the other end of it, a flight of stairs that led him down.

Justin crept slowly, keeping an ear tuned for anyone approaching. Despite all the noise he'd made, it seemed he had gone unnoticed—for now.

Okay. Mr. Rand is in here somewhere. Maybe Libby too. I've got to find him.

Below the stairs was the mansion's second or third floor—Justin couldn't be sure. There was a hallway of rooms ahead of him, and he busied himself with checking each one.

Curiously, each room was empty, devoid of any furniture. He worked his way along, door by door until he arrived at another set of stairs.

Then he heard a commotion from downstairs. And voices.

Justin crept to the staircase banister and looked over.

From where he stood, he could see down to the first floor of the mansion. Justin was apparently on the third.

Mr. Rand was down there with two other men that Justin didn't recognize.

"Deckard, please. We are only here to help you," Simon said.

"No! You are only here to defy Azora." Deckard spat back.

"Rand!" Miller shouted. "Behind you!"

Rand turned just in time to see Hoby charging at him. The big man brought his fist back and swung, but Rand ducked out of the way.

Hoby rounded on him again. His chest and shoulders bulged in his tight t-shirt. His fists were clenched, popping the veins in his forearms.

Hoby grabbed Rand from behind, massive arms like a vise. Rand struggled and gasped as Hoby squeezed him tighter, like a boa constrictor, forcing the air out of his lungs.

"Nice work, Hoby," Deckard said. "Now tie him up again and we'll prepare to give him to Azora. I'll deal with these other two in the meantime."

Simon and Miller stood tense as they watched Rand struggle against Hoby's hold.

"Little help?" Rand barely managed the words through his breathlessness.

Simon yanked one of the crosses from Miller's bag and thrust it toward Deckard. "Hazul, in the name of the Lord, I command you to show yourself!"

Deckard recoiled from the cross as if struck by an invisible bullet.

Simon sure has priorities, Rand thought. He could no longer feel his arms.

"Hazul!" Simon shouted, voice loud and firm. "Leave the body of this man and show yourself!"

Deckard cried out. He clawed at his body like his insides were burning. Then his eyes glowed red, just as they had the first time Rand had fought with him. He lifted his head, opened his mouth, and vomited out a black, amorphous cloud. It streamed from his throat, Deckard screaming as the entity separated itself from him.

The dark cloud drifted to the top of the stairs. It hung there, then took shape. The arms and legs formed, then the body, and finally the head, punctuated by two blood-red eyes. Tendrils of black sprouted from the back of his head, resembling hair. He leaned on his front hands, like a silverback gorilla.

Rand felt himself released from Hoby's grip. His knees buckled and he fell to the side, landing hard on his hip. He quickly sucked in as much air as he could.

That's one way to free me, Rand thought as Hoby fled from the creature that had appeared. The large man burst through the door and was gone without looking back.

Miller rushed over to his side. "That's him, Rand. His name's Hazul."

"I'm fine, Miller, thanks." Rand pushed himself into a sitting position, arms and back still aching.

Hazul leapt from the top of the stairs and landed a few feet from

Rand and Miller. Miller yelped and scurried away. Hazul kept his red, burning red eyes on Rand.

This one moves quick.

Rand shuffled away while trying to get back onto his feet.

"Hazul!" Simon was behind the demon, arm outstretched, gripping the cross. "In the name of—"

Hazul pivoted and swiped his shadowy arm, striking Simon in the chest, and battering him backward. His cane and cross spiraled across the room and he landed hard in a heap.

Rand scrambled around Hazul while the demon was distracted. The duffel bag lay on the floor.

Rand dug inside and pulled out the first things he grabbed—a cross and a bottle of holy water.

The hairs on his neck rose. He felt those red eyes on him.

"Rand!" Miller shouted. "Watch out!"

Behind Rand, Hazul's mouth gaped open, a black hole, and in the back of his throat, a ball of fire formed. The heat blasted into Rand's face as if he were looking into a crater to the center of the earth.

The fires of Azora, Deckard had said.

Rand dodged out of the way just in time. A stream of fire erupted from Hazul's mouth like a flamethrower, engulfing the entire area where he'd been a moment before. The fire consumed the duffle bag, burning the crosses, the sage, and the Bibles.

All of their supplies were gone, except for what Rand held in his hand.

The flames, hot and powerful, spread throughout the room, filling it with unbearable heat.

Hazul rounded on Rand again, red eyes following him like magnets.

But Rand had his weapons now. He could finally fight back.

Rand raised the cross between them like a shield.

And then Hazul began to grow. His black body expanded—eight, maybe nine feet tall.

Rand craned his neck to look up, becoming smaller and more pathetic in Hazul's presence.

Oh, no...

A demon's power was relative to his size. Rand should have guessed Hazul had been hiding his true form—only an extremely powerful entity would be capable of perfect possession.

Rand's outstretched hand lowered against his will as if Hazul's dark presence pushed it down. The cross he gripped seemed so small and weak now.

This is too much, Rand thought. He'd underestimated his foe.

Behind Hazul, Miller had helped Simon to his feet and was inching him toward the exit.

Good, Rand thought. *You two get out while you still can.*

Your God has willed for you to die tonight. The voice was in his head, sharp and dark—Hazul communicating with him directly and telepathically.

"No," Rand said, although he doubted.

You are God's plaything. A sacrifice. You think you are a fighting man, but your life is a joke to him.

The flames licked at the ceiling, growing wild and out of control. Smoke billowed throughout the room now, making it hard for Rand to breathe. He'd have to escape from the mansion soon.

But Hazul was not going to get out of his way, and had grown too large to simply run from.

Rand tried to ignore what Hazul said to him, but in his own heart, he felt the truth of it. He'd prepared for so long with Simon, and God had still been silent.

Miller and Simon made it to the door and stumbled through it. At least they would survive the fight.

Hazul opened his mouth again, the ball of fire forming once more.

Rand knew it was impossible to command demons when his faith was so low. But that didn't mean he had to stand there and be burned alive.

If not for God, then for everyone else, Rand thought, tightening his sweaty palm on the cross in his hand. *Libby. Miller. My future clients. They all need me.* He thought of Georgia and those he'd helped in the past, who all would have been so much worse off if he had given up on them.

Just because he felt God had abandoned him didn't mean he had to abandon himself.

The cross, Rand realized, looking down at what he held in his hand. Although it was small compared to Hazul, it still contained power.

Hazul had immediately left Deckard's body when Simon had used it to command him.

Deckard had slapped it out of Rand's hand the first time they'd fought.

At Gerald's house, Hazul had quickly fled, seeming terrified of it.

As powerful as Hazul was, he truly feared the symbol of the Lord.

Rand couldn't go around Hazul, so instead, he went under. Just before the torrent of flame swept over him, Rand charged, sprinting between Hazul's two arms that he leaned on. The demon's gorilla-like body had grown large enough that Rand could fit underneath it.

He thrust the cross over his head, and as soon as it touched Hazul, the demon let out an ear-splitting roar.

Rand dragged the top of the cross along Hazul's belly, a white line appearing where it traced, like a sword cutting into flesh.

He rolled through Hazul's legs just before the demon collapsed. Hazul shrieked in pain from the touch of the holy object.

Rand got back onto his feet and removed the top from the bottle of holy water he clutched in his other hand.

Hazul was trying to stand again, but Rand did not give him the chance. He threw the water, a wide trail of liquid, and it burned Hazul like acid.

As the demon screamed in pain, his body began to dematerialize. The black form shrank and then folded in on itself. Then it became a pillar of black smoke which sucked into the floor and vanished. Fleeing back to hell.

With lungs filling with smoke and unbearable heat nearly

cooking him alive, Rand headed for the door to follow Miller and Simon back to freedom.

Sharp, blunt pain took him in the base of the skull. His vision blurred, and he stumbled and hit the floor.

His hand went to where he'd been hit. Warm blood met his fingers.

Rand rolled over onto his back. Deckard Arcan stood above him, pointing the barrel of his own gun at him.

47

Deckard was partly obscured by the billowing smoke. Rand started to cough and the pain in the back of his skull throbbed. The only thing he could think of was getting out of the house before it came crashing down around him.

He started to drag himself away from Deckard.

"I said I'd give you to the fires of Azora, and I will," Deckard said.

"We need to get out." It took all of Rand's breath to speak. Hazul no longer possessed the man, so Deckard was as vulnerable to the fire as Rand was—whether he realized it or not.

"We are not going anywhere."

Rand's strength gave out, and he found he could not even slide away anymore. A coughing fit overtook him, the smoke burned his eyes, and the mansion had become an oven around him.

"In the name of Azora, I offer this sacrifice," Deckard intoned. "A sinner delivered to the fires of the angel."

No, Rand tried to call out, to plead, but there were no words left in his dry throat.

Movement out of the corner of Rand's eye. Someone else was there.

Who—

Deckard was too focused on Rand to notice. "May your blessings return to us as we give this evil man—"

Then Rand recognized him.

Justin Tidwell burst through a cloud of smoke, Simon Cole's discarded cane raised above his head. He brought it down—hard— on Deckard's outstretched arm, directly onto the elbow.

A shot fired, zipping to Rand's right and barely missing him. The gun dropped and Deckard went down, grabbing the crook of his arm.

Then someone tried to scoop Rand up from underneath his arms.

"I gotcha," Miller said. He tried to lift Rand, but he was too heavy.

Justin rushed to Miller's side and assisted the shorter man. Rand leaned on the strength of the two, nearly dead weight, as he was dragged from the burning mansion.

Rand coughed and sucked in the clean, cool air. The chills spiked his sweaty skin, and the relief from the heat made him feel as if he'd been delivered straight from hell.

"Dad!" He heard Libby's voice, but couldn't see through his watery vision. He felt her hands on his chest.

Rand's lungs burned, but he finally managed to stop coughing. He swiped at his teary eyes. Libby and Miller crouched down beside him, and Simon and Justin stood over Miller's shoulder.

"You all right, Rando?" Miller asked. "The preacher shot at you. Did he get you?"

I don't think so. Rand still didn't have the strength to speak.

"What the hell were you doing in there?" Libby rounded on Justin.

"Deckard's still inside," Simon said. "We need to—"

There was a loud crack and a crash—the roof of the mansion gave way and collapsed in on itself. Sparks and smoke rose high into the sky, lighting up the night.

The fires of Azora, Rand thought. *Seems suitable for you, Deckard.*

In a few more minutes, the entire mansion would be a pile of ashes.

Once Rand managed to get his breath back, he sat up. Everyone surrounded him now—Libby, Miller, Simon, and Justin. If any one of them hadn't come to his aid that night, he would not have survived.

Rand held out his hand. Miller clasped it and Rand pulled against him to get back to his feet. A wave of light-headedness came over him, but it passed after a momentary pause.

"Happy Sunday, y'all," Rand said. "Let's get out of here."

48

O'Conner's was the only cigar bar in the city, and Rand went there with his buddies about twice a year. The bill he racked up in the joint was always substantial, so he tried to limit himself.

It didn't surprise him, though, to learn that Charles Tidwell, Justin's father, frequented it at least once a week. When Rand had called Charles, he told Rand to come.

Inside, the sweet smell of cigars and oak blanketed him, and his mind began trying to convince him to pick out a nice cigar.

The lounge was small and intimate, with dim lighting and dark furniture. A group of three men in suits were lounging and smoking and sipping whiskey. Charles was among them, and when Rand walked in, Charles excused himself from his friends and went over to him.

"It was good to finally hear from you when you called. You had me worried."

"I've been hearing that a lot today," Rand said, thinking back to all he'd endured.

"What'd they say at the college?"

Rand had just come from there. He'd had a meeting with the

dean. "The dean's a friend. I helped him out with a haunting before. That's how I got the job, actually. But a week was a bit too long, and it forced his hand. I'm on probation for a while."

Charles winced. "Sorry to hear that. I feel like it's my fault. I put you up to his, after all."

"Don't feel that way. Everything will be fine."

"Still." Charles took a drag on his cigar. "Can I get you a drink? As a token of gratitude."

"No, thank you."

"Really? Then why did you want to meet me here? I figured O'Conner's would be your kind of place."

"It is," Rand said. "I love it. But I only wanted to tell you that everything is done. You have nothing to worry about anymore."

Charles Tidwell scratched at his chin, cigar between his fingers, a trail of smoke drifting from the tip. His brow furrowed, and Rand knew he had something to say, or perhaps ask. He could already guess what it was.

"I've seen the news sites," he said, voice low. He glanced at the nearby bar. The young girl behind it was busy mixing a drink for one of Charles's friends. "About the fire. They're saying it was an accident. Maybe a suicide. Do I even want to know what happened down there?"

"No, you don't."

"Were you there?"

"It was almost me inside that burning house."

Charles winced. "And Justin? He got home very late that night, and wouldn't say where he'd been..."

"He was with me," Rand said. "Let's just say you should be very proud of your son."

That seemed to give Charles some comfort. A hint of a smile formed on his face.

But it was gone the next instant when something behind Rand caught Charles's eye. "Oh my God." Rand followed his gaze.

Justin Tidwell had come in and looked completely different. His long, disheveled hair was cut short and neatly styled to the side. His dark and baggy clothes had been replaced with well-fitted khakis and a tucked-in collared shirt.

"What do you think?" Justin asked his dad.

It took Charles a few moments to find his words. "Very nice and refined. Why did you..." He caught himself, probably thinking it was better to not even ask. "What are you doing here?"

"Mom said you were here." Then he acknowledged Rand for the first time. "Hey, Mr. Rand."

"Is everything all right?" Charles asked.

"Yeah. Just... wanted to hang out, is all. If that's okay with you." Justin looked down at the ground, embarrassed. "Maybe try a cigar. They're not supposed to let me in here, but I know you're friends with the owner, and—"

"We're sitting over there, son," Charles said, pointing to the corner of the lounge. "Of course you're welcome to join us." Now he had a full-blown smile on his face.

"I'll leave you to it," Rand said. "I hope y'all have a good evening."

"Oh, you're not staying?" Justin asked.

That surprised Rand. Despite everything they'd been through, Rand never figured they'd be friends. "O'Conner's just isn't in the budget this month."

"And he refuses to accept a gift," Charles added.

"Can I talk to you before you go, Mr. Rand?" Justin asked.

"Sure," Rand said.

Charles nodded and returned to his friends to give the two of them some privacy.

"I wanted to thank you again," Justin said. "For showing me the truth of everything."

"I should be saying that to you," Rand told him. "Without you, I would be dead."

"I feel so dumb. How could I have bought into all that?"

"He was a convincing man. Don't beat yourself up too much."

But Justin didn't seem comforted. Rand was looking at a different kid, one who looked a bit older than he had the week before, a little wiser after going through what he had.

"What will you do now?" Rand asked. "Find another church?"

Justin shook his head. "I'm done with all that."

"Really?"

"I think my dad was right all along. Maybe it's best to invest in ourselves rather than wait for a make-believe guy in the sky to fix us."

Rand nodded. It was the reaction he would've expected anyone to have after learning the truth about Deckard Arcan.

"What about you?" Justin asked.

It was such a simple question, but for Rand, it ran deep.

"I'm still struggling with own my faith. Hopefully, I'll find it one day."

Besides the demons and kidnappings and life-threatening situations, the most difficult aspect of the past week, for Rand, was the hollow sensation in his heart—a place where God should have been, but wasn't.

"I hope you do," Justin said.

"Go be with your dad," Rand told him. "He's missed you."

Justin nodded and started walking away, but stopped. "Oh, you won't be seeing me around anymore."

"What do you mean?"

"Just talk to Libby. I'm sure she'll tell you."

Justin joined his father and his friends. When he sat among them, he seemed to fit right in.

Rand frowned. For the first time over the past several months, he would've been okay with Justin dating his daughter. But he would be silly to expect a high school relationship to endure past what both Justin and Libby had been through.

He took one last deep breath of the sweet cigar smell and left O'Conner's.

"It is my prayer that we never forget Jesus Christ is the one true savior of mankind."

Rand had always known Simon Cole's voice was surprisingly strong for an elderly guy, but it was twice as powerful when he was preaching.

It was Sunday morning, and Rand and Libby sat in the pew closest to the door. They were squeezed in together—the sanctuary was crowded, and there were even a few people standing in the back of the room.

Rand wasn't surprised by the turnout. It was the first Sunday that Deckard Arcan's church was not available.

"The enemy will send many pretenders," Simon continued, making eye contact with everyone in his congregation. "Because it is the enemy's prerogative to deceive. But always remember: there is only one savior, and that is Jesus Christ. Only through him can we find redemption. No other is worth our devotion and praise."

When the sermon ended, Simon Cole stood outside the doors of the sanctuary and shook hands with every member of the congregation who filed out of his church. Rand lingered nearby and watched. It was a chilly morning even though the sun was shining. The storms had passed.

"He's great," Libby said.

"You coming back next week?"

"Eh. It's a long drive, don't you think?"

A man shook hands with Simon and then buttoned his suit coat as he walked. He caught Rand's eye, and the two looked at each other for a few lingering moments. Rand recognized Sheriff Jones, who looked quite different out of uniform. Rand's stomach flopped with sudden nerves.

Jones only gave a short nod, expressionless, and turned his attention away.

I guess he knows now who the real enemy was.

After the congregation had dispersed, Simon made his way over to Rand.

"Good morning," Simon said. "I was glad to spot you in the back when I started my sermon."

"Wouldn't miss it," Rand said. "How are you?"

Simon had taken quite a wallop from Hazul. He'd already walked with a limp and cane, but now his gait was even slower and more lopsided than it had been before.

"I'll recover," he said, smiling. "The pain comes with the territory."

"I suppose." Rand remembered all the times in the past he'd been beaten, bruised, and knocked out by demonic entities.

"How's the town?" Rand asked. "Ever since…"

"This was the largest attendance I've seen in my church in years," Simon said. "Most of them are from Deckard's. They're seeking answers. They want to know what they saw that day with Chloe. And they want the truth about the man."

"Sounds like you have your work cut out for you."

Simon smirked. "And what about you, Rand? How are you?"

"Little banged up. In a bit of trouble at the university for missing a bunch of classes, but it could have been a lot worse."

"No," Simon said. "I asked how *you* are." He gave Rand a soft look.

Rand swallowed. He remembered Justin. And Georgia Collins. And all the people he'd helped in the past, all those who had nowhere else to turn, except toward him. He wondered how long he could take on all the burdens of others before he was finally crushed underneath it.

"I'll always be here if you need encouragement," Simon said. "It's not an easy job. But you are clearly the one chosen for it."

"I wish there was a little more encouragement from God himself," Rand said.

"God must really trust you if he stays out of your way."

Rand smiled.

"I hope you join us here on Sundays in the future. Oh, and bring your friend, Miller. A bit of an oddball, but I like him."

ONCE THEY WERE on the road and heading back home, Libby reached over and put her hand on his arm. "I'm proud of you, Dad. Thanks for everything you do."

"Even if you get caught up in it?"

"I can take care of myself."

"I wish your mother felt the same."

"Now that everyone's okay, she'll get over it. Eventually."

Rand smiled. He knew that no matter how dark the road ahead, as long as he had family and good people with him by his side, he would get through it all.

THE BLACK-EYED KIDS

RANDOLPH CASEY HORROR THRILLERS
BOOK 3

PROLOGUE

Somethin' ain't right.

Wayne Swanson peered out the window of his front door, studying his vast yard as best he could in the pitch-black night. There were no streetlights in the rural area where he lived, so the only light came from the moon. Wind whipped at the trees, blowing the dead brown leaves all over his lawn. Old Pat on the news channel had said the wind speeds were low, but to Wayne's eyes it looked like a hurricane was coming. He'd endured plenty of those in his long life.

He sipped his whiskey, savoring the burn in his mouth and the back of his throat. He didn't drink often, but that night he needed to calm his nerves.

"It's the weather, Wayne," his wife Geraldine said behind him. "The weather guys can't predict it no matter how much they try, and neither can you. Stop obsessing."

It wasn't the weather that bothered him, though. He was on the lookout for something else. Twice in the past week he'd had trespassers on his property, and they'd come around the same time both nights.

"The weather ain't the problem, Gerry," Wayne said, never taking his eyes from the window.

His wife sighed. "Honestly, Wayne. You can't call the police *again.*"

Wayne pressed his lips together. He'd called the police after both occurrences, but they'd turned up nothing. The second time, the officer had given Wayne that look he'd come to recognize. The one that seemed to say, "just another old-timer losing it." Not even Geraldine believed he'd seen anyone.

Boss, Wayne's bullmastiff, whined and scratched at the back door, wanting to go out. Wayne checked his watch. It was 9:49 PM. Close to the time the trespassers had come the last two times.

Wayne downed the rest of his whiskey in a single gulp and went to the kitchen. Boss looked over his shoulder at Wayne, eyes big and pleading.

"Yeah, yeah." Wayne placed his empty glass on the nearby counter and crouched down to lace up his boots. Even at eighty-one, he could still bend, sit, and work. He was blessed. Sadly, his wife couldn't say the same.

"Are you taking the dog out?" Geraldine's voice came from the living room.

"Yup," Wayne said. He finished tightening his boots and straightened up.

Geraldine appeared in the kitchen. Her long, white hair was tied up in a loose bun and she wore her white nightgown, ready for bed. "Try to keep him calm. He'll wake the neighbors."

"We ain't got neighbors," Wayne said, annoyed at how often he had to remind her. The residents of Plaster Road, the Swansons included, owned large plots of land. Their nearest neighbor on one side was about a mile away. On the other side, two miles away. There had once been a closer house, but it had been demolished, leaving behind a vast, unused portion of land. Wayne wondered when the owner—whoever it was—was going to build something there.

Wayne opened the closet next to the back door. His shotgun

leaned against the wall. He grabbed it and checked to make sure it was loaded. It was.

"Wayne." Geraldine's hand went to her collarbone. "What in God's name?"

"Somethin' ain't right, Geraldine." He grabbed the flashlight off the closet shelf, checked that it worked, and opened the back door. Boss bolted outside.

Wayne knew Geraldine didn't like his gun. Knew she didn't believe that he'd seen anyone on their property. The police had failed him twice, so if these goons were going to keep harassing him, he would have to take matters into his own hands. Wayne Swanson did not like to take chances if he could avoid it.

Forty years ago, burglars had broken into their home and made off with a bunch of stuff. The most valuable had been some of Geraldine's family jewelry. His wife had cried for days after losing things with such sentimental value. Wayne had sympathized with her, but he always knew it could have ended up so much worse. What if they'd come home during the burglary? And if they had, what if those criminals had been armed?

The nighttime walk around the house had been a ritual ever since Boss was a pup. Wayne called it "the patrol." Boss couldn't, and wouldn't, settle down to sleep until he sniffed around the perimeter of the house, circling the entire property and scoping everything out. He would pee here and there, drink a bit from his outdoor water bowl, and when they returned inside he'd curl up on his cushion in the corner and snore until dawn. Innocent enough, at least until recently, when the patrol had become a lot more sinister.

That's what had frightened Wayne the most. Both times, the trespassers had come during the nightly walk, as if they knew Wayne would be outside. If they knew his routine, that meant they'd been lurking around for a lot longer than a week.

The wind whistled past Wayne's ears and whipped at his shirt. It was unusually cold for autumn in the south, and the chill pierced through the thin cotton material. He trained the flashlight's beam onto the ground in front of him. Boss dipped in and out of the light, sniffing around and leading the way. Wayne's boots crunched through piles of dead leaves so thick that they bunched around his ankles. He'd have to rake them in the morning before they rose to the roof.

The roof. That means the gutter's gonna be full, too. He didn't mind cleaning those out, but it was always a pain because Geraldine didn't like it when he climbed the ladder. She would no doubt shout at him all day, telling him to come down and pay someone to do that before he fell and broke his neck.

Wayne and Boss circled the house and came to the empty lot next door, the one where the abandoned house had been demolished by the new owner. Boss never wandered too far onto it, as if he knew the property line. He sniffed the ground and looked around, then paused with one leg up, poised to pee.

Suddenly, Boss's entire body stiffened. He started growling.

Wayne pointed his flashlight toward where his dog was looking. The beam illuminated only an empty field.

"Who's there?" he shouted. Wayne tightened his grip on his shotgun.

Boss backed up against Wayne's ankles. The dog was usually fearsome and wanted nothing more than to tear the mailman apart, and no visitor had ever scared him. But whatever Boss sensed in the empty lot next door turned him into a cowering mess.

"T-this is trespassing," Wayne shouted. "I'll c-call the police."

No response.

Wayne's flashlight blinked out like an extinguished torch, plunging him and Boss into darkness. Wayne mashed the button several times, thinking he'd pressed it by accident, but it didn't come back on.

"What the hell?" he muttered. He'd just changed the damn batteries.

Boss let out a single, aggressive bark. Wayne dropped his useless flashlight and gripped his shotgun in both hands.

Then, even though it was dark, Wayne saw them. The two

familiar black shadows stood in the middle of the empty lot, side-by-side, one taller than the other.

Wayne raised his shotgun and pointed it straight at the pair. "I've got a gun. You'd better leave." His aim was unsteady in his trembling hand.

They remained completely still, like statues.

Wayne Swanson wasn't seeing things. He was eighty-one years old, but Dr. Hays praised his eyesight every year when he went in for his checkup. Yet how could those shadows be there in the first place? It made no sense. You had to have light to make shadows. It was like the shadows were darker than the night.

Wayne pumped the shotgun, hoping the sound would frighten the trespassers. "I'm warnin' you. This is private property."

Boss started whimpering and crying.

Wayne considered firing a warning shot. Far up and to the left, of course, only to scare the bastards off. But if he did shoot, he'd never hear the end of it from Geraldine, who'd likely think he was only firing at figments of his imagination.

A sharp gust of wind almost knocked Wayne off his feet. It was like something from a storm, though Old Pat hadn't said anything about a storm coming in. The leaves whipped around Wayne, lifted from the ground, and were carried up like a mass migration of birds, breaking his line of sight on the trespassers.

Boss relaxed. When the leaves settled, Wayne saw that he and Boss were alone. The intruders had run away again.

Wayne scooped up his flashlight, pressed the button. It turned on as if nothing had been wrong before. He aimed the beam at where the figures had stood. Definitely gone. He pivoted and shone his light toward his house. He illuminated the back door, the windows, anywhere the intruders could be breaking in.

They weren't there.

"How the hell do they move so fast?" he whispered to Boss. And so quietly? He hadn't even heard running footsteps crunching the leaves. It was like they'd simply vanished rather than fled.

There was no telling how long these thugs would be satisfied just by scaring an old man and his dog. Eventually, they'd do something worse. Hurt him, or Geraldine. Wayne had to get to the bottom of this before that happened, with or without the police's help.

Wayne made a final sweep of the empty lot with his flashlight. He shivered and said, "Come on, Boss. Let's go back inside."

He returned to the house, already dreading tomorrow night's patrol.

Somethin' definitely ain't right.

1

There was always at least one, though this year there were three students dressed in Halloween costumes.

Rand Casey rarely got distracted when he was teaching, but he couldn't take his eyes off the outfits. He had a Taylor Swift, a guy in a gorilla suit complete with an oversized banana, and someone who he assumed was a character from a popular television show he didn't watch but had caught glimpses of when his daughter Libby had it on.

I really *hate Halloween*, Rand thought to himself as he clicked the button on his remote. The image on the screen at the front of the classroom changed to show two identical men wearing black suits and sunglasses.

"What do you think of when you see this picture?" Rand asked the class.

"Men in Black," someone said. Others snickered, likely assuming that wasn't the answer he was looking for.

"Correct," Rand said. "I think there is a considerable lack of evidence around this topic and it's safe to say that Men in Black do *not* exist."

This was one of Rand's favorite lessons in his Intro to Supernatural Studies course, and he always gave it near Halloween time. After all the supernatural and spiritual phenomena he taught in his class, he would eventually get the inevitable question: Is there anything you *don't* believe in?

Yes. Plenty. He'd put together an entire presentation on topics he considered nothing more than myths and urban legends. It usually turned into an interesting debate when he brushed up against someone's favorite conspiracy theory.

Rand felt strongly about this lesson. First, it was good to bring some lighthearted relief to the terrifying subject matter he usually taught. Second, if the purpose of his course was to equip his students with the knowledge they needed to defend themselves against dark supernatural forces, then it was equally important for them to know what *didn't* exist.

"You mean, like, the movie with Will Smith?" the student asked. "Of course that isn't real."

"The movie borrowed from the popular urban legend," Rand explained. "The Men in Black story has been around for a while. Just like in that film, it's said that they come in pairs, always dressed in black suits."

The student, the supposed Will Smith expert, seemed confused. "What do they want?"

"There are plenty of theories," Rand said. "People who claim to have been abducted by UFOs say Men in Black visited them and threatened them to keep quiet about what they experienced. Most believe the Men in Black work for a branch of government involved in secrecy and intelligence."

"Seems believable to me," the student said.

"Standard government secrecy and intelligence are believable," Rand said. "But sinister thugs that threaten UFO fanatics? No. The original abduction claims are shifty in the first place, so why would we believe that Men in Black approached them?"

A familiar hand in the front row shot into the air. "Is any of this going to be on the midterm?"

Rand chuckled. He'd tried to have a light lesson, but as always,

Stacy Thompson still worried about her 4.0. She eyed him through wide blue eyes, nervously fingering her shoulder-length blonde hair as she waited for his answer.

"No, Stacy. It wouldn't make sense to test you on myths and legends, don't you think?"

Stacy seemed to consider his words while lowering her hand.

Rand appreciated Stacy. Sometimes, she was the only person in the class to ask questions or participate in discussions.

The stadium classroom was more empty than full that day. Over half the students that had enrolled in his class at the beginning of the semester had dropped. That was common. Intro to Supernatural Studies wasn't difficult, but most students found it frightening.

"Next," Rand said, clicking his remote. The following image was of a tall humanoid wearing a suit. Its arms and legs were extra long, and it had a white, featureless face.

"Slenderman," muttered several students.

"Precisely. This guy's popular around the internet and arguably the most mainstream creepypasta out there."

"Creepypasta?" Stacy asked.

"Creepypasta is an internet slang term. It's from the word 'copy pasta,' which referred to text that went viral through emails and message boards back when the internet was young. Creepypasta refers to popular stories that circulate online that tell personal accounts of scary stories, strange incidents, and unexplained experiences, all of which are fictional, but written as if true." Rand gestured to the screen. "This guy took the 'net by storm in the early 2000s, and since then has launched an entire franchise—books, movies, and video games. It shows you the power of the internet these days. For as long as humans have been around, urban legends have been handed down orally. Now, with a few clicks, a story can spread across the globe in less than an hour."

Rand clicked the remote again and Slenderman disappeared. He was replaced by two young children standing side-by-side, one taller than the other. They looked normal except for their eyes, which were completely black.

A student wearing sweatpants and an oversized t-shirt raised his hand. "Is it true you hate Halloween, Mr. Casey?"

"I'm glad you asked," Rand said, turning his back on the ominous-looking kids that loomed on the screen behind him. "Yes. Halloween is the most dangerous day of the year, and even though I know I can't control anyone, I would urge you all to stay inside."

Dozens of blank eyes stared at him. A few chuckles and murmurs flowed through the room.

"Oh… you're serious." The student smirked.

"Make fun of me all you like," Rand told them. He was used to it. He had a sense of humor about most things, but Halloween was not one of them. "After all these months in this class, after all these lectures, what makes you think celebrating a day dedicated to witchcraft is a good idea? It's the one time of year when the world of the living and the dead are nearest, and only evil can come from that."

He was met by silence. The girl dressed as Taylor Swift was trying her best to stifle her laughter.

Rand ignored her and checked his watch. "Okay, that's it for today. You can all go."

"What about that?" Stacy asked, pointing toward the screen.

Rand looked over his shoulder. "Oh yeah. The black-eyed kids." He glanced at the time again. There were five minutes left in the class, but he wanted to get out of there early. "We can cover them tomorrow. Or maybe not. They say once you know about the black-eyed kids, you'll encounter them, so perhaps it's best if we ignore them altogether."

Stacy's face went white.

"Don't freak out, Stacy. This whole lesson is about things that *aren't* real, remember?"

Stacy didn't seem comforted. She couldn't look away from the picture. The black pools of their eyes seemed to draw her in.

Rand picked up on Stacy's fear and felt a pang of guilt. His class was for educational purposes, not a place to come for cheap, spooky thrills.

Rand used his remote to turn the screen off.

As the students gathered their belongings and filed out of the room, Rand packed his laptop and books into his bag, slung it over his shoulder, and followed them out.

Rand had finished class early because he needed to check up on his daughter Libby and Tessa, Libby's mother, just to make sure they weren't planning anything for Halloween. Like his students, they also thought his distrust of Halloween was a bit over the top. He worried they might try to throw a costume party or plan something behind his back.

In Rand's opinion, the holiday was more dangerous than a category-five hurricane. And just like a hurricane, he had to make sure his family stayed indoors and safe.

2

The kitchen table was covered in notebooks and flashcards. A computer and a tablet rested near two Starbucks cups, one empty, the other half full. Stacy Thompson stared at all her study materials, feeling overwhelmed.

"This is too intense," Kim said. Stacy's roommate joined her at the kitchen table, sporting only a single notebook and a highlighter. She wore purple pajama pants and a white t-shirt. She used her hand to toss her wavy brown hair aside and out of her face. "How can you even find anything in all this stuff?"

"It's my ritual," Stacy shot back.

Kim looked confused as she scanned the paraphernalia. "Your ritual has gotten out of control. You need to rein it in. I don't know how you get stuff done."

Every semester, Stacy told herself she'd get more organized. Or maybe she needed to get more streamlined. She spent so much time prepping for study that she didn't actually get much studying done.

Less is more, she tried to tell herself. Though she stressed every semester before midterms, her process had yet to let her down. The dreaded B had never found its way into her grades.

"Are we studying or are you just going to make fun of me?" Stacy asked.

Kim opened her notebook and removed the cap from her highlighter, ready to go.

Stacy scanned through her supplies. On the edge of the table was the notebook she used for her Religion class, the only elective she had room for in her schedule that semester. The class was called Intro to Supernatural Studies, which was a misnomer because there wasn't a follow-up course. She'd chosen it because it had a reputation for being easy. So far the tests had been simple, but studying was a challenge because the material frightened her.

"You can't be serious," Kim said.

Stacy looked up. "What?"

Kim had spotted Stacy's clearly labeled notebook. "You have a midterm in your ghost class? How is that even possible?"

"I think all classes are required to have a midterm."

"What could possibly be on a test in a class like that?" Kim went on, then smirked. "Or maybe you study for that class so much because of your huge teacher crush."

"Shut up," Stacy said. "I still need to study."

Kim rolled her eyes. "You have a photographic memory, and you've never made a B in your life."

While that sounded like an accomplishment, it only increased the pressure. Stacy had gotten straight As since she was five years old. The last thing she needed was to get her first B now.

"Are you going to the Boyd Street block party tomorrow night?" Kim asked, her notebook forgotten.

"Are you serious? There's no way I have time for that."

"Me neither, but I wouldn't miss it. It's a blast every year. I heard a group of students petitioned the university to move midterms away from Halloween weekend specifically because of the block party, but they got shot down."

"Midterms aren't something we can change, Kim. We need to study."

Kim sighed. "You sound just like one of *them*."

"One of who?"

The doorbell rang, taking Stacy by surprise.

"Did you invite Craig over?" she asked, then frowned and tossed aside her highlighter. "I thought we were supposed to focus on midterms tonight *without* extra company."

"Relax. I didn't invite him."

But Craig, Kim's current boyfriend, did have a habit of showing up unannounced. Stacy actually liked Craig, but that night he would be too much of a distraction.

Stacy pushed her chair out, the wooden legs screeching against the tile floor. She marched into the living room and threw open the front door.

"Craig, tonight isn't—"

No one was there.

Stacy stomped onto the porch and looked around. There was a chill in the air and a light breeze, so Stacy folded her arms and hunched her shoulders as she scanned the yard and street.

"Idiots," she whispered under her breath.

She and Kim rented a house in a small neighborhood near campus. The other houses nearby were also occupied by university students, which meant the area was far from peaceful. Every weekend so far that semester, one of their dumbass neighbors had thrown a party with enough booze to fuel it until the late morning hours. Stacy had wanted to move for a long time, but Kim liked the house. Stacy wanted to keep Kim as a roommate, so Stacy had to tolerate the noise. But that night, with midterms looming, she just couldn't handle any distractions.

But now, so close to Halloween, some extra disturbances were inevitable, starting with some immature moron ringing the doorbell and running away.

"You're only embarrassing yourself," Stacy called into the night, then went back inside, slamming the door behind her.

Another knock sounded at the door.

Stacy stopped dead. She slowly turned, furrowing her brow.

Impossible, she thought. The porch had been empty. How had someone come to the door that quickly?

She reached for the knob, but hesitated. A strange tingle blossomed at the base of her neck. She didn't know why, but this time she could sense a presence on the other side of the door.

Stacy took her hand away from the knob and leaned toward the peephole instead. Someone—no, *two* people, stood on her porch. Two *short* people, like children.

Maybe early trick-or-treaters? Stacy thought. There weren't any kids in their college neighborhood.

Stacy gripped the knob, turned it slowly. She cracked open the door.

She'd been right about them being children. The older boy looked about ten years old with unwashed, greasy brown hair. The red-and-white striped t-shirt and blue shorts he wore were smudged with grime as if he'd been rolling around in a dumpster. The other boy, who looked to be about eight and was a head shorter, wore a black shirt and shorts with a thick mop of ginger hair, tangled and unkempt. Both were barefoot.

Where are their parents? Stacy wondered. *Where are their shoes?* Both kids had bare feet and their toes and ankles were caked with dried mud.

"Umm," Stacy began. "Hi." She peered over their heads and into the yard and street, searching for any sign of their parents.

"We need to come in and use your telephone," said the taller boy, staring straight at Stacy's chest. The other kid stared at her chest, too, although his hair hung over his eyes.

Perverts, Stacy thought, folding her arms over her chest.

"Where did you come from?" Stacy asked. "Where are your parents?"

"Your telephone," the older one said, as if growing angry.

"Umm... I don't have one. I only have a cell phone. It's in the kitchen, but if you wait here—"

"We need to come inside and use your telephone!" he shouted at her now, still staring at her chest. "We won't hurt you. We're not bad people."

Stacy recoiled at the sudden outburst. "I didn't say you were…"

Stacy's pulse thudded in her ears. Something wasn't right. Neither of the boys had moved since they'd arrived. They also didn't seem to mind the cold while wearing hardly any clothes, and their request sounded more like a threat.

"You're going to turn us away? We're two young kids who need help. Why would you do that?"

A roiling sensation in Stacy's gut left her wanting to vomit. She closed her eyes and swallowed, trying to fight off the sickness that had come over her so suddenly.

When she opened her eyes, both the boys met her gaze.

Stacy froze.

Their eyes were completely black. No iris, no pupil, no whites. Like two soulless black holes staring through her.

Stacy couldn't look away, drawn into their seemingly endless depth. She gripped the doorframe; in that moment, she just needed to touch something that she knew was grounded.

"You have to let us in," the older boy said. He spoke slowly, as if luring Stacy to obey. "We need help."

"No," she snapped. She grabbed the door and slammed it shut in their creepy faces. She threw the lock and deadbolt.

Now that the little freaks were out of sight, the feeling of nausea began to fade. She backed away from the door, expecting to hear another knock. Maybe some shouts from them. But so far, the boys hadn't reacted.

Stacy went to the living room window that had a view of the front porch. She nudged the curtain and peeked through. The little freaks were gone.

She exhaled a breath, letting the curtain fall back into place.

Stacy bolted to the kitchen, mind reeling from the bizarre occurrence on the porch.

"Kim."

Kim looked up from her notebook and cast Stacy a strange look.

"Oh. You came back? I figured you gave up on studying and—" Kim straightened in her chair, eyes wide with alarm. "Stacy, are you all right? You look—"

Stacy jabbed her finger toward the door. "T-The kids from my class. The ones with black eyes."

"What are you talking about? What kids—"

"Kim, they're there. It's…"

Stacy felt tears coming. She had too much to say, but couldn't get it out fast enough.

Kim stood and went over to Stacy. She put her hands on Stacy's arms, and Stacy welcomed the touch—something that felt normal.

"You're shaking." Kim's face was close, concerned. "Slow down. Start at the beginning. Tell me where you went for so long."

"So long?" Stacy took a step backward out of Kim's embrace. "Wh… what do you mean?"

Kim's eyebrows pulled together. "Stacy, you were gone for two hours."

3

Rand crossed the quad and headed toward Campus Corner, the university's main coffee shop, with his bag slung over his shoulder. He breathed in the clear air of the chilly morning. It was shaping up to be a nice fall day, except for one major problem.

Halloween. It had finally arrived.

That alone kept Rand on edge. Anything could happen on Halloween. Whatever thin veil kept the world of the living and dead separate, it was thinnest on that night, and all manner of dark entities delighted in coming for him.

Shindael. The demon was never far behind. Rand hadn't seen him in a few days, but Rand was no idiot. Shindael would never give up tormenting him, and Halloween was the perfect opportunity.

Rand's plan was to approach the day as if it were normal and hope nothing went wrong. Coffee first, classes second, then make sure Libby and Tessa were safe inside for the night, and finally return home and stay there until the next morning.

Simple. Except it rarely ever was on Halloween.

Campus Corner was a small place with a relaxed vibe, if a bit pretentious. The manager regularly rotated mediocre paintings by the university's art students, and as usual, some guy plucked away at his guitar in the corner, soft notes filling the cafe. Rand hoped he wouldn't start singing.

When Rand walked in, he was met with a decorative plastic skeleton and ghost dangling from the ceiling, swaying in the breeze that snuck in from outside. Rand glided around them, keeping his distance as if they were diseased.

"Good morning, Mr. Rand," said the barista Cassie, who was always there for the morning shift. She must've only taken afternoon classes. She'd added a pink streak to her short blonde hair since Rand had seen her last. "Happy Halloween."

"What have you done to the place?" Rand gestured toward the hanging decorations—pumpkins, spiders, monsters, zombies. "It's usually so nice in here."

"Ted made me put all that up before we opened this morning," Cassie said, rolling her eyes. "But whatever. It's Halloween. I guess we can have some fun."

Rand grimaced. Cassie rang up his black Americano from memory.

"I'll bring it out to you," Cassie said as Rand handed her cash.

"Thanks, Cassie."

Rand went to the patio to enjoy the nice weather—and to get away from the guitar player who'd started humming into the microphone. The outdoor section was adorned with plants and had a stone water feature that Rand found particularly relaxing.

Rand sat down at the only remaining empty table and leaned back in his chair. His phone chimed in his pocket. When he slid it out, he had a text from his friend Miller.

Happy Halloween Rando.

The text was followed by all the possible relevant emojis: ghosts, devils, zombies, aliens, pumpkins.

Rand rolled his eyes. Even Miller made fun of him for his hatred of Halloween, though the man knew first-hand how dangerous it could be.

He'd better stay inside tonight, too, Rand thought. He made a mental note to swing by Miller's shop and make sure he wasn't making plans for the night.

Cassie brought his coffee, and the warm cup in his hand felt pleasant against the chilly morning. Rand sipped it, savoring the steaming bitterness.

"Is it okay?" Cassie asked.

"It always is when you make it, Cassie," Rand said.

The girl beamed and lingered near his table. "So what are you going to be for Halloween this year, Mr. Rand?"

"I'm going to be asleep with the doors locked and the lights off."

"Oh, that's no fun. Why don't you come to the Boyd Street block party? That's where I'll be." She glanced toward the unattended counter inside the coffee shop. A line was forming in her absence.

"I think I'm a little old for something like that."

"I saw Mr. Galway there last year. He was dressed like a mummy."

Rand didn't know Jim Galway from the Math department personally, but was aware of his reputation for perving on young female students. Boyd Street would be right up that guy's alley.

"Please be careful tonight, Cassie," Rand said. He wanted to lecture her about how she would be better off staying indoors, but didn't feel like opening that can of worms while his coffee was still hot.

"Of course. But not *too* careful. I don't want to miss all the fun." She gave Rand a wry smile before she went back inside.

Rand shook his head. Cassie was another lost cause, a Halloween lover. He couldn't save them all.

Rand picked up his phone to respond to Miller. But before he could, someone else appeared by his side.

It was Stacy Thompson. Her face was pinched and her eyes glistened with tears.

"Oh. Hey, Stacy. Are you—"

"Mr. Casey, I need to talk to you." She seemed a bit more on edge than usual.

"Is it about the midterm? Stacy, I don't think you need to worry—"

"No, it isn't about the midterm," she shrieked. She caught herself and looked over her shoulder to see if she'd drawn any attention. A few nearby heads had turned. When she looked back to Rand, she forced a whisper. "Please. I need to talk to you right now."

"Okay," Rand said, softening his tone and straightening in his chair. "Have a seat."

Stacy again scanned the other students filling the nearby tables. "Can we go somewhere more private?"

"Oh. Um... sure." Rand grabbed his coffee cup and followed Stacy through the coffee shop's patio entrance and out onto the street where no one else was around.

"What's going on?" Rand asked her.

Stacy wiped away a tear. "I saw them last night."

"Saw who?"

"Those kids you had on the screen in class yesterday. The ones with black eyes. They showed up at my door."

"But Stacy," Rand said. "Those things aren't real."

Stacy Thompson deflated. "Come on. After everything you've taught us, *you're* going to be the one to not believe me?"

"Whoa," Rand said. "It's not that I don't believe you, it's just..." She seemed on the verge of breaking down, and he realized perhaps he'd been too thoughtless with what he'd said. His daughter *had* told him dozens of times that he sometimes didn't think before he spoke. "Why don't you tell me the whole story."

Stacy shuddered. "I don't even want to think about it."

"The only way I can help you is if I hear your story. Don't leave anything out."

The way Stacy had come to Rand just now was the same way his past clients did after they'd had a terrifying encounter they couldn't explain. Rand needed to start off the same way he always did: by hearing the story. Often, supernatural explanations could be debunked just from the stories alone.

The lanky, curly-haired guitar player from the coffee shop

passed through the patio's gate and in between Rand and Stacy. He carried his guitar case and focused on his cell phone, texting as he walked by, oblivious to the tense silence he'd just disrupted.

Stacy waited until he was out of earshot. "I was at home. My roommate Kim was with me. We were supposed to study, but the doorbell rang."

They most often arrive at the door, Rand thought, remembering the few stories of the black-eyed kids he'd studied.

"I thought it was Kim's boyfriend, so I got up to answer the door, and they were standing there. No, wait." She paused. "No one was there the first time. I thought it was someone playing a prank, so I went back inside and closed the door, but then someone knocked. And it was weird, Mr. Casey, because no one was there and then the knock just happened. Like, there wasn't even time for someone to come up to the door."

Rand frowned. What Stacy had just described was quite common with supernatural phenomena. He'd experienced it himself many times. Entities didn't need to walk up to your door. They just appeared.

"When I opened the door again, they were there." A tear escaped from her eye and she wiped it away.

"When did you notice their eyes were black?" he asked. Stacy seemed thrown off by the sudden question. To Rand, her response mattered.

"Um... Not right away. I don't know how I missed it. They weren't looking me in the eye at first. Just kind of staring straight ahead. And I just started to feel weird. Sick. Like I wanted to throw up. Or like they were hypnotizing me. Something like that."

Rand pursed his lips. These were all details that he'd studied in previous sightings. The victim always reported a trance-like state that began once the kids had appeared. This caused them to not immediately notice the black eyes. After the encounter was over, the victim surmised that the black-eyed kids were trying to keep the victim from noticing their eyes. As if the kids knew that their unnatural eyes were what would keep the victim from allowing them inside.

"Did they speak to you?" Rand asked. *And did they say they needed a telephone*, he thought.

"Yes. They wanted to come in and use my telephone."

Stacy watched him, waiting for his next question. Rand knew what he needed to ask next, and he dreaded the answer.

"Did you let them in?"

"No."

Rand let out the breath he'd been holding.

"Why? What happens when you let them in?"

He didn't know. No one seemed to know. In the few accounts of the black-eyed kids that existed, all the victims had been able to break out of the so-called trance and refuse to let the kids in. That was one reason why Rand had always considered the black-eyed kids to be a myth. There were no *real* endings to the stories. No one had ever let them in, so he didn't know what happened when they came inside, or what the black-eyed kids wanted in the first place.

"They freaked me out so bad that I slammed the door on them. Then they disappeared. But then…"

"Then what?" Rand asked.

"But when I went back to the kitchen, my roommate Kim said I'd been gone for two whole hours. And according to the clock, she was right. But my conversation with the kids felt like it had only lasted for a few minutes. It was so weird."

Distorted time, Rand thought. That was never a good sign. He'd experienced it himself on a number of occasions.

"Say something," Stacy pleaded.

"What you've told me sounds a lot like the accounts I've studied," Rand replied, speaking slowly and carefully. He didn't want to frighten Stacy more than she already was.

"I thought you said they weren't real."

"I've never encountered them in my practice," Rand said. "And the stories I've come across need a… lot more corroboration, in my opinion."

"Well, I have all the corroboration you need now."

This was an interesting situation. Rand had never before worked with a client that he'd known personally. For that reason, all were subject to a little bit of skepticism before he began a full-blown investigation into their claims. But Stacy Thompson was different. He'd never known the girl to make up stories, lie, or seek attention.

"Did you do any more reading about the black-eyed kids after class?" Rand asked.

"No," she said. Her eyes honed in on him. "You don't believe me."

"I do believe that you saw something that made you feel that way," Rand said, choosing his words carefully. "But you have to keep in mind that there's a process I follow when someone approaches me with stories like this."

Stacy rubbed her fingers into her eyes. "Fine. Can you at least tell me what I should do?"

"What were you planning to do tonight?" Rand asked.

"Hide in my room."

"If you hadn't seen anything last night, what would you have done?"

"Study, of course."

"Okay. That sounds good. But I wouldn't recommend you to be alone. You need to be around people." Any entity seeking to frighten or attack their target almost always waited until the individual was alone.

Stacy's gaze lingered on the fall display that had been set up near the entrance to the coffee shop's patio. Stacked blocks of hay were topped with jack-o'-lanterns. "My roommate has been begging me to go with her to the Boyd Street block party."

Rand grimaced. "That won't work. You need to stay inside where it's safe."

"But if I stay home, then I'll be alone. You just said I needed to be around people. There'll be *hundreds* of people on Boyd Street tonight."

"Right, but..."

"But what?"

"You shouldn't leave the house on Halloween."

"That's just you being paranoid about the holiday. You told us yesterday in class that you hate it. The problem is these kids, not the day of the year."

"Can you talk your roommate or another one of your friends into staying home with you tonight?" Rand asked.

Stacy scoffed. "Yeah right. It's the biggest party of the year."

"Well…"

Maybe the Boyd Street block party would be the lesser of two evils for Stacy, Rand thought. *Just this once.*

"Will you help me?" Stacy's face softened as if she was nervous that he might tell her no.

"Of course," Rand said. "There's a reason for what you saw, and we'll get to the bottom of it."

"How? What will you do? Is this going to be like…"

Be like the cases I talk about in class? Rand thought. *I hope not. But I can't yet say for sure.*

"Don't tell me you don't know what to do," she said.

"I do," Rand said. Actually, it would be more accurate to say that he knew where to start.

Miller.

Rand's friend Miller Landingham had dug up info on every urban legend known to man. Surely he had some information or insight pertaining to the black-eyed kids.

"I'll discuss this with a colleague. We'll make a plan of action and go from there."

Stacy deflated. That didn't seem to be practical enough for her. "But what if they come back before you can do anything?"

"That's why I'm urging you to be around people," Rand said. "Just for tonight. Tomorrow, I'll have something more concrete for you."

Rand understood Stacy's dissatisfaction. He truly did. But he had to approach this carefully. If Stacy had indeed had an encounter with the black-eyed kids, then the situation was unprecedented to Rand.

His own fear had begun to creep in, as if he were absorbing it from Stacy. He would have taken it all from her if he could have. Despite all that he'd experienced, Rand had never claimed to be immune to fear, and he never would. But when a brand-new situation caused him to feel fear, he knew that was just another liability —entities could, and would use it against him. They had before.

Stacy looked at her watch. Her knees buckled. "I'm late for Calculus. Ugh. Today was supposed to be a midterm review class."

"Go," Rand told her. "I'll be in touch after I speak with my colleague. Call me if anything happens. Anything at all."

"I need your number."

Stacy handed Rand her phone and he typed in his number. He handed it back to her and she called his phone. When her number popped up on Rand's screen, he declined the call and saved her as a contact.

"Don't leave your phone on silent tonight," Stacy said.

"Try to relax, Stacy. Everything is going to be okay."

She flashed a hint of an eye roll, as if she'd like to believe what he said, but didn't. "You sound just like Kim. I can't even relax when creepy kids *don't* show up at my door." She sighed. "Anyway. Just help me. I still feel really weird about what happened."

"I'm here for you, Stacy."

She tried to smile, but it only came out as a small twitch of her lips.

Rand watched her go, frowning. He always hated it when someone had their first negative interaction with the spiritual world. The trauma could last a lifetime. Stacy Thompson didn't deserve what had happened to her, and he would do anything he could to help her.

Fucking Halloween, he thought.

4

The final bell rang and the halls of Denton High School filled with teenagers clamoring for the freedom of the Halloween weekend. Libby Casey was among them. She rummaged through her locker, skimming the spines of her textbooks. Her teachers had been generous and hadn't assigned much homework for Halloween night, but Libby started shoving half her books into her backpack, anyway.

Her locker slammed closed, almost catching her arm like a biting steel trap. Her friend Bailey's hand was pressed on the locker door, fingers spread.

"He asked me," Bailey said, beaming.

"Terrence?"

"Yes. Finally. It took him long enough. I was *this* close to flexing my inner modern woman and asking him to the Halloween dance myself."

A black-and-orange banner hung above Libby's locker.

"DENTON HIGH HALLOWEEN DANCE. ALL GOBLINS AND GHOULS INVITED."

Bailey had had her eye on Terrance as a date for two weeks. She'd dropped all kinds of hints, and Libby had had to hear about every single one. As the dance drew closer, she'd started to get para-noid that he wouldn't ask her. She'd even started dressing up more for school—today she wore a hint of mascara and she'd curled her brown hair, eschewing her normal single braid.

"That's what I told you to do in the first place," Libby said. "You knew he was shy. You could've just shown him how it's done and not wasted a bunch of time."

"Doesn't matter now," Bailey said. "Oh, and he's cool with going in our group." She eyed Libby's full backpack. "Planning on getting much homework done at the dance?"

"I need the books for the plan," Libby said. She opened her locker again and crammed more textbooks into her backpack. Bailey watched with an amused grin as Libby struggled to pull the zipper over the protruding edges of the hardcovers.

"Right. The *plan*. It's all about the *plan*. You've been telling me all week that you needed a plan. Do you finally have one?"

"I do. So listen up, because if it doesn't go just right, then I won't be able to go to the dance."

They started down the hall toward the exit, shouldering past thick groups of students like they were trying to push to the front of a concert crowd. Libby had to raise her voice over the din of conversations so her friend could hear her.

"First, we'll go to Bill's house." Bill was Libby's soon-to-be step-dad, and her mom had moved into his house. "I'll lay all these books and notebooks out on the table like the most intense study session you've ever seen. When my dad shows up, the story is that we're staying in all night to study."

Bailey listened, waiting for more. When she realized that was the end, she shot Libby a confused look. "That's it? Libby, that's called a lie, not a plan."

"That's just the first part," Libby said. "If my dad buys it, then we're done. But I've also planned for other... contingencies."

Bailey lifted her eyebrows. "Like?"

"Well, if he lurks around Bill's house like a prison guard and makes sure no one leaves, then we'll have to sneak out the back door, in costume, and cross the neighbor's yard to get out of the neighborhood. Then, we'll walk to your house, where you'll have parked your car, and we can use it to get to the dance.

"There's also a chance he'll show up to the dance and look for me if he finds out about it, though right now he doesn't know. I've already paid Victoria Lansing fifty bucks to be on the lookout." Victoria was the student body president and had organized the Halloween dance. She'd told Libby that she planned to spend the entire dance at the door checking to make sure costumes weren't inappropriate or that no one was trying to come into the dance drunk. "I gave her a picture of my dad, so she'll know what he looks like. She'll send me a warning text if she sees him, then I'll run out the gym's back door by the locker rooms.

"Oh, then there's my mom. She and Bill have their own party tonight at Bill's office, so if my dad catches them instead, there's a chance he can convince my mom to tell him—"

"Jeez, Libby," Bailey said. "Seriously? I always thought Mr. Rand was a cool dad."

"Three hundred and sixty-four days a year, he's the best I could ever hope for," Libby said. "But when it comes to Halloween, he has a strict no-tolerance policy. No celebrating, no leaving the house. I'm the only person I know who's never been trick-or-treating."

Bailey may never understand, but Libby *absolutely* needed a plan if she was going to make it to that Halloween dance. All throughout the week, every time Libby's attention in class had drifted off and she'd considered each potential way her dad could catch her out of the house on Halloween night, a heavy load of guilt burdened her. She, more than anyone else, understood why her dad was so averse to Halloween. What most people considered a fun holiday was a perfect time for evil spirits to stir.

When Libby had firmly decided to seize Halloween for herself that year, to finally experience it like a normal person for once, she knew she'd need a well-thought-out plan to get away with it.

The stakes were high. If she was caught, then not only would her dad be very angry, he would also be very hurt. He had the highest expectations for Libby, and she knew he would feel very betrayed.

Mrs. Worsham, the oldest teacher on staff and a decade past normal retirement age, stood at the front door of the school in the middle of the exit, forcing the students to divert around her as if she were a rock in a river.

"Don't drink and drive. Don't do drugs," she shouted through hands cupped around her mouth. Everyone, including Libby and Bailey, tuned her out as they left the building.

The afternoon was clear, and Libby welcomed the chilled air as she emerged from the stuffy, crowded hallway. Outside, some students dispersed to their cars while others piled into the school buses lined up at the edge of the parking lot. Libby could smell their familiar exhaust.

"I still think you're giving too much thought to this plan," Bailey said. They could hear each other better now that they didn't have to talk over the crowd of students and Mrs. Worsham's dire warnings. "Oh, I forgot to tell you that Terrence and I are going to dress up as skeletons for the dance. After he asked me, he told me he didn't have a costume, so I said he could borrow the skeleton outfit my brother wore last year. I'll wear mine again and we can match."

"Oh, about the costumes," Libby began. "We'll need to pack a bag of normal clothes to change into in case my dad—"

Strong arms wrapped around Libby from behind, and she shrieked. An icy chill shot through her body as she scrambled out of the unwelcome grasp. She whirled around and saw Parker Haney behind her, confused yet amused.

"Whoa. You okay?" he said. His smile widened, showing his perfectly straight teeth.

"Parker. Sorry. You scared the crap out of me." Libby's skin prickled as the sudden, sharp dose of adrenaline began to fade. She rubbed at her arms to make the icky feeling go away.

"My bad." Although he didn't seem too sorry.

Libby herself was surprised by the fierce, instinctive reaction. It was more than just being startled. The last time she'd been grabbed from behind, she'd been locked up in an attic by a psychotic man during her dad's previous case.

"We all good for tonight?" Parker asked.

"Yeah." She took a calming breath to settle her nerves.

Parker Haney was captain of the swim team, had wavy, sandy-colored hair and an athletic body, and made good grades. According to Bailey, Parker was utterly perfect. Libby wasn't that single-minded about him, but she did like him. When word began percolating through the school that she and Justin Tidwell had broken up, Parker wasted no time inviting her to the Halloween dance.

"You said you'd be at your stepdad's house, right?" Parker said. "You still need to text me his address."

"Yes." But then Libby remembered the intricate parts of her plan that she hadn't shared with Parker. "Or we might be at Bailey's."

"But I thought…" He shrugged. "Whatever. Just let me know. See you later on."

Parker left them and joined a group of his buddies on the other side of the parking lot.

"What's with the freak-out?" Bailey asked, giving her a look. "It's physically impossible to be repulsed by Parker Haney."

"It reminded me of that time… He just scared me. Forget it."

"And I see you haven't clued him in on your little plan," Bailey said as they walked toward Libby's car.

"We barely know each other. I don't want him thinking I have a crazy dad. It's only today that he's like this. The rest of the time, he's fine. But I'd like to make a good impression on Parker, so if you don't mind keeping my dad's paranoia a little secret between us, that'd be great."

"You got it," Bailey said.

"So we'll go to Bill's house now," Libby said. "I'll call my dad from the landline so he knows I'm there, give him the cover story, and have Mom talk to him so she can corroborate. She'll get a lecture about how I'm not to leave the house, blah, blah, blah." Bailey started scrolling her phone as Libby continued explaining. "Meanwhile, we'll set up the living room to look like we're studying, because no matter what my mom says, my dad *will* still show up. Then, we'll—"

Libby's phone vibrated in her back pocket. When she checked the text message, she saw it was from her friend, Georgia Collins.

"Hey Libby! I need u to meet me at the hospital. I need to talk to u…"

Libby's heart thudded. Georgia had cystic fibrosis and spent most of her time at St. Mary's Hospital. Libby had first met Georgia when Libby's dad removed a demon that had attached itself to the sick girl.

"Is everything okay?" Libby sent the response, and immediately the three dots started bouncing on the screen.

"Can u come by the hospital? Like now? Ur out of school right? I've been waiting all day."

Libby chewed her lip. That didn't really work with her plans.

"Can I call you?"

"I want to tell u in person."

"What's wrong?" Libby heard Bailey ask. "Who texted you?"

Libby's tight plan hadn't allowed any room for diversions. Visiting Georgia now would put her behind schedule.

But what if Georgia had gotten some bad news about her health? Or was she experiencing supernatural activity again? Was it both?

"It won't take long." Georgia texted again. But Libby knew how talkative Georgia could be.

Libby decided she had to go see Georgia at St. Mary's. It was the right thing to do.

"Be there in 15."

Georgia sent back a thumbs-up emoji.

"Um, Bailey," Libby said. "Little change of plans. I have a quick errand to run."

"You said you'd drive me home." Bailey's face fell.

"I know, but this is an emergency. I think."

Georgia was usually fine with texts, calls, Instagram messages, video chats—all of it. But now she wanted to speak to Libby in person. Given the terrifying circumstances that had brought them together, Libby just couldn't put her friend off when she seemed so desperate.

"What about your big scheme to trick your dad?" Bailey asked.

"I'll just have to risk it." Libby popped her trunk and her backpack, heavy with textbooks, made a loud *thunk* when she dropped it in.

"Just don't leave me hanging," Bailey said as Libby climbed into her car. "As Parker Haney's date to the Halloween dance, you have a responsibility to all females at Denton High to—"

Libby couldn't help but grin as she closed the car door, cutting off her friend's speech.

5

St. Mary's Medical Center was the largest hospital in the city. It was pristine, highly regarded, and seemed protected by an aura of Catholic iconography and signs that promised faith-based healing combined with the practices of modern medicine. As Libby walked down those familiar, pristine hallways, only terrible memories came back to her. She passed the chapel and chills coursed through her body. It wasn't so long ago that a horrible demon had chased her and Georgia through those same corridors.

Georgia had told Libby to meet her in the "Healing Garden," which was a huge outdoor area behind the hospital, filled with trees, fountains, and flowers in the spring. Libby followed the cobbled sidewalk, searching for her friend. Other patients were out and about, going for a stroll with a nurse in attendance.

Libby spotted her friend off the main walkway. Georgia sat on a bench underneath a sprawling oak tree, reading a book. Her eyes were shaded by large sunglasses that made her look like a fly. Her oxygen tank leaned against the bench beside her, cannula running from its spout to her nostrils.

Georgia looked up as Libby approached, smiled, and then stood.

"I haven't seen you in forever," Georgia said when they hugged.

Apparently, to Georgia, "forever" meant a few weeks.

"Sorry. School's been crazy," Libby said.

"You mentioned you got caught up in your dad's last case," Georgia said. "But you never told me the story. I posted, like, eleven things on Instagram and you didn't comment on any of them. That was my first clue that you were in trouble. Sorry I didn't come and rescue you myself. Are you all right?"

"More or less. But what about you? You were really freaking me out with those messages. What's going on?"

The light went out of Georgia's eyes just a little. Georgia sat on the bench and Libby joined her. Georgia *seemed* normal, at least. Or, rather, as normal as could be expected. She didn't look weaker, or sicker, or like she was struggling.

Georgia peered ahead toward the garden's small pond, and Libby followed her gaze. Next to it, an elderly man wearing a hospital gown lifted his hand and waved. Georgia returned the gesture. "That's Mr. Vincent."

She's stalling, Libby realized. "Close friend of yours?"

"We chat when we bump into each other. He likes to feed the fish in that pond."

Georgia adjusted her nasal cannula. "I actually wanted to talk to your dad about this, but I thought I'd run it by you first."

"Have there been any other *incidents*?" Libby asked, the words coming slowly.

"Nothing like that," Georgia said, fingering the plastic tube. "Thank God. But there have been other interesting changes..."

"Like..."

Georgia watched an elderly woman being pushed along the walkway in her wheelchair by a caretaker. She waited for the woman to pass out of earshot. "I see things."

"What do you see?"

"People."

Libby now realized where this was probably going. "And... what kind of people?"

"Are you *really* going to make me quote *The Sixth Sense*? I think you know what I mean."

"Yeah, I do, but is it like last time?"

"No no no. Not at all."

Georgia Collins had been through a lot. Libby had first met the girl through a series of unfortunate circumstances that led Georgia's parents to contact Libby's dad. There was a demonic infestation in St. Mary's, and Georgia was the one who'd discovered the entity. The situation had quickly spiraled out of control.

"Last time, it was that asshole demon talking directly to me," Georgia explained. "Now, I only see... well, I'm not sure how to describe it. They're just happening, like a movie. I'll see an old man walking down the hall, and he doesn't look like he belongs. Sometimes I see people dressed up in old-fashioned nurse uniforms. They're going about their business, ignoring me and everyone else."

"Ghosts," Libby said.

"Yeah. Your dad mentioned once that there are probably tons of ghosts here because lots of people die in hospitals."

"He's right. This place is overflowing with highly charged emotional energy here."

That was how Libby's dad had explained it to her. The ghosts, the spirits of the people that Georgia was seeing, had a strong connection to St. Mary's during their lives. By the sounds of it, she was seeing both patients and employees that had passed.

"I remember when you brought that medium to my room for a séance," Georgia went on. She rhythmically traced the edge of the bench with the tip of her index finger. "She could see the spirits all around us, and she communicated with them, too."

Georgia was talking about Katie, who used to work with Libby's dad on cases. Katie was sensitive to the spiritual world and could contact spirits more readily than her dad could. Katie and Libby's dad had also dated for a short time, though it had been one of his messier breakups.

"Some people, like that medium, are very sensitive to things that most people cannot see," Libby said.

Georgia stopped tracing the edge of the bench and wiped her hand on her jeans. "What if I'm one of them?"

"It's possible," Libby said. "Because..."

"Because why?"

Libby hesitated.

"Because I'm so close to the end?"

Georgia didn't have a problem calling it like it was. Because of her cystic fibrosis, Georgia was never meant to have a long life. If she were lucky and didn't have any serious complications, she could expect to live until her thirties.

"That's not always the case," Libby said, "but yes, people who are closer to death often see those who have already passed on but are still lingering."

"I did some internet research and read the same thing online."

"Be careful with what you read online about that kind of stuff. There are some crazies out there who don't really understand what they're talking about. Or what they're messing around with."

"My doctors say the same thing when I tell them I read about my symptoms online."

"If they're just ghosts, then they won't hurt you. Like the lady in the nurse's uniform you're talking about. She probably worked here when she was alive. When she died, her spirit wasn't ready to let go. Now she walks the halls, repeating her day-to-day activities because she doesn't even realize she's dead."

Libby knew that demons, on the other hand, were far worse. They were inhuman spirits that intentionally caused chaos, fear, and sometimes even death.

"That's really sad," Georgia said, voice dropping.

"Yeah."

"Do you think since I can see her, I could also talk to her? Maybe help her move on to the next life? Isn't that what mediums do?"

I have to be careful how I respond, Libby thought. Her dad always advised people to never mess around with the other world, and he was right. The realms of the living and the dead were never meant to intersect.

"I don't think that's a good idea," Libby said. "Once you do that, you'll give off a certain aura. Other spirits will pick up on it and know that you are able and willing to communicate with them. They won't leave you alone. They might reach out, and you definitely don't want that. Because once you start, you can't stop it."

Libby's dad had dealt with dozens of cases that started just like that—people who were clairvoyant enough to see spirits making efforts to communicate with them.

Georgia stared at the grass between her feet, considering. The sun had begun to set, and Libby rubbed the goosebumps that had sprouted on her arms.

"What if I *do* want to communicate with these spirits?" Georgia asked.

Libby hesitated while she chose her words carefully. "That's a huge decision, Georgia. Once you open those doors, they're hard to close."

Georgia sniffled, and the first tears appeared at the corners of her eyes.

"Oh." Libby put a hand on her friend's shoulder. "Are you okay?"

"Yeah, yeah," Georgia said, wiping her eyes. "It's just... I'm going to die. Well, everyone dies, but I'm going to die before everyone else. I'm sick and that's not going to change. I won't grow up and be a politician who makes all these laws that fix the country. I won't get to be a famous artist or musician. Or a police officer, or a teacher, or the greatest female boxer to ever live. I'm *never* going to grow up."

Libby's own eyes began to fill with tears. Her friend had come to terms with her short life, and Libby had always assumed that Georgia had also handled all the emotions that came with it. Libby now realized that she'd been mistaken.

"Maybe this is a way I can help people. Kind of like your dad, except with less scary stuff. That medium he brought over... she helps people. Since I have this ability, I can start helping people. Because if I'm going to give anything back to the world, it has to be now. Otherwise, what did my life mean? I was born sick, lived sick, sucked up a bunch of valuable food and water and air, all to just die.

I can't do that." She wiped her eyes and cheeks with her shirt. "I accepted a long time ago that I'm going to die, but what I haven't accepted is me dying without doing something great."

Libby took a deep breath before answering. "I hear you. Everything you said makes sense. But before you make any decisions, talk to my dad. He can guide you better than me."

"Yeah. But I wanted to tell you first. Just to get your take on it."

"You were right to do that," Libby said. "My dad is crazy right now, with Halloween coming up. He always loses his mind this time of year."

"He's not a fan, is he?"

"The understatement of the century."

"I'll call him November first, then."

"Make it November second."

"If you say so. Oh, it looks like Mr. Victor made a new friend." The man was chatting to another patient who had walked near the pond. "Other people can see Victor. That means he's not a ghost. See? I'm already an expert medium."

Libby smirked. "Just promise me you won't try to reach out to any of those spirits until you speak to my dad," Libby said.

"Fine. I promise." Georgia held out her pinky and Libby wrapped it with her own. "So, wait, you have a new boyfriend now. Already?"

"He isn't a boyfriend."

"What happened to the last guy?" Georgia asked. Libby winced. "Oh, wait... he's the reason you got kidnapped, right? Yeah, definitely a good thing y'all aren't together anymore. You never sent me a picture of this one."

"I'll show you one quickly before I go." Libby pulled her phone out of her pocket and opened her camera roll. "Denton's Halloween dance is tonight and I have a whole thing planned out so my dad doesn't catch me."

Libby showed Georgia the picture Parker used for his Instagram profile. He faced off-center with a blurry background. The lighting was just right.

Georgia studied it. "No. Don't like him."

Libby's mouth fell open. "You're literally the first person who's said that about him."

"Don't care. He's not right for you."

Libby chuckled at her friend's staunch declaration. "And how do you know?"

"I can just tell."

Libby stood and put her phone back into her pocket. "As much as I'd love to stick around and hear why,"—and admittedly she *was* curious about Georgia's reasoning—"I have to be on my way. If my dad finds out what I'm up to, he'll kill me."

"Good luck with that," Georgia said. "And if he does kill you, it won't be the worst thing in the world. At least I'll still be able to talk to you."

6

Rand drove straight from campus to Miller Landingham's bookstore. He'd wanted to cancel his classes and get there sooner because he considered what Stacy had told him an emergency. However, with his recent and extended absence due to his previous case, he was already on thin ice with the department head.

Rand burst through the bookshop door, nearly knocking the jingling bell out from where it was bolted into the ceiling. For possibly the first time, he was not the only person there. A single shopper—a middle-aged woman—was browsing the shelves of used books. Miller stood nearby, hovering awkwardly, waiting for some sort of query. Rand knew Miller was not accustomed to having shoppers and didn't quite know how to act.

The frantic jingling got Miller's attention. His annoyed gaze darted between Rand and the bell, no doubt wondering why his friend had nearly ripped the thing from the plaster.

Rand jabbed his finger toward Miller's office. Miller nodded toward his precious customer. Rand, however, ignored him and charged behind the checkout counter and through the door that led to the back of the bookshop.

The office contained Miller's whole life. All the documents for his business overflowed from drawers in his computer desk. Boxes of books he hadn't yet shelved were stacked along the wall. His single mattress and comforter were in the corner, the closest thing he had to a bedroom at the moment. A phone charger dangled from the nearby plug. The smell of fried food, likely from lunchtime, lingered.

Miller shuffled inside the office behind Rand. His black, disheveled hair was greasier than usual and his cheeks and neck were covered in coarse stubble. "I have a customer. Can't this wait until after she's gone?"

"One of my students had an encounter."

Miller paused and appeared to digest what Rand had said. He closed the office door. "An encounter with what?"

"Do you know anything about the black-eyed kids?"

Miller waved his hand. "Those are just an urban legend, Rando."

"That's what I thought," Rand said. "They're in my 'stuff I don't believe in' lecture I gave yesterday. This morning, though, one of my students approached me in the campus coffee shop, scared out of her mind, saying black-eyed kids showed up on her doorstep the night before."

"You're kidding." Miller took off his glasses and rubbed each lens with a section of his red-and-white plaid shirt pinched between two fingers. "You sure she was telling the truth? Not just trying to mess with you? I know not all your students believe in the stuff you teach."

"Stacy Thompson would be the last person to do something like that," Rand said.

Miller replaced his glasses and sat in his chair near the computer. "She didn't let them in, did she?"

"No, thank God. That's their thing, right? They always want to come inside the house."

"It's not in all the stories, but it features prominently in most."

"What stories have you read?"

"I've found accounts online of people who've encountered these things. Most are very similar. There's a knock at the door, doesn't matter what time of day, and it's two kids. They usually stand out in a jarring way. Like their clothes don't match the current fashion trends, or they look dirty. Sometimes they even smell. But they always say they need to come inside your house."

"That's about all I cover in my lecture," Rand said. "Although I know there has to be more to it."

On a nearby table was a box that did not match the others in the office. It was plain brown, while all the rest were stamped with the blue logo of Miller's bookstore's distributor. The cardboard flaps were not sealed. Curious, Rand flipped one open.

"Don't look in there!" Miller shouted.

Rand jerked his hand back as if burned and gave Miller a questioning look. "What is it?"

"It's an early Christmas gift." Miller rubbed the back of his head. "For you."

"Since when can you afford gifts?"

"I can't. So you better smile and love it when you get it."

Rand distanced himself from the off-limits box in two long, deliberate strides. "Anyway. Have you collected any information about these kids?"

"I've gathered some things, but I tend to skip over most." Miller swiveled in his chair and jiggled the computer mouse to wake up the screen. "Since the stories are almost identical, it feels like they're from internet trolls." He double-clicked through a maze of folders on his hard drive.

"Why do they ask to come in? Why don't they just walk in?"

"It seems they have to be invited," Miller said.

"Like vampires?"

"Yeah, but we both know vampires aren't real."

Rand raised his eyebrows. "Well, yesterday I said the same thing about black-eyed kids. What happens if you let them in?"

Miller straightened in his chair and slowly turned to face him. "Now that I think about it, I've never seen an account where that's happened."

"Stacy asked me the same thing, and I didn't have an answer."

"Here's something," Miller said, opening a document. It took several seconds to load on the aged, lagging machine. Once it appeared, Miller skimmed the text, lips moving as he read. "What I have here is the first credited online post about them that appeared in 1996."

"That's why I'd always considered them an urban legend," Rand said. "Real demons have been known for millennia, but the black-eyed kids weren't ever written about until the internet came around."

"I agree," Miller said. "This story is interesting because it doesn't have them coming to the door. They approached the guy while he was waiting in his parked car. The kids knocked on the window and asked him for a ride. He tried to ask them questions, but they wouldn't answer. They only demanded that he let them into the car. Then he noticed their eyes were completely black. He was so scared he drove off right away."

"Same basic concept," Rand said. "They wanted inside."

"Exactly. What else..." Miller skimmed the document. "They often come in pairs. That's another common fixture of the stories."

"Like the world's worst missionaries."

"They're usually boys, but occasionally you'll encounter a girl." Miller scrolled his mouse wheel. "Many of these people say the black-eyed kids can communicate both aloud and telepathically. Some of these writers claim to hear the kids' voices inside their heads rather than with their ears. So, that's a difference in some stories."

As Rand listened and absorbed the information, he scrubbed at a patch of dried food that had spilled onto the floor with the toe of his shoe.

"But also, those who had these experiences say that the black-eyed kids only visited them once. It seems that if the kids fail to get inside your house the first time, they give up and try someone else." Miller looked at Rand. "Do you think you're worrying too much?

Maybe it was a one-off thing, and since your student didn't give them what they wanted, they'll just leave her alone."

"Hopefully. But I don't want to take any chances. I need to do something for her because…"

"You feel responsible," Miller said, as if reading his mind.

"Yes."

"I get why you feel that way, but I don't think it's true."

"The timing was too coincidental for me. I even said at the end of the lesson that once you know about the black-eyed kids, you'll have an encounter."

Miller rolled his eyes. "I know about them and they've never shown up here looking for some light reading."

Rand ignored that bit of sarcasm. "Even if they don't show up at Stacy's house again, a cleansing ceremony in her home is the least I can do. Maybe put up some wards, too. That would make both she and I feel better."

"I think that's the best thing to do," Miller said. "Also, you should probably remove them from your 'stuff-you-don't-believe-in' lecture and put them into the 'stuff-that-might-be-real' lecture."

"Maybe you're right," Rand sighed.

Miller's old computer fan whirred as he searched through more folders. An idea came to Rand.

"What if these things are coming after Stacy as a way to get to me? That's what *he* would do."

Shindael.

"When was the last time you saw him?" Miller didn't have to ask who *he* referred to.

"It's been a while. Maybe a week?" He usually paid Rand a visit at least once a day. "I know he isn't losing interest in me. He's probably waiting for something. Planning his next strike. Maybe this is it, and Stacy's the target."

Miller swiveled his chair to face his friend fully, computer forgotten. He rested his elbow on the desk. "How have you been holding up? After all that stuff that happened in Finnick? I haven't talked to you much since then."

"Good," Rand said. "As well as can be expected, I guess." His last case had been a week-long ordeal, battling the possession of a charismatic preacher in the small town of Finnick. He'd had more than one chance to surrender to Shindael and give himself up so that all others in his life could be spared. He hadn't, of course. Rand didn't make deals with demons.

"No matter what you think," Miller said, "and no matter what Shindael makes you feel, you did the right thing in fighting back. Because I'm sure that these things would have come regardless."

Rand tried to force himself to snap out of his downward spiral before it got too bad. "You're right. If they come back, I'll deal with them. This is my mission. This is what I do. If I don't, then who else will?"

"Exactly."

Rand checked his watch. "I'll head to Tessa's, and then I'll give Stacy a call and set up a time to visit her home to cleanse it."

"Why are you going to Tessa's?" Miller asked.

"Libby's supposed to stay there tonight. I have to make sure she's actually staying there. That they all are."

"Why wouldn't they? Everyone knows how you feel about Halloween."

"They do, but that doesn't mean they'll take me seriously."

Miller rose from his chair to accompany Rand to the front of the store. The woman who had been there when Rand had arrived was still browsing the shelves.

"Oh good. She's still here," Miller whispered to Rand. "Maybe I'll actually sell something today."

"What are you up to tonight?" Rand asked.

"I'll stay up and finish some accounting. Been a while since I've done the books."

"Good man," Rand said, grabbing his friend's shoulder. "Stay inside. With this black-eyed kid thing, I have a bad feeling about Halloween this year."

"You have a bad feeling about it every year."

AFTER HIS FRIEND LEFT, Miller emerged from the office to find the woman waiting at the cash register. He rang up her books, making his first and likely final sale of the day. When he was alone again, he returned to his office where he eyed the box that Rand had almost opened.

Stupid, Miller chastised himself. *I should've known he'd come by. Why did I leave this out?*

He flipped open the cardboard flap and pulled out an adult XXL portable toilet Halloween costume. He'd seen it online and knew it was perfect. Miller unfolded and studied it with a smile on his face. It looked even better in person than it had on the internet.

There was no way he was missing the Boyd Street block party tonight. Rand was his good friend, sure, but the man's paranoia toward Halloween was too much.

Rand wouldn't stop Miller from hitting the biggest Halloween party in the city.

7

Libby's mom lived with her fiancé, Bill, in his massive house located in the city's finest, most exclusive neighborhood. The smooth roads curved alongside tranquil lakes. The houses, some of which were legitimate mansions, were spread out on generous plots of land that resembled the greens of golf courses.

"I always forget how freaking huge Bill's place is," Bailey said as they pulled up the driveway, peering out and up through the windshield. Now that school was over, she'd tied her brown hair into a loose bun and had changed into a grey, oversized t-shirt.

As much as Libby wanted to focus on the fun night ahead of her, she couldn't get Georgia's words out of her mind.

What if I do want to communicate with these spirits?

Libby had seen many terrible and frightening things, and even Georgia had experienced what these dark entities were capable of. Libby could not fathom what would drive someone to willingly step into the ring with them.

"How much space does Bill need?" Bailey asked. "Didn't he live here alone before he met your mom?"

After leaving the hospital, Libby had picked Bailey up from her house. Luckily, she didn't live far from Bill's.

"I still haven't seen every room," Libby said, pushing Georgia from her mind as they got out of her Mini Cooper, a gift from Bill. The girls took their backpacks from the trunk.

"Next time I'm here, you need to take me on the grand tour."

"Don't tell my mom, but I prefer being at my dad's. It feels more... normal." Libby used her key on the front door and they entered the high-ceilinged living room. A black, L-shaped leather couch faced a seventy-two-inch television. In front of it was a dark brown, mahogany coffee table.

"We'll set up our books and stuff here," Libby said, gesturing toward the tidy living room. *The cleaners must have come earlier,* she thought. She hated to clutter it up so soon, especially since she knew Bill liked everything spotless. But it was necessary to make the story she'd tell her dad believable.

"I still don't understand why your dad would just show up here," Bailey said. "I mean, he and your mom aren't together anymore, and she lives here with her new fiancé. It doesn't make sense."

Libby's phone chimed with a text message and she looked at the screen. It was from her dad's friend, Miller Landingham.

"Warning: your dad was just here. He's headed to Tessa's."

"Oh crap," Libby said. "My dad's on the way."

"Really?" Bailey asked.

"Yes. Quick, make this place look like it's supposed to."

Libby and Bailey opened their backpacks and spread out their books, notebooks, and pens all over the coffee table and couch. A few minutes later, the once-tidy living room looked like a full-blown study party.

Bailey stood up and examined the scene, hands on her hips. "You sure he'll fall for this? It almost looks *too* exaggerated."

"The more, the better," Libby said.

"Oh, good, you're home, Libby." Libby's mother's voice came from above. Tessa stood on the landing at the top of the stairwell that looked down into the living room. She wore a black dress, striped stockings, and a pointed hat—her witch costume for Bill's company's Halloween party. Makeup completely caked Tessa's face. She spread her arms and smiled. "What do you think?"

"Mom, you have to change out of that *right now*," Libby said. "Dad's on the way."

Libby had already told her mom about the dance and the plan to sneak around her dad. Since Tessa was attending Bill's company's costume party that night, she and Libby had a shared interest in tricking Rand.

Tessa's face fell. "Really? How do you know?"

"Miller just texted me a heads up."

Tessa swore under her breath and retreated to her bedroom.

"She looks great," Bailey said. "What are her plans for tonight?"

"She has Bill's company's party."

Libby rubbed at her forehead. That was a close call. If her dad had shown up while her mom was in costume, the cat would've been out of the bag for sure.

"I can't imagine Bill dressing up in a costume," Bailey said as she sat down on the couch. The puffy leather cushion and backrest enveloped her.

"Mom said he wasn't planning to since he had to host, but she convinced him to go as Frankenstein."

"Oh, I *have* to see that. Bill always seems so serious."

The front door burst open, startling Libby. Her dad spilled in and paused as he surveyed the entire room, as if investigating something. He wore dark blue jeans, a black v-neck t-shirt, and a light brown jacket.

Bailey twisted in her seat to see who had barged in. When she spotted who it was, she quickly looked away and stiffened.

"Why are you coming through the door like that?" Libby asked, exasperated. Her heart pounded from the sudden fright.

Nerves also took their hold. It was go time. Now or never. Libby's plan would either work, or her dad would figure out she was hiding something.

"This should be locked," Rand said, closing the door behind him.

Libby tried to force herself to relax and act like she had nothing to hide. "You got here fast."

"Were you expecting me?"

Libby bit her lip, realizing her mistake. "You know Mom hates it when you let yourself in."

"Anywhere my daughter lives is automatically an extension of my own home. Hey, Bailey."

Bailey raised a rigid hand in an awkward wave. She definitely looked like she was hiding something. Libby wished her friend was better under pressure.

Rand's attention went to the school supplies spread out all over the coffee table and couch. "What's all this?"

Good, Libby thought. "What's it look like?" Libby replied, hands on her hips. "We have tests coming up and we're going to study tonight."

Bailey nodded.

Her dad considered this for a moment, as if trying to detect deception. Libby maintained her poker face.

Tessa appeared at the top of the stairwell again, this time dressed in jeans and a t-shirt with her blonde hair pulled up in a bun. She glowered at Rand. "I didn't hear a knock or a doorbell."

"Anywhere my daughter lives is automatically an extension of my own home," Rand repeated.

"It's more like home invasion." Tessa came down the stairs. "What are you doing here?"

"Checking on my family," Rand said.

"You could simply call. Or text. Or do many other things that respect Bill's house and privacy."

Rand narrowed his eyes. "Have you started wearing black lipstick again?"

Libby saw it too. A dark smudge remained on the corner of her mom's lips from where she'd wiped it off too hastily and missed a spot. Tessa pivoted and walked briskly toward the kitchen.

"Don't tell me that's part of a Halloween costume," Rand said, following her.

"Are we busted?" Bailey whispered.

"Maybe Mom is," Libby said. "But I think he believes our story." She heard her parents' voices in the kitchen, but couldn't make out what they were saying. "Hopefully we'll be fine. We'll know in a few minutes…"

TESSA GRABBED a dish towel and wetted it under the sink. She scrubbed her lips while keeping her back to Rand.

"What's going on?" Rand knew when he'd come in that something was up. He could sense it in the air. That was why he'd barged in—to give himself a better chance of catching his family unawares.

"Don't you think it's time for you to lay off this whole Halloween thing?" Tessa dropped the dish towel and turned to face him. "This is getting ridiculous."

"You know it's for everyone's protection."

"We wouldn't *need* protection if you would stop doing all the crazy stuff you do."

That cut Rand deeper than he allowed himself to let on. He'd spent many late nights agonizing over that very fact.

"I've been chosen for this and I can't quit. You know that." Rand began surveying the kitchen for any evidence of Halloween celebrations. He walked along the length of the counters, opening cabinets and drawers. "It wouldn't be fair to the people who need me."

"And what about *us*? How is it fair to us? Especially after your daughter went missing for *days* after your last little—what are you looking for?"

Rand opened the pantry. In Bill's massive kitchen, the pantry was twice the size of his own, but he quickly spotted the contraband on the bottom shelf—two big bags of Halloween candy. He grabbed one in each hand and held them up for Tessa to see.

She folded her arms. "The neighborhood kids are also suspended from Halloween because you say so?"

"Trick-or-treating is part of the celebration, Tessa. We've been over this."

"Bill is very active in this neighborhood community and he knows all the families. He can't just turn his porch lights off and refuse the children tonight."

Rand tore open both bags of candy and upended them into the trash can while Tessa watched.

"You've really lost it, Rand," Tessa said. "You're usually crazy, but this is going too far. Not everyone agrees with your little anti-Halloween thing."

"Just in case anyone here is planning something behind my back, I wanted to let you know that there's already been an incident."

Tessa seemed skeptical. "An incident?"

"One of my students came to me this morning and told me that last night she encountered two beings that I believe could be demonic."

"Jesus, Rand, even your students are suffering now because of you? At what point will you give it up so everyone you know can live in peace?"

Tessa had always known how to harness the guilt Rand struggled with and grind it even further. It was like his ex could read his mind and use what she found in there against him.

"Luckily, the girl did the right thing and didn't take their bait, so they left," Rand explained, sidestepping Tessa's comment. "I spoke to Miller about it. He's familiar with the beings and thinks that since she didn't fall for it, they'll just leave her alone. But still, you never know…"

"I don't want to hear any of this, Rand," Tessa said. "Stop bringing it into my life."

"I'm telling you this so you can be prepared," Rand said. "I'm just looking out for all of you."

Tessa scoffed. "If you really want to look out for us, then maybe you should move *very* far away from here."

Rand sighed and his shoulders fell. He'd also considered that particular solution. It could potentially be safer for his family, but he couldn't stand the thought of not seeing Libby regularly.

Did that make him selfish? Almost certainly. It put his desire to be in his daughter's life over her safety.

"Are you satisfied with your little checkup?" Tessa's glare had not softened after her last painful jibe. "It's time for you to go."

Rand *wasn't* satisfied, but he couldn't linger and police his family all night. He was well aware that he was getting on everyone's nerves, but it was all for their protection, whether they understood it or not. On November first, he'd chill out.

Tessa escorted him to the front door as if she were a bouncer tossing him out of a bar. Libby and Bailey sat on the couch with their textbooks and notebooks.

"Bye, girls," Rand said. "I'll text you later, Libby, to see how the studying's coming along."

"Sure," she said.

Tessa opened the door for him, but before leaving, Rand faced her again. "By the way," he said, lowering his voice. "You should totally start wearing black lipstick again. I miss those days when you wore all black and dyed your hair pink."

Tessa shoved him hard on the shoulder. "Goodbye, Rand."

"I bet Bill's never seen those pictures."

"Happy Halloween, Randolph."

She closed the door in his face.

8

The sun drifted below the horizon, leaving the sky a splotch of orange and blue. It also left a chill in the autumn air, and Stacy shivered as she rushed toward the campus library.

Inside, she found it pleasantly warm, but eerily empty. The stale smell of decades-old books was familiar and calming to her.

Although midterms were coming, no one else seemed to share her enthusiasm for studying. Or maybe everyone was preparing for the Boyd Street party that would begin later that night.

Mr. Casey had told her to go. Insisted, actually, so she wouldn't be alone. Her incident had alarmed Mr. Casey just as much as Stacy, and she'd agreed with the idea of being surrounded by people.

But first, I'll cram in a few hours of review, she thought.

She just wished the library wasn't so empty.

Stacy went to the study rooms on the second floor. Mrs. Karen was at the desk, tapping on the computer keyboard, and she looked over the tops of her glasses at Stacy when she came in.

"What are you doing here tonight?" Mrs. Karen whispered.

"The usual."

"Shouldn't you be out having fun somewhere?"

"Shouldn't you?"

Mrs. Karen only chuckled. "I'm too old for that now." She handed Stacy the sign-in book and she wrote her name. She was the only one on the page.

"All the rooms are free," Mrs. Karen said.

Stacy found her favorite, which she considered lucky. Deep down, she knew that was ridiculous, but it wasn't bad to have rituals. She unpacked her books, feeling guilty for disobeying Mr. Casey.

The study room was so quiet that when her phone rang, it scared the hell out of her. She fished it out of her pocket and checked the screen.

It was him. Mr. Casey had promised to check up on her that night.

"Hello?" Stacy felt busted—as if her teacher knew she was alone when she shouldn't be.

"Stacy. It's Rand."

"Hi, Mr. Casey."

"Just calling to make sure you're okay."

"Everything's fine so far."

"Why are you whispering?"

Stacy cleared her throat. "Sorry." She spoke normally, which sounded like screaming in the silent study room. She felt like a hypocrite—she always hated it when others answered their phones in the no-talking area of the library.

"Are you still going to the block party tonight?"

"Yes, sir."

"Good. I never tell anyone to leave the house on Halloween, but in your case, you need to be with friends."

"That's my plan." Stacy glanced around the study room, feeling just how empty the place was. Perhaps she hadn't been thinking when she'd decided to study in the library. She'd never been alone in the silent study rooms before. It hadn't even occurred to her that they'd be deserted on Halloween night. Now, it seemed obvious.

"Please call me if something happens, although I don't think it will. I've spoken with someone who is familiar with the type of encounter you had, and he said because you didn't fall for their trick, they should leave you alone."

"That's good to hear," Stacy said.

"All right, Stacy. Take care."

"You too, Mr. Casey."

She hung up and placed the phone on the table.

Mr. Casey was more than just a good teacher; he was a great man, and Stacy was very thankful for him.

Although Stacy always denied it when Kim teased her, it was true Stacy had a small crush on her teacher, and him being so thoughtful during her time of need only made it worse. She wouldn't mind if he kept calling her even after the night was over.

Hopefully Mr. Casey was correct and what had happened was an isolated incident. Stacy still wasn't over it. She had barely slept the previous night.

Stacy turned to her books. Reviewing math problems would take her mind off of things.

But instead, she reached for her Intro to Supernatural Studies notebook. On the inside of the cover, she'd written two notes that Mr. Casey had told them would be the answers to questions on every test of the semester, because the information was so important.

Your authority over an evil spirit is greatest when you call them by name and command them to leave in the name of the Lord, Stacy read. She'd highlighted the note in three different colors and circled it with a marker.

The second note was equally as highlighted as the first. *Under no circumstances should you ever make a deal with any demonic entity. Although it may seem tempting, there is always a catch. Demons are masters of deception.*

True to his word, Mr. Casey had included the questions on every one of his tests and Stacy had answered each with the exact responses that she'd memorized.

Despite knowing the information by heart, she reviewed it yet again. Because if Mr. Casey was wrong and those creepy kids didn't leave her alone, then having the information memorized wouldn't be enough; she'd actually need to use it.

9

K im's face was inches from the bathroom mirror, eyelids pulled apart, the contact lens balancing precariously on the edge of her finger.

One. Two. Three.

She placed it over her cornea and blinked away the brief discomfort as the contact settled into place. Kim didn't normally wear contact lenses, so she wasn't used to touching her own eyeball. However, her costume wouldn't be complete without them.

One down. One to go.

She did the same on the left eye, which was easier than the first. Once the tears dissipated, she checked herself in the mirror. Feline eyes looked back at her. Although painful to put in, they were the best part of her costume.

Kim's cat outfit was admittedly sparse. The pointy ears on top her of head completed the illusion, complementing the black leotard and leggings that made up the rest of her costume.

Buster, the real black cat of the house, jumped up on the toilet and inspected her.

"What do you think, Buster?" Kim asked, bringing her face close to his to show off her similar eyes. "I look just like you, don't I?"

She patted his head and ran her fingernails down his back, which he arched, as she surveyed herself in the mirror. All she had left to do was draw whiskers on her cheeks with makeup.

But first I need to figure out where Stacy is, she thought.

She picked up her phone from the side of the bathroom sink and called Stacy. It rang four times before her roommate answered.

"Hey." Stacy's voice was hushed.

"Why are you whispering?"

"I'm in the library on campus."

Kim paused for a moment. "Why are you there? I thought you were coming to Boyd Street."

"I am. But..."

"But you figured you'd study first."

"Sorry. I'm just so nervous about these tests."

Kim had been excited when Stacy had texted her at noon, saying she'd changed her mind and would go with her to the block party. Kim assumed it was because of the weird experience Stacy had had the night before. *She probably doesn't want to be alone on Halloween.* It was understandable, even though Kim thought Stacy was playing up whatever it was she claimed to have seen.

"Are you *really* going to come? Or are you going to study all night?"

"I'm coming."

"Well, I'm ready. Like, completely dressed. And Craig is supposed to meet me here soon."

"You go ahead," Stacy said. "I'll see you there."

"I've heard that before. Many times."

"I'm serious, Kim. I'm leaving right now." Kim heard rustling papers, closing books, and a zipping backpack. "Packing up and walking home. I'll be there in fifteen minutes."

"Do you want me and Craig to wait for you?" Kim asked.

The doorbell rang.

"No, y'all go ahead," Stacy said.

"You can't walk all the way to Boyd Street on your own," Kim said as she approached the front door. When she opened it, she was greeted by three young children dressed as a pumpkin, a ghost, and a vampire.

"Trick or treat!" they shouted in unison.

"Wow," Kim said to the group. "Cool costumes."

"You too," said the vampire. "You're a cat!"

"I am. I love cats." Kim used her shoulder to tuck the phone to her ear as she grabbed the nearby bowl of candy and dropped handfuls into the open and waiting bags.

"We have a dog," the vampire replied. "See?"

He pointed behind them. The kids' parents waited in the front yard, their black lab on a leash. They smiled and waved at Kim as she finished handing out the candy.

"What do you say?" prodded the kids' mother when the kids turned their backs.

"Thank you," they shouted back at her in unison.

Kim closed the door. "Did you hear that, Stacy? Everyone's out enjoying Halloween except for you."

"I'm glad you remembered to get candy," Stacy said. "I forgot. Anyway, don't wait up. See you soon."

They hung up. *Good. Stacy's on the way. Now, where the hell is my boyfriend?*

She dialed Craig. It rang and rang, and she thought it was about to go to voicemail when he picked up.

"Hey, baby," he shouted into the phone, though his voice was barely audible over the commotion in the background.

"Uh, *where* are you?"

"On Boyd Street."

Kim's mouth fell open. "You're not coming to get me?"

There was a long pause. "You said earlier that I should go ahead and you'd meet me."

No. What she'd said when Craig had asked if he could go early with his buddies was, "Yeah, you can if you want." She figured her annoyed tone had given off all the clues in the world as to how she really felt about that.

"So I'm just supposed to walk to Boyd Street by myself?"

"But you said—"

The doorbell rang again.

"Forget it, Craig. Stacy and I will walk together. Hope we don't get mugged and molested by axe murderers on the way."

She hung up on him. There were no axe murderers in the short distance between her house and Boyd Street, but she wanted to make Craig feel bad for not picking up on her feelings. She opened the door, and this time she had a zombie clown and a fairy dressed in a frilly pink dress.

"Trick or treat!"

"Oh, wow. You're way too scary for me," Kim told the clown. Fake blood smeared his bright-colored costume. "I think I'll have nightmares tonight."

She dumped a bunch of candy in the clown's bag as he giggled. He turned and ran off the porch back to his waiting parents, leaving his little sister. Kim crouched down to her level. "You're very pretty. Much better than that creepy clown. Here, take more." She scooped three handfuls into the girl's bag, and the child beamed.

It was imperative that Kim have no candy remaining in the house after the night was over—she didn't pay for gym classes four times a week just to have her hard work undone. "Promise you won't tell him?"

"I promise," the fairy said, elated at their little conspiracy.

"Good. Have a happy Halloween."

"Thank you."

She returned to her parents, and Kim waved at them before closing the door behind her.

Right. Where was I?

The whiskers. She'd draw those on, have a beer, and wait for Stacy to arrive. Now that she was pissed at Craig, there was no reason to rush.

The doorbell rang again.

Ugh. I need to turn off the porch lights. I'll never finish getting ready with all these interruptions.

She opened the door. Two young boys stood side-by-side.

"Happy Halloween," she said, reaching for the bowl of candy. When she turned back to them, she saw that neither of them wore a costume. Only simple, dirty clothes and, oddly, no shoes.

"What are you two supposed to be?" she asked.

Neither responded. They stared ahead, past her and into the house.

"No costumes, huh? I like your style. Skip the hard work and go straight for the candy." Kim glanced over their heads but found no parents in the yard.

In fact, everything was now much quieter than it had been when she'd opened the door a minute before. The groups of trick-or-treaters that had filled the sidewalks had all gone away.

"How did you convince your parents to let you out without them?" No response.

Whatever.

"Here you go." She lowered the bowl. "Take however much you want." Neither of them carried a bag to collect their candy. "No candy? Fine. Have a happy Halloween." She went to close the door.

"We need to come in and use your telephone," the older of the two boys said.

Kim froze. "You both were here last night, weren't you?" Neither responded. "You met my friend Stacy. You asked her the same question."

"We just need to come in and use your telephone," the older boy said. "We aren't bad people. We aren't going to hurt you."

Something was very off-putting about the way he spoke. He sounded so *proper* for such a young kid.

Kim set the bowl of candy down. "You scared my friend pretty badly last night."

"We're sorry." His response was flat and emotionless, like reading a line off a cue card.

"Doesn't seem so, but whatever. Look, she'll be here in a few minutes. Why don't you come in? You can apologize to her when she gets here."

The two boys stepped inside.

10

They walked evenly side-by-side, stiff and rigid, as if wearing a back brace. Kim watched them as they turned into the kitchen.

Weirdos, she thought.

She closed the front door. At least Stacy could see that they were harmless and that there was nothing for her to be afraid of. Then Kim would kick them out, head to the party, and have a good night.

When Kim returned to the kitchen, she found the boys sitting at the table, looking into their laps. Their shaggy, greasy hair hung low over their foreheads. They must have been siblings, although not twins—the one that had spoken was older than the other. But all their movements were in unison.

"Well, make yourself at home, why don't you?" No response. "You two aren't staying for long. You're just here to apologize to my friend, then you're out. I'm not babysitting tonight."

She picked up her eyeliner from where she'd left it on the kitchen table and used the magnetized mirror on the refrigerator door to draw whiskers on her cheeks.

"I don't know why you're wasting your Halloween. Soon you'll be too old to go trick-or-treating."

She finished her last whisker and glanced at them in the mirror. They were both looking at her.

Kim turned to face them, but when she did, she found them looking down again.

"Hopefully you'll be less shy when you grow up. Do you want something to drink?"

She opened the fridge and grabbed a can of beer and it hissed as she pulled the tab. She took a sip. "You can't have this, but I have water. I might also have some juice. Wait, forget it. It's expired."

Kim took the bottle of juice and carried it to the sink. She poured it out and threw the bottle in the trash. She leaned on the counter, tapped Stacy's name in the recent calls list, and brought the phone to her ear. "Do you still need to use my phone? I'll let you after I call my friend."

"Hey, I'm almost there," Stacy said when she answered.

"Good. Because we have visitors."

"Craig and his friend? I told you, I'm not interested in Steve."

"I know you're not interested in Steve. You're too obsessed with your ghost teacher. But there are two other young gentlemen who want to meet you."

"What do you mean? Who?"

A grotesque smell filled Kim's nostrils, and she coughed. It smelled like a combination of sulfur and feces.

"Jesus," she said, pushing herself from the counter. She walked into the living room to get away from the stench.

Aren't they too old to shit their pants?

"Jesus?"

"Not him. It's the two boys from last night. They came back."

There was a long silence on the other end of the phone.

"Hello?"

"The kids with black eyes?" Stacy said, almost too low to hear.

Kim realized she hadn't actually made eye contact with them yet. They seemed to avoid it. "I don't think so. But they're barefoot, and they asked to use my telephone. Just like you said."

"Oh my God," Stacy said.

"Relax. They're fine."

"What do you mean?"

Something moved in Kim's periphery—Buster. The black cat emerged from the hallway and walked into the living room. He peeked around the corner and spotted the two boys at the kitchen table. He hissed loudly. His back arched, his hair rose, and he opened his mouth to display his fangs.

"Buster," Kim shouted.

Buster only turned tail and sprinted down the hallway, meowing as he went.

"Kim, what do you mean they're fine?" Stacy asked again. "You told them to leave, didn't you?"

"No. They're sitting right here in the kitchen."

Kim flipped the light on in the hallway, looking for where Buster had run off to. Something had really pissed him off.

"Kim, you have to get out of there." Stacy sounded so serious that it was almost funny.

"Relax. I brought them in here to make them apologize to you for scaring you."

"Leave the house *right now*."

Kim rolled her eyes. "Stacy, come on." She turned the light off in the hall and went back to the living room. "You can't seriously—"

When Kim looked into the kitchen, she noticed the two boys had gotten up from the table and were standing side-by-side, just as they had been on the porch.

Underneath their shaggy hair were eyes blacker than the darkest night. Four voids that seemed to compel her to stare back.

"Kim. I'm serious. You need to leave."

Stacy's voice was distant now. The connection on the line turned to garbled static.

Kim wanted to move, to look away, but her body felt as if trapped in a block of ice. Her fingers loosened and the phone fell from her palm, clattering on the hardwood floor.

The two boys gave her a ghastly smile.

11

Stacy Thompson had never run so fast in her life. She sprinted down the sidewalk, her heavy, full backpack bouncing up and down.

She kept her phone to her ear as she ran. "Kim. You need to get out there."

No response. She checked the screen and saw that the line had disconnected. She called back.

It rang and rang.

"Hey. This is Kim. Sorry I missed your call, but if you—" Stacy hung up and called again.

Pick up, Kim!

She turned the corner into the neighborhood and tore down the sidewalk, feet landing heavily on the cracked and uneven concrete. She darted around families of trick-or-treaters who looked at her strangely as she zipped past them.

The front door of her house was open. She bounded up the steps.

All the lights were on and everything was silent and still. The only sound was the buzzing of Kim's phone on the floor.

Stacy hung up and Kim's phone stopped buzzing. It lay in a puddle of beer, the can nearby and on its side.

"Kim?"

Stacy's pulse pounded in her ears.

The kitchen was empty. The room smelled terrible, and there was a black fluid smeared all over the floor.

She turned on the light in the hallway. Nothing. Only the door at the end of the hall—her bedroom—was open.

Stacy didn't want to be there. What if the black-eyed kids were hiding somewhere inside?

"Kim, where are you?"

Stacy crept forward, and the aged hardwood floor creaked beneath her feet. She went into her bedroom and heard meowing underneath her bed. Stacy got down and saw Buster curled into a ball. His green eyes were wide and his entire body was shaking.

Stacy straightened and checked Kim's room and the bathroom, but she was nowhere to be found. The house was empty.

Tears formed as her mind raced with all kinds of thoughts and possibilities.

I need to call the police.

She lifted her phone but wondered what she would say. That her friend let in two kids with black eyes, and now she was missing?

The dispatcher answered. "Nine-one-one, what's your emergency?"

"My roommate is missing and I think she was taken."

"Where was her last known location?"

Stacy gave her address.

"I'll send an officer. Where are you now?"

"I'm here at my house."

"Are you alone in the home?"

"No one's here. I checked."

"Good. Please remain calm until someone arrives."

Stacy hung up on the dispatcher and immediately called Mr. Casey.

12

R and slid his fingers between the blinds and spread them apart. His neighborhood was usually quiet at that hour, but there were still some families and their costumed children going door to door, trick-or-treating.

Mrs. Blatch, who lived across the street, was posted up on a lawn chair in her yard with a big bowl of candy in her lap. As long as Rand had lived there, Mrs. Blatch had always been enthusiastic about Halloween.

A pair of kids started up Rand's driveway. Before they got too far, their parents shouted after them and gestured for them to move along. The kids sulked back to the road where they continued on to the next house. Rand's porch lights were off, as they always were on Halloween night. No trick-or-treaters welcome.

Rand turned away from the window. On the coffee table, Rand's large, leather-bound Bible lay open from when he'd tried reading it earlier. It beckoned to him now, drawing his gaze. He forced himself to sit on the couch and lean toward it. But still he felt disconnected.

Rand always spent Halloween reading his Bible and praying. He drew comfort from its holy words and the powerful promises of God to save mankind from the clutches of hell.

But this Halloween seemed darker than the ones before. This year, Rand found that the Scriptures no longer shed the hopeful light that they once had.

His Bible was open to the first page of the book of Job. Rand related to the story a bit too well. In it, God allowed Satan to test Job, a faithful man, by afflicting him with a series of horrible misfortunes. In the end, Job stood strong and his faith in God never faltered.

That night, though, Rand couldn't even get through the first paragraph. He could no longer claim to be like Job. Rand had failed his test of faith.

When Rand looked at the heavy tome that contained the words of God, he couldn't help but remember his previous case. Deckard Arcan, a false preacher who was possessed by a demon from hell, had been leading all the faithful in the small town of Finnick down a dark path. At least he had been until Rand stopped Deckard and banished the demon back to hell.

That case had tested Rand more than any other had before. Rand had mustered all of his faith and hope that God would finally intervene on his behalf and help him in the spiritual battle.

Yet God had been silent.

Rand had barely escaped from that demonic battle with his life. He'd only survived because of help from his friend Miller and an old preacher named Simon. Since that point, Rand had struggled to trust God for anything. Here he was, fighting on the front lines against the devil's servants, risking his life and family, without a single sign that God was grateful.

Rand bowed his head and closed his eyes and clasped his hands together between his knees.

God, he prayed. *On this evil night, please protect my—*

He found himself unable to go any further. It must've been his tenth failed attempt at prayer that night. If he'd learned anything from his last case, it was that he was alone in the fight against evil. God had no intention of making himself known.

Rand was the only one who was going to lift a finger to protect his family and fight for his clients. Even though Rand was doing what he thought would have been God's job, the creator of the universe remained silent and distant.

But Rand had pulled through without God's help on his last case. He figured he'd probably have to do it again on his next. That was the reason he drove his family crazy with his overprotection on Halloween—because he was only one man and he could only do so much if something went wrong.

God could not be counted on.

Rand turned away from his Bible and leaned back on his couch. He drummed his fingers on his thighs. The pattering of them hitting his jeans was the only sound in his deathly silent house.

It's too quiet, he thought. He was starting to feel like he was inside of a tomb.

Rand picked up the remote and turned the television on. He scanned the channels, but everything showing was related to Halloween: zombies, slashers, monster movies. One station was even having a twenty-four-hour marathon of *The Exorcist*.

Definitely not watching that, Rand thought. *That movie isn't fictional.*

He ended up leaving the TV on the weather radar.

Rand got up from the couch and went to his bedroom. He'd already changed the bed sheets and vacuumed the carpet. His nervous energy had made him quite productive. Rand opened his top drawer and started matching his socks. He swore that after a long enough period of time, socks took on a natural fit to his left or right foot. He liked to pair them accordingly.

Tomorrow morning couldn't come soon enough.

Rand's cell phone rang, causing a jolt of anxiety. He rushed to where he'd left it on the coffee table in the living room, next to his Bible.

It was Libby. His heart sank.

"Libby, is everything okay?"

"Relax, Dad. Jeez."

"You're okay?"

"Yes. I'm checking on you. Clearly you're the one who's not okay."

Rand took in a quick deep breath and let it out, settling himself. "You can't scare me like that."

"How? By calling? You need to chill."

"You know how I feel about tonight."

"Yeah, which is why I'm seeing if you're all right."

Rand dropped onto the couch. His legs had grown weak and rubbery. "As good as can be expected." *Even if I am a little anxious*, he thought. "What are you doing?"

"Bailey and I are taking a study break. Watching a horror movie."

"Which one?" he asked, hoping to catch her off guard if she was lying.

"*Halloween II*," she answered without hesitation.

Rand snatched up the remote control and brought up the menu on his television. He jumped to the movie channels and scrolled. Sure enough, *Halloween II* was beginning.

"You still there?" Libby asked.

"Yeah. Do you and Bailey need anything?"

"Only for you to relax and take a load off. You're stressing me out."

"I'll try. Be good and stay indoors."

"Right."

Rand could practically hear her rolling her eyes through the phone. "Where's your mother?"

"Upstairs. Or in the back. Somewhere in this huge house."

"But she's home?"

"Yes, Dad," Libby droned. "She and Bill are both here."

"Maybe I'll call her."

"Don't you think you've annoyed her enough for one day?"

Probably, he thought.

"Call me if you need me," Rand said.

"I'd say the same, but you're starting to irritate me. Good night, Dad."

"Night."

Rand dropped the phone onto the couch near his thigh.

A few seconds later, the phone rang, and once again the sound startled him. He figured it was just Libby calling again about something she'd forgotten to mention.

But when Rand checked the screen, he saw it was Stacy Thompson. His other hand gripped the couch cushion. "Oh no."

He straightened, his entire body sick with worry.

Rand brought the phone to his ear. "Hey, Stacy. Are you—"

"Mr. Casey. She's gone," Stacy replied, sounding hysterical.

Rand shot to his feet. "Stacy, what's going on?"

Stacy rambled on, but she was crying too hard and nothing she said was clear.

"Stacy. Try to calm down. I can't understand anything you're saying."

She took several frantic breaths, making the line sound like static. "Mr. Casey, she's gone, Kim's *gone*. Disappeared. She let the kids in and now she's *gone*."

There were other incoherent words thrown in between the sobs, but Rand had heard what he needed to.

"Stacy," Rand said. "Where are you right now?"

"I'm at home and Kim's missing."

Rand remembered Kim was Stacy's roommate. She'd been there when Stacy had first encountered the black-eyed kids.

"When did you discover she was missing?" Rand strived to keep calm.

"Just a few minutes ago. She called and said she let the kids in, and I told her to leave but she wouldn't believe me and then I ran back here but I wasn't fast enough and now she's gone."

Someone finally let them in, Rand thought. He remembered the conversation he'd had with Miller earlier.

No one knew what happened once you let them in.

Rand could only hope that Kim had run away. Hiding at a neighbor's house or something.

"Mr. Casey!" Stacy shouted; he'd been silent too long.

"Okay. I'm coming over. Send me a pin of your location."

"Are you coming now? I don't know what to do. I called the police, but I don't know what—"

"Whoa," Rand interrupted. "Stacy, listen to me. Call the police back right now and tell them *not* to come."

Stacy was silent for a moment, probably wondering if she'd heard correctly. "What?"

"Yes. Call them back and tell them not to come."

"But I already told them that my roommate was missing."

"Tell them it was a bad Halloween prank and she's there and everything's fine."

In cases where the supernatural was concerned, calling the police only made things worse. Rand had learned that lesson the hard way several years ago. Cops investigated their cases with logic and deductive reasoning. That was a good thing, to be sure, but it simply wasn't the best solution in supernatural situations.

"Are you sure?" Stacy asked.

"Yes. Do it. Then send me a pin of your location. I'm heading to my car now."

"Okay…"

"Stay put. I'm coming."

"You promise?"

"Yes. I am already on the way."

13

Although Libby had played countless volleyball games inside the high school gymnasium, that night she hadn't recognized it all when she'd arrived. It had completely transformed. Heavy beats boomed as a DJ played songs at the front of the gym. Strobe lights flashed a wide array of colors around the room. The costumed students congregated either on the dance floor or off to the sides in groups.

Now, Libby was near the speakers, dancing close with Parker Haney, who was dressed like a giant deer. Libby wore a camouflage hunting outfit, complete with an orange vest and a bow. When she and Parker had gone to take their picture, Vicky Stuart had told them she was entering them as finalists for the costume contest.

As they danced, Libby remembered to check on her friend. She spotted Bailey and Terrance, both wearing matching skeleton costumes, standing near the wall and chatting. As usual, Bailey was doing all the gabbing while Terrance stood there, nervous and nodding along.

Libby felt Parker's hands slide too low down her backside. *Time for a break,* she thought. She leaned back and shouted in his ear, "I'm going to check on them."

Parker glanced over at Bailey and Terrance. "They're fine. Let them be."

Libby pulled out of Parker's arms and shouldered her way out of the circle of dancing students. As she distanced herself from the speakers, her eardrums rang, muffling all other sounds besides the music.

"Libby," Bailey said when she saw Libby approach. "Terrance just told me he wants to study abroad in Italy for a semester in college. Haven't I always talked about wanting to do that too?"

"Yeah, you won't shut up about it, actually," Libby said, casting Terrance a small smile. He still seemed awkward and tense around them.

"It's *muy bene*," Bailey said.

"Excuse me," Terrance said. "I need to use the bathroom. I'll be right back." He left them alone.

"Do you think he's having fun?" Bailey asked as she watched him go. "This doesn't seem like his thing."

"I've noticed you doing all the talking. Maybe he has something to say, but he's just waiting for you to zip it."

Bailey shrugged. "Wouldn't surprise me. He's a really interesting dude. I can't believe I've never really had a conversation with him before now. His dad flies airplanes and is teaching him how. They go up almost every weekend and he promised to take me sometime. Isn't that cool?"

"That *is* pretty neat," Libby said.

"How are things going with Mr. Swim Team?"

"Even dressed as a deer he's super-hot." Libby looked back to where they'd been dancing, but he wasn't there anymore.

"Tell me about it," Bailey said.

Libby scanned the gym until she found Parker again. He was with two of his friends and they were talking amongst themselves.

"Have you checked in with your dad?" Bailey asked.

"Only once before we left," Libby said. "I haven't since then, and probably won't again tonight. I don't want to overdo it, you know?

He sounded reassured when we talked, so I think he'll be fine until morning."

"So we'll get away with this after all."

"Looks that way. Thank God. It's good to finally spend Halloween like a normal person."

She hated having to lie to her dad, but now that it was all said and done, she was enjoying herself.

Nothing bad has happened at all, she thought. *All that drama for what?*

Parker Haney left his friends and crossed the dance floor to where Bailey and Libby stood. The big antlers of his costume protruded to either side of his head.

"You all right?" Parker asked.

"All good," Libby said.

"Excellent. So listen…" He licked his lips. "Me and the boys are thinking we should get out of here."

That took Libby by surprise. "Oh."

"I mean all of us," Parker added. "As a group. Us three and them. And Terrance."

To Libby, this sounded like it had been Parker's plan before they'd even arrived at the Halloween dance, and she wished Parker had mentioned it. "And go where, exactly?"

Parker hesitated a second before answering. "The Boyd Street block party."

"Oh my gosh, *yes!*" Bailey shouted.

"No way," Libby said.

Bailey and Parker looked at her.

"What's wrong?" Parker asked.

"Yeah," Bailey said. "What's the deal?"

"You guys can go if you want. I'm not."

"Why not?"

"Too risky."

"Risky how?" Bailey said. "Do you mean your dad? You told me it was a done deal. All obstacles avoided."

"Still. Just coming here is pushing my luck. I know if I try to do too much, then I'll get found out."

"Is your old man at the block party?" Parker asked.

"No."

"Where is he right now?"

"Home."

"Exactly," Parker said. Libby hated that he'd led her down his trap. "He's home for the night. There's no way he'll find out."

"Well, what if one of his students sees me? It's a college thing."

"Do they know what you look like?" Bailey asked.

I'm going to thrash her later for taking Parker's side on this, Libby thought. "I've been to his class once or twice."

"They'll recognize you at night, in a huge crowd, *and* in costume?" Parker flashed his charming smile. "Not buying it."

Libby sighed. She knew her arguments weren't holding a lot of water, but there was no other way to explain the bad gut feeling she had about the idea. She could fool her dad for a little while, but he was always crafty enough to eventually figure it out.

"She's got no other excuses," Bailey said. "I think that means she's in."

Terrance rejoined them from the bathroom. He glanced at each of them in turn as they stood in silence. "What's going on?"

"How does the Boyd Street block party sound?" Bailey asked him.

Terrance seemed surprised. "Uh… sure?"

"Good man." Bailey punched his arm playfully, and Terrace recoiled. "You see, Libby? That's three against one. You're outvoted."

Libby was *definitely* going to give her friend an earful about this in the morning. Bailey knew how risky it was, but Boyd Street was just the kind of thing Bailey would be into—she couldn't wait to go to college and was always angling to get invites to parties.

Libby sighed. *Dad should be asleep. Maybe I* am *being paranoid.*

"In that case, who's driving?"

14

Soon after Rand left, his phone chimed with a text—Stacy's location. He put it into his phone's GPS and sped along, hoping to not pass any police officers on the way.

Fifteen minutes later, Rand almost put his Jeep on two wheels as he turned into Stacy's neighborhood while barely braking. The sides of the narrow streets were filled with the residents' parked cars, leaving no space for Rand's. So, Rand parked his car in the middle of the road in front of Stacy's house and bolted out.

He stopped short. Rand saw Stacy sitting on her front porch steps, knees pulled up to her chest and face buried into her jeans. The front door was wide open behind her.

His heart broke for her. *This is all my fault*, he thought. Rand wished these ghosts and demons would only come after him. But they knew the best way to harm him was to target the other people in his life.

Stacy looked up as he approached. Her eyes were puffy and her face red, streaked from her tears. She stood up and threw her arms around Rand's neck in a tight hug, and then she pulled away from him just as suddenly. "Sorry. I'm just…"

"It's okay," Rand said. "Let's sit back down."

Rand sat down with Stacy on the top porch step.

"I didn't know what else to do, so I called you," Stacy said.

"You did the right thing. Did you call the police back?" She nodded. "Any problems?"

She wiped her nose and sniffled. "They asked if I was sure everything was okay, and I said yes. They said they'll cancel their dispatch and told me to tell my friends that pranks like that aren't funny on Halloween."

"Okay, good."

"But Mr. Casey. If... something's happened to Kim, why can't we call the police?"

"You're just going to have to trust me on that one," Rand said. "When supernatural stuff happens, the cops always make things worse. Now, I want to hear your story."

Stacy looked away as she recollected. "Well, I was at the library on campus... I know you told me to go to Boyd Street, and I swear I was going to, but I wanted to get some studying in before I did. Anyway, I was on the way home and Kim called me and said..." She swallowed. "That *they* had come back and she'd let them in. I tried to tell her to get out of the house, but the call disconnected. And when I got back, she was gone."

As Rand listened, his dread grew. He had a serious problem on his hands. Stacy looked at him with new tears glistening in her eyes. "Can you help me? Can you help Kim?"

"Yes, I can," Rand said. "First, though, I'll take a look around."

He rose and walked into the house, stepping carefully like a detective at a crime scene wary of spoiling any evidence. A cell phone—Kim's, he presumed—lay on the floor in the living room in a puddle of spilled beer. The can was nearby, indicating that she'd dropped both at the same time.

The house smelled awful, like a combination of sulfur and animal feces. That lingering stench, he knew, was from the entities. There was black residue on the floor in the kitchen and living room. Rand followed it, making sure not to step in it, and found puddles of the same stuff on two of the four chairs at the kitchen table.

They sat here, he thought.

He pictured the black-eyed kids coming in and taking a seat while Kim spoke to Stacy on the phone. At some point, they must have attacked her and taken her away.

Rand went down the hallway and checked the bedrooms and bathroom, but everything seemed normal. All the action had occurred in the living room and kitchen.

When he returned to the living room, he saw Stacy had come back inside. Her arms were folded and she looked worried. "Well?"

Rand crouched down next to the black stuff puddled on the hardwood floor. It had the consistency of muddy rainwater that had been tracked in on the bottom of dirty shoes. He dipped his finger into it and rubbed it between the pads of his thumb and forefinger, then sniffed it shortly, the horrific odor assaulting him.

"This is where the smell is coming from."

"Plasma," Stacy said. Rand eyed her. "The stuff left behind by demons. You taught us about it in class."

"That's right," Rand said.

"It's not anything that will ever be found naturally on Earth," Stacy continued. "It's an entirely new substance from another world." She rattled off the information as if it were common knowledge. The girl had studied for his class so much that, by now, these facts about dark entities probably *were* common knowledge to her.

"Precisely," Rand said, standing.

"So these two kids *are* demons."

"It seems so. The way they appear and disappear, as well as the smell and plasma they leave behind."

"The black eyes," Stacy added.

"That also."

"You taught us they can't take on a complete human form. There will always be a flaw in their disguise. For these kids, the flaw is their eyes."

"Correct."

Stacy chewed her lip as she looked around the room. "And what about Kim?" She appeared sick with worry.

Rand realized what Stacy was asking. *No blood. No body. No signs of injury.*

"I don't believe they've hurt her," Rand said. "I think they've only taken her."

"If that's the case… taken her where?"

"That's what I need to figure out."

Although Rand was trying his best to maintain the appearance of the stalwart professional, he knew he was treading into unknown waters with this one. He'd cleansed haunted houses. He'd guided lost spirits to the afterlife. He'd cast out demons from possessed people. But up until that morning when Stacy had told him her story, Rand had believed the black-eyed kids to be nothing more than an urban legend. He didn't know what these entities wanted, and he didn't know what they were capable of.

Rand remembered the Bible he'd left open to the book of Job on his coffee table. It seemed the black-eyed kids would be yet another deadly test dropped on Rand's shoulders. And he was already sure that God would remain silent the entire time.

Regardless, Stacy needed his help. He had to push forward with or without God's support. He had to figure out how to get Kim back from the black-eyed kids.

Rand followed the trail of plasma outside and onto the porch. He spotted something on the concrete path leading up to Stacy's house. "Do you have a flashlight?"

Stacy opened the drawer near the door and pulled out a long, black flashlight. She clicked it on to see if it still worked, and when it lit up she handed it to Rand. He shined the beam on the ground. The residue left behind by the black-eyed kids was less concentrated there, but now that he scrutinized it with a light, he saw that there was something else.

"Did you touch any of this stuff?" he asked Stacy over his shoulder.

"No. I stepped over it." Stacy joined Rand and studied the sludge alongside him.

"Do you see what I see?" Rand asked.

"It looks like a child's footprint. Wait, there's two feet." She pointed toward the sidewalk where there were, in fact, two sets of footprints. Two sets of *left* footprints.

"Both of them were barefoot when I saw them," Stacy said.

"Demonic entities leave footprints behind sometimes, but they tend to only be left-sided footprints," Rand said.

"Because left is associated with things that are backward, wrong, and evil?" Stacy recited.

"Correct," Rand said, impressed.

The footprints led all the way to the street and then turned left where they continued down the sidewalk. But the direction of the footprints indicated that the kids had walked *toward* Stacy's house, not away.

"These were made before they arrived at my house," Stacy said. "They came from that direction." She pointed down the street, to the left. "Which means…"

Rand and Stacy looked at each other as the thought dawned on them at the same time.

"Your house wasn't the first place they visited tonight," Rand said.

15

The group returned to Parker's car, where he removed his deer head and put it in the trunk so he could fit inside. Libby got into the passenger seat and the two skeletons climbed into the back.

"I'm glad you came around," Parker said as he started the ignition. "Where we're going will be way better than a school dance."

"We were finalists for the costume contest, you know," Libby told him.

Parker fished a small hip flask out of the center console. He unscrewed the top and went to take a sip, but Libby swiped it out of his hands before it reached his lips.

"Hey," he said.

"Just drive. Save this for later."

Parker gave her mock puppy eyes, but she only pointed ahead. "Come on." She screwed the lid back onto the flask and tucked it into the breast pocket of her camo shirt.

Parker drove fast and recklessly toward the university. Boyd Street was adjacent to campus, and many college students lived in the area, which was why it had become such a popular spot for the huge

Halloween party over the years. Libby had never been, but she'd heard about it, and figured she'd try it out if she stayed in state for college. She still had her reservations about going there, but as she rode along, listening to Parker's loud music and holding on when he took sharp turns, she realized that maybe she was being overly cautious.

"Ah, crap," Parker said after he turned onto one of the narrow neighborhood roads. Cars lined the street on both sides and throngs of pedestrians in costumes blocked the way forward.

He inched behind them, but they made no effort to get out of his way. Many of them held drinks, and some of them even swayed. Parker flashed his brights at them, but a guy dressed as a caveman only gave him the finger.

"Are we here?" Libby asked. She didn't know her way around the neighborhoods near campus.

"We're five blocks away," Parker said, "and already it's packed."

"We have to park and walk like everyone else," Bailey said.

Parker groaned. He swerved into an empty space between two cars, parallel parking with surprising swiftness. He leaned over the console and gave Libby a big, goofy grin. "I got us here in one piece. *Now* can I have my flask for the long hike in?"

"How are you planning to drive us home?" Libby said.

"You're a stickler for the rules, I see." He flashed his smile and then threw open his door.

Libby got out and slung her hunting bow over her back, while Parker collected his antlers from the trunk.

"Do you mean five long blocks or five short blocks?" Bailey asked.

"Either way, you're here now," Parker said. "May as well put in the legwork and have a good time."

Bailey looked at Terrance. "You okay with walking?" He shrugged.

Seems like Terrance just goes with the flow, Libby thought.

Parker opened a text on his phone. "Ah. My friends are already on Boyd Street." Since Parker's car didn't have enough room for everyone, his friends had ridden with someone else. "We'll meet up with them."

The group started the trek, and Libby was immediately thankful her costume had called for comfortable boots. Her thick camo hunting shirt and pants also kept her warm in the chilly night.

She pulled her phone from her pocket and checked. It was nine-thirty and there was no message from her dad.

"I heard that last year the cops had to shut this down because some guy drank too much and ran around naked," Parker said. "When they arrested him, he kept saying it was part of his costume."

"I heard that story," Bailey said, "but I think it was just a rumor."

"Oh, maybe." Parker shrugged. "It's still funny, though."

"What about you?" Libby asked him. "How do you act when you're drunk?"

"Give me my flask and find out."

"I think I'd rather not."

"Maybe you should," Bailey said. "If there are cops here and they catch you with it, you'll get an MIP."

Minor in possession. Libby hadn't considered that.

"Good point, Bailey," Parker said. "Lib, feel free to hang onto it for me."

"Ha," Libby said. "Here, you—"

They walked by two young boys standing side-by-side near the sidewalk. Libby had not seen them at first, and it was like they had appeared from nowhere. They stood unmoving, staring straight ahead, and seemed to blend in with the night.

One wore a filthy red-and-white striped t-shirt and blue shorts, the other a black shirt and shorts. Both had shaggy hair and, for some reason, they were barefoot, even though it was chilly.

Libby and her three friends fell silent as they passed.

Something about them gave Libby the creeps, and she wanted to get away as quickly as possible. Once they were past the kids, the other three burst out laughing.

"That was awkward," Bailey said.

"Did anyone even see where they came from?" Parker asked.

"No. It was like they just suddenly appeared..."

"Creepy as hell."

Libby didn't find it funny. She'd felt something very off about them.

"I'll go back and invite them to the party," Parker said.

"Shut up," Bailey told him. "They were like five years old."

"Nah. Maybe nine or ten. I might just ask them to hold my flask for me. The cops wouldn't get them in trouble—"

"Uh, guys." Terrance spoke up for the first time since they'd left the car.

Libby turned and followed Terrance's gaze as he looked behind them. The two boys were on the sidewalk, looking at them, and about ten paces away.

"Are they following us?" Bailey whispered.

Libby watched them back. She didn't like the way they stood so still, or how they seemed to extend from the darkness that surrounded them. Her gut told her to get as far from them as possible.

Parker pushed between Bailey and Terrance and shouted at them. "Hey. Why don't you two fuck off?"

Bailey shoved him. "Parker. They're just kids."

The kids said nothing. Nor did they move.

"Come on," Parker told them.

They started walking again.

"You can't curse at kids like that," Bailey said.

"Why not?"

"Because they'll pick it up and start saying it."

"I'm sure they've heard their mom and dad say worse. I mean, they must have crappy parents. Who lets their kids wander around by themselves at this time of night on Halloween?"

"Guys," Terrance said again.

They all halted and looked behind them. The kids were still the same distance away as they had been the last time they'd paused.

Parker straightened and went to shout at them again, but Bailey only put her hand on his shoulder and stopped him.

"Are y'all okay?" she asked them, concerned.

"We need you to take us to your house," answered one of the kids. It was so dark that Libby couldn't see which of the two had spoken.

"Our house?" Parker whispered.

"We... don't live around here," Bailey said. "Where are your parents?"

"Please," the kid said, louder. "We need you to take us to your house. Now."

"Guys, they aren't wearing shoes," Terrance said.

Libby glanced at their feet. Terrance was right. In fact, they were only wearing shorts and t-shirts. It was way too cold to be dressed like that.

"Something's wrong," Libby said, although it was barely more than a whisper, and no one paid her any attention.

"I said we don't live near here," Bailey said. "But you can use my phone to call your parents."

"Why won't you listen to me?" the kid shouted, causing Bailey to flinch. "We just need you to take us to your house. We aren't going to hurt you."

Libby didn't like the way they were talking. It wasn't normal— their diction was too precise, their movements too still and not like children at all. "Guys." She grabbed Bailey's and Parker's arms. "We have to go."

"We have to help them," Terrance said. "They're alone out here."

Libby froze when the shorter of the two boys looked right at her. She knew he was because she could *feel* his gaze pierce through her. A heaviness of despair washed over her, and for the first time, she saw his eyes were completely black. They were like portals that sucked her in.

'You know he isn't real, don't you?'

Libby heard the voice in her head. It was a dark, gleeful voice that delighted in her fear.

She knew the voice had come from those kids, speaking telepathically. And if they were speaking telepathically, then they were not of this world.

She and her friends had to get away from them.

"Come on." Libby pulled her friends along as she turned and ran. The others were so startled by her reaction that they didn't think, and only ran with her.

"Where are we going?" Terrance shouted from the back of the group. "What about the kids?"

They bounded down the street, turning left and zipping between the parked cars along the side of the road. Libby was in front but didn't even know if she was heading in the right direction toward Boyd Street. She didn't care. All she knew was she had to get away from those kids.

"I can't run anymore," Terrance called.

Although Libby had the stamina to keep going, she slowed and stopped. The other three gasped for breath.

Libby looked behind them, then all around. The kids had not followed.

"What was that?" Bailey said to Libby, almost angry. "What if they needed us?"

"They didn't, Bailey. I got a terrible feeling from them."

"A bad feeling?" Terrance said. "They were only kids."

"They weren't," Libby said. Her pulse felt as if pounding through her entire body, not only from the sudden sprinting but also from the fear.

"What does that mean?" Terrance asked.

Libby looked at Bailey. "It was a *really* bad feeling. Do you know what I'm saying?"

"You mean..."

"Yeah."

She put her hand on her forehead, eyes wide. "Just like that? Walking along the side of the road?"

"What are you two talking about?" Parker asked.

"Come on," Libby said. "Let's keep moving."

"I'm going back," Terrance said. "They're in trouble." He walked away from the group.

"Terrance, wait," Bailey called.

"Let him go," Libby said. "They won't be there when he gets there."

"How do you know?" Parker asked.

Libby didn't respond.

They waited several minutes until Terrance returned. When he came back, he only shrugged. "They're gone."

They walked in silence the rest of the way toward the block party. All Libby could think about was how she wanted to go home. She also knew she should call her dad and tell him what she'd seen. But that would mean getting into loads of trouble.

Dad was right, she thought. *I ended up having an encounter.*

She prayed she could go the rest of the night without another.

"What was all that about?" Parker asked.

Libby really didn't want to get into it. Bailey had understood her, but Bailey knew a lot more about her than Parker did.

"I'll explain it to you later," she said.

"What's wrong with now?"

Libby dug the flask from her pocket and handed it to Parker. He took it from her, and that seemed to placate him. He unscrewed the top and took a long swig.

16

Your house was not the first place they visited tonight," Rand said.

Stacy looked as if she wanted to shrivel up into a little ball. "What do we do?"

"Let's see where these tracks lead," Rand said. He had to make sure everyone else on the block was all right.

Rand began following the black footprints along the sidewalk—two left feet with the small stride of a young child—while Stacy reluctantly stayed one step behind. Rand swept the flashlight beam over the path, making sure to not lose the trail.

They took a sharp left and turned up the walkway toward Stacy's neighbor's front door. The tracks led to the porch.

"Looks like they were ringing a few different doorbells tonight." He glanced at Stacy, who looked at the line of footprints with a worried expression. She kept her arms folded across her stomach and the sleeves of her thin white sweater were pulled over her hands. "Do you know who lives here?"

She wiped at her eyes again, removing the last of the remaining tears. "Chris. He's got two roommates, but I don't remember their names."

Rand looked around. They were the only ones outside—all the trick-or-treaters had wrapped up.

"Let's pay Chris a visit."

And hope that nothing terrible happened here.

Stacy followed Rand up to the front door and he rang the doorbell. Music boomed from inside the house. The door opened and a college-aged guy in a blue-collared shirt appeared in the threshold. He gave Rand a weird look, but then he spotted Stacy. "Oh. Hey, Stacy. Happy Halloween."

"Hi, Chris."

"You okay?" He glanced at Rand.

"Yeah, I'm fine," Stacy said, turning her head away. Chris's eyes softened with concern.

"Rand Casey," Rand said, holding out his hand. Chris paused and then shook it.

"Hi. What can I do for you?"

"Did a couple of kids knock on your door earlier? Or ring your doorbell?"

"It's Halloween, man. Kids have been ringing my doorbell all night."

"I'm talking about two very specific kids. If they did, then you'd know what I mean."

Recognition dawned in Chris's eyes. "Maybe you ought to talk to Matt. He had some wild story about two creepy children who weren't wearing costumes. We all laughed at him."

"Is he here?" Rand asked.

"Yeah. Keep in mind that he's had about nine beers, even though he says he hasn't. Wait here."

Chris went to find his roommate.

"I can't believe this," Stacy whispered. "I'm not the only one this happened to."

Matt came to the door wearing nothing but a pair of shorts and flip-flops and his skinny chest was pasty white. He carried a can of beer. He squinted at Rand as if he couldn't quite see him clearly.

"Are you Matt?" Rand asked.

"Who wants to know?"

"My name's Rand. I was talking to your buddy Chris just now. He said you answered the door when two strange kids rang your doorbell earlier this evening."

Matt's eyes went wide. "Man, those little fuckers freaked me out."

"What did they say to you?"

"They wanted to come in and use my telephone."

Stacy shot Rand a look. "And then?" he prodded.

"I thought they were lost because they weren't wearing any costumes and I couldn't see their parents anywhere. They... they also didn't have any shoes. I don't know, it was just weird."

"You didn't let them in, did you?"

"Hell no. I told them to ask someone else because I lost my cell phone earlier today. Then they got mad at me. Started yelling at me. I had a bad feeling, so I slammed the door in their faces." Matt paused. "Wait, you're not, like, their dad or something, are you?"

"I'm not. The neighbors had a similar problem with these kids."

"Oh. Well, I hope they found their telephone. Who are they, anyway?"

"No one special. If they come back, don't let them in no matter what they say."

Matt scrunched his face. "Sure. If you say so, man."

"Have a good night. Try not to drink too much."

Matt took a long swig of his beer as he closed the door.

"That guy didn't fall for it," Stacy said. "Why did Kim have to?"

"If they knock on enough doors, then statistically speaking they're bound to find one person to let them in."

"Why did it have to be Kim?"

They returned to the street and once again picked up the trail of black footprints, which headed off the sidewalk and onto the road.

"Damn," Rand said.

"What?"

He swept the beam of light over the asphalt. "They've crossed here, but since their prints are black, it makes them hard to see."

Stacy stood beside him and helped him search. "Don't move the light so fast." She grabbed his hand with the flashlight and guided it slower along the street. She stopped it. "Right there. Is that it?"

Rand kept the light trained on the spot and leaned down. He could barely make out the black slime and the two footprints in them. "Yeah. Good work. Go slow and don't lose the trail."

The prints led them across the block and to the left. Rand stepped carefully, making sure to not accidentally smudge the tracks with his own shoe.

"These are getting thinner," Rand said.

"Look." Stacy grabbed his hand with the flashlight again and pointed it up. The bright beam illuminated one of the parked cars on the road—a white sedan. The plasma was streaked on the driver's side of the car. Children's black handprints were pressed onto the window. They contrasted with the car's white paint job.

Rand pointed his light toward the house that corresponded to where the vehicle was parked. "Looks like this person had a car visit."

"Do they approach people in cars, too?" Stacy asked.

"It's not unheard of," Rand said. "Come on."

Stacy followed Rand to the door and he rang the bell.

The person who came peeked out from behind the curtain and studied him for a long time.

The door cracked open and a college-aged girl looked at him through the sliver of space. "Do I know you?"

"My name is Rand Casey, and I wanted to ask you about your car."

The girl scrutinized him for a short while, then opened up the door a bit more. "What about my car?" She peered around her yard, surveying the area.

"Are you all right? You seem upset."

"It's just been a weird night," she said. "Sorry. I hate Halloween."

"I hate Halloween too. Again, I'm Rand, and this is Stacy."

"Veronica," said the girl.

Rand gestured over his shoulder. "I noticed your car is covered in something nasty."

Veronica folded her arms. "Yeah. I wanted to wash it off, but I don't want to be out here tonight. I'll do it in the morning."

"Did something happen to you earlier?" Veronica looked away and tucked a loose strand of hair behind her ear. "I'm asking because we also had some weird things happen."

"Seems there's someone going around the neighborhood," Veronica said.

"Do you mind telling me what happened?" Rand kept his voice gentle. He could see the girl was on edge.

"I…" She searched for her words. "I came home from a friend's house and parked there. I looked down for a second because my purse was on the floor of the passenger seat. Then two little kids knocked on my window. It scared the crap out of me because I hadn't seen them and then they were just there all of a sudden. I rolled down the window, and they wanted to get into my car because they needed a ride somewhere."

"Where did they want you to take them?"

"I don't know. They never said. I kept asking them where they needed to go, but then they yelled at me, telling me I was bad for not letting two innocent kids into my car, or something like that." Veronica shivered and looked as if she might cry. "I wanted to help them because I figured they were lost. But then they freaked me out when they got angry. So I ran out of my car and into my house and locked the door."

"You did the right thing," Rand said. "These same boys have been knocking on other doors up and down the block, saying similar things. They're just Halloween pranksters."

"Well, whoever they are, they're really freaky. I still feel weird."

"They're gone now, but if they come back, don't let them in."

"If you say so," Veronica said.

"Thank you for your time. I hope the rest of your night goes better."

Veronica went back inside as if she couldn't stand being exposed for another minute.

"What does it all mean?" Stacy asked Rand.

He didn't answer, and instead pondered Veronica's story as he returned to her white sedan. Once there, he shone his light around and scoped out the area, looking for the trail of footprints. "Do you see any more tracks?"

"No," Stacy said.

"It looks like they originated here. This was their first target."

"And it was a car instead of a house," Stacy added.

"Yeah."

It wasn't just about getting into the car, Rand thought. *They specifically asked to be taken somewhere...*

"What are you thinking?" Stacy asked.

Rand realized he'd been lost in thought for a long time. "I'm wondering about their request to be driven somewhere, rather than just wanting to get inside the car."

"What about it? Do you think..."

"Yeah," Rand said, meeting Stacy's worried gaze. "I think the next step is finding out *where* these kids wanted to go. If it's a specific location, we might find Kim there because she didn't just vanish into thin air."

That was impossible. If she was alive, that meant they took her. If the kids were looking for other victims to take, then that meant they had somewhere to keep them. Demonic entities were almost always tied to a place with a negative energy that attracted them and anchored them there.

Stacy looked like she was going to be sick. Rand anticipated her next question.

"And how do we find out?" she asked.

In every case Rand had been involved in, there always came a time to transition from an outside observer to a direct participant. At some point, if he was going to make progress, he had to get his hands dirty.

"I'll have to ask those two kids myself."

17

R and and Stacy left Veronica's house and returned to where Rand had parked his Jeep in the middle of the road. It was about eleven o'clock. Lights in the windows of the surrounding houses had been turned off, leaving the neighborhood darker than it had been before.

"What will you do?" Stacy asked him.

Rand withdrew his car keys from his pocket. "I'll drive around the neighborhood until the kids come for me."

Stacy looked at him like he was crazy. "How do you know they will?"

"They're demonic entities, so chances are they know who I am. Demons show themselves to me when I *don't* want them, so I assume they'll be more than happy to oblige now that I do."

"Aren't you scared?"

"I'm trying not to think about that." Yes, the idea of seeking out the black-eyed kids chilled him inside. But he couldn't run away from his fear. "How far back does this neighborhood go?"

Stacy pointed down the block. "If you head this way, you can go either right or left. Both circle around on each other. It eventually opens up to the edge of campus on the other end."

"Got it."

"What about me? What should I do?"

"I think it's best if you come with me." He hated telling her that, but it was true.

"I knew you would say that." She closed her eyes and took a deep breath, as if psyching herself up. "I guess that's better than staying home alone."

"Exactly."

"But do we have to *look* for them?" Stacy asked. "Can't we just wait inside for them to knock?"

"We need to be in the car when they show up," Rand said. "From what we've heard tonight, if we're in the house, then they'll ask to come inside. But if we're driving, then they'll ask for a ride. Hopefully I can use that to find out where they want to go."

Miller said that the first reported account of a black-eyed kid sighting had happened to a person while he was in his car.

"I'm going to vomit," Stacy muttered.

"Let's get moving before we freak ourselves out too much."

"You mean you're not already scared enough?" Stacy went around to the passenger side of his Jeep.

Rand fired up the engine and began to cruise down the street, in no rush at all. As he drove, he kept his eyes peeled. The houses in the neighborhood were simple and clustered together, mostly rented by college kids. To Rand, it felt strange to seek out demonic entities in such an unassuming, ordinary place.

"Is this the kind of stuff you do for your cases?" Stacy asked.

"Yes. Although I've never done anything quite like this before."

Since Rand had never encountered black-eyed kids before, he was pretty much making things up as he went along. He didn't want to tell Stacy that, though.

Stacy peered out the window and shook her head. "I can't believe I'm part of one of your cases. How did that happen?"

Rand didn't respond. The question sounded rhetorical.

"How do you live like this?" Stacy asked him, her voice forlorn.

Rand had been asked that quite often. "I've been chosen. It's my job to help those who encounter the supernatural."

He came to an intersection and took a left turn. The compact houses continued on, and he drove carefully to avoid sideswiping any of the parked cars along the road.

"Chosen?" Stacy snorted. "Sounds more like you're cursed."

"That's what most people say. I've had to do a lot of soul-searching to turn my perspective around. So now, I consider myself chosen."

"You always tell us we shouldn't mess with the occult," Stacy said. "You said if we do, then we attract these things into our lives. Maybe being in your class is enough. You fill my head with scary stories and images during your lessons, and then I go home and study the material. So now my whole life is math problems, balancing chemical equations, and demons."

Rand looked at her in the passenger seat. She still gazed out the window. "You should take a break. My tests are easy, and you're a straight-A student. You don't need to study to do well in my class."

"I have to study no matter what," Stacy said. "I've never had a B on any report card or transcript in my whole life. My older sister went all the way through medical school without getting a B in a single class, and my parents expect me to do the same. I'm not a gifted test taker like her, so I have to study my butt off to get the same results.

"I took your class because they said it was an easy A, but they also said the same thing about Biology 101 with Dr. Fraser. I focused on other classes since Bio was supposed to be a given. But then the first test came and I realized I'd underestimated it too much. I made a C. I then realized that I'd have to give it *some* time. But the final grade was only averaged from three tests, so I over-prepared for the next two. I ended up with an A in the class, but it was the closest to a B I'd ever been. So when you say your class is an easy A... I've been burned by that before."

"How about this," Rand said. "You don't have to take the

midterm. I'll just give you an A. After everything you've been through tonight, you've earned it."

Stacy sighed. "What I should've done was take Ms. Sharma's class instead of yours. World Religions. I've heard her essays are killers, but at least there are no black-eyed kids."

Rand felt deflated. All the girl wanted to do was pass school and live up to her own steep expectations for herself. And here he was, the "chosen one," screwing it all up.

Something in his periphery caught his attention. He halted the Jeep at a four-way stop. There were no other cars at the intersection, so Rand idled there for a bit.

Stacy looked at him when she realized they weren't continuing on. "Why are you stopping? What do you see?"

Rand stared toward the side yard of the house on the corner. There was an oak tree there, and he could just make out a shadowy figure standing near it. Rand could recognize that shape anywhere.

Looks like Shindael is doing some trick-or-treating, he thought.

"Wait here," Rand said, throwing the Jeep in park. "Lock the doors."

"Where are you going?"

Rand left the Jeep idling at the four-way stop and crossed in front of the headlights, walking toward the tree where he'd spotted the demon. When he got there, Shindael wasn't there anymore, having disappeared the moment Rand took his eyes off him.

Typical, Rand thought.

He approached the oak tree and checked around the other side of the trunk. Nothing. The nearby streetlight was burned out, leaving the area in darkness. The only light came from inside the house. In the single window that looked out into the yard, Rand spotted a shadowy outline peering at him from behind the glass. Rand stared at the demon for a long time, the figure unmoving.

"Come out here and face me," Rand said out loud.

He turned his back on the window. Shindael had reappeared inches from him, just as Rand knew he would. The familiar feeling of dread and despair that he experienced whenever the demon was near bubbled up inside of him.

"Happy Halloween," Rand said.

Shindael remained still.

Rand understood Shindael to be different from the demons he usually encountered in his cases. Shindael ranked highly in hell, favored by the devil, and therefore commanded a legion of servants that did his bidding. He even had a unique appearance—common demons appeared as black shadows or as a combination of animals, while Shindael's skin was light blue as if he were frozen. The back of his smooth head was elongated, which Rand thought resembled an alien's, and his eyes were small, slanted, and completely black.

Although Rand was never happy to see his nemesis, the sudden presence gave him an important clue.

"I assume you're behind all this. That the black-eyed kids are your servants." Shindael did not respond. "Where is the girl?" he demanded.

'God has abandoned you.' As always, Shindael communicated with Rand telepathically. The voice was a breathy whisper in his mind. *'You cannot bring yourself to read holy Scripture. You can no longer pray. That is because you know God has forsaken you. He will not protect you from me.'*

Rand ground his teeth together and held Shindael's black gaze, even though the dark pools made him want to turn away.

Rand knew Shindael could read his innermost thoughts, so he strived to keep his mind blank. He did not want to react, even if Shindael was right. The more separated Rand became from God, the more vulnerable he became. Shindael was well aware of that.

"I asked you a question," Rand said through clenched teeth. "Where is the girl?"

'I cannot give you what I do not have.'

"Why Kim? Why Stacy? What do either of them have to do with you? I'm the one you want, right? Why hurt them?"

'You are my plaything, Randolph. You have opposed my master, and for

that you will pay. Your life is not enough. I have vowed to torment both you and those close to you as punishment for your actions.'

Rand had heard as much before. Shindael had made that clear on the night they'd first encountered each other.

What frightened Rand about Shindael the most was the depth of the demon's power. It was clear he was in a position of authority in the hierarchy of hell, since all the demons that Rand had faced lately were direct servants of Shindael. Such power meant that Shindael could reach out and kill Rand whenever he desired.

But with the demonic, it would never be that simple. Shindael desired more than mere death; he wanted chaos and destruction.

'I care nothing for the girl. Only you. She is nothing more than a piece of our game. When the sun rises, I will command my servants to deliver her into the hands of my master in hell.'

Rand swallowed. Kim was alive, but if Rand couldn't find her and rescue her before dawn...

It was exactly what Rand had come to expect from Shindael. He'd likely grown bored with killing humans thousands of years ago. Now he used them for his twisted amusement.

"Tell me where your servants are," Rand demanded.

'If you seek my servants, you will find them.'

"Yeah, that's what I'm doing. So if you can call them up and have them meet me, that'd be great. I don't have—"

Shindael's eyes flared red and his mouth gaped open, exposing sharp teeth. The demon's shadowy apparition lunged toward Rand as if leaping to take a bite out of him. Rand flinched and covered his face with his arm, dropping onto the ground, bracing for the pain.

It never came.

"Mr. Casey."

Rand uncovered his eyes. Shindael had vanished and he was unharmed.

He's never come at me like that before, Rand thought. *Maybe he didn't appreciate the sass.*

"Mr. Casey!"

Rand looked toward Stacy's voice. She'd rolled down the car

window and was shouting at him. Rand got up and returned to the Jeep, scanning the intersection for any sign of Shindael, but the demon had left him.

"Are you okay?" Stacy asked as he approached.

"Yes. I'm fine."

"Who were you talking to?" Stacy asked.

"An old friend."

"But... there's nobody there."

Rand wiped at his face. It was slick with sweat.

"Were you seeing someone? Or something?" Stacy gave him a sympathetic yet questioning look.

Rand exhaled. Given what Stacy had been through so far that night, it seemed fair to let her know what they were dealing with.

"Shindael." Even uttering the name took his breath away.

"What?"

"A demon that follows me. He punishes me for all the times I've defeated his servants."

Stacy's eyes fell to her lap as she pursed her lips. "This demon has something to do with what's going on tonight?"

"Yes."

"He's making the black-eyed kids do this?"

Rand nodded.

"Does he know where Kim is?"

Rand had to be careful with his words. He wanted Stacy to be informed, but to still remain as calm as she could manage. "We have to find her before dawn."

Stacy kept her eyes down. She sniffled and cleared her throat. "Or else what?"

"There's plenty of time." Rand forced his tone to sound confident and sure. "We'll get to her. I promise."

Stacy wiped at her eyes and glanced at the digital clock on the dashboard.

It was just after midnight.

"But—" Something caught her eye further down the street. "Oh my God." She pointed.

Two child-sized shadows stood side-by-side about twenty yards down the road. The streetlight ahead spilled a yellow glow onto them, but they still only looked like black figures, as if they were immune to the illumination.

"That's them," Rand said.

Rand rushed around the front of the Jeep and got behind the wheel.

"Don't do it, Mr. Casey," Stacy begged, unable to take her eyes off the two kids. "There has to be another way."

"They won't hurt you as long as I'm with you." It wasn't necessarily true, but he hoped that would reassure her.

He inched the Jeep forward toward the pair. They stood in the middle of the street, making no effort to get out of his way. When he'd closed the distance, his headlights flickered, blinked, and then went out.

"What did you do that for?" Stacy asked, voice tense.

"I didn't."

The streetlight extinguished.

Demons didn't like the light. They shut them off whenever possible.

Rand gripped the steering wheel, wondering if he should make the first move. Beside him, Stacy breathed in sharp, terrified gasps.

The two walked around the side of the Jeep toward the driver's-side window. The taller of the pair lifted his hand and knocked three times.

Although every instinct in Rand's body implored him not to, he rolled down the window.

"We need you to give us a ride."

It was the taller one who spoke. His voice was high-pitched like a child's, but he sounded very... off. His words were very clear, precise, and direct, unlike a normal kid.

"Get in," Rand said.

18

Boyd Street was chaos.

Hundreds of costumed college students crammed onto the narrow road. Music blared from the nearby houses, from the parked cars, and from speakers set up on the front lawns. Although the night was chilly, the dense crowds generated heat, causing Libby to sweat underneath her heavy costume.

Libby and her friends arrived at the party in silence and confusion. The incident with the kids had killed their mood.

Libby surveyed the area. There was so much going on, but none of it distracted her from the horrible feeling she had. The hunting bow slung over her shoulder seemed heavy now, and although her boots were comfortable, her feet ached; she'd been standing for hours and her sudden spike of fear had left her emotionally drained and fatigued.

She felt a hand on her arm. "You okay?" Bailey asked, concerned.

"I don't think so," she said, keeping her voice low so that Parker wouldn't hear. "That was just…"

"I know. Come on. We can forget about it now."

Terrance was also subdued. He had not liked how they had

blown off the kids. Libby admired him for his concern, but she knew it was misplaced.

Parker, who led the group into the Boyd Street crowds, turned and clapped his hands to command their attention. "Enough of this downer stuff. We're here for a good time, and we're going to have it. My buddies are around somewhere, so we'll hook up with them and get tonight started right. Come on."

He pushed through the crowds, his broad antlers coming close to striking other partiers.

Libby and Bailey followed, arms linked, with Terrance a few steps behind. Libby appreciated that Parker was attempting to fix the mood, but she knew she was too far gone to get a second wind.

They passed by a group of people surrounding a beer keg. Three guys lifted the legs of a large, costumed man, trying to position him to do a keg stand, but they weren't strong enough to support his weight. Two others orbited around them, filming on their cell phones while laughing.

"Come on, lift him up." one of them shouted.

The rest of the crowd chanted. "Mill-er. Mill-er. Mill-er."

Libby paused. She stared at the upside-down man, wondering if she was seeing things. His costume kept her from seeing if it was really him.

"Libby?" Bailey said. Parker had not realized she'd stopped and had trudged onward.

"You go ahead," Libby told her. "I'll catch up with you in a minute."

Bailey and Terrance followed Parker and disappeared into the crowd.

Libby approached the keg-stand fiasco. The three bros finally got the legs high enough and the big man put the spout into his mouth and drank while the crowds whooped in encouragement. One of the supporting guys lost his strength and dropped out. The sudden shift in weight caused the other two to lose control and their friend fell, landing hard on his side and then rolling onto his back. Beer sprayed from his lips in a foamy mess. Everyone cheered and laughed, and the guy filming on his cell phone zoomed in on the fallen man.

After a few moments, a couple of guys helped him up. He was dressed like a portable toilet, and it was definitely him.

They met eyes at the same time. Libby saw the confusion that crossed Miller Landingham's face.

Libby walked over to him. "Miller? What are you doing here?"

"Umm..." Miller looked around, wiping beer from his chin. "Maybe I could ask you the same thing."

Libby folded her arms. "Are you going to tell on me?"

"Not if you don't tell on me."

Libby stuck out her hand, and they shook.

"We were at the school's Halloween dance, but then we came here," Libby said. "I don't feel like being here, though. I'd rather go home."

"Does your dad know you're here?"

"Of course not. You?"

"Hell no. He stopped by the shop earlier and made sure I wasn't going to leave. I lied to him."

"Same, but at my mom's house. Mom and Bill are going to Bill's company's party, so everyone is sneaking around behind Dad's back."

Miller shrugged. His entire costume shifted up when he did. "We have to. Otherwise, no one gets to have any Halloween fun. What's Rando up to tonight, anyway?"

"He said was staying in, same as every year."

She imagined her dad at home, peeking through the windows like a paranoid person. He was likely proud of himself for forcing his family and friends to stay inside like him when in reality none of them were obeying.

She remembered the two boys she had seen and hated to admit that maybe, this time, her dad had been right.

Libby eyed Miller's group. There were about seven college guys, and they were upending another of their friends over the beer keg. This guy went more easily than Miller had.

"How do you know these dudes?"

"Long story."

"Come on."

"Uh... well, the bookstore is strapped for cash. I do a couple of things on the side to make extra money. I buy them alcohol from time to time, and charge them a fee."

Libby only shook her head. "Seriously?"

"I gotta do what I gotta do."

"But... that doesn't explain why you're here."

"They invited me. How else were they going to get a keg? And besides, what else was I going to do tonight? Oh, and your dad has no idea about this little side hustle, so that stays between you and me, all right?"

"Sure."

Miller eyed her. "You okay?"

"Yeah..." She debated telling him about the creepy kids. He'd believe her; they'd both had plenty of run-ins with evil. But a single isolated encounter was not always something to worry about. It came with the territory when you associated with Randolph Casey. Besides, she didn't want to put a damper on Miller's Halloween. He had worked just as hard to maneuver around her dad.

"I'm fine. Just tired."

"Head home, then. This place is crazy and gets more intense every year."

"I'll try. But I'm with a group."

"If you want me to find you a way home, let me know."

"Thanks, Miller. And nice costume."

He patted his chest. "Couldn't pass it up."

Libby left him and pushed through the crowds, searching for her friends. As she got closer to the middle of Boyd Street, she realized the party was far more crowded than she'd thought. All around her, she saw witches, zombies, and more than a handful of partygoers dressed up like the president. She brushed past a girl in a sexy devil costume who spilled some beer on Libby's camo shirt. A soldier and a cowboy erupted into a fistfight. The surrounding people reacted instantly and swarmed to form a circle around them, shouting and cheering. Libby got caught up in their motion, her entire body shifted by the sudden force of the crowds. She fought to regain control and pushed against the masses, getting as far from the brawl as she could.

When she burst through, a wave of light-headedness passed through her. Cold sweat broke out on her forehead, and she closed her eyes.

I don't feel well. It had come on suddenly. Maybe she was feeling claustrophobic. Or perhaps she was just more tired than she thought and all the people were causing too much chaos.

I'll never find my friends like this. I need to call them and set a place to meet—

She felt a small hand slide into her palm and clasped her fingers. Like that of a child.

Libby opened her eyes. When she looked down, she saw him— the younger of the two kids they had encountered on the way to Boyd Street. Only his mop of long, tangled hair was visible. He did not look up at her, only straight ahead.

Sudden pain pounded in her temples. The sounds of the party around her lessened as if she'd put in earplugs. Libby was frozen in place. She wanted to pull away from the kid, but couldn't for some reason. She should've been much stronger than him.

The boy started walking. He pulled Libby along by the hand and she had to follow. That, or be dragged. He had surprising strength, and when she finally found the will inside her to resist, he only clutched her fingers tighter, sending crushing pain into her bones.

Libby was led through the crowds. The edges of her vision blurred, and she felt like she was about to faint. The crowds parted for the kid. People did not seem to see either Libby or the boy.

Where are you taking me?

Somehow, she knew the boy could read her thoughts. But there was no answer. Then another frightening thought occurred to her.

Where is the other one?

Although she struggled to see clearly, some people they passed struck her as odd. They wore costumes that looked like throwbacks —maybe to the 1980s.

They stopped walking, and Libby immediately saw the other boy straight ahead of her. He stood ten paces away with his hands by his side. His black eyes bored into Libby, and an icy chill spread through her entire body. She knew without a doubt that these two kids were evil and that she had to flee from them. The smaller one still clasped her hand.

There was a girl standing beside the other black-eyed kid. She wore a cheerleader Halloween costume and held a beer. She leaned against a guy whose arm was around her while he talked to one of his friends and paid her no mind. The girl looked down at the kid, eyes wide and filled with fear.

She can see him, too, Libby realized.

The girl, without taking her gaze from the boy beside her, used her free hand to slap her boyfriend's side, trying to get his attention. He ignored her.

Run, Libby tried to shout, but she couldn't hear her own voice. All the sounds around her had somehow drained away.

The cheerleader couldn't hear Libby either.

The older boy smiled at Libby.

'Do you want to see me hurt her?' The voice filled Libby's head, loud and dark like an otherworldly growl.

In her desperation, Libby remembered what she needed to do— what her dad had always taught her to do. *In the name of Jesus Christ, I command you to leave.*

If they truly were evil, they were compelled to obey if commanded in the name of the Lord. But Libby's voice was muted once again.

The boy opened his mouth wide, revealing sharp and jagged teeth. Black smoke spilled from his throat. He turned and clamped down hard on the cheerleader's leg just beneath the hem of her skirt. She screamed, dropped her beer, and collapsed to the ground. Everyone around her was startled by her sudden outburst.

Libby wanted to cry out, and she quickly looked to her side. The younger kid who held Libby's hand snarled up at her now, his black eyes narrowed in anger.

In the name—

The kid swiped at Libby with his free hand, moving at blinding speed. Pain erupted in her arm as if she'd been sliced with a knife, and she shrieked. A moment later, the boy was gone.

Libby fell to her knees, clasping her left elbow where it hurt. The other evil boy had also vanished.

Everyone surrounded the cheerleader, who had collapsed and was holding her bitten thigh.

Libby looked down at her own arm. Three long gashes were ripped into the sleeve of her camo shirt and blood seeped from the burning wounds.

She stood and rushed over to the crying cheerleader.

"What the hell did you do to yourself?" demanded the guy she'd been leaning on.

Libby dropped to where the injured girl sat on the pavement. "Are you okay?"

"He bit me," the girl said through her tears.

"I saw him too."

Terror filled her eyes. "Really?"

"Yes." Libby held out her bloodied, scratched arm. "He did this to me."

"Who was he? Why did he do this?"

The girl's boyfriend hoisted her up, forcing her to stand. Libby also stood. "She needs to go home."

"Yeah, no shit," he said, annoyed. "She's drunk and somehow cut herself." He rolled his eyes. "She's always ruining the night because she can't hold her liquor." The guy pulled her away.

"What was that thing?" the girl called to Libby as she was dragged, but soon the couple disappeared into the crowd.

The pain in Libby's head was gone, as was her blurry vision. The sound of the party returned in full force, and the only sign that the evil kids had ever been there were the bloody scratches on her left arm.

Libby knew that something was terribly wrong. These creatures were not only going to appear once as an isolated incident.

Miller.

She rushed back the way she'd come, pushing past drunken guys and girls, not caring about shoving them.

"Libby."

She saw Bailey standing with Terrance and Parker. Parker was talking to one of his friends, the same one from the dance earlier. Libby kept running. She had to find Miller.

When she got back to the place with the beer keg, the big portable toilet was nowhere to be found. Libby recognized the guy who'd been filming with his cell phone, and she grabbed him with both hands.

"Where's Miller?"

"Whoa. Chill, girl."

"Where is he?"

"He's right there. Let go of me."

Libby followed his pointing finger and spotted Miller near a parked truck. He and two other guys had lined up a bunch of shots on the lowered tailgate.

Libby rushed over, and just before Miller got the small glass to his mouth, she swatted it out of his hands. It shattered on the asphalt. She threw her arms around him and hugged him tightly, relieved to be in the presence of a friendly face.

"Libby? Are you okay? What happened?"

"There's something here, Miller," she said between sobs. "I don't know what it is, but it's evil."

Miller pulled her away from his friends. "What do you mean? Oh, you're bleeding?"

"He scratched me," Libby showed him her arm. She rolled up her ripped sleeve to reveal three red, glistening wounds.

Miller held her wrist and inspected them. Fear crossed his face. "This happened just now?"

"Yes. There are two of them. One did this to me, and the other made me watch while he bit someone else."

Miller pursed his lips and looked away. Libby knew what he was about to say because she was thinking the same thing.

"We have to call your dad."

19

"Get in," Rand said.

The two boys opened the Jeep's back door and slid into the seat behind Rand and Stacy. The door closed by itself, as if with magic.

Rand idled for a minute, waiting for the kid to speak again. An uneasy tension bloomed. Stacy was stiff in the passenger seat, eyes fixed ahead.

"Where are we going?" Rand asked.

"We need you to take us home."

Rand waited for more information. He used his mirror to peer into the backseat, but the pair was covered in a darkness that did not seem natural.

"We're just two little kids!" the boy shouted at Rand as if frustrated they weren't moving. Both Rand and Stacy jolted at the outburst. "We aren't going to hurt you."

To Rand, it sounded like the boy was reading off a cue card with no other context.

"Right," Rand said. "We'll take you home."

Rand shifted into drive and coasted down the road. As he did, he noticed that Stacy had started trembling and seemed to be trying her best to hold it together.

Rand drove down a street that led him out of the neighborhood and onto a boulevard. He idled at the stop sign and allowed two cars to pass before he turned left.

"Where is home?" Rand asked. "Where exactly am I taking you?"

Rand tightened his grip on the steering wheel. He could feel the two kids in the backseat; their presence was powerful and heavy as if some invisible force was pulling his entire body toward the ground underneath his Jeep. Rand had experienced that feeling many times in the past. Evil spirits often had an aura of negativity surrounding them that grew more distinct the closer they were.

"Where are we going?" Rand asked again.

I can honestly say I never thought I'd give a demon a lift, he thought.

As they drove, Rand tried his best to keep his attention on the two shadows in the rear. Although he ran over bumps and uneven patches in the road, causing him and Stacy to sway with the moving of the vehicle, the kids remained completely still as if the forces of physics did not apply to them.

He passed Gavin's Deli on his left. Rand was so surprised that his focus on the black-eyed kids faltered. He looked over his shoulder as the fast-food joint faded in the distance.

"What?" Stacy whispered, alarmed.

"Nothing," Rand said. He thought Gavin's Deli had gone out of business and no longer existed. *Miller used to love that place.*

Something else caught Rand's eye in the rearview mirror. It was a car far behind him on the boulevard, speeding up and gaining on him fast.

The black sedan flashed its lights, signaling for Rand to move out of the way. There was an empty lane on either side of him, though, so Rand stayed put. The car tailgated Rand, lights flashing on and off and horn blaring.

"What's going on?" Stacy asked. "Mr. Casey, he's crazy, just get out of his way."

Rand realized what was happening and held his ground. It had been a long time since he'd encountered a phantom vehicle. It was a common demonic trick. The black-eyed kids were using it to attack him.

"Mr. Casey," Stacy said.

"This won't work on me," Rand said, glaring into the rearview mirror.

Finally, the black car swerved around him and sped past. It drifted recklessly across all the boulevard lanes, then disappeared into the distance ahead. As it went, Rand looked for a license plate. Just as he'd predicted, there was none.

"What in the world?" Stacy said. She gripped the center console and the passenger door's armrest.

"It wasn't real," Rand told her.

Stacy gasped. "You mean that was one of those ghost cars you teach us about?"

"Yes." Rand checked the two kids in the backseat again. They were still there, unmoving. "We can thank our little friends for that."

"Oh my God," she whispered.

Rand had occasionally seen phantom cars when he was involved in a case. They appeared to drive insanely and did whatever they could to get him to crash. The key to handling them was to recognize what they were as soon as possible, understand that they weren't real, and hold your ground.

There had been a handful of other cars on the boulevard when Rand had first turned onto it, but now it was empty. *Too* empty. It was late at night, sure, but this main thoroughfare usually had at least a few motorists during the night.

Two bright lights flashed in the distance ahead.

"Mr. Casey." Stacy reached over and grabbed Rand's arm.

The headlights grew brighter as the car sped toward them, going the wrong way in their lane.

"It's back," Rand told her. "Close your eyes, Stacy."

"What are you doing?"

Rand heard the sounds of the oncoming car's revving engine as it zoomed toward his Jeep. Rand grasped his steering wheel with both hands, knuckles white, and maintained his course.

"It's going to ram us!" Stacy shouted.

"No it won't, Stacy. Close your eyes."

Rand leaned forward, ready for what appeared to be a head-on collision.

It'll go right through us, he thought. *They always do. It isn't real.*

The phantom vehicle wanted him to swerve. To dodge. To flip his car or crash. But Rand would not fall for its trick.

The black sedan made no signs of diverting.

At the last moment, Stacy screamed and lunged, grabbing the steering wheel and yanking it to the right. The Jeep jerked into the other lane just as the phantom vehicle sped past, narrowly missing them. Rubber squealed on the road as Rand tried to regain control of the skidding Jeep. He turned into the swerve, trying not to panic, and then he straightened out.

An icy chill passed through Rand's entire body, the sickening nerves sprouting from a disaster just nearly avoided.

"What are you doing?" Rand shouted. "I told you to close your eyes."

"I'm sorry. I couldn't—" Tears leaked from Stacy's eyes.

Rand caught himself and contained his anger. Stacy had never been in such a situation before. She had reacted instinctively, and he couldn't blame her.

"How can you be sure that it wasn't real? It looked like it was. I'm *so* sorry, Mr. Casey, but—"

Rand gripped her forearm. "It's okay. We're fine. It doesn't matter now."

Stacy wiped her eyes and sniffled, exhaling slowly.

"Everything's all right now," Rand said.

Red and blue lights flashed behind him, followed by the single blare of a police car's siren.

20

R and swore.

    Stacy looked into her side mirror. The bright lights lit up her face. "Is it another ghost car?"

"I don't think so."

Of course the cops are out tonight, Rand thought. *And here I am, swerving all over the place.*

Rand honestly would have preferred to deal with another phantom vehicle. At least he could predict those. Rand had had very bad experiences when the police got involved in his supernatural cases.

"Mr. Casey?" Stacy prodded.

Rand put on his blinker and drifted to the shoulder. He would comply and work his best charm to convince the officer that nothing was wrong. Hopefully before the black-eyed kids caused any issues.

The police cruiser followed Rand and came to a stop several feet behind the Jeep. The two shadows remained silent and still. The bright lights from the police car did not seem to reach them. Rand waited for what felt like an eternity for the officer to make his move.

"What do we do?" Stacy whispered.

"Just be cool. I'll handle it."

The police officer approached, and Rand rolled down the window. "Evening, officer."

"License and registration." The officer shone his flashlight inside the Jeep. He was a young man with a slight build and a gentle face, even though he tried to exude authority.

Rand reached into his glove box and withdrew the registration papers, then pulled his driver's license from his wallet and handed them over.

The officer inspected them with his flashlight. "Do you know why I pulled you over, Mr. Casey?"

"I'm guessing because of that little swerve. I had one hell of a sneeze."

The officer shone the light back on Rand and eyed him. "Have you had anything to drink tonight, Mr. Casey?"

"Nothing."

He aimed the light at Stacy, inspected her for a moment, and then checked the rear of the vehicle. The officer's stony expression melted away and was replaced by uncertainty. Rand assumed the officer was starting to feel the dark aura that emanated from the black-eyed kids.

The flashlight blinked out.

Shit, Rand thought.

The officer slapped and shook it, jiggling the batteries. He clicked the button on and off, but it did not light up. He took a step back from the Jeep, and his hand went to the gun on his belt. Rand knew the other man's gut was telling him that something was off.

"Get out of the car, Mr. Casey."

Rand lifted his palms. "Is there a problem, officer?"

"I said get out of the car." A stern command this time.

Rand had no choice. He opened the car and slowly climbed out of the Jeep.

"Keep those hands where I can see them." The officer gripped

Rand's arm and guided him toward the front of the car. "Hands on the hood."

Rand complied. The officer began to pat Rand down, first his jacket, then his jeans, then his ankles.

"Carrying anything I need to know about?" the officer asked.

"No, sir."

"Who's the girl?"

"My girlfriend." Rand hated to lie, but the truth—that she was his student—sounded worse.

The officer's hands paused when he said that. "She looks young. Am I going to find something I don't like if I check her ID?"

"No, sir. Check it if you want."

The officer hesitated as if considering whether to verify that or move on. He walked toward the back of the Jeep and spoke into the radio that was clipped onto on his shirt at the shoulder. "Barry, can you run a plate for me?"

"Go ahead, Joe."

Officer Joe read off Rand's license plate number.

"Got it," Barry said.

Joe returned to Rand. Rand saw the shadowed heads of the black-eyed kids turning in unison as they tracked Joe's movement. Watching him.

"Who are the kids?" Joe asked.

"Stacy's brothers." He nodded his head toward the passenger seat. "We took them trick-or-treating."

"Bit late for that, don't you think?"

The radio burst with static. "Hey Joe."

The officer reached to his shoulder and pushed the button. "What you got for me?"

The radio garbled. Barry's voice cut in and out.

Joe pressed the button again. "Repeat."

Rand glanced at the black-eyed kids again. They still watched Joe.

Oh, no.

He knew well how demons interfered with electronic equipment. Especially radios.

"The Jeep is registered to Randolph Casey," Barry said. His voice sounded different this time. Flat and distant. "Louisiana resident, address eight-one-three Plaster Road."

Rand's ears perked up. That wasn't his address.

"Anything on record?" Joe asked.

"He's been busy," Barry said. "Lots on his file. Murder, rape, incest, fornication with animals."

Joe froze, then furrowed his brow. "What was that?"

Barry's voice grew louder. "That's right, Joe. Randolph Casey likes to *fuck* animals."

Barry started to laugh. An inhuman, mirthless laugh.

"That isn't—" Rand began.

"Barry, what—"

"You need to shoot him, Joe. You need to shoot him *right now*." Barry cackled again.

Rand could tell Joe was both frightened and confused and didn't know what to do. So he drew his gun and pointed it at Rand. "Get on the ground."

"Whoa." Rand's body wanted to dodge out of the way of the gun barrel, but he forced himself to remain still. Stacy shrieked inside the car.

"On the ground!"

"Okay, okay." Rand flattened himself on the pavement. "Listen to me, Joe. That isn't your colleague on the radio."

"You're messing with my radio somehow," Joe said, although he sounded unconvinced. Like he was merely trying to make sense of what was happening.

"I didn't do anything," Rand said.

"I'm taking you in," Joe said.

"Don't arrest him," the radio blared. It wasn't Barry's voice at all anymore. It was inhuman. "Kill him. Shoot him, Joe. Kill him. Kill him *now*."

Joe ripped the radio from his shirt and threw it to the pavement as if the voice grated unbearably on his ears. "What the hell is this?"

A deep, otherworldly roar bellowed from inside Rand's Jeep. Both he and Joe snapped their heads toward it, caught off guard. The entire car lurched, rocking side to side as if two monsters were fighting inside.

"Stacy," Rand called out, and almost pushed himself up off the asphalt.

"Don't move," Joe shouted, bringing his gun closer to Rand's back.

Another growl, louder than the first. Stacy shrieked inside the car.

Joe's wide eyes darted back and forth between the Jeep and Rand.

"What are you waiting for?" Rand shouted at Joe. "Get her out of there."

"Stay right where you are." Joe lowered his gun and rushed to the passenger side of the Jeep. Rand heard him throw open the door.

"Ma'am, are you—"

"Let me out of here!" Stacy screamed.

From where Rand lay, he saw Stacy's feet land on the street and run around the front of the Jeep. She was kneeling over him and clawing desperately at his clothes, trying to get him to stand up.

"Where are those kids?" Joe asked.

Stacy forced Rand to his feet with surprising strength. He wanted to stay on the ground to avoid more trouble, but Stacy was no longer acting rationally. Her face was flushed red and her blonde hair was disheveled. The black-eyed kids had done something to her.

"Hey," Joe barked. Rand and Stacy froze, standing together, eyes on Joe. "Where the hell are the kids? Where did they go?"

Rand had no idea. But whatever the kids had done, they had scared Stacy almost to death. *Maybe even hurt her.*

"They…" Stacy began, her voice trembling.

A black shadow began to leak from the open doors of Rand's Jeep and float up toward the sky like smoke. The tendrils blended with the darkness of the night and seemed to vanish toward the sky.

They're leaving, Rand thought. He'd seen many demons leave behind a shadowy, smoke-like substance when they disappeared.

Joe watched the shadow as it drifted toward the sky, transfixed. His mouth moved as if trying to say something, but no words came out.

When the shadow had vanished from sight, Joe cast Rand and Stacy a frightened, helpless look. He now seemed deeply disturbed.

Joe turned and fled. He leapt back into his police cruiser and sped away.

"Are you okay?" Rand asked Stacy. "What the hell happened?"

Stacy lifted a trembling hand and gripped the collar of her t-shirt. She pulled it down, revealing a dark red handprint seared into the skin on her shoulder. A fresh wave of sobs came when she saw it.

"Fuck. One of them touched you," Rand said.

Rand had suffered many marks just like it. They tended to burn pretty badly at first, but the pain usually subsided after a few hours.

Stacy swallowed and fought to calm down so she could speak. "I'm sorry, but I didn't know what else to do. Those kids were making all that stuff happen with the police officer, so I started praying and commanding them to leave in the name of Jesus like you taught us in class and they got mad and started growling and rocking the car and one of them grabbed me and—"

"Shh... shh... it's okay," Rand said. "You were absolutely right that they were causing this, and you did the right thing."

Stacy sniffed and tried to suppress her tears. She still held her shirt away from the handprint, appearing nervous the cotton would irritate it.

A horn blew and a car swerved around Rand's parked Jeep. Then another.

After a long time of the boulevard being devoid of any other cars, the other motorists had finally reappeared, seemingly all at once.

"Where did all these cars come from?" Rand asked as he guided Stacy toward the passenger seat. He wondered if the black-eyed kids had also somehow caused the boulevard to clear with some kind of supernatural ability. Likely, but he didn't have time to think about it just then. "Come on. Let's get off the road." He helped Stacy in and closed her door.

As he walked around to the driver's side, another car maneuvered around his Jeep. This one slowed, and the man behind the wheel gave Rand a look of concern through his rolled-down window. "You all right?"

"All good, thanks," Rand said, giving a polite wave.

The man seemed unconvinced, but Rand hopped back into his Jeep, fired up the engine, and pulled off into the nearby parking lot of a hotel.

Rand rested on the back of his car seat. Fire still pumped through his body. His heart seemed to bang in his ears. Nervous sweat dampened his flesh.

When he turned toward Stacy, he caught her examining the red handprint on her shoulder again.

"I've had dozens of those. It'll fade."

"I can't believe it," she said, not taking her eyes away. "It's just like those pictures you show us in class."

Rand wished he could take that mark from her. If it weren't for him, that never would have happened.

"I screwed up the plan," Stacy said.

Rand twisted in his seat to face her more fully. "What do you mean? You *saved* me back there. I was about to be arrested."

Stacy let the collar of her shirt fall back over the handprint as if she could no longer bear to look at it. "We had a plan. Find the black-eyed kids, and make them take us to Kim. But when I saw how they were tricking that police officer and how much trouble you were in, the only thing I could think to do was chase them away with the commands you taught us in class. And now they're gone and we don't know where Kim is." She shook her head and fumbled with a frayed strand of denim on her jeans, as if ashamed to make eye contact.

"Eight-one-three Plaster Road," Rand said, surprising himself by how the memory seemed to spill from his mouth.

Stacy looked at him. "Huh?"

"Eight-one-three Plaster Road," Rand repeated. "When the black-eyed kids were projecting their voices over the officer's radio, that was the address they gave for me. But that isn't my address."

Rand slid his phone from his pocket and typed the address into the GPS app. The map zoomed onto a location at the edge of the city.

"It's a real address," Rand said.

From what Rand could tell, Plaster Road was a long, rural highway with many curves and bends through a heavily wooded area.

"I've never heard of it." Stacy shifted to get a better look at Rand's phone.

He held it out so she could see. "Me either. But look, it's way out there in the northern part of town. I think it actually might be outside the city limits."

"Why here?" Stacy asked. Her and Rand's faces were inches apart as they studied the map.

Rand could only come up with one explanation. "Demons are master liars, as you've learned in class, but that doesn't necessarily mean they just pull stuff out of their asses. The things they say are either things that they know or are meaningful to them in some way." Rand used his thumbs to zoom in on the area, but there wasn't much detail on the map. "If they spouted off this address, that means this location is important to them for some reason."

"Do you think that's where they're keeping Kim?" A hopeful note had slipped into Stacy's tone.

"I can't say for sure," Rand said. "But this is the best clue I have."

Rand's phone started ringing in his hand, displacing the GPS app.

Libby.

His heart dropped. It was after midnight and there *should* be no reason for her to call at that hour.

"Libby," he said, bringing the phone to his ear, voice cracking.

"Dad." Her voice sounded like she'd been crying. "Something's happened."

21

Rand waited in that hotel parking lot for what felt like ages. Libby had wanted to explain what had happened over the phone, but once Rand realized she was out of the house and with Miller, he told her to come to him.

He paced back and forth near his Jeep, Stacy watching him worriedly. She'd stopped asking him questions once she'd realized how upset he was.

Rand wondered if they did this every year. Told him they were going to stay in and behave just to placate him, only to go out and party on the most dangerous night of the year.

He felt angry and betrayed, but he had to file that away for later. For now, he needed to make sure his daughter was okay.

Miller's old pickup truck turned into the hotel parking lot. Before it came to a complete stop, Libby bolted from the passenger seat and ran over to Rand, throwing her arms around his neck and pulling him into a tight squeeze.

"Are you okay?" Rand asked.

"I don't know," she said, the tears starting again.

"Tell me what happened."

Miller killed the engine and joined them. Rand gave his friend's portable toilet Halloween costume a single irritated glance before turning his attention back to his daughter.

He saw her arm. Three scratches had torn through her camo shirt, leaving red lines on her pale skin. "You were attacked."

"I'm sorry," she said, wiping her tears away. "It's just—"

"Just tell me what happened. And the truth this time, please."

Libby exhaled. "I wanted to go to the Halloween dance at school. You know, do something normal on Halloween for once. I knew you'd never let me, so I didn't tell you. Bailey and Mom were in on it too.

"Anyway, I predicted you'd come check everything out, so we set up a fake study party at Mom's house. As soon as you were gone, Bailey and I got into our costumes and went to the dance.

"The guy who took me to the dance wanted to go to Boyd Street, so we went. On the way to the party, we ran into these two creepy kids. I got a really bad feeling from them. Like, I knew there was just something totally *wrong* about them and that they didn't belong. We ended up running away.

"We got to the party and I saw Miller there." Miller hung his head like a kid getting ratted out for misbehavior. "I hoped that nothing else was going to happen, but then the kids appeared again. One of them grabbed my hand and I couldn't get away. It was like I was frozen. I did what you've always told me to do—I commanded them to leave in the name of God, and that's when the one holding my hand scratched me and vanished. The other one bit a girl on the leg. Then I ran and found Miller, and now we're here."

Rand rubbed at his temples with his fingers, pressing into them. A headache had started to form behind his eyes, and not because of his proximity to demonic entities. This one was from fatigue and mental exhaustion from all the adrenaline rushes he'd had that night.

"What have you been doing, Rando?" Miller asked. "You look like hell."

"Why haven't you taken off that costume?" Rand said. "You look ridiculous."

Miller shed the portable toilet, leaving him in nothing but faded blue jeans and a white t-shirt covered in sweat. As he did, Rand shared his side of the events.

"So this has escalated beyond ringing doorbells," Miller said.

"We have a legitimate emergency," Rand said.

"And you said you have an address?"

Rand held up his phone, GPS flashing the location. "Stacy and I were just about to head out there, but then y'all called."

Miller ran a hand through his sweaty hair. "I can't believe you invited them into your car. You specifically did what I told you *not* to do."

"So did both of you," Rand said, glaring.

"Lecture us later," Miller shot back. "What's the address you managed to get?"

"Eight-one-three Plaster Road," Rand said.

Miller whistled. "Plaster Road, huh? That's a blast from the past."

"You know it?"

"You don't? It's one of the oldest areas in town. They fought hard decades ago to not be included in the city limits. Those properties have been there for generations."

Old homes, Rand thought. *This is starting to make more sense.* Old homes were far more likely to attract negative spirits.

"What should Libby and I do?" Miller asked.

"You both are coming with me," Rand said. Miller and Libby exchanged a glance. "That's right. Being alone and separated seems to provoke more encounters. If we stay as a group, we decrease those chances."

Rand would have preferred to send them home and keep them as far away from this mess as possible. But after hearing about Libby's encounter, Rand realized that the black-eyed kids could appear anywhere. The best place for Miller and Libby, at least at the moment, was where he could keep an eye on them.

Rand got behind the wheel of his Jeep while Miller climbed into the passenger seat. Libby and Stacy crawled into the back, occupying the spaces where the black-eyed kids had been just twenty minutes before.

When Rand fired up the ignition, the digital clock on the center console lit up. It read 12:43.

He tapped the clock with his index finger, drawing Miller's attention to it.

"The blue bastard showed up," Rand said, keeping his voice low. "We have until dawn."

Miller's expression became grim.

As Rand pulled out of the parking lot, he hoped he would find something useful on Plaster Road. Something that would give him a clue as to what to do next. Hopefully it would lead him to Kim.

Deep down, he knew it would not be that simple.

22

As Rand drove, a heavy silence fell over them all, one punctuated by anxiety, exhaustion, and fear.

It was only broken when Libby said to Stacy. "I'm Libby. His daughter."

"I'm Stacy. I take his class."

Rand followed the blue highlighted road on his phone's GPS outside of the city limits, and soon enough, he came to an intersection. An old street sign, small and barely legible in the night, indicated that it was Plaster Road. He turned right.

Miller was correct—Rand could tell it was one of the oldest roads in the region. It was narrow, curved, and not well maintained. There were no streetlights, so Rand had to switch on his brights and take the turns very slowly. Trees lined the road on either side; it had been paved through the woods. They created the illusion of driving through a darkened tunnel. Fallen brown leaves covered the pavement. There were houses along the way, built on large swaths of property, which kept the neighboring houses at a distance.

Rand followed the highlighted route down the curvy pathway on the GPS, the tension inside him growing as he neared.

The blue line ran out. "You have arrived at your destination," the GPS announced.

When Rand slowed to a stop, he saw only darkness. He turned the Jeep and drove into the lot to point his high beams, confirming what he feared.

No driveway. No house. The address was for an empty lot of overgrown grass and dead leaves.

Rand grabbed the flashlight and got out of the car and looked around. Miller followed his lead while the girls waited behind.

There was a house, 811 Plaster Road, to his left. The next, presumably 815, was off in the distance. The lot between them was large enough for a house and had probably contained 813 at some point. But now it was gone.

"This can't be happening," Rand muttered.

"The demonic are experts at these kinds of tricks," Miller said. The bright headlights cast long, ominous shadows on the leaf-covered ground.

Rand's headache was growing worse. "A dead end."

"Not yet," Miller said. "Let's at least have a look around. Maybe there's something we can discover here."

The two men walked farther onto the property, the leaves crunching underneath their shoes. Rand swept his flashlight around the area, looking for anything.

"No trees," he said. "That means this lot was cleared, and the house was probably here at some point. But it's not anymore."

"Wonder why," Miller said.

"This has to mean something," Rand said, as if trying to force it to be true. "All the houses on Plaster Road are still intact, right? Except for this address. The odd factor is always what we should consider."

"I guess," Miller said. "But again, what does it mean?"

Then he heard it—coming from the darkness to his left.

The loud clicks of someone cocking a shotgun.

23

Miller's hands shot up toward the sky, a knee-jerk reaction. Rand followed suit, still holding the flashlight. He froze, but out of the corner of his eye, he could make out the shadow of a man who was pointing the barrel of his shotgun right at them.

"Hey, take it easy. We're not here to hurt you," Rand said.

"I finally caught you, you son of a bitch."

"You have the wrong guy," Rand said.

"Wrong guy, huh?" The man spoke with a thick southern accent. "I don't think so."

"I'm here to help you."

"Here's what we're gonna do," the man said. "I'm calling the police, and you're not gonna move until they get here. I'm sick of all the commotion you're causin' and I won't stand for it anymore, so you'd better not move, or else—"

"You can't shoot us," Miller said. "This technically isn't your property. Property defense doesn't apply here."

The man shifted his gun to Miller and he fell silent.

"You there," the man said to Rand. "You live around here? I don't recognize you."

"I don't," Rand said. "I've been dealing with some pests who've led me here. If you put down your gun, we can talk about this and get to the bottom of it."

The man considered his words for a few moments, then lowered his gun. Rand and Miller dropped their hands.

The man stepped forward, and the bright beam from Rand's flashlight revealed him. He was old, perhaps in his seventies, and wore boots, tan cargo pants, and a loose-fitting, button-down shirt with his long sleeves rolled over his forearm. His face was wrinkled and stern.

"Name's Randolph Casey. Friends call me Rand." He held out his hand, and the man shook it.

"Wayne Swanson."

"This is Miller." Miller opted not to shake, but lifted his palm in an awkward wave, seemingly still dazed from the close call.

Footsteps rustled the dead leaves on the ground. Rand shined his light—Libby and Stacy rushed over to him.

"Is everything okay?" Libby asked.

"Everything's fine now," Rand answered for Wayne, hoping to force that narrative. "Everyone was just a little spooked, which is understandable since it's late and we're not supposed to be here. But it's all good. Wayne, this is my daughter Libby."

"What you folks doin' here in the middle of the night?" Wayne asked. "You picked the wrong place to poke around. I almost blasted y'all."

"We're interested in this house," Rand said. "Eight-one-three Plaster Road. Except it doesn't seem to be here anymore."

"Interested? Why?"

"Long story, my friend. We've been chasing down some nasty Halloween pranksters. Wanted to teach them a lesson, you know. Talk to their parents and tell them what their kids were up to. We thought this was where they lived, but as you can see..."

In most of Rand's cases, there always seemed to come a time when he needed help from a third party. He didn't like to lie to these people about what he was doing, but it was useful to leave out the "hard-to-believe" details. If he began every conversation disclosing he was a demonologist and paranormal investigator, he'd never get very far.

"Maybe you and I have the same nuisance," Wayne said.

"What problems have you been having?"

"Well..." Wayne adjusted his cap. "Truth is, I don't know. Trespassers, but they're real slippery. Can't seem to corner 'em."

"What do you mean?" Rand asked.

"Past couple weeks, they been showin' up. I'll take the dog out at night before me and Geraldine head to bed, and then Boss will spot 'em. They usually stand in this lot, right around there." He pointed. "Sometimes in those trees. Man, Boss goes nuts. Barkin', hollerin', slobberin' everywhere. But he won't go over, which is weird, 'cause Boss ain't usually afraid of no one."

Rand and Miller exchanged a glance.

"Did you ever see what these guys looked like?" Miller asked.

"Nope. They always standin' in the dark, and they run off before I can get a look at 'em. I called the cops a few times and they check around, but they never find nothin'. They won't come out anymore, 'cause now they think crazy old Wayne is seein' things."

Libby looked worried, as did Miller. Rand knew what was going on. There was definitely supernatural activity in this area, and Wayne was catching glimpses. While that definitely wasn't good for Wayne, it meant progress for Rand.

The vacant lot was not the dead end he'd thought it was.

"What's the deal with this place?" Rand said. "What happened to the house?"

"Oh yeah," Wayne said. "This was where the Erlich family lived."

"Who are the Erlichs?"

Wayne stared at him. "You serious? The Erlich family murders from 1984?"

"I would have been seven years old in 1984," Rand said.

"Ah. Either way, no one seems to remember that except for me and Geraldine. Maybe 'cause I lived here this whole time, so it's impossible to forget."

"What happened?"

"The Erlichs were my neighbors. They had a daughter and she had two young kids, each from a different fella. That girl had a boyfriend who was the father of neither, and one night he went crazy and broke in and shot all of 'em, then himself. I heard the shots and called the police. But by the time they got here, it was all said and done."

"Oh my God," Libby whispered under her breath.

"That sounds familiar," Miller said. "Pretty sure I read about it somewhere. One of the worst crimes in the city's history."

"It was," Wayne said. "They were a nice family, if a bit messy with the lawn upkeep. Those two kids always had their toys in the yard. Anyway, that doesn't mean they deserved what happened to 'em. Tragic shame, really."

"So what about the house?" Rand asked.

"Well, as you can imagine, no one wanted to live there after that, and I don't blame 'em. The place started to fall apart. If I ever had a moment, I'd go in there and fix up some things, but time went on, I got older, and it became too much. It eventually turned into an eyesore, so I wrote to the city council to do something about it, but they don't pay any attention to us folks way out here on Plaster.

"Anyway, about two years ago, I heard someone had purchased the land. Probably got it for a steal. I figured they would show up and assess the place, but they didn't for the longest time until one day men showed up with their bulldozers. Said the new owner wanted the house demolished. I watched as they tore it all down. Good riddance."

"Any idea who bought the property?" Rand asked.

Wayne only shrugged. "Not the foggiest."

Rand had not even lived in the city in 1984, so he'd never heard of the Erlich family murders. However, an event like that was sure to leave behind a huge surge of negative energy. Honestly, Rand was surprised that Wayne hadn't experienced anything strange until only recently.

The daughter had two young boys, Rand thought.

"So I don't know," Wayne said. "Only thing I can figure is someone's picked up on this spot and wrote about it or somethin'. You know these true crime books and these podcast things? Murderers and tragedies—folks eat that stuff up nowadays. Boggles me. But anyway, maybe some nuts want to see the place. Whoever bought it should set it up as a tourist attraction. But I hope he does somethin' soon because these people are drivin' me crazy and upsettin' my dog."

"I'm sorry all this is happening to you," Rand said. "But I think I can help."

"How? And why?" Wayne's eyes narrowed, and Rand could see the realization dawn on him. "Oh… You're one of those nuts, aren't you? Which are you? Murderer fan or ghost hunter?"

Rand let the question linger for a moment before he answered, trying to decide his best course of action. He figured he'd developed enough of a rapport with Wayne by then to go with the truth. "Ghost hunter."

Wayne scoffed. "I don't know which is worse."

"This is why I can help you. The things you're seeing—"

Wayne waved his hand at him. "Don't even start with me. My wife Geraldine's the one who believes in all that spirit nonsense, not me."

"I was serious when I said I had the same problems as you. I have intruders that always vanish, and I think this place has something to do with them."

Wayne rubbed his forehead and adjusted his cap again. "Look, you seem like a nice guy, but I ain't about to get into it with you. I wish you'd just leave."

"Give us the rest of the night," Rand said. "I want to search more around here. After tonight, I won't come back, and you'll never see me again. But if I find what I'm looking for, you'll stop having trespassers on your property."

Wayne looked at him and sighed. "Whatever, man. If you wanna waste your time, go ahead. But I'll take you up on your offer. If I catch you here again after tonight, I'll call the police."

"Deal. Also, if anyone knocks on your door tonight, don't answer it. And definitely don't let anyone inside. Just please trust me on that."

Wayne eyed them all in turn, clearly skeptical. "You folks have yourselves a good night." The leaves crunched under his boots as he headed back to his house.

"Charming guy," Miller muttered.

"A bad tragedy happened here," Stacy said, "and that's what attracts the spirits and negative energy. Just like what you teach us in class." Rand nodded. "He said the family had two boys."

"Exactly."

"But what does that have to do with Kim?"

"That's the part I have to figure out." Rand swept his flashlight across the empty lot. There was nothing but dead leaves and broken sticks covering the ground.

"You have less than five hours to do it, Rando," Miller said, checking his watch.

"Dad," Libby said. She held her buzzing phone. "Mom's calling. She's probably home and wondering where I am."

"Let her know."

Libby answered and took a few steps away to speak to Tessa.

"So what do we do?" Miller asked.

"It's obvious that something is going on here," Rand said. "This lot is a hotbed of spiritual activity, and I got the address straight from the black-eyed kids. It's all connected somehow."

He already knew the best solution when he needed to uncover what was hidden from the naked eye.

"I need to bring in a medium."

24

Wayne closed the door behind him, glad to shut out the midnight chill and the crazies that had wandered onto the empty lot next door.

"Lunatics," he muttered as he walked toward the closet near the back door to drop off his shotgun.

A figure stood in the center of the living room. Wayne let out a yelp and leapt back, instinctively grabbing his shotgun into both hands. Only after a moment did he realize it was Geraldine.

"You gonna shoot me now, Wayne?" His wife placed her hands on her hips.

"What the hell are you doin' standin' around in the dark like that?" Wayne barked, heart pounding from the sudden fright. "I thought you went to bed."

"I'm trying to figure out why you're running around the neighbor's property in the middle of the night."

"We ain't got no neighbors."

Geraldine clicked on a lamp. "Seriously, Wayne. What's going on?"

Wayne jabbed his thumb over his shoulder. "There's some nut jobs outside. Paranormal seekers or some such."

Geraldine had appeared annoyed, but now her face softened. "Really? What do they want?"

Wayne sighed. He really should have been more careful with his words. "Nothin'"

"What do they want, Wayne?" Geraldine said.

Wayne adjusted his cap, really not in the mood to talk about it. "They're interested in the Erlichs."

Wayne avoided talking about the family that used to live next door. His wife had become attached to the two boys. She'd always wanted children, but it had never happened for them, so those two had filled that void.

Geraldine still carried the pain of losing the Erlich children to such a horrific crime. Many years had passed since then, but something had changed in Geraldine that night, and that broken piece of her had never been the same.

"Do they know something about the boys?" Geraldine asked, a hopeful hint behind her voice.

Wayne had to be gentle here, yet firm. When it came to the two boys next door, Geraldine never thought sensibly. "Let those people do what they need to do so they can leave. Ain't no sense gettin' involved."

"But Wayne—"

There came three knocks on the front door.

Wayne whirled around. He couldn't believe it. "Are they *seriously* bangin' on my door? I already told 'em everythin' I knew."

"Let them in," Geraldine said.

Wayne glanced back at his wife. "You crazy?"

"It's cold out there, Wayne," she said. "Let them inside."

Wayne muttered a curse under his breath. The last thing he wanted was Geraldine meeting paranormal nuts. His wife was already a half-step away from being one of them herself, what with all the spirituality books she read and ghost-hunting TV programs she watched.

I'll just shoo 'em away, Wayne thought. *There's nothin' else I can tell them anyhow.*

Wayne opened the door, expecting to see the ghost-hunting man and his heavyset friend. But there, standing on his porch, were two young boys.

Wayne took a startled step backward. They resembled the two boys that used to live next door.

No, Wayne thought. *This is impossible. They've been dead for years.*

The pair looked like they hadn't had a bath in a fortnight and wore summer clothes even though it was cold outside. Wayne wondered why they weren't wearing any shoes.

Wayne tried to speak, but his voice only came out as a dry croak. The two boys stared into the house without looking at him.

"We need to use your telegraph," the older boy said.

"Pardon?" Wayne finally managed to say. Wayne was old, but even he hadn't ever seen a telegraph machine.

"Who is it?" Geraldine called behind him. "Is it the paranormal guy?"

Wayne heard Geraldine's bare feet on the floor as she began to walk toward him, but a strong instinct seized his gut, one that he couldn't explain.

"Don't come any closer, Geraldine," Wayne shouted.

"We aren't going to hurt you." The older boy spoke louder now, angry. "We just need to come inside and use your telegraph. We're only two young children, so you can trust us."

Wayne did not like the way the kids were speaking to him. Rudeness aside, something was giving him a very adverse feeling to their presence. A horrible stench had also risen to his nose.

Somethin' ain't right, he thought.

Geraldine gasped, suddenly beside Wayne. He hadn't heard his wife walk up to the door.

"It's them," she whispered.

"Let us in!" the older boy shouted.

"Get out of their way, Wayne," Geraldine said, gripping his arm. "They must be freezing."

Wayne was not one to believe in anything supernatural, and these two boys were not an exception. But he now remembered that the paranormal nut had warned him not to answer the door if anyone came knocking, nor to let anyone in.

And despite everything else that raced through Wayne's mind, his horrible gut feeling took over. He slammed the door in the kids' faces, feeling instant relief the moment they were out of sight.

"What are you doing, Wayne?" Geraldine cried. "Have you lost your mind?"

Geraldine shoved Wayne out of the way and opened the front door again.

The front porch was empty.

Geraldine fell silent and walked out onto the porch. Wayne readied his gun and stood close behind her. The two of them scanned the dark front yard.

"Where did they go?" Geraldine shivered.

There hadn't been enough time for the two boys to walk away that fast. It seemed they'd simply vanished into thin air.

"Wayne, what's going on?" Geraldine asked, her voice more hesitant now.

"I don't know," he said. "But if that paranormal nut comes back later, I'll have a thing or two to say to him."

25

Tessa had reclined her car seat and was hoping to doze off, but it was too uncomfortable. The clock on the dashboard read 1:36 AM. She couldn't wait to change out of her witch costume, wash off all her makeup, and crawl into her king-sized bed. Bill drove. He still wore the bolts in his neck from his low-effort Frankenstein Halloween costume.

"You okay?" Bill asked as he turned into the neighborhood.

"Just tired."

Tessa had been to a few parties for Southern Finance, Bill's company. "Party" was hardly the word to describe them. Bill's employees and colleagues were all nice enough, but not exactly thrilling. They discussed work, difficult clients, and industry trends while Tessa would simply nod and smile and be supportive.

Life with Bill was quiet, but good. Structured and stable. A far cry from her past relationship. Their wedding was in a few months, and Tessa was looking forward to solidifying her new life.

"Did you have fun?"

"Yeah," she said, although her voice spiked up, which happened whenever she told a white lie.

"Good. Me too."

Bill was never much for reading between the lines.

"You were right," Bill went on. "The Halloween party was a good idea. I didn't believe they'd be into it, but they were. Some of those costumes were wild, don't you think?"

"Yeah." In truth, everyone's costumes were basic. Creative dressing was not in these peoples' skill sets. Costumes and parties weren't numbers or sales or interest rates. But at least they'd tried.

"And did you hear Terry tell that story about his client in Indonesia?" Bill started laughing all over again. Tessa had heard it but hadn't understood all its technicalities or why it was funny.

Bill pulled into the empty driveway, and Tessa shot up straight, alarmed. "Where's Libby's car? She's not here."

"Umm…" Bill struggled to put words together. "I'm sure she's fine."

Tessa fished her phone from her purse. No missed calls or text messages. She unlocked it and dialed her daughter's number. As it rang, she threw off her seatbelt and left the car.

"Hey, Mom," Libby answered.

"Are you okay? I just got home and you're not here. You said you'd be back before midnight."

"Yeah, I'm fine."

"What's going on? Where are you? Who are you with?"

Libby hesitated. "I'm with Dad."

Bill stood with Tessa in the driveway as she talked, looking on worriedly.

"With your dad? How did that happen?" she asked. Bill furrowed his brow in confusion.

"There's been an incident."

That word. It had been the same one Rand had used earlier that day when he'd barged into the house. Tessa had dismissed it then, but now she could hear how serious Libby was. "What do you mean?"

"It's kind of a long story, but I can tell you about it later."

"No!" Tessa barked. "Libby, you need to come home right this instant." She headed up the driveway and toward the front door. Bill followed.

"But Mom—"

"I don't want you involved in whatever your dad is doing. Not after what happened last time."

"What's going on?" Bill asked, but Tessa didn't answer him.

"I'm with Dad. I'm safe," Libby pleaded.

"Do you have your car? I'm coming to get you if you don't. Where are you? Where's Bailey and your other friends?"

"Mom." Libby's eye roll could be heard in her voice, and that infuriated Tessa even more.

"Put your father on."

"Hang on."

Bill unlocked and opened the front door, and he and Tessa went inside. The living room was warm and the outside chill melted off.

"Tess," Rand said.

"What the *hell* do you think you're doing?"

"I could say the same thing to you. You allowed her out of the house, and now something's happened."

"I am so *sick* of his crap, Rand. Where are you? Are you going to bring her here, or should I come there?"

"Let me call you back in five minutes and we can figure out how to get her home," Rand said.

"No. I want to help you, Dad," came Libby's voice in the background.

"I swear, Randolph, if you hang up this phone—"

Bill closed the door behind her. As soon as he did, someone knocked.

Tessa paused. Bill gave her a confused look.

"Did you see anyone when we were out there?" Bill asked.

For a moment, Tessa forgot about Rand. "No. Did you?"

Bill shook his head. "Must be some late-night trick-or-treaters. Why are they out at this time? I'll get rid of them."

"Are you talking to me or Bill?" Rand asked.

"Bill," Tessa said, turning her attention back to the conversation. "Someone just knocked."

"Seriously? Tessa, don't—"

The line went dead. When she checked the screen, the empty battery indicator flashed.

That's weird. She'd known her phone battery was low, but not enough to die on her.

Bill opened the door. Two young children were on the doorstep. One was a head taller than the other and they were dressed similarly in shorts and t-shirts. For some strange reason... they were barefoot.

When Tessa saw them, she recoiled, though she couldn't pinpoint why. Something about them was *very* off.

"We need to come in and use your telephone," the oldest boy said.

Even the way he spoke was wrong. It was too clear, too precise, as if there was a ventriloquist standing off to the side, speaking for him.

"Umm..." Bill glanced back at Tessa, then to the kids. "Where are your parents? Are you okay?"

"We only need to come in and use your telephone. We're just two kids and we aren't going to hurt you."

An overwhelming sense of foreboding swirled through Tessa's body. It was a feeling she had not felt in a long time, but she remembered it well. She felt it during the years she was with Rand when the monsters from his cases paid her little visits.

There's been an incident, he'd said.

"I guess that would be all right," Bill said. "You can call your parents and wait here until they come to pick you up."

Since she was frozen in fear, it took Tessa a few moments to realize what Bill had just said. Her instinct seized control. She bolted toward the door and slammed it shut in the kids' faces.

"What are you doing?" Bill looked at her like she'd gone nuts. Maybe she had.

"Don't let them in," she said.

"What are you talking about? They're kids and they need our help."

"No. I have a terrible feeling about them. And Rand said—"

"Come on, Tess." Bill gave her an exasperated look. "How many times do I have to tell you? You can't let Rand keep getting in your head. You're *free* from that now."

"This is different, Bill. Those kids aren't right."

Bill regarded her for a moment before choosing to ignore her and open the door again. But when he did, the two kids were gone.

He walked out onto the porch and looked around the yard. Then he came back in, confused. "They sure walk fast."

They vanished, Tessa thought. *The yard is way too big for them to get out of sight that quickly.*

"Well, I hope they get home," Bill said, closing the door again.

As soon as he did, there were another three knocks.

Bill backed away from the door. Tessa grabbed his arm and squeezed it.

"What in the world?" he whispered.

"Don't answer it."

They waited, staring at the door in silence. A minute later, three more knocks, louder than the ones before.

Bill stiffened beside her. "Will they go away?" he asked.

"I think so."

Tessa heard footsteps on the other side of the door. It sounded like the two kids were rapidly pacing back and forth.

Then their footsteps started stamping *on* the door as if they were kicking it. Then continued up the length of the door.

Tessa realized the two kids were walking *up* the door.

The steps continued along the outside wall of the house. Tessa and Bill followed the sounds with their eyes.

The kids reached the roof. Tessa went to the kitchen in the back of the house, following them. Bill was right behind her.

The two sets of footsteps traversed the entire roof and began their steady climb down the opposite wall. They walked down the rear side of the house and halted just outside the back door of the kitchen.

A moment later, there came another three knocks.

"How do we get rid of them?" Bill whispered.

"Go away!" Tessa shouted at them.

Three more pounds, harder than before, which rattled the door on its hinges.

"Leave us alone."

Another strike, this one sounding like a battering ram. The door shook and the wood cracked. Tessa and Bill leapt back, startled.

The house fell silent again.

Bill had his arm around Tessa, and in that moment she wondered which of the two of them were more afraid.

"I think they're gone," Tessa whispered after the silence had lingered.

"Are you sure?"

She removed herself from Bill's embrace and inched toward the door, holding her breath.

"Don't open it," Bill said.

There was only one way to be sure. She gripped the knob, working up her courage, and then flung the door open.

No one was there. The outside surface of the door had been bashed in, the paint chipped and cracked.

Bill joined Tessa and inspected the door. It would have taken a huge force to cause that kind of damage. No kid was strong enough to do that.

The silence broke sharply when Bill's cell phone rang. He glanced at the screen, then answered. "Hey, Rand." He listened. "Actually, no, everything is not okay. I think you should come over."

26

For the first time in a long while, Rand felt overwhelmed. He just couldn't keep up.

He sped through town in his Jeep, Miller and Libby and Stacy riding with him. It seemed like the more he dug into solving the mystery, the more the black-eyed kids attacked. They were spreading their reach, forcing Rand to stretch himself thin as he addressed each event.

When he got to Bill's house, Bill and Tessa were waiting on the expansive front porch. Tessa wore jeans and a sweatshirt, but still had on the black lipstick that Rand had caught her wearing earlier. Bill's thinning black hair was standing on end, and he'd forgotten to remove the plastic bolts from his neck that Rand assumed had been part of a Frankenstein costume.

Tessa rushed to Libby and hugged her. "Are you okay? Oh my God, what happened to your arm?"

"I'm fine, Mom."

Bill was paler than usual. "What happened here?" Rand asked him.

"Come see."

Rand followed Bill into the kitchen and to the back door where he showed him the damage. It looked like a cannonball had been fired into the door.

"They came to the front door first. You were on the phone with Tess, and the phone died just after they knocked. I was about to let them in, but Tess got a really bad feeling from them, so she slammed the door on them. When I opened it up again, they were gone."

Rand was relieved. Tessa had developed a sense for evil entities when they had been together—it was almost inevitable for anyone who dated him for long enough. Seems like it had served her well here.

"They knocked again, but I didn't answer. After that, they climbed straight up the door and wall and onto the roof, then down this wall here." Bill pointed as he explained. "They were right outside the back door. When they realized we weren't going to answer, they gave it one last pound before leaving us alone. That's where this damage came from."

Rand grew sick as he listened. "This is what I've been dealing with all night. They're popping up everywhere. You did the right thing by not letting them in."

"I almost did," Bill said. "Tessa stopped me at the last second. She said they didn't feel right."

I taught her well, Rand thought.

Rand and Bill returned to the living room, where everyone gathered. Stacy, Miller, Libby, and Tessa. All eyes turned to him, weary and frightened and confused, all waiting for him to guide them.

It was nearing three o'clock in the morning, and the adrenaline spikes Rand had been experiencing all night were fading. His mind was foggy, his focus torn in many directions. He wanted to stop, regroup, and reassess, but there was no time. He *needed* to figure this out before sunrise—Shindael had promised that Kim's life depended on it.

"What does it mean, Rand?" Tessa asked him. "What are these things, and what do they want?"

"They want us," Rand said. "As far as I know. They've already taken Stacy's friend."

"Where did they take her?"

"Long explanation, but it has something to do with an empty lot on Plaster Road." He glanced at Miller. "As I said before Tessa called, I think the best course of action is to bring in a medium."

Miller nodded. "I agree. But that means…"

Rand sighed. *It means I have to call Katie.*

She was the only medium he knew in town, but she'd stopped working with Rand when the pressure of always communicating with the other side had gotten to be too much.

"I promised to not call her for any more cases," Rand said.

"What other option do you have?" Miller asked him. "You have to try."

Miller was right. Rand glanced at Libby, who shrugged in agreement.

He took out his phone and brought up her number from his list of contacts. She would be furious that he was waking her up.

The phone rang and rang, not going to voice mail. Everyone watched Rand as he waited for her to pick up.

He was about to hang up when her familiar voice answered. "Rand?"

"Katie. Hey. Sorry to call so late."

"What do you want?" Her tone was guarded and skeptical.

"There's been an incident." It was quickly becoming his motto for the evening.

"Are you okay?"

"Listen… a case has come up."

"You promised me we were finished. I'm out of it."

"I know, but…"

"We've talked about this," she said. "My world is different these days, and I like it. The last time we worked together was my worst experience by far."

Rand remembered that well. It was only a short while ago the demon Karax had wreaked havoc through St. Mary's Medical Center.

"I know, Katie, and I'm sorry, but—"

"Besides, even if I wanted to help you, I couldn't. I'm not in town."

"Oh."

"I'm in New York City with Mitch. He's here for business and he invited me along. I won't be back for another week."

That was definitely a problem. He needed her now.

"Right. Sorry to bother you."

"Good luck, Rand. I understand it's not easy."

"It never is." He hung up the phone and faced the roomful of people who were counting on him to figure something out. "She isn't in town."

"So what do we do?" Miller asked.

"I don't know." He looked at his daughter, but she only stared at the ground, looking lost in thought.

"Maybe you can try to do it yourself," Miller said.

"I'm not sensitive enough," Rand said. "I've tried before."

"Yeah, but what other option do you have? You're running out of time."

"You've told us before in class you sometimes see and communicate with the spiritual world," Stacy said.

"That's true, but usually only by accident. It's not something I'm able to turn on and off at will, like an experienced medium."

"Can you please try?" Stacy begged.

"The empty lot definitely has spiritual activity," Rand said, "but when we were there, I couldn't perceive it."

"But—"

"Dad," Libby spoke up. Everyone looked at her. "I…"

"What?" Rand asked.

"I think I know someone who can help."

27

W hat came out of Libby's mouth was the last thing Rand
had expected to hear.

"Georgia?" Rand said, and she nodded. "What are
you talking about?"

"She called me earlier today," Libby said. She looked like she was
making a troubling confession. "She planned to talk to you about
this but wanted to tell me first. I met her at St. Mary's and she
admitted that she sees spirits now. Not like the demon from last
time," she added quickly. "But, you know, benign spirits. Ones of
people who passed away at the hospital, or used to work there a
long time ago."

"Seriously?" Rand asked. His daughter nodded. He rubbed at his
temples and closed his eyes.

He never liked learning that someone had begun experiencing
the spiritual world, much less someone he knew. As much as he
hated to admit it, Georgia seeing spirits made perfect sense to Rand.
Georgia was terminally ill, and those close to death were often more
in tune with the spiritual world that was normally invisible to most
people.

Plus, Georgia had had a recent brush with spiritual warfare. All of those factors combined were very likely to make her sensitive.

"Why didn't she tell me?" Rand asked.

"She was going to," Libby said. "But I suggested she wait until after Halloween since you were being your usual crazy self."

"I don't think Georgia will understand the seriousness of this."

"I tried to explain it to her, but she told me she wanted to embrace it," Libby said. "She saw the way you and Katie helped her, and she was hoping she could use this ability to also help other people."

"Absolutely not." Tessa stepped in between Rand and Libby. "You will *not* bring this girl into your mess."

"I actually agree," Rand said. "Georgia shouldn't get involved in this."

"But Dad, what else are you going to do?" Libby said. "There's no other option."

"There has to be," Tessa said.

"Even if she wants to embrace being sensitive, she is untrained and inexperienced," Rand said. "And these beings we've encountered tonight are very powerful. It isn't safe."

"No," Tessa said. "She *won't* embrace being sensitive, she *won't* get involved with your shenanigans, and you will not—"

Libby brushed past her Mom, stepping closer to Rand. "There's something going on in that empty lot. You can't figure it out on your own. You always used to call in Katie, but now she can't come. What else can you do if you don't call Georgia?"

"Libby," Tessa chastised.

Rand sighed. His daughter was right. He was in a corner and out of options. He glanced at Miller, who only shrugged. Then he looked at Stacy, who only watched him pleadingly, begging him to conjure up some sort of plan.

"She already told me that this was something she wanted," Libby said. "If you ask her, she'll try to help you."

He checked his watch. It was very late—or early in the morning —but he knew Georgia had a habit of staying up well into the night.

"Call her," Rand finally said.

As Libby pulled out her phone and stepped into the kitchen to place the call, Tessa rushed over to Rand and shoved his shoulder. "You are unbelievable. How many people do you have to expose to this insanity?"

"We're desperate right now, Tessa."

Bill put a hand on Tessa's arm as she continued to glare at Rand. Libby returned to the living room and held out her cell toward Rand. He took the phone and hesitated for a moment, reconsidering if he truly wanted to go down this road. He didn't, but he needed to.

"Hey, Georgia."

"Happy Halloween, Ghost Man." Despite the late hour, she sounded chipper. The familiar voice would have made him smile under normal circumstances.

"What are you still doing up?" Rand asked.

"Are you serious? It's Halloween night and *all* the good movies are on. I just watched *The Texas Chainsaw Massacre* and *Child's Play*. I'm not going to sleep for a week. Why do I do this to myself?"

"You're a brave girl," Rand said.

"I know. So, Libby told me she told you what I told her." She paused. "Did you get that? I confused myself."

"I got it. Do you realize this is very serious?"

"Yes. Libby said you're in the middle of a situation right now. Kind of like what happened to me."

"Similar, but different. I need Katie, but she's out of town."

"So I'm your second string."

"I don't want you to be. This would be a huge burden for you to take on."

"But I owe you, Ghost Man. You saved my life."

"You don't owe me anything for that."

"I'm fifteen, so I'm practically an adult, which means I can decide for myself."

"Fifteen isn't even close to being an adult."

"Wrong. You know about dog years, right? When a dog is six,

they say he's forty in dog years. I get to do the same thing because of my disease. So really, I'm the same age as you."

Rand had to chuckle. Georgia's short life expectancy saddened him, but the girl handled it well, all things considered.

"Besides," she went on, more serious. "I told Libby this, and I'll tell you too. I want to use the time I have left to help people. There isn't much they let a fifteen-year-old do, because adults don't understand the concept of dog years, so maybe this is my thing. If I have this ability, I may as well embrace it."

Even though Rand wanted to shelter Georgia from the spiritual world, it was hard to argue with her line of thinking. "Where are your parents right now?" he asked.

"They're at home. I'm at the hospital."

"Can you leave?"

"You remember Harold the security guard? He'll allow me out. Especially if I tell him I'm going to see you. He likes you a lot, and he always asks me when you're coming to visit."

"After this is over, I promise I'll drop by and visit both you and him. Let him know."

"Cool. So, are you picking me up? Where are we going? What are we doing? Is it another demon?"

"I'll send Libby to get you. She'll explain everything on the way."

"Sounds good, Ghost Man."

"Be sure to dress warm. It's cold out there."

She hung up and Rand gave the phone back to Libby. "Take your mother's car and grab Georgia. Then meet me at the empty lot."

"So now you're helping yourself to our vehicles?" Tessa folded her arms.

Rand noticed Stacy was no longer in the room. "Wait... where's Stacy?"

Bill pointed toward the front door. "She went outside while you were on the phone. She seemed upset."

Rand hadn't seen her leave. "Right. I'll talk to her."

"Mom," Libby said, holding out her hand. "Can I borrow your keys? Please?"

Tessa stared at her daughter in disbelief. "Why do you insist on staying involved? You remember what happened last time. You were *kidnapped.*"

"Yeah, it's dangerous and scary, but what you don't see is that Dad helps a lot of people who wouldn't know what to do if he wasn't there for them. I've seen these monsters, and you have too. They're really bad, and they hurt people. They have to be stopped. We both know Dad is the only one who can do it."

Tessa eyed the rips in Libby's sleeves and the red gashes on her skin. She didn't budge, apparently unmoved by her daughter's speech.

Bill dropped his own keys into Libby's hand. "Promise to come home if things get too out of control."

Tessa glared at Bill, incredulous.

"Thanks, Bill." Libby rushed out of the house before anyone could stop her.

"I can't believe you," Tessa rounded on Bill. He started to explain himself, but Tessa spoke over him, drowning out his excuses.

Rand eyed Miller, who frowned at him. "Any other suggestions before Libby springs a cystic fibrosis teenager from the hospital in the middle of the night so she can speak to spirits?"

"You're doing the best you can with what you have."

Rand went outside onto Bill's front porch. He found Stacy sitting on the steps, staring into the night. Libby was backing Bill's BMW out of the driveway onto the street.

Rand lowered himself next to Stacy. Under the porch light, he could see she'd been crying again.

"Is your daughter going to get that girl?" Stacy asked.

"Yes."

Stacy grimaced. Rand assumed she blamed herself for another person getting roped into her situation.

"I'm the one bringing Georgia into this," Rand said, trying to shift the responsibility onto himself. Stacy didn't respond. She wasn't buying it. "How are you holding up?"

The question made Stacy sniff, threatening to bring on a fresh wave of new tears. "This is all my fault."

"You can't say that," Rand said. "It isn't true."

"But it is," Stacy said. "They came for me that first night. If I had just done more to make Kim understand what they were, then she would've known to not let them in. She didn't take me seriously, and I should have insisted."

"You're thinking about it too much," Rand said. "You can't predict what someone will do, especially when the supernatural is involved."

Stacy wiped away a tear that escaped her eye. "Even if that's true, *I* was the one who invited them to the house."

"What do you mean?" Rand asked.

"It finally dawned on me when you were on the phone with that girl. You always repeated the most important rule about dark spirits. If you invite them, they will come. I studied and obsessed over your class just like all my other ones. I mean, I read about this stuff every day. I thought about it when I wasn't studying. I even dreamed about it sometimes. After all that, *of course* I was inviting them."

"This will be all over soon," Rand said, hoping it was true. "We'll get Kim back."

Stacy looked at him, eyes still wet. He could read the silent question on her face.

What if we don't?

In Rand's experience, that was never something to consider.

"We'll be strong," he said. "We'll fight hard."

28

L ibby drove into the familiar parking garage and glided Bill's BMW, smooth and seamless, into one of the many spots by the hospital entrance. The empty garage was vast, capable of housing the cars of all the visitors that St. Mary's welcomed during the day. But now, Libby felt alone and isolated.

She took out her phone and tapped out a text to Georgia. The clicking from the phone's touchscreen keyboard was loud against the silence.

"Hey, I'm here in the garage. Do you want to meet me here?"

Three dots appeared as Georgia typed back.

"Sure. Be there in a minute."

As Libby waited in the idling car, the parking garage seemed to grow dimmer, as if not all the lights were being used. There were a few other cars, but they were parked far from where she was. She couldn't see anyone else around.

She thought there was movement in the rearview mirror. She glanced up, but the shape zipped out of view in the reflection. Libby twisted in her seat and looked over her shoulder.

Maybe it had been her imagination. Libby couldn't see anyone else in the parking garage, though she no longer felt she was alone. She didn't want to be there anymore.

Libby took her phone out and sent another text to Georgia.

"Actually, I'm coming in. Meet you by the main elevator."

She got out of the car and hurried inside the hospital.

The expansive lobby was devoid of personnel. Only an elderly volunteer sat at the desk, and she put her book down and straightened in her chair as if expecting Libby to ask for directions. Libby avoided eye contact and continued down the main corridor.

When she reached the elevator, it dinged and opened, and Georgia came out before Libby could go in. She wore jeans and a zipped-up hoodie, her blonde hair tied up in a messy bun on the back of her head.

"I thought you were waiting for me in the car," Georgia said. She rolled her portable oxygen cylinder behind her, the clear plastic nasal cannula dangling from her nostrils.

"I got freaked out," Libby admitted.

"You look terrible," Georgia said.

"It's been a long night."

Georgia eyed the three gashes in Libby's sleeve. Although they had stopped bleeding, her blood still marred the camouflage pattern. "I guess this is what we're dealing with."

"Before we go," Libby said, "I just want to make sure you've given this plenty of thought. This is all happening very fast, and you haven't had a lot of time to really consider."

"I'm sure," Georgia said. "As a matter of fact, I feel like I didn't get a fair fight last time. That demon just possessed me and your dad had to save me. *Now* I have a chance to take one on for real."

"This isn't a game," Libby said.

Georgia grabbed Libby's hand and pulled her along down the hallway. "Come on, let's get moving."

A few minutes later, they passed the hospital's chapel, and Libby froze. The memories came back to her. Not that long ago, the demon Karax had chased her and Georgia through those same corridors. He'd cornered them in the chapel, which he could not enter. That was when Georgia had collapsed in Libby's arms, and when Georgia woke up, Karax had possessed her.

"You okay?" Georgia asked.

"Maybe we should pray before we go," Libby said. Her dad always tried to pray before taking on the demonic.

"I thought we didn't have time." Georgia paused, then said, "Actually, you're right."

She flung open the chapel doors and marched inside. It resembled a miniature church, with pews on either side of a carpeted aisle and an altar at the front. The place had been repaired since Karax had destroyed it. Libby remembered how the demon had turned the entire chapel to rubble in the span of a few seconds.

Georgia approached the altar and took the cross that was there.

"Stealing from the chapel?" Libby asked.

"Father Calvin won't mind if we *borrow* this for the night."

Georgia was right. Any kind of religious icon was a defense against the demonic.

When they returned to the parking garage, Libby noticed it had grown even darker. A shiver went up her spine, and it wasn't from the chilly night.

"This place gives me the creeps when it's empty," Georgia said.

"Come on. Let's get out of here."

They got into the car, but when Libby turned the key, the ignition wouldn't start.

"Oh, no." She tried again, but the battery only clicked.

"Did you leave the headlights on or something?" Georgia asked.

"No. And even if I did, I wasn't inside long enough to kill the battery."

Libby realized what was going on. She knew it even before the shadow darted across the rearview mirror.

She and Georgia saw it at the same time and simultaneously looked behind them through the back window.

Nothing.

"Did you see that?" Georgia whispered.

"Yes."

"Try to start the car again."

Libby twisted the key again and again. The engine struggled to turn over, and the lights on the dashboard dimly blinked, searching for a source of power from the battery.

"Come on," Libby said through gritted teeth.

"Uh, Libby." Georgia's voice was clipped.

Libby looked up from the ignition and followed Georgia's gaze through the passenger window.

The two black-eyed kids stood about ten paces from the car.

"Is that…"

"Shit. That's them." Libby twisted the key again, her hand trembling.

"They just teleported or something. What the hell?"

When Libby looked again, the two kids were closer, half the distance they were before.

Georgia gripped Libby's arm. "Go!"

"I'm trying."

The battery finally took and the car fired up.

Georgia shrieked again. The older kid was now right outside Georgia's window, peering in with his pure-black eyes. Through Libby's window was the younger one who'd scratched her. He smiled in at her, seemingly amused by their fear.

Libby threw the car into drive and stomped on the gas pedal. The BMW took off, jolting both her and Georgia. Libby jerked the steering wheel to the left and spun to make a U-turn while the tires squealed on the pavement.

Libby sped toward the garage exit, thankful that the barrier wasn't down. She blew over the speed bump, bottoming out Bill's BMW with a rough grinding sound. Both Libby and Georgia bounced in their seats since neither of them had had a chance to put their seatbelts on.

"Ugh, that was so freaky," Georgia said.

Libby glanced into the rearview mirror. The two boys had reappeared, standing on the edge of the parking garage entrance and watching the girls go. They faded from view as Libby put more distance between them.

"Now you've met what we've been dealing with all night," Libby said. "I told you this wasn't a game."

"They gave me such a bad feeling." Georgia put her hand over her heart, just under her throat. "Right here. Like I had a giant hole in my chest."

Libby's pulse pounded as she merged onto Arnold Road. It was the quickest way to get to Plaster Road. Thankfully, they were the only car on the road in the early morning hours.

"They were a lot different from Karax," Georgia said. "I guess demons come in all shapes and sizes."

"You got that right. But they are equally as dangerous."

"Does that mean they know what we're planning to do?"

"For sure." Libby kept both hands on the wheel. She focused on the road ahead, hoping a cop didn't pull her over for speeding.

The painted lines on the road fell away underneath the car. Libby's breathing and pounding heart finally leveled out. All she wanted was to get back to the others. She and Georgia would be a lot safer with her dad and Miller.

"Libby…" Georgia stared into the passenger-side mirror.

Libby checked the rearview. There were sharp movements in the dark distance behind them.

The two black-eyed kids were sprinting after the car. Their legs were only a blur, like a cheetah bounding across the savannah. The streetlights extinguished one after the other as the kids passed them.

They were catching up.

29

"Hold on." Libby pushed the gas all the way to the floor. The BMW revved and picked up. Sixty miles per hour, then seventy.

"Faster!" Georgia shouted, watching the black-eyed kids get closer in the mirror.

"They're going to catch us," Libby said. She couldn't outrun them.

Libby watched in horror as the younger kid fell forward and began running on his hands and feet like an animal. He leapt into the air, momentarily vanishing from sight. A heavy thump landed on the roof of the car, denting it.

The older kid appeared beside Libby's window, keeping pace, glaring in at her.

Libby swerved at him, but the kid dodged to the side. He snarled at her in response. He leapt closer and struck the window. The glass shattered and the entire car lurched to the right from the force of his inhuman strength.

The younger kid reappeared, his head dipping upside-down from atop the car, looking in through the windshield. He pounded his fists on the glass, causing it to splinter and crack more and more with each blow.

"Seatbelt," Libby said, reaching for hers and clicking it into place. As soon as she heard Georgia do the same, Libby jammed both feet onto the brakes.

The seatbelt locked around Libby, biting into the soft skin of her throat. The kid on top hurled forward while the older kid sprinted ahead.

As the tires screeched on the road, Libby lost control of the car. It spun in circles, kicking up smoke. The world blurred in the windows, and Libby squeezed her eyes shut, praying the car wouldn't flip.

When they came to a halt, Libby hesitated before opening her eyes again. The smell of burned rubber assaulted her nostrils.

"Are you okay?" she asked Georgia. Georgia panted and gasped, trying to catch her breath through her oxygen tube.

"Where are we?" Georgia asked.

It took Libby a few moments to understand what Georgia was asking. "What the hell?"

They were off-road somewhere, parked in the grass. There was a smattering of trees around them.

Libby twisted in her seat and scanned the area, looking for Arnold Road. Had they spun off the street entirely? That wasn't possible. Everything had happened very quickly, yes, but where they were now looked entirely different from where they had been.

Libby opened the door, but Georgia reached over and gripped her arm.

"Where are you going?"

"To figure out where we are and how to get back to the road."

"What if they're still out there?"

"They probably are," Libby said. "That means we have to find the way back even faster."

Libby climbed out of the car and surveyed her environment. Arnold Road was nowhere in sight.

Georgia got out, reinserting her nasal cannula. "I don't get it. Where the hell are we?"

"It's them," Libby said. "They're doing this to us." It was the only reasonable explanation.

Scratches completely marked up the sides of Bill's BMW. Some were small, while others reached all along the side of the car. All were in sets of three.

There was movement above. Something rustled in the tree branches overhead. It sounded like a squirrel jumping from one limb to the other.

A terrible feeling came over Libby. Georgia rushed to Libby's side and linked arms with her, and the two girls stood together as the sounds continued.

"You were right. Let's get back in the car," Libby said.

But as soon as she turned, they were there. The black-eyed kids leaned from behind a thick tree trunk, one on each side, peeking around at them as if playing a game of hide and seek.

"Go away. Leave us alone," Libby demanded.

The two kids popped back behind the trunk, hidden from view again.

Georgia leaned into the BMW through the driver's side and emerged with the cross she'd taken from the chapel. She clutched it close to her chest.

She pointed. "There."

Libby turned. The kids had reappeared. They sprinted directly toward the girls.

The kids jumped into the air in unison, springing high, arcing toward them with hands outstretched, ready to grab. Their mouths were open, baring sharp teeth.

Libby turned away and shielded her face. Georgia thrust the cross between them and the pouncing demons.

Before the kids' extended hands could touch Libby and Georgia, the pair vanished in a burst of black smoke. The cloud engulfed both Libby and Georgia, blocking their vision and making them cough. It smelled strongly of sulfur.

Libby waved her hands, dissipating the smoke.

A car horn blared.

Libby and Georgia now stood in the middle of Arnold Road, holding each other. The wide lanes, asphalt, and painted lines had all returned. Georgia still had the cross extended in front of them.

A honking car swerved around them.

"We're back," Georgia said.

Bill's BMW was parked nearby, both car doors open. The dents, scratches, and cracked glass still marred its once-sleek body.

"I don't get it," Georgia said.

"It was all an illusion created by the kids," Libby said. "You saved us."

Georgia looked down at the cross in her hands. "I remember your dad always saying religious icons would work."

"Come on. We need to get to him."

30

R and knew he was driving too fast for the winding Plaster Road. There were no streetlights; he could only see what was within the range of his headlights.

The clock on his center console drew his eye. It read 4:17 AM.

He took a curve a bit too fast, only letting up on the gas rather than tapping the brakes. The box-like form of his Jeep tipped precariously at the top of the curve.

"Why don't you slow down a bit, Rando?" Miller said from the backseat.

"Libby and Georgia are probably already there," Rand said flatly. At that point, he was not particularly in the mood to be told what to do. Beside him, Stacy shifted uncomfortably in the passenger seat. She stared out the window, arms folded.

Rand wondered what was tumbling through her head. Probably more of the same—blaming herself and wondering what she did wrong. Although Rand had tried to console her, he knew Stacy would only continue to feel it was her fault, at least until this whole situation could be resolved. Or maybe she would never forgive herself for what she'd put her friend Kim through.

Despite the pothole's size, Rand saw it too late. It looked like a crater on the surface of the moon. Because of his speed, Rand didn't have time to swerve. His front driver's-side tire fell into the hole with a crash, jolting his Jeep sharply to the left. Rand swore as he gripped the wheel with both hands and pressed on his brake for the first time since being on Plaster Road.

The tire underneath rumbled loose as it deflated, and the entire car leaned. Rand eased to the side of the road and stopped.

"What did you run over?" Miller asked.

Rand threw off his seatbelt and stepped out to inspect the damage. As he thought, his tire was completely flat.

He stared at it for a long time. As he did, an angry energy began to well up inside him. It seemed to sprout in the back of his head and spread slowly down his chest and take root in his heart.

Rand had seen many flat tires before, but this one was different. This *meant* something. Of all the bad luck he'd had in his life, this might have been the worst timed.

Rand surprised himself when he started chuckling because nothing about what was happening was remotely funny. The mirth seemed to come from nowhere. Perhaps it was his body trying to combat the seething anger that was about to boil over.

He couldn't stop himself. Before he knew what was happening, he was laughing so hard that tears came to his eyes.

"Mr. Casey?"

He was aware that Stacy had gotten out of the car and was now looking at him as if he'd lost his mind. Maybe he had. Couldn't she see why this was funny?

"Rando." Miller was there too. Rand hadn't seen either of them get out of the car. "Are you all right?"

Rand thrust his hand toward the tire. "Look, Miller. We have a flat." He wiped the edges of his eyes.

"Yeah," Miller said, his tone cautious, as if he was speaking to someone who'd just escaped from an asylum. "You hit a pretty nasty pothole. Why are you laughing?"

"Can't you see?" Rand said, but when he looked at his friend, then at Stacy, he saw that neither of them were laughing along. "A *pothole*, Miller. A hole in the road has blown out my tire. At the *worst* possible time."

"Yeah, buddy," Miller said, venturing to put his hand on Rand's shoulder. Rand recoiled. In that moment, the thought of being touched repulsed him. It belittled his frustration. Miller slowly lowered his hand as if it were a weapon. "These things happen. Especially out here on Plaster Road, where they never repave the streets."

Rand felt another wave of laughter coming on. "I've had demons blow out my tires. Or knock them off completely. Sometimes all four at once. I've had phantom cars try to run me off the road." He gesticulated wildly as he made his point. "I've had apparitions appear right in front of my path, trying to get me to swerve. All of it."

"Yeah..."

"And now that we're in such a big hurry... now that timing matters more than anything... there's a *pothole*. Just a *pothole*."

He caught a glimpse of Stacy. The girl had worn a fearful expression for most of the night, but now it was aimed at him.

"It's okay, Rando," Miller said. "We'll put the spare on, then—"

"It *isn't* okay, Miller," Rand snapped, and his friend took a step back. His laughter was gone now, disappearing as fast as it had come. "It *isn't* just a pothole. If *God* is on our side, don't you think he's powerful enough to help me miss a stupid little *pothole* right when it fucking counts?"

Miller looked confused. He ventured to speak. "I see what you mean, but—"

"No, you don't." Rand could see his friend was only placating him, trying to get him to shut up and continue on, but what was the point?

"So this is about the God thing, then."

"It's *always* been about that."

Rand knew he wasn't going to win. That was clear to him now. If God was just going to throw potholes, of all things, in his way, then how could he count on God to be there when he faced not just one, but *two* demons from hell?

And who knew when Shindael would make another surprise appearance?

Rand started walking, passing in front of the headlights and cutting the beams of light with his shadow. He needed to get away. Just for a minute. He'd been running around frantically all night without stopping and he finally needed a time out.

"Where are you going?" Miller shouted after him.

"I just need a fucking break," Rand shouted without looking back.

He strode into the woods that lined the side of Plaster Road. The thick mounds of leaves brushed up against his ankles as he plowed through them.

The farther Rand got away from his headlights, the darker it became. Soon, he couldn't see anything. His shoe caught on a thick tree root. Rand flailed his arms to keep his balance, but it was too late. Gravity took him. He fell forward onto his stomach and ate dead leaves and dirt as the air was knocked from his lungs.

He rolled onto his back and stared up into the darkness. The treetops blocked out the night sky, so he couldn't even see the stars or the moon. He felt like he was in a coffin, buried alive.

Fitting. At least if he were six feet under, he wouldn't be around to bring pain to everyone around him.

Ever since his last case, Rand had considered the idea that God was not with him at all. Never had been. He was alone in his fight against the demonic.

This night confirmed it.

He remembered what Tessa had said. *Maybe you should move very far away from us.*

Fine. He didn't need any more convincing. As soon as the sun came up, he'd pack a bag and be on his way. It was in everyone's best interest. He saw that now, thanks to a pothole.

Rand thought about how huge that hole had been. Maybe it had taken years to grow to that size. He imagined God sitting on his throne, watching that hole in the street get wider and deeper with every tire that ran over it, knowing it was being cultivated for this very moment.

He heard something between the trees.

Rand rolled over onto his stomach and looked deeper into the woods. A bright light had appeared in the distance between the thick tree trunks, white and shimmering.

Rand clenched his eyes shut and opened them again. The light was still there. Coming closer, even. As if floating toward him.

Now I'm seeing things, he thought.

As the light neared, his muscles relaxed. The tension eased from his limbs. His heart rate slowed. The overpowering negative thoughts left him as if chased away.

Am I dying?

There was certainly a white light. He had guided lost spirits toward the white light a countless number of times. Was this the same white light?

It felt so good. It had to be death.

But why am I dying? Did I hit my head when I fell?

The light was closer now. It was too radiant to look at directly, and Rand had to squint.

Somewhere in the back of his mind, he knew he couldn't die. Not now. If he did, who would help Stacy? Who would save Kim?

"Mr. Casey?"

The sound of his name came from behind him. He twisted where he lay on the ground and followed the voice. He was met by an even brighter light, but one far less comforting. A flashlight from a cell phone.

Stacy wielded it as she approached. "Mr. Casey, what are you doing on the ground?"

Rand pushed himself to a sitting position and looked behind him again. The white light was gone, and now there was only darkness.

"Did you see that?" Rand asked.

"See what?"

He pointed. "There was a—" He paused. He didn't know *what* it had been.

"Mr. Casey, you're scaring me."

Rand looked back to Stacy, his hallucinations forgotten. What she'd just said dropped him back into reality like a ten-ton stone. Of all the things that she'd experienced tonight, *he* was the one scaring her?

He climbed to his feet and brushed off the leaves that clung to his jacket. Smudges of dirt remained on his jeans and his palms. "I..."

Stacy slung her arms around his torso and buried her cheek into his chest, pulling him into a tight hug. Rand was dumbfounded, wondering what he'd done to deserve that. Nothing. She was just comforting him the only way she knew how.

"You're at your breaking point," Stacy said, her voice shaking. "You've been doing so much for me all night and it isn't fair." She looked up at him now. "Go home, Mr. Casey. I'll go meet Georgia at the lot and find Kim."

Rand wondered where this was coming from. "What do you mean? You can't go alone."

"And you can't keep on like this," Stacy said, taking a step away from him. "I'm sorry I asked you to do all this for me. You've already done so much, but this is my problem. Not yours. I can take it from here."

Rand could hear how hard Stacy was trying to sound strong. Despite her valiant words, she still looked stricken with fear. Despite that, Rand realized she was resolved to take the matter into her own hands.

"Stacy, no. I'm not going to leave you."

"But—"

"I lost it for a minute." He still wasn't quite over that pothole. "I'm sorry you had to see that. But I'm here for you until the end."

"Are you sure?"

"Yes. Come on," Rand said.

They walked together out of the woods and back to Plaster Road while Stacy used the phone flashlight to illuminate their way. Rand spotted the gnarled root that had brought him down.

When they got back to the road, Rand saw Miller leaning against the Jeep, holding the jack that Rand kept in his trunk. "You good, Rando?"

"Yeah," Rand said. "I just needed a minute." He wiped at his face and ran his hand through his hair. "Let's get this spare on."

Miller thrust the jack into Rand's chest, the metal tool stabbing into his sternum. "Already done."

"You changed the tire?"

Miller gave him an incredulous look. "You haven't figured out how this works yet? We're a team, Rando. You fight the demons while I hide away scared. You ask questions about a case while I find the answers. You have a breakdown in the forest while I change the tire. Got it? Now, can we get moving?"

31

Libby steered the car into the empty lot on Plaster Road. The uneven terrain caused the BMW—not being designed for off-roading—to rock and bounce.

When the headlights cut through the darkness, she did not see her dad's orange Jeep.

She'd figured her dad would have arrived already, given their little detour on the Arnold Road Extension.

"Hmm... I hope nothing's happened," Libby said, pulling her cell phone from her pocket. Then Georgia's breathing turned into sharp, rapid gasps. "What's wrong? Are you out of oxygen in your tank?"

Georgia shook her head. She looked petrified. "It's this lot. There's..."

"Do you sense something? Already?"

Georgia looked at her. "What happened here? I've never felt anything like this. This is *way* worse than anything at the hospital." Georgia threw open her car door and climbed out.

"Hey, where are you going?" Libby said, following the other girl. "Maybe we should wait for my dad."

Georgia walked deeper into the empty lot, pulling her oxygen tank on wheels behind her. The headlights from the BMW cast Georgia's long shadow onto the dead grass.

Libby didn't follow her friend. She'd seen enough mediums to know that once they got going, it was best to leave them alone and not interrupt.

Georgia paused in the center of the lot. She looked from side-to-side, up and down. Then she turned right and walked deliberately, as if following a faint trail. She stopped and pivoted on her heel, as if whatever she was tracking had suddenly changed directions. She followed the new path for a bit before halting again. She twisted her head in each direction, as if trying to pay attention to many things at once.

Libby folded her arms and shivered as she watched the other girl. The workings of the spiritual realm never ceased to amaze Libby. Georgia looked like she was playing a game of tag with a bunch of imaginary friends.

Even though Georgia was many paces away from Libby, she heard sobbing. Something had upset Georgia.

Libby started walking farther onto the lot. When Georgia heard her coming, she paused.

"Something horrible happened here," Georgia said, wiping her eyes.

"What did you see?" Libby asked.

"I don't really know. There's a bunch of spirits here. They all feel different, and they're all moving."

"Moving?"

"Yeah."

"What are they doing?" Libby asked.

"I don't know. I can't see those details." She paused. "But I can feel. There's *so* much negative energy in this place."

"You should stop." Libby was sterner with her suggestion this time. "We shouldn't mess around with this until my dad gets here. He can help you figure out what you're sensing."

"But there's one that's not like the others." Georgia took several long, deliberate paces to the side and planted herself in a certain spot. "She's right here. All the others are moving around the lot, but this one hasn't left this place the whole time."

Libby shrugged. "I don't know what that means. Again, my dad—"

"I can't communicate with it," Georgia said. "I tried and no one's answering me. But I can just barely see..."

Georgia closed her eyes. She hesitated like that for several long moments. Her brow furrowed. "Hmm... That can't be right."

"What do you see?"

Georgia's eyes sprang open, and she looked confused. "That's weird."

"What is it?"

"I saw—"

Another car pulled onto the lot. The orange Jeep's headlights pierced through the darkness.

"Oh, good," Libby said. "Come on. You can tell my dad everything you just told me."

32

Bill's BMW was already there when Rand pulled into the empty lot. He parked next to the car. He immediately noticed the long scratches gouged into the car's black paint. The BMW had been beaten to hell and back.

"What the hell?"

He leapt from the car seat and took a closer look. The windshield was cracked, the top of the roof had a huge dent, and there were more scratches on the other side of the car.

"Dad." His daughter approached him from the other side of the lot. Georgia Collins was behind her, oxygen tank trailing.

"Libby, are you two okay?"

"Yes, we're fine."

"What happened to Bill's car?"

"The black-eyed kids came after us. We got away, though."

Miller and Stacy came around, both eyeing the car.

"Good to see you again, Ghost Man," Georgia said.

"You too. Sorry to ruin your Halloween."

"Hey, man. I owe you big time. So anything you need, I'm here to help you out."

I wish she wasn't so enthusiastic about this, Rand thought. "Why didn't you tell me as soon as you started having clairvoyant visions?" His tone was scolding.

"I was going to," Georgia said, rolling her eyes. "But Libby told me to wait until after Halloween because you apparently turn into a psycho."

Rand glared at Libby. She shrugged. "Right. We'll hash this out later. For now, we need to get to work." He started walking deep into the lot, but Georgia grabbed his arm and stopped him.

"I've already sensed things."

Rand looked down at her. "Really?"

"The spiritual activity here is really strong. I felt it as soon as we got here."

"What did you see?"

"There are lots of presences here. They're moving around all over the place. I don't know what they're doing, but there's a lot of negativity."

"No surprise there," Miller chimed in.

"Tell him what you told me," Libby said. "About there being one that's different."

"Oh yeah. One of them isn't like the rest. It's standing still while all the others are moving around the area."

To Rand, that was a step in the right direction. Whenever groups of spirits were present, it was usually helpful to focus on the one that was most different from the others. The outlier was usually able to give the best information.

He was quite impressed with how much Georgia was able to discern without having had much practice.

"Do you know anything about this one that's standing still?" Rand asked. "Were you able to communicate, or…"

"I saw something, but it doesn't make sense," Georgia said, looking at the ground. "I'm new at this, remember? It's probably a mistake."

"What did you see?"

Georgia looked up at him and hesitated. "A black cat." She shrugged. "I don't know what it means. Maybe a symbol. Maybe nothing. I do like cats, so maybe I was just trying to think of something to make me feel better from all the—"

"That's Kim!" Stacy said.

Rand and the others turned. All eyes were on Stacy now. "What?"

"Kim was going to be a black cat for Halloween," Stacy explained. "She was getting ready for the Boyd Street party when I was on the phone with her. She would have been wearing her costume when she got taken."

Rand turned back to Georgia. "A black cat. You're sure?"

"Yes. Wait, you mean I'm not wrong?"

"Where did you sense the black cat?"

Georgia led the way to a point near the back of the lot. Rand and all the others followed her. She stopped in a very precise location, as if she had followed a treasure map to a spot marked with an X.

"Here."

Rand looked around. So did the others.

"So Kim is here," Stacy said, "but also not here?"

"The black-eyed kids brought her," Rand said. "But we can't see her."

"She's invisible or something?" Stacy asked.

"She's standing right where I am," Georgia said. "I can feel it. And I can see the black cat again. It's very clear."

"What does it mean, Miller?" Rand asked.

"Maybe she was taken to the spiritual dimension," Miller said. "It's possible to be alive and visit there."

"How do we get her back?" Stacy asked.

"It has to do with time," Libby said.

Everyone looked at her.

"Time for what?" Miller asked.

Libby ignored him. "Dad, when was the Arnold Road Extension built?"

"I don't know," Rand said, wondering what his daughter was thinking. "Why?"

"Arnold Road's been there forever," Miller said.

"Not Arnold Road," Libby said. "The *extension*. That new part. When was that built?"

"Oh. Umm..." Miller scratched at his stubbled chin. "I don't know. A few decades ago. But the road itself was—"

"When the black-eyed kids attacked us on the extension, our car spun out and we suddenly weren't on the road anymore. The whole thing had disappeared."

"Oh yeah," Georgia said. "That was weird."

"And then when Georgia chased them away with the cross, the road reappeared."

It took Rand a few moments to piece together what Libby was telling him. "Time distortion."

"What?" Libby asked.

"When the black-eyed kids were in my car, I passed a Gavin's Deli."

"Impossible," Miller said. "They went out of business years ago. Which is a shame because their roast beef melt—"

"I knew that was strange, but I didn't make the connection earlier. I was seeing the past."

"And when I saw the black-eyed kids at the party," Libby added, "everyone around me looked like they were from the eighties. I thought it was a bunch of Halloween costumes, but..."

"That's it," Rand said, a surge of energy coursing through him. "The black-eyed kids are anchored to the Erlich family murders from 1984. When we're near them, sometimes we see what the world looked like at that time." Rand looked at Stacy. "And Stacy, you lost two hours the first time the black-eyed kids came to your door, right?" Stacy nodded.

Rand was almost embarrassed he'd missed it. It made so much sense. Time distortion was a common side effect of being near a demonic entity. Usually, it seemed more like a slowing or a quickening of the present time, but every so often, one could glimpse the past. Other times, the future.

"So Kim is trapped in the past?" Stacy asked. She still looked confused.

"The black-eyed kids brought her there," Rand said. "Those other spirits that Georgia senses must be the Erlich family. The one that feels different is Kim."

"She's still right here," Georgia said, pointing at her feet. "But you're saying she's in this spot as it existed thirty years ago, right?"

"Yes," Rand said.

"So, how do we get into the past?"

Rand knew the answer. Judging by the silence that descended on the group, he figured everyone else had arrived at the same conclusion.

The past could be accessed when the black-eyed kids were near. That meant he needed them to come.

"Mr. Casey..." Stacy peered toward the cars. She pointed a trembling finger.

Two black figures stood in the beams of the Jeep's headlights, swallowing the light.

33

G et behind me," Rand said as he stepped forward. The others obeyed.

Both the Jeep and BMW still had their headlights on. The four bright beams were broken only by the black forms of the two kids, standing side-by-side. None of their features were visible.

"Georgia," Libby whispered behind Rand. "Where's the cross?"

"I left it in the car."

Rand took another step forward. "Hey! I'm here. I'm who you came for, right? So go ahead."

"Dad," Libby said.

"Mr. Casey, what are you doing?"

Neither of the black-eyed kids moved. They stood still, like mannequins.

"What are you afraid of?" Rand shouted.

The two shadows took a step forward in unison. As soon as they did, all four headlights shut off. The entire lot was plunged into total darkness.

Rand could no longer see them. He heard frantic shuffling behind him. One cell phone light turned on, followed by another.

Then a third. Those beams swept the area, but it was very hard to see anything. They weren't powerful enough for the expansive lot.

Rand heard footsteps to his left. Then whispers to his right. Then rustling in the trees overhead.

"Stop playing games," he called into the darkness. He spread his arms wide. "I'm here. Come and take me."

Leaves rustled somewhere in front of him. The others must have heard it too, because all three cell phone lights turned in that direction at the same time.

The beams lit up one of the black-eyed kids—the younger one—as he sprinted toward Rand.

He leapt forward like some kind of animal, then opened his mouth and bared his teeth.

Libby cried out. Stacy screamed.

Rand's instincts told him to shield himself or dodge, but he resisted. Instead, he waited for the child to make contact so he could be taken to the past.

The force of the demon struck him in the chest like a battering ram. Rand was knocked off his feet. Before he even hit the ground, his entire world went black.

34

S tacy had only seen the younger black-eyed kid at the last second.

He'd soared through the air, arms outstretched, illuminated only by the meager beam of her cell phone. She'd been knocked off her feet. She remembered pain that disappeared just as quickly as it had come. Her vision had darkened and her mind had quieted, and Stacy wondered if that was what it felt like to die.

But she was awake now, lying flat on her back.

As clarity returned, Stacy used her elbows to force herself into a seated position. The effort it took to sit up was astounding, leaving her fatigued.

"What happened?" Speaking took more strength than sitting.

Stacy's eyes adjusted. She looked around. She was alone.

Mr. Casey was gone. So was his friend Miller, and his daughter. Georgia as well.

"Mr. Casey?" Panic crept in. "Mr. Casey?"

Stacy looked behind her. Everything had changed. The empty lot was no longer just a barren patch of land. A house had appeared. It was simple, small, and plain. Children's toys were scattered in the yard and the grass was overgrown. There were no lights on inside.

"Mr. Casey?" Stacy whispered again, her voice trembling.

"Stacy." Mr. Casey's voice was loud behind her, and it startled her. She twisted around in the grass, relieved that her teacher had found her.

But it was Georgia who was standing behind her. But there was something strange about her. Georgia was alone, back straight and hands by her side. Her eyes were closed, as if she was sleeping. And although it was suddenly very windy, her clothes or hair were not blowing.

"Stacy, can you hear me?"

It sounded like Mr. Casey's voice was coming from Georgia. Georgia's mouth did not move.

"Yes, I'm here," Stacy said. "Where are you?"

"I'm communicating with you through Georgia," Mr. Casey said.

It took Stacy a few moments to make sense of it all. She was in the past, and the others were still in the present. Georgia, with her sensitive abilities, was able to communicate with the past from the present. Stacy figured this was what it felt like to be a ghost speaking to a medium that was reaching out to the spiritual world during a séance.

"Listen to me, Stacy," Mr. Casey said. "They took you."

"I know. I can see the past. The Erlich house is here."

After a few seconds of silence, Mr. Casey said, "We can get you out of there."

"How?"

Georgia moved for the first time since she'd appeared. She extended her hand straight ahead of her, palm stretched toward the sky. Her eyes remained closed, trance-like.

"Can you see Georgia?" Mr. Casey asked.

"Yeah. She's right in front of me."

"Good. Take her hand," Mr. Casey said. "She is a bridge between the two time periods. If you take her hand, you'll come back to the present."

"What? How?"

"Your body and soul belong here, so when they are displaced like they are right now, they will always look for a way back. Connecting with your true world will return you to where you belong. Take Georgia's hand. You'll see."

Stacy pushed herself to a standing position. Georgia remained still, hand outstretched, offering her a way back to the present.

Could it really be that simple? Stacy wondered. Mr. Casey sounded very certain. He'd probably experienced this situation before in one of his cases.

"Mr. Casey, Kim is inside the house," Stacy said.

"I know. But so are the black-eyed kids. That house is where they are anchored, remember? As soon as you come back, then I can find a way to access the past."

Stacy did remember, and she felt ill at being reminded. It was like being in enemy territory. Here, in this illusion that surrounded her, the black-eyed kids were in charge. But still, she hesitated to take Georgia's hand.

"Stacy?" Mr. Casey asked. "What are you waiting for?"

"I'm sorry, but I can't." The words tumbled out, surprising even her.

"What do you mean? It's simple. Just touch Georgia."

"It isn't that. It's just..."

"Stacy." Mr. Casey's voice was stern. A warning. He probably knew what she was thinking.

It wasn't fair. Kim being taken was Stacy's fault. Mr. Casey running all over town trying to help Kim was *also* Stacy's fault. Libby and her mother had also seen the black-eyed kids. Georgia was now involved. Stacy deserved all the blame. She remembered how broken Mr. Casey had become on the side of Plaster Road. The events of the night had pushed him to the edge. She simply wouldn't be able to live with herself if something happened to him.

"I'm going inside the house to get Kim," Stacy announced.

"You can't do that," Mr. Casey said. "It's too dangerous. You need to come back and let me go instead."

"I was the one they wanted in the first place," Stacy said. "This is where they meant to bring me. Well, I'm here now. I can fix this."

"Stacy." Mr. Casey's voice was steady, trying to reason with her. "You won't just walk inside that house and get Kim. It won't be that simple. There is *always* a trick."

"I know. I take your class, remember?"

"Stacy. Don't do this. Please."

"I'm sorry, Mr. Casey. I'll come back, I promise. And when I do, Kim will be with me."

She turned away from Georgia and started walking toward the house.

Mr. Casey's protests grew quieter as Stacy got farther away from Georgia until they were just a noise in the distance. Soon, Stacy couldn't hear him at all.

Then came the first sign of movement from the house. Someone jogged from around the back, along the side, and toward Stacy. She froze where she stood.

It was the younger black-eyed kid. His bare feet pattered on the grass. He still wore his grimy black t-shirt and shorts.

He stopped a few feet from her and looked up at her with his pure-black eyes. Then, smiling, he lifted his hand and pointed at the house.

35

Stacy walked toward the house. When she reached the front porch, she turned around, but the child had vanished. Georgia remained in the distance, her hand outstretched, waiting for Stacy to return.

The black-eyed kids were here. At least, the younger one was. They were watching her. What would they do when she got close to Kim?

When Stacy approached the front door, it opened by itself, as if the house was pleased to welcome her into a nightmare. Stacy took a steadying breath. She was just about to step inside when she heard a car behind her.

A pickup truck barreled off the road and into the yard, zipping narrowly past where Georgia still stood. It ran over a yellow toy car before it ground to a stop.

The door flew open and a round, stocky guy spilled out. He was haggard, with disheveled black hair and sweat stains on his white t-shirt. The man upended a bottle of whiskey into his mouth and drained what remained, then tossed the empty bottle to the other side of the yard. He reached into the bed of his truck and pulled out a shotgun.

He marched forward, directly toward Stacy. Fear seized her entire body, but the man seemed to not see her.

The armed, drunken man brushed past Stacy and went inside, not acknowledging her at all. He turned right and disappeared into the darkened house.

"Carl?" a man's voice called out. "Why do you have that gun?"

A gunshot rang out from within. A woman screamed. She was silenced by another shot. Stacy recoiled after each blast.

Stacy understood what she was seeing. She'd learned in Mr. Casey's class that spirits would sometimes play out the tragic circumstances of their deaths over and over again. Mr. Casey had told them he'd experienced it many times before, and he'd learned that often the best way to learn what kept the spirits trapped on Earth was to follow the events.

Stacy steeled herself, then went the same way the gunman had gone toward the back of the house. She walked through a simple kitchen, then behind it, a hallway. The door to the first bedroom was open.

Stacy glanced inside for only a millisecond before tearing her eyes away.

A man sprawled out on the floor. A woman crumpled in the corner. Dark red had been spattered on the wall.

Stacy backed away, hand over her mouth to keep herself from vomiting as tears leaked from her eyes.

Stay strong, she thought. *I have to stay strong for Kim.*

"Bonnie," Carl barked from somewhere else in the house.

The parents, their daughter, and her two kids, Stacy remembered. *Those were the victims.*

She'd just seen the parents in the bedroom. Bonnie must be the daughter—Carl's girlfriend.

Every part of Stacy wanted to stop Carl from continuing on his rampage, but she knew it was futile.

She'd asked that very question in class when Mr. Casey had spoken of this phenomenon. He'd told her it was indeed tempting to want to alter the course of these tragic events, but it was impossible.

They had already happened. Even though they still replayed over and over, there was nothing that could be done to change the past. The tragedy replaying itself on a loop was what kept the negative energy in a location long after the events had happened. That negative energy attracted the demons that fed off of it.

"Where are you, Bonnie?" Carl roared, drunk and angry.

Stacy realized that someone was behind her—a young girl, perhaps only a few years older than Stacy. On either side of her were two kids, her arms protectively around their shoulders. They had shaggy hair, old clothes, and bare feet.

They looked identical to the black-eyed kids, though their wide, fearful eyes were not black. The girl crouched down and whispered something to them.

The girl hurried her sons into the hallway and past Stacy, none of them aware of her presence. The girl reached up and pulled open the hallway attic door. She unfolded the ladder and ushered her two kids up. She closed them up in their hiding place.

"Bonnie!"

The girl looked in both directions down the hall, trying to decide which way to go. From what Stacy could tell, the house was one story, but large. The rooms all seemed connected, and every path led back on itself. It was a deadly labyrinth, and Stacy already knew that Bonnie would lose the game.

"Bonnie," Stacy said. Her voice echoed unnaturally, reverberating back at her, reminding her she didn't belong there. She was an intruder in their place in time.

Stacy wasn't sure, but she thought Bonnie spared her the smallest of glances before darting forward and disappearing through a door at the end of the hallway.

Did she hear me? Stacy thought.

Stacy followed. Bonnie had retreated into what looked like the living room. She tip-toed around a large sofa, quietly advancing toward the foyer and front door, where Stacy had entered—the only escape.

But Carl appeared around the corner, his shotgun aimed at her chest. Bonnie lifted her palms and backed away from Carl, but he only pressed forward.

"Carl, what are you doing?" Bonnie said through her sobs.

"Where are the kids?" Carl's speech was slurred.

"Please leave us alone," she pleaded.

Carl struck Bonnie on the chin with the butt of his shotgun and pointed it at her again.

Bonnie did not wipe the blood from her lip.

"Where are they, Bonnie?" Carl screamed at her, shaking the gun in his drunken rage.

Stacy couldn't stop herself. "Put the gun down." Although she put as much energy behind her command as she could, it still came out muted and distant.

But Stacy's voice seemed to catch Bonnie's attention. As if she could barely hear Stacy.

She can *hear me,* Stacy realized. *Even if we are in different dimensions.*

Mr. Casey had said it was impossible to change the past, but Stacy couldn't just stand by and watch Carl murder this poor girl.

"Put down the gun," Stacy yelled again.

Bonnie turned to look at Stacy. Their eyes met, and Bonnie seemed to have a moment of clarity.

"Who's there?" Bonnie whispered.

"What are you looking at?" Carl demanded.

"I'm looking for my friend," Stacy said. "My friend is here somewhere."

Bonnie's brow furrowed. "A girl?"

"Who are you talking to?" Carl spat. "Tell me where the kids are."

"Yes!" Stacy said. "Where is she?"

Carl cocked his shotgun. "Answer me!"

"In the attic," Bonnie finally whispered.

Carl smirked. Stacy knew the response was for her, but Carl thought it was for him.

Stacy looked away just in time as the blast went off. Bonnie collapsed, her body falling limp to the floor.

Stacy began to weep. What had she been thinking? Maybe Mr. Casey was right. Maybe she *should* have let him handle this. She didn't have the stomach for all this violence.

Carl stepped over Bonnie's body and went into the hallway. He eyed the attic door.

But then he turned and went the other direction, placing his gun over his shoulder. He went to the kitchen and opened a cabinet above the sink, which was filled with liquor.

"Your old man always said I was a drunk," Carl muttered to himself. "Well, takes one to know one. He won't be saying that again."

While Carl was distracted by his whiskey, Stacy took the chance to rush to the hallway, lower the attic door, and unfold the ladder.

Stacy climbed up. The attic was filled with boxes and old furniture, clutter from a family that had lived in the house for a long time. There was a path through the middle of the junk that led to the back of the attic.

The two young boys were huddled together in the corner, the older one's arms wrapped around the younger. They trembled as they watched the door.

"I'm not here to hurt you," Stacy whispered to them. They did not respond.

They can't see me.

"Who's there?" a voice called out. It was raspy and weak, as if on the verge of giving out. But it was familiar.

Stacy rushed over and around the boxes.

36

R and had never felt so helpless.

He paced the same small stretch of the lot over and over, waiting and worrying. Every few seconds, he glanced at Georgia. She stood still, eyes closed as if she was in a trance, arm outstretched toward nothing.

Rand checked his watch. It was 5:09 in the morning.

"All that pacing is making me nervous," Miller said.

"You *should* be nervous," Rand said. "Stacy has no idea what she'll encounter where she is. I don't even know."

"She'll be okay, Dad," Libby offered. But her words sounded hollow.

"Stacy's your star student, right?" Miller said. "You've taught her well."

"It's not the same," Rand said. "You know it isn't." Sitting through his lectures was one thing. Coming face-to-face with the demonic was something else entirely.

Footsteps crunched the dry leaves somewhere in the darkness. A flashlight beam danced on the ground as someone approached. "Who's there?" Rand called, halting his pacing and standing alert.

Wayne Swanson shone the light onto his own face. He had his shotgun in the other hand.

"We're almost done here, Mr. Swanson," Rand said.

"Somethin' ain't right," Wayne said.

"I know," Rand said. "We're working on it." He glanced again at Georgia. To Wayne, she probably looked insane.

"It ain't that," Wayne said. "You've gone and done somethin' else."

Rand could see that Wayne wasn't just annoyed—he was afraid. "What's wrong?"

"You tell me. What have you stirred up 'round here?"

Rand exchanged a glance with Miller, then looked back to Wayne. "Has something happened?"

"My wife's scared out of her wits, that's what's happened," he said. "And I gotta be honest, I never seen anythin' quite like that before."

"What did you see?"

"Exactly what you said I would. You told me if anyone knocks at the door, don't let 'em in."

Rand sighed and shook his head. "Tell me what happened. I can help you."

"You don't need to tell me," Wayne said. "You need to tell my wife. She's the one losin' it right now."

"Sure. Is she inside?"

Wayne hesitated and appraised Rand for a few seconds, probably debating whether or not to let him into the house. "Come with me." Wayne turned and started walking toward his house, shotgun resting over his shoulder, resembling a soldier.

"You two stay here and keep an eye on Georgia," Rand instructed. "If Stacy comes back, or anything happens, come and get me."

Miller nodded. Libby chewed her lip nervously.

Rand followed Wayne, wondering what the black-eyed kids had done this time.

37

Kim still wore the leotard and leggings of her black cat Halloween costume. A metal cuff was around her right ankle, attached to a short chain bolted to the wooden attic floor.

"Stacy!"

Stacy ran over to her friend and wrapped her in a tight hug. Kim squeezed her back.

"What's going on?" Kim said, sobbing into Stacy's neck. "What is this place?"

"I'll explain everything, but first, let's get out of here."

Kim's black hair was disheveled and tangled. Her skin was milky pale. Her black makeup was streaked from her tears.

"Why am I here, Stacy?" Kim's voice shook. "I don't want to be here anymore."

Stacy touched her friend's wet cheeks with both her hands. Her skin was like ice. "You don't have to be. I'm bringing you out."

"I don't want to see it anymore."

"See what?"

Kim only stared back at her through wide, bloodshot eyes.

Escape first, talk later, Stacy thought.

Stacy knelt and investigated the clamp around Kim's ankle and where the chain was fastened to the floorboard. She gave it a few yanks and the wood bent a bit.

"The floor is weak," Stacy said. "Maybe if we both pull on it—"

Kim wasn't listening. Her eyes were on the two frightened boys in the opposite corner of the attic. They were oblivious to what was happening.

"Please save them," Kim whispered.

It struck Stacy why Kim was traumatized.

The spirits of the Erlich family were reliving their tragedy on a repeating loop, Stacy thought. *Kim has watched these boys get murdered over and over again.*

Stacy was sickened at what those demons had done to Kim. They'd trapped her right where she'd be forced to repeatedly witness one of the most horrific things imaginable.

"Listen to me." Stacy snapped her fingers in front of Kim's face, commanding her focus. "This isn't real. None of this is real."

"But—"

"If you don't want to see it happen again, then we need to get out of here. But we can't get out of here unless you help me. Do you understand?"

Kim's lip quivered. She nodded.

"Good. Grab this chain and help me pull it up."

Stacy and Kim both gripped the metal chain. "One. Two. Three." They pulled together and the floorboard bent farther than the first time.

"Keep going," Stacy said through clenched teeth.

The wood cracked, then gave way. The girls stumbled as the chain ripped free.

"Follow me."

Before they could flee, however, footsteps came from the other side of the attic—heavy boots on the wooden floor. The boys started whimpering.

"Please don't," said the elder boy.

"It's happening again," Kim whispered.

Stacy set her jaw. She grabbed Kim's face and buried it into her shoulder. She clenched her own eyes shut. The shotgun went off, and the noise was deafening in the tight confines of the attic.

Kim tensed in Stacy's arms. Stacy held her friend tighter.

The gun fired again.

A few seconds after that, there was a third shot, followed by a heavy thud. The attic fell silent except for the ringing in Stacy's ears.

"Come on," Stacy whispered to Kim. "Don't look in the corner."

The two of them went for the door. Stacy refused to glance at the small bodies. What she couldn't miss, though, was Carl, sprawled out in the middle of the attic like a starfish, his shotgun lying beside him. Blood pooled around what was left of his head. Stacy and Kim stepped over him and climbed down the wooden ladder, returning to the main section of the house.

After they got down, Kim could no longer hold it together and started sobbing. "Why does that keep happening? It never stops."

Stacy half dragged Kim along as they entered the living room. Bonnie's body should have been on the floor, but it had vanished.

The front door was still open from when she'd entered the house earlier.

"Come on," Stacy said, taking Kim by the hand. "We're almost there. I'll explain everything when—"

The door slammed shut by itself.

"Oh no."

Stacy twisted the doorknob, but it would not budge. It was as if someone were holding it closed from the other side.

"Um… Stacy."

Something had caught Kim's attention behind them. Stacy followed her friend's gaze.

The younger black-eyed kid had appeared.

38

Wayne Swanson's front door creaked as he opened it. Rand followed the older man. The sudden warmth inside the home wrapped around Rand like a blanket. Wayne's dog, Boss, who'd been lying on his bed in the corner, rose when Rand entered.

The living room was lit only by a single reading lamp that cast a dim, eerie glow. An elderly woman stood from where she sat on the sofa. She wore a white nightgown and her silver hair was disheveled from sleep.

"This is my wife, Geraldine," Wayne said.

"You must be freezing." Geraldine seemed frazzled. "It's so cold outside tonight. I'll make you some coffee. Black, or with milk and sugar?"

"Cool it, Gerry," Wayne said. "The paranormal nut ain't got time for coffee. He's only here so we can tell him what we seen."

Rand could live with being the paranormal nut, as long as these two were okay. "Mrs. Swanson, I understand you had some visitors earlier this evening."

Geraldine gestured to the old sofa, and Rand sat. She lowered herself onto the cushion next to him while Wayne stood nearby. He still clutched his gun.

"They knocked on the door," Geraldine began. "I was wary, because we rarely get guests, and we never have them late at night."

"They came only a few minutes after me and you spoke," Wayne interjected, "so I figured you'd followed me to ask me somethin' else."

"Who was at your door?" Rand asked, although he already knew the answer.

"The neighbor boys."

Wayne groaned. "This is what I've been tryin' to tell her," he said to Rand. "They ain't the neighbor boys. They've been dead for years, God rest their souls."

Geraldine dabbed the corner of her eye with a crumpled tissue.

When Rand had learned that the Erlich family had two boys who had died in the shooting, it made sense that the black-eyed kids were mimicking their appearance.

"I believe you, Geraldine," Rand said. "But even though those two boys looked like the ones you knew, they weren't."

"They were the spitting image," Geraldine said. "Except…" She sniffled.

"Except what?" Rand prodded.

"Their *eyes*. They were so… dark. It wasn't natural. And the way they made me feel… There was something very wrong about them."

"You didn't let them in, did you?" Rand asked.

"Hell no!" Wayne barked. "Gerry was beggin' me to, but I slammed the door in their faces. They ain't normal, and there's no chance they're comin' into my house."

"You did the right thing. Did they leave you alone after that?"

"I opened up the door again a second later, and they'd disappeared."

Rand was glad he'd remembered to warn Wayne about the black-eyed kids earlier. Otherwise, he might have let them in, especially if Geraldine thought she knew them.

"So what do we do?" Wayne asked. "I don't know much about all this, and I can't say I really believe it. But we had no issues before you showed up. Now we have a problem, and I expect you to fix it."

"I will," Rand said.

"Seems to me all you're doin' is standin' around in the lot next door shiverin' your tail off."

"I know what it looks like, but trust me, everything is under—"

Three knocks sounded on the door.

Geraldine gasped. Wayne readied his gun. Boss stiffened, ears back, a low growl rumbling from his throat.

"They're back," Geraldine whispered.

Rand rose from the couch. He stepped toward the front door.

"What do you think you're doin'?" Wayne said in a harsh whisper. Geraldine went to her husband's side and linked her arm through his.

"I'll handle everything," Rand said. "Don't do anything rash."

Rand opened the door.

The older black-eyed kid stood on the porch, alone. He glared at Rand with his dark eyes.

"Let me guess," Rand said. "You need to come inside and use my telephone."

39

Stacy gasped and grabbed her friend's arm, squeezing it.

"That's one of those kids who came to the door," Kim said. "He brought me here."

"We're leaving now," Stacy declared to the kid. "This is over." She tried to make herself sound sure and authoritative. Demons had to listen, right?

'Bring me Randolph Casey.'

The words were in Stacy's head, clear as if they had come from the boy's mouth. His words were deep and dark, unlike any normal human speech. Kim looked at her, frightfully perplexed—she'd heard it too.

'Bring me Randolph Casey, and I will let you both go.'

"Why is he talking about your teacher?" Kim whispered.

Mr. Casey would be more than happy to take their place and face off against the boy. He'd wanted to be the one to enter the house and rescue Kim, after all.

Stacy caught herself, realizing what was going on. The demon had offered a deal, and she was considering it. Suddenly, she remembered the note scribbled on the inside cover of her notebook, circled and highlighted.

Not a chance, she thought.

The blank expression on the boy's face shifted into one of irritation. Stacy knew he could see into her mind and that she had figured out his bluff. He snarled at her, quick to anger.

"I will *not* bring Mr. Casey to you. We are leaving here together, and you will let us go."

The boy began to change. His human body and features dissolved away. His arms and legs became thin, wiry appendages, culminating in three sharp claws, each half a foot long. His mouth grew wider and gaping, filled with pointed teeth. The entire black form stood several feet taller than Stacy.

As the boy transformed into his true appearance, Kim squeezed Stacy's arm so hard that it began to ache. "What do we do?"

Stacy tried the door again, but it was still stuck.

The demon lifted one of his arms, poised to attack. Stacy shoved Kim away from the door while Stacy dove in the opposite direction. The claws swiped the air where the two of them had been standing a moment before. The sharp points ripped into the door, grinding three jagged marks into the wood. Stacy remembered the bloody marks on Mr. Casey's daughter's arm.

The demon turned his attention to Stacy, appearing uninterested in Kim.

Good, Stacy thought.

Stacy backed into the dining room area, moving farther away from the exit. The demon stalked toward her.

Stacy's back bumped against a large table, blocking her retreat. The demon lifted its hand again and swiped down with incredible speed, but Stacy leapt aside.

The claw struck the table, splintering it into a bunch of wooden pieces. The table's legs buckled and snapped off, and a nearby chair caught in the crossfire also crumbled.

Stacy lost her footing and fell. She landed hard on the floor near the destroyed table. She glanced at the remains, astounded. If he had hit her instead, there would have been nothing left of her body.

"Stacy!" Kim shrieked from somewhere. "Get up!"

Stacy had to return to her feet. She couldn't maneuver if she was on the ground. The demon was already glaring at her, ready to strike again. Stacy shuffled away into the corner, now out of places to flee.

What would Mr. Casey do? Her mind raced with his stories from class. In them, he'd always been prepared. *Bibles. Holy water. Crosses.* She had none of those things.

But when she looked again at the pile of wood that remained of the table, she got an idea.

The demon lifted his clawed hand again.

Stacy didn't hesitate. She lunged forward and grabbed one of the table legs along with a piece from the chair that had been crushed. She stood and held them together to form the sign of the cross.

Immediately, the demon recoiled from it. Stacy pressed forward with her makeshift cross. The demon cowered down, pulling his arms close to his body, repelled by the holy symbol.

Now, Stacy was the one pursuing. She pushed him to the far side of the room, into the other corner. He glared at her, furious, waiting for her to drop the cross so he could strike again.

"I command you to let my friend and me go."

The demon growled at her in protest.

Mr. Casey had taught her that the most powerful force against a demon was his own name. By using it, she could command them more authoritatively.

But I don't know his name... Stacy thought.

Mr. Casey *had* told her that this demon served a master. Given the hierarchy of hell, it made sense to Stacy that the master's name also commanded authority. Perhaps this demon even feared his master.

"You have failed, and your master,"—what was the name Mr. Casey had told her?—"*Shindael* will be very unhappy."

The demon let out a low groan.

Stacy had sent the kids away once, earlier in the night. She could do it again.

She took another step forward, still holding the cross as a barrier between her and the demon.

"There will be a terrible punishment for your failure. You should leave the real work to your superiors."

The demon snarled at her and then began to dissipate. His body turned into black smoke that sank through the floor, sucking in through the cracks in the floorboards.

Stacy waited a few seconds after he'd vanished to make sure he was really gone, then dropped the two broken pieces of wood.

Kim had watched the whole thing from around the corner, half hidden behind the wall. "Is it gone?"

"Yes."

Her friend looked at her as if she were from another planet. "How did you know how to do all that?"

"I pay attention in class."

40

Rand moved aside, and the black-eyed kid did not hesitate. He stepped inside, his bare feet pattering on the hardwood floor as he walked into the living room and around the sofa toward the back of the house. He moved as if he'd lived in the house his whole life and knew where he was going.

Wayne and Geraldine watched him with wide-eyed fear, and Boss growled at him from Wayne's side. The kid didn't acknowledge any of them as he turned the corner and walked out of sight.

"What are you doin'?" Wayne whispered. "Why'd you let him into my house? Get rid of him."

Rand went into the kitchen. The black-eyed kid sat at the head of the table, his back to Rand. Rand pulled up a chair and sat down facing the kid. The demon turned toward Rand, fixing black eyes on him again.

"Where's your friend?" Rand asked.

The black-eyed kid smirked.

'He's with the girl.'

The voice echoed in Rand's head. Telepathic communication, just like Shindael used.

Stacy, Rand thought.

His mouth went dry and dread settled in the pit of his stomach. The boy continued to smirk.

Wayne appeared at the entrance of the kitchen, still holding his gun. Rand lifted his hand toward him, though, and the man stopped where he was.

"You've finally got me here," Rand said. "What is it you want from me?"

'It doesn't work like that.'

Rand set his jaw. The demon could read his mind. See his plan. That meant Rand had to coerce him a little more.

"You don't want to miss your opportunity," Rand said. "You're just another one of Shindael's slaves."

The kid's smirk was replaced by a glare. Even his eyes seemed to grow darker than they had been before.

"What better way to gain favor with the devil than to capture me right here and now? What are you waiting for?"

Rand knew demons were fiercely prideful. There was a clear hierarchy in hell, and the lower ones despised those who were favored by the devil.

The kid bared his teeth and leaned forward, placing his palms flat on the table. Black plasma leaked from the corners of his mouth.

"Shindael will always use you," Rand pressed, "At least until you do something meaningful, like take me. Shindael himself could not even do that. Imagine the rewards."

The black-eyed kid began to transform, and his childlike disguise melted away. He grew in height until his head almost touched the ceiling. The black plasma oozed off his body and dripped onto the floor, leaving puddles between his feet. Each of his hands was made up of three long claws.

Rand stood and backed away. The demon roared at Rand so loudly that he had to cover his ears to block out the pain in his head.

The horrible sound was cut short by a gunshot.

A hole appeared in the demon's body and rancid plasma splattered across Rand's face and clothes. Wayne stood at the kitchen's entrance, smoke drifting from the barrel of his gun.

The demon crumpled over and lost his footing, his clawed hands going to the wound in his stomach, as if surprised to be attacked from behind.

Human weapons would never be effective against a creature like this, but there was no way Wayne Swanson would know that.

Rand rushed to the other side of the kitchen and lowered Wayne's shotgun. "Come on."

He yanked Wayne back into the living room. Geraldine trembled in the corner, covering her ears with her hands, shielding them from the loud gunshots. Rand gripped her by the elbow. He hurried the elderly couple toward the front door.

Behind them, Rand heard the demon's feet stomping in pursuit. The furniture crashed as he knocked it out of his path.

Rand threw open the door and the three of them burst out into the cold. Boss brushed by Rand's leg as the dog bolted from the house alongside them.

Miller was in the yard. "What the hell is going on in there? I heard a gunshot." Something behind Rand caught Miller's eye, and he froze.

Rand turned. The demon stood just on the other side of the door but no longer chased them. He lingered there for a moment before dipping back inside the dark house. The door closed by itself.

"W-what the hell was that thing?" Wayne pointed a trembling finger toward his house.

"Are you crazy?" Rand shouted at Wayne. "Guns won't hurt them. You'll just piss them off."

"Rand," Miller said, a cautioning tone in his voice.

"What do you expect me to do?" Wayne shot back. "Just sit there? Did you see what I saw?"

"Of course. It's—"

"Rand." Miller grasped Rand's shoulder. Rand took a breath and forced himself to calm.

He reminded himself that if he'd been in Wayne's shoes, he'd probably have done the same thing. He removed his jacket and placed it on Geraldine's bare shoulders.

"I got him right in the chest and it didn't even slow him down," Wayne muttered.

Geraldine started sobbing. Wayne put his arm around his wife and she leaned into him.

"I assume that's the black-eyed kid's true form," Miller said.

"Yes. One of them's in the house, and the other is with Stacy," Rand told Miller. "Has she come back yet?"

Miller only shook his head, and Rand sighed. The longer Stacy was gone, the higher the likelihood she'd gotten hurt.

"I tried to get that one to capture me and bring me to where Stacy is, but he refused."

"Of course he did," Miller said. "He knows your plan. It isn't going to be that simple." He reached out and dabbed his fingertip into a glob of plasma that remained on Rand's jacket. He rubbed it between his fingers as he inspected it. "These guys are so disgusting."

"I need to get them to take me," Rand said.

"How?" Miller asked. "They won't do it. They want Stacy separated from you. So unless you have a time machine…"

Rand ran a hand through his hair. Miller was right.

"She's your best student, right?" Miller asked. "Do you think she knows how to handle herself?"

Rand blew out his breath and put his hands on his hips as he thought. "If anyone does, it would be her."

"Then maybe you're worrying too much," Miller said. "If you've taught her well…"

"Still. It should be me in there, not her."

"True. But it *isn't* you in there."

"So what do I do?" Rand asked, more to himself than to Miller. "I can't just stand around here waiting." He turned toward the house. "I have to go back in there."

"Are you *nuts?*" Wayne said.

"He won't leave your house until he's forcefully removed."

Wayne exchanged a worried glance with his wife.

"I may as well do what I can while we wait for Stacy to make it back," Rand muttered. All he could do was pray that the girl was okay.

"Here." Miller held out the cross that Georgia had brought with her from the hospital. "This is the only thing we have." Rand took it. "Do you want me to come in with you?" The question came out thin and tense.

"No. Stay out here with Libby and Georgia," Rand said. He turned to Wayne. "No matter what happens, don't go back inside your house until I come out. Do you understand?"

Wayne nodded.

Rand had never been completely without fear when entering a place where a known demon was waiting and lurking. He probably never would be. But his cases always came to this. He was the one who had to fight so that the demon's victims could be freed.

When Rand went back inside the house, the living room was dark. The lamp that had lit the room earlier must have been smashed during the demon's pursuit.

The door behind him slammed shut by itself. Rand whirled, startled. He tried the knob, already knowing what he'd find. It was stuck, held closed by an unseen force that didn't want him to leave.

When Rand turned around again, the house had changed.

There was an old, box-style television at the front of the living room. It had not been there before. The lamp was on, when seconds before it had been broken. The furniture was completely different from what had been there minutes ago.

It took Rand a few moments to realize what was going on. He was seeing the Swansons' house as it had been in the past.

He was *in* the past.

Finally, the demon's presence had brought Rand to the point in time where the negative spirit was anchored.

Then he heard voices coming from the kitchen.

41

When Kim tried the door again, it opened without resistance. In the front yard, the truck that Carl had arrived in was gone. All the pieces of the event were vanishing, undoing themselves, setting up for the next time the horrific loop would begin again.

Georgia was still there. She waited in the same spot she had been before, palm outstretched, beckoning for them to return.

"Who is that?" Kim asked, wary as she fell behind Stacy's shoulder.

"Relax. She's our way out of here."

"How?" Kim asked.

Stacy and Kim crossed the yard. The wind blew mercilessly, whipping Stacy's hair into her face.

"If we touch her, we'll be transported back," Stacy explained.

"Transported where?" Kim asked.

"To reality."

"What—oh, Stacy. Look." Kim pointed behind them toward the house they had just escaped.

Five people stood in a line, watching them go. Bonnie and her two kids and Bonnie's parents. They had a peaceful, light-blue glow surrounding them. The two boys held hands with their mother, one on each side. Even from a distance, Stacy could see the gore that marred their bodies. Bloody holes gaped in their chests and stomachs, left behind from the close-range shotgun blasts.

"They're looking at us," Kim whispered, voice quivering.

"It's okay. We don't need to be afraid of them."

"But what about—"

"That other thing was different. These are friendly."

The family's presence gave Stacy a sense of peace, finally displacing the dread that had filled her all throughout the night.

Kim looked at Georgia and her outstretched hand. "Let's do it before something else weird happens."

"Give me a minute," Stacy said.

Kim glared at her. "For what? We're almost out of here."

Her friend was right. But Stacy remembered something else she had learned from Mr. Casey. These people, brutally killed long before their time, would replay their tragedy over and over, forever.

Unless they're set free.

Stacy crossed the yard again and approached the ghostly family. All five of them kept their gazes on her as she neared. None of them reacted. They only seemed curious about Stacy, as if knowing she didn't belong, but couldn't figure out where she'd come from.

Guiding spirits to the afterlife had been on the second test of the semester. It didn't take much—usually gentle encouragement. Sometimes the spirits just needed permission to forget the evil that kept them anchored to the world of the living.

"There is no need for you to suffer anymore," Stacy said, meeting the eyes of each member of the Erlich family. "I know you all died long before your time. There is a better place waiting for you in the afterlife. You should go there now. There isn't any reason left for you to stay here."

Stacy looked at Bonnie. Although the girl's face was unclear—a common characteristic of a ghostly apparition—Stacy could've sworn the woman was smiling at her.

"If you see the light, go toward it," Stacy instructed. "That's where you belong. That's where you can finally rest."

Each member of the Erlich family looked up into the sky. Stacy followed their gaze but saw nothing besides the dark grey clouds rolling by.

Their apparitions lost shape. The five transformed into orbs of blue light, lifted into the air, and rose higher and higher until Stacy could no longer see them.

They can now be at peace, she thought.

Stacy returned to the other side of the yard where Kim stood beside Georgia.

"I feel like I don't even know you anymore," Kim said, shaking her head in amazement.

"Come on." Stacy took her friend's hand and felt Kim squeeze it.

Stacy reached out to clasp Georgia's outstretched palm.

42

Rand followed the voices to the kitchen, where he found two women sitting at a table. A tall candle burned between them.

Rand had experience with witnessing past events. It happened sometimes when dealing with certain ghosts or entities, especially if he went to a location that had been significant to them during their lifetime.

Who are these two ladies? Rand thought.

"It's important for you to do exactly what I say," one woman said to the other. "This isn't a game, and it can be dangerous if we break the rules. Do you understand, Gerry?"

The other woman, whose back was to Rand, nodded.

Rand realized he was witnessing a younger Geraldine. He went closer to the table and looked at her face. It was definitely her, except her hair was darker and there were far fewer wrinkles.

The two women could not see him, and the scene before him was not real—it had already happened. Rand was a mere spectator.

The other woman paused and glanced at Rand's feet. She blinked twice.

"Do you see something?" Geraldine whispered.

The woman didn't answer at first, but only continued to listen. "I think there's someone here."

She's a medium, Rand realized. This woman could probably feel Rand's distant presence, even though he was visiting from a different time.

Rand was watching a séance.

Oh no, he thought. Things were starting to make a lot more sense.

The woman broke her attention away from where Rand stood. "Okay. Let's begin."

"Will this take long, Helen?" Geraldine asked. "Wayne has no idea what I'm up to, and if he comes home and sees this, he'll be very upset."

"We can't put a time limit on the spiritual world," Helen said.

Geraldine didn't seem to like that answer, but she nodded regardless.

Helen laid her arms over the table, palms up, and Geraldine took Helen's hands.

"Close your eyes," Helen said. Geraldine obeyed.

"We are here tonight to reach out to the two little boys that we recently lost," Helen said. She paused for a few moments. "They were a very important part of Geraldine's life. She saw them as her own children, and they were cruelly taken from her."

Rand only shook his head. It was no accident that he was seeing this particular moment of the past. Geraldine probably thought that a medium could help her communicate with the two neighbor boys, but instead, they'd made contact with the demonic entities that disguised themselves as the children.

If you invite them, they will come. It was the warning he gave repeatedly in his class.

"Johnny and William, if you are here and you are listening, give us a sign."

Geraldine's face clenched up as if the mere mention of the two boys' names brought her grief.

"We wish to feel your presence once again. Please come to us."

Helen let the silence linger for a long time. Rand gripped the cross in his hands, on edge, waiting for something to happen. He knew that Johnny and William weren't the spirits that eventually answered Helen's call.

"Johnny and William, we are listening. We are here for you. Please come and speak with us. Give us a sign that you are present."

Footsteps came from above. Light and staccato, like running, barefoot children. Rand and Geraldine looked up at the ceiling at the same time.

"Stay focused," Helen told Geraldine, tightening her grip on the other woman's hands—Geraldine had almost broken the circle.

"That's them," Geraldine whispered. "They always liked to play in the upstairs loft when they came over."

The loft, Rand thought, making a mental note.

"That's our sign," Helen said. "They've come. It makes sense for them to arrive in the loft first since they have a strong memory of that location. But we want them to come down here and speak with us. Give them more time. When they're comfortable, they'll come."

Helen isn't wrong, Rand thought. *But she doesn't realize that the demonic are very good at impersonating what people want to hear.*

"Johnny and William, thank you for giving us a sign of your presence. We hear you upstairs, and we invite you to come down and join us."

The pitter-patter of footsteps came again. Soft children's laughter accompanied them.

Rand craned his head toward the ceiling and followed the sounds of the footsteps. He would have to find the stairs and go up there. If what Geraldine said was true and the loft had been significant to the boys when they were alive, that meant the loft was where Rand needed to go.

Rand turned his back on the séance and started walking from the kitchen to the living room. There was no point watching more when the spirits he was hunting were upstairs.

"Oh. There's someone else here. This presence is *very* strong."

Rand turned and immediately spotted Shindael, who stood just over Helen's shoulder. An ice-cold wave flushed through Rand's entire body.

"Who is it?" Geraldine asked.

Helen's eyebrows pressed together and her lips tightened. "Umm... I don't know." She lifted her chin to speak. "New spirit who has joined us... We welcome you. Please identify yourself."

Rand thought he could see an amused smile behind Shindael's small, black eyes.

"Leave them alone," Rand said.

Shindael grasped Helen's shoulder, his thin-fingered hand seeming to crush the woman's petite frame. Helen gasped and shot up from her seat, yanking her hands from Geraldine's.

Shindael vanished.

"What's wrong?" Geraldine asked.

Helen rubbed the shoulder that Shindael had touched. "I have to go." She looked like she was about to cry.

"Helen, wait."

Helen stormed right past Rand, not seeing him or sensing his presence. She scooped up her purse from the coffee table with a trembling hand. "Something feels wrong. I'm sorry." Then she rushed out the door, leaving Geraldine alone and confused.

Once Helen was gone, Geraldine blew out the candle.

They did not close the ceremony properly, Rand thought. Shindael and the two entities that had responded to Helen's call would remain. Rand was honestly surprised it had taken entire decades for the Swansons to start having problems.

Rand crossed the living room and entered another part of the house, which he had not previously seen. Off to the side, he found the stairwell. The darkness seemed to grow thicker with each step up.

Geraldine appeared beside him. She was oblivious to his presence. She also gazed upstairs, seeming confused and intrigued at the same time.

"Don't go," Rand whispered to her. He knew what was going through the woman's head.

Geraldine started climbing, intent on discovering the source of the children's footsteps.

The loft's darkness swallowed Geraldine.

43

Each step creaked underneath Rand's shoe. When he reached the top, the room lit up—Geraldine had turned on a lamp that sat atop a nearby table.

The loft above the Swansons' house appeared to be for storage and was filled with boxes and extra furniture. The ceiling slanted and came to its highest point in the center.

Geraldine looked around. Johnny and William were not there.

But something was making those noises, Rand thought. *Something is up here.*

Rand then grew extremely cold. The chill was familiar to him. Something evil was present—something Geraldine could not see.

Geraldine rubbed her palms along her arms, trying to warm up. She must have also felt the unnatural chill in the air. She also looked wary.

It seemed to become too much for Geraldine to bear. She rushed down the stairs, leaving Rand alone in the loft.

Rand surveyed the loft—and found the demon behind him. It was the elder black-eyed kid. He still retained his true, shadowy form. The creature was nestled in the corner of the ceiling.

Rand backed away as icy needles prickled his skin.

He'd said the other kid was with Stacy, Rand thought. *This one has come for me.*

The demon climbed down from the ceiling corner, long legs and arms moving like an insect. His substantial body blocked the top of the stairs, trapping Rand inside the loft.

Rand sensed the wall growing closer behind him. The loft was a small space. Keeping his distance would be impossible. It was going to be a close-quarters fight.

Rand raised the cross and placed it between him and the approaching demon. With one swift movement from his clawed hand, the demon swiped at the cross and snapped it in half, leaving Rand holding only a small piece of splintered wood.

Before Rand could fully comprehend what had happened, the demon zipped behind Rand and wrapped his long arms around Rand's body.

The air was forced from Rand's lungs. His sternum and ribs bent under the demon's strength, and he knew any tighter of a squeeze would shatter them. The pressure built in his throat and face like his head was in danger of popping off.

Rand's instinct took over like a drowning man struggling for the water's surface. He clawed at the arms but found no relief.

He had never been attacked like this before. This was far worse than the scratches and beatings he'd endured from other demons.

A new pain bloomed. Rand realized the entity's touch was so cold it burned like dry ice searing into his skin. He didn't have the breath to scream.

Then Shindael was in front of him, having materialized from thin air.

He was inches away from Rand, watching the man struggle in his servant's grasp.

'You're not praying.' Shindael's words filled Rand's head. *'Perhaps you should start.'*

What was the point? When had it ever helped before?

Shindael smirked. He'd read that thought.

Rand realized he was right where Shindael had always wanted. Trapped, hopeless, and worst of all, faithless.

'It has been my pleasure to torment you, Randolph. But the time has come for us to finish this. You bested Karax. You prevailed over Hazul. You have foiled the plans of my master, the devil, for too long, and now he commands your death.'

Because of the pain, it took Rand a few moments to comprehend what Shindael was saying.

The game was over. The end had come. The long-armed demon had captured Rand so easily and was crushing him to death. Rand had never had a chance.

The edges of his vision blurred and his consciousness began to flicker out. The only thing he saw clearly now was a white light that had appeared behind Shindael.

There it was again. The same white light Rand had seen in the woods. Now he knew he was dying.

Except… he hadn't been dying when he'd seen the light the first time.

This is something else, Rand realized.

With the only remaining air in his lungs, he forced out two words. "Behind you."

The oldest trick in the book.

Shindael turned.

The light started to morph. It took the form of a girl with silver, flowing hair who wore a white dress. Her striking eyes were also completely white.

Shindael roared. It was a deep and powerful sound that Rand had never heard from the demon before. Shindael had always been stoic, but when he saw the girl, his calm demeanor broke.

Shindael was *afraid* of her.

Shindael's apparition dissolved into a cloud of smoke. That cloud vanished from the room in the next instant. He'd fled from the girl.

Rand felt the shadowy arms around him relax. The appearance of the white-eyed girl and the abandonment of the demon's master had caused him to slip.

Rand's mind worked fast. Shindael feared the white-eyed girl. That meant the demon that held him did as well.

Rand twisted out of the demon's loosened grasp and broke free. In the next instant, he grabbed the black arm and pulled. The demon's strength and resolve had left him.

Rand shoved the demon toward the girl. The white-eyed girl lifted her hands, as if to catch the creature. As soon as the two made contact, the demon unleashed a guttural howl.

Then he burst into a splatter of black plasma. The disgusting fluid painted the walls, the floor, and even sprayed onto Rand's clothes.

None of it touched the white-eyed girl.

The spike of adrenaline faded all at once. Rand dropped to his hands and knees, gasping for air to fill his lungs. His bones ached, and the cold burning from the demon's touch had seared through his jacket and shirt and left stinging red marks on his flesh underneath his tattered clothes. His palms burned too, from having grabbed the demon's arms.

Rand looked up. He was at the feet of the girl. She seemed about ten years old, but it was hard to see clearly now. Her light was so radiant Rand found it difficult to look directly at her.

Despite the pain in Rand's body, an overwhelming comfort flowed through him. He felt peace and calm. Somehow, he knew the feelings were coming from the white-eyed girl. He didn't ever want to leave. Tears welled up in his eyes. He felt unworthy of being in her presence.

"Who are you?" Rand managed.

The two pieces of the broken cross that lay on the ground moved by themselves. They zipped over and sealed themselves together at the girl's bare feet, reattaching and mending themselves as if it had never been broken.

'You are a faithful servant.'

Her voice filled Rand's head. It sounded like the most beautiful music he'd ever heard.

'Now go and rest.'

The light that emanated from the girl grew brighter, blinding Rand and forcing him to cover his eyes with his arm. When he could see again, he was somewhere else.

44

Rand lay supine, looking up into the starry sky. The cross, now whole, rested on his chest.

He found the strength to push himself onto his elbows and looked around. He was in the front yard of Wayne Swanson's house. A group of people were nearby.

His eyes adjusted, and he spotted Miller, Libby, Wayne, and Geraldine. The group didn't know he was there. They spoke amongst themselves and hadn't yet noticed his sudden reappearance.

"Hey," Rand called out.

All of their heads snapped toward him at once, startled.

"It's Rand!" Miller's voice. The group rushed over.

Miller looped his forearms into Rand's armpits and pulled him to his feet. A wave of dizziness hit him. "Easy, Miller."

The cross tumbled off his chest and landed in a pile of leaves. Libby picked it up.

"How did you get out here?" Miller asked. "We just watched you walk inside the house."

Rand rubbed at his eyes. His fingertips came away wet. The last of the tears were still there. "That's time distortion for you."

"Are you okay, Dad?" Libby asked. "What happened in there?"

"Your clothes are all ripped up," Miller said.

Everyone looked at him expectantly, waiting for his answers. Wayne Swanson still held his shotgun.

"That entity won't be bothering you anymore," Rand told Wayne. "Wait... Stacy. Where's Stacy?"

He was met by grim silence.

If Stacy hadn't returned yet, then surely she was in trouble. *I have to find a way back to the past,* he thought.

There was movement—someone was coming toward them. Everyone turned toward the sound of footsteps crunching through the leaves. Wayne readied his gun.

As they neared, Rand realized it was actually three people approaching. He recognized Stacy first, and she was with a girl dressed in a black leotard. Georgia was behind them, pulling her oxygen tank along.

Rand rushed over to his student. "Are you okay?"

Stacy didn't answer, and instead wrapped him in a tight hug. Rand felt the tension in her body. It eased out of her as they embraced.

"Are *you* okay?" Stacy asked him. "Your clothes are ripped. What happened to you?"

"I had a little standoff with one of the black-eyed kids," Rand said.

"I was with the younger one," Stacy said.

Rand pulled away from Stacy and gripped her shoulders. "And?"

"I beat him. And I got Kim back."

The girl beside Stacy looked haggard and spent as if she'd just been released from a torture chamber. Rand could only imagine what Kim must have experienced while being held captive.

"I'm sorry you went through this," Rand told Kim. The apology sounded hopelessly hollow to his ears.

Kim couldn't seem to muster the strength to respond. She only leaned against Stacy for support.

Kim's brokenness weighed heavily on Rand. The girl was yet

another innocent who had been harmed for the sole purpose of tormenting him.

Wayne Swanson appeared at Rand's side. "This is all very touch-in', but it's way past my bedtime. Are you tellin' me that I don't have anythin' to worry about anymore with those... things? They scare my dog."

"Your dog will be happy to know that they're gone," Rand said.

It seemed to take all of Wayne's willpower to force his hand out toward Rand. He shook it. Maybe Rand *was* a paranormal nut, but he was happy to help.

The Swansons returned to their home while shouting at Boss to follow them. The cold dog was more than happy to run back inside.

Georgia held up her hand to Rand, and Rand high-fived her. "Next time I'm going to charge you, Ghost Man."

Rand smirked. "Deal."

"You sure everything's good?" Libby asked.

Rand nodded. "I'm sure. And I'm exhausted. Let's all go home. Libby, can you take Georgia back to the hospital?"

"Yeah," Libby said. "Come on, Georgia."

"Can I drive this time?" Georgia asked.

"Have you ever driven a car before?" Libby asked.

"Sure. In video games." Libby gave Georgia a look. "Come on, what's the worst that can happen at this point? I crash it?"

"Ugh, I know. Bill's going to freak out when he sees this."

"He can just buy another one, can't he? Isn't he a billionaire?"

The two girls continued talking as they walked toward Bill's half-destroyed BMW. They got in and drove away.

Rand, Miller, Stacy, and Kim returned to Rand's Jeep. The two girls climbed into the backseat.

"Hey." Miller eyed Rand over the Jeep's hood. "What happened in there? To us, you were only gone for a few minutes."

"It was a white-eyed girl," Rand said.

Miller blinked. "A what?"

"Yeah. The demon had me trapped. Shindael was there too. They were just about to kill me. And then she appeared."

"Do you think…"

"I do," Rand said.

Miller's mouth fell open. "That's *huge*. Have you ever seen an angel before?"

"No."

Miller smirked. "I *told* you God hasn't abandoned you."

He sure did wait until the last possible minute, Rand thought. "But that's not all. When I escaped, I threw the demon toward the girl. She touched him, and when she did, he…" He gestured with his hands as he sought the right word. "Exploded."

"Exploded?"

"Yeah. Black plasma went everywhere." He gestured to the black stains on his clothes. "He was just gone, like a popped balloon."

Miller digested that information for a few moments. "This is a big deal, Rando."

"She was an angel and all she had to do was touch the demon. She killed him."

"If you're right, then this is a *huge* breakthrough."

Miller was right. In all his encounters, Rand had only ever been able to send the demonic entities back to hell. They were free to return to Earth whenever they wanted. He'd even encountered some demons more than once.

Never before had he been able to actually *kill* them. That was supposed to be impossible. Demons weren't alive—they were merely spirits. How could you kill something that wasn't technically alive? But demons fled from anything holy for a reason.

Now, Rand had seen that reason with his own two eyes.

That was how Rand was sure that the girl he'd seen was an angel of the Lord.

He was filled with hope. This changed everything. If only the angel had touched Shindael, too. But Shindael had taken off as soon as he'd glimpsed the girl.

"We'll talk more about it later," Rand said. "For now, let's go home."

"Are you in a rush?" Miller asked. "Can we stop for breakfast?"

Rand rolled his eyes.

The first rays of dawn broke. Finally, after the long hours of cold darkness, the world was brightening.

Rand and Miller climbed into the Jeep and Rand started off down Plaster Road. As he drove, the sky became a brighter blue, chasing away the stars until the top of the orange sun peeked over the horizon.

IT WAS APPROACHING eight in the morning by the time Rand got home after dropping off Stacy and Kim, then Miller. The weather radar was still on the television from when he'd rushed out after Stacy had called.

He started walking toward his bedroom but halted when the Bible on the coffee table caught his eye.

Something was different. He approached it slowly, trying to place it.

Then it occurred to him. It was turned to a different page than he'd left it. The previous night, he'd been reading the story of Job. Now, the Bible was open to the very end of the Book of Revelation.

Long ago, Rand had highlighted and underlined a verse in those final chapters.

"And the devil that deceived them was cast into the lake of fire and brimstone, where the beast and the false prophet are, and shall be tormented day and night for ever and ever."

Rand couldn't help but smile.

Lord, Rand prayed, *thank you for revealing your power to me. I know my faith has been fragile, but I am your servant and warrior.*

The prayer was short, but that was okay. It was the most authentic prayer he'd managed in a long, long time.

RAND PACED the front of the classroom as his students busied themselves with their midterm. It was the same test he gave every semester, and it was easy. Certainly, the students in the other religion classes were stressing out over their essay tests. Rand's students, however, were soaring through, flipping the pages and circling the obvious answers to the multiple-choice questions.

But Rand's gaze kept returning to the empty desk in the front row—the one usually occupied by Stacy Thompson. He hadn't heard from her at all since he'd dropped her off at home a few nights before.

One by one the students finished and walked to the front to hand in their exams. Rand stacked them. Toward the end of the class, the only person left was Garrett, the lone student in the class who had a failing grade. He scratched at his head as he read and reread the questions, flipping the pages back and forth.

Eventually, Garrett gave up, making his guesses with big, frenzied circles on his paper, then went to the front of the room to turn in his test.

Rand shoved the tests into his bag and slung it over his shoulder. He'd grade them that night. Or maybe give Libby a couple bucks to do it.

He stopped by his office first on the way to the parking lot. There, he had a visitor waiting for him in the hall by his office door.

Stacy sat with her knees up to her chest, arms wrapped around her legs. She looked very distressed, and she stood as soon as she saw him.

"I was worried about you," Rand said. "Everything okay?"

Stacy shrugged.

Rand unlocked his office and the two went in together. He took his seat behind his desk and Stacy sat in the chair opposite him.

"I'm giving you an A on the test even though you skipped it," Rand said. "After everything that happened, you've earned—"

"I dropped your class."

Rand immediately felt deflated. Within the first few weeks of the semester, anyone could drop a class without repercussions to their

GPA. But Stacy would receive a W on her transcript, which stood for "Withdraw." It was worse than an F.

"Why? You didn't have to do that. You should have talked to me first."

"I had to do it, Mr. Casey. I can't spend another minute in your class, absorbing all the stuff you teach. Not after what happened the other night. And if I stay in the class, I know I'll study for it, which means I'll be thinking about the material all the time. I have to drop it. It's better that way."

Rand sighed. They could have worked something out. He would have been happy to have let her never come back and still give her an A.

But he remembered how traumatized Stacy had been on Halloween night. She'd stepped up and saved her friend when it mattered, yet the whole ordeal would leave a lasting scar on her for the rest of her life.

"But what about the easy A?" Rand asked.

Stacy shook her head. "I don't care about my GPA anymore. There are some things that are more important. Like guarding myself against these things that you teach us about."

"I suppose you have a point," Rand said. A brief silence fell between them. "How's your shoulder?"

Stacy stretched the collar of her shirt down to show where the black-eyed kid had grabbed her. The handprint was still visible, but the redness had started to fade.

"Almost gone," Rand said. He could hear the guilt behind his tone. Stacy should have never suffered an injury like that in the first place.

Stacy slung her backpack over her shoulder and stood. "Thank you for being there for me when I needed you. You're the best teacher I've ever had." She held out her hand, and Rand shook it.

Stacy left his office, and just like that, his star student was gone. He collapsed back into his chair and let out a deep sigh. Even when he won, he still lost.

Rand logged into his computer and brought up the presentation he'd given the other day—the lesson on the things he didn't believe in. He navigated to the slide on the black-eyed kids. The picture he'd pasted on the slide had nowhere near the same effect as the kids in real life.

Rand studied the picture for a few seconds. Then he selected the entire slide and pressed the delete key.

The black-eyed kids vanished from the screen.

Randolph Casey returns in The Herron House, the **fourth book** in the Randolph Casey Horror Thrillers series.
<u>Start reading now</u>!

HEY THERE.

Thank you for spending your valuable time reading my book, and I hope you enjoyed it.

As you may know, reviews are one of the best ways readers can support their favorite authors. They help get the word out and convince potential readers to take a chance on me.

I would like to ask that you consider leaving a review on Amazon or Goodreads. I would be very grateful, and of course, it is always valuable to me to hear what my readers think of my work.

Thank you in advance to everyone who chooses to do so, and I hope to see you back in my pages soon.

Sincerely,

- Rockwell

ALSO BY ROCKWELL SCOTT

A Haunting in Silver Falls

A quiet town. A cursed statue. An ancient evil claiming its next victim...

Sixteen-year-old Kara Mills expects her summer in Silver Falls to be dull—
spent in a small town she doesn't care for with an aunt she barely knows.
But boredom quickly turns to dread when Aunt Adrienne brings home an
eerie statue from a local thrift shop. What starts as a strange curiosity soon
takes on a life of its own.

The statue vanishes and reappears in different places around the house,
leaving Kara to question her own senses. While she assumes it's her aunt
playing tricks, Adrienne, a deeply spiritual woman, insists that a powerful
spirit resides within the statue—and she welcomes it.

At first, Kara is skeptical. She can only watch as her quirky aunt offers small
gifts to the statue and talks to it as if it's listening. But as the days pass,

Adrienne's fascination turns into obsession and devotion. She grows cold and distant toward Kara, her behavior more erratic—and dangerous.

Soon Kara can no longer deny that something is very wrong. Terrified and alone, she witnesses her aunt falling deeper under the influence of a dark force. As evil begins to pervade Adrienne's entire home, Kara must confront the truth behind the statue before it consumes them both. But the malevolent entity within won't let go without a fight—and the cost of saving Adrienne could be more than Kara is prepared to pay.

ALSO BY ROCKWELL SCOTT

A Haunting in Rose Grove

A malevolent entity. A violent haunting. A house with a bloody history. Jake Nolan left it all behind, but now he must return.

Jake has it all — a new home, an amazing girlfriend, and nearing a promotion at work. Best of all, he feels he's finally moved on from the horrors of his traumatic past. But when he learns that his estranged brother, Trevor, has moved back into their haunted childhood home, Jake knows his past is not quite finished with him yet.

Jake rushes to the old house in Rose Grove — a small town with a tragic history — to pull his brother from that dangerous place. But it's too late. There, he finds Trevor trying to make contact with the spirit that tormented them years ago.

And Trevor refuses to leave. He is determined to cleanse the house and remove the entity. But the supernatural activity becomes too much to handle, and Jake knows they are both unprepared for the fight. Worse, the entity targets Daniel, Jake's young nephew, and wants to bring him harm. And when the intelligent haunting shows signs of demonic infestation, Jake realizes they aren't dealing with a mere ghost.

Jake attributes the evil spirit for driving his parents to an early grave. Now it wants to claim the rest of the family, and the only way Jake and Trevor will survive is to send the entity back to hell.

A Haunting in Rose Grove is a supernatural horror novel for readers who love stories about haunted houses and battles with the demonic — the truest form of evil that exists in our world.

ALSO BY ROCKWELL SCOTT

The Gravewatcher

Every night at 3 AM, he visits the graveyard and speaks to someone who isn't there.

Eleanor has created an ideal life for herself in New York City with a career that keeps her too busy, just as she likes it. But when she receives an anonymous message that her estranged brother Dennis is dead, her fast-paced routine grinds to a halt. She rushes to Finnick, Louisiana — the small, backward town where her brother lived and temporarily settles into his creepy, turn-of-the-century house until she can figure out how he died.

But that night, Eleanor spots a young boy in the cemetery behind Dennis's house, speaking to the gravestones. When she approaches him, Eleanor's interruption of the boy's ritual sets off a chain reaction of horror she could have never prepared for. The footsteps, the voices, and the shadowy apparitions are only the beginning.

Eleanor learns that the boy, Walter, is being oppressed by a demonic entity that compels him to visit the graveyard every night. She suspects Dennis also discovered this nightly ritual and tried to stop it, and that is why he died. Because there are others in Finnick who know about Walter's involvement with the evil spirit and want it to continue, and they will do whatever it takes to stop Eleanor from ruining their carefully laid plans. Now Eleanor must finish what her brother started — to rescue the boy from the clutches of hell before he loses his soul forever.

The Gravewatcher is a supernatural horror novel for readers who love stories about haunted houses, creepy graveyards, and battles with the demonic - the truest form of evil that exists in our world.

ABOUT THE AUTHOR

Rockwell Scott is an author of supernatural horror fiction.

When not writing, he can be found working out, enjoying beer and whiskey with friends, and traveling internationally.

Feel free to get in touch!

Instagram
https://www.instagram.com/rockwellscottauthor/

Facebook
www.facebook.com/rockwellscottauthor

X
@rockwell_scott

www.rockwellscott.com

rockwellscottauthor@gmail.com

www.ingramcontent.com/pod-product-compliance
Lightning Source LLC
Chambersburg PA
CBHW060207030726
47499CB00004B/951